DUAL CLASS

II

ARTHUR INVERSE

MoonQuill

Dual Class
Book 2

Copyright © 2025 Arthur Inverse

ISBN (paperback): 979-8-88993-040-2
ISBN (hardcover): 979-8-88993-047-1
ISBN (e-book): 979-8-88993-052-5

Cover by BeeBros Team
Interior Design by Tangcu LLC

Published 2025 by MoonQuill
Arlington, VA
www.moonquill.com

Table of Contents

Chapter 1
It Might be Time to Visit Some Old Friends

The sun was reaching its apex as the day droned on. A man sat at the top of a wooden guard tower, his legs dangling as he looked out into the vast forest beyond. His shoulder-length black hair swayed in the midday breeze, his black and gold trimmed robes fluttering ever so slightly.

In his hands were a few items he was having a hard time not complaining about.

"Ahhh! Why is this thing in the middle of the fucking Ant's Hive?! How did that sad excuse for a King even get it there?!" Drake shouted into the air, raising the piece of paper that he'd looked at time and time again for the past week with both hands.

Drake Wallen, also known as Shot in the tutorial—or more accurately now as "The Tyrant" by the system—was doing his best to not run off and loot the pitiful Goblin King Moth's Treasure Hoard.

"Perhaps they placed it there prior to the ants arriving?" Natto offered, placing a roasted nut into her mouth. "Ish naut like shew cannot just go there youshelf lahtah..." she continued through her chewing.

"Why have you still not learned to *not* talk with your mouth full? It's so unladylike." Drake snorted, looking down at the little pink-haired construct who wore a Miko outfit.

"I get it from you! All of my bad habits, all of them!" she snapped back.

Doesn't that mean she got all my bad traits and none of my good ones when they made her? Wait... Drake thought.

"That makes no sense. I don't do that."

Natto gave him a side stink eye as she took a large bite out of another nut, the sides of her cheeks puffing up as she chewed.

Drake coughed, then went back to checking some of the new items he'd acquired.

He'd won the fight against the Goblin King at the cost of a very painful recovery, a near-death experience, and a very loud scolding from several different people.

Drake had been bedridden for three days even after being healed by Jacqueline. Then he'd had another four days of "No doin' nothing," as Jacqueline had ordered him.

He'd been disgruntled about it, immediately saying he didn't need to rest and that he would be fine. But his body's unwillingness to move even his head from his pillow had forced him to comply.

Fortunately, Drake had a plethora of notifications to go through and catch up on, including titles, quest updates, and rewards.

One specific title in the seemingly numerous updates he'd received had filled him with boyish joy. He opened it, scanning over his entire status in the process.

Drake Wallen

Tutorial Alias: Shot

Race: Human [F-Rank]

Profession: Miner P2 (7%) [F-Rank], Empty

Class: [Unique] Elemental Miller Level 19

VIT: 310 (15%)

STR: 338 (20 + 15%)

DEX: 280 (40 + 25%) + (40)

INT: 648 (15 + 20%)

WIS: 324 (29%)

END: 274 (20 + 20%)

Free Points: 40

Skills Branches

Primary

Elementalist P2 (49%) [F-Rank] 5/5
Magic Sight P2 (62%) [F-Rank]
Heretical Mind P2 (68%) [F-Rank]
Multiplicative P3 (0%) [F-Rank]
Elemental Endowment P2 (41%) [F-Rank]
Elemental Conflux P2 (32%) [F-Rank]

Secondary
Shield Miller P2 (5%) [F-Rank] 4/5
Warrior's Stamina P2 (50%) [F-Rank]
Guardian's Reprieve P2 (2%) [F-Rank]
Aura of Command P1 (5%) [F-Rank]
Martial Strike P2 (35%) [F-Rank]
Empty

Primary Subtree
Internal Mastery [F-Rank] 5/5
Of the Apex P2 (20%) [F-Rank]
Weak Point P2 (17%) [F-Rank]
Tempered in Flames P2 (41%) [F-Rank]
Tyrannical Aura P2 (33%) [F-Rank]
Tyrant's Indomitability P1 (26%) [F-Rank]

Secondary Subtree
Soul Mastery [F-Rank] 5/5
Mana Manipulation P2 (88%) [F-Rank]
Atrophy of the Mind P1 (45%) [F-Rank]
Cower P1 (30%) [F-Rank]
Sound Body and Mind P2 (60%) [F-Rank]
Purity of Soul P2 (18%) [F-Rank]

Tertiary Subtree
Weapon Mastery [F-Rank] 5/5
Hoarder P2 (31%) [F-Rank]
Fully Loaded P1 (18%) [F-Rank]

Weapon of Choice P2 (34%) [F-Rank]
Adrenaline Acuity P2 (43%) [F-Rank]
Magic Exposure P1 (51%) [F-Rank]

Quaternary Subtree

Empty

Titles: First Blood, Two Versus One, One Versus Many, Monkey Slayer, Living on the Edge, Close Call, Dead Man Walking, Dual Class, Punching Up, Improbability, Rounded, Dog Hater, One-Man Army, Dog Killer, Battle of Attrition, First of Your Kind, Goblin Hater, Goblin Slayer, Murderer, Serial Killer, Well on Your Way, Highest Contributor, Vanquisher of Kings, Tutorial Forerunner, First of Many, Glory of the Patriarch, Expectations of the Host, The Dawning of a Tyrant

Highest Contributor

During a large-scale quest event, you contributed the most to the quest's completion. Your deeds have earned you many a reward and accolade.
+15% to all damage dealt.

When Drake had seen the title, he'd done a head shimmy in his bed. Though that was only because the single thing he could move was his head—and only barely at the time.

The next few titles were also nothing to scoff at.

Vanquisher of Kings

You have dealt 99% of the total damage to a royal. As the usurper of the Goblin Throne, you are forever hated by the goblin race.
+10% damage to Royal Bloodlines. +50% damage to all goblinoid races.

Tutorial Forerunner

You have proven yourself to be one of great strength and steel, reaching heights very few of your tutorial group have managed.
+20 to all stats. +5% to Aura Effects.

Well on Your Way

Obtain the first fully progressed skill of your rank, reaching Proficiency 3.
+1% to all stats.

First of Many

Having contributed to the death of a Royal, you have set in motion your vie for power and glory. May the path to the top be bloody and long.
+5% damage to beings above your rank.

Glory of the Patriarch
Substantial enough deeds have been performed by an individual for the system to recognize them by name.
+15% to all Aura Effects. +10% damage to any beings below your rank.

Expectations of the Host
The sponsor of your tutorial has noticed your accomplishments and expects great things from you.

Drake had winced slightly at the last one when he'd read it from his bed a day after waking up from healing. He was beginning to pile up a lot of unwanted attention, but that was what happened when you started to make progress anywhere. Be that games, life, or a death tutorial, it seemed.

Finally, there was one title he somewhat knew was coming, but even his cringiest of bones couldn't handle it.

The Dawning of a Tyrant
Your will and ideals have been thrust upon the world. Your views will not be opposed, and those that have opposed them have perished underfoot. Your rule is law under penalty of death.
+15% to all Aura skill effects. +15 to all stats.

When Drake had finished looking at all the titles the system had given him for the quest, he was overjoyed but also melancholy, as he was unable to put them to any use while bedridden.

Placing the map that he'd received from the Royal Knight Quest back into his inventory, he pulled out two pairs of violet-colored crystals in his left hand.

Communication Crystal [F-Grade]
These two mana-linked crystals can be used to communicate over far distances.
Infuse mana into the crystal to establish a connection.
Can only be used with its uniquely paired counterpart.

He currently didn't have a use for the items, but he was happy to receive them for later. The crystals were a reward for completing two of the last few quests he'd had yet to finish earlier: the Red Cap Goblins and the Goblin Scouts.

After Drake's seven-day pause from any physical exercise, he was ready to go. He especially wanted to go back to the site where he'd fought the King, as he hadn't had time to collect any of the loot. Thankfully, he'd gotten some of the rewards from the quest completion and from the King himself, even though Claire had been the one to finish the sad excuse for a monster leader.

When Drake had recovered enough, he immediately ran off to stretch his legs. There were no more armies that he could find, but he soon came upon the remnants of the goblin camp where he'd rescued the first batch of captives.

There, he found a wasteland. Leftover camps, war equipment, and cages.

Thankfully, most of the people who'd been left behind—the small number that there were—had been able to survive off the rations they had stored away. They were all severely dehydrated and malnourished, but thanks to their levels, they'd been able to go beyond their old human limits.

For once, Drake was thanked as a savior. The faces of the thirty-some-odd people lit up with tears of joy the moment they saw him and he opened their cages. Drake had to kill a small number of goblins that remained, but they were no threat to him as he was now, resulting in a quick and timely death for the monsters.

The people, once saved, returned with him to his outpost. The outpost was now more than amply fortified thanks to Hudson gaining some more levels, allowing for even more robots to line the walls and for his big boys to get up and running.

Snapping back to reality from his reminiscing, Drake placed the crystals into his inventory and pulled another item from his recently expanded inventory full of goodies.

In his hand was a skill stone. A very controversial one.

Skill Stone: Blood [Rare]
Unlocks 1 random skill from the Blood tree.
Requires 1 open skill slot.

"I'm not so sure how I feel about using a stone like this, even if it *is* rare..." Drake mused.

Natto tapped his side with a roasted snack as she swallowed her most recent bite.

"I would not worry about such things now. It has been an adequate amount of time since you have consumed any stones, and you have calmed down a great degree since that fight," she said. "You will need all the strong stones you can acquire to complete your goal regardless of how you feel about where the stone came from. Or was all that talk just such—talk?"

"I don't like it when you tell me things I already know..." Drake smiled wearily.

Natto snorted, a grin creasing her lips before she went back to snacking.

Drake took a long look at the horizon before turning his attention to the rampart below him. He saw an increasingly familiar face, one that had continued to follow him since he'd returned that day.

"What do you want, Mom?" Drake asked sarcastically.

"Who's your mom?!" Claire pouted. "It's past lunchtime, and Sherry is throwing another fit! And you didn't even sleep last night either! Don't think I didn't notice!"

Drake rolled his eyes.

"I'll be right there. I thought I was the big strong guy protecting the outpost, but instead, I'm the place's personal chef at this point." He laughed.

Claire crossed her arms as she looked up at him, her dirty-blonde hair tied into a side ponytail that was draped over her left shoulder. She stood leaning on one leg to the side.

Drake looked down and snorted, waving her away.

"I said I'll get to it. You know I'm a man of my word, so off you go."

Claire pursed her lips but knew by now that arguing wouldn't do much with Drake. She quickly turned and walked down the rampart steps, heading for the camp.

"You really should put a stop to that. It will only end in her being more heartbroken," Natto chided, looking at the back of the young woman.

"Believe me, I've tried. But she's become as attached as Chelsea has, and I want nothing to do with either of them romantically. I've said as much. There's just too much to do right now, and I don't have a reason to lead them on. They know that." Drake sighed, placing the stone inside his inventory.

Drake stuffed his hands into the pockets of a new pair of uncommon pants that he'd obtained from the quest as he thought about how the two had started to dote on him following the completion of the quest.

He was surprised, to say the least, that Chelsea of all people would flip on her head from hating him to actually going out of her way to please him. And this was after he'd allowed her to get injured during the fight.

Thankfully, she'd made a full recovery thanks to Jacqueline. But on the other side of the coin...

Drake looked to his right shoulder where his earthen arm still remained.

The cooldown on Jacqueline's spell was far longer than she had let on. Her healing spells had been used to mend both Chelsea and Julia. The problem was her most powerful spell; it had healed Drake from the brink of death, but that was also the issue.

While the spell had healed Drake, because his arm wasn't technically injured, it hadn't been remade during the process.

He'd been more than a little annoyed when he'd heard the reasoning, saying he would just slice off part of his shoulder like a holiday ham if that's what it took. But then she'd told him of her cooldown, which had annoyed him even further.

Drake was truly irritated, but there was nothing to be done until the cooldown was up, which would be tomorrow. But he had another problem.

Turning his head to the rest of the camp, he remembered another one of his promises.

He had to bring the camp to Shigure's, and he was well overdue to do so. Most of the people in the camp had been understanding of the delays, especially now that he had so many comrades willing to stick up for him. It was a welcome feeling after so much animosity previously.

But a deal was a deal, and his word had to be kept. After all, he was only as good as his word if he wanted to keep people's trust.

And I may or may not want to go see how Bjorn is doing. Annnnd may or may not want to try to beat him up, Drake thought, opening up the leaderboards.

Top Level Leaderboard
Rank 1, Level 27: Bear
Rank 2, Level 24: Shigure Kenzo
Rank 3, Level 22: Joker
Rank 4, Level 19: Shot
Rank 5, Level 18: Super Megan
Rank 6, Level 17: Jimina Seinen

...

Tutorial Points Leaderboard
Rank 1: Shot [23,664,505 TP]
Rank 2: Bear [7,465,355 TP]
Rank 3: Shigure Kenzo [2,483,945 TP]

...

Drake smiled widely as he looked at the results of the rewards from the quest. He'd gained a whopping ten million TP from his contributions and thankfully also managed to level up from finishing the other quests. The only ones he still needed to complete were the Tyrant Ants and the Goblin Knights.

Encounters with the goblins had become less frequent, but by no means had they ended. Some of the regular Goblin Knights and Lieutenants had survived and rallied the scattered forces, trying to find new prey in the tutorial. Drake had been having some trouble finding the last remnants of their forces, but he was close to finishing. He only needed two more Knights for the quest reward.

Speaking of other rewards, thanks to his kill count, Drake had also received a large sum of enhancing pills. He'd consumed them the moment they'd popped into his room on top of him, laughing while he forced Natto to feed him.

In total, he'd received more than the quest had initially offered. From the wording, it sounded like the requirement for the reward was only killing the bare minimum—five thousand. Drake had killed more and, to his delight, received more pills as compensation. A total of thirty of each pill.

Each pill gave one free point. The Strengthening Pill increased his strength and dexterity by one, and the Mana Pill increased his intelligence and wisdom by one each as well. The result was a full thirty points to four different stats.

With all the stat bonuses from his titles and the pills, he'd essentially picked up a few more levels outside of what it said on paper. And what's more, one of the most needed rewards was the rare piece of equipment he'd selected.

The options had been vast, including both weapons and jewelry, but he'd picked the bracers that now donned his person.

Bracers of the Desert Wanderer [F-Grade, Rare]
Bracers made from the hide of the Desert Wildbacks: roaming monsters of the treacherous open desert of the Red Sands. Their natural carapace allows them to withstand not only the heat and uninhabitable conditions, but also retain water for extended periods of time.

125 – 142 Physical Damage Reduction.
93 – 127 Magic Damage Reduction.
1% Critical Hit Damage Reduction.
Increases stamina by 10% and stamina regeneration by 20%.

The bracers were the only option he could find in the selection that allowed him to increase one of his lowest resources at the moment: his stamina.

Drake hopped up to his feet, popping the Blood skill stone into his hand once more. His left hand stretched for the sky as he let out a relieved groan.

"Alright, guess it's time to see to some food. I'm getting hungry myself," he said, looking down at Natto. Her ears twitched at the word.

"Food?" she said, stopping mid-bite.

"Yup. Then I think it's about time we go visit an old friend." Drake smiled, his hand gripping the stone tightly.

You wish to consume Skill Stone: Blood [Rare].

Confirm?

Yes < No

You have learned Ruler's Constitution [F-Rank].

Ruler's Constitution [F-Rank] P1 (0%)
May your reign be long and as strong as thee.
This skill enhances one's body, bringing it to the brink of what is possible and allowing its user to live and prosper while their Kingdom grows under their watchful eye.

Passive: Your health pool is now doubled. Increases based on proficiency.
Extra: You now gain an additional 2 vitality per level.

Drake felt the enjoyable surge of cold to warm that he'd almost forgotten over the past week, the wave of overwhelming power a sweet reminder of what consuming skills entailed.

But he quickly cocked an eyebrow at the skill description.

"Wait, I never signed up to do kingdom building..."

Chapter 2
The Next Step

"Haa..." Chelsea sighed as she scrubbed down her armor and wiped her bow with a lightly-damp cloth, her eyes distant while her hands continued to move mechanically.

"Chels, you've been doing that for half an hour now. What's wrong?" Megan asked, taking a sip from her canteen in the midday sun.

They were both on the 'soccer field' that Tom and Drake had made, spending a bit of time relaxing in between going out and hunting now that there were no major quests. Many of the goblins had scattered, leaving relatively sparse amounts of them around.

Chelsea jerked slightly at her name being called.

"Oh... Um... You know, just reminiscing on how many mistakes I've made and how I would do things differently..." she said, giving a wry smile.

"Chels, it isn't really about *him* again, is it...? I thought he turned you down." Megan scoffed, the constant mention of the man giving her a sour face.

"Megs, you need to let that stuff go. Chris was a piece of shit. We all know it. And Shot did it because I asked him to in return for healing his arm, so if you have to blame anyone, blame me."

Megan pursed her lips, using her forearm to wipe away some of the sweat she'd managed to build up despite her stats being stronger than most at her level.

"I'm not blind to it anymore, Chels. It's been more than a week, and I've seen what he's done for people around here. But he could have been a little... *nicer* about it..." she grumbled.

Chelsea stood up from her seat, placing her equipment into her inventory, then threw her arms around her unsuspecting friend as she pulled her in for a hug. Megan yelped briefly, but she didn't pull away from Chelsea.

"Megs. Sometimes we need the tough love. If I've learned anything from being here and in a party with him, it's that he's a good guy. Even if he's got a foul mouth sometimes."

Megan scoffed again. "You're only saying that because you like the asshole. The rest of us..." Megan trailed off. Suddenly, she poured the rest of her canteen on Chelsea to get her off of her.

Chelsea drew backwards, her mouth open in a gasp of disbelief before her face soon twisted into a smirk.

"The rest of us just see him as the guy in charge," Megan finished, sneering.

"You bitc—" Chelsea was about to yell back, her face a feral smile, but she was interrupted by another voice before she could grab Megan.

"Heyyyyy... Shot wants everyone to come to the rampart," Sherry said in a long drawn-out huff. "He says he needs to talk to everyone about something important, and we get to eat after so stop messing around and hurry up or I'll have Hudson's big boy here just carry you there," she finished, one hand slapping the metal monster, the other pushing up her slipping glasses by the brim, a gleam in her eye.

Both Megan and Chelsea recoiled slightly at the large automaton that stood twice the size of Sherry. It was a sleek black and had a smaller head marked with yellow eyes and red lines that were present all over its body like circuitry.

"G-Got it, we'll be there in a minute," Chelsea answered wearily. Megan agreed with several sharp nods.

Sherry soon departed, her big boy bodyguard following along.

"Jeez, she is scary when she's hungry," Chelsea said, standing straight up and shaking some of the water off herself.

"Yeah, you could say she isn't herself when she's hungry..." Megan added.

Both girls looked at each other for a moment, then burst out in laughter before beginning to walk towards the aforementioned meeting place.

* * *

"I thought you said you were going to make food. Not a meeting and *then* make food!" Claire admonished.

"It will be pretty quick, just hold your horses," Drake said, giving a wry smile, his mask now at the side of his head.

"I would very much enjoy food..." Sherry agreed, rubbing her stomach.

"Well, what exactly you got us all here for, pup? More monsters looking to kill us? Might as well be any given Sunday at this rate." Hudson huffed, his arms crossed as he leaned against his second big boy, the other standing behind Sherry.

Drake chuckled but held up his hand.

"Just give it a minute, we're missing a few people. And we have an extra," Drake added, looking over at Megan who gave him a scoff before looking away.

"Sorry... I just thought she could help if it came to it. Her class is very beneficial," Chelsea said sheepishly.

"That would be true, if she actually gave me any information about her class. But as it stands she's nothing but a *Malandi* who keeps giving me the stink eye, unless she would like to change that before we start getting into the thick of it?" Drake asked, giving Megan an olive branch.

Megan's head turned back. She opened her mouth apprehensively, but then turned once again to face the other direction.

Seems she's still holding a grudge, Drake thought.

"You did kill the person she thought of as a protector, although she is certainly wrong and being quite a bitch as you said," Natto answered.

Look at you. Surprised you knew that one, I haven't used it yet. Drake smiled internally, then turned his focus back to the concerned Chelsea and the stubborn Megan.

"Then you can leave, Miss Megan. I have no use or tolerance anymore for people who are unproductive or willfully stubborn to what I have to do. You are here under my protection, and you will receive it until we reach Shigure's.

But I won't put up with your behavior—I don't have time for it," Drake said evenly.

Megan's face paled. Her eyebrows furrowed like she was about to say something, but she was stopped by Chelsea and an icy glare from Claire.

"I'm a Priest, you know! I could help if I wanted!" she spat over her shoulder.

Drake gave her an even look. "Do I look like I need a healer? And if you don't want to help, you're no more a Priest than Tom is," Drake said, thumbing to the side.

"Hey! I help! What about that thing yesterday?!" Tom shouted back, his new kiteshield raised with his arms.

Megan's jaw dropped. She growled, but she ended up turning away to leave, passing by Jacqueline, Theodore, Amir, and Harley on the way.

"My lord, what in the name hast thou done to she?" Theodore said, his head following her down the steps.

"I don't know," Drake said, shrugging his shoulders with a smirk. "I just told her she's useless. She didn't seem to like that."

Theodore sighed but moved to stand next to Drake, Harley following and covering her mouth to hide her snicker.

Amir and Jacqueline fell in next to Claire and Chelsea, giving nods and greetings to the rest of the group.

"Sir, what exactly is the news that's so important it requires all of us?" Amir asked, looking around.

Drake scanned over the group before he spoke, surprised by how much they had all changed over the last week they had been together. They'd gone from combative captives to worthwhile party members who would come to defend him at a moment's notice.

"Yeah, what in the bloody hell are ya waking us up for, you sob? It's only noon!" Jacqueline asked snarkily, her hand on her hip as she rubbed some of the tiredness away from her eyes.

Well, almost everyone. Drake smiled.

"Good morning sunshine. Don't worry, I'll be quick so you can go back to sleeping. You really look like you could use the beauty sleep. Wouldn't want your age showing more than it already is." Drake laughed.

"W-What?!" Jacqueline stammered before the rest of the group gave a small awkward chuckle.

"Don't worry, I'll be out of all your hair before you know it," Drake said, switching to a more serious tone. "I wanted you all here so I could explain what'll be happening over the next day and a half."

Drake pulled the treasure map from his inventory, showing it to everyone.

"This was one of the rewards for killing the Royal Knights. It's a treasure map to the King's hoard, and I'm going to go get it," Drake started explaining, everyone's face lifting slightly in intrigue. "But, I'll be going alone," he added. The group's collective expressions contorted into a frown, save for Sherry who was still rubbing her stomach.

"What do you mean? Are you going to just leave us here and go off fighting again?" Claire asked, her scowl deepening.

"No, I'm not," Drake explained, and her face relaxed. "I'm going to leave you at Shigure's."

Claire's mouth instantly turned into a deep frown, but before she could complain, Drake cut her off.

"I know what you'll probably say, but it's going to be the safest place without me here in the outpost. I've got a good friend there," Drake said, looking over to Theodore, his eyes raising with understanding, "and if anything happens, I know he'll make sure you're all safe while I go get whatever is in that hoard."

"Sir, why wouldn't we be able to come?" Amir asked.

Drake looked over to Tom, then back to Amir. "Well, being honest, I'm not confident I can keep you safe on my own. And even with all the progress little Tommy boy has been making, I can't say I'm sure I'll be able to protect anyone other than myself from a swarm of Tyrant Ants, based on what Natto's told me."

Tom's face twisted, conflicted on whether he should feel proud that he had improved or sad that he had missed the mark of Drake's expectations.

"Tom, don't be like that my man. You've come a long way, and if we weren't up against a hive probably five times the size of the goblin army, I wouldn't hesitate to take you and everyone else along. This is one fight I need to take, but I won't be able to take you all with me," Drake explained.

"What are you going to do without my buffs!" Claire protested.

"You damned hothead. You know my little boys would be a godsend against things like that," Hudson added.

"Sir, you can't very well expect us to just agree to you going out alone again. What if you are injured like with the King? Not to mention against that many monsters, my experience buff would only help!" Amir said, also chiming in.

Drake had expected some resistance from them, but he was pleased to know they wanted to tag along. He was most surprised, though, with Chelsea. She looked him in the eyes.

"Shot. You need to take Megan."

"Huh?" Drake replied, raising a brow. "Why would I take her? Didn't you hear what I *just* said?"

"Oh, I heard it and that's exactly why you should take her," Chelsea said, her eyes now struggling to find a place to look. "She... I shouldn't be saying this, but she has very strong combat buffs that would help you."

Drake's interest was piqued.

"What buffs? And if they're so strong, why in the world would she not come forward to help earlier or even try to strike a deal like you and Miss Grumpy did?" Drake asked.

"I'm not grumpy you fucking daft idiot! I just bloody hate you!" Jacqueline shouted.

"See, grumpy. But my point still stands."

Chelsea seemed to struggle for words, but she eventually found her voice again.

"I know you understand people's trauma enough to not fault her for it, but she had a bit of a breakdown when the tutorial started like the majority of us. I mean, everything changed so quickly, and then there were monsters and people killing each other. It was horrific for everyone..." Chelsea began, her face darkening, "and Megan was no exception."

"Yes, but you certainly were, were you not? Mr. Run-into-the-forest-with-no-magic-mage," Natto giggled.

Not now, she's being serious, Drake thought, trying to deflect Natto's jab, his eyebrow twitching ever so slightly from his dark past being brought to light.

Chelsea continued, not knowing about Drake and Natto's conversation within his head.

"When she was pulled in, she was ripped from her boyfriend's apartment right from their bed in the middle of the night. She had already been battling with chronic depression, and he was her rock. So when that bastard Chris came around, he replaced him, and she obviously resents you for killing him, like I'm sure you know. Thankfully, the system and the skill stones she's used have helped a bit with her mental strength, but she still hates you," Chelsea said.

"Where are you going with this?" Drake asked during her pause.

"I mean that you won't pull your punches when you speak to her, and I think she needs that to break through whatever mental block she has keeping her from moving forward. And to boot, her skill set as a buffing healer could only help you. Her, Jacky, and Julia were the main reasons we even got so far. Her buffs are that strong, and they'll only continue to get stronger. I won't ask to come because I know what kind of dead weight I would be in that situation, but at least bring someone who can help you," Chelsea finished.

Drake smiled and placed his hand on her shoulder. Her head tilted upwards to focus on him as a small smile pulled at her lips.

"Well, at least you know you're useless unlike some people here," Drake said. Her smile quickly turned into a frown.

"You're a fucking asshole!" she shouted.

Chapter 3

I'll Think About It

Drake stood at odds with the group, his arms crossed as he stared back at several of them, not wanting to give them any ground.

"I'll think about it," he finally said.

Everyone breathed out a brief sigh of relief, but Theodore soon followed up.

"My lord, what compendium did Lady Natto divulge to you on the temperament and abilities of the Tyrant Ants that hast thee so wary?"

Drake pursed his lips for a moment, recalling the information.

"Tyrant Ants on their own wouldn't be much of a hassle—I'm sure even Sherry could beat one alone if she really had to," he said, pointing to the grumbling little ball of hangriness with his chin. "The problems are one: there are more ants than there were goblins, and even with my stores of mana, I don't think I could keep going nonstop. I'm just not experienced enough. And two: the variety of ants that may be there is troubling."

"How wouldeth that be, my lord? This one hast yet to witness a situation that thou couldst not overcome," Theodore replied.

"That's very flattering, Theo, but the problem is more the ants' levels *and* their classes. From what Natto said, the tutorial isn't allowed to pass a certain number of monsters and monster levels initially and during these ramp up phases," Drake said. He paused, then put up a finger, looking at everyone in turn. "But that's only initially. Whoever or whatever is sponsoring this particular nuthouse of a tutorial was an extra special kind of dick."

"How do you figure that?" Tom asked.

"I will tell you, my good chap! They've selected only monsters that reproduce at an alarming rate. The goblins, apes and now the ants. Everything except the gnolls have exploded past the limit because technically the system doesn't see it as a violation of the rules. Now, that isn't the only problem. It's the fact that this also means the variants are going to be different here in what's essentially captivity compared to in their natural homes. Remember the goblins? How many knights and everything there were?" Drake asked the group.

Everyone nodded, Claire giving a particularly deep scowl as she remembered the nasty monsters.

"Well, I asked Natto about it, and that isn't how it normally is. In any region the goblins normally inhabit, there are multiple kings, and they're constantly at war with each other for resources. Namely breeding rights with the local species..." Drake said, slightly trailing off, but began again after mentally wiping his mouth of the distasteful words. "And this means they die regularly, leaving only a small handful of the variants we saw. Let alone the number of knights this king had. They normally wouldn't have enough resources to form Royal Knights because the knights would die so often, so it has me thinking the Ant Hive might be worse."

"Well, way to spit in our pea soup there, pup. Alright, I'm gonna haul my ass out of going in on this one. I know I'm just a stationary target, and my little guys would only be able to kill so many," Hudson said reluctantly, scratching his growing beard.

"I just want food... You go do whatever you want man, just make lunch already!" Sherry shouted.

Claire looked hesitant, but she stood firm in her desire to come along.

"I'm still coming. You need my buffs if Chelsea's friend doesn't come."

Wow, she won't even use Megan's name. She must really dislike her... Drake thought.

"*I believe the word you are looking for is 'hate.'*" Natto laughed. "*Although I do agree you should take some of them along. If your plans are to stay the same, you will need them to be as strong as possible later on.*"

Yeah, but it also requires them to stay the fuck alive, Drake added.

"Break a few eggs to make omelet rice."

That isn't the saying, and that isn't what we're going for here, Natto. I know you care more about my improvement and well-being but try to give a little thought to other people... Drake sighed.

He changed his focus, bringing his attention back to the group.

"Like I said, I'll think about it. But onto the next issue. We're going to move everyone over to Shigure's, and honestly I want to say it's going to go smoothly, but there're still some knights lurking around somewhere. I'm going to need Theo and Chelsea to scout for us while we move. Hudson, Tom, and Jacqueline are going to have to help me watch the surroundings. Hudson's drones are going to be put to the grindstone for this little move, and your big Tonka T's are going to be lifesavers with their arsenals if anything tries to show up."

Jacqueline spoke up after this, surprisingly voicing her concern for Drake.

"You sure you want to be doing that gov? Don't want to wait another day so I can fix ya arm there?" she asked.

"I would, if I didn't have other plans. We only have around ninety days left as it is, and I don't know how long my plans will take at Shigure's camp or how long it might take to go through the Hive. I've managed this far without an arm," Drake said, raising his jet black earthen one, "and I don't think a few more hours is going to make a difference here. Besides," he said, smiling at Jacqueline, "a deal's a deal, and I know you won't run off before you heal me back good as new. Well, old new. You know what I mean."

Jacqueline rolled her eyes, accepting his reasoning because she didn't want to bother arguing, but the rest of the group still showed some slight concerns.

"Are you really sure, Mr. Shot? You've done so much for everyone. I don't think anyone would fault you for waiting a bit longer for your arm," Harley said from Theodore's side.

"Thank you for your concern, Harley, but it's alright. There is only one direction I can go, and that's forward. And right now that points me at Shigure's. I have something I need to do when we get there, and a person I need to have a good rematch with," Drake said, smiling wider. "Oh! And for everyone here, as thanks for putting up with me, I want to show my trust in you all. *Yes*, even you, Tom." Drake pointed with a smirk.

"Hey! I'm trustworthy!" Tom fired back.

"Right. Anyway, as you all know, Shot is my tutorial alias. And to make it easier for you all to find me if you wish after this tutorial is all said and done, my real name is Jugemu Jugemu Go-Kō-no-Surikire Kaijari-suigyo—" Before Drake could continue the joke, Natto shot out of the side of his head and onto his shoulder.

"You stop right there if you wish to keep your face intact," she threatened.

"Okay, you don't have to be so snippy. Must be the lack of food…" Drake laughed nervously, slowly pushing down her knife from his face. "My real name is Drake Wallen, and I hope to see you all after the tutorial when we someday reunite."

"Wait, was that a death flag…" Tom whispered, his face furrowed, hand meeting his chin in deep thought. "That was a flag, right?"

* * *

With the meeting over, Drake and the group headed to the area that was now deemed the 'kitchen' for the outpost. Most of the outpost had settled down and gotten used to life here over the week, especially with the addition of more normal activities to do like the sports fields Tom and Drake had made.

Some even took it upon themselves to put many tents together to make indoor arenas for other games. One such game was an interesting card game involving monsters that they'd seen in the tutorial along with many of the more prominent figures in the outpost.

Drake had gotten to watch some of the people play with them and was surprised to see that the cards were made out of actual thick paper—well, mana paper. The cards came in a similar form as the trading cards that they had before the system, but the illustrations were more manga-esque. Some even moved.

What made him give a giddy internal squeal of boyish delight was when he saw a card modeled after himself. But it quickly turned to confusion when he saw the scene on the card. It was of him fighting the Goblin King in his Septanarus Heretical Endowment Form, which no one should have been a witness to.

Drake shrugged it off as a good way to spread misinformation and let it be. No one should've been able to witness what he'd done during that fight, and he'd sown enough seeds that no one besides his inner circle knew of his real abilities and class.

That and the card was so cool looking that he couldn't bring himself to take it from the owner and destroy it.

The cards were very interesting to Drake; he'd begun collecting them himself in his pastime, trading skill stones for his initial deck.

Refocusing, Drake and the group began prepping the food for lunch.

Since his return, he'd had to have some of the other people help with cooking. He'd been bedridden for several days, after all. They'd learned quickly, but it seemed Drake still had the magic touch that people craved.

"Why does it always taste better when you cook? We do the same exact thing," Claire grumbled as she began slicing chunks of boar into small cubes.

"I'm just that good at everything I do. These hands here," Drake said, showing his spice covered fingers, "*these* are magic."

Claire rolled her eyes, going back to cutting the meat.

"*The only magic you have is the supernatural ability to ward off the opposite sex.*" Natto giggled from inside his head.

Oh, we shall see. Don't think I've forgotten about our little bet. Just you wait till I find a girl to my standards. Drake chuckled.

"*I hardly think your standards matter. Certainly you will have to wait lifetimes before you find someone willing to tolerate you,*" Natto countered.

I think I've already found plenty. Drake smiled, looking to his left and right at the line of people cutting, prepping food with him, and chatting happily to one another.

"Alright, let's start the stew then. It's a shame we don't have rice though... I miss my rice cooker..." Drake sighed, bringing over his pot of prepped spices to the cauldrons and placing a small amount in each one.

The rest of the line followed him, putting each of their ingredients into the respective pots. Others placed the skewered meat onto the grill screens that Hudson had made using his old welding skills.

Drake nodded, looking at the operations going smoothly.

"Good, that should set us for food for a bit. I'm going to the mines until we're ready to leave tomorrow. Theo has his instructions on getting everyone ready. Claire, you're in charge of the food till it's done, and if you would please bring some into the mines for me later, I'd appreciate it," Drake directed, turning to the mines without waiting for an answer.

After a few moments of walking, he reached the entrance of the mine where a gruff man waited with a pickaxe resting on his shoulder.

"Took you long enough, ya damned idjit. You like cookin' too much, but that food does be mighty tasty so can't blame ya. Either way, ya ready pup?" Hudson asked.

Drake gave a scoff, then pulled out his own pickaxe from his quest.

"Oh I'm very ready to pick this place clean. Let's get to it, ya old bastard!" Drake laughed back.

"Old? The hell you think I'm old fer? I'm only damn near twenty-two."

"*Liar! Falsehoods and deceit!*" Natto shouted, deafening Drake's ears.

Shielding his ears out of habit, Drake winced and looked back up to Hudson.

"There's no way you're that young. What's with calling everyone pup if you're younger than 90% of the tutorial?" Drake asked.

Hudson rubbed his nose and walked to the mine's door.

"Just something I picked up working with older dogs in the machine shop. Thought it made me sound more manly. Works, don't it?" Hudson said, smiling.

"It—Yeah, I guess it does, huh... Imagine that, speech doing such things, pup," Drake said, trying the word out.

"Don't do that. That's mine," Hudson said flatly. His face was deadpan, and his accent was somehow gone.

Chapter 4
Familiar Faces

The grunts of the two men echoed through the tunnel as they struck the wall of treasure, excavating the valuable gems, stones, and materials with each blow.

"Just about finished, I think, Hudson. Can't believe we got through it all," Drake chimed in between his strikes.

"Truth be told, didn't think we'd manage to get all of it. But did we really have to get all of it?" Hudson asked over his shoulder, hitting his portion of the wall.

You have increased Mining to Proficiency 5.
You have reached max Profession Proficiency.
Increase your Overall Rank to move on to the next Rank. Any additional Profession Experience will be lost.

You have increased Material Identification to Proficiency 5.
You have reached max Profession Proficiency.
Increase your Overall Rank to move on to the next Rank. Any additional Profession Experience will be lost.

"And that's what I've been waiting for, baby! Wooo!" Drake yelled, his voice reverberating off the walls.

Hudson recoiled, covering his ears.

"God damn it ya idjit, did ya have to holler like that? I'm right next to ya, ya bastard! And why in Sam Hill did you amplify it with your gosh darn magic?" Hudson growled.

"For extra effect!" Drake said with a smile and began waving. "Come on you old-goat-who's-technically-a-young-goat, if you're not a lying goat. Let's go see some daylight. I think we have enough materials to build a Death Star." Drake finished waving his hand, splashing water over his head to cool himself and wash off some of the sweat.

Drake offered a ball of water to Hudson as well, but Hudson waved him off with his hand and a shake of his head.

"I'll do it myself, thank ya. Water you use is always too cold, and I'd rather not turn inside out," he said.

Drake raised his eyebrow for a moment but then let the comment pass, not wanting to even acknowledge the awkward joke. He remembered what he'd done to a Goblin Knight not so long ago.

Both of them placed their pickaxes back into their inventory and made their way through the main shaft of the mines, working their way to the door. Neither one talked much until they reached the exit, where Hudson spoke up.

"So, pup. I don't think I ever got a chance to ask ya, but what're your plans when we eventually get out of this damned infernal death scenario?"

Drake tilted his head, giving it a bit of thought.

"As far as what?" Drake asked.

"Don't beat around the bush. Far as everything. Do you think, strong as you are, it'll be enough? Are ya going to keep going on killing sprees even on Earth or whatever hellish version of it it is now?" Hudson clarified.

Drake moved to lean on the wall, his hands behind his head.

"I think it'll pretty much be the same. I won't know exactly until we leave, but my main plan is to find my family and make a place where they can be safe. I have two brothers who can take care of themselves, but I don't think they'll do very well in what the system is doing on Earth..." Drake mused, his face dimming slightly. "But I have confidence they and my mom are going to make it. And if they somehow don't," he paused, his face going steely, "whoever touched them better pray to whatever god they can that I don't find them."

Hudson shivered. Not from the statement or its contents, but from the expression Drake had on his face as he spoke.

"R-Right. Well, what are you going to call this place of yours? I would be remiss if I didn't turn up eventually," he asked, trying to change the topic.

"Hmm," Drake thought, humming for a moment. "I have a few names but nothing concrete. Lots to still figure out, and Natto can only tell me so much before we leave the tutorial apparently, or the big scary system might smite her."

"It can do that?"

"I haven't seen anything yet, but if she's barred from saying something, I trust it's for a good reason."

"Well shit, ain't that a coyote taking the house cat type of situation if I ever heard it."

Drake's face screwed up into a mess of confusion.

"Huh? Punyeta, what in the world is that saying?" Drake laughed, finally opening the door, the light of the next day beaming through and forcing the pair to shield their eyes.

"Just means a fucked up, ass-backward situation, pup." Hudson chuckled, stepping through the door into the outpost.

"I might have to use that one. Confuse the hell out of someone," Drake said, his face curling into a grin.

Both the men gave a chuckle then looked out into the outpost.

The entirety of the camps had been packed up, only the sports fields remaining along with some remnants of campfire pits here and there. An ocean of people stood near the gate of the outpost milling about.

"Looks like Theo did a bang up job." Drake whistled.

"This one is pleased thou feels that way, my lord," Theodore said, shimmering into view next to Drake, his head in a half-bow.

Drake had gotten used to Theodore appearing whenever his name was spoken in true butler fashion. Hudson, on the other hand, jumped at the sudden appearance of the man.

"God damn it! Do you all have to do that?! Just because y'all have invisibility skills don't mean you got to use them like that all the damned time!" he croaked.

"What do you mean, Hudson?" a voice from behind him said as Chelsea also shimmered out of her cloaking ability.

"Son of a bitch! I said stop it, you damned idiots!" he shouted, storming off to the crowd in the distance.

"You two are going to have to do that more often." Drake laughed.

"It *is* pretty fun since he doesn't have a detection skill." Chelsea giggled. "So, how were the mines? Get everything you wanted?" she asked.

"Everything and more, which will be good for when I have to trade some of it at the outpost. And now I can finally get that rare trading card fucking Jimmy has been holding out on..."

"Rare what, my lord?" Theodore asked, not hearing him clearly.

Drake cleared his throat.

"Nothing, some rare equipment I was looking for. Anyway, is everything going smoothly?" Drake asked back.

"Yeah, everyone was just waiting for you two to come out. Claire and Harley have been making sure everyone's in line. Theo's been on top of making sure people are packed and prepared as well," Chelsea answered.

"Thank you, *Theodore*, for your amazing report," Drake said, looking at Chelsea, her face reddening as she winced slightly with an awkward giggle. "As long as everything's ready, I think it's about time we get moving. Theo, did you get the person I asked for?"

Theodore nodded. "The woman 'tis thitherward, my lord," he said, pointing to the gate.

Drake nodded. "Good! Then let's get this train a-chugging! Next stop: tomato town!"

"*I hate it here...*" Natto sighed.

* * *

"Alright! Everyone settled?" Drake shouted over the crowd of people as he stood on top of his usual guard tower. "This is only going to be a few hours' journey, but everyone stay calm and vigilant! Those of you with identification, observation, and aura sense skills and the like will be on the outside of the group to identify any threats! I've placed members of my group within the caravan to help with anything. You all know who they are and what they're capable of, so there's no need to worry! Hudson has gone all out with his skills to give us the utmost protection with his little dudes. And if anything shows up that might even *look* at us the wrong way, you can rest assured I will make sure it regrets it!" Drake finished with a booming voice, using his magic to make it reach the entire group.

"Color me surprised, that was actually not a bad speech. Usually you'd say something mad," Jacqueline jabbed.

"Yeah well, something like this is going to have tensions high, so no need to joke around. But don't worry; I have some *spicy* ones ready if anyone tries to do anything." Drake laughed.

Jacqueline rolled her eyes and scoffed, looking over the crowd below them. Harley and Sherry were also with them. Sherry needed protection and so did Jacqueline as their sole high-potency healer.

With the addition of Julia and Megan, they had some more powerful healers now, but Jacqueline far outstripped them in raw healing efficiency. It may also be that Drake didn't want to lose the only person who could heal his arm right now. There were of course other healers within their mass of people, but they unfortunately paled in comparison to the ones he knew personally.

A byproduct of Drake and his team protecting the majority of the outpost was that many of the people within had stalled on levels, the average being around level 12. Most also only had common or uncommon classes. Anyone with a rare or better class was unwilling to join Drake.

Those people, as well as many of the other survivors of the horrors of the goblin invasion, had been scared and traumatized to the point that they wished to never see another monster. And Drake could understand.

He didn't like to mention it, but many of the women he'd saved from the goblin camps had given birth to the creatures during their time in the outpost.

Wincing at the thought, Drake remembered how hectic it had been when the first incident had happened. Since then they'd set up measures, but every event was not a pleasant one and only fueled his anger and vindication for killing the king.

Despite all of this, many of the survivors had progressed leaps and bounds since then. The system, if good for nothing else, had helped many of them become resilient to the mental traumas, albeit only slightly. Claire had also helped by forming a group where the survivors could speak and express their traumas to others safely.

The entire ordeal was the worst of the issues the outpost had dealt with over the week that Drake was essentially out of commission.

Some people had taken him not being in full capacity as a green light to do whatever they wanted in the camp, but it was quickly snuffed out by the rest of his party members. The rulebreakers were placed into the cage with the rest of the naughty naughty people.

Unfortunately, Drake didn't have the heart to do away with them and instead placed them under the watch of Tom, Hudson, and Amir at the end of the group. The worst of the culprits were placed under an oath made by Sherry to not flee and to cooperate on the way to Shigure's camp, where they would be tried for their crimes by a third party.

With everything settled, Drake gave one last booming shout outward as he moved to the center of the group. There, he was in reach of his party for the initial move.

"My soldiers, rage. My soldiers, scream. My soldiers, fight!" Drake chanted as his aura spread out from him, encompassing and flowing over tens of people as he increased the proficiency to 2. This allowed him to double the number of people, effectively reducing the cooldown by several minutes and increasing the effects and duration for several minutes as well.

Drake nodded to his party members around him, and they all moved to their designated positions. Chelsea and Theodore shimmered out of vision, cloaking themselves in their skills. Harley moved to the front to help with scouting alongside Drake, Sherry, and Jacqueline.

Hudson, Amir, and Tom moved to the rear. Hudson's robots dispersed as drones began to hover overhead, his two big boys spreading out evenly in the rest of the group.

Drake opened the gate, then turned to the woman that Theodore had found for him.

"Miss Braun, pleasure to meet you. After you," Drake said, offering her the lead to guide the way.

The brown-haired, average height woman nodded tersely as she kept her distance from Drake, not bothering to speak while shaking ever so slightly.

"Ugh, another one..." Natto sighed.

She is hardly being aggressive. She was one of the victims of the goblins; I can't very well be mad that she's apprehensive to be near me and to have to guide us, Drake shot back.

"Why even ask her to lead, we know where we are going do we not?"

It's about having everyone feel included and participating. They may not like it now, but once we get to the camp, I hope they'll feel at least some accomplishment and relief from making and contributing to the journey. I'm trying to build people up, not have a flock of mindless followers who just fall in line like chicks. Besides, if I've noticed, I'm sure you have as well. There are a few people here that shouldn't be. I need them to think we're spread thin, and people within the group are easy targets. Why do you think I had Theo and Chelsea 'scout' ahead? Drake mused.

Drake followed in tandem with Miss Braun as the rest of the makeshift caravan of people moved with them. He made sure to stay alert, scanning the surroundings and stretching his Aura sense as far as possible as he looked for anything out of the ordinary.

"Hey... I'm hungry, Shot. Do you have any more snacks dude?" Sherry grumbled, dragging her feet.

"Didn't ya just eat? Damned endless black hole of a stomach you got there, Sherry. Wish I could eat as much as all that," Jacqueline said, her face wrinkling and turning a tinge green.

"I just use up a lot of mental energy... Uhhh..." Sherry continued to groan as she picked up the pace and grabbed at Drake's sleeve.

"Fine, fine. Don't pull at me. You're a grown woman, why do you act like a little pet?" Drake chuckled wryly, pulling out some pork skewers he had saved. "Here, now ju—"

Drake cut himself off when he felt a disturbance in his sphere. His eyes honed in on a person with a cloaking skill on.

Drake quickly snapped his fingers and changed to his Lightning Endowment, his hair cascading into a bright yellow hue and his tattoo shimmering in a similar fashion as he surged forward, his left arm gripping at the air.

"Who are you?" Drake asked evenly, startling the surrounding people in the caravan as he appeared.

For a moment, Drake glared at the invisible person as they refused to reveal themselves. He clicked his tongue, gripping his fingers more tightly around whatever he had a hold of. Beads of red quickly flowed from under his fingertips, outlining the form of a person from the waist down as a scream shrieked out.

The person quickly lost their concentration under Drake's pressure. The skill dispersed, revealing a man in all black, his face covered by a familiar mask that Drake had seen before. And his identification skill was useless.

Cw%odi2n Level *1nC

The man coughed and struggled under Drake's ironclad grip, both of his hands clawing at Drake's before he spoke in a seething tone.

"You're too late... Thanks for finally leaving your damned hole with such juicy experience and TP!"

Drake's head turned as a scream rang out from the back of the group.

"Shit."

Chapter 5
Copycat Joker

Drake rushed in the direction of the scream, the man within his grip in tow.

What awaited him was beyond what he'd expected. More than ten people were lined up, each one holding a person hostage with blades of all shapes and sizes against their necks.

More people with high level stealth skills. God, I hate stealth classes! Everyone picks them! Drake cursed.

In the hands of the familiar-looking people were members of the caravan, and in particular, one Drake recognized by name stood in the center.

Megan.

Somehow, she'd been taken by the man in the middle, who struck Drake as familiar, but he couldn't place why. His identification skill wasn't able to glean any information either.

The man in Drake's grip continued to struggle in vain. Drake's fingers burrowed deeper into the man's flesh.

"Oi, jackass. Let my guy go, unless you want to see the pretty miss here bite the dust in a very painful way," the man said, a smirk on his face.

Out of the ten people lined up, he was the only one showing his face, but Drake couldn't place why.

Drake took in the surroundings. Megan was the only one he personally knew that was taken hostage—the rest he didn't know by name, but they were under his protection all the same.

Drake began to relax, but he didn't let go of his Endowment. The man seemed to not know that it was a spell, so he planned to use that to his advantage.

He did as the man asked, slowly releasing the man in his grip, His left hand dotted red from the puncture wounds he'd inflicted.

The man gave a scream and a yelp when he was dropped to the ground, but quickly scrambled to make his way over to the rest of the group.

"Dumbass. Don't you know ya never negotiate?" The man sneered, slowly moving his knife to the side of Megan's face. She gave a sharp muffled scream that came out in a whine. "Now, what are we gonna do with all of you? Went and gave us some nice stuff here on a silver platter, huh?"

Drake stayed silent, biding his time. His experience with Stewart had taught him that it was better to just let the crazy ones talk while looking for an opening.

The man's brow twitched, apparently not getting the reaction he wished for from Drake.

"I'm talking to you, asshole! The fuck are you, an NPC?! How did someone like you kill Stewart anyway?" he shouted in anger.

Drake's body subtly stiffened at the mention of Stewart's name.

He knows Stewart? Drake thought, keeping his eyes locked on the man now.

"Is he perhaps another worker from your job, Drake?" Natto asked, slightly confused as well.

No, I've never met him, but he looks familiar. I can't place it... Is it from his rank up?

"Doesn't matter. You've got quite a big bag of TP on ya, don't ya, Shot, little buddy!" The man laughed. "But, seems like you've gained a few levels recently, so you can't all be show. Strip," said the man, deadpan.

Drake's brows raised.

Is this guy a pervert?

"You heard me prick, strip. All that armor and gear, take it off," the man said again. "That is, unless you want us to kill everyone ahead of schedule?"

After the man spoke, more people began to walk out from the crowd, placing black masks over their faces and changing into gear Drake hadn't seen in the camp before.

"Little insects... Do not dare do what he is asking," Natto demanded. *"You do not need to put yourself in the way of what is happening. Kill that man now before he simply demands more and more."*

No. It'll be fine. I've looked at the leaderboards. Worst case he's level 22, Joker. But I don't think anyone at that level can compete with me even without gear; my base stats are just too high. And he doesn't seem to know I can change my stats through my spells. I've said it before, but I won't willingly accept loss of life, Drake thought firmly.

Drake questioned the man's motives but didn't protest, slowly removing pieces of equipment one item at a time.

"What the fuck is that?" the man muttered after Drake had begun removing his robe and shirt, revealing his bare chest full of scars and his earthen black arm attached at the shoulder.

Drake said nothing, continuing to remove his equipment until he was in his trunks.

"I said everything, ya deaf moron! Ya undies too—can't be too safe on what might be an item nowadays. Come now, don't be shy." The man sneered.

Drake frowned, but assented.

Alright, maybe he's taking it a bit too far, he thought.

Drake removed his last remaining piece of clothing, standing stark naked in front of hundreds of people. His body had changed since his rank up, and outside of his scars and missing arm, not a blemish was on him. His body was lean and muscular, his face strong and stoic as he looked back at the man.

"Good." The man pointed over to someone from the crowd. "You, grab his shit." He then pointed back to Drake. "And you, pretty boy, come closer so I can touch ya."

Drake again furrowed his brows in confusion, but took measured steps forward until he was within an arm's length of the man holding Megan. Her eyes averted from Drake in embarrassment.

Oh, that might be awkward later... Hope it doesn't traumatize her, Drake thought, mentally shrugging.

"Nice. Now just a little touch, and we can have some good old-fashioned experience farming!" the man said with glee, reaching his knife hand out to touch Drake's cheek.

But this was what Drake had been waiting for. The moment the man's hand made contact with his flesh, he sprung into action.

Using his Martial Skill, he put power into his left arm, throwing it past Megan's head right for the man's. It shot forward like a bullet, near instantaneously connecting with the man's face.

Rocketing backward, Megan was left unharmed in the same position, but Drake couldn't stop there.

Before the rest could react, he quickly dropped his Endowment and snapped his fingers to summon bolts of lightning, allowing one to hold more mana than the others.

"Heretical Endowment! Single!" Drake chanted as he snapped. The powerful bolt of lightning pushed his Endowment effect even further as he moved with speed incomparable to before.

Moving between the ten hostages, he placed ten lightning bolts into the skulls of the people in masks, the small holes smoking from their heads as they fell to the ground—instantly dead.

You have killed participant Raymond Howley Level 16.
Experience earned. 46,255 TP have been awarded.

You have killed participant Roberta Hernandez Level 14.
Experience earned. 39,255 TP have been awarded.

You have killed participant Omar Abbar Level 16.
Experience earned. 86,255 TP have been awarded.

You have killed participant William Lanken Level 12.
Experience earned. 26,465 TP have been awarded.

...

The notifications poured in as Drake moved to gather the people who had been captured. Making sure to handle them with care, he used his wind magic to gently herd them back into the caravan of people.

"Thank you... but don't touch me! You're still naked!" Megan hollered, her face turning a shade of red.

Drake scoffed, dropping his head a bit.

Really... Can't I get just a thank you once in a while? he thought bittersweetly, once again surprised that he'd felt nothing while killing the captors.

Drake's eyes went to the man who'd gathered his equipment.

"Those are mine," he said evenly, his aura flexing as the man fell backwards, dropping the equipment.

"All yours bro! Just don't kill me!" he shouted back, looking at Drake like he was a monster.

"Depends on if you continue to be a dumbass," he said. He reached for his robe, his hand lowering to grab it. "That goes for the re—" Drake was suddenly cut off by someone grabbing his wrist.

Looking up, it was the man he had punched before, his hair a vibrant yellow. The same color as Drake's.

"Oi, this shit is fire! No wonder you can move so fast!" the man cackled, wild-eyed.

Drake looked at the man, confused for only a second before the man tried to strike him. With his increased dexterity, Drake dodged the first blow, then the second and the third. The pair was suddenly locked into a rapid exchange of fists as Drake tried to parse what was going on. He was able to maintain pace with the man even without his equipment, making him even more confused.

After a few seconds of exchanging punches, Drake began casting spells which the man mirrored, laughing all the while.

Drake again furrowed his brows in surprise. The man was able to keep up with Drake as far as spell capacity, but Drake's spells were winning out handily, obviously more powerful, and soon he began to push the man back.

"Oh?! So that's how you do it, huh? This is just like that one game!" The man laughed with glee. "More mana, more power, huh?!"

The man barked another laugh as he jumped backward, his hair cascading into a pure snow white as he summoned a large white fireball.

Drake's eyes widened in understanding.

He has all my skills? Punyeta, what is going on?! He didn't steal them. Did he copy them?! he shouted internally.

Drake quickly summoned ice to do the same, cursing that he couldn't bring out his staff without his shawl. Clicking his tongue, he made a large earthen wall that covered him and the people around him. He'd have to make do.

The fireball collided with the jet-black wall, which barely held up as it drained Drake's mana. Eventually, the wall melted down in a bombardment of white flames.

Through the center of the wall that was melting like liquid taffy, Drake saw the man grinning ear to ear.

"Guess you're probably wondering what's going on, aren't cha? Ya dumb fucking mongrel!" the man shouted as he summoned another two fireballs into his hands.

"No, I've pretty much got it. You're some kind of weak copycat version, right?" Drake said, his expression showing how unimpressed he was.

The man's face contorted in indignation, then bloomed into a shade of red-hot anger that Drake had never seen before.

"W-Weak?! Motherfucker, I'm the main character of this fucking shit-hole story! You aren't going to stop me! I'm going to fucking kill everyone around you while you fucking watch! Then I'm going to kill you slowly as I savor your last breaths! That sweet TP'll push me straight to the top! I'm Joker! *I'm Death, straight up!* A better version of you than you could ever be!"

Drake scoffed, snapping his fingers as his Endowment and his right arm faded away, dust in the wind.

He glared daggers at the man, his aura coming to bear as he flexed it against him.

"*Marked,*" Drake whispered. The man winced under his gaze, but soon found his smile again.

"Two can play it, you stupid bastard! *Marked!*" the man repeated, mirroring Drake word for word.

The feeling of his own skill hit him, but it wasn't as impactful as Drake would have thought.

Does he not have the same proficiency as I do through his class? My Indomitability didn't go off, so I guess this type of status effect isn't counted as a debuff.

Drake began summoning all the elements at his disposal, preparing for his spell. He then quickly began chanting all of his skills.

"*I am the shield, I am the rampart! Bulwark! I am the wall on which my enemies billow. Unbreakable! On blessed wings! Guardian's Reprieve!*" Drake shouted in succession, his naked body shimmering in three flashes of green.

Joker followed Drake's chants word for word, his own body flashing with green light as he completed each skill.

Then Drake finished his original spell.

"*Heretical Endowment! Septenarius!*"

Drake's body shone in a kaleidoscope of cascading colors, his hair and tattoos shifting back and forth before finally finding equilibrium in the even shifting of the spell.

Joker smiled and followed suit, casting the same spell.

"*Heretical Endowment! Septenarius!*"

But the spell didn't activate. The elements that Joker had conjured all continued to float around him as he looked on, dumbfounded.

Drake moved to meet him face to face in all his birthday suit glory.

"Thought so. You can wear my shoes, but you'll *never* fill them." Drake grinned and threw a quick jab, his fist connecting with the center of Joker's face.

Joker lurched backward from the impact of the blow, blood and teeth spattering the surroundings.

Drake shook his hand for a moment. His own defensive skills used against him were a tough wall to break through, even with his Endowment.

But he didn't stop there. Drake collected himself and moved quickly, stepping behind Joker. He threw an upward kick, sending Joker flying into the air with a thunderous boom, the spells Joker had conjured evaporating as they couldn't keep up with the speed at which he was launched upward.

Drake bent down, sending a small pellet of earth into the floor below him. Using his earth magic, he manipulated the ground. It fully engulfed him, then hurtled him upward to follow Joker, leaving the forest floor in chaos.

He skyrocketed upwards, eventually passing Joker's body that was now bent into an upside down 'U' as it fought against the momentum of his kick.

Now above Joker, Drake wound his fist backwards, using his might to propel it into the flying man. His strength collided with the rocketing body.

Drake heard an audible crack from his own fist as he caught a glimpse of Joker's hair shifting to brown.

Bastard's still lucid enough to switch Endowments. But he's going to run out soon! Drake laughed internally.

Joker's body flew toward the ground at an unparalleled speed, the blow from Drake changing his trajectory. Drake quickly used his wind magic in tandem with his fire to shoot himself downward as well.

Joker careened towards the earth like a falling star. A moment before he hit the ground, he vanished.

Fuck. Never thought I'd be upset about having a movement skill. Drake cursed, but he quickly found where Joker had moved to using Marked from earlier.

Drake's head snapped above him as he used his own magic to steady himself, killing his momentum.

"Y-You fuhkin! Peece of shit! I told shew dis is my shtory!" Joker yelled through his broken jaw and missing teeth, his hands raised in a very familiar anime stance.

A lightbulb went up in Drake's mind as he saw the glowing ball of white forming above Joker, illuminating his broken face enough for him to recognize the man.

"Wait, you're the guy from the start of the tutorial?! You're a weeb?!" Drake said, honestly surprised.

"I'm nauht a weeb! I'm a fuhking Otahku you fuhking prick!" Joker screamed in hysteria as the ball of white magic began expanding outward.

"I don't care what you are, you're disrespecting the source material! How dare you use that move as a villain!" Drake shouted back, shaking his head and forming a platform of earth below him to stand on in the air.

Joker screeched in frustration as he looked down at Drake with blood-thirst in his eyes.

"*Sperit! Boh—*" Joker tried to shout, but he was interrupted by a deep voice that somehow reached him and reverberated in his chest, breaking his concentration.

"*Ka-me-ha-me...*" Drake began chanting slowly, his voice growing into a roar, eyes flashing between the colors of his skills: a brilliant blue, green and yellow.

In Drake's left hand, a pure white ball of condensed fire formed. Drake added a layer of lightning around the ball, the magic crackling in anticipation of release as his hair continued to cascade in the color of his elements.

Drake turned his head up, staring at Joker with a laughing smile.

"Let's see who the real protagonist is, you filthy villain side character!" Drake yelled almost in a cackle. "*Haaaaa!!*"

Drake threw his only arm forward, the ball of fire and lightning extending forward like a beam of light, hurtling toward Joker.

In a panic, Joker threw his spell forward as well, not bothering to finish the incantation as the huge ball of white fire loomed over him.

Within moments, the two spells collided, each one vying for ground against the other. Both Drake and Joker screamed as they poured their will and mana into the spells.

Drake slowly began to win out, his spell and Endowments helping him inch forward. Joker began to struggle as he apparently became more and more exhausted as the back and forth went on.

But Drake wasn't done. He knew his victory was certain, but now of all times, he desired a complete and total victory.

"And this! This is how you break through limits as the main character, you fucking joke!" Drake shouted. He dumped his spare FP into his intelligence, pushing it to 684. A new bolt of lightning and a gust of wind formed below him. "*This is to go even further beyond! Kaioken! Times Ten!!!*" Drake roared as he used his new lightning and wind spell to form a lightning aura around himself, his hair blowing wildly from the upward gust.

Drake's spell surged forward, colliding with Joker's at the point of impact before traveling through it and piercing through the man. His final words rang out through the air, reaching Drake even through the cacophony of booms and explosions.

"KA-KA-ROTTTTTTTT!!"

You have killed participant Joker - Richard Fuerle Level 22. Experience earned. 4,573,425 TP have been awarded.

Congratulations! You have reached Elemental Miller level 20. 40 FP have been awarded.

Chapter 6
Cleaning Up

The platform that Drake had formed with his magic slowly crumbled under the pressure of his spell. As he fell through the splitting cracks at the center, his Heretical Endowment faded, leaving only his Water Endowment to recover his status.

Plummeting to the ground, Drake made out that no one had moved from their positions prior to him leaping into the air after Joker. Even the man Drake had caught before the incident was somehow still there, his mouth agape in bewilderment at the fight that had just ensued.

Drake landed safely, his status slowly recovering, but he was still in a fragile state from his spell's backlash. Thankfully the spell wasn't as crippling as the first time he'd used it—the extra use of the potion played a big part in that.

Looking around, he again spotted his equipment right where he'd left it next to a shivering and frightened man.

"W-What are you?!" the man shouted loudly as Drake walked towards him. His shout snapped the surrounding people out of their trances, and everyone began to let go of their held breaths.

Drake lifted an eyebrow, unsure how to answer.

"I'm still human, can be an asshole when it suits me though. And right now. At this very moment. Slightly chilly. Now let me put my clothes back on, will you? Can cut diamonds with these things," Drake said, looking down at his chest with a snarky grin.

Drake reached down, pulling up his trunks as he heard a shout from behind him. The familiar voice of the auburn-haired archer rang clearly through the area.

"What happened?! Megan! Are you okay?! Shot! Why are you naked?! Put some clothes on you weirdo!" she shouted as Drake turned to face her, her hand going up to block her eyes, but Drake didn't fail to notice that she was still looking through the cracks between her fingers.

Drake rolled his eyes and put on his shawl first, then placed the rest of his equipment into his inventory to put them all on at once through the inventory window.

"I was forced to strip, *thank you very much*, and I have about two hundred witnesses that can attest to that, Judge Judy," Drake quipped. "Thanks for your concern..."

Shimmering into view next was Theodore, his face concerned as Harley and Claire ran from the front and finally caught up with Drake and the rest of his group. Sherry wobbled back and forth many steps behind them.

"W-What happened?" Claire asked, out of breath as she leaned on her staff.

"Oh, you know," Drake said, turning to give her a quick wave of his hand. "Differing opinions on story importance." He smiled.

Drake flicked his shawl, a red potion falling out of the air which he grabbed and downed in a single gulp.

"Ugh, tastes like rotten strawberries. What I wouldn't do for one of Bear's potions..."

"*You call fighting over imaginary characters a difference of opinions?*" Natto scoffed.

Hey, he's like the OG. Not everyone can use that move. Especially some half-wit villain. The guy was my childhood hero! Drake countered, looking around at the still mostly-stunned people.

"*A man who ate his body weight several times over every other episode, neglected his children until he needed them to 'train,' beat the shit out of them on a regular basis, put a six-year-old on a different planet to fight a super-powered alien, and lest we certainly forget, another alien was also a better father figure than he was to his own children. That childhood hero?"* Natto asked.

Yep, that one. And don't you forget it! And hey, beating the shit out of your kids and putting them in traumatizing near-death experiences is standard for anime dads! Drake defended.

Drake was forced to put his back and forth on hold as he saw some of the people in black who had revealed themselves begin trying to chant spells and skills to escape.

Moving quickly to intercept them, Drake snapped his hand, replacing his missing arm with one made of ice. Leaping forward, he began placing ice collars on each person and attaching them to the next until he had well over twenty people in icy collars.

"Oh no, none of you are going anywhere, not after the risk I just took to get you all to show your true colors. All of you and I are going to become very close friends until we reach the camp," Drake said, his eyes flaring through each skill color. "*Very* close friends." He smiled.

"What in the back alley, tomcat hell was that explosion we just seen?" Hudson said, finally joining the group from the back of the caravan, several of his drones flying above him.

"Is everyone going to ask the same question? Bad guys show up, I went *pew pew* with magic, I win, bad guys die," Drake said sarcastically, miming a gun with his left hand and firing off a few imaginary bullets.

"Oh... that right, is it?" Hudson replied, taking a look around at the rubble in the middle of the ground and at Drake holding a line of people in ice shackles. "Must have been a big bullet then, pup."

"Oh you know me, flashy, flashy." Drake chuckled. "Now, do we have chains for these guys or do I really have to haul them around?" he asked, his playful mood fading as he looked around. "If I wasn't such a bleeding heart for fairness, I'd just do it myself, but it's only right that they're tried by an objective third party..." Drake finished reluctantly.

"They hardly deserve such rights. They have been a part of a group that has killed since the start of the tutorial," Natto said, confronting Drake.

True. But this way, they'll be put to trial in front of thousands of people instead of just hundreds, showing the rest of the tutorial what happens to people who indiscriminately kill others for whatever reason, Drake amended.

"I must take back my previous statement. You might be far more evil than I have given you credit for," Natto conceded, a sliver of concern in her voice.

Call it what you will, but it's a good deterrent for anyone thinking of doing the same just because they're a little stronger than others. I'm sure it won't be the last time I'll have to make an example of others... Drake thought, his face visibly dimming.

"Sire?" Theodore asked, moving from one of the people he was placing chains onto to get closer to Drake. "Art thou feeling adverse from thy spells?"

Drake shook his head. "No, I'm just... a little disappointed in people, that's all."

"What? For what bloody reason? Don't try to level with me and say you think these cunts deserve anything other than what's coming to them?" Jacqueline said, finally entering the conversation.

"Oh, aren't you just a peach, Jacqueline. Always know what to say in the moment," Drake said sarcastically, melting his ice spell from around the necks of the now chained prisoners.

"I do, don't I? Bout bloody time yo—Wait, you're being sarcastic aren't you?" she realized.

Drake snorted then readdressed the group.

"Alright everyone, we're going to take a moment to reorganize. Anyone who's hurt beyond your regenerative abilities, please come forward to get what you need to heal. Then we're going to keep moving; we have a few more hours until we reach the camp, and we want to make it there before noon!" Drake shouted over the group, earning him some distant gazes.

Drake tilted his head, wondering what was going on.

Turning to Claire, he asked, "Is something wrong?"

She shrugged her shoulders, unsure herself.

"Are we really not going to talk about it?" Tom said, suddenly speaking up.

"Talk about what?" Drake asked.

"About how you basically fla—" Tom tried to explain before Amir put his hand to his mouth.

"No, we will not speak of it. Please ignore Tom, sir. He doesn't know what he's saying," Amir said, cutting him off.

Drake caught most of what Tom was getting at and simply shrugged. He noticed some glances coming from Chelsea and even more embarrassed and confused ones from Megan. Both had seen him stark naked.

"Eh, doesn't bother me. I'm sure I have a picture or two on the internet showing it off. In fact, I'd be surprised if I didn't," Drake said, honestly unperturbed.

Trying to change the conversation, Drake turned to their guide.

"Miss Braun, once everyone is settled, please lead us the rest of the way," Drake said, giving her a knowing glare, his aura spreading out ever so slightly.

"Y-Yes, of course!" she answered.

"*Drake?*" asked Natto.

Oh, you didn't know? She's part of their group. You said it yourself; I don't need a guide to get to the camp. But I did need someone to lead us astray or, you know, into a trap, Drake replied.

"*Then what was that all about cohesion and participation?*"

It's still true, but killing a few birds with one very large, oversized rock is also good.

"*Do you not mean two birds, one stone?*"

Nope, many many birds, Drake said, using his thumb to point at the small group of perpetrators now being corralled to the back with the rest of the criminals from his own outpost. One of Hudson's big boys and other drones escorted them from above.

I get to clean up our group somewhat, and those that didn't fight in the initial attack with Joker get to assume I'm either incompetent and falling into their plan by following their guide, or they think I'm a genius for foiling their plans. Or, ya know, just think I'm a monster in human skin from how I trashed their leader naked, Drake mused, a smile cracking his even stare at Miss Braun. Her brow began to sweat.

"Then what will you do with this woman later?" Natto asked.

She will get tried like the rest, but we didn't lose anyone in the attack, thankfully. I wasn't expecting Megan to get held hostage, though. She's level 18; you'd think she'd be a little more attentive... He turned around to the group.

Chelsea, Harley, Theodore, and Jacqueline were standing around a few people, a glow of white around them as they were healed. Once the light dimmed, Drake caught Megan's eyes. Her face turned scarlet, but she moved to him despite that.

Drake raised his brow, looking down at the blonde woman.

"A-Are you hurt also?" Megan asked, not meeting his eyes.

"Oh, yeah I'm fine. My hand is slowly healing, no need for a healing spell. The potion I took will do just fine," he told her.

She nodded and turned away quickly.

"Th-Thank you for saving me. Chelsea was right, you might be an asshole, but you aren't all bad..." she mumbled before running back to their small group, finding her way into Chelsea's arms.

Drake snorted.

"Gross, it's making me itchy being thanked like that." He sighed as he felt another person approach him from the side.

Turning his head, he saw another woman he had tersely interacted with when he had saved Megan and the others.

Julia.

"I'd like to also thank you, sir. I didn't feel comfortable disturbing you when you got back from fighting the Goblin King, so I've been waiting for a good time to say it... but it's been one thing after another with this group. And seeing how you fought, it's so much different than how you fought with Chris. Can I ask what class you are?" Julia asked.

Drake chuckled lightly. "I thought you were thanking me, not interrogating me." He grinned.

Julia winced. "Sorry, my curiosity got the better of me."

"It's alright. I'm sure most people are trying to figure out my class just like you," he said, waving his hand dismissively. "I can't tell you, unfortunately, at least not yet. And a thanks isn't needed. I was simply helping a party member when all of that happened. But I do appreciate you helping the hostages with your barriers; it helped when saving them."

Julia's expression became confused.

"How did you know? That spell has no visual indication, and I wasn't in range for you to hear me," she wondered aloud.

Drake pointed to his eyes.

"I have a pretty good magic sensing skill. Seeing that much mana shifting kind of gives it away. So no saying thanks. We're even, and it makes me itchy." Drake laughed, scratching his sides.

Julia relaxed from Drake's casual manner and nodded.

"Alright, that's comforting to know," she replied.

"What is?"

"Knowing you aren't as big an asshole as Chelsea, Megan, and Jacqueline make you out to be."

"Ha! I knew you had a special ability to piss off women!" Natto laughed inside his head.

Drake sighed.

"Can I ask one more thing, though?" Julia asked, speaking up again.

"Sure, we have some time before we have to move. Shoot."

"What's with the pink ears and tail? I thought you said you were human?" she asked.

Drake cringed, completely forgetting that Natto had him wearing her squirrel ears and tail to help sow confusion.

"Ah, those... Let's just say it's from one of my items. It doesn't help much, eats a lot of food, and tends to be very loud and annoying, but every so often it gives a gem of advice." Drake grinned wryly.

"Screw you, idiot!" Natto shouted.

Guess I do have superpowers. Drake laughed internally.

Chapter 7
No Need For Alarm, It's Just My Smartass Talking

"Shit's been pretty quiet since that big quest ended huh, Bert?" a man said, leaning onto his claymore.

"Well yeah, Tom. Isn't that how those shows do it? Little break from big event to big event?" Bert replied as he used his rifle's scope to look out into the treeline of the forest.

"Bert... we aren't in a TV show. What the hell is wrong with you?" Tom chuckled.

"A lot of things, but I thought we were talking about the quiet peace we've got now, not my crippling depression and bad habits," Bert said nonchalantly.

Tom looked over, his face gibe.

"Good thing too, we would be here all day if we were."

Bert turned from his scope to Tom, a smirk on his face.

"Tom, we *are* here all day, remember? We got in trouble for slacking on guard duty last time, and I don't need Bear standing five feet above me looking down on me again. Being above average height felt like being as small as a mouse next to him." Bert shivered visibly, remembering the experience.

Tom shook his head, his arms suddenly wrapping around his body.

"Yeah, never mind, you're right on that one. Guy's built like a tank if the tank had an old, estranged uncle that just came out of prison," he said, his body giving a quick jerk. "But he's a nice guy though, gave out those potions that tasted like grape juice. Remember that?"

"Oh yeah, nice guy. Can kill you with his pinky toe, but a nice guy. He would be a smash at parties," Bert agreed.

Suddenly, a new voice chimed into their conversation.

"Aw, well that's nice of you to say, guys. I'll make some more of those potions for ya," the voice said from behind them.

"Oh no problem, thanks," the pair said before realizing they hadn't answered the other but someone entirely new. Their heads slowly tilted upwards to meet the eyes of the new man.

Behind them stood Bjorn, a smile on his face, matte gray armor covering most of his body. Only his right arm showed any skin, the muscles of his shoulder rippling. The handle of his enormous two-handed sword peeked over his left shoulder, eerily glowing a faint white.

"Bear! Sir! We weren't slacking! Just a little guard duty chat!" Bert said, scrambling for an excuse, a high-pitched laughing groan escaping his lips.

Bjorn waved them off as he turned his focus to the forest.

"Don't worry about it, bro. I'm not going to hurt you for talking about me. Takes a lot more than that to get under my skin." He laughed. "And I'm going to have to ask you to go grab everyone. I think we have visitors."

The pair of guards changed from an expression of panic to one of confusion. They both followed his gaze back to the forest, where a single man and woman walked out from the tree line, both lit by the orange dusk of the setting sun.

"Are they enemies? It's only two," Tom said.

Bjorn smiled. "Oh no, there's more. But I'm more excited about seeing an old friend," he said to the two, his eyes flashing white for a moment as he utilized his legendary skill, revealing the man's name despite his alias.

Drake Wallen Level 20

* * *

"Oh, looks like they spotted us. What a wonderful welcome party," Drake said, giving a soft whistle at the people pouring out of the extended rampart. "Look at that, they even put up an extra barricade. That's some points to Shigure," he mused. The worried Miss Braun looked over her shoulder.

"Yes, it seems to be a new addition from when I was here. I'll be goi—" she started, but Drake didn't let her excuse herself.

"No no, I insist you meet them with us. After all, you were such a wonderful guide," he said evenly. "You can stand at the head of the other ones we've captured, explain how and why you decided to try and kill over 200 people for your own gain and pleasure."

The woman began running for the camp, her cover blown and the cat now fully out of the bag.

Drake sighed, knowing this was going to become a problem, but nevertheless he had to stop her before she could cause more trouble.

Stepping forward, Drake moved quickly to intercept her. Miss Braun's stats paled in comparison to his own, and he easily gripped her by the wrist. In front of the entire camp. And the rest of his group moving out of the tree line.

Within seconds, he felt the stares of Shigure's camp fall on him, all hostile.

Saw that coming. Now if someone—Drake thought just as a shout sounded over the crowds.

"Let that woman go!" a voice yelled.

Why. Why is this happening? I've been a good person, right? I've built up my good karma, right? Drake cursed inwardly against Natto's high-pitched giggling in the background.

Drake turned, expecting to see a younger person based on the pitch of the voice. He wasn't surprised when he saw exactly that.

The teen in front of him wore a loose robe not unlike Drake's, but it was in a more Oriental style. The robe or kimono was well fitted to the teen's figure, leaving enough room for movement but not enough to become a hindrance. On his side sat two swords, one much longer than the other, in pure black scabbards accented by rose gold markings. The handles of the swords were covered in just as dark a black as the scabbards, the rose gold hilts beautifully shimmering.

Drake took a moment to focus on the man, his eyes staying a clear blue.

Shigure Kenzo Level 24

Drake also turned his attention to the smiling giant sticking out like a sore thumb behind the crowd of people from the camp.

Bear Level 27

Did Bjorn not tell the kid who I am? Or does he have a hero complex? Drake thought, looking back at the teen glowering at him, his hand on his sword hilt.

"You are by far the last person to suggest anyone has any sort of complex," Natto said pointedly.

Drake opened his mouth underneath his mask, then closed it, unable to argue.

"No, she's a criminal," Drake said, finally addressing Shigure.

"Regardless of her crime, you should not treat her as such. She is still human," Shigure countered.

Drake raised a brow. "Have you not dealt with people in the tutorial who've killed swaths of innocents just for the hell of it? She's no better than a monster killing indiscriminately for their own pleasure," Drake explained evenly, hearing murmurs coming from his own group as they now fully exited the forest into the opening of the outpost.

"There's that boss music again. Please someone else tell me they hear it and it's not just me," Tom whispered from behind Drake.

Drake ignored Tom and kept his focus on Shigure.

Should I goad him? I wanted to fight him anyway, and it seems like Bjorn is making sure no one else is going to step in, Drake thought, going through his options.

He decided to have some fun.

"I'm here at the request of Bear. This woman is a criminal and responsible for nearly killing all of the people you see behind me," Drake said pointedly. "Are you going to let her run around free? If so, then I may have made a mistake coming here. I expected too much from a *child* playing at being a leader."

Shigure's face instantly darkened into a fierce scowl at the jab.

Uh oh. Too far? Drake's eyes flashed yellow, his aura beginning to boil, ready to be released.

"Imbecile! Must you make every person you meet hate you instantly? It makes doing anything we need incredibly difficult!" Natto yelled.

Drake mentally shrugged as he kept his eyes fixed on Shigure.

"I *know* who you are, Shot. And you may be welcome by Sir Bear, but he is not a member of the coalition and holds no power here. He is simply a guest. Regardless of what preconceived notions you hold of my leadership, I am in charge, and if you wish to enter, you will have to adhere to what *I* say. So let the woman go and *we* will take it from here," Shigure growled out, his hand almost quaking as it gripped his sword.

Oh, he's surprisingly calm despite himself, Drake thought, impressed.

"*Certainly leagues ahead of yourself.*" Natto snickered.

Rude.

"I only came here because of my friendship with Bear and the promise I made with him. These people behind me are here for shelter and protection. Are you going to deny them that because I refuse to give up a criminal? What about the rest of the ones I have captive who've done just as much as her, if not worse? Are you really going to demand I give them freedom when they've forcibly and violently tried to take that same freedom from these innocent people? How do you expect to protect anyone with such a soft attitude?" Drake jabbed.

Shigure's face contorted into true anger at his last words. He lowered his stance.

"You know nothing of what I will do to protect these people and my family! I won't allow you to continue to insult me and my honor as a leader of this coalition. Let her go—this is the last time I will ask!"

Drake smirked under his mask.

"Theo."

Shimmering into existence next to him was Theodore in all his butler glory, his mustache a work of art as it stayed picturesque on his face.

"Yes, my lord?" Theodore answered, his body in a slight bow.

"Take Miss Braun to the other prisoners. Everyone who wants to stay with this *child* can stay. The criminals will have to be judged for their crimes by someone more *competent,* it seems," Drake said, making sure to keep eye contact with Shigure as he spoke.

Shigure's eyes cracked with malicious intent at the final jab, his honor insulted for the last time by Drake.

"*First Strike, Blood Moon Style, Ket—*" Shigure began to whisper, his sword and drawing hand moving as he twisted his body, but he was interrupted by just the man Drake wanted to see.

"Okay, okay! That's enough," Bjorn said, holding Shigure by the shoulder. "Ever at your own pace huh, bro?" Bjorn's smile was still as large as it had been moments ago from the crowd.

"You know me, Bear, I like to make an entrance," Drake said, breaking his evil facade and turning back to Theo. "Thank you for playing along, Theo. Can you please go get the rest of the prisoners from Hudson? I'd like to hand them over like we planned."

Shigure relaxed slightly, but he still glared daggers at Drake.

Drake chuckled. "Sorry, I couldn't help myself," he said, holding out his left hand. "I just wanted to get a gauge on who you were, and I'm glad you are who I thought you'd be."

Bjorn, not Shigure, raised a brow, curious.

"Oh? And what's that?"

Drake moved his mask so his face showed his large smile. "A snot-nosed brat." He laughed sarcastically.

The surroundings suddenly crackled with dense mana, Shigure's visage turning dark.

Bjorn snorted, shrugging as his hand came off Shigure's shoulder and he looked at Drake.

"Hey bro, I tried."

Chapter 8
Shigure vs Drake — And I Took That Personally

Drake stood his ground, looking at the teen as he began to channel some sort of skill. He gave a nod to Theodore and Bjorn as they took Miss Braun away and removed themselves from the surroundings.

"Is this really how you act when you're goaded by a stranger?" Drake asked, admitting that he had intentionally insulted the teen. "How in the world did you become the leader of such a large group when you can't even discern friend from foe."

Shigure lowered his stance and growled back, "Because it is you who said it!"

"What?" Drake said, confused.

Bjorn spoke up from behind in the crowd.

"My bad! Might have said a few things about you to him! Don't take it personally!" he shouted.

Drake tilted his head in confusion, not sure what exactly he could have told the teen about him that would have him this upset.

"I'm not sure I get what you mean?" Drake said honestly, his weight shifting to one leg as he crossed his earthen arm, his other moving to pick at his ear.

"That! That's what it is! Sir Bear has told me everything about you, everything I need to know! How you started the tutorial alone. How you went off on your own, selfishly ignoring the plight of others within the tutorial!" Shigure shouted.

"Oh no, here we go again. And he wants to say he hates anime, but he always monologues like he has main character syndrome..." a man wearing glasses said, polishing a gun that reminded Drake of a certain vampire in a red cloak.

"You're mad I prioritized myself over others? In what world are strangers my responsibility over my own safety? If you haven't noticed, we're in a life-and-death situation. Not only that," Drake said, thumbing to the rest of his group, "but I think I've gone out of my way to help others a fair amount."

"You could have done more! Sir Bear has told me of how you struck down a named monster! How you rampaged on the other side of the forest and captured an Outpost on your own! Do you—Do you know how many people we had to sacrifice for this outpost?! And you gained one on your own! Why did you not use that strength for others sooner?! The amount of lives you could've saved might have been many times more!" Shigure continued, his eyes thinning to points.

"Listen here. I'm not the moral authority, and I don't owe it to you to affirm your morals. I do what I want when it suits me and when *I* feel it's right. My life, my decisions. I take what comes with it and accept every consequence and loss, learning from every mistake as best as I can and moving forward for me and for those I hold dear. Even if that means killing someone to protect my own family or stepping on some shithead monster who thinks they can harm people close to me." Drake scoffed. "So don't come at me with those anime protagonist lines of self-loathing and projecting your inadequacies onto me. You lost people either because they were weak, or because you suck ass as a leader and didn't plan enough ahead. So enough of this guilt-tripping from some imaginary moral high ground—it's getting old real fast. Especially when you can't even back it up."

"You are going to compare me to a fictional character?! This is real life, not some game or show! Real people died because you lacked the empathy to help them when you could!"

"*Excuse me*? What the fuck do you know about my struggles? I may have jabbed at you, but I never once assumed you didn't struggle like everyone else who's still standing here," Drake growled. "And those fictional characters hold a very special place in my heart, so watch your *fucking* mouth."

"Then you're a fool! Those shows are meant for children and imbeciles!" Shigure shot back.

"*Ha! I like this kid; he certainly understands it!*" Natto chimed in.

"Okay, no more talking. That last comment *I took personally.*" Drake's eyes flashed yellow.

* * *

Shigure lowered his stance, steadying himself against the ground as he eyed his opponent. The man before him, Shot, was an insult to everything he had gone through in the tutorial and before.

Being who he was, a Kenzo, he had to meet his family and peers' every expectation in every capacity and more. There was no failing. There was no less than.

And this man had flagrantly gone against everything Shigure himself had gone through. He had ignored expectations and done anything and everything he wanted, not caring for anyone but himself.

Shigure was disgusted. Throughout his entire life, he was expected to live for the clan, for everyone as a whole. It was his duty and his greatest pride.

Helping his friends in school. Helping his family during Kendo lessons. Excelling in every area he could and taking on more and more responsibilities to prove to himself and everyone else that he was better, that he could go above and beyond.

He had been the head of the Kendo Club, winning the National Tournament as the youngest competitor in years to the shock and awe of his entire school. Even more so to the delight of his parents, who'd said he was their pride and joy.

But this man, he had done everything Shigure had done in the tutorial and more, all while following his own whims! It wasn't fair, it wasn't right! How was he any better than him? How was he any more deserving of the number one in the tutorial's adoration over him?

Shigure gripped his sword in anger and frustration. He took a quick glance at Bear, the man who still hadn't trusted him enough to give him his real name. The man who would not stop singing the praises of this man, Shot.

Shigure had been calming down and internalizing his anger since that day Bear had returned saying he soon wouldn't be able to beat Shot. But when the notification came a week ago of the Goblin King being slain, his mental limit had been reached. A man he had never met had far surpassed him in contribution to the quest and even surpassed Bear.

When they both saw the notification, Shigure was devastated, expecting Bear to be the same. But instead, Bear had been smiling, even going as far as to say, "It was only a matter of time before he blew past me." He, the number one in the tutorial. Bear was not frustrated or angered but expectant like it was only natural that the man had passed him.

Shigure wouldn't have it. Not this man, not a man of his caliber that had done nothing before the tutorial, not a man who played the song only to his own desires. He was not a man of stature, not a man of rock-solid morals, not a man at all in Shigure's eyes. He was nothing but a filthy degenerate.

Shigure shouted, activating his skill before striking, using every resource available to him from his skills. He was assured in his win: he was a one-on-one specialist, and his skills reflected it.

"Kenzo, Shigure! Kensei! Maeru!" he announced, activating his Shogun's authority for a duel and increasing his attack by a full 100%.

"First Strike, Blood Moon Style, Ketsu Iai," Shigure whispered, his eyes trained on Drake.

Leaping forward with the last word of his skill, Shigure drew his o-katana from his saya, the ring of the metal sounding through the area.

Shigure expected the battle to be finished immediately, but he was struck in sheer surprise when he saw Shot standing there, his hair changed to a radiant orange, hand holding Shigure's blade in between his fingers, and his expression even as Shot's eyes shifted from blue to green to yellow.

"Ah, so you got a funny nickname too, huh? And you're pretty fast. Expected nothing less of someone above level 20," Drake stated while Shigure struggled to remove his blade from Drake's grip.

Shigure's eyes widened in surprise as he continued struggling to wrench his blade from Drake. The man's arm was painted in a fiery orange and covered in a deep blue glow.

Shit! How can he be so strong?! I'm four levels above him! Does he have an epic or higher class?! Shigure cursed. His hand released his blade to instead unsheathe his smaller daisho blade, his wakizashi.

"Fifth Strike, Blood Moon Style, Ketsushouku!" Shigure shouted, trying to use his smaller blade to force Drake to release his primary blade, his former reddening with the skill.

Although the strike was awkward from his position and with his wakizashi, he was able to force Shot to release his o-katana. Shigure's skill cut upward, the sword aura screeching with power from the skill.

Shigure looked at the man who now stepped backward, his hair turning a brilliant yellow hue and his arm changing color with it. A low whistle fell from Drake's lips.

"Wow, got some nice skills there. Are they part of your class skills? Having that many individual skills would take up a lot of slots," Drake mused. He flicked his wrist while snapping his finger simultaneously, a staff appearing in front of the man which he grabbed and spun into position. A shard of ice formed from a white magic circle at his side.

Shigure was again surprised, his eyes widening.

"You're a mage?! But how? You stopped my strike cold?!" Shigure growled, holding his two swords at the ready.

"I'm just full of surprises, don't you worry. Or, well, you know. Do." Drake laughed. "Regardless, let me enjoy humiliating you a bit more."

"You're nothing but a self-centered bastard! Why would Sir Bear ever say you were better than I?!" Shigure yelled. "You dare say you are going to humiliate me after trying to stand on your own ideals, mocking my own? You are a hypocrite!"

"Only when it suits me! And I never said I wasn't." Drake sneered, the shard of ice vanishing as his hair turned ghostly white and the changing flames on his left arm disappeared. Drake began chanting.

"I am the storm that is approaching..."

"I won't let you! *Eighth Strike, Blood Moon: Nitoryu no Ogi, Mugen no Chi no Mai!"* Shigure screamed, both of his blades lighting up a deep blood red as he surged forward to chase Shot. The man somehow deftly dodged each swing of the swords with a hair's margin, continuing to cast his spell.

"Why! Why are you so fast!" Shigure screamed, his blade striking downward as Shot lightly stepped to the side.

"A good magician never reveals his secrets! And you seem to be struggling there, Sword Saint! Very secret technique-esque, just to not land a single blow," Drake answered, goading Shigure further before continuing his chant. *"Provoking, black clouds in isolation!"*

Shigure continued to swing, struggling to land a blow as his stamina began dropping from the prolonged expenditure of his skill. Meanwhile, Shot seemed to be in good spirits, the yellow circle that was forming under him beginning to crackle and snap with each word he spoke.

"Stop with your foolishness! Will you not even take me seriously?!" Shigure spat, continuing to chase forward and beginning to swing more and more wildly as his emotions flared.

"Finally noticed? I told you! I'm going to put you in your place. No one insults my heroes. Let the true meaning of fear and power be etched into your very being!" Shot howled. His eyes flashed again to yellow, and Shigure stiffened.

Shigure suddenly couldn't move, his breath stalling as he could barely feel his hands gripping his swords. As if everything had stopped and his blood had gone cold. He felt Shot's eyes on him.

Never before had he felt this small under someone's gaze, the feeling of vulnerability increasing as the slow realization washed over him that he was outclassed.

You are now under the effect of the skill: Of The Apex.

Hardened Body has been disabled. Loss of 50% defensive effectiveness.

Shogun's Authority has been disabled. Loss of 100% overall damage increase.

What?! Shigure shouted internally, looking back at the eyes of the predator before him. Cold sweat pooled over his body as he shook, struggling to move.

"I have a nickname too, apparently. Shall I share it?" Drake asked evenly, his eyes never leaving Shigure.

"F-Fu-Fuck you!" Shigure managed to growl out of his clenched jaw.

"It's the Tyrant. Reap what you sow for challenging me!" Drake cackled, his arms spreading. "*I am the reclaimer of my name! Born in flames!*" Drake shouted. The circle below him burst into light as a thunderous crash sounded, the lightning forming into lashes of electricity reaching behind him. "*I have been blessed!*" Drake continued, his figure illuminated by the blinding light of the dense lightning magic behind him. "*My family crest is a demon of death!*" he roared, the magic circle forming a huge Oni behind him, filling Shigure with awe as he finally regained control of his body.

The massive amount of mana and the size of the spell dropped Shigure to his knees.

"It's not fair!" he screamed, trying to reject the reality in front of him.

"The world was never fair. And now, *you shall die,*" Drake proclaimed. He cast his spell, the figure of lightning magic changing into a dense sword of lightning mana.

Drake ran his staff against the crackling blade, then pointed it directly at Shigure.

Shigure looked up, his loss evident now, the reality hitting him as he contemplated the regret in his heart for being so blind to think he was stronger.

"There's always someone stronger. I became conceited. If only..." Shigure's eyes looked into Shot's, the acceptance of his fate plain on his face.

Drake raised the sword of lightning high above his head, and Shigure closed his eyes, waiting for the inevitable. A snap was heard, but the blow never came.

After a few seconds, Shigure finally cracked his eyes open slowly, seeing Shot standing there, no longer the tyrant of death that he saw before closing his eyes.

"Good, that's what I wanted to hear. You got some good convictions, kid. Even in the face of an insurmountable opponent, you accepted your mistake and realized your shortcomings. Good stuff," Drake said, moving his mask to the side and revealing a smile as he bent down to give Shigure a pat on the shoulder.

"You aren't going to kill me?" Shigure questioned.

"No, of course not. Wouldn't be a very good first impression, and I still need you to take care of all my people," Drake said. Shigure visibly relaxed with a sigh. "*But,* I still have to kick your ass for insulting anime." Drake laughed, snapping his fingers next to Shigure's head. The staff in Drake's hands vanished, replaced by a single ring in the air and a small fireball that vanished just as quickly as it had appeared. "Clench your teeth kid!" Drake howled as he laughed, his open hand moving to equip the ring on its way to Shigure's face.

Drake's hair shimmered to red, condensing around his fist as the last enhancement from his tattoo rings encompassed his blow in a bright blue just moments before impact.

Shigure had one thought before he was struck.

This... asshole!

Chapter 9

Don't Interrupt the Dazzling God!

Whispers and murmurs were heard all around Aono, but her eyes were honed in on the individual standing at the front of the crowd who was holding a woman by the arm.

"Is this the 'what are you doing' scene?" Aono whispered. She pulled her stylus from thin air, her mana paper slowly materializing in front of her.

"What is it, Miss Aono?" a man next to her asked, pushing up his glasses.

"Shhh!" another snapped. "Do not interrupt our god when she holds the holy stylus!"

Several other men pulled the louder man backward, melding into the crowd. The one who reprimanded the man stood tall and proud next to Miss Aono, silently guarding her.

"Oh, ohhhhhh!" Aono squealed, wildly tracing her stylus from one side of the paper to the next. "The approach of the stout-hearted but foolish boy! Magnificent! How will my knight respond?!"

On the field before them, more and more people gathered on Shigure's side as both he and Drake discussed something in the center. Soon a chill fell on the air and an enormous man appeared between them, holding back the teen.

"And a third? Is it a love triangle moment?! I must record this!" Aono murmured, her hand increasing in pace as the scene unfolded on her paper.

On her mana paper, she depicted a drastically different picture than the events she was witnessing. Flowery scenery and chiseled jawlines reflected the gleam of the morning sun. Drake and Shigure were torn apart by the hulking figure of the third man, his dark orange hair, beard, and matted gray armor appearing as an imposing mountain between them.

Suddenly the chill in the air lifted, and it seemed all was fine. There was no following battle, leaving Aono surprised.

"It is shtill fine," she said, slurring the word as she wiped the drool from her mouth with her sleeve. She looked down at the masterpiece she had just created. "This will do *just* fine..."

But once again, she was left surprised as a howl sounded from the center of the field.

"*Kenzo, Shigure! Kensei! Maeru!*"

Aono's head snapped to attention, the paper she had just been admiring ripped from the mana board it was attached to and flying backward in the air where the man next to her grabbed it and placing it into his inventory.

She looked on, hyper focused as best as her stats would allow. She saw Shigure disappear, then heard a clash of thunderous proportions.

Her head jerked, following the sound and seeing Drake holding Shigure's blade. His red mask smiled with its pearly whites, the blade held within them.

A shriek of joy escaped Aono's lips as she forgot herself. Her thumb found her teeth and she bit down on her nail, unable to reel in her anticipation.

Shigure suddenly unsheathed his secondary blade, forcing Drake to release the previous one. With a sharp, soft whistle, Drake shifted his hair color, and a stylish staff materialized in front of him.

"You're a mage?!"

"I'm just full of surprises... Let me enjoy humiliating you!"

Aono only heard bits and pieces of the verbal exchange, but the motion and back and forth of the battle left her breathless. Her head suddenly snapped back as her sleeve went to her nose.

"Miss Aono?!" the man next to her asked, concerned.

"I have a nosebleed... B-But, no matter!" she shouted, suddenly attracting the attention of the people around her, their looks filled with concern.

Aono ignored the sudden expulsion of vital energy due to her excitement, switching drawing hands and using her blood-soaked sleeve to clog the flow.

Her eyes stayed peeled on the battle and their exchange of words, taking it all in, marking it down with one stroke after another of her stylus.

"I am the storm that..." Drake began, but he was forced to move as Shigure gave chase.

Aono continued to lose blood as she watched the battle unfold, every passing moment filled with Drake dodging and running as he appeared and disappeared from view. The magic circle below him expanded and brightened.

"The spell is changing color?! He has become even more elegant in his use of mana manipulation! As expected of my knight!" Aono shouted gleefully.

Then the mood on the battlefield shifted once again as Drake was locked in a standoff against Shigure.

Shigure refused to, or possibly couldn't, move. Just like on the battlefield, a wave of fear and deathly cold crashed over the crowd, momentarily freezing Aono in her tracks. But her artist's will would not let her be impeded for long. She forced her way from the grip of the fear, making sure to recount the events *accurately*.

The magic around Drake flexed and molded, turning into an enormous ball of lightning. In moments, it shifted, forming the face of a demon behind him.

But within that time, Shigure had surrendered. He dropped to his knees in clear despair.

Aono could take no more, her body on the brink of collapse as she illustrated the last thing she saw, her vision darkening, her hand desperately putting the image to paper.

"Such elegance, my dazzling god!"

Chapter 10

What Do You Mean I'm Not Allowed?

"**I**s he dead?" Claire asked, standing over the teen who had just been launched in their direction by Drake.

"I don't think so...? Mr. Shot did hit him pretty hard, though," Harley added.

"My liege may have gone well past whateth was necessary this time." Theodore sighed, looking down at the boy with pity.

Drake waltzed over to the people surrounding Shigure, taking his time with relaxed steps.

"I hit him hard, yeah. But I didn't hit him *that* hard. Come on, give me some credit! I'm not an assh—" he tried to say, but several pairs of eyes glaring back at him stopped him.

"Either way, Jacqueline, would you please heal him up? I still need to talk to him," Drake said, clearing his throat with a cough.

"Yeah, I can do that, but ya sure? He isn't going to go on a mad rampage again, is he?" Jacqueline asked. She reached out her hand before she felt a gust of wind blow her hair back.

Looking up, she saw a blade inches from her face, stopped only by Drake's hand gripping it, his fingers glowing an ethereal blue.

"And who the fuck are you?" Drake asked. He held the blade firmly in one hand, his other gripping the small black-haired girl in a ninja outfit by her throat.

"*Drake, she is a construct! And a combat one at that,*" Natto reported, making Drake raise his eyebrow in interest.

Drake looked down at the girl as she stared daggers back at him.

"H-How dare y-you!" she growled. "D-Do not touch m-my master again!"

Well then, I've never heard you call me master. Is that a construct thing? Drake asked.

"*And you certainly never will, ape. No, it is a result of her being a part of him as well. I believe it to be a cultural preference of sorts,*" Natto replied back.

"That's awfully rude to say to the person who's going to heal him, don't you think?" Drake said, glaring right back at the seething construct. He loosened his grip just enough that the girl could speak without issue but kept his hand around her neck to make sure she wouldn't slip away.

After a slight cough, she shouted back at them.

"We do not need your help! You have done enough harm and are no longer welcome here! Get out, and get away from my noble lord!"

Drake's face scrunched up in irritation.

"You know, ambushes are for commoners. And who's 'we?'"

Feeling people move into his sphere, he turned, hand still around the girl's neck.

"Release Uta and Lord Shigure! Or we wil—" the voice began shouting before it was cut short by Drake's aura-infused stare.

"*Or you'll what, prick?*" Drake said evenly, his arm beginning to glow a deeper blue as he funneled mana into it.

"Okay, okay! No need for that," Bjorn said, making his way through the crowd of Shigure's camp. "Shot, tell them to calm down as well, will you bro? Last thing we need is another mess after you just got here. And did you really have to go so hard on the guy? He's still a kid. You're supposed to be an adult."

Drake looked behind him, seeing Hudson and his robots aiming back at Shigure's camp and Harley and Chelsea doing the same with their bows. Theodore was nowhere to be seen, assumed to have gone invisible.

Amir, Tom, and Claire stood close behind Jacqueline, their weapons drawn as well. The only one not assembled was the relaxing Sherry, who looked on with an uninterested yawn.

"Damn, really missed a chance for an Avengers Assemble call right there. And no! I'm a man-child, just ask anyone. *Besides*, he started it," Drake replied, now letting go of the small girl named Uta. His hand moved to pacify his group as well.

"No, I'm pretty sure you started that whole argument," Bjorn said, pulling Uta to his side. She desperately struggled to get free to see Shigure.

"No, I started the first argument, but then we finished that. Then he insulted my hobbies, so he started it again. Believe me, I kept count." Drake nodded to himself.

Bjorn shook his head despite a grin creasing his face.

"I didn't know you were so petty, but at least you didn't kill him. After our last figh—*spar*, I expected you to go too far and I'd have to step in." Bjorn chuckled.

"I said I was a man-child, not a toddler. I know when to stop. Okay, I know when to stop *sometimes*," Drake amended, feeling the stares on the back of his neck. "Jacqueline, please heal him now that we have the *commoner* under control," Drake jabbed.

Jacqueline nodded, keeping her eye on Uta for a moment before casting a light healing spell on Shigure, mending his tattered and bruised face.

"*May the wounds of the injured be reversed by my command. I offer up this prayer in good faith of the Mother and her healing grace,*" Jacqueline chanted.

"You know," Drake interjected after the cast was completed, "who do you pray to exactly when you do that?"

Jacqueline shrugged her shoulders, her hand glowing brightly above Shigure's head.

"Hell if I bloody know. I just cast the spell and it does its wacky healing. Brilliant, really, that I don't have to know much as long as I have the skill, ya know?" she answered.

Drake pursed his lips under his mask, not sure how to take the answer. He would have to ask Natto about it later when he had a moment, but first, he had some other things to address.

"Now," Drake began, turning back to Bjorn and Shigure's group, which seemed to have come out in full force. "What exactly do you mean I'm no longer welcomed? Are you really saying that you're going to reject *all* these people?" Drake asked, his arm fanning backward and presenting the caravan of two hundred-odd people.

"No, I don't think—" Bjorn tried to say before being cut off by a hefty man in full plate armor.

"That's exactly what we're saying, you fucking monster! You think after what you just did that we're going to let you or any one of your followers into this place?" shouted the portly man, his hand moving to lift his large hammer to his shoulder.

Drake laughed. "Followers? My man, about 99% of the people behind me don't even like me," Drake said pointing with his thumb. "And who might you be, anyway? The dude in charge of the rations but always says there isn't any food left?"

The stout man's face reddened, but he reluctantly held his tongue as another person from Shigure's group stepped forward and spoke. This time a woman.

"*We* are leaders of our own respective groups here at this outpost, and we have deemed it too dangerous to let someone like you into these walls. We need to protect our own people, and you are clearly unhinged."

Drake scoffed.

"*Clearly*. That's why I let the little leader of your group live, right?" Drake sighed.

"N-No. Unfortunately, I will have to agree with them," Shigure finally managed to say after returning to consciousness. He unsteadily sat up with some effort. "I have lost and need to improve further as a leader, but you intentionally goading me into conflict will not be tolerated. However," Shigure added, turning back to his group, "it will only be him. I will not abandon innocent people. As he has said, my only grudge is with him, not the people that are unfortunate enough to be in his care as a result of circumstance," Shigure added, struggling to get to his feet.

Bjorn released Uta, and she rushed over in a flash to support him. Completely ignoring everyone around them, she shouldered the teen boy, her face twisted in deep concern.

Drake was slightly conflicted about being barred from entering the place he'd wanted to come for in the first place, but he did dig his own grave on this one for his bit of fun.

"That's fine. That was what I originally came here to do regardless. I owed Bear that much after what he did for me," Drake conceded. He turned around and gave a small speech to his caravan, his head bowing slightly. "Everyone who wishes to stay here is free to do so. Our time was short, but I wish you all the best and that while you were under my care, you felt at the very least protected."

What Drake wasn't expecting was the thanks and gratitude that came from the crowd as they passed him while moving to the outpost. Genuine thanks and tears of relief found him, and he stood in shock.

He had thought most of the people that were forced to be with him had only done so because there was no other option. He was sure it was the case with how many of them fought tooth and nail to go against him.

But he hadn't been as observant as he'd thought, his focus and time taken up by defending the outpost during their time with him. He hadn't seen the change in the massive camp he'd created. Hadn't seen the shift to heartfelt gratitude after days of him risking his life, offering food and shelter, and accommodating them day after day.

He could understand the emotions from their words. His body felt itchy, but not in the awkward way he was used to where it crawled when the thanks was an obligation from the other party. No, this time they had no reason to thank him for his assistance. He had simply done what he needed to do to keep his promise to Bjorn.

The other shoe dropping for him wasn't these people he'd helped out of obligation. It was the eight people who hadn't moved.

Tom, Chelsea, Hudson, Amir, Harley, Claire, Theodore, and even Jacqueline had stayed.

Sherry, on the other hand, was lazily moving her feet with the crowd of people, mumbling about food, to which Theodore shimmered into existence to grab her by the shoulder and turn her around. She began walking back to the group in the same food-deprived daze that had her going with the flow previously.

"If he's not allowed, I won't be going," Claire said, her arms crossed as she stuck up her nose.

"Damn straight, little lady. Might not've liked this damned idjit when we met, but it's been one hell of a time, I'd say," Hudson added.

"Agreed. He's still an asshole, but he's our asshole!" Chelsea said, then blushed when she realized what she had just said. "Wait, I didn't mean it like that!"

"I still think he's a right prick, but I'd be a bloody idiot to not stay with someone who can push the third strongest in this right mad place around like a rag doll. So I'll be staying whether ya like it or not, gov. I do still owe you an arm after all, yeah?" Jacqueline said, shifting her weight onto one hip.

"I promised to help sir, and that still stands. Only with you have I felt so motivated and pushed to do better. Your hard exterior and jokes can not fool us! We know you care deeply for others," Amir said excitedly.

Drake snorted, not sure how to answer as the rest started talking as well.

"I know very well that Theo would not leave you, Mr. Shot, so I guess you are stuck with me also!" Harley laughed, giving a small bow.

"'Tis but undeniable fact, my lord! Thou shalt not remove this one from his side! Thou hast yet to tell the boundless secrets of magic and dark arts to this unworthy apprentice! And 'twouldn't be proper for a lord to not have his loyal knight!" Theodore cried out.

"This is the way," Tom said, his eyes closed as he dipped his head.

"Tom, you're just afraid to go alone, aren't you," Drake quipped.

"Come on, man! Let me be cool for once!" Tom shouted back.

Drake laughed. "In due time, youngling!"

"Then we'll just be camping out here, then! And speaking of arms," Drake began, gritting his teeth and getting ready to do what he really did not want to, "I'll be collecting now."

Drake canceled the magic holding his earthen arm in place, a little regretful to lose the multifaceted ability that had become second nature to him, but he quickly removed his garb and revealed his burnt shoulder to the crowd. Some gasped, shocked at the many scars on his body.

Forming a blade of ice in his left hand, Drake steeled himself, then sliced off the cauterized flesh in one swoop, a muffled scream coming from his throat.

"Fucking *ow!*"

Chapter 11
Khajiit Has Skill Stones if You Have Coin

Drake sat up, a beam of light from the crack in his tent's entrance alerting him to the sunrise.

It was the first time in weeks that he had decided to sleep through the night, and it was well worth it. He finally felt refreshed, and considerably so.

Drake raised his arms, looking curiously at his replaced right arm for the umpteenth time with a smile on his face. He flexed his fingers, not having to manipulate them any longer to do the gesture.

"Good to have you back, Vanessa," Drake joked.

"Did you *really* name your right hand Vanessa?" Natto said as she rose from the adjacent bed, rubbing her eyes to remove her grogginess.

"Don't disrespect my ex-girlfriend like that. We may have broken up, but she treated me very well, I'll have you know," Drake continued sarcastically.

"I am assuming this is some kind of joke or reference, and I certainly feel like I do not wish to understand it," Natto answered with her face going even.

"It certainly is." Drake laughed. "But now to start the day! Lots to do, many people to beat the snot out of!"

"What about food?" Natto asked expectantly.

"Yes, food too. I got a lot of good stuff left over, and I have a feeling I can get a bunch of new stuff from Shigure's camp today if I can get some people to trade with," Drake said. Suddenly, he felt someone move outside his tent.

Raising his brow, he got up and began to walk to the front of the tent, Natto hopping onto his shoulder and merging with him once again. His hand moved the tent entrance, and a flood of morning sun bloomed into the room, momentarily blinding him.

Blinking a few times, he saw the hulking figure of a familiar walking mountain holding a meat skewer as it waved at him.

"Rise and shine, bro. Thought you would never wake up," Bjorn grunted through a mouth full of boar meat.

"Why are you here so early in the morning? Don't you have, like, Shigure camp things to do?" Drake said, snorting.

"He certainly does, but I can not get him to stay and do them since you are here now," a shorter black-haired teen said from his side.

"Oh, you're here too? It's just a party now, or should I say a trial? You aren't going to try to kick me off your lawn now, are you Shigure? And shouldn't you be doing camp leader stuff?" Drake said, exasperated.

Shigure coughed but answered nonetheless.

"I am taking a day for recuperation. I also had some things to discuss with you," he said in an even tone.

"Kid wants to fight again. He's all twisted up about losing that hard, bro." Bjorn chuckled.

Drake smirked.

"Well, he's going to have to take a rain check. I have some things to do, namely breakfast before a certain someone stabs me."

"Is food awake yet...?" a dazed voice called out. A hand moved to open a tent across from Drake's.

Stepping out of the tent was a woman in a plain white tee with no pants, her hair a mess and her cracked glasses slanted at a very awkward angle.

"Sherry, what have we told you about walking around like that?" Drake shook his head and walked to the woman, pushing her back into her tent.

"You said it was really hot. What about food?" she answered.

"True, but I also said to stop doing it. I can only take so much visual stimu-lation..." Drake mumbled before coughing. "I mean, I said it's unlady-like. Now dress up first and brush your hair, okay? Then I'll have food ready, I promise." Drake sighed.

Bjorn laughed loudly as Shigure turned his gaze downward, his face going crimson.

"You have some real quirky people in your group, don't you bro. Where did you pick them up? Also, like the new digs. Are they from the quest completion?" Bjorn asked.

Drake smiled, happy to be in Bjorn's friendly and casual presence once again. The pressure of being a leader lifted as he felt the man's unobligated friendship.

"It's a long story, but the armor and stuff is kind of from it. Do subsequent quests prior to the big one count?" Drake asked, answering Bjorn's question with another.

"Don't worry, we got a good ninety-some days left, bro. I gots time. And I suppose it does? Seems like you got a good haul from everything, *Mr. Number One*," Bjorn jabbed, finishing off his skewer. "So what exactly are your plans? Anything I can tag along on? I've been pretty bored since the tutorial-wide quest ended."

Drake pursed his lips, but he quickly took him up on his offer.

"Actually, yeah, and that also includes the little angst-filled super teen here. Do you guys trade for stones? I need some food and possibly some rare stones to fill out some people's skill trees before I go out again. And I'm also looking for a person. Or, well, people maybe," Drake answered.

Shigure's mouth opened to argue, but he quickly closed it as he took in a deep breath.

"We do trade, but that is only within the camp, so you will have to have Sir Bear or I do it for you. And what type of people may I ask? We do not do *that type* of thing here," Shigure answered, his eyes moving to Sherry's tent.

"Bro, please. I don't need to pay, and I don't shit where I eat, so I've never touched Sherry. If you like her, I could tell you how to get to her heart. I'm sure it's really hard to figure out, but I'll tell you the secret." Drake leaned in and whispered, "*It's through her stomach.*"

Bjorn chuckled lightly at their exchange, his face in nearly a permanent smile since Drake had arrived.

"So, who are you looking for then? Can't imagine you need anyone in particular for your group, seeing how many members you have now. You have your regular old Uta as well with that mustache guy," Bjorn said.

"Oh, Theo?"

"You called, my Lord?" Theodore said, winking into existence.

"Yeah. How ya been, Theo? Looks like you've picked up some new tricks."

"This one has been splendid, Sir Bear. Thou hast been in good health as well, it seems? Thy armor is quite impressive. 'Tis a quest reward?" Theodore asked.

Bjorn slapped his chest, hitting the black-matted armor.

"Not exactly. Grabbed this off one of the Goblin Knights. This baby, though?" He pointed to a purple inlaid ring that somehow fit around his right hand's thick sausage-like finger. "This I got from the tutorial-wide quest reward. A real sweet piece to add to my fighting style."

Drake raised a brow in curiosity.

"Hmm, why do I have a feeling your item is better than the one I got?" Drake voiced, staring at the item.

"Just how it goes, bro." Bjorn laughed.

Drake sighed, knowing Bjorn was completely right. Sometimes you just got the short end of the stick.

"Anyway, I'm looking for basically anyone with formal martial arts or military training. Also, I'd like to trade or help out here if I can with the extra skill stones I have," Drake explained, looking over to Shigure.

The teen thought over what Drake wanted for a moment, obviously thinking of several people.

"What are you going to offer in return for these people? And what do you need them for? If you wish to spar, we have plenty of people that would like to give you a piece of their mind, myself included," Shigure said, his hand moving slowly to his sword.

"Look, I know you probably want to reclaim your honor or something, but I just want to learn proper fighting. Like most people, I was just a normal guy before the tutorial, and I have a lot of gaps in my fighting knowledge. As for what I can give? How about some of this." Drake began to empty a fraction of the gear and stones he had accumulated over the past weeks he had been fighting.

Shigure's eyes went from pretentious to surprised, then to outward shock.

"I knew you had killed many from the final count on the tutorial quest, but this is absurd," Shigure muttered.

"And there's more where that came from. Now about those stones I need and those people I want to see?" Drake asked, a smug smile inching its way onto his face.

Shigure nodded.

"I have a few people I will ask, but it will be their decision. If you have any alcohol, that would be good,"

"Alcohol? Can't say I've come across any... Do you guys have booze?" Drake asked, looking over to Bjorn. Bjorn shook his head.

"I wish I had some. There's one guy in the camp who was a brewer before the tutorial and somehow got a class for it, but he won't share it with anyone. Damn shame too. I could use some good whiskey."

"What would I need the slick and loose for?" Drake asked, turning back to Shigure.

"We have a very... *particular* person who enjoys alcohol. We've had to stop him from strangling the brewer several times for refusing to sell to him. He is an ample fighter, but he refuses to do much without receiving the substance." Shigure sighed. "If we had him fighting regularly, we would have been able to do much more during the quest."

That's interesting. You know anything about making booze, Natto? Drake thought.

"I would be able to tell you roughly how to make rice wine, but unfortunately there is no substance here able to replace rice. It would also take you several weeks. You are alone in this endeavor, I am afraid," Natto said regretfully.

"I'll ask about it with everyone later, see if we can't work something out. Now let's get to eating some food," Drake said. A head popped out of Sherry's tent.

"Food?!" she shouted, a comb still stuck in the tangled mess of her hair.

"Yes food, Bottomless Pit Number Two." Drake sighed, moving past her tent with Bjorn, Theodore, and Shigure in tow.

"Who's number one?" Shigure asked.

Drake gave Bjorn and Theodore a look, all three chuckling.

"Oh, you know if you know," Drake said.

* * *

Drake went from tent to tent, waking up his group for breakfast. Surprisingly, most were already awake or hadn't slept.

Almost all of them had formed the habit of staying awake regardless. The endless random attacks at any time from the goblins over the two weeks had ingrained it in them.

"What's for breakfast? Can we help?" Claire asked, her hair tied to the side of her head in a single side ponytail.

"Is it something new? Stew has been getting a little old," Chelsea said. Her double ponytails were tied in front of her in a braid as she leaned over the table Drake had pulled out.

"This time I'm going to try something a little *extra*," he said, smiling. "I had Hudson make a tinfoil equivalent, so we can make a few new cool things now with a bit of slow cooking!" Drake said excitedly.

He began taking out ingredients, some white powder that looked like flour, a bit of yellow mix that would replace the yeast as far as he knew from Natto's explanation, and some purple-shelled eggs that he had looted from one of the Goblin Lieutenants's bags.

Quickly mixing and kneading the mixture, he plopped twenty evenly split pieces of dough to the side, letting them rise.

"Now for the protein," Drake said, taking out the last of the boar that he had stocked.

Bjorn looked on expectantly as Shigure watched in disbelief.

"Is he actually cooking?" Shigure asked, whispering to Bjorn.

"Damn straight. Man's might be shit at a bunch of things, but he's a wonder boy at cooking," Bjorn answered.

Drake gave a sarcastic snort from the table as he sliced the boar into large roast chunks, placing each into a separate pan that stood on top of several fire pits.

"That's some big talk coming from someone who came in *seconddd*," Drake said, elongating the word.

Bjorn chuckled. "I'm still the highest level here, bro. And don't forget who lost last time." He smiled back.

Drake deflated, remembering the events after Bjorn had left right after their fight.

"Ugh, don't remind me. I'll have to tell you what happened while I had your little debuff," Drake said as he flash-seared the pieces of boar meat.

Bjorn winced slightly.

"Oof, yeah, sorry about that. Did something bad happen?" he asked, watching Drake work the pans.

"Oh, nothing. You know, people getting tortured, meeting a mortal enemy. Nothing I couldn't handle with a little spit and elbow grease." Drake smirked back, taking the now-seared pieces of meat off the pans.

Drake then took out some pieces of makeshift foil. He extinguished one of the fires, using his earth magic to move the coals out enough to stay warm but not lit, then placed the roasts into the foils with some deer fat and whatever veggies he could manage, tightly bundling them together in the wrapped foil. He then placed the bundles into the coals, erecting a cover of earth above them.

Taking another firepit and doing the same, he then wrapped the fresh dough in foil and placed them inside as well.

Wiping the nonexistent sweat from his brow, Drake turned over to Shigure and the rest of the group looking on eagerly.

"Okay, we have about an hour till the bread and meat is done, so how about a little sparring session? It's why you came along, right, Shigure?"

Shigure jerked at the mention of a spar, but his pride wouldn't let him back down.

"I-if it is what you wish for, I shall abide. Experience is a growing warrior's most treasured ally," he said shakily.

"Good! Then let's get to it!"

Both the men moved to a clearing beyond the tents as everyone but Sherry looked on.

At the sound to start, both instantly moved into action, but Drake was not trying to be flashy this time around. He quickly KO'd Shigure, knocking him unconscious.

"Jacqueline! Clean up aisle two!" Drake shouted.

Chapter 12
Curiosity Killed the Cat

"Come on, it isn't even noon yet and you're giving up?" Drake said, looming over Shigure as he sat on his haunches next to the teen. "I-I can't breathe! L-Let me rest!" Shigure panted.

"What's there to rest for? We have Jacqueline; she'll fix you right up no problem, right Jacqueline?" Drake said, looking over his shoulder.

"Yeah, whatever gov. Oh, Chelsea, pass me some more of that bread. It's bloody spectacular!" she said, chewing on a bite of meat.

"Noo! You already ate yours! This is mine!" Chelsea spat, pulling her loaf away from her reaching arm. Drake shook his head.

"I don't want to see that vile woman ever again," Shigure murmured. "I'll have nightmares of being healed over and over again for weeks…"

"Aw, don't sweat it. A good man goes through pain and trauma as they say, right? What better place than here, where you have your good buddies and an above-average-looking woman to heal you?" Drake said, moving his mask over to show his bright and totally-not-menacing smile.

"Who's my buddy? Is this really just because I made fun of your stupid cartoons?! You're just like Sato!" Shigure replied, barely able to lift his head to glare at Drake.

"What?" Drake moved his eyes to avoid Shigure's eye contact. "Of course it isn't… I just want to help you learn how to fight against someone like me."

"I *hate* you," Shigure spat, his head thumping back onto the ground.

"Okay, looks like he's kaput." Drake laughed. He looked up at Bjorn who was also finishing his food at the table with the others. "How about we give it a go then, Bear? It's been a whole two weeks since we sparred. What do you say?"

Bjorn polished off his roast boar before answering, giving his mouth a wipe.

"I'd rather not. I'm trying to get away from proving people right that I'm a big scary guy, remember?" Bjorn said, eyeing another loaf of bread and chuck boar roast.

"I don't think we get to really decide that anymore with how things are, Bear. You were the one who told me I had to be more, and I think you need to hear the same. If anyone has the right to do more and be more for people, it's you, my friend. I wouldn't have gone as far as I did for the people that were taken by the goblins if it wasn't for your little promise. And now, after everything, I think it's time for you to step up just like you made me step up."

Bjorn sighed as he stood up from the table, many eyes following him as he did.

"I've been trying to stay away from fighting for so long, but this tutorial keeps throwing me in situations without any other options. Maybe I should consider just embracing it. I *am* pretty good at it. Beat the shit out of you, after all." He smiled, but his expression turned melancholy. "Maybe it's just me. I think we need to talk anyway. Don't think I didn't notice you've been avoiding explaining what's happened with you."

Drake turned, trying not to meet the big man's gaze.

"Fine, but only after I get to knock you around a bit. You know, for old time's sake," Drake said reluctantly, but he grinned back nonetheless.

"Yeah, yeah." Bjorn waved and shouldered his enormous sword. "We'll see about that."

"Wait!" Shigure shouted from his lying position. "I would like to ask if we may spectate your fight? It would be a great learning experience to see."

"I don't see why not. Most people have seen what I can do by now, not that they can really figure out what exactly I'm doing, so I don't mind," Drake said, agreeing.

"Yeah, should be a good show if Shot here does anything like last time." Bjorn chuckled.

"I had a bone to pick. I've matured since then," Drake said, earning him a loud guffaw from his group at the table. "Okay"—he coughed—"I've matured a *little* bit."

"Only one way to find out, so let's get this done," Bjorn insisted.

"Then I will gather some of the people from the coalition to observe. Uta?" Shigure said to no one in particular.

The construct materialized next to him in a wisp of inky black smoke, her hands pressed in greeting as she knelt on one leg.

"Yes, Lord Shigure?" she asked.

"Will you please go grab the heads of the coalition for me? Allow them to bring anyone they wish to observe the fight between Sir Bear and Shot," he directed.

"By your will." She bowed and disappeared in a puff of smoke.

Drake looked over to Theodore. "Why can't you do that?"

"My lord, this one is a Dark Magician, one of the gentleman arts. This one doth not wisp in a charade of smoke, this one melds, and quite eloquently at that," Theodore said, putting a piece of boar gingerly to his mouth.

"That's fair. But maybe adding some flair to it will give you some variation. Could give you a more dramatic and knightly feel if you came when the surroundings darkened and all that," Drake suggested, crossing his arms in thought.

"This one will consider it, my liege."

"Shot," Bjorn said, nudging him with his heavily armored elbow.

"Ow, what?" Drake answered.

"We got some time now, bro. Here. Lend me your ear for a bit before we start. I need some advice from the little voice in your head," Bjorn said, turning a bit away from the rest of the group and holding his hand up to stop Shigure and the others from following them for the moment.

"Sorry peeps. Private meeting before the fight," Bjorn said, smiling.

* * *

Bjorn and Drake moved away from the group and took a few minutes to distance themselves, not wanting to risk being in earshot of someone who may have increased hearing.

"So what's the deal? You're usually more open and straight with me, Bjorn," Drake said, his brow raised.

"I need to speak to Natto about something that's been going on," Bjorn offered, getting to the point.

Drake nodded, and a small pink construct materialized on Drake's shoulder.

"I am against helping this oaf after what has happened previously," Natto said, tilting her nose up.

"Come on, Natto, he's coming to us for help. Least we can do is hear him out," Drake said, trying his best to be diplomatic.

Natto simply huffed and kept her head turned and tilted upwards in defiance. Drake smiled gently and turned to give Bjorn a nod.

"Thanks. Let me get straight to it before we get interrupted like always. I've been having some strange dreams since I finished using my skill stones. I have some of the highest rarity stones, and let me tell you, they were not fun to use," Bjorn began. Natto's head turned slightly at the mention of skill stones, her interest piqued.

Bjorn continued, "They started right after we fought. I just finished using them and was practicing. After the initial use and dealing with the power increase, it was going well. Then a few nights after, I started getting weird dreams, almost lucid visions of a forest."

Drake looked around, trying to hide his smile as he placed his eyes on the surrounding forest.

"No, I thought the same when I first saw it, but this forest was different. The trees reach the sky. Literally. There's a mist about the ground that never leaves. There... were giants in the mist. Eventually I got through the forest in some sort of... The only way I can explain it is another body. I came to a mountain, tallest thing I've ever seen, bro. Its snowy peaks were surrounded by clouds and monsters I've never seen before."

Drake whistled. "That's a pretty crazy dream alright."

"That's not the end, bro. The mountain. It moved."

"Drake," Natto said, her face now glaring at Bjorn more than she ever had. Drake turned to her, his eyebrow cocked in confusion.

"Yeah?" he asked.

"Do not fight him," she said.

"What?"

"*Kill him.*"

Drake's face contorted in anger, but he reeled it in a moment later.

"Why?" he said through gritted teeth.

"He can not be allowed to reach E-Rank."

"What do you mean?" Drake questioned.

"This oaf has consumed more than one legendary stone, or he was not born human. No, I am sure of it," Natto said flatly.

Drake's head snapped to Bjorn in surprise.

Bjorn's face was even, but his eyes showed his confusion and his mind working in the background.

"Those visions—or dreams, as he calls them—are his psyche changing. They will get stronger the closer he gets to reaching level 30 and finishing his rank up quest," Natto explained, not taking her eyes off Bjorn.

"Wait wait, how do you know that? Aren't you limited to things within F-Rank at the moment?" Drake asked.

"Legendary stones can be used in F-Rank, you idiot! Of course I know how they would affect someone. Do you remember how your epic and rare stones changed you? Legendary stones are of a different dimension entirely. How he has not gone mad is beyond me; his mental fortitude is impressive, I will concede that at least. But if he is allowed to completely change into what I suspect he will, you and your planet will regret it." Natto growled the last few words, the hair on her tail and ears standing on end.

"What is he going to turn into that's going to be so scary? I'm sure we can—"

"You can not! They are worse than what we already suspected we are dealing with! Do you wish to add to the problems we have to face?! The race he is going to turn into cares not for friendship nor worldly desires. They only respect and vie for power and destruction. They are the consumers of worlds, the destroyers of universes, they are—"

"*Titans*," Bjorn said, finishing Natto's sentence.

"Wait, like mythological titans?" Drake asked, becoming more and more confused.

"No. These are not like the titans of your lore from Earth, although some of their race are seen as such. These are world-enders, massive beings of power, destruction, and endless hunger. You know of the gods from mythology, I assume? Or at least the basic ones from history?" Natto asked.

"Yeah, of course. I've seen enough movies and anime to remember a few, at least," Drake answered.

"Those are meant to depict these titans. Those gods, as you have known them, were no mere small men and women. They are enormous containers of mana, and they only wish to consume to grow. They continue to roam until they have been killed or continue to eat after they have grown to a point they can not be stopped. There is no in-between," Natto said.

Drake turned to look back at Bjorn.

"Him? Do that? You have to be joking, Natto. He barely wants to fight, let alone see entire worlds blown to bits. Right, Bjorn?" Drake asked, but Bjorn stayed silent in contemplation.

"Bjorn...?" he muttered in concern.

"I don't know if what she is saying is true, but... I've been slipping," Bjorn conceded.

"Slipping?" Drake asked.

"I used to abhor violence, bro. I would only fight when I was forced into a corner or needed to defend myself or others. Now... I don't know, it's different. I'm looking for it. And not in a good way. I may have said I didn't want to fight, but honestly, I was looking forward to it when you asked," Bjorn said, scratching the back of his head.

"That's normal, isn't it? We're all in a situation now where we need that strength, that drive to get stronger and be able to protect what we hold dear, right?" Drake said, trying to offer him a leg to stand on.

Bjorn shook his head.

"I don't have anything like that, Drake. My parents passed away shortly before the tutorial started up. I only had my dog and some very distant friends where I lived. Sure, the townsfolk warmed up to me, but we weren't friends. I have no girlfriend because, well, I think they're a pain in the ass, and honestly I haven't found one I liked for more than a few minutes. No kids or siblings to speak of. I try my best to be giving, and that's what I strived to do when the tutorial happened and I got on my own two feet," he said solemnly. "But if what the little miss said is right, you're going to have to kill me."

Chapter 13

I Refuse

"I don't care what Natto says. Why would I agree to something as stupid as killing you before you've even done anything?" Drake scoffed.

"Drake! This is not the same laughing matter as what we have dealt with before! This is a Primordial race that even the other Primordial races are afraid of. Their entire lineage has had to be kept in check since before the fall of the first system!" Natto pleaded.

"Don't care. Is he doing anything now? Is Bjorn a threat now?" Drake demanded.

"He is a potential threat that could end your universe before you are ever able to go forward! Yes, he is a threat!"

"That's later. I mean right now, in this moment. Is my friend, the person who saved me—is he a danger to me, my friends, or family?" Drake asked again.

"No... not this very second. But! He certainly will be! His future race is known as world enders! They devour entire systems!" she shouted.

"Then," Drake began, smiling and looking back at Bjorn in the eyes, "I'll just have to get strong enough to keep him in check. I've already had more than enough reasons to reach the top. This is just one more thing lighting a fire under my ass to keep going!" Drake laughed, his smile widening as he spread his arms, Natto nearly losing balance and falling off. "Bjorn! I refuse!"

"Drake... I don't think you can even stop me now. How are you going to stop me when I'm some super monster who wants to eat and kill everything, bro?" Bjorn asked.

"Shaddup! I'll figure it out! And who says I can't stop your big red-pubed ass? Are you going to make me go all out again to prove you wrong?" Drake sneered.

Bjorn's eyes thinned.

"This is serious, Drake. And no, this time is different. I have better control over my skills than before, and I'm leagues ahead of you in levels and stats. I have an epic rank class as well. There is no stopping me now; what hope do you have later?" Bjorn said, his eyes serious.

"Don't think you're the only one with a special class. When we last fought, I hadn't even had a chance to practice my skills. I won't be so easy to beat this time around. I'm willing to bet my life on saving yours. So let me do it, you stubborn frotch," Drake spat.

"I can't let you risk your life for me man. It isn't right. We're friends, but how do you think I would feel knowing I put that all on your shoulders? What if the worst happens? I wouldn't be able to live with mysel—"

"Don't care! I'll take it all. All the responsibility, all of the weight. I'm still learning and muddling through becoming a better person, but you started it Bjorn. You made me take the first step forward after I thought I had no chance and was stuck wallowing in self-pity. You're the second person to save my life with words alone. So shut the fuck up already," Drake said, smiling and throwing his fist into Bjorn's chest, "and let me save you for once."

Bjorn sighed. "And you call me the stubborn bastard? You're like a child," Bjorn conceded, a smile creasing his face.

"I am what I ea—Wait, no, I'm just a kid when it suits me. And not listening to things I don't want to hear suits me just fine when it comes to those important to me. You're stuck with me now, man. For life. This is our Naruto-Sasuke moment," Drake said, giving a big grin.

"I do not understand why you will not listen to me... I was quite literally made to help advise you on things of this nature," Natto said, slumping down into a sitting position on Drake's shoulder, her head in her hands.

"Don't worry, you'll get used to it Natto. We only have thousands of years together." Drake laughed.

"Do not remind me! Thousands of years listening to pointless and awful references! Please! Take me now! What did I do to deserve such a fate?!" she pleaded to the sky.

"*No one is coming to save you,*" Drake said in a deep voice. He broke out in a chuckle. Bjorn shook his head.

"How did I end up enabling such a moron? And who the hell is Naruto?" he asked.

Drake recoiled.

"You can't be serious? You know Vash but you're telling me you don't know him? I take it back, you might be a lost cause." Drake deflated.

"Please, leave me with the yappy ones at the food table... I care not for this nonsense anymore," Natto asked.

"You know we can't do that, but I'll tell you what. I'll have Claire bring you to a tent to eat. I snagged some of the finished food for you anyway," Drake answered. Natto's eyes brimmed to life, and she nodded vigorously.

Bjorn gave a belly laugh. "Are you sure you two aren't related? You act more like siblings than any I've ever seen, bro."

"I mean technically?" Drake said, wincing slightly.

"Oh? Wait, really dude?"

"It's a weird system thing. Maybe I'll explain it later. Anyway, let's get back. There's a crowd forming over there, and I'm getting a hole drilled into the back of my head from someone with a long vision skill of some sort," Drake explained.

"You can tell that from here?" Bjorn asked.

"Yeah, my mana perception has gone up a bit since I started getting accustomed to my skills. You telling me you can't, Mr. Legendary Skills?" Drake countered.

"Never said that." Bjorn smiled and walked back with Drake to the group.

"Hope you aren't lying for your sake, or I'm going to knock the snot out of you."

"Yeah, yeah. We'll see..." Bjorn answered, his voice trailing off a bit.

* * *

"You twats hug it out?" Jacqueline asked, smirking.

"Yeah. You jealous, sweetie?" Drake asked, smiling back.

"W-Who's fucking jealous?! Bloody wanker!" She reddened.

"I think you have a thing for me, Jacqueline. But I already said I don't like aged wine," Drake jabbed again.

"I'm twenty-six, you dumb nob!" she growled.

Drake shrugged, turning back to the growing group and Shigure.

"So, who did we sell tickets to?" Drake asked.

Shigure raised a brow, confused, and took a moment to understand what Drake meant.

"We have gathered all of the leaders of the coalition. Some of them were absent when we... *fought*," Shigure said.

"You mean when I kicked your shit in?" Drake grinned, amused.

Shigure grit his teeth, but held his tongue.

"You don't need to be so insulting to the boy, Mr. Shot. You should know better," Harley said, waving her finger at him.

Drake shirked backward slightly, a nervous grin on his face.

"Yes ma'm, I'll tone it back a bit. Just trying to haze him a little, you know how it is." Drake chuckled.

"That's just how he is, Harley. We all know he's an asshole; it's like his key character trait," Chelsea said, chiming in.

"I don't deny it." Drake shrugged and looked around at the faces present. He spotted most of his group, save Hudson and Sherry. Drake also saw some faces that weren't here yesterday.

Megan and Julia had turned up, surprisingly. Amongst the crowd, there were many he didn't know, and he also saw the exchanging of skill stones and monster cores in the background.

Oh, people are taking bets? Maybe we should get in on that, Drake thought.

"*Your first priority should be my meal! Have the zappy zappy girl feed me— be quick about it!*" Natto grumbled.

Alright, alright.

"Claire, can I see you in my tent for a moment?" Drake asked. The woman's face lit up, but she was slightly confused.

"U-Um, sure?" she answered, walking with him to the tent.

Entering quickly, Natto also appeared on Drake's shoulder. Claire's expression quickly deflated.

"Really, again?! I'm not a babysitter, Drake!" Claire shouted. "I wanted to see the fight just like everyone else!"

Drake put up his hands placidly.

"I know, I know, but I need someone to watch Natto, and you're one of the only people she doesn't seem to be annoyed with."

"Then why don't you just do it? I'm not her keeper!" She frowned.

"Can you just do this for me? Look, I've been thinking about who can come with us when I go to take down the nest. And I think Bear might come, so that means I can take more people. Just let her eat like she normally does and I'll let you tag along, alright?" Drake offered.

"Promise...?" Claire asked, still huffy.

Drake nodded. He placed the food out for Natto, her eyes drilling into him expectantly.

"Fine," Claire said reluctantly. "But! You need to get Chelsea in here too. It isn't fair if she gets to watch and I don't."

Really? Why are women so competitive over this kind of thing? Drake sighed.

"Alright, fine. Then just watch her and make sure no one comes in, alright?" Drake asked once more.

Claire nodded, satisfied. Her hand went for a piece of bread, but she was quickly stopped by a knife landing inches from her hand. Drake laughed as he exited the tent.

"Chelsea, Claire wants to speak to you," he lied.

Chelsea's ears perked up, but her brows showed her confusion.

"About what?" she asked. "The fight is just about to start."

"I don't know. Something about settling the score or something," Drake fibbed again, walking past her and to the crowd.

Chelsea looked at him skeptically, then nodded and moved to the tent. Drake let out a breath.

Now that that's over...

"Now then..." Drake addressed the crowd. "Are you normies ready for a little shock and awe!" he roared.

"Who are you calling a normie, Raijuu mei!" a person screamed from the crowd, his glasses reflecting the sheen of the pristine silver gun he held in his hands.

Drake's eyes widened at the familiar slang, surprised it was used against him.

"Sato, will you please shut up for once," Shigure said, his head in his hand.

"How dare you call me a normie!" Drake said, hurt.

"You just put two gorgeous women in your tent. Of course you're a raijuu!" Sato spat.

Well, when he puts it that way... I wonder what he would say if he knew I turned them both down. Drake laughed at the thought.

"Is this another one of the coalition leaders?" Drake asked curiously, eyeing the gun.

"No. This is my childhood friend, Sato," Shigure said, showing a bit of embarrassment.

"I told you, it's xXxGunLover69xXx! Why are you ruining my immersion, Kenzo?!" Sato cried.

"Well, so much for an alias..." Drake mumbled inspecting the teen.

xXxGunLover69xXx Level 18

Oh, he's actually pretty high up there, Drake thought, surprised.

"Say, Sato, what can you trade me for these?" Drake said, pulling out the guns he was still saving from the cowboy gnoll. He smiled. "Look like a certain someone's gun, don't they?"

The teen's eyes bloomed wide as he spotted the steampunk guns.

"It's Jinx's pistol! And two of them?! My lord, I will do anything for them!" Sato said, his attitude taking a full 180.

"Ah, otaku are so easily swayed." Drake smirked. "Show me your wares, junior."

"I've been collecting many stones, but I can see I was mistaken about you, good sir. If my guess is correct, you know what..." Sato said, slipping a playing card from his pocket and showing it to Drake.

"This is..." Drake's hand shook as he looked at the card. For the first time in a long time, he dropped to his knees. "Where did you get this?!"

"I know a guy and won it off him in a match!" Sato puffed his chest proudly. "Well? What do you say?"

Drake jumped at the card, dropping the pistols at his feet.

"Done!" Drake shouted, looking at the card.

Trading Card Illustration: The Dazzling Tyrant [F-Grade, Rare]
Limited edition trading card made by the Artist. Only five copies were made. The card depicts the Grand Tyrant within the forest in all his glory. It is a sought-after collectible for all traders.
First limited edition card of the Dazzling Tyrant Series. One of five.

Bjorn looked on, finally forced to say something.

"Hey, are we fighting or can I go back to eating?"

"IN A MINUTE!!" Drake howled.

Chapter 14
Shock and Awe

Drake coughed embarrassedly.

"My bad, I didn't mean to get so caught up about that *collectible*. I just couldn't help asking, seeing how cultured your friend Sato was," Drake said.

"Cultured? He is the least cultured person here," Shigure spat, his eyes frowning. "I wish he would grow up! We've almost died many times, and all he does is make stupid anime references!"

Drake coughed again. *Oh, I'm going to piss this guy off for sure,* he thought.

"Grow up? Kenzo, I'm a year older than you!" Sato snapped back.

"Yes, but mentally you are several years behind! How many times must I tell you those cartoons do not apply to the real world!" Shigure shouted.

If only this guy knew I've been using those shows as a basis for everything in this tutorial. If it wasn't for them, I might have died several times over. Not to mention almost all of my spells are a reference to one show, manga, light novel or another, Drake thought, laughing to himself.

"Then," Drake said, looking at Shigure and Sato, "how do you explain me kicking the shit out of you?" He chuckled.

"Excuse me?" Shigure spat, unsure of Drake's meaning.

"Everything I hit you with is from a show or game I've experienced. Yet you seem to think they were useless." Drake smiled.

"W-What?"

Sato smiled triumphantly next to Shigure.

"What I think you are failing to realize is that everything is a means of growing stronger and maturing. You're dismissing something Sato and I feel passionately about on the basis of some preconception or other," Drake said, shaking his head dramatically. "That's going to become fatal in this new world.

"Your construct," Drake continued, pointing his thumb behind him, "that is going into my tent right now should have told you."

Shigure winced. His face then contorted into knowing as he realized Drake had some sort of perception ability.

"We are not the only ones this system has uprooted and thrown into the blender. You think our old world was a melting pot of diversity? You should know that it pales in comparison to the myriad of races we will see once we leave this place. And shutting out what is going to be a clash of times, cultures, and more importantly people is going to hurt you and the people you lead. I'm not saying that you have to like anime, but understanding the things you hate to solidify your position on it is vital to a good foundation for tolerance and mutual respect," Drake explained. He paused from his long-winded speech to take a breath. *I really need to cut back on the preaching.*

"Not to mention, those shows are great. I mean have you even watched SlayerS? That alone would help you live through half the shit in this tutorial. And don't get me started on that dude that slays goblins. Chef's kiss, my man," Drake said while making the gesture.

Shigure was so taken by surprise by the sermon that he stayed silent, essentially conceding the point. His eyes showed that his mind was turning as it consumed the words.

Drake was somewhat surprised that the teen didn't argue more. He honestly thought that he would be more adamant as most younger people were with their beliefs. It seemed the multiple beatings Drake had dished out had at least opened the kid's mind.

Figuratively speaking.

Drake turned to the crowd, many of them scowling back at him. Ignoring them, Drake's eyes fell on Megan and Julia.

"I'm pleasantly surprised to see you both again. Even if one of you seems to disdain me." Drake chuckled and walked over to the pair, ignoring the other scowling faces.

"Hello again, *Lord Shot*," Julia said, giving a small bow.

"Are you making fun of me?" Drake asked incredulously.

"I wouldn't think of doing such a thing, *Lord Shot*," Julia said again, a smile on her face.

Drake sighed, looking over to Megan who was eerily silent compared to Julia. Her face was scrunched in a mix of frustrated emotions.

"So, what's the deal? You two came to watch the fight as well? Pretty sure you've both seen what I can do," Drake said, leaning on one leg.

"I was unconscious. And no, I would like to extend my gratitude again and ask to join your inner circle. I know my skills will be of use," Julia said evenly, then nudged Megan with her elbow.

"I... I'd also like to offer my service. I have been missing my friends. And I—" Megan looked downward before continuing. "—I know I've been giving you a hard time. On the way here, you saved me, saved *us* again. And I've talked to Chels, Jacky, even Tom more while we traveled. I want to see with my own two eyes who you are. If you really *are* just a cold-hearted killer with a gentle face like... Chris... or if you're the savior they all make you out to be," Megan finished, her eyes still on the ground.

"Hey Megan," Drake said, "my eyes are up here." He snorted, waiting for the woman to face him.

She stared back at him shakily, her eyes darting back and forth, but Drake stayed silent until she was able to keep relative eye contact.

"When you ask for a favor, you need to look the person in the eye and be sincere. The eye is the window to the soul, and if you can't even look me in them, how will I ever be able to trust you?" Drake said, waiting for her response.

Megan was slightly shaken, but apparently determined. She stared back, her eyes tearing up slightly as she did.

"I am asking to join your party like the rest. I want to learn more about you—to make my own decision if I should leave my friends to you!" she said, her voice growing to a shout.

Drake smiled, impressed by the boom of her voice.

"Nope! No can do. All full up," Drake sneered back.

Both women looked at him in disbelief, their mouths hanging wide open.

"What do you mean you don't have room?!" both yelled.

Drake laughed then shrugged.

"I'm only kidding. Sure, both of you can come with us. We could always use more support classes."

"You're such an asshole!" Megan snapped. Julia, on the other hand, laughed with Drake.

"I think I will enjoy being in this group. Always keeping me on my toes. It feels like home," she said.

"We can talk about the details later. Right now, I need to put on a show. It was good talking to you two, and I'm thankful for your straightforwardness. Welcome aboard Team Shot." He smiled.

"I'm never saying I'm a part of a team named that," Megan mumbled, crossing her arms.

Drake snorted and walked past them, making his way to the other star of the show.

"Sorry for the wait, man, crazy how much you get pulled left and right with knowing people," Drake said, apologizing to Bjorn.

"All good bro, I'm used to it. Forget I was a CEO? Sometimes you need to have meetings even when you don't have time," Bjorn replied nonchalantly with a wave of his unarmored hand. "Then, should we get started? I'll clear some space." Bjorn smiled and pulled his sword from his back.

He walked away from the congregation of people, finding a relatively open area for him to swing his sword in a manner that seemed to take no effort despite the size of the weapon. With the swing, he felled enough trees to open up the forest in front of him.

"Jeez, who are you, frigging Scandinavian Cell?" Drake said, giving a brief whistle.

"I don't know who that is," Bjorn said, cocking an eyebrow.

"Alright, that's it." Drake sighed. "Everyone is going to have to go through anime rehabilitation when we get back to Earth, I've had enough of people not getting my references! You are all so uncultured and deprived..."

"I got that one!" Sato screamed from behind them. Drake gave him a thumbs up.

"At least there's *one* real one among us."

Bjorn turned, pointing his sword tip at Drake with one hand.

"Should we get started then, *Lord* Shot?" Bjorn smirked.

Drake's eyes lit up with eagerness as they flashed through his ocular skills.

"*Marked.* I'm more than ready," Drake replied, his stance going low as he snapped his freshly returned right hand's fingers and summoned bolts of lightning to either side of him.

"Don't think this is going to go the same way as last time, Bear!" he roared. Another snap of his fingers hurtled the lightning bolts forward, and they flew straight for Bjorn.

The bolts screeched towards Bjorn, but he only smirked as he stood in the open area he had created.

Drake didn't wait for the impact. Once the bolts blocked Bjorn's vision of him, he shot to the side, snapping his fingers once again. His tattoo rings slipped into his inventory, and he summoned his Morning Glory Staff.

Bjorn's eyes somehow tracked Drake as Drake came into view around the bolts of lightning on his left side.

Again with his nuts perception. But he isn't the only one who can see through things! Drake roared internally.

The bolts of lightning finally met with Bjorn, but unexpectedly, Bjorn dodged one of the two. One passed over his shoulder harmlessly, his free hand stopping the other bolt in its tracks as he gripped it like it was a mere twig of electricity.

Bjorn then crushed the bolt in his hands, the lightning mana dissipating into the air as he kept his eyes fixed on Drake.

Drake skidded to a stop, pointing his staff at Bjorn.

"The halls of the underworld welcome you! Cocytus!" Drake roared, a white magic circle forming below his feet.

With the creation of his unique spell, the increased mana made the magic flourish. The magic circle spread to encompass the surroundings, moving far enough to bring itself under Bjorn. Suddenly, it erected a massive door of ice, flecks of purple-tinted ice-like glass adorning the inside.

Drake smiled behind his mask, his free hand raised high in the air as he roared, *"Shut the Gate!"*

Instantly the door slammed shut like an iron maiden around Bjorn. The thunderous boom silenced the surroundings.

"W-What? Is Bear...?" someone murmured from the crowd.

"Just... like that?" another said in disbelief.

Drake remained vigilant through the crowd's commotion. He'd received no notification, and he knew his friend better than that.

Just a warm-up, huh? he thought, feeling the spell struggle to hold together around Bjorn.

The next moment, Drake felt something bubbling behind the closed door, sending a shiver down his spine.

Quickly snapping his fingers, he summoned lightning and switched his Endowment. He bolted from the spot he was just standing on, throwing his staff into the air as it vanished into his inventory. Two rings materialized in front of him that he quickly threw his fingers into, the tattoos on his arm flaring to life as brilliant yellow cascaded over them, accompanied by the deepening blue of the mana being infused.

A split second after Drake's foot left position, a white blade of mana erupted from the door of ice, rending the ground he was just standing on into a gaping valley.

The ice spell fell apart, shattering into shards of shimmering splinters that reflected the light of the morning. A mist of both dust and cold snow covered the man inside as he stood, waiting for Drake's next move.

"I thought I told you how I felt about your gimmicks, Shot," Bjorn said evenly, his eyes flaring white in the shadows of the falling ice.

Drake smiled wider, hearing the familiar statement.

"And I thought I told you my inspiration is anything but!" he roared back. "And I'll prove it! Those inspirations will be your salvation, Bear!"

Drake threw his hand forward.

"*Heretical Symphony of Elements!*" he yelled, commanding his every spell to be used, all eleven instances, Proficiency 3 Multiplicative skill shining.

Drake didn't finish with just that as he charged his defensive skills, ready to enter a brawl as well.

"*I am the shield! I am the rampart! Bulwark! I am the wall on which my enemies billow! Unbreakable!*"

The green sheen of the skills covered Drake in a cloak of security.

"He's using defensive skills?! Isn't he a mage?!" someone roared over the grounds.

"How can he summon that many spells? That isn't possible!" another added.

Drake ignored the shouts and complaints coming from the peanut gallery, instead locking his gaze on the red outline of Bjorn within the smoke of ice and dust that his Weak Point Skill helped him faintly see and feel.

"*On blessed wings! Guardian's Reprieve!*" Drake shouted, finishing chanting his defensive skills and shooting forward with the help of his wind and fire spells used in tandem to increase his speed. He reached Bjorn in an instant with his fist outstretched.

Drake's fist was covered in both the blue from his imbued mana and the red of his Martial Skill as it careened toward Bjorn's face. The ice around them fell in chunks and crashed like a recently demolished building.

But once again, Bjorn's tenacity and perception showed. In the last moment, a metal-gloved hand stopped Drake's. The booming sound and force of the impact shattered the ice around them, blowing the remains of the enormous ice door apart and sending pieces flying outward.

Drake clicked his tongue. *He has one hell of a reaction time. But what about this!* Drake bellowed internally, using the rest of his spells.

Drake moved his lightning behind Bjorn to his blind spot, continuing to throw punch after punch at Bjorn's head. Bjorn effortlessly blocked each punch with his free hand.

Is he getting faster?! Drake thought in amazement.

He began imbuing more and more mana into his tattoos, their blue glow deepening as it started to overtake the red of his Martial Skill.

His bolt of lightning took its chance now that Bjorn was distracted and screamed forward, but Bjorn somehow again knew it was coming. He moved his sword to deflect the spell. It ricocheted off and impaled the ground in a red-hot molten hole. Bjorn smiled back at Drake.

Drake cursed, but he didn't give up. Continuing to channel his mana into his spells, he began bombarding Bjorn with the elements at his disposal.

Spears of lightning, water, fire, earth, magma, and wind began shooting forward in every direction, but to no avail. Drake could not land a single blow.

What the fuck is this? Is he omniscient?! I can't even scratch him this time around!

Drake continued his assault as Bjorn remained calm, deflecting each of the spells with his large claymore, his movements so precise and casual that he made the blade seem weightless.

Bjorn apparently had enough and finally went on the offensive. Using a large sweeping motion, he cut right through the spell circles, surprising Drake.

"Who are you, fucking Asta?!" Drake spat, pushing backward just moments before the blade struck him.

"Always with the random references." Bjorn smirked and held his blade's tip toward Drake.

"The sword itself isn't doing it, it just happens to be part of one of my skills," Bjorn said, refusing to move.

"Just like last time, you aren't going to move unless I make you, huh?" Drake scoffed.

"You couldn't make me even if you wanted to this time. The skill has improved well beyond what you have seen, and I've reached the max proficiency in some of my skills." Bjorn laughed. "Let me show you."

The mana surrounding Bjorn's body began to shift, taking on a bright hue as he raised his sword to the heavens.

"*The world has borne witness to my absolute power,*" Bjorn muttered, the density of the white mana spiking as his sword became a heavenly white.

"*Rend the skies! Heaven Splitting Blade!*" Bjorn shouted, his sword lowering with such speed that Drake was almost unable to move out of the way in time.

He had no time for his charade of fake casting. Immediately, he used his fire and wind spells to propel him to the side. Part of his robes were caught in the blade's mana-infused swing.

Drake shot to the side, colliding with the ground and rolling across it. He eventually found himself upright and looked at the destruction wrought by Bjorn's strike.

He stared at his smoldering robe, part of it erased, the fabric singed by the swing. It was still usable, but almost half of it had been destroyed.

Looking to the ground, he saw what was now a chasm separating him from the camp. And from the expressions he saw on the spectators, they had no idea what Bjorn was capable of.

"Well, you ruined my favorite robes," Drake muttered.

"Happens," Bjorn said, resting his sword on his shoulder.

Drake frowned.

"Well, since we're going all out here, allow me to oblige!" Drake rose to his feet, his hand arching in front of him as seven magic circles formed for his elements. Two more yellow magic circles formed on either side of him, and they began to slowly deepen into a wondrous violet color.

"*Heretical Endowment of the Elementist! Septenarius!*" Drake cried, the seven elements vanishing as his hair and tattoos began to shift in color into a glorious cascading show of the elements.

Bjorn looked taken aback at the display.

"You can do them all at once? That's new, bro."

"I'm not done yet. This might have been meant to be a spar, but apparently

I need to show you just how far I've come." Drake smirked, his body glowing in the shifting colors of his elements.

"*Heretical Asura! Duo!*" Drake howled. His two lightning spells embedded themselves in his back just above his shoulders, turning into two additional arms that now slammed together, sparks crackling from the impact as the sound of thunder cracked through the surroundings.

"And for the finale! You're the first who gets to see it firsthand, Bear!" Drake shouted across the field, a primal smile creasing his face under the mask, his eyes turning to points as he reveled in the battle.

Drake clapped his hands together, and when they separated, two white burning balls of fire formed in the palms of his hands.

"*Heretical Attunement, Fire!*"

Drake crushed the flames in his hands. They leaked from his fingers and spiraled up his arms, forming breathing gauntlets of flames around his tattoos.

"I'm coming at you full force! No backing down! I'll prove I can keep my word, my friend. I won't let you become a monster, even if I have to become one myself to stop you!"

Chapter 15
Friendship Always Prevails

Drake surged forward, his speed allowing him to close the gap between him and Bjorn in an instant. The combination of all of his Endowments doubled his stats on top of his new attunement to his tattoos, which raised his strength through fire even further.

Moving quickly to Bjorn's blind spot, he threw his fist forward, aiming for his right side—exactly where his liver was.

Drake's flame and lightning-fueled fists careened for its target, but again, Bjorn's own hand moved, stopping Drake in his tracks.

"What?! Do you have eyes in the back of your head?" Drake spat, measuring Bjorn's gaze. Surprise was painted over Bjorn's face, forcing a similar expression from Drake.

What? He's surprised? Does that mean he didn't do it consciously?! Drake stepped again, changing his direction of attack.

Moving with speed even Bjorn could not follow, Drake attacked from all sides, using his Asura spell to strike from four different directions.

But it was to no avail. He was unable to find a gap in Bjorn's defenses.

Not all was lost, though, as Drake slowly began damaging Bjorn's armor. The marks of his searing strikes began to appear across the metal, and Bjorn's breath became more and more labored as the fight went on.

Slipping in and out of Bjorn's guard, Drake threw everything he had at him. But like before, his every straight, every jab, every blow was met with the wall that was Bjorn's hand or blade deflecting or blocking Drake's strikes.

He's not doing it on his own, that I'm sure of. It must be his skill. He basically has an automated defense, Drake thought. He zipped backwards, one of his arms moving from his shoulder and forming a dense lance of lightning.

"You've reached your cap on your defensive buff. I can tell. Your speed has stopped increasing as well," Drake conjectured.

Bjorn looked back at Drake, silent, neither confirming nor denying his statement.

"Bear, you've lost. You can't keep up with me anymore! And your skill won't let you move without losing your stacked up buffs! I've won this time. You can trust me to keep you in check. So... so don't give up and tell me to kill you ever again!" Drake shouted across the field, many of the spectators gasping in confusion.

"Kill him?"

"What does he mean? Bear wants to die?"

"Why in the world would he do that?"

Bjorn's eyes snapped to Drake, his body glowing with a black aura.

"Who said I can't move?" Bjorn growled. "Just let me do what I think is right! I don't want to hurt people! My life has been nothing but one long fight. Let me just give up. I can't do it anymore, Shot. I tried to push through, to adapt like I always have, bro. But this time, the faces of the people I've had to kill to save my own life... They keep appearing! Every time I close my eyes, they're there! I can't take it! What's even worse is I'm starting—I'm starting to enjoy it! The cruelty, the savagery. It's something that's becoming instinctively pleasurable. I don't want that!"

"And what's wrong with that?" Drake said. "What's wrong with feeling remorse for taking a life, what's wrong with not wanting to be at constant war with others?"

His lightning spell crackled louder with every passing word.

"But you don't have to worry about that anymore, Bear. I'll take all of that responsibility on. You'll never have to worry again about slipping. I'll show you how strong I've become, and if it isn't enough, I'll just reach out and grab the power I need to keep you from falling further. So don't say you've given up! Because I won't let you give up. You have so much more to do for the world.

Just like you've told me I might be needed, I *know* you will be for this wild world we're about to enter," Drake said, staring back at him.

"I-I don't think you understand. There is a monster in me, bro! You don't know what that feels like!" Bjorn spat back.

"Fuck if I don't! There's something inside both of us! That's the responsibility of the strong: to quell the monster inside. Do you think it's painful having to deal with the thought of it being let loose?" Drake asked.

"Yes. I don't need this anymore. I don't need to keep going, man…"

"Bullshit!" Drake shouted. "Do you know what hurts more? What's really painful? It's the feeling of regret! The feeling of giving up before the end of the line. Not giving it your all before your last breath, knowing you can take one more step to change things. Change it with me, Bear! You don't have to be the monster, because *I* will be."

Drake flexed his aura, encompassing the area and Bjorn.

The spectators all gasped in surprise as their beneficial abilities were wiped clean by his Tyrannical Aura. Some were unable to bear the brunt of the force, passing out in a frothing white mess.

Targeted beneficial skill outranks current skill.
Targeted beneficial skill outranks current skill.
Targeted beneficial ski…

Drake didn't give up, focusing his aura on Bjorn and doing his utmost to strip away the defensive skill.

Bjorn reacted almost instinctively as he began marching forward, each step embedding him deeper into the ground as if the gravity around him was flexing and weighing him down.

Fuck! My skill can't compete with his legendary skill. I'll just have to brute force it then! Drake cursed.

"Brace your teeth, buddy! I'm not holding back!" Drake warned, but Bjorn seemed to ignore it, continuing to walk slowly forward, entranced.

Drake quickly slipped his rings into his inventory, extinguishing the flames around his fists. A staff of four petals appeared in front of him.

"Heretical Attunement! Lightning!" Drake shouted, merging his violet lightning with the staff as it grew in size, becoming a blade of iridescent sparks.

"Darkness beyond blackest pitch," Drake began, staring down his friend, the blade of lightning snapping and roaring as it licked the ground and crackled back and forth. *"Deeper than the deepest night!"*

He continued to chant, but Bjorn was not about to allow him to do so freely. He suddenly shot forward, his hand outstretched to grab Drake.

Drake wouldn't allow himself to go down, though, and desperately dodged, his speed still greater than Bjorn's. But the casting of his spell had slowed Drake to the point where he was only barely dodging Bjorn's hand and the subsequent strikes from his sword.

I can't let his sword touch me or it's over! Drake shouted internally. He desperately continued his chant.

"Lord as vast as the largest ocean." Each word condensed the mana further into the blade of lightning, but now Drake needed more.

"Heretical Attunement! Fire!" he shouted, adding a second element to the spell. He felt the drain as forcing the concurrent spells caused his status to drop, but he needed to continue regardless.

Still being chased, Drake dodged and tumbled across the ground, scrambling any way he could to not be hit by Bjorn's sword.

"Colder than the coldest ice!" Drake roared, adding another element to the blade. *"Heretical Attunement! Ice!"*

A shard of ice shimmered to life under the fire as it contained the lightning within the frozen crystal.

Drake coughed suddenly, the strain catching up with him. A bead of red liquid escaped the edges of his mask.

"King of Darkness who shines like gold upon the Sea of Chaos! I call upon thee and swear myself to thee! I stand ready to bear the strength you give me!" Drake screamed rapidly. His consciousness was beginning to falter, his movements starting to slow.

Drake forced himself to stay awake as he bolted in every direction, keeping ahead of the relentless Bjorn. His fists and swings of his sword carved the ground below them in enormous divots and craters.

"*Let the fools wh—*" Drake tried to continue, but his body faltered for only a moment.

But that moment was enough for Bjorn to catch him. His sword swung down, and his fist came down from the side.

I can't dodge!

Drake had no choice. He had to take one of the blows.

So he bet on which one he thought was best.

Bjorn's fist collided with Drake's face as Drake turned mid-air, narrowly dodging his sword swing but taking the full brunt of the punch as Bjorn's fist slammed against him.

Gained Reprieval charge.
Gained Reprieval charge.
Gained Reprieval charge.
Max charges stored, charge lost.

Drake flew backward like a bullet, tumbling against the ground until he came to a stop. Struggling to stand, Drake smiled underneath his mask, his fight with the Warrior Vampiric Ape flashing in his mind.

He had gained just enough distance to finish his spell.

Bjorn rushed forward to follow up, but he was too late.

"*—who stand before me be destroyed by the power you and I possess!*" Drake howled at the top of his lungs, his breath coming out as visible steam from his mask.

Bjorn was just inches from Drake.

Drake teleported at the last second, straight into the air above Bjorn, his massive spell expanding as it whipped wildly in the magnificent shifting colors of his combined elements. His hair and robes snapped against the wind the spell produced as he shouted the last words.

"*Giga! Slaveeeeeeee!!!!*"

Drake put all his force into bringing down the tremendous spell. It lit up the sky as it screeched forward toward the ground, the brilliance of the spell so bright that it outshone the sun and cast shadows all around it.

The spell roared toward Bjorn, the man standing stoically as he stared back at the spell, a smile creasing his face as he mouthed two simple words.

"Thanks, bro."

"No problem," Drake said. He used his last Reprieval charge to teleport down next to Bjorn. "Now no more saying stupid shit, or this spell really will hit you." Drake chuckled and snapped his fingers, the spell winking out of existence. "Now lend me an overly muscular arm of yours—I'm about to pass out. I need to at least stay cool-looking for a bit longer."

He chuckled before he fell forward against Bjorn's arm.

Bjorn looked over in disbelief, mouth opening and closing as he tried to find the words. His face slowly relaxed and turned into a smirk.

"Fine, you win. Stubborn bastard just has to win," he chuckled.

* * *

"What's going on outside?" Chelsea asked from her seat across Claire's, her face staying in a perpetual scowl.

"I don't know, probably Drake going crazy again. But we'll never know since we're on baby duty," Claire replied, scowling back.

"You mean *you* were on baby duty! Why did I have to get dragged into this," Chelsea grumbled.

"Because it would have been unfair if it was just me!"

"That's not my problem, Claire! It was unfair you got to go into the tent! Here I thought I lost..." Chelsea mumbled.

"W-What?! He doesn't even see me like that!" Claire pouted.

"Y-Yeah. He doesn't seem to have a thing for me either, but I did dig into him a lot before... He isn't gay, is he?"

"I—I don't think so? I catch him looking all the time... I'm not sure if he just doesn't want... dirty goods..." Claire said, turning despondent.

"What? If that asshole ever said anything like that, we would tear him apart! Seriously. That wasn't even your fault!" Chelsea said, consoling her.

"Thanks," Claire said, smiling slightly. "Ah, did he tell you the same thing about not being interested?" Claire finally asked.

Chelsea blushed, but answered timidly.

"Y-Yeah. He was a gentleman about it, but I really didn't expect him to turn me down. I mean, look at us," she said, her face turning into a smirk. "He's got to be gay or too stupid to say no."

Claire laughed. Before she could respond, they both heard a loud crunch interrupting them.

"Are you two quite done? The aforementioned *baby* is trying to eat in peace," Natto said. She bit into a piece of boar and ripped a portion of bread away from the loaf with an audible crunch and tear.

"Uh, sorry. Just, you know, girl talk," Chelsea said sheepishly.

"I am also a woman, you know." Natto sneered back.

Claire coughed, breaking her silence, then quickly turned away to fix her hair, not wanting to meet Natto's eyes.

"I applaud you both for not giving up on the fool, but my advice to you *is* to give up. He has no need for a relationship right now, at least until he has decided on his future plans. Furthermore, I do not believe he has told you how his last endeavor with the opposite sex had gone," Natto explained.

"Okay, so he isn't gay. Good," Claire whispered under her breath.

Natto cocked her eye but ignored the comment, continuing her line of thought aloud.

"Your best course of action is to either forget about him and find another man, or, I suppose, simply wait," Natto said, taking another bite of boar. "But regardless of how you feel, know that he is a man of his word and will at least protect you as the contract stipulates until the end of the tutorial. After that, he has not even shared with me what his thoughts are for the most part, so we will all have to wait for an answer there..."

Natto trailed off, her attention going elsewhere as the sounds of fighting outside began to increase.

"Your name is Uta, yes?" Natto said to no one in particular.

Instantly Chelsea's eyes snapped to the corner of the room, where a small black-haired girl inched out into view. Chelsea drew her bow and trained it on the girl. Claire moved to Chelsea's side, pulling her staff out at the ready. Only Natto remained calm, continuing to eat.

"It is alright, you two. She simply wants to speak—although she could most likely kill one of you if she had to. But she knows as well as I that the repercussions of such an action would spell a very ugly end for her beloved master." Natto sneered. "Then? What is it you wish to discuss? I am surprised you did not out my owner for having a construct in public... I am assuming your group does not know you are a construct as well, then?"

Both Chelsea and Claire drew in a quick breath at the information but maintained their vigilance toward the girl.

"You would be correct. My name is Uta. May I ask for yours as well?" Uta asked.

"Natto. Well?" she replied.

"I can tell you are a Territory Assistant; that means you have information I do not. I simply wish to ask questions in aid of my master."

"Oh?" Natto cooed, intrigued. "And what is in it for us? You seem to forget how poorly you treated my owner when we arrived. What makes you think I would even want to deal with you?"

Uta ignored Natto's question, instead asking her own.

"You called him your owner and not master. Why do you not show respect to him?"

Natto scoffed, her face turning a shade of red.

"Because that dumb ape would take it too far if I did!" She coughed. "Call it a precaution to keep his ego in check. You have seen how he likes to fly off the handle."

Natto pointed her fork, boar meat and all, at Uta. "Now, enough of dodging my question. What reason would we have to give you any sort of information?"

Uta ground her teeth like she was chewing on something unpleasant.

"I have advised my master as best I can, but I simply am not equipped to aid him in what is to come after the tutorial. Seeing how he was so soundly defeated by your... *owner*, I realize now that even with all his skills, he is sorely lacking in ability and will need every advantage to survive once the tutorial is finished," Uta explained.

"And?" Natto urged, growing tired as she ripped another piece of boar and bread.

"My master has permitted the use of an alliance. In return for your information, he will do his best to help your owner outside of the tutorial," Uta continued.

"That does not help us when we would be the ones protecting you, do you not agree? Seems that you are the only ones benefiting if that is truly the *only* thing you offer."

"Natto is kind of scary right now, don't you think Chelsea?" Claire whispered.

"Yeah... She's usually never like this. I mean she's a little intimidating when it comes to the skill stones, but this is different. I can feel the tension," Chelsea whispered back.

"Y-You know of the coming fight and the vote for the planet's leaders in the conference before the war. My master will vouch for your owner, meaning the rest of the coalition will as well!"

"Oh, now *that* sounds like a good deal." Natto smiled.

Chapter 16

The System Summits

"Where did you get this information?" Natto asked pointedly, licking the scraps from her meal off her fingers.

"Pardon?" Uta replied.

"*Please*. You do not wish to believe I am ignorant enough to not know you are a combat construct and thus not privileged to this information? This is information only an F-Rank Information or Administrative Construct would know. I only have it available because the ape happened to gain a forerunner title in the last quest. So again, I ask you: where did you obtain this information from?" Natto reiterated.

Uta looked down nervously, her body language hesitant as she seemed to think over the question.

"Then," Natto suddenly said, "if you do not wish to give up such information, we are done here."

Uta raised her hand and voice in objection.

"Wait! I—We—"

"Yes?" Natto pressed, crossing her legs on the edge of the bed she was eating on.

Gritting her teeth, Uta explained.

"My master... my master had another friend within the tutorial when they were brought here. A woman named... Haru. She was a Priest at the beginning, and during her time progressing, she eventually became as invaluable to the group as she was to my Master," she explained. She clenched her hands around her leather pants. "On her rank up, she received an Information Construct. Through the construct, we learned quite the amount of information to progress us through the quests, avoiding pitfalls and allowing the core group to optimize their skills and stats. But she was taken by a crazy man named Kohoo."

Natto flinched at the mention of the name, her memories of the events at the outpost flashing in her mind. Her subconscious hate for the man that caused Drake such grief burned like a rekindled ember in the back of her mind, but she stayed silent, allowing Uta to continue her explanation.

"The man was just a regular member of the initial group and seemed relatively useful. But once Haru changed classes and became more and more important to the group, he swiftly changed. He suddenly became more attached to her—even obsessed. And one day, while we were surrounded by gnolls, he took her from the back lines. We desperately searched for her for days, but we couldn't find a trace of her or Kohoo," Uta recalled, taking a moment for a breath. "Then, after we took the outpost we currently reside in, the morning after we found a body at the gate. Battered, bruised, and mutilated. It was obvious who it was and what... what they had done to her..."

Gasps came from Claire and Chelsea's side of the tent. Claire struggled to keep her composure as she felt the same violation of what Haru had most likely gone through.

"I see. So from her construct, you obtained information about the World and System Summit. But of what else do you know?" Natto asked.

"Is that not enough?" Uta replied.

"It is not, for you are missing a large part of what leads up to those summits. And if you do not understand the process, the end result is pointless," Natto said with a wave of her hand. "Is your master prepared to fall in line in the truest sense?"

Uta frowned.

"What is your meaning?"

"I am telling you that if your master will not bend the knee, all of this is pointless in the first place. There can only be one King," Natto said, her face turning to a scowl, "and it *will* be mine."

As if in tune with the outside, the tent lit up in brilliant white, the sound of thunder reverberating through the tent.

"What was that? What's going on out there!" Chelsea shrieked, turning to the entrance.

"We have to go see. Miss Natto, we will be right back!" Claire called back over her shoulder. Natto nodded briefly as she kept her eyes on Uta.

Both the girls exited the tent, leaving Uta and Natto in a staring match until Natto sighed.

"It would seem that we are at odds, then. Whether your master decides to fall in line willingly or has to be forced, it does not matter. He can not compete with Shot," she mused.

"Th-That is not true!" Uta snapped. She pulled her blade from her back and rushed forward, holding it to Natto's neck.

Natto remained still, unperturbed, a sneer on her face as she looked back at Uta's slightly quivering body.

"It is. And you should be glad, for he will take on everything our new home will have to bear in the coming years. Do you think your master can compete with Primordials? Does he have what it takes to slog through the blood and dirt that is required to take the second planet? What of the system, the other universes, the tournament of ranks? Shot may be a fool, but he is a pragmatic and intelligent one when required. And most of all, he is a tenacious brute." Natto smiled.

Uta clicked her tongue, cursing under her breath. A moment later, she vanished into a wisp of inky shadows. Left alone, Natto touched her neck gingerly.

"I do hope this does not scar..."

* * *

"Shot! Shot! Damn it, he's out cold." Bjorn chuckled.

Drake's group quickly surrounded Bjorn and Drake, their faces filled with concern.

"Here, love, let me see him. Ahh, what a bloody mess. Does he have to always go wildin' about like this?" Jacqueline scoffed. She placed her hands over his chest, a faint glow of white exuding from them.

"Well hot damn, miss, that sounds like some genuine concern there." Hudson laughed, kneeling down next to Drake. "Pup's got balls, that's a sure thing. Putting the number one on his ass"

"I'm still standing, bro," Bjorn countered.

"Eh, we all know you woulda lost. Don't be such an idjit," Hudson fired back.

Bjorn scoffed, shaking his head.

"Are all the people around this guy like this?" He chuckled wryly, looking down at Drake.

"I happen to be quite normal, sir," Amir piped up, standing behind Hudson.

"I would like to say I'm also part of the normal club," Tom added, but the turning of the group's heads to give him confused looks forced him to cough. "Okay, relatively normal?"

A light chuckle sounded from the group, but it was quickly deafened by the shouts coming from the other crowd.

"What is the meaning of this? What was he talking about, Sir Bear? Why would he want to kill you?" Shigure roared, his face frowning deeply as he inched his hand toward his sword.

"Whoa whoa whoa," Bjorn said, trying to pacify Shigure. "It's not like that."

"Then what is it? Explain!"

Bjorn scratched his beard, thinking over how to respond.

"It's a long story, and I can't tell you the full story. You'll just have to trust me, bro. It's nothing to worry about."

"Of course I need to be concerned! What he just displayed, he clearly could have killed you! What is going on, and why can you not explain it?" Shigure shouted back.

"Because I won't!" Bjorn roared, suddenly snapping. "Enough badgering!"

Shigure recoiled from the shout, but he quickly recovered and stood his ground.

"I need to understand if he is a threat to the people under our care," he said evenly this time, his head cooled slightly from Bjorn's shout. "If he is capable of fighting beyond even you, what is stopping him from turning on the rest of us at any time?"

"Mr. Shot would never do something like that!" Harley interjected.

"Yes, my lord would never feeleth the need to slaughter the weak and defenseless. Quite the contrary; he hath giveth them safe harbor," Theodore added.

"How am I supposed to believe something like that from his followers?" Shigure asked. "I am responsible for the safety of everyone within these walls. How am I supposed to guarantee that while he is still breathing?"

The air chilled at that moment.

"Are you saying you want to kill him?" Bjorn asked coldly.

"N-No! I just need a guarantee that he will not turn against us!" Shigure asked again desperately. "I do not wish to lose anyone else!"

"How about the fact that he hasn't done it already?" Bjorn replied pointedly.

"That does not mean he will not do it later!" Shigure shouted back.

"Th-Then… how about a contract?" Drake said, raising himself from the ground shakily. "Thank you, Jacqueline. I didn't know you cared like that," he said, smiling.

"Piss off," she spat. She turned her head away.

Giving a quick laugh, Drake patted Bjorn's shoulder. "It's alright, man. Honestly I'd be more concerned if he *didn't* get this uptight. It's kind of his thing."

"Contract?" Shigure asked, his posture relaxing slightly.

"Yeah sure, we can just make a mutual agreement for the remainder of the tutorial. No killing each other. If we do, mutual destruction. Sounds cool, right? We'll be like two superpowers pointing nukes at each other." Drake grinned behind his mask.

"That joke is in bad taste, bro," Bjorn said, a slight grin replacing his previously scowling face. Drake waved him off.

"Well, Shigure? How about it?" Drake asked.

"How do I know this is not a trick of some kind?" Shigure countered.

"Wow, ever the by-the-books stickler, huh? Because everyone in my group—well, besides Bear here—has one with me already," Drake answered casually as he rolled his arm, wincing slightly from the fatigue.

"What are the details of these said contracts?"

"Basically, I can't hurt them, but they can hurt me. They could even kill me and I wouldn't be able to do a damned thing about it," Drake replied, moving his mask to the side of his head.

"Are you a fool? Why would you do such a thing? It's absurd!" Shigure shouted.

"That's rude. And maybe, but I needed to force myself to trust those around me. Just like you, I have some problems with trusting others. So what's the word, yes or no?"

Shigure looked at the rest of Drake's group, scanning their faces.

"Is this true?" Shigure asked.

Nods came from the other side, no one denying what Drake had said.

Shigure did not fully relax, but he gave a huff of air and sighed.

"How would we go about doing this contract?" Shigure finally asked, relinquishing his suspicion enough to go further. The fact that he was now against a fully awake Drake and a still-able Bjorn had totally no influence on him. None at all.

"Great. Sherry!" Drake shouted.

A somewhat short black-haired girl with a side bob and broken glasses stepped forward from their group.

"Is it lunchtime yet?" she asked.

Drake sighed, shaking his head.

"You just had breakfast! Double portions!"

"Yeah, but we skipped second breakfast," she grumbled.

"Susmaryosep, daughter of a Took," Drake said, exacerbated. "Fine, more food when you do this, okay?"

Sherry gave a very lazy double thumbs up, the corners of her mouth curling upwards then going back to their usual even position. "Nice, sounds good dude."

Drake walked forward, his head beginning to hurt for who knows what. But he quickly shook himself and directed his focus to Shigure.

"Then let's get started," Drake said, extending his hand.

Not fully clear of his suspicion, Shigure pensively extended his hand to meet Drake's. Drake wasted no time, though, snatching Shigure's hand in his and tightening his grip so the teen couldn't run away.

Seeing them grip hands, Sherry began chanting.

"Infallible Mistress of Truth and Law. Be my witness in the writing of this tying of destiny. Form Creation. Of Truth and Law."

The spell began with a bright light, ending with the dimming of the blinding light around Drake and Shigure.

Would you like to form a contract with Shigure Kenzo?

Details of this contract are as follows:
You may not deal fatal damage to the contractor.
You may only instigate harm or damage with mutual agreement.
The parties of the contract will receive lethal retribution for killing the other party.
The recipients will be required to maintain the contract for the full duration of the tutorial, under penalty of death.

"And there we go! That's not so bad, is it?" Drake said, giving a soft chuckle.

Chapter 17

Lines That Won't Be Crossed

Shigure might have accepted the contract, but he was still skeptical about the whole premise of Drake. Sherry was, after all, part of his group. But for now, it seemed it was enough.

Shigure simply wasn't able to press the matter. It seemed that Bjorn and Drake had a better relationship than he had with Bjorn, even after their time together, and this truly aggravated Shigure.

He thought he'd gotten over the jealousy he was feeling, but it somehow boiled up once again, and what was coming did not help.

"Alright, so we all good now? No more at each other's throats for the time being, 'kay?" Drake said casually, his hair shimmering from his original black to blue.

Drake addressed Shigure, but his eyes glanced to the rest of the group from Shigure's camp standing behind him. Some recoiled from the stare while others still struggled to get up from the ground, Drake's and Bjorn's auras having done significant damage to their posture and egos. They scowled back at him.

Then two voices came from Drake's side.

"What happened? What was that light?!" Claire shouted, stopping next to Drake, her hands finding her knees as she gasped for breath.

"Seriously, that sounded like lightning struck right next to us! What in the world did you do?" Chelsea asked, pointing at Drake.

"Why is it *my* fault?" Drake asked.

"Because it's always something you did!" Chelsea snapped back.

"Okay, fair. Guilty as charged. Sue me!" Drake laughed, shrugging.

"We would if we could!" they both screamed.

"Okay, calm down. I didn't know I had three moms, jeez." Drake snorted. "Where's you know who?" Drake asked, suddenly realizing they had left the tent without Natto.

"Oh. Um, we left her to see what was going on. She's with the girl called Uta," Claire answered sheepishly.

Drake's eyes snapped to Shigure. The teen paled under Drake's primal stare.

"Explain," Drake said, bloodlust spilling off the single word. "Explain why she is still there."

"Wait! We only wanted to tal—" Shigure tried explaining, but he was cut off by a lightning spear passing his cheek close enough to burn the hair on it.

"Then speak to me," Drake growled. "If even a hair on her head is out of place, you will find out just how *tyrannical* I can become."

Drake's threat was not empty. Once again his aura pressed outward, chilling Shigure's entire side of the field.

"Y-You wouldn't dare! You would ha—" someone from behind Shigure spat, but they were stopped by another bolt of lightning crackling past the person's face—this time taking off their right ear as they shrieked in pain.

"I'm speaking to Shigure. Do not interrupt. *It's rude*," Drake said, scowling.

Drake slowly moved his mask back into place, his eyes shimmering from color to color.

"Well, I'm listening," Drake pressed.

"I—We wanted to trade voting for you at the world summit in exchange for information. We would help you outside the tutorial," Shigure explained quickly.

"World summit...? This is the first I'm hearing of it." Drake paused.

"Don't move. I'll be right back," Drake stated tersely, his hair shimmering to a brilliant yellow with a snap of his fingers as he took a step and moved out of view.

An instant later he returned, seemingly the same, but he had recovered Natto who was now merged with him. And Drake was not pleased.

Uta had held her at knifepoint, and even with Natto doing her best to dismiss the action as irrelevant, Drake was livid.

"Where is she?" Drake asked.

"W-Why?" Shigure stammered.

"She has harmed someone dear to me. I knew she entered the tent to speak, but she went too far. So either you bring her here to deal with the consequences of her actions, or I go find her. And let me tell you. Waldo never hides for long," Drake joked, but his demeanor, aura, and glare were anything but amused.

"I will not—" Shigure tried to say, but Drake moved as the words left his mouth. His arm paused only inches from Shigure's face, glowing a deep azure above the brilliant yellow of his tattoo.

Drake looked over at the man who had stopped him. "Bear, he volunteered to take the punishment. Let go."

"Come on, bro, you don't need to kill him. Is the little lady alright?" Bjorn asked, honestly concerned.

"She has a scratch," Drake replied tersely, his eyes still trained on the shivering Shigure despite their casual conversation.

"Then you're going way overboard. At least only give him a scratch. We can have a calm discussion where everyone isn't trying to kill each other after," Bjorn said, his eyes moving to Shigure, disappointed with the teen.

"Fine," Drake let out. "Just a scratch then," he growled. He extended his finger from his closed fist, the air pressure pushing past Shigure, blowing his hair wildly but not harming the teen. Instead, it hit the mess of people behind him, pushing them backward in a gust of wind.

Drake relaxed, and Bjorn released him as Drake moved his mask to the side of his head again so that Shigure could see his expression.

"Just kidding; I can't hurt him anyway. But the contract doesn't say anything about anyone else now, does it, *Shigure*?" Drake insinuated.

The teen's head moved eerily slow from left to right, his face pale. Sweat pooled down his forehead as he looked back at Drake.

"If you touch my family again, you will not like what happens. Next time you want to talk, you talk to *me* and me alone," Drake said, pausing afterward to drive home the point.

"Now, get me those people I need. But you lost the reward of skill stones. From now on, if you want something, it will be fair and square from us. No more beneficial trades, nothing. Only business."

Shigure stepped back, color slowly returning to his face and a scowl creasing it, but he nodded nonetheless.

"And if I see Uta," Drake added, "she better have a spectacular apology, or it will be the last time you see her." He looked to the stout man behind Shigure who had spoken up earlier. "And *that* is a threat."

The short man snorted in fear, his hand going for the hammer that had fallen next to him. Drake only looked on, waiting for him to grab it, but the man noticed the stare. He decided against it and turned his head away from Drake's gaze.

Finally, Drake looked at Shigure.

"There are just some lines you don't cross. This is going to be your only warning."

Drake let the words hang as he turned away, moving past the rest of his group wordlessly towards his tent.

* * *

"How dare he threaten us! He is only one man!" the stout man cried once Drake was fully out of view and he knew he was safe.

"Yes, Darius. It seems that he is getting too large for his britches, if I do say," a thin-looking man said next to him.

"Enough. Darius, Adam, do you think we have a chance of going against him when he also has Sir Bear on his side?" Shigure said, deflating as he looked to Bjorn who walked not to Shigure's camp, but to Drake's.

Why... What is so different?! And now I have burned a bridge that I could not afford to! Shigure cursed.

"How is it enough? The man-child threw a tantrum, and we are supposed to just take it?" Adam crossed his thin pale arms across his chest.

"Then what would you have us do?" Shigure asked.

"We simply take one of his people hostage and force him to cooperate," Adam said nonchalantly.

"Adam! That is not how we do things! Even if Uta had hurt their companion, I know she would not do so without good reason. And this is only for a scratch! What do you think would happen if you managed to take one of his compatriots?!" Shigure snapped. "Your personality has darkened since you changed races. I only allowed you to stay because you are an invaluable fighter, but remember your place!"

Adam scoffed. "Big talk coming from someone who just ran with his tail between his legs."

Shigure placed his hand on his weapon. Adam raised his hands placidly, not wanting to push Shigure too far.

"Yes yes then, leader. Whatever you say," Adam answered, giving a sidelong glance at some of the women following behind Bjorn and the now gone Drake. "Whatever you say..."

* * *

"Drake, what was that display out there? You know you can not simply act on your emotions. I thought you were well past this when you received your new skills," Natto asked from the bed where Jacqueline was standing next to her, gently touching the near-insignificant wound on her neck.

"No. I don't care about the reason. If they hurt you, then I will not stand for it. I can work around and bend on a lot of things, but my family, my loved ones, those who I hold dear. If someone touches what is mine..." Drake murmured, his vision reddening.

"What? What did you just say? Yours? Very presumptuous, I must say," Natto scoffed, but she turned her head, her face turning a shade of scarlet.

"Huh? W-Why did I say that? I just meant that people won't be doing what they want with the people I care about anymore. I don't want people I hold dear to ever have to go through the types of things I did or might still have to go through," Drake clarified, pushing the slip of words to the back of his mind.

I thought my Tyrant's Indomitability solved this whole shitshow of emotional polarity. And I haven't consumed any legendary stones like Bjorn has, so what's the deal? Is it just a matter of the person? Am I just that mentally weak? Drake asked himself, but he was pulled from his thoughts when Claire spoke up.

"I'm sorry we left her alone. I-I thought it would be fine, and we were just concerned about what was going on outside," she offered.

Drake sighed. He knew it wasn't entirely their fault, but he had to hold them responsible. Natto wasn't a combat-oriented assistant, and they had left her basically defenseless with a Combat Assistant. It didn't take an anime protagonist to understand where that was going.

"Look, I know I asked a lot, but you two," Drake said, addressing Claire and Chelsea who both looked down in embarrassment, "I'm disappointed. I won't allow you to take the blame for how I reacted, and I won't say it's your fault I had to put my foot down with that kid, but you severely lost points with me for that mistake."

Drake sighed again.

"We're sorry, but we were just concerned," Chelsea said, looking to Jacqueline in hopes of a lifeline, but the woman just shook her head, her expression blatantly saying, 'I want no part of that mess, love.'

"Don't let your infatuation with me detract from what I've asked you to do," Drake said firmly, looking at them both. The pair shirked backward slightly, their embarrassment plain despite their turning away.

"I've told you both I'm not interested, and that's how it is. I'm too busy for either of you, and I have no plans of fooling around with anyone for now. You want me to take an interest? Then do what I'm asking of you next time. I don't need someone who can't do the simple task of watching a one-foot garbage disposal, let alone a lover who can't listen to a word I say," Drake said, crossing his arms before adding in a whisper, "How is that supposed to work in bed if you can't even listen outside of it…"

Both their faces flushed even more, but they nodded reluctantly.

"Then," Drake added, his face relaxing, "thank you for worrying about me."

He smiled. "But don't do it again, alright? Now go to your own tents before Shigure gets any wild ideas. And can you send in Bjorn? I'd like to have another conversation with him."

The pair brightened at the words of gratitude, nodding sheepishly before exiting.

"You got some real serious lovesick birds there, gov," Jacqueline teased, finishing up her healing of Natto.

"Oh, and that doesn't include you?" Drake teased back.

"Damn right it doesn't, ya daft bastard." She scoffed. "Besides, I don't like to share," Jacqueline whispered, walking out of the tent.

"Hm, I may have made a mistake teasing her too much..." Drake laughed nervously.

"Imbecile." Natto scoffed.

"What can I say? I'm a hands-on learner." Drake laughed back, but his face turned serious. "I'm glad you weren't hurt badly, Natto. But never do that again."

"It is fine—"

"*Never*," Drake said again firmly. "I don't care if you can come back or whatever. I won't allow anyone to hurt you. If it wasn't for the contract, that boy would be on the ground with a hole in his chest the size of his ego."

The tent entrance flap whipped open, and a hulking figure entered.

"Oh, am I interrupting that serious movie moment thing you do? My bad, bro, I'll come back in like five minutes," Bjorn said, turning around.

"I-I don't do that!" Drake shouted, his hand gripping Bjorn's shoulder desperately.

Chapter 18
The Kings of the World

After the altercation outside with Shigure and reprimanding Claire and Chelsea while Natto was being healed, only Drake, Natto, and Bjorn remained in Drake's tent.

Drake looked over at Natto.

"So, what was this whole conversation you had with Uta about?" Drake asked, doing his best to hide his irritation.

"Would you like the long or short version?" Natto asked.

"I would like the *whole* version, thank you," Drake replied, his finger tapping on his arm.

"Then, we should start at why she came here in the first place," Natto began explaining. "Uta was sent here by Shigure to offer an alliance within and continued outside the tutorial in exchange for information and, essentially, protection."

Drake's brow rose.

"What does he need protection for?" Drake asked.

"From people like you, dolt!" Natto sighed. "You seem to be under the impression that you are the only Dual Class within the countless worlds and systems that inhabit the expansive multiverse, but you would be sorely mistaken. I have confidence that you will grow to be ever stronger and progress to the top. Again, I have no doubt in this, but you will face challenges you cannot yet see. It seems, even for all the faults we have seen from him so far, Shigure is planning ahead and predicts that. Especially after the 'fight' you put him through, he knows he is not yet capable of defending himself to the degree he wishes for. That is where you and the oaf come in," Natto explained.

Drake pursed his lips. He'd started becoming complacent ever so slightly after his fight with the Goblin King, but he wasn't fool enough to believe he was the strongest. He was still the lowest rank on the ladder; it was only natural that there would be stronger beings in the multiverse.

Wait, that means even with everything I can do now, there are people that can blow me out of the water? Drake thought, shivering slightly.

"What's this got to do with me now?" Bjorn asked.

"You have chosen a side, even if you are too inept to realize it. Shigure sees that and went for a desperate olive branch by extending his offer to us," Natto responded.

"I haven't chosen any side, bro," Bjorn said.

"That matters not. It only matters how Shigure sees it, and I assure you, that is certainly how he does." Natto scoffed, then continued. "Regardless, his offer was worthless, and I told Uta as much."

"Why's that? If all he wanted was a no-fighting pact, it seems fine with me. I'm not trying to kill people all willy-nilly," Drake replied, waving his hand.

"But that is not your choice anymore," Natto explained pointedly. "Drake, you told me before that you wanted the power to protect those you hold dear. And I told you what that requires. You seem to have forgotten that conflict is a staple of the system. There is no way around it. You may have whimsically allowed the oaf to live, which I might remind you is a mistake, but your impulsive nature will only be allowed for so long. You are now a forerunner, which means that you must stand at the top above others, always. If you slip and fall, you will be trampled underfoot by those who are more determined than you. Those with ambition that far outstrips your own. The game of kings has already started," Natto said, looking right into Drake's eyes. "Well, in a sense. It is certainly a leadership role at the very least."

"You lost me at not being impulsive." Drake chuckled.

"Drake! This is serious!" Natto shouted, her teeth bared.

"Okay, okay! I get it," Drake said.

"Do you?! This no longer pertains only to the ones inside the tutorial. Once the small world you are forced into here ends, there are fights you will *need* to win, or it will cause loss of life incomparable to what you have already witnessed here," Natto said, her tone as serious as possible.

"What do you mean?" Drake asked, Bjorn also leaning forward in interest.

"The tutorial is for several purposes. One is to thin the herd, so to speak, by allowing the ones who will progress the furthest to stand and obtain the means to do so," Natto explained, raising a finger. "The next is to set in relative stone areas of influence for when the population exits the tutorial."

"How would they be set in stone? Aren't we all from different places and areas outside of the tutorial?" Drake countered.

"Yes, but that is not my meaning," Natto continued. She raised a second finger. "Each tutorial raises or establishes a ruler, in a sense. They would be at the top of each respective tutorial in both level and points. These participants, almost without fail, have constructs leading them, which means that they are privy to advanced information at all stages, giving them an edge as well as a well-thought-out plan after the tutorial."

Drake's eyes lit up in understanding.

"So you mean to say these people or forerunners are the ones that're going to establish these 'areas of influence,' and the people from their tutorials are essentially their followers?"

"Certainly so." Natto nodded. "This is done deliberately to create areas for new system-sanctioned towns headed by those individuals through a quest endorsed at the system centers. But we are getting ahead of ourselves."

Natto sighed.

A moment passed, giving everyone a breather to internalize the information, before Natto continued, keeping the conversation on track.

"With that, I will speak on why the child's offer was meaningless," Natto began. "Ignoring how these system-sanctioned areas are made and progressed, what you need to focus on, Drake, is why it pertains to you."

Drake gulped, anticipation beginning to creep up in his mind. He had known for a long time that the road to his goal was long and painful, but imagination and reality were always such lengths apart that it was hard to accept.

"These towns force you to be a leader, a figurehead, a monument to the people under your influence. And it will not accept less than that," Natto said, glaring. "These areas will compete for the right to be a World Capital, and any of the system-sanctioned areas that compete must either rise or submit."

Natto gave Drake a moment before she added, "Not only this, prior to taking power, you must receive the title of ruler through the World Summit."

"World Summit? Like a conference?" Drake questioned.

"Yes, exactly so. The summit will allow the top one hundred of the potential World Capitals to vote on the decision," Natto explained.

"Decision on what?" Bjorn interjected.

"The decision on which of the system-sanctioned cities will become the World Capital. The decision can be made through one-on-one combat, all-out war, competition through system-assigned quests, or something as simple as a democratic vote, to name a few. Your world is far more expansive than either of you apes could possibly comprehend." Natto scoffed.

"If all we need is to secure enough votes to decide the competition, why not just accept his offer? Is there something I'm missing?" Drake asked.

"Yes," Natto answered. "It will depend on the amount of sanctioned areas made, but it is possible that there may be a tie, in which case the voting will need to happen again at a later date. This also means that the voters can jump ship to another boat in that time period, so you need to have the loyalty of each voter in some way."

Drake nodded, understanding now.

"So you are saying Shigure wouldn't be loyal enough to follow through," Drake conjectured. Natto nodded. "What about if we use Sherry to just force him to do it?"

Natto shook her head. "Unfortunately, system events like these null and void such arrangements. Even Primordials cannot tamper with them. These summits are freedom in its purest form, as no one is allowed to be harmed during the period that they are in play. Though I am sure many have tried."

"What stops them, exactly? Just the system doing system things?" Drake asked.

"I do not know the specifics other than that physical, mental, and spiritual attacks do nothing. But this is all I can reveal on the matter. Without leaving the tutorial or increasing your race rank, there is no more that I can divulge."

Drake leaned against the supporting pillar of the tent, immersed deeply in thought.

"Drake. I'm not sure where you're going to go with this, bro, but I won't be a part of something like fighting a war for you. I only stepped in when Shigure threatened to kill you because it was uncalled for and you were exhausted at my expense," Bjorn explained. "I won't speak on what I've heard from the little miss, but as for what comes next, consider me a friend, not a soldier. If this is all we're talking about, I think it's time I leave."

Drake turned and nodded, then stopped Bjorn before he could exit, remembering what he needed him for.

"Ah! Hold up, Bjorn," Drake said, outstretching a hand. "I needed to ask you about a little adventure I'm going to go on."

Bjorn stopped, raising a brow.

"What adventure? Aren't we already full on those right now?" he asked, giving a hearty chuckle.

"You would think, but I have something you might be interested in." Drake smiled, holding up a map. "This is a map to the Goblin King's Hoard, my friend, and I want you to come with."

"What's the catch?" Bjorn looked the map up and down, his hand on his chin.

"It's going to be a little bit of a magic school bus adventure," Drake explained. "And it's only going to be after I get settled with what I came to do here. You in?"

Bjorn stood back and paused.

"Hmm, are we talking present time Magic School Bus or OG Miss Frizzle?" Bjorn questioned.

"OG, of course. It's going to be one very educational time!" Drake laughed.

Bjorn gave Drake a pat on the shoulder, then turned and left the tent.

"Was that a yes or no?" Drake wondered aloud.

"I do not speak moron, so you will have to guess on your own," Natto said, shrugging.

"I'm going to say it was a yes. It felt like a yes."

* * *

Once Bjorn had left, Drake took the rest of the day to practice within his tent, making sure to keep an eye on the small camp his party had set up.

Opting not to sleep, he was determined to keep skilling up while maintaining a watchful eye. He had found a few people snooping about the camp, and he quickly sent them on their way during the night with the help of Theodore and Harley.

No cawing of roosters or bright sunlight woke Drake this time. He continued to train at the edge of his bed silently, Natto snoring louder than any of his spells.

Drake had found out during the night that he was able to include Natto in his training as well. Even though the construct was technically an item, she was still considered a party member at all times regardless of the ten member restriction the system seemed to have in place.

Good to know I can pull one over on the system now and then. Drake chuckled internally.

The discovery had given Natto quite a fright during the night when Drake had used his Aura of Command without warning. The sleeping girl woke as she felt the effects, Drake snickering like a hyena at her reaction.

After a few attempted stabbings and ghastly laughs, Natto had gotten used to the skill activating off cooldown and began to sleep through it, only waking up when she became hungry enough to extort some food from Drake.

What surprised Drake during the night the most out of everything, though, was that Sherry had also tried to sneak into his tent. Not for anything illicit, but for food as well. She'd smelled the cooking in her tent across from him.

That girl has a better nose than bomb dogs, Drake reflected.

The final thing that interrupted Drake during the night was the snooping around of a pair of women. Thankfully, Harley was able to stop them before they did something drastic. Also, Megan had apparently joined Chelsea and Jacqueline in their tent, and she came out and dragged Chelsea away from Drake's tent, shouting reprimands the entire way.

Drake stretched his arms and closed his fist around a ball of water that he was playing with, his Endowment switching from Fire to Water to replenish his status.

"I think I might have to have Hudson put up some sentries after what happened last night. I'll have to let Shigure know, too... I don't really feel like I should have to talk to the little prick right now, but it wouldn't be fair to whoever is snooping around at night if they just upped and died."

The few people that Drake had actually found during the night were rather different. Their skin was pale, and their arms were gangly. What was more was that they weren't actually people, at least not what he would consider people. But with the amount of races that were apparently going to show up when they left the tutorial, he could be very wrong.

What Drake had found were ghouls.

"First titans, gods, and demigods are real. Now Twilight might be coming to town. I really hope there aren't going to be any dumb romance plotlines with werewolves and vampires..." Drake sighed.

He turned slowly as he got up, hearing Natto yawn as she apparently roused awake.

"Is it breakfast time yet?" she asked.

"No it's not, and don't invoke the word of power, you're going to summon—" Drake tried to say, but then a familiar black-haired girl poked her bed head through his tent.

"Breakfast?" Sherry asked, one of her eyes still half asleep.

"Ha, too late..." Drake chuckled wryly.

Chapter 19

New Day, New Questions

Drake sat in front of a cauldron, stirring a pot of food as he looked off into the distance thinking.

"So the agenda today is…" He sighed. "Well, nothing in particular if Shigure doesn't come through. And after yesterday, I don't think it would be a good idea to just barge into his camp demanding what I want either."

"*Less talking, more stirring!*" Natto yelled from inside his head.

"Yes yes, your gluttonous majesty." Drake yawned with a wave of his free hand, then looked to his side, seeing a drooling Sherry. "How is it I ended up with two of the same person in a tutorial that's made for five thousand, when the world has billions of people in it? Does this system hate me?"

"*Everyone hates you. It is the only reason you are special, you ape.*" Natto laughed.

Drake got up and placed the pot into his inventory. Sherry gasped before she devolved into a banshee-like wail.

"*I was only jesting! Yes, only a joke!*" Natto screamed.

Drake sat back down, taking out the cauldron and casually starting to stir once more. He used his other hand to practice his aim with his spells along with some of his other skills that were falling behind.

He chanted skill after skill whenever one came off cooldown. His body flashed green while his arms stayed a solid red as they were encased in his Martial Skill.

Drake assumed today would be a solid resting day of training and upping his skills, but trouble soon found him in more ways than one.

"And I'm telling you, you should not lower yourself to trying to sneak into a man's tent at night! It is disgusting behavior, Chels!" Megan snapped.

Drake looked out from the corner of his eye, still sitting down and lazily stirring the food. He could tell that Chelsea was tired of hearing the words, apparent from her eyes rolling.

"Meg, I'm not lowering myself to anything. You think I'd do that just for any guy? I messed up with Drake, and now I have to put in that extra effort!" she said, giving a small arm pump.

Drake chuckled as silently as he could, amazed she was still so gung ho about him.

It really is about just not showing any interest, huh? Who knew Timmy Turner's bus episode would come in so handy? Drake laughed internally.

"I do not believe that is the full extent of what is going on here, Drake." Natto scoffed.

You're right, it must be my massively good looks and my being an overall impeccable male specimen of the human species, Drake fired back jokingly.

"The only species you are the ideal for is the one that drags knuckles and hoots in the jungle, eating ants with sticks." Natto laughed.

That is an oddly specific insult... Also, silverback gorillas are majestic. I thought we went over this?

Natto ignored Drake as the conversation died down, the pair soon joining them.

"Well? Sleep alright you two? Surprised Megan decided to join us out here roughing it." Drake grinned sarcastically.

"She decided to come after some things, and apparently seeing you fight Bear put the final nail in the coffin. Right now she's bunking with Jacky, Julia, and me," Chelsea said as she sat down next to Drake.

"Oh," Drake said, wiggling his eyebrows, "sounds like a gay old time."

Chelsea frowned while Megan growled back.

"Take a joke." Drake laughed, but slipped in his question after. "So, what was the reason? Does it have to do with the people, er, *things* we found yesterday night?"

"It does." Megan sighed and stretched her arms above her head. "There are some problems here that are apparently an open secret."

Drake stopped his stirring for a moment to focus on Megan, the sounds of footsteps coming up behind him.

"What kind of secret?" Drake asked seriously.

Megan pulled back slightly, adjusting herself from her stretch.

"The kind where people go missing on hunts for monsters, then start to show back up during the night for a few days," Megan explained.

"That doesn't sound like too much of a problem? Couldn't they just have gotten lost fighting monsters, then made their way back a few days later?" Drake offered.

"Well, the problem is that they're changed when they come back. Small things at first: they're paler, don't eat, don't go out in the daytime. But then it gets worse and weirder. They stop responding to healing magic, and after a few days, they disappear again," Megan said.

"Okay, maybe my vampire theory isn't so crazy now," Drake thought aloud.

"Vampires? Are we talking like 1900s Dracula or 2000s Edward?" Bjorn said, thumping down on the other side of Drake while Hudson, Amir, Theodore, and Harley found chairs.

"I'm thinking big ooga booga scary vamps from like, games and fantasy fiction. There aren't any in the tutorial though, I thought?" Drake asked.

"There are no monster vampires that we have seen, no. But that does not rule out the possibility that they could have recently appeared, or we may have a variant that someone has changed into," Natto interjected.

"Oh, there is one that I know of," Bjorn said, pulling a canteen of something sweet smelling from his inventory.

The group's eyes landed on him, waiting for an explanation after the bomb he'd just dropped, but he seemed to willfully ignore them or just not notice as he took a long swig of his canteen. Several seconds passed as they all waited, Bjorn finally letting go of the container with a satisfied gasp.

"Yeah, I hate the guy, but you probably saw him yesterday. Adam. Pale, scraggly guy. He's a Strigoi Viu, if I'm not wrong," Bjorn explained.

"And he's still alive, why?" Chelsea asked.

"Well, honestly?" Bjorn sighed, looking down into the fire of the pit. "He shouldn't be. I tried to kill him once I saw his race," Bjorn said, pointing towards his eyes. "It should be alright to say since you're all with Shot. My perception skill is very useful, and I can see past aliases and learn more information than the standard identification."

Drake gasped, covering his body.

"Pervert," he said in faux disgust. "That explains some things then. That's probably why you think you could've won in that fight; you got better raw stats than I have, huh?"

Bjorn chuckled.

"Yeah, that's part of it. I told you though bro, I also have two legendary skills, and honestly they're pretty bangin'." Bjorn laughed then became serious. "But Adam hasn't really been a problem, at least not how you would think. He's a good fighter; he specializes in plague magic and curse magic. I haven't exactly figured out the difference. All I know is it's nasty and hard to deal with."

"That does seem like a problem," Drake thought. "So that's why you didn't or *couldn't* kill him?"

Bjorn shook his head.

"No, I can kill him. He's a mage type." He looked up back to Drake. "A real, normal, ordinary mage type. The problem is Shigure needed him to help with the goblins. Even with Shigure and myself, there were a lot of goblins, man, and his magic allows him to section off most of the forest if he wants. So I had to stop because Shigure physically wouldn't let me."

"Art thou implying he can barrier thou from slaying him?" Theodore asked, his face showing disbelief.

"Not exactly. Adam was one of Shigure's first team members, and now he follows him around all over the place. So when I tried, he just stood in front of Adam each time. I can't very well kill the kid for not wanting me to kill Adam, so I gave up. And Adam hasn't been a nuisance with anything I've seen. Those missing people you're talking about could be him, but I have no evidence to back it up. Adam's always stayed within the walls of the camp. And before Shot asks about doubles and illusions, yes I'm sure it's actually him. My skill can see through that stuff, and I know he only changed races because of an item, it wasn't a stone. Or at least, that's what Shigure's told me. If he's lying then I've been played, but I doubt it."

"Well," Drake said, finally getting back to his pot and beginning to stir again, "as long as he stays out of our shit, it's not our business. That's Shigure's problem until they want to make it mine. But just to make sure, everyone stay in pairs and find a buddy. Speaking of which, where are Tom, Jacqueline, Julia, and Claire?"

Chelsea raised her hand from her seat on the ground next to Drake. "Jacky is still sleeping in the tent with Julia. They both like to sleep in. Tom I have no clue though."

"Okay, anyone seen Tom? Claire?" Drake asked again.

"Tom is back in my tent. Guy couldn't find anyone to bunk with, so I had to let the idjit sleep in mine. Either that or I'd have to hear him cry like some lost puppy outside all damned night," Hudson chimed in, his arms crossed. "Think the poor bastard is still sleeping in there, but he should be fine. I set up some of the little guys back there since we had those wacko visitors last night. There's the big un' in there as well, so they're welcome to try to get him."

Drake nodded. "Then I'll go check for Claire. Chelsea, would you mind taking over for the food?"

"Yeah no problem, I don't mind," Chelsea replied, scooting over a bit so she could grab the ladle.

"I'll be right back then." Drake waved, walking to the back end of their small camp. He sighed. "Why didn't she just bunk up with Sherry..."

A few moments later, Drake stretched out his aura and saw that someone was still in her tent, which he assumed was Claire. Getting to the edge of the tent entrance, he stopped.

"Do I knock? There isn't exactly a doorbell. Ah, I know!" Drake smiled and flexed his aura, thankful he had done more practice with it through the night.

A second later, he heard a yelp and the crashing of some metal objects. After another several seconds passed, he saw a woman come to the tent entrance, her staff ready and dirty-blonde shoulder-length hair a mess, blue eyes staring at him in fear.

Drake stood there smiling back. Her face relaxed slowly, then scrunched in anger.

"Do you have to do that? I swear I almost died of fright!" Claire huffed.

"Well, I didn't want to go into your tent without asking," Drake said honestly, "and screaming at the top of my lungs felt inappropriate."

"So you decided to scare me to death instead? I thought we were being attacked again!"

Drake winced, feeling awful for forgetting that she may still have issues from what had happened to her.

"Would you forgive me if I said I just didn't want to ruin my singing voice by screaming?" Drake said, cringing back slightly.

"Fuck you. Next time just come in and wake me up," Claire said flatly, folding her arms as she blew a strand of hair out of her face.

"Excuse me?"

"I meant what I said. You're welcome to come in and wake me. I trust you," Claire reiterated.

"Nah, no thanks. Not interested," Drake replied.

"Not like that!" Claire said in a rage, but she quickly deflated and looked at her feet, the mood changing drastically now that they were alone. "I mean, I wouldn't mind... but you just don't... I mean... is it because I'm dirty...?"

Drake recoiled, honestly shaken by the question.

"What? Of course not. I'm just not interested in anyone right now, I told you that," he explained.

"That just means I'm not good enough! Right? What is it then, why am I not good enough for you?!"

Drake looked back at Claire, his mind trying to untangle how she could even ask that question. He had told her exactly why already.

"It isn't you, it's me," Drake said, then slapped himself as the words exited his mouth. "I can't believe I said that, but it is. Look, I'm not ready right now, especially after everything that's happened to me. I'm just not looking for anything. Maybe after the tutorial when everything settles down."

"*Drake, it will never settle down, not really,*" Natto said, muscling her way into the conversation for a moment.

Yeah, but she doesn't know that, Drake thought. He could feel Natto shake her head, but she went back to being silent.

"Then," Claire said, looking upwards, "when I find you after the tutorial, will you take me then?" she asked with pouting lips and puppy dog eyes.

Drake sighed. "I'll think about it."

"Yay!" Claire said, more animated than ever. "Then it's a promise!" she added, sticking out her pinky.

Drake laughed and met her hand with his own, but when their fingers touched, she tried to pull him in, her face coming inches close to him.

But Drake was ready for it, his reaction speed too fast for her priest-based class. After his many battles, his instincts took over and he pulled her past him, flipping her on her ass.

She fell forward with a yelp after being somersaulted, landing with a thump on the ground. Her face now pointed towards the blue sky, she let out a long exhale.

Drake turned around and looked down.

"You really thought that was going to work?" Drake smiled.

"You're so mean," Claire whined.

"You're the one who tried to assault me, but I'm the dick?" Drake laughed, helping her up.

"I was shooting my shot!" Claire argued.

Drake snorted but pulled her into his arms, giving her a soft embrace of a hug. Their height difference allowed him to rest his head on hers.

"I'm proud you've come so far. You still need to tell me about your brother sometime though," Drake said softly.

Claire was surprised by the embrace and shrank in his arms, just nodding.

"Also, sorry for scaring you." Drake laughed. "My bad, Claire."

Drake gave her a pat then let her go after a moment, walking back to the fireplace. A loud click of the tongue sounded in Drake's head.

"Damn it, I might be losing this bet," Natto cursed. Drake chuckled lightly and put his hands behind his head.

Chapter 20
Meeting the People Who Can Kick My Ass

Drake walked to the campfire, many eyes following him as he sat back down. Chelsea had finished the morning stew and handed it out to the group.

"So, how was your mini-date, bro?" Bjorn asked, scooping a spoonful of stew into his gullet.

"Went okay. We'll find out how great it was in about nine months," Drake said, deadpan.

Drake could hear several forks drop as heads turned to focus on him.

Bjorn laughed, the others of the group not taking the joke quite so light-heartedly.

"What the fuck do you mean nine months? I thought you didn't have any interest!" Chelsea spat, rising to her feet.

Megan slightly choked on her food and coughed while hitting her chest. Harley offered her a cup of water, grinning wryly.

Amir turned his head away, mumbling something under his breath as he decided to continue eating.

Theodore looked on with a smile.

"My lord, shall thou be siring heirs already? My, what a wondrous day it is!" he shouted before Harley could hit him in the side.

"He's joking, love," she whispered.

Theodore's eyes widened before he slumped slightly.

"This one sees. So there will be no heirs of the great lord to serve, then..."

Drake sighed.

"What is wrong with all of you? Do you think this is some romantic comedy or something?" Drake laughed and sat down, grabbing his own share of the food.

He remembered to grab a good portion for the black hole that was currently residing in his head as well when she gave a reminder. A very loud and dramatic reminder.

"S-So you didn't do anything?" Chelsea stammered, lowering herself to pick up her spoon.

Drake snorted. "No, I'm an innocent church-going boy. Never once have I done anything." He chuckled.

"Hey, too far," Bjorn said, nudging his left shoulder.

"Sex jokes are fine but that's too far?" Drake asked.

"Hell yeah, bro, we know literal anciently-described gods are actual things now. Who are you to say the big man upstairs won't actually come down now to put you on your ass if it tickles his big fancy?" Bjorn laughed half-jokingly.

Drake paused, thinking about it seriously for a moment.

"Well, that is true. From what Natto told me, dragons, liches, and a bunch of other things are real as well, so he could definitely be real in some form." Drake chuckled and took a scoop from his bowl.

"'Tis true? The mystical beasts of legend art not tales of grand adventure, but living breathing monoliths of destruction?!" Theodore asked in glee.

"Well they technically stand on two legs, from what she said, but yeah. Breathe fire, super strong, kill you by looking at you, like shiny things. Whole shabang," Drake explained.

"Pup, you might be too used to all this system hub-bubbery, but do you realize what ya just said? Them dragons are real? Doesn't that moisten your leggings?" Hudson said, his brow raised.

"Yeah of course it does, but we won't be dying for another ten years, so it's all good!" Drake said.

Now he had everyone's attention again.

"Oh, right, I haven't told you all this." Drake chuckled, looking around the fire. "Well, the short of it is that when we get out of the tutorial, we have, like, solar system witness protection. Only for ten years though—then the big baddies can come get us. And from what Natto said, those dragons I mentioned are maybe hosting this thing, and they'll come take what they gave us and more in this tutorial."

"Huh... so even the stones?" Bjorn asked, tilting his head and ruffling his beard in curiosity.

"Yup, even those. Crazy right?" Drake answered.

"Eh. Mine now, bro," Bjorn laughed, going back to eating.

"How can you two be so calm about this?" Megan asked.

"Oh, I'm shaking in my boots. Just look at my feet," Drake said, shaking his dented boots "See? Shaking."

"Mr. Shot, I feel like this is no laughing matter. Are we going to be alright?" Harley asked.

"I would honestly give us a... thirty percent chance of living after the ten years, if I'm being optimistic. Around ten percent if we're speaking realistically," he said.

Theodore smiled next to Harley, placing his hand on her lap comfortingly.

"My lord, what dost *thou* think of our chances of longevity after said time period?"

Drake smiled back. "One hundred percent, Theo my good man."

"How can you say that?" Megan asked.

"Because I'm here," Drake replied seriously, his smile gone. "I have too many people I care about to just lie down and take it from some old gatekeepers. The system might be cruel, but it's never given me zero chance of survival. If there's even a sliver of hope for us to make it," he said, looking around, "then don't any of you worry. I'll grab it."

Drake broke his serious expression quickly, going back to eating. The rest of the group mulled over the information he had just given them, but their faces relaxed as they heard his following words. It had been tough, that was certain, but Drake had seen them through it all so far.

"You're kinda preachy aren't you, bro," Bjorn said, filling another bowl.

"You aren't supposed to talk about it, man. Way to ruin the moment." Drake snorted.

"Talk about what?" Claire said, walking to the group and sitting down next to Drake, albeit slightly sheepishly. Her hair was damp, and her clothes were different from when Drake had seen her earlier.

Amir turned scarlet. His mind apparently went wild as whatever fantasy he had in there grew or found the piece that completed the puzzle.

"Morning after shower... Haram..." Amir mumbled.

Drake sipped the broth of his soup, pretending he didn't hear him. Harley and Chelsea seemingly did the same as they had excellent hearing from their classes and stats. Chelsea, though, was far more interested and invested than Harley was, leaning over and lightly bumping shoulders with Drake.

Drake ignored it, continuing to eat.

This is going to be a problem now, isn't it, he thought.

"If you continue to not take one of them, I would certainly say so." Natto laughed.

Thankfully, Drake was saved.

Tom had woken up, and him being him, he pushed his way through and sat right next to Drake, forcing Chelsea to move. Her face turned into a deathly scowl.

"Oh, stew again?" Tom sighed.

"What, don't like it?" Drake asked.

"No, all your food is amazing for some reason, but we've been eating it a lot lately," Tom complained.

"That's fair," Drake said, pulling the pot of food back into his inventory.

"What?! No, I didn't mea—"

"You said you were eating too much, so try my new recipe: 'no soup for you' a la mode." Drake smiled.

"But—but—" Tom said, his face crumbling into a frown.

Drake enjoyed teasing the guy, but he was stopped by an approaching group of people coming from Shigure's camp. He dropped the food back down, Tom bowing in thanks. Bjorn and Drake both left to meet them.

"Good morning, Shigure," Bjorn greeted.

"It is nice to see you as well, Sir Bear. Shot," Shigure said reluctantly.

"Watch it. I'm not the one on thin ice, kid. Are these the people I asked for?" Drake pointed with his chin.

Looking over the group, Drake was able to see several people of decent level. Some were around level 15, others at level 14, and one individual was at 16. They were no match for Bjorn or Drake, but that was not the point.

"Yes, these are several of the people from our camp with formal martial arts or military training. I am also included in this, as I have formal Kendo experience as well as Judo," Shigure explained, fixing his attitude.

"Thank you. But before that, what do you know about the people or ghouls that showed up last night?" Drake asked pointedly.

"I-I am uncertain as to what you mean. We have no one who is of that race, and I can assur—"

"Don't want assurances, especially not when I had to snuff four of them out last night when they tried to enter our tents. Where's this Adam guy?"

Shigure glanced at Bjorn, but Drake redirected him with a small flex of Aura, chilling Shigure for a moment.

"He... He is within the camp. Apparently he is sensitive to light at his current rank and doesn't want to exhaust himself after having to come out yesterday. But I am certain he was not the culprit," Shigure offered.

"Okay, I'll bite. Why?"

"Because we have also suffered losses from these attacks. Even Adam's own group has lost people to them when they are out at night."

"Why exactly are they out at—oh, vampire, right. Well, that doesn't exonerate him from the attacks. He's the only vampy we know of. And don't forget you and your little friend stepped on my toes, so I'm only going to be nice one last time. If I get a whiff of stinky dead people again, he. Is. Mine," Drake growled, his eyes shifting colors.

"I will... pass the message along."

"Make sure that you do." Drake smiled, then looked past him at the group.

"Alright, hello people I don't know. But you might know me!" Drake said, spreading his arms. "I am in need of someone to kick my ass."

The group began mumbling to each other, some of their eyes widening and some smiling.

"I know what you're all thinking. 'Oh, how are we supposed to do that to you?' Well, it's going to work like this. I will be lowering my perceived stats to match yours. And yes, it works; I tried it a bit yesterday with some trial and error. I will move slightly slower, hit slightly weaker, and no magic. I need to gain experience in martial arts and self-defense because I'm a novice. So who's up to beat the crap out of me?" Drake asked.

The entire group looked confused, doing nothing but standing there silently. Shigure, on the other hand, shot his arm up excitedly.

Drake laughed and sighed at the same time.

Does Shigure think he's at school or something? he thought.

"Okay, whoever agrees to help me will get a few thousand F-Grade monster cores as well as a rare skill stone of their choice from my inventory," Drake added.

Every hand in the group shot up like he'd just offered his weight in gold with a sports car on top. Drake smiled.

"Good. Now, who's first?"

Chapter 21

Training Sucks Donkey Nuts

"Alright, I—I can't anymore. Ahhh..." Drake gasped, writhing on the ground.

"What's wrong, prick? Can't handle a little ass whoopin'?" the man standing said as he sneered down at him.

"Apparently not." Drake huffed, looking back up at the man. "I never imagined people actually trained to kill would be so hard to fight..."

I can still beat them in a fight at full power though. Just want to slide that in here... Drake thought, trying to nurse his bruised ego.

"I will say I am impressed with how well they are pummeling you. I did not think that your military was so well trained." Natto giggled, laughing at Drake's expense.

I'm going to refrain from saying something very rude, and it's totally not because I'm exhausted from holding back while getting my ass kicked.

Drake huffed and heaved a breath, drawing in some much-needed air as he sat his body back up. He was getting shafted left and right when it came to technique, and his self-imposed handicap made it even harder. But he had kept his vitality at its peak for the most part, also allowing his Aura to continually scan the field.

He wasn't so foolish as to believe that telling Shigure to control his people would result in them actually listening. The more Drake interacted with the teen, the more he questioned if the boy was actually in charge or just a powerful ally people were manipulating.

Drake had noticed quite a few onlookers come and go. Thankfully, after witnessing his entrance yesterday and seeing Bjorn camped nearby laughing at Drake being smacked around, they decided against doing anything for now.

"All done, buttercup?" the man jeered, again throwing an insult at Drake.

"I consider myself more of a Bubbles, thank you. Let's go again. I'm slowly getting it." Drake sneered back.

"You call that getting it?" a woman from the side said, pointing and laughing. Drake ignored the jab, taking his stance once more.

The man across from him did the same, opting for a more adaptive, loose form, attesting to his mastery of his MMA style.

Drake scoffed. He knew the man was also playing loose because he didn't respect Drake as an opponent.

It's taking all my willpower to not just put my hand through his head...

Drake only knew his fighting styles from shows and anime, the most in detail being boxing.

They both rushed forward, meeting in a clash of jabs and strikes.

Drake kept his arms up, doing his best to cover his head as he used his nimbleness to dodge as best he could.

But the man was faster. Using his experience and quick thinking, he feinted for Drake's left, then quickly swept his back leg, taking Drake to the ground once more.

The man barked a laugh, bringing down the heel of his metal boot in an attempt to crush Drake's head.

Falling to the ground, Drake let out a puff of air but recovered, tumbling out of the way of the stomp. With his now increased dexterity, he sprang back up with a handstand from the ground, collecting himself and going in close again.

Drake moved in towards the center of the man, doing his best to use the same feint the man had and throwing a quick jab to his left. Unfortunately, Drake's arm was caught in an arm lock, the man laughing as he used his knee to kick upwards.

But Drake wasn't about to be undone. And he wasn't about to let his Adrenaline Acuity go to waste.

So he cheated.

Seeing the knee strike coming in slow motion, Drake pushed himself off the ground and over the man's right shoulder, pulling him into a headlock, then wrestling him to the ground.

"Gotcha, bitch!" Drake chuckled, holding the man in a tight headlock.

After a few more struggling seconds, the man finally tapped out. Drake released him and got to his feet.

"See? Learning!" he huffed.

The man grumbled something and went back to the spectators, another person walking forward.

"Not bad, rookie, but keep in mind going to the ground in a real fight is death. You won't just be dealing with one opponent." The man smiled.

"Good to know. Then let's go with two, then," Drake said, pointing to the woman who had insulted him earlier. "You seem to want to get in on the action, so let's see what you got, Blossom. Or, wait, you're probably a Buttercup in this situation," Drake said, tilting his head in a momentary debate.

The woman growled and glared back at Drake.

"I'm goin' to enjoy kicking your sorry ass, kid!" she spat, cracking her knuckles.

Drake gasped in faux fright.

"Oh no! Mojo Jojo is angry; whatever am I going to do?"

* * *

Adam looked from the rampart of the camp down into the field, a group of people sparring while onlookers formed a circle around those currently fighting.

"Hmm, at least he's shit at hand-to-hand combat," Adam mused. "His magic was rather extraordinary, but it's nothing I can't handle."

Adam looked beside the ring of spectators to a smaller group near Bear. There, the rest of Shot's party looked on, laughing and pointing, some still eating while others moved back and forth between the tents of their little camp.

"I don't see why they would want to follow an idiot like him when we are obviously the better choice. It's rather sad that such beauties are wasted on a fool." He scoffed.

Next to Adam, a small magic circle appeared. From it, a pale gangly man rose up from the ground.

"Yes, what is it?" Adam asked.

"Master, we were unable to infiltrate their camp in the night," the ghoul gurgled.

"I can see that. I'm more interested in what you learned, you dumb fucking lesser."

The Ghoul shrank back, bowing deeply.

"We have mapped out their camp. The leader sleeps alone in a tent at the far end while the rest have decided to form pairs or larger groups in the others. The man in charge seems to have a perception skill that lets him notice us within a certain distance," the Ghoul replied.

Adam sensed a 'but' within the pause.

"And what's the but? Out with it—I don't want to be seen with something like you. It will ruin my plan," Adam spat.

"Yes... There is a woman who is on the edge of the camp. She is far enough away that we believe we can grab her in time, even if we were to alert their leader. But we will suffer great losses."

Adam waved his hand.

"I don't care, do it. I can always make more of you filth. Don't fail this time, or you will be *changing employers*."

The ghoul gurgled a grunt and sank back down into the magic circle.

Adam scoffed, placing a sleeve to his nose.

"Filthy lessers... If only I could be with the purebloods where I belong. I wouldn't have to deal with their disgusting stench, and I could have all the pleasures and riches I want," Adam thought aloud, his eyes moving again to the group below. "But soon... Very soon, I will have an obedient workhorse." He sneered, a smile creasing his pale lips.

* * *

Chelsea moved closer to Claire, inch by inch, with only one clear goal in her mind.

I need to find out what happened! I might have set myself back by being a bitch early on, but I won't be beat! she thought, her eyes focusing on the blonde woman who sat across from her looking at the sparring.

"What are you doing?" Tom asked. He chewed on a piece of jerky, his eyebrow raised.

"Don't fucking worry about it, Tom!" Chelsea said, snapping at the poor man.

Tom recoiled, gulping down the rest of his jerky in one bite and suddenly choking.

Claire heard the ruckus and turned her head, furrowing her brows in curiosity.

"What are you two doing?" she asked, almost parroting Tom.

"That's what I would like to know!" Tom said, coughing.

"We aren't doing anything, but what are *you* doing?" Chelsea huffed, scooting over even closer to Claire before whispering, "I thought we had an unspoken deal not to get ahead!"

Claire scoffed. "Hmph, how are we supposed to have a deal if it's unspoken? Sounds really stupid. And... I didn't get ahead," Claire said, suddenly deflating.

"What? What happened, exactly?"

Tom inched closer only to be hit square in the face by Chelsea's fist. Tom was unharmed, but he got the message and walked away.

Claire squirmed a bit under Chelsea's intense stare, but she eventually folded, spilling the beans on what had transpired between her and Drake.

"He hugged you?!" Chelsea shrieked, her face turning green.

"Shhh! It isn't a big deal! I feel like he mostly did it because he felt bad that I tried to kiss him," she murmured.

"Yeah, maybe, but are you sure you're alright? After..." Chelsea struggled to find the words uncomfortably sitting on the end of her tongue. "After what happened?" she finally said meekly.

Claire pursed her lips, struggling to answer.

"I don't know... I wasn't even thinking about that when it happened. I just felt... safe?" Claire said, her eyes relaxing as she stared out into the field and watched Drake get hit in the face for the umpteenth time.

It was Chelsea's turn to squirm in her seat, feeling awkward now.

"Ahh, that's not fair." She sighed. "I'm happy for you after everything—we all need something like that with what we're going through—but I can't help but be jealous..."

Claire snickered.

"You're a surprisingly pure maiden at heart, huh, Chelsea? It isn't like we're dating," Claire said. Chelsea's eyes brightened at the answer. Claire smirked. "At least not yet."

Chelsea shifted again in her seat, pulling her legs up to her chest as she pouted.

"I wish I knew how to make things better; I feel awful for all the things I said when I first met him. When he saved us, all I saw was another empty hope and hollow promises. Chris, the guy who used to lead our group..."

"What? Was he like Drake?" Claire asked.

"No. When I first met him, before I knew him, Chris was honestly better. The picture of the perfect guy. Charismatic, charming, always knew what to say and when to say it. Firm but soft and always understanding enough to listen first," Chelsea explained, rattling off details. "But behind it, he was a monster. A real monster. And that's all I saw behind Drake when he swooped in and gave us a way out of that nightmare. It was wrong, I know, but I was afraid." Chelsea chuckled lightly, admonishing herself.

Claire reached her hand out to touch Chelsea's shoulder.

"I was lucky, then. I saw Drake as a monster as well," Claire began, looking again over at Drake and then back to Chelsea. "The only difference was I needed that monster to get back at those goblins for what they did. I haven't even told Drake this yet, but my brother died protecting me from them. When we were taken into this insane godforsaken place, all I had was him. All I had was Jared. But he could only protect me for so long against the hordes of goblins, and eventually, they took us..." Claire paused, her arm shaking as she pulled it away. Her mouth quivered and tears quickly filled her eyes. "They pitted us against each other in the ring, but he refused to fight me. The goblins... Those sick animals... Th-They made me kill him," Claire sobbed. "It was him or me, and they would have killed us if we both refused. We saw it happen before, and Jared knew. So he died... to protect me. I would have ki-killed myself, but I was just too scared, too weak..."

Claire's face stiffened, her eyes burning in rage thinking back on it.

"Then he saved us. At first, when I saw him, I didn't want to believe he was real either. Just another light going to be snuffed out by those monsters no matter how strong he appeared to be. So I tried to run. But instead, he stopped me, protected me, fed me, and gave me a reason to keep going. And now. Now that he let me kill not only the goblin that forced my brother and me to fight but also the one that started it all, the king—I want him. I want Drake to be my reason to keep going." Claire smiled.

"Damn it, stop!" Chelsea said, wiping the tears from her eyes. "How am I supposed to beat that? Let me be angry for a bit, will you? Or at least let me compete!" She sighed. "Now I can't help but cheer for you too. Why are all the women around here so perfect? I feel so inadequate now... First Harley, then you. Who's next, huh? When's my turn!" Chelsea roared, throwing her hands into the air.

Chapter 22
Finding the Thing—I Mean Crafter—I'm Looking For

The day progressed with Drake going back and forth between the challengers, each one defeating him handily for a few hours until the forms and strikes were beaten into him, allowing him to slowly improve.

Eventually they broke at meal times, not because Drake was particularly hungry, but because of two certain bottomless pits—comparable to the abyss—who wouldn't allow him to continue.

During the first break at lunch, he invited the people who'd participated to join him so long as they provided some food.

Most of them declined, opting to just eat their meals near the camp while they waited to get back to training as soon as Drake was ready. All of them were eager to resume venting their frustrations on Drake, not to mention they enjoyed the old-world challenge of fighting like regular people once more.

Drake and his group began cooking, and the aroma suddenly attracted the nearby people who had declined earlier. The smell of the food was all too enticing for them, as they were used to eating jerky and essentially prison rations of poorly made soup, bread, or whatever else was being served in the camp.

This wasn't to say no one was cooking good food inside Shigure's camp, but it was a luxury, meaning it was expensive to purchase. And Drake was offering to cook as long as you provided the food.

He and his group quickly finished eating, sharing some time going over what he had missed during his hours of sparring. Once they finished their small talk, he once again got back to the grindstone, but he needed to up the difficulty.

During their session before dinner, Drake began using magic. Not to use it against his opponents, but to simply train his multitasking and skills. He cursed when he realized he couldn't use certain skills due to them giving him a clear advantage, but he quickly found a workaround.

Having several people stay within eyesight and relative earshot, Drake was able to further push his abilities and multitasking by using his Aura of Command for both his opponents and the party members when it was available.

Drake was also somehow able to convince some bystanders to let him use his ocular skills on them. Eventually, Bjorn jumped in and asked for him to train using him as the target. Bjorn wanted to train his own skills by resisting the skill.

Progress was slow, but he was without a doubt getting there, even on the first day. Drake was finally able to start progressing on the skills he'd been sorely lacking in due to limited time and an inability to utilize them.

This again continued until dinner before he was interrupted by a cranky Sherry and a complaining Natto. Both whined incessantly about how he wasn't paying attention to their food dilemma—the dilemma being that there wasn't constant food being prepared for them.

Dinner was a bigger event this time around, as all the people who'd declined before now happily brought ingredients, wanting to have a good warm meal for dinner.

Drake and his party prepared the meals for everyone. They honestly felt slightly nostalgic cooking for more people after weeks of having to cook for hundreds. They chatted and laughed while serving the food, reminiscing about how just a few days ago, they would spend their time doing the same thing but for several times the amount.

The meal progressed normally, but Drake didn't fail to notice some penetrating gazes coming from both the forests as well as Shigure's outpost. His thoughts turned to how tonight might be more bothersome than the last. He might have to make an example out of people tomorrow during their sparring.

Thankfully, there were no incidents after dinner outside of Sherry wandering into his tent grumbling about food and Chelsea trying to sneak in only to be pulled back by a chastising mother hen named Megan.

Drake was now practicing in his bed, looking at the canvas above him as his hand twirled and melded magic to the side.

"I'm getting pretty good at this; I kinda feel like a Grand Mage at this point," Drake mused, smiling to himself.

"Please, you are still only F-Rank. While you are progressing well, do not allow it to go to your head. The higher-ranked pure mage classes will still be able to outperform you in mana manipulation for the time being. We must remember that your skills, while strong, are still meant for general use. Hopefully we are able to get an epic subtree stone from that wretched goblin's horde, or we will be forced to wait until the tutorial shop," Natto explained from the bed at his side, her eyes still closed as she breathed softly.

"It would be nice not having to spend everything on just stones at the end... but I'm curious what else is in the store. I don't particularly need anything desperately outside of stones, but it's always nice to have shiny new equipment," Drake thought aloud, his desire to upgrade his equipment coming through.

Drake might not be playing games anymore thanks to the tutorial, but his habit of wanting the next big upgrade for the nice high damage numbers was ever-present.

"There are several categories within the shop. Cultivation pills, for example, like the ones you used for increasing your stats. There will certainly be exquisite equipment to be found, I am sure, since we have all but confirmed that this tutorial is sponsored by the dragons. There are also accessories, skill stones, maps, quests, and system-sanctioned buildings. You will even most likely find other constructs such as myself there," Natto said, pausing a bit.

"Hmm, that's quite the selection, but I think I'll pass on the other constructs," Drake said, taking her pause as a hint of nervous insecurity. "I only need one pesky little glutton by my side right now." He smiled.

"What do you mean, pesky?" Natto huffed. "And what is 'right now' supposed to mean, might I ask!" she continued to jab in faux offense, raising her hands into the air, but she was still lying down with her eyes closed.

Drake chuckled and let the back and forth die. He continued to look upward, training his spells as he thought about the day and went over the fights he'd had, trying to fix his mistakes in his head.

Throughout the night, this continued. Drake gave himself no rest, diligently increasing his skills until morning.

Finally, the light began to pierce through the canvas bit by bit as the sun outside rose. That gave Drake a passing thought.

"I wonder, where exactly are we? I thought about it before, but there aren't any stars, but we have a sun. Is the sun fake? Natto mentioned it before, but I wish I had some way to confirm it," he thought aloud.

Drake looked over, surprised when he didn't hear a reply from Natto— only to see her snoring, sound asleep, a line of drool coming from her slightly open mouth.

"I don't know what's more surprising, her drooling like an old man after a drunk night out or her actually needing sleep. She's usually awake and asking for food by now, not to mention she's a construct..." He chuckled and rose from his bed.

Drake quietly stepped out of the tent, stretching as he did. The morning light and dew reminded him of his father's home far out from the city.

"Man, I really miss this type of scenery in the morning. Only thing missing are singing birds."

"You called?" Bjorn slapped Drake on the shoulder, a big grin on his face.

"What the fuck kind of bird would you be? And I asked for singing, not ear-shattering chalkboard scratching." Drake laughed back, pretending his back was not stinging. Bjorn gasped in faux offense.

"I used to be the best singer at company karaoke," Bjorn said, his face filled with confidence.

"Bjorn." Drake laughed. "You were the CEO of your company at a company event." His eyebrow raised.

Bjorn's confidence deflated quickly as he got the message, but he still asked, "Yeah? So what, bro?"

"You don't think they just said you were good because they were afraid of getting fired?" Drake laughed again. He began to step out behind his tent, summoning a ball of water as he did.

"What are you trying to say? I'm a bad singer? And do you really see me as someone who would fire an employee over saying that?"

Drake pursed his lips, taking a minute to reply.

"Drake, bro, really?" Bjorn said.

"I'm kidding. No, I don't take you as a tyrannical corporate leader from a tech company in California," Drake said, making sure his voice was as sarcastic as possible.

"That one stung, man. I'm a good singer," Bjorn said defensively.

"Wait, you're not going to say you wouldn't fire people for that? Instead you're getting mad about me insulting your vocal expertise?" Drake asked, aghast.

Bjorn shrugged.

Drake shook his head, not sure if he should laugh or sigh at the man admitting to being a terror at the office.

Behind his tent and out of view of most of the camp, Drake placed a majority of his belongings into his inventory, spilling the lukewarm water over himself.

"Ahh! I've said it before, I'll say it again. My kingdom for a bar of soap..." Drake sighed.

"Here," Bjorn said, offering up just that.

"What?! Where did you get it?" Drake exclaimed.

"Guy inside makes it. They have a good amount of craftsmen in the camp, ya know," Bjorn said nonchalantly.

"Why didn't you tell me this sooner, man?!" Drake yelled as he dripped water from head to toe.

"I dunno, you didn't ask?" Bjorn shrugged once more, a grin on his face.

"Also, you should cover up bro. There's some wandering eyes," Bjorn said, pointing with his chin.

Drake was already aware from his Aura sense, but he decided to joke around.

"Ahh! Perverts!" he screamed in embarrassment. He quickly summoned his robe to cover himself, recoiling in disgust.

"W-What?! I was just looking since I was passing by!" Megan shouted, peeking out from behind the tent. "Besides, I've already seen it all…" she mumbled, surprisingly blushing.

Fuck, is it another one? Damn it's hard being me sometimes. Drake laughed to himself.

"I know, I'm only kidding. Do you need anything, Megan, or are you just hungry like the rest of the vultures?" Drake asked, blow-drying himself with his magic.

"I, um, I wanted to ask if I could join your sparring sessions?" she asked tentatively. "After everything, I realized I'm not really able to defend myself as a healer, but also just in general I feel very vulnerable. So I thought learning a bit might help."

Drake mulled it over briefly, looking to Bjorn behind him who shrugged with his eyes.

He's so very very helpful… Drake sighed internally.

"I don't see why not. Just make sure to not overdo it, and don't let people know what class you are," Drake reminded.

"Why's that?"

"Because I don't want anyone getting any ideas about taking advantage of you or one of our other support classes. Your stats and skills are oriented for non-combat support just like Claire and Amir, so you wouldn't last long in a fight, but for sparring I don't see it being a problem. But if they know you're a vulnerable class, I don't know what they would do. And frankly, based on what's been going on, I don't trust most of them. So let's just say I want to cover all my bases and stay on the safe side. Don't want to have to save you three times in one tutorial, after all," Drake explained, smiling.

Megan nodded silently before adding to her question.

"Also, most of the others in the group were talking about joining too. A lot of us were watching and feeling like we weren't doing enough, so I'll relay the message, if that's alright?" Megan asked.

"Yeah, that would be very helpful, thank you. Wow, look at you being part of the team already after one day!" Drake said sarcastically.

Megan braced a bit from the jab, but she nodded all the same and went in the other direction towards her own tent. Drake raised his brows, honestly surprised that she hadn't snapped back at him.

"Is it just me, or are all the women that hated me starting to... Naw, couldn't be. This isn't some romance novel or anime. Or are they all masochists..." Drake mumbled.

"Brother." Bjorn chuckled. "You are in for some trouble in the future; I can already tell."

Drake laughed wryly. "I don't know what you're talking about. I'm just a naive innocent young man. Just looking at the opposite sex makes me feel all itchy."

Bjorn shook his head before changing the conversation.

"You seemed interested in those craftsmen. Any reason for that?"

Drake paused and remembered one of his major goals that he hadn't really been able to voice yet.

"Yeah. I need someone who can make accessories, specifically jewelry if possible. Rings would be perfect," Drake explained.

"Oh? Trying to fill out your professions while you're here?" Bjorn asked.

"Yup, exactly. I'm thinking of making a status concealment item. I've seen it enough times with the PKers, but I haven't been able to get my hands on the item itself." Drake said, sighing, "so I want to make one myself if the profession will allow me. Not to mention with my item sets and fighting style, explosive stat switching is a must. And I need to snag some different stat multipliers if I want to continue that."

"Hmm, I think I know a guy. Well, thing. Actually, yeah, guy works." Bjorn smiled.

Drake gave him a questioning glance.

"Am I not going to like this?"

"Don't worry about it, bro. Long as you don't look him in the face, it'll be fine. Probably." Bjorn laughed and slapped Drake's bare back.

Chapter 23

Making Progress and the Thing?

You have reached Atrophy of the Mind Proficiency 2.
You have reached Cower Proficiency 2.

Drake paused, holding his hand up to stop his sparring partner when he heard the sound of the increased proficiency notification in his ear. A smile creased his face.

Nice. These ones took way longer than they should have, but can you blame me when I can one-shot everything already? Haven't had to use the debuffs too often because of it, Drake thought before another notification promptly followed the others.

You have reached Tyrant's Indomitability Proficiency 2.

The third notification he received was one that he felt. His mind cleared noticeably, like dirt scraped from a windshield or dust removed from a long forgotten book. He felt his thoughts move more quickly and precisely, and his breathing felt smoother and more relaxed. Overall, his being felt—well, felt *better*.

Drake took a long breath, exhaling out before he looked back to his sparring partner, feeling genuinely refreshed.

"Wow, that was amazing. If only every skill up felt that good," Drake said, taking his stance again.

On the other side of Drake was Shigure, his foot tapping impatiently on the ground. He sighed, finally seeing Drake ready once more. Shigure took his own stance and looked Drake in the eyes dubiously.

"You have just increased a skill?" Shigure asked.

"Yeah. Are you surprised? I've been using them on and off the entire time we've been sparring," Drake answered.

"Yes, but proficiency two to three takes a significant amount of time to advance. Are you saying that you still have proficiency one skills?" Shigure asked again, his stance slackening as he was overcome with surprise.

"A few. Some of them I still can't increase, really. I have one that I'm sort of cheating on," he said, thinking about his Fully Loaded skill.

The skill required all of his equipment slots to be filled, and he technically was able to do this thanks to his Hoarder skill. Drake wasn't wearing any necklaces, but he had an extra ring on each hand, which apparently counted for the missing slot. But he could observe the noticeably slower progress the skill made compared to his other passive skills, leading him to believe that he needed to properly equip every slot to make the skill progress faster.

"That's all you're getting out of me. Now get your dukes up, pretty boy." Drake laughed.

Shigure scowled back and lunged forward, his stance low as he went for a takedown.

Drake had become accustomed to Shigure's opening for the fights. The teen was a good fighter—precise and strategic. Almost too much so, as he continued to use the same maneuvers over and over again as if he were reading line by line from a book.

Shigure closed the gap, looking for a grip on one of Drake's blocking arms. Drake knew it was coming and stepped to the side, instead grabbing Shigure's arm to the teen's surprise.

In one swift motion, Drake used the move that Shigure had been practicing on him for the past several hours. He pulled Shigure in close, bringing his arm over his shoulder as he gripped his hakama by the flap, then flipped Shigure over his shoulder.

Shigure slammed into the ground, the air leaving his body with a gruff grunt.

Drake pressed his counter. He jumped into the air comically and laid his elbow down on Shigure's stomach, resulting in Shigure yelping as Drake bent into the impact.

He got up, laughing. "Shigure, you really need to work on your hothead-edness. That's like the tenth time I've flung a comment at you and gotten you to charge in first. What's the deal? I understand you don't like me, but this is going a bit far, man," Drake said, offering his hand to the teen.

Shigure wiped the drool from his mouth, slapping away Drake's hand in the same motion.

"Bro, that's not only rude, it's unsanitary. Your mouth is already dirty, and who *knows* where it's been," Drake joked, waving his hand to clean the spit from it.

"To hell with you! All you have done is insult me since you have gotten here! That is more than enough reason to dislike you," Shigure spat. He got to his feet shakily.

Drake used one of his hands to summon water to clean his other hand. He looked back at Shigure and dropped an eye, his expression saying, 'really?'

"If that's what you're sticking with, it's whatever. Just know I don't believe you." Drake sighed. "Are you ready for another round, or do I have to go find someone more motivated to really kick my ass?" He laughed, raising his arm to beckon Shigure again.

Shigure roared and lunged forward.

"Did I not just explain this?" Drake snorted in disbelief.

* * *

Several more hours passed as Shigure and Drake sparred back and forth, only stopped eventually by angry gluttons demanding their dinner.

As one would expect, Shigure refused to stay, opting to go back to his camp to eat whatever the leader of a coalition eats.

"He really doesn't like you, huh? Rocks up every time to try to kick you into the dirt, but won't eat notin," Jacqueline said, bringing a spoon to her mouth.

"Yeah, sir, it seems that he has a particular hatred for you. Do you happen to know why?" Amir asked, sitting down at the table next to Hudson.

Drake pursed his lips and rocked back in his chair.

"If I had to guess? I really don't know. It could be almost anything. I had a guy hate me before because I talked to a girl he had a crush on. I've had people hate me because I like a show they don't. Hell, I've had people hate me for saving their asses from death camps," he jabbed. A few wry chuckles sounded around him. He smirked. "What? Too soon? Did I cross a line with that one?"

"I thought we were past that?" Chelsea said, frowning.

"Oh we are. I'll die for anyone here, but that doesn't mean I can't be petty and bring it up once in a while," Drake continued with a smile.

"Mr. Shot, you should really be more forgiving with those things," Harley admonished, shaking her finger at him.

"Why's that?" Drake asked, raising his hands in mock surrender.

"What do you think will happen when they get dirt on you and it's reversed?" she replied.

Drake winced.

"Good point. Alright everyone, I take that back. I am a reformed individual that will never bring up how you all hated me again, even though I saved you all, gave you food, skill stones, and tolerated you being insulting, disrespectful, and all-around insufferable," Drake said sarcastically, bowing his head slightly.

"Ain't that a bit much there even for you, pup? Something got ya on edge?" Hudson asked as he tore a piece of bread from his loaf.

"I can always count on you to be emotionally in tune with me, Hudson. You sure you weren't a therapist before all this?" Drake smiled. "Or perhaps an FBI agent?" he added, squinting his eyes at him.

Hudson stayed silent, bringing his food to his mouth.

"I knew it!" Drake joked, pointing his spoon at him. Then he answered seriously as his eyes wandered to the surroundings. "But really, I don't know. I've been getting a bad feeling. Like someone is testing me."

"Such as, my lord?" Theodore asked.

Drake summoned a small bolt of lightning to the end of his finger, pointing it upward. A bullet of earth fell from his pinky in the next moment and embedded itself into the ground. The earth behind him molded into a slab.

"I'm going to be very clear about this, so here's a visual." Drake winked. "Here is me," he said, engraving a scorch mark on the slab. "Here is the area I can sense with my skill." Drake put a circle around him that took up most of the slab.

"Now, here are all of you next to me," Drake began again, scoring extra dots in the circle close to the original one, "and here are the people around us right now." He placed several dots on the edge of the circle and some within the circle.

"Anyone notice what's going on here?" Drake asked.

The faces around the table looked intensely at the slab, though a few remained blank.

"That's a lot of dots on the edge there," Claire offered, pointing to the cluster on the edge.

"Good." Drake nodded and brought up another slab to his right. "Here is what it looked like yesterday."

Drake took a moment to form a circle and dots representing people around the larger dot in the middle. This time the dots were more scattered and less oriented at the edge of the circle.

"Notice the difference?" he asked.

"The dots of said persons art less centered than the ones today. As if these persons do not understand thine are within the sensory circle," Theodore offered.

"Good, Theo. This is why you're my number two. And not *that* number two—you would need an eyepatch for that, not the monocle. And I don't particularly look as good bald. But yes, what I'm getting at is, I can't tell who these people are or if they're monsters: my skill doesn't differentiate. But I can tell when a living being is within a certain distance. What I didn't know was if the sensing itself gave off any sort of notification that it was being used. I believed it was just when I used the full extent of my Aura that I was influencing my surroundings, but apparently I was wrong, and now someone is trying to find out where my limit is." Drake's eyes thinned.

"Is that what that weird tingling is? You think someone is planning something?" Tom asked, a spoon poking out from his mouth.

"I don't know. I don't think Shigure would be stupid enough even if he's angry, but I don't know enough about the other members of the camp," Drake thought aloud.

"What will you do if it's someone from the camp and not just monsters?" Megan asked.

"Shh, you. You're a probation member; you don't get a say," Drake snapped jokingly. She frowned. "I'm only hazing you a bit, Megan. I don't know if you've noticed, but I'm an acquired taste." Drake grinned.

"Very acquired," everyone at the table said except Theodore, who looked around confused.

"Hmm? My lord is a splendid individual!" he exclaimed. Theodore raised a brow. "This one does not see the problem with his humor? Is it not obvious he is merely jesting?"

Harley nudged him with her shoulder, whispering in his ear, but thanks to everyone's enhanced senses she might as well have been speaking normally.

"No love, it's not," she said.

Drake snorted and brought the attention back to him. "Anyway, if it's just monsters, though I'm kinda doubting it, I'll take care of them when they decide to do something or get closer. But if it's not..." Drake sighed, looking off distantly as he stared at his two titles.

Murderer

Kill five of your own race. This title permanently marks you as a murderer.

Serial Killer

Kill ten of your own race. This title permanently marks you as a serial killer. Though the world may not approve, the system smiles upon you and the forthright journey ahead of you.

Drake recoiled at the explanation of the titles, but he refocused and answered Megan's question.

"But if it really is some*one* and not some*thing* trying to harm us, then I will make the same decision I made before." His eyes turned to points, his aura flaring. "I will protect mine. Whatever may come."

Bjorn plopped his bowl down on the table, breaking the tension immediately.

"Shot, I know where you're coming from, but tone it down there bro," Bjorn said, chuckling. "You're going to scare off the dude you were looking for if ya do that." He pointed over to the space between their camp and Shigure's.

In that open space, a hulking figure lugged itself over. The outline of the person—or thing—was twice the size of even Bjorn.

"The bloody hell is that ting?" Jacqueline asked.

"Don't look him in his eye; he doesn't really like being stared at," Bjorn said nervously. He scratched his beard. "He's pretty sensitive about it. It took a bit of convincing to get him out."

"Wait, you weren't kidding when you said *thing*?" Drake said incredulously, his brows raising as he identified the person—or thing.

Lamar Youngston Level 14

Chapter 24

Lamar

"**H**ow is there someone larger than you, exactly?" Drake asked Bjorn in a whisper.

Bjorn snorted. "Hey now, I'm not *that* tall. And he's a craftsman who picked up a non-combat class. He apparently got a hold of a hammer that changed his race."

"*Dude*, you're like six-foot-seven. Do you even realize how enviously tall you are?" Drake chuckled. "And where are all these items? I haven't seen one yet that does that," he mused, looking at the incoming figure. "So? What race is he now?"

"He's a cyclops," Bjorn said tersely. He gave the incoming man a wave.

"Like the *Odyssey*?" Drake asked, raising an eyebrow.

"Yup. He's a little brusque about certain things now that his race changed, is what I'm told, so don't get offended," Bjorn warned.

"Me? Offended?" Drake said. Bjorn gave him a look.

"Fine... Long as he doesn't insult my mother or my height, it's whatever."

The ground began to rumble with every step Lamar took as he closed in on the camp. Now that he was closer, Drake could make out his features and clothing better.

Lamar was tall. Very tall. Seemingly around ten feet or higher—Drake wasn't able to measure exactly from his perspective.

Lamar wore a classic leather apron around himself, some soot and dirt here and there on his sleeveless shirt, and his skin was a shade of pink that Drake hadn't seen outside of fantasy palettes. A small protruding nub on his forehead led to his bald head. On his waist sat a hammer made of what looked like steel from a fiction movie, its sheen so eye-catching that Drake had trouble pulling his gaze from it. And finally, Drake saw Lamar's eye—singular eye.

"Hey there," Drake said, giving a shallow wave. Lamar ignored Drake, instead looking over to Bjorn.

"How are you, Bear? Thank you for earlier. Short stuff here the guy?" Lamar said, his face in a frown.

Drake gritted his teeth. A tinge of frustration immediately bubbled up.

"*I like him,*" Natto said approvingly.

Drake pushed down his frustration and did his best to keep his smile.

Why do all the new people I meet immediately know what my sore spots are? This guy is lucky I need him for crafting... Drake mumbled internally.

"Excuse me, don't you think insulting someone as soon as you meet them is a bit rude?" Drake said with his smile, but the smile didn't, *couldn't*, reach his eyes.

Lamar raised his single brow, a bit surprised.

"This one a bit mouthy, ain't he?" Lamar chuckled and pointed with his thumb at Drake.

"I'll kill you," Drake said quickly.

"What?"

"I said, I'll *keep* you. I like a man who's upfront with his insults. Too many people going around with this passive-aggressive stuff lately," Drake amended.

Lamar raised his chin to look down at Drake, a smile slowly creasing his lips and revealing his sharp fangs for teeth.

"Is that right? You'll *keep* me, will ya?" Lamar grunted. His voice was deep and low, almost like the crackling of coals being raked. "How are ya gonna be doing that?"

Drake smiled back, extending his hand facing palm out towards the cyclops.

"Shot..." Bjorn warned, inching closer.

"If you think threatening is going to work here, you got another thing coming, ya bastard. I'm a master craftsman. You know how many wannabe tyrants have threatened me?" Lamar snorted.

"Well one, I'm a *real* tyrant: I have the title to prove it. And two," Drake said, still smiling, "I just wanted to offer some things!" With that, Drake poured out every last raw gemstone he had in his inventory along with piles and piles of materials from his mines, completely covering the cyclops.

Lamar roared beneath the pile, his head popping out of the staggering number of materials with a 'pwah.'

"What the fuck is all this, ya bastard?! Where in the world did you get this all?" he shouted, his eyes going from gem to gem and material to material.

"Let's just say I was well endowed." Drake chuckled. "So? Ready to hear my proposal?"

Lamar took a moment to unlodge himself from the overwhelming pile of materials that he was currently stuck under. Eventually, he dusted himself off, his head turning side to side as he looked for his now-missing hammer.

Casually, he jabbed his hand into the pile of materials, pulling out the tool and spinning it briefly before slipping it back into his belt.

"I'll bite. What's it ya want? A weapon, armor, accessory?" Lamar asked, crossing his arms.

"*I*," Drake said, stepping forward, "want a teacher." Drake bowed his head slightly. "Please teach me to craft jewelry, *shishou*!"

Silence.

Drake was hit with utter silence, forcing him to bring his head up to meet Lamar's eye.

Lamar had an expression of disgust as he looked down from his towering stature.

"Oh, you're one of *those*," Lamar spat. "Lamar is fine. If you call me that shit again, it won't matter how much stuff you got; you're gonna be finding some third-rate crafter instead."

Drake smirked.

So the big man doesn't like weeby stuff? Well, that's disappointing, but now I know how to annoy him, Drake thought, laughing.

"Of course. I would never dream of doing it if you disliked it," he lied, thinking of ways to piss him off just enough to be annoying, but not enough to go overboard. "Now then, about my offer. I'd like to be taught, and I will give you half of the pile as pay."

"All of it," Lamar countered.

"Are you trying to rob me?"

"Might be. I want all of it."

"*Fuck you.* No."

"Then find another cyclops with a pure crafting class to help, *dumbass.*" Drake gritted his teeth.

"Half and I'll cook your every meal. And I'll promise protection," he offered.

"What good is food going to do? And no one is dumb enough to try and harm me. They couldn't get what they wanted if they did," Lamar said.

"I'm not talking about just you. Have someone important to you? Say, someone who can't defend themselves or isn't *quite* as *valuable*?" Drake explained.

"You wouldn't fucking dare, you bastard!" Lamar roared.

"Shot, that's going a bit far even for you," Bjorn interjected.

"You're right, it's going too far. But who said I was ever going to do that? Who do you think I am, Bear? I'm talking about protection for them. I might not be that scummy, but we both know there are people who are."

Lamar stepped back from his outburst and looked down at Drake.

"What makes you think you could stop anyone, pipsqueak." He sneered. Drake looked up incredulously.

"Have you not been here the past two days, or do you live under a rock?" Drake asked.

"I live in a workshop, and I don't leave it unless very select people ask me to," Lamar said, looking at Bjorn.

Drake shook his head, then stepped past Lamar. After a few trots, Drake moved into the open part of the field and pointed his hand into the air. Looking over at Lamar, he scoffed.

"*Ignis,*" Drake whispered. A crimson magic circle formed below him as a ball of orange flame sparked to life in his hand. It quickly deepened, shifting hue to blue. The next moment, it snapped back and forth, now turned to pure white.

Drake willed the fireball to launch from his hand. It screeched into the air, the ball of white-hot fire lighting up the surroundings even in the brightness of the waning sun.

The ball shot upwards, roaring until it reached well above them and the outpost.

Drake snapped his fingers. The ball exploded, sending sparks and fragments of fire in every direction. The explosion looked like something had been hit by a ballistic missile in the air, and the fragments careened to the ground.

Next, Drake clapped his hands, the magic circle below him shifting to pure white.

"*Gelum,*" Drake said evenly. His hands separated into an arc, revealing fourteen shards of ice. Drake then rested one hand at his side, the other held to snap his fingers. The instant the snap sounded, each shard of ice shot off—trained right at the fragments of fire. Once an ice shard surged out from Drake, another quickly formed and took its place, shooting forward in the same manner to hit its target.

The pieces of ice swiftly cut through the air, meeting their targets and exploding into bursts of water crystals that put on a wondrous show in the twilight. The forming droplets were enough to produce a rainbow in the air.

Drake snapped his hands once more, his hair shifting to blue as he changed Endowments to regenerate.

"Good enough?" Drake asked.

"Nice light show, bro," Bjorn said. His hand was held above his eyes as a visor while he whistled.

"I've seen better," Lamar said, scoffing.

Drake recoiled, aghast.

"W-Where?!"

"Oh, I don't remember. Just ain't impressed. But I think it'll do if that's what you're offering." Lamar sneered.

This fucking guy! Drake seethed internally.

"I will say it again: I like him! He will be a great addition to the group of Anti-Drake cringeness!" Natto cheered.

Not helping...

Natto snickered but ceased her verbal taunting.

"Then if it's good enough... Who is this person? Family?" Drake asked, sighing.

"Yeah, I got a sister," Lamar answered.

"Is she as ugly as you are?" Drake asked, his intrusive thoughts winning.

"Screw you, freak! She's twelve and still human!" he snapped.

"Whoa whoa, okay!" Drake chuckled. "I was just asking. So she's under sixteen, which means she didn't join the tutorial. That's good. It means she was excused from experiencing this nightmare."

"What? Since when is that a thing?" Lamar asked.

"Oh, I forgot most people don't know. Or maybe only the dumb ones haven't noticed there isn't anyone here under sixteen." Drake rolled his eyes.

Lamar scowled at him.

"Don't call me stupid, ya bastard. How was I supposed to know that?"

"Oh, I thought we were still on the insulting-each-other train. My bad." Drake laughed, then cleared his throat. "Well, my completely unobservant, vision-impaired friend. If you agree to my terms, then a wild new world awaits you! For I have the key to the kingdom in the form of a snippy, wonderful, sometimes detestable little glutton all rolled into a tight little one-foot package!" Drake exclaimed, spreading his arms.

Lamar scrunched his face up and turned to Bjorn.

"Is this guy alright in the head?"

"Everyone's a little crazy at this point, bro, you're a cyclopean for crying out loud." Bjorn chuckled and gave the big man a pat on the arm.

Lamar shrugged, reluctantly agreeing as he couldn't argue that point. The world had become a madhouse, and they still weren't even in the 'real' world yet.

"Then if I agree, I get half, and you're going to just share all this information with me? What's stopping you from learning how to craft what you want in the first place if you have all this knowledge?" Lamar asked.

Drake laughed wearily.

"Well, she isn't exactly the best informed in that department. System restrictions and all that," Drake jabbed.

"Hey!" Natto yelled, stepping into the conversation. *"I have insurmountable knowledge on all things within the system!"*

But do you know how to teach me to make shiny jewelry? Drake asked.

"N-No..."

Point made. Drake laughed.

"Fine. I'm not dumb enough to think I can defend my sister once the world starts up again. But how exactly are you going to help her? And are you going to tell me what's going to happen once the tutorial ends?" Lamar said, beginning to rattle off question after question.

"Ah, ah, ah, nope." Drake placed a hand out and up to the cyclopean, stopping him in place. "First, handshake. Then you get the deets."

Lamar stayed silent for a prolonged minute. Drake kept his hand raised, waiting for him to finish parsing through whatever decision he would make.

After a few more moments, a rumbling sigh sounded from Lamar's throat.

"I don't see why not. The deal's too good to say no to," Lamar grumbled, "but I feel like I'm getting involved with someone I shouldn't..."

"Ha! Even he knows!" Natto shouted.

Chapter 25

Movement

"Let me get this straight." Lamar leaned on the table, the wood underneath beginning to crack.

"Whoa whoa whoa! Lamar! What did I say, man? This thing is going to break if you keep doing that every time I tell you something you don't know!" Drake shouted, his hands up as he pushed the cyclops off the table.

"Right, my bad... Still though, how do you know so much about the outside of the tutorial?" Lamar asked. His voice was low, but his disposition was much more amenable now that he was slowly being informed by Drake.

"I have a little"—Drake coughed—"*lovely* little bird in my ear that tells me things." He smiled. "But more importantly, where were you in the real world before all this?"

Lamar leaned back on the custom seat that he'd brought out, the object creaking under his weight.

"We were over in Virginia, but what does that have to do with anything?" he asked.

"That isn't that far... but we don't know how the world will be affected after it's been merged. From what I've been told, it'll increase in size, but even I don't know by how much." Drake sighed and put his hands behind his head, tilting his seat back.

"Now that you mention it, Shot, what are all of us going to do when the tutorial is over? How are we all going to meet up?" Chelsea asked from the end of the table.

"Well, it's a bit complicated."

"Complicated, my lord?" Theodore asked this time.

"Yeah. From what my little birdy has told me, we don't actually have a way, or at least she can't tell me. It's outside the scope of what she can do because it doesn't pertain to the quests she's privy to or the other things she's allowed to divulge." Drake sighed.

"I do not appreciate that sigh; that is insinuating I am useless!" Natto shouted.

I didn't even say anything. Sensitive, much? Drake snickered under his breath.

"If I am, it is because of you! I am half your personality, remember?" she replied, obviously sneering although Drake couldn't actually see it.

Rolling his eyes, he focused back on Lamar and the group in front of him.

"I would like to say I have a concrete plan, but without more information on what's going to happen—specifically when the tutorial ends—the best I got? Is that we all meet up somewhere in the middle of all our locations prior to the system." Drake sighed and pursed his lips in contemplation.

Suddenly, Natto said something he didn't expect.

"Forgive me, Drake. I wish to be of more help, but sadly I cannot in this instance."

It's alright. Don't sweat the little details. The whole purpose of forming this group is to make them strong enough to be on their own two feet after we all separate, Drake explained, grinning slightly at Natto apologizing.

"Either way, I'll figure it out. Everyone's priority is to level up and get stronger; we still have around eighty-some-odd days before we're out of this mess, and I plan to have us going into that ant's nest ASAP," Drake said.

"There's the other thing we need to talk about, idjit. Who exactly is going on this backwater mud trip down a brown hole?" Hudson asked.

Drake tipped back and forth on his chair, thinking for a moment. "Honestly, I'm still thinking. We only have ten slots for a party unless we can find a support class here that allows us to extend the party, but I don't think we will. I don't think Shigure will want us to keep taking important people away from their camp..." Drake sighed.

"Tis very astute, my lord. Thou hast been diminishing their personnel by quite the number. Acquiring Sir Bear alone was a great blow to their fighting forces, this one would assume," Theodore said.

Drake nodded.

"Yeah. Big, tall, grumbling fire head is probably their strongest fighter," Drake said, looking at Bjorn, "and I'm sure Shigure is dealing with a whole slew of nonsense with his coalition now that he's gone. These types of alliances, as far as I'm concerned, only last as long as it's mutually beneficial. That's what I'm getting worried about. The movement we've seen, that Adam guy, how Shigure seems to have a stick up his ass about my general existence—it's a recipe for something very bad. So I want everyone"—Drake looked over to Claire and Sherry—"and I mean *everyone* in pairs from now on. That includes tents and sleeping arrangements. They're testing my range of detection, and I don't want anyone going it alone or too far out. Is that clear?"

"Jeez, yes Dad." Jacqueline scoffed.

Drake smiled.

"Good. Then, I'm going to talk privately with Lamar. Need to know the bells and whistles of how to make the good shit!" Drake stood up and walked over to the enormous lug. "Let's get going, new bestie."

"Don't fucking call me that, freak." Lamar scowled.

"Aw, come on pal! Don't be so cold," Drake wheedled.

"I'm not your pal, you psycho! It's a business deal," Lamar grumbled.

"Ohh call me a psycho again. It gets me all *tingly* when we give each other nicknames."

Lamar and Drake walked away and toward Drake's tent. All the while, they went back and forth, Lamar spitting insults towards Drake as Drake continued to tease him now that they had a deal and Lamar couldn't get out of it.

"Think they're going to be okay?" Chelsea asked the group.

"I think Sir Shot will quickly wear on the cyclops. Perhaps we should send someone to keep him civil?" Amir asked, sipping his food from his bowl.

Everyone looked around. Everyone raised their hand.

"Not it," they all said in unison.

* * *

"Lord Shigure, we cannot continue to allow that man to take important figures from our camp! It is weakening our position by the day, and we do not even know when the next tutorial-wide quest may happen!" Darius pleaded.

"Darius, I understand your concern, but what would you have me do?" Shigure sighed, his hand gripping the sword at his side. "Would you like me to go over there and *tell* him to cease? Would you like me to demand that he stop? If you don't remember, we banned him from our outpost, yet he didn't care and simply set up shop outside! If he wanted, he could likely kill every last one of us! I've only been civil because I have no other choice in the matter."

"There is always my option," mused Adam as he moved closer from the side.

"No! I can only imagine what would happen if we harmed someone from his side. Do you want to doom us all?! I told you no before, Adam. Do not make me tell you again," Shigure shouted back.

"Shigure... Adam does have a point, though," a female voice chimed in. "If we can't beat him in a straight-up fight, why not even the playing field with some leverage?"

"Savannah... Not you too?" Shigure grimaced. "I will have no part in poking a beehive. We are responsible for more than just ourselves as leaders of this coalition. We are not tyrants or criminals, and we will not bar people from choosing where they go or who they associate with," Shigure said reluctantly, doing his best to not let his inner thoughts come to light.

Despite hating Drake fervently, Shigure knew some of the advice he'd given rang true. Shigure was far too easily emotionally manipulated, and only after getting his ass handed to him for the entire day did that start to sink in— whether he liked it or not.

"That's rich coming from someone who fought the man on a whim the first time they met." Adam sneered.

"Do you have a problem with how I run things, Adam?" Shigure asked, his focus turning to him.

"Not at all, fearless leader! I'm just concerned there won't be anyone left to lead once that man, Shot, takes everyone of value from us," Adam answered.

"You've done nothing but whine for the past several days since he has been here. I won't continue to hear you scheme openly about harming his group. I will not and *can*not start a war with him. We will not win. We are going to play nice until he and his group leave. If you dare to do anything else that jeopardizes that, Adam," Shigure said, the sound of him drawing his blade from his saya ringing sharply as an undertone to his voice, "I will *personally* take care of you."

Adam held up his hands. "Fine. I don't want to go it on my own just yet. I'll play nice," he mumbled.

"Good," Shigure said sternly. He looked at the other two. "You both as well. Do not forget who is the actual leader of this coalition or why you made me leader. If you want continued protection, you will fall in line."

All three nodded—even if some were disgruntled—in agreement. Each one eventually left the area with only Adam staying. Adam had his own plans regardless of what he told Shigure and the others.

A few moments later, a hiss sounded, and Adam turned to one of his ghouls.

"My lord," it hissed. "Our preparations are ready, but there is a change in their camp."

"What change? Out with it, already! I don't have time for this," Adam spat.

"They have moved the woman we were targeting. She is now with another and much closer to the leader. If we were to move forward with our plan, we will not be able to capture her," the ghoul grumbled.

Adam clicked his tongue in frustration, his mind spinning away on what to do.

"This is fine. We have mapped out his sensory skill, yes?" he asked, to which the ghoul nodded. "Good. Have a group pull him and Bear away while another goes for the woman. Use as many of our stockpiles as you need. Once the tutorial is over, it won't matter either way. I will simply make more."

The ghoul slinked backward into the darkness, leaving Adam alone once more.

"Finally, I'll have a competent pawn, and the Master will be happy... I wonder how he will reward me for catching such a strong one?" Adam laughed.

Chapter 26

Fool

Lamar and Drake talked for a few more hours while the sun set in the distance. Eventually, the two decided to finish up the conversation tomorrow. Lamar would come back in the morning with his equipment and more patience than he had today.

Drake had spent the majority of the time explaining more of what he knew about the system and what could possibly happen outside of the tutorial. More specifically—what he could do to help Lamar and his sister once they were out of the tutorial.

He may or may not have kept jabbing at the cyclops because it was enjoyable to tease him, which wore on the poor crafter's mental state. But Drake had already cemented that Lamar was a man of his word, and once they came to an agreement, he would not go back on it.

Drake waved Lamar off as the night had already settled in a few hours ago. Lamar waved a very large middle finger over his shoulder.

"Good man, that guy. Well, good cyclops I mean," Drake said.

Stretching a bit, he gazed around the camp. It seemed that mostly everyone was in their tents by now, save Bjorn who was still walking around. Drake raised his brow as he spotted the not-as-large-as-Lamar but still quite enormous man crossing his path.

"Bear, what're you doing?" Drake asked. His aura sense picked up on a figure behind him.

"Ah, Adam here said Shigure needs to see me," Bjorn answered, jabbing a thumb to the pencil thin man.

"Yes. Lord Shigure is deciding what to do about"—Adam gave a terse glance at Drake before turning back to Bjorn—"our squatters. Also, he wants to decide how to proceed within the tutorial," he continued. He looked back at Drake, a slight red shimmer in his eyes as he did so. "It would seem more and more people are going... *missing*."

Drake pressed Adam with his aura, scowling for added effect.

"Are you insinuating something?"

Adam visibly jerked, his shoulders beginning to shiver, but he still smiled back at Drake despite the bodily reaction.

"Of course not. I would never," Adam answered. "I am simply saying that the folks that have gone missing have increased with your appearance. Whether that is a coincidence or not, who am I to say?"

Before Drake could press the issue, Bjorn shook his head and took Adam by the arm.

"Knock it off, Adam. You're already lucky I haven't killed you, and Shot here has a shorter temper than I do. So unless you actually want to die, I'd shut the fuck up, bro," Bjorn cautioned. He looked back at Drake. "I'll be fast, so no worries."

Bjorn gave Drake a quick nod, then dragged Adam with him toward Shigure's outpost.

Drake watched the two walk off into the distance until he was unable to make out their features in the dark. He turned his head, stretching out his aura and sighing.

"Is everyone really that much of a prick, or is it the system bringing out the worst in people," Drake asked aloud.

"*The system surely has a part in it. But certainly, that thing is just a rotten one,*" Natto replied.

"Well," Drake digressed, feeling out the camp with his aura, "seems like everyone's where they're supposed to be. There's only a few people on the edge of the circle, but that's normal now. Guess it's time to just sit and practice till something happens."

Drake moved back into his tent and took a seat on the floor as Natto popped out onto his shoulder, then rolled out onto the bed with some snacks in hand.

"Natto," Drake began to ask, "this might be a weird question, but how likely is it that I won't be human anymore when we leave the tutorial? If I can even be considered human *now*, that is," he said, chuckling wryly.

Natto paused mid-bite into her snack, her face stiffening then relaxing before she sighed.

"What brought this on? Normally you are so aloof and laid back about these things," she asked back.

Drake looked up at the tent's ceiling, his hands conjuring elements that he molded and shifted as he thought.

"I was just wondering is all. I was thinking about my family again. My youngest brother is fourteen, so he won't be in the tutorial, thankfully. But that has me thinking about what he'll think of me when I meet him again, ya know? Is he going to recognize the... the monster I'm becoming? I don't think he's old enough to understand that what I'm doing is because I don't have a choice, but I'm more worried about how they'll all feel once I see them again. Am I still going to be my mom's little boy? My brother's older dependable bro? Or am I just going to be a monster none of us can even recognize," Drake professed.

Natto scoffed.

"You are thinking too much, you moron. You are far from being a monster. The multiverse is filled with true oppressive scum, tyrants of unimaginable scale, and unspeakable evils. And I am reiterating, *real* evils. There are powers that be and command universes like they are children playing in a toy shop, killing billions simply for the fun of it. You are no monster. At least, not yet," she said softly. "I do not know of your family well enough to say, but... I *do* know you and what you have done here, what you have been *forced* to do. No one can fault you for such. And I will not let them. Your family has seen you through hard times already. What is a little system compared to that?"

Drake blinked, confused, his magic extinguishing as he did.

"Wow, that is the nicest thing I think I've ever heard you say. Are you dying or something?" Drake looked upward, his hands splayed out. "Is it going to snow? Maybe a category three?"

"Shut up!" Natto blushed and threw a roasted nut at the back of his head. "I am simply stating a fact! If your assistant does not stick by you, then who will? For all our bickering, I am still your ally, no matter how much you incessantly irritate me with every fiber of your being!"

"Aw, Natto, I didn't know you cared."

"Shut up!"

"It's okay to talk about your feelings. I'm here for you."

"I said shut up!"

Drake laughed and relaxed, his shoulders slackening as he formed a small magic circle of white between his hands.

He molded and melded the ice magic, making a small group of figurines to represent his family: his mother, youngest brother, younger brother, and his father. All happily laughing together.

Natto scooched forward to see the piece, looking over his shoulder.

"That is quite detailed," she murmured.

"Well, I did use to draw for a living. Switching from 2D to 3D is a bit weird, but I think I'll get the hang of it. At least I can get some of the details right, and the ice makes it easy to sculpt," Drake replied, looking at the figurines.

Before their conversation could continue, Drake felt a large group appear at the end of his senses, forcing him to snap his head in that direction.

"That's bigger than the usual group..." Drake mumbled.

"How many is considered bigger than usual?" Natto asked, hopping onto his shoulder.

"I count about twenty that I can feel. Might be monsters or the ghouls from before, I can't tell," Drake answered. "I'm going to wake up Hudson, let him know to set up sentries."

Drake quickly exited his tent and made his way hastily to Hudson and Tom's tent, entering without notice to wake them up.

"Tom, Hudson!" Drake shouted.

"W-Wha?!" Tom yelled, grabbing his blanket and throwing it off.

"The hell are you doing, idjit," Hudson spat as he exited his bed half-naked.

"Bunch of monsters, maybe ghouls, are gathering outside. I need you to set up some more sentries—get your big boys out as well just to be safe. I'm going to go check it out myself.

Drake took no more time to explain before he shot off and disappeared.

"Did you get all that?" Tom asked.

"I heard set up the lil 'uns, and that's all I need. Get dressed, you damned fool." Husdon scoffed. He took out his clothes and armor from his inventory.

"*Someone* isn't a morning person..." Tom mumbled.

* * *

Claire stared aimlessly at the top of the tent, the sound of Sherry snoring and mumbling about dinner in the background. She let out a sigh.

"How much longer are we going to be doing this... I finally found a guy I like, and I can't even do anything until after the tutorial," she lamented.

Putting her hands up into the air, she remembered the warmth of Drake's body and embrace, a small smile creasing her lips.

"Maybe I'll sneak into his tent. He wouldn't mind, right? We're practically dating since he hugged me." She snickered and slowly got out of her bed.

"Food...?" Sherry suddenly said, snapping to attention.

Claire yelped softly, the surprising movement making her recoil. She quickly collected herself and sighed.

"Is my nickname going to be food or something? Well, I *am* kind of a snack," Claire joked to herself before turning to Sherry. "No, I'm just going out to take care of some business."

Sherry nodded. "Okay, say hi to Drake for me." She grinned then plopped back onto the bed, the sound of her snoring getting louder with each breath. Claire was shocked, her mouth opening and closing absently.

"Is it that obvious?" She shook her head but made her way to the tent entrance nonetheless.

She heard the rustling of tent canvas as she exited, briefly spotting Drake exiting Hudson's tent and leaving the area.

"Where is he going?" She pouted.

"Claire, you're awake?" Tom said, asking the obvious.

"Um, yeah, I just couldn't sleep. What's going on?" she asked back.

"There's some monsters a little way off, so Drake went to take care of them. Shouldn't be a problem, but he asked Hudson to put up some more sentries. Might want to stay inside or go find the others just to be safe," Tom answered. He gave her a wave as he went to another tent.

Claire sighed, crossing her arms.

"That guy just keeps going off on his own. I wish he would ask us for help more often..."

"The strong do not pity the weak, unfortunately, dear woman. But you will work well for your intended use," a raspy hissing voice suddenly said from behind her.

"Wha—" Claire tried to exclaim before a hand shot out from the tent and pulled her back into the dark.

* * *

Drake took long strides toward the group of people, almost making his way there in a matter of seconds thanks to his Lightning Endowment.

But something was wrong. The group he was chasing continued to run from him without attempting to fight. They weren't outrunning him, but their fleeing made it take longer to deal with them than it should have—if only by a few seconds.

Finally catching up to the group, Drake saw what he had expected: people with pale skin, sunken eyes, and tattered clothes. Ghouls.

"Poor people," Drake said sympathetically, his eyes gazing on the pack of monsters who were once humans.

"Do not pity us, fool," one spat. He pulled a blade from his side.

"Oh, they can talk? And it's rude... Were you mean before or after being turned into a thriller video reject?" Drake asked as he formed a javelin of white fire in both of his hands, trying his best to get some information out of the monsters.

"We will tell you nothing! Our job is already at its end," another hissed.

The hairs on Drake's neck stood on end. His eyes widened.

"What did you say?" he growled.

"Fool, we have done our job. Kill us if you wish, but it wi—" one tried to snap, but his head was torn from his shoulders by a searing white heat before he could finish.

Drake threw and expanded his javelin, enveloping the twenty or so monsters in a brilliant white glow as they shrieked and screamed. All of them melted and turned into ash on the ground.

You have killed ghoul Mary Winshaw Level 12
Experience earned. 30,000 TP have been awarded.

You have killed ghoul Joe Koy Level 11
Experience earned. 20,000 TP have been awarded.

You have killed ghoul Dwane Cavalier Level 10
Experience earned. 10,000 TP have been awarded.

...

Subjugation Quest: 27 of 100 Converted Ghouls [F-Rank]
Reward: Experience and an F-Grade Accessory of your choice.

Drake had already taken off back to the camp as the notifications rolled in and his quest updated. He only prayed he wasn't too late—that his foolishness hadn't cost him his friends' lives.

Drake canceled and recast his Endowment in an instant.

"*Flash Step!*" he shouted. His Lightning Endowment empowered him again, this time many times stronger as he made the journey back in a fraction of the time.

Spreading his aura, he looked for anything out of place. He noticed only one tent that had what seemed like a struggle going on.

Sherry! Claire! Drake shouted in his head. His feet moved with unprecedented conviction toward the tent.

Drake shot past the entrance, arriving at the last remnants of the struggle in progress. His eyes took in the surroundings in a mere moment, his Adrenaline Acuity going to work.

He saw blood on the floor, ripped and broken clothes and equipment. Sherry was on the ground, blood dripping from her head where she lay limp. Drake's eyes met Claire's just as she was sucked into a shimmering magic circle, a pale and gangly hand wrapped around her mouth. Her eyes showed abject horror.

Drake rushed forward, his hand outstretched, but he was barely not in time. Claire vanished into the circle as it disappeared.

Time froze for Drake. His hand grasped at the dirt, and his body began to shake. His mind was a pot of emotions quickly boiling over as his clenched jaw was slowly forced open.

A guttural roar infused with aura and mana pierced through the camp. *"NOOOO!!!!!"*

Drake howled, his aura and mana-infused scream going wild as he drove his fists into the ground.

A fraction of a second later, his head snapped to Sherry. Drake's anger only rose as he moved to her, pulling a potion from his inventory that he gently slipped into her mouth.

Sherry coughed, but she was still well enough to swallow the liquid on her own. Drake could see the gash the blood was coming from close as he placed her on a new bed carefully.

His mind continued to swirl in chaos, but on the outside, he was calm and collected. His eyes glazed over as he looked in one direction.

Shigure's camp.

Chapter 27

The Monster You Wanted

"What are you talking about? I haven't asked for anyone to be here," Shigure said, his face filled with confusion. "What is this about?"

"Adam said you needed me to talk about the future and Shot?" Bjorn looked over to the pale man.

Adam laughed, his hand going to his forehead as the laughing grew louder. Soon he had a congregation of ghouls summoned to his side along with many of the other coalition leaders, including Darius and Savannah.

"I just took the matter into my own hands!" Adam shouted. "You were slipping, Shigure. You allowed some stranger to come here and slowly take over your camp bit by bit. Something had to be done, and I've done just that."

Bjorn and Shigure's faces twisted into scowls.

"What have you done?" Bjorn asked, his aura's pressure beginning to press down on the group of people and ghouls in the tent.

Shigure flinched under the sudden pressure, but he stood steadfast as Uta appeared in front of him, her kunai at the ready.

"Adam, you couldn't have been so foolish! And Darius, Savannah! I expected better!" Shigure spat.

"*Please*, enough of you and your high horse, Shigure. We all knew the game when we came together," Savannah said. "As long as we were in control, we got what we all wanted. Power. And now that is slowly slipping away thanks to that Shot character that you're too soft to kick out."

"Agreed, we had to do something. And Adam gave a solution." Darius nodded, many of the other leaders agreeing as well.

"Besides," Adam said, leaning forward, "we all know you don't like the guy either, not to mention he took your dear precious friend Bear away. Now we will have him under my control, and everything will go back to normal. Just with me at the tippy top!" Adam cackled.

Bjorn stepped forward, but he was stopped by Adam's open hand.

"Ah ah ah, not so fast. You wouldn't want to kill innocent people, would you?" Adam snapped his fingers, and three magic circles formed next to him, three more ghouls holding hostages slowly emerging from them.

Bjorn stopped in his tracks, his eyes turning fierce.

"Shigure... If only you just let me kill him," Bjorn said, his shoulders slumping as he walked back toward the end of the tent.

"Where are you going, Bear?" Shigure asked.

"I won't be part of what is going to happen. You brought this on yourself." Bjorn sighed and opened the tent flap, exiting.

"Well, that was no fun," Adam tried to say casually, but he was stopped by the chill that overcame the tent.

The blood of everyone inside ran cold as the air was choked from them. None of them—living or dead—spoke, moved, or breathed a single puff of air. The tent had turned dead silent.

Through the entrance that Bjorn had just exited, another person replaced him and walked through.

His hair was as white as snow save for the blotches of red that spattered it here and there. His eyes were a stunningly deep and clear blue that radiated power as they shifted first to a striking yellow, then to a serene, shining green and back.

The man's clothes, although tattered in some places, still gave an intimidating form to him, pure black embroidered and trimmed with gold. His hands were covered with bright white flames cascading across his finely toned muscles.

In one hand was the head of a ghoul. In the other, an unconscious man.

"S-Sir Shot?!" Shigure's voice was almost a whisper, and his tone cracked as if refusing to make noise in the situation.

Drake threw the man to the floor, burning the ghoul in his other hand's skull to nothing but ash in a flash of white fire a moment later.

"This prick told me I could find Shigure here," Drake said. "So it's *Sir Shot* now that you fucked up, huh?" Drake continued, his voice even and cold as ice. "Where is she?"

"W-Where is who?" Shigure asked.

Drake looked Shigure in the eyes, holding his gaze for a moment, before his eyes shifted to one of the other leaders of the coalition.

Adam.

"*Marked.*"

Without warning, Drake shot a jet-black earthen spike into the man's chest, opening up a hole the size of a bowling ball.

"Where is she?" Drake asked again, looking back into Shigure's eyes.

"I don't know who you are talking about! Please stop this, we can talk this out!" Shigure said, his mouth agape as he looked at Adam on the floor, his innards and blood pooling on the ground around him.

Drake raised his hand again.

"Your little vampire isn't dead, but what about the next one I try this with? *Where. Is. She.*"

This time Darius somehow obtained the nerve to speak.

"You can't just come in here and demand something like that! What kind of monster—"

Darius didn't get to finish his thought. Drake moved in an instant from his position to Darius, his hand now wrapped around the man's mouth.

Drake pulled him in close—close enough to see the pores in his skin, the cold sweat pooling out of them.

"So, you know what I'm talking about then. You have five seconds. Where is she?" Drake said coldly, his eyes sharpening to points.

Darius mumbled in Drake's grip, unable to speak.

"Ah, you can't speak like that, can you? I'll fix that," Drake said, moving his hand to grip his skull from the top. "Now. *Five.*"

Drake's hair shifted to a crimson red. He began slowly gripping tighter down on the man's head.

"I don't know, I swear! Please! I'm sorry, please! Stop this!" Darius pleaded.

"*Four.*"

Drake began tightening his grip, and the sound of bone cracking and bowing under pressure filled the room. Everyone's eyes shakily watched Drake as he one-sidedly began punishing the coalition leader and one of their most prominent fighters.

"Pleash! Ahh, ahhh!!!! I donsh know anyshinggg!!!"

"*Three.*"

"Sir Shot! Please, he doesn't know anything! You've made your point!" Shigure shouted, trying to step forward.

Drake conjured a lightning bolt, the spell flying instantly to spear the ground in front of Shigure.

Shigure's eyes went from the bolt to Drake. Drake's eyes were cold as he continued to lock his gaze with Shigure. His hand gripped the now-shaking man above the ground, lifting him into the air, Drake's fingers visibly beginning to pierce the man's skin.

"*Two.*"

A laugh began again.

Drake paused his tightening grip and looked down at the body of Adam as it began shifting and convulsing.

The body laughed and sat straight up on the ground.

"Oh, that was a trip! Did you intentionally not kill me and leave me with just enough health?" Adam said, the hole in his chest beginning to mend right in front of the others.

Drake dropped Darius to the ground. The moment the man landed, he squirmed in pain, gripping his head as blood spurted out from the finger holes Drake had put there.

"Where is she. I'm done asking," Drake said, repeating himself one last time.

"She's right where I put her: somewhere you will never find, unless you do what I say," Adam said, standing up.

Drake moved forward, getting within Adam's immediate space in an instant. Plunging his hand into the man's stomach, Drake lifted him into the air.

Adam gave a gruff gurgle. With a forced grunt, he coughed out a splattering of blood but somehow kept a smile on his face.

"*Ow...*" he said sarcastically before sneering. "But you won't get anything out of me like that. Not to mention if you keep this up, I might just tell my little goons to kill my hostages."

"Go ahead," Drake said coldly.

"W-What?" Adam said, surprised.

Drake threw Adam to the floor, still holding his intestines in his hand before burning them to ash.

"I'm here for Claire, and I'll kill every single one of you until she is returned," Drake said, his voice bringing the temperature down several more degrees as he began freezing the ground below him. A white magic circle formed and expanded to encompass the tent.

"You can't really mean that?" Adam said, a bead of sweat forming on his forehead as he began to realize he had severely miscalculated.

Drake raised his hand, pointing it at the still-dithering Darius. Drake's hair shimmered back to white, a crimson-red magic circle forming at his fingertip.

"*Fire Bullet,*" Drake chanted.

A flame sparked to life at the end of his fingertip, soon contorting and spinning into a ball as it roared to life. It condensed, shimmering to blue before paling to a bright white.

Drake fired the bullet, the spell piercing through Darius and into the ground. The air hissed as water evaporated from the heated ice in a white vapor cloud. The ground steamed as it warmed, a pool of magma beginning to

form while the body sank and began to sear against it. The bystanders scrambled to get out of the area.

Drake looked coldly at Adam, his face silently saying it all.

Where is she?

Adam looked back, his face contorting into fear. But he should have no
reason to be afraid: he had the upper hand. He also had a trump card with her
as a hostage.

"Y-You don't scare me. I kno—" Adam started to say, but he was silenced
by the sound of thunder hammering down into the tent.

A flash of light blinded the room, and when visibility came back, half of
the onlookers had suddenly turned to black smoldering ashen remains.

"W-What have you done?!" Shigure screamed. "They had nothing to do
with this!"

Drake turned his head to Shigure.

"Don't be an idiot, kid. They chose what side they were on the moment
they were behind him and not you. I'm done being nice. No more mercy, no
more excuses," Drake said. He took slow measured steps toward Adam, who
was still aghast on the floor, his arm covering his healing stomach.

"Does it hurt?" Drake asked.

"W-What? Of cours—Ahhh!!!" Adam shrieked. The place where Drake
gripped his hand turned slowly to ice.

"*Good.* But now you're going to make me repeat myself. *Where is she?*"
Drake gripped tighter as he shattered Adam's hand, using fire to melt the
stump so it couldn't grow back.

"I w-won't tell you!" Adam spat. "What are you all doing?! Get him!" The
remaining coalition leaders hesitated after witnessing what Drake had just
done to the others, but the remnants of the ghouls within the tent rushed forward mechanically at the word of their master.

Drake didn't even have to turn around as he embedded his hand into the
ground.

"*Dug Haut,*" Drake whispered.

The ground shook and cracked. Spikes of black earth shot upward, skewering the ghouls in an instant and putting their attempts at a counterattack to rest.

Drake then gripped Adam's shoulder, his hand beginning to heat up, and melted through his clothes and flesh. The fire crackled and popped as it seared through.

Adam howled in pain, trying his best to wrench himself from Drake's hand to no avail.

"Where."

Drake placed his hand on his kneecap.

"Is."

Then the other.

"She."

Adam continued to howl in pain, unable to pass out due to either his skills or his race not allowing him.

Adam's limbs didn't reform after being seared, so Drake took a blade of ice and severed them once again, waiting for them to heal so he could repeat the process.

"Sir Shot... No one deserves this," Shigure murmured.

"Shut your mouth. What would you know of what he deserves?" Drake's aura flexed again in anger. "You didn't see her face. The fear in it. You didn't promise her you would keep her safe!" Drake shouted, his control slipping as both his aura and mana leaked from him.

"This sorry piece of shit is mine to judge! *Or do you want to try and stop me*?!" Drake scoffed, his face turning into a sneer.

He turned back to Adam, disgust in his eyes as the man finished healing. The moment he did, Drake gripped him by the throat, pulling him away from the tent and back to their camp.

* * *

A few moments later, Drake arrived with Adam in tow, the group coming to meet him.

"Did you find her?!" Chelsea and Harley asked in tandem.

Drake looked down grimly.

"No. I need Jacqueline's help," Drake said, tilting his head back up and scanning for her.

"Yeah?" Jacqueline asked, stepping forward. Drake didn't beat around the bush.

"You're the only one who has direct healing spells that I know of. I need you to do something for me," Drake said evenly.

"What's that, yeah?" Jacqueline asked, raising a brow.

"Heal him," Drake said, pointing down to Adam.

"What? Are you mad?"

Drake shook his head.

"It's either going to cause him immense pain, as he's an undead, or it will keep him alive long enough for me to torture him into giving Claire back."

"My lord..." Theodore muttered from the side. "Thou dost not hast to bear this burden alone..."

"No. This is my responsibility, Theo. I'll get her back and keep her safe, just like I promised her."

Drake looked back to Jacqueline, who was still pondering, her mouth trembling.

"Well?" he asked.

"I-I don't know how I feel about this. He's a piece of shit tosser, but torture...?"

"Fine. I understand." Drake pulled the man out of sight and into his own tent, the sounds of screaming continuing.

"He's really torturing that guy?" Tom asked aloud.

"What do ya expect him to do? Claire got snatched up, and he doesn't have many options," Hudson sympathized, crossing his arms.

"Drake..." Chelsea muttered from behind them, her arms wrapping around herself with a grimace. A warm embrace came from behind her as Harley hugged her.

"Don't worry, Chelsea, Mr. Drake is going to be fine. He's always alright after, right?" Harely consoled.

"Yeah, but this seems different... I've never seen him so cold, not even with the goblins."

"My lord is stout of heart. This one is sure he will prevail over this trial as well," Theodore added, putting his hand on Harley's shoulder.

The only ones not present were Sherry and Amir. Sherry was still recovering, and Amir had taken it upon himself to watch over her.

Megan and Julia had come out from their tent, finding the rest of the group talking amongst themselves. Both moved to Chelsea and heard the story of what had transpired in the last couple of minutes, consoling her as well once they heard the news.

After a few minutes of the group hearing the screams from Drake's tent, Bjorn stepped into the camp.

"Sir Bear?" Theodore asked, surprised to see him coming from outside of the camp.

"Hey there, Theo. Where's Drake?" Bjorn asked, but he shook his head when he overheard the shrieking and crying suddenly coming from his tent again. "Never mind." He sighed. "Looks like he's still at it."

"What dost thou mean, Sir Bear?" Theodore asked.

"It happened pretty fast, but... he went on a rampage in Shigure's outpost. Killed more than half of the coalition leaders," Bjorn explained.

The group's faces widened in surprise.

"And it looks like he won't stop until he gets what he wants out of Adam," Bjorn added.

"You didn't stop him?" Chelsea asked.

"Why would I? I knew Adam was a bad apple when I met him, and I warned Shigure what might happen. I don't want to see people die, but everyone in that tent knew what they were doing. As for the hostages... I overheard him talking. He might've said he didn't care, but I saw how he saved them regardless," Bjorn said, giving a forlorn grin. "I'm not sure how Adam communicates with his ghouls, but hopefully that's the last of the hostages besides Claire that he has."

More screams came from Drake's tent. The group's heads all turned to it.

* * *

"I-I can't... Please just kill me..." Adam moaned, his body slumping to the floor.

"Give her back then." Drake sneered.

"I—Ahhh!!! Pleaseee, enough!!" Adam screamed as Drake embedded another elemental spear into his thigh.

Drake had been using all of his elements to torture Adam, and this time he had impaled him with a spear of water. Allowing the water to flow into Adam's veins, he slowly ballooned them until they popped from the increased pressure within. He then slowed the flow, allowing them to heal, only to do it all over again.

"Bring her here," Drake said tersely.

"F-Fine! Promise me you will just kill me after! Promise me!"

Drake didn't answer, only glaring back.

Adam shrunk back, but he waved his hand, a silver magic circle forming and a woman with a ghoul behind her emerging slowly from the circle.

The moment they were fully out of the circle, Drake quickly dispatched of the ghoul, crushing it into the ground and catching Claire as she fell.

Drake held her close, pulling her into his embrace, his shoulders shaking ever so slightly.

"I'm sorry... I'm—I'm so sorry..."

Chapter 28

A Tomorrow Problem

Shigure was stunned, frozen in place as he looked at the remnants of the people that had survived the true one-sided smiting from Drake. Whimpers and cries filled the room, and the smell of burning flesh and charred earth wafted through the air.

"—rd Shigure! Lord Shigure!" Uta shouted at him, shaking him back into the present. Her voice started out as a muffled, distant tune, but it eventually came into focus.

"W-What happened?" he asked, startled.

"That man... he went crazy." Uta gripped her sleeves, shaking. "My lord, I understand more than ever that we have made a mistake in making him an enemy. I-I apologize for contributing to this."

Shigure was momentarily dumbfounded, but he was forced to compose himself, not wanting Uta to feel solely responsible for the situation.

"No, I am to blame for asking you to speak to his assistant alone. I should have addressed him myself. As for this"—he looked again at the carnage that filled the tent—"this was Adam's foolish doing. He played with a beast more dangerous than we could possibly imagine."

Continuing to scan the area, Shigure spotted Savannah somehow still alive despite being directly involved. He quickly stormed over, his face twisting into a scowl as he passed the survivors of the incident as well as the now-freed hostages. But they were not his priority right now.

Grabbing her from the ground and forcing her to face him, he roared in anger.

"What were you imbeciles thinking?! Did you not see what that man was already capable of when he fought both me and Bear?!" Shigure shouted.

"W-W-We... We just didn't want to lose our power... We thought he wouldn't dare do anything if we had one of his team members! How were we supposed to know he would kill everyone?! Would anyone in their right mind do that?" she shouted back, trying to deflect.

"Does it look like that man is in his right mind? Or that he conforms to the old world's way of thinking! You've all done nothing but doom us!" Shigure spat, throwing her back to the ground as he bit his lip.

Fuck! Just looking at this mess, that man wasn't even slightly serious when he faced me! If he can wipe out nearly the entirety of our fighting force without breaking a sweat, we stand no chance! And we don't even know the capabilities of his teammates, Shigure thought, his face paling and his brow breaking into a cold sweat.

"My lord..." Uta asked, concerned.

"We have to go to him immediately. If we don't make this right, we're all as good as dead. That man, Shot. He's less human than I believed, and he doesn't bat an eye at killing those he deems an obstacle. All we can do is *hope* that we can appease him," Shigure said, his face curling into a grim smile as he chuckled nervously.

* * *

"K-Kill me... You have her, so keep your promise! Kill me!" Adam pleaded.

Drake pulled Claire into his arms, making sure she was fine and completely ignoring Adam for now. He heard her breathing steady.

She seems fine, but how can I be sure nothing was done to her? Drake wondered.

"You will have to ask for a healer to cleanse her, or perhaps the oaf has a potion to do so," Natto offered.

Drake nodded, his eyes snapping back to Adam as they turned to hateful points.

"You think we're done here?" Drake said in a low growl, standing slowly so as not to jostle Claire.

"Y-You promised!" Adam wailed.

Drake scoffed. "I never said a word about you dying painlessly. We are going to have a long chat about what a complete piece of shit you are."

Drake moved over to the bed in the tent and placed Claire down.

"Natto, you can come out. Watch her please," Drake instructed before turning back to Adam.

Natto rolled out onto the bed, stopping next to Claire as Drake strolled back over to the pale man whimpering on the ground for his life to end.

"I couldn't tell you anything even if I wanted to! I'm bound by a magical contract!" Adam screamed.

A deep orange magic circle formed in front of Drake's hand. It began to bubble and slither up his arm.

Drake slowly brought the arm closer and closer to Adam's face. "We'll just have to put that to the test, won't we? Because I don't believe a single word coming out of your mouth."

Adam stared at the hand inching closer and closer to himself, the sweat from his face quickly evaporating as it dripped down onto the hand covered in magma.

"I—I just wanted to bring you under my wing! I needed someone as strong as you! You should take it as a compliment!" Adam stammered.

"More like an insult," Drake said coldly. His glowing orange hand was now just millimeters away from Adam, painting the man's pale skin a light auburn.

"I have a master! He's very strong! If you keep this up, he isn't going to be happy!" Adam said, making a 180-degree turn in demeanor.

Natto scoffed from the bed. "The filth has cracked..." she murmured.

Drake moved quickly, his hand going to Adam's exposed shoulder. He ran his hand down his arm, the sound of searing flesh hissing the entire way as Adam shrieked again in pain. His flesh curdled and charred as it slowly began to regenerate only to be burned once again.

"What makes you think I give a shit about some old decrepit dude who can't even fight me himself? You touched someone important to me. This is between you and me, and I'm going to make sure you die in the most painful way I can possibly imagine. This isn't business or part of the tutorial anymore. This is *personal*," Drake spat venomously.

Snapping his fingers, Drake conjured slivers of earth above every major pain point he could think of. And with a quick flick of his wrist, countless spikes began to embed themselves into Adam.

"Ahhh! W-Why! It was just one girl?! I didn't even do anything to her! You have so many more!" Adam squealed.

Drake physically cringed hearing the phrase 'have so many more,' but something twinged inside of him.

Were they not his? Why shouldn't they be his? They should belong to him just like everything else. That's why he was so angry, no? They tried to take *his* possession.

Drake quickly shook his head.

"Is that what you think of people? As things? They are people I've promised protection to. You violated their peace, which makes it my job to make it right and *more*," Drake spat.

His fingers expanded, the tips finding the ends of the stone spikes. One by one he turned them into magma, and they began searing Adam, increasing the pain he felt several times over.

"Since you brought it up, who is this big mysterious bad guy behind you?" Drake asked, crouching down. The magma from his hand melted away and burned the ground below before a blue magic circle shifted to replace the orange, a long spear of water manifesting.

"I-I can't tell you!" Adam wailed.

"Not good enough." Drake sighed, embedding the spear into Adam's stomach.

This back and forth went on for several more minutes, but Drake was unable to glean any useful information outside of a stronger and more dangerous person or thing behind Adam.

The pattern broke only due to Natto speaking up.

"Drake, Claire is regaining consciousness," she told him.

He was forced to stop, turning away from Adam, but he made sure to keep a watchful eye on him through his aura sense.

"Claire?" Drake said pensively, hearing her groan as she slowly roused.

"W-Where am I...? Drake?" she mumbled, sitting up slowly in the bed.

"You're safe," Drake said, smiling behind his mask. "Do you remember anything? How do you feel?"

Claire put her hand to her head, noticing Natto next to her as well. She gave a small grin.

"I just remember being taken into a dark place... After that, I'm not sure. I-I feel alright? Should I not?" she said, somewhat chuckling.

Drake was taken aback by how nonchalant about the whole thing she was being, but if she couldn't even recall what had happened, it might be for the best.

He snorted. "You're much stronger than I gave you credit for... I'm glad you're safe, I—"

Drake caught himself, not sure what to say. But before he could find the words, his Magic Sight and Aura picked up Adam attempting to move and cast something.

He instantly whipped around, his arms flaring to life as he shot forward with deadly precision, giving the makeshift vampire no time to react.

Drake had moved so swiftly and with such instinct that he only realized that he was holding Adam's head in his hand after hearing a gag coming from Claire behind him.

You have killed participant Adam Savage Level 15.
Experience earned. 1,373,425 TP have been awarded.

"Shit, I still wanted information out of him." Drake sighed, more concerned with killing his only lead on who was manipulating the poor sap behind the scene than with actually taking his life.

But another surprise awaited Drake as Adam's body suddenly burst into blue flames.

"What? I'm not doing that..." Drake said, his face twisting with confusion. He dropped the head on the ground, and it burst into blue light as well.

What came next was the sound of an ethereal far-off voice that was annoyingly familiar and condescending.

"*Haha! Finally! It took you long enough! Too bad for you, but one of my skills is a cheat death! So I'll be safe and sound outside the tutorial once it's over,*" Adam said, the sneer in his voice obvious.

Drake wasn't sure how to respond, so he just talked to the air.

"That's great. Means I get to kill you twice." He smiled.

"*Such arrogance! I hope you can keep that up when you're in the face of my master and the whole army of the undead! You're going to pay, you bastard! And I'm going to ravage that girl in front of you next time we meet. I promise you that!*" Adam screamed.

Drake's aura and mana flared, his teeth grinding.

"You better keep your promise and come at me with everything, you filthy, sorry asshat! You're going to need all that and more to take someone from me again! When I see you, I'll leave nothing left. Not a soul, not an atom of you will exist! So bring your big scary wannabe overlord—it'll take all of that and more for you to have a shot in hell at beating me! No one, not you, not some hiding little bitch off on some planet playing with themselves, not the system, not even some fucking god is going to take her from me! She's mine!" Drake snarled, his eyes humming yellow as they flashed with power.

It turned quiet in the tent. The connection Adam had with them was either broken or running out.

"Um..." Claire whispered behind Drake, breaking the uncomfortable silence that fell on the tent.

"Well, that was quite the statement." Natto snorted behind her hand and turned away from Drake.

There is something wrong with me... Why do I keep referring to people as mine? Is it another effect of the stones? I have to get a handle on this. Drake sighed, but he turned to meet his figurative maker.

"Yeah, I may have gotten a bit heated there... My bad," Drake said.

"Oh, it's okay. So..." Claire murmured, tapping her fingers together. "I'm yours...?" She grinned, her face turning a shade of red.

Drake scratched the back of his head.

"Look, I'm genuinely glad you're fine. My statement that I'm going to wait until after the tutorial is going to stand. But I'm truly sorry; I couldn't protect you like I promised," he admitted. "It will never happen again," he said, moving over to the bed.

Drake pulled her into his embrace. This time his desire to protect her was not out of obligation, but because he truly didn't want to see her hurt like before.

"So stay close to me," Drake whispered.

Claire was stunned. She nodded into his chest, not sure how to answer.

Drake chuckled, giving her a pat on the head with his clean hand, the other snapping his mask to the side so he could show his full smile.

"How else am I going to keep an eye on you? You're a bigger troublemaker than my little brothers. Who gets themselves kidnapped like that?" Drake sighed in mock disappointment, shaking his head.

"It isn't like I planned on it!" Claire shot back, pinching his side.

Drake laughed it off, his expression relaxing. He was truly glad she was alright and that it had worked out with him finding her unharmed. Not only because she was safe, but because he feared what he might've done had something happened.

Drake's exterior might have been soft, but inside, his thoughts were struggling to deal with the new cold thoughts and emotions that began to stir. His inner thoughts told him to wipe out Shigure and the coalition leaders, aware of the threat they posed if he allowed them to stay alive. His thoughts pleaded with him to eliminate anything that may stand in his way or possibly take any of his *possessions* from him again.

But he fought back, bottling up the thoughts and emotions that screamed at him to fight, to kill any and all threats. He muffled them into soft whispers in the back of his mind.

This is turning into a bad anime music video; I don't think I can handle it if I suddenly get a voice in the back of my head screaming to kill everything. Although Sukuna was pretty badass. Drake sighed.

Breaking the moment, a small pink construct began gagging on the bed behind Claire, making both her and Drake turn at the noise.

"Guhhhh, can you get another tent? I feel I may lose my precious snacks if this continues any further. It is like watching a trainwreck, but one you cannot tear your eyes from. If anything, I wish to tear my eyes out!" she howled, pulling at her eyelids.

"Well that's just rude." Drake laughed and let go of a reluctant Claire. Drake gave a smile to Natto, but his thoughts still poked at the back of his mind.

It's a problem for tomorrow... It's alright to just be happy right now, isn't it? Drake thought, sighing.

Chapter 29
Ultimatum

Drake wanted nothing more than to relax for the remainder of the night; the 'excitement' was just a little too much for him. Sure, he had done some daring do, but he would much rather sit and practice his magic at this point.

Not to mention he was sure Claire would appreciate not being traumatized more than she already had been recently.

Getting kidnapped can do that to a person, he thought.

Which brought up another point Drake was going to have to deal with soon. Quickly after everything was said and done, Natto poked fun at them both. Claire had fallen asleep on Drake's bed—Drake was sure it was from mental exhaustion this time and not the overwhelming stack of trauma she was accumulating.

The problem was that she had fallen asleep holding onto Drake, making it incredibly difficult to do anything.

"Man, it feels like I'm back in high school. All the responsibilities of having a significant other but a very, very, *very* small amount of the benefits..." Drake sighed.

"You had a girlfriend in school, did you?" Natto asked in disbelief.

Drake let out another sigh, already regretting saying something about it.

"Kind of?" he answered, looking down at the soundly sleeping Claire. Her chest raised and lowered gently.

Natto's head turned in confusion. "What exactly is 'kind of?'" she wondered.

"I was a pretty naive kid back in school, even that late into the game," Drake said, reminiscing, "and a girl I knew basically said we were a couple when we went to piss off another guy. The one she really wanted."

Drake ignored Natto, who was currently holding her hands to her mouth and trying not to laugh, and continued with his story.

"Basically it ruined my entire high school social life, and I didn't even know it was happening. I thought we were just friends hanging out." Drake shrugged with his free arm. "I only found out through other friends who were asking about why she and I broke up. Was a real fun time learning I'd been used like that."

Natto gave a deep exhale before she spoke.

"Th-That is very unfortunate," she said, half giggling.

"Fuck you."

That's part of the reason it took me so long to actually start dating after high school... Well, it is what it is. At least it was a good life lesson, Drake thought somberly.

Their conversation was interrupted by three figures stepping into Drake's Aura sphere. His head turned in that direction. He was relaxed despite what had just happened, but only because one of the figures was too large in size to be anyone other than someone he had come to trust implicitly.

The familiar voice came from the tent entrance a moment later.

"Cool to come in? I don't hear anymore screaming, so I'm assuming you finished up?" Bjorn asked through the canvas.

Drake summoned a light green magic circle in front of his face and whispered into it.

"Yeah, all done. Big happy ending and smiles all around. Just keep it down a bit: someone in here is sleeping," Drake said, hoping his little magic trick worked.

When no one responded out loud and they instead walked inside as quietly as they could, he knew it had. But his casual demeanor quickly changed to one of cold, calculated ferocity, his eyes shifting colors.

"Honestly, I thought it was going to be Theo and maybe Chelsea. But bringing these two? Is it supposed to be a present, or am I about to get snuffed?" Drake asked sarcastically.

Bjorn shook his head.

"Look bro, I'm all for you defending your party and getting vengeance. I don't like people dying, but I'm not dumb enough to not realize things have changed, and they weren't the best standards for human decency," Bjorn explained. "But Shigure here. Even if he's young, he still leads a bunch of people, so I can't have you flying off the handle and trying to kill him."

Drake scoffed. "I couldn't even if I wanted to, but the rest of the so-called 'leaders' and the little assistant that still owes me an apology—that's a different story," he said, his every word dripping with icy venom.

Shigure quickly stepped forward in front of Uta, his hand pushing her behind him.

"I know you are still angry, and I am sorry that this has happened. But as I said, we had no part in it!" he said desperately.

"No, you just happened to try and go behind my back, resulting in one of my most dear friends and someone I consider family—even if they try to eat me out of the house on a daily basis—getting injured by your own negligence because you were too cowardly to just ask me yourself," Drake spat. His wind magic circle sputtered with a little more power.

"I-I understand that," Shigure said, bowing his head down slightly.

"Yeah, but does *she?*" Drake asked, a second magic circle forming under his feet. An earthy brown shifted with power, spikes of jet black erupting and pointing themselves at Uta and Shigure.

Bjorn whistled. "Neat trick."

"I'm becoming more creative," Drake chuckled in passing, still staring at the pair between his spell.

Uta growled and glared behind Shigure, staring daggers into Drake.

"What she said insulted my master! I would be remiss to not retaliate!" she spat.

"Wrong answer," Drake said, one of the spikes inching closer as Shigure maneuvered in front of it. "Try again."

Shigure began to sweat, his emotions painted clearly on his face: he wasn't sure if he would be allowed to live at this rate.

"Sir Shot," he tried to say, but he was cut off by another spike inching closer. Drake obviously hadn't enjoyed the conditionally added word of respect now that Shigure wasn't in control of the situation.

"Stop with the sir, we've been over that you don't like me. And I'm sure after today you like me a lot less, especially after I killed half of the coalition leaders. Even if they were dirty. Also, before you ask, yes Adam is dead. It's a bit unfortunate he didn't let me hurt him more after everything," Drake explained, his face showing just how much mentioning the name disgusted him.

"W-What did you do to him?" Shigure asked, not able to help his curiosity.

"I ripped his head off and he burst into blue flames. Was something right out of Legend of Zelda when you beat the creepy witch bosses, same weird voice and everything."

Shigure's face twisted in confusion, obviously not understanding the reference.

"Oh come on, that game isn't that old! Even speedrunners still play it. Fine, Breath of the Wild?" Drake amended. Shigure's face showed understanding now. Drake scoffed, but his aura refocused and pressed on the pair again.

"Back to it. I've lost most of my gentle heart for the night, and don't get it twisted. I'm going to kill the rest of those sack-of-shit leaders the moment Claire feels better because people like that will just continue to cause problems. I've seen those movies, and everyone hates those characters. So either she can own up, or she can go night night for however long it takes an Assistant to come back," Drake explained.

"Can we not talk this out...?" Shigure asked.

"Are you really trying *that* hard to not apologize for something that's your fault? Honestly..." Drake sighed, the spikes disintegrating around them. "You're going to die before you're able to learn to own up to your mistakes, man. Do you not understand that this whole situation is directly your fault?"

Shigure frowned as Uta's scowl deepened.

"What do you mean? It was Adam that did this along with the other conspiring leaders vying for power. I had nothing to do with it!" he said, raising his voice.

"Shh," Drake said, using his aura to press down on him to shut him up. "I said keep it down." He sighed and shook his head, Shigure and Uta nearly falling backward from the pressure. "You are the leader of this little gang, that means anyone under you is your responsibility. When a snot-nosed little bastard hits your kid, you don't blame the kid, you blame the moron who raised him. Get where I'm going with this?"

Shigure ground his teeth despite the overwhelming points Drake had made. But he stayed silent.

Drake shook his head, giving Bjorn a glance as he shrugged.

"You can't be serious," Drake said, tipping his head back into a sneer. "Then I'm going to give you a choice. You are either going to fall in line, or you are going to leave."

Shigure and Uta's eyes widened.

"What? What makes you think you have the authority to do that?!" he said, panicking.

"I'm stronger than you, and you refuse to take responsibility for your subordinates despite being in the head honcho position. You can't enjoy all the benefits without shouldering the responsibility that comes with it. Leaders must be held accountable for the actions of the ones they hold power over," Drake said evenly.

"Nonsense! I won't be held responsible for what a few idiots did; I told them to back off! I told them it was a mistake!" Shigure said, his voice beginning to rise again with his emotions.

"It's still your pile of shit to scoop up. You may not be able to keep your people in line, but I sure as hell will," Drake finished.

"You sincerely intend to take the entirety of the outpost I built up because of this?!" Shigure questioned.

Drake scoffed. "Either that, or I kill your Assistant and put you out on your ass alone for the rest of the tutorial. I can't *hurt you* hurt you, but as you can see, my Aura works just fine at suppressing you. So suffering because of it seems to be a gray area."

Claire began to shift on the bed, her hand finally releasing Drake's. She rolled onto her side, somehow catching Natto by surprise when she pulled her in like a hug pillow despite the construct's struggle to get away once caught.

"Ah! Unhand me, wench! I am not a thing to be hugged! Although I am cute and fluffy enough to be considered one... But unhand me!" Natto protested.

Drake laughed momentarily, rubbing his wrist.

"God that girl has an iron grip..." he mumbled. He turned back to Shigure, finally able to close the distance now that he was free. "So what's it going to be, Shigure? Fall in line, or lose everything?"

Shigure grimaced and recoiled, shrinking under Drake's eyes.

"You are a demon in human skin! Do you not understand what you have already done to this camp tonight?" Shigure spat, trying his best to deflect and shift the blame.

"See," Drake said, leaning in, "that's the difference. I know full well what I have done, and I accept the consequences. When my penance comes, I will bear the full responsibility as I should. But it won't be today, and it won't be from *you*."

Shigure tried to look to Bjorn for help, but the tall brawny giant only shook his head.

"Sorry bro, I have no dog in this fight. I was never a part of the coalition in the first place. Just wanted to help out and save people. But after tonight, with so many people dead and turned into ghouls that could've been stopped had you not prevented me from killing Adam earlier"—Bjorn's expression turned serious—"you reap what you sow, and you're getting off easy."

With no one to turn to, Shigure slumped to the ground. Uta put her hands around him, concerned.

"Fine, I give up... The outpost is yours, and the people are now for you to lead and protect," he finally conceded. His head burrowed a hole into the dirt, his teeth gnawing at his bottom lip in frustration.

"That's good, but I still need an apology from her," Drake said, pointing at Uta.

"Is it not enough that you have dishonored my master to such a degree? Now you wish to disgrace my honor as well?" Uta sneered.

"He did that all on his own, same as you when you lost it and decided to injure my family. I've killed people for less, so count yourself lucky," Drake spat, his hair shifting to a brilliant yellow as he moved and pulled her away from Shigure in an instant. "Because if I was truly the demon you say I am, you would already be dead."

Uta's eyes grew several sizes when she realized what had happened. Finally, she conceded the point like her master had.

"I'm... I apologize for my transgressions. Please do not separate me from my lord," she muttered.

Drake looked over to Natto, who was struggling to dodge the growing trail of saliva dripping from Claire's mouth above her head. They caught each other's eyes, and Natto nodded, finding the words adequate.

"Well, I think it was a shit sorry, but she says it's good enough." Drake sighed, his hair going back to black as he released Uta's arm from his grip.

A voice creaked out in a high-pitched plea from behind Drake a moment later.

"P-Please, save me from this blasted woman... Shot! Do not turn away! Shot... Ahh, the drool, the droooooool..." Natto wailed.

Chapter 30
Cleaning Up Before Breakfast

"What? I said I was sorry," Drake said, honestly not sorry, but he had to say at least that.

"*Then... why are you smiling! I could have drowned! That foul woman drools more than the Niagara Falls!*" Natto said from within Drake.

"Yeah, she does sleep with her mouth slightly open, doesn't she," Drake said, putting his arms behind his head as he mused aloud.

Drake had finished his threat—*business* with Shigure and saw him and Uta off to their outpost. He was now pacing the length of his own camp, making sure that everything was well and good for the time being.

He looked into the distance, waiting for the sun to rise and lamenting what was to come when it finally rose into view.

"You know, I don't want to do it, I really don't," Drake said, clenching his fists. He remembered the feeling of crushing the skulls of some of the men.

"*I cannot tell you how to feel, Drake, only that it is justified and necessary,*" Natto responded.

"Is it? If I had been more stern and open with how strong I was, if I just displayed my power sooner and threatened them with more consequences, would that have stopped them from even contemplating the thought of going against me? How do leaders prevent tragedy? I wish I knew, but there isn't an anime out there that encompasses the subject. Hell, there're hardly any books I've read that really capture the true nature of the greatest leaders in history," Drake said, scorning his own inexperience. "I know what it means to take responsibility, but leading others, punishing those who go against you, and putting those who step out back into line… I'm still muddling my way through it all."

"Through what?" a voice said behind him.

"Oh, you're still awake? Did you sleep, Chelsea?" Drake asked, turning his focus behind him. He had known someone was approaching, but he only knew who it was now that they had spoken up.

"No, not many of us have. We didn't know what to think when we saw you walk back into camp with that guy. Is—Is Claire alright?" she asked.

Drake exhaled a breath. "Yeah, she's better than I thought. Or at least appears to be. She's sleeping right now in my tent. Which reminds me, I need to talk to Jacqueline and your friend Megan. And where the hell is Bear when I actually need him? I need to know if that flower child has some *good goods* that can possibly cleanse status ailments…"

"Some what…? Never mind. She's in your tent? You didn't do anything to her, did you?" Chelsea asked leadingly.

Do I really need to do this now? I'm thankful for Chelsea as a party member, but I'm not interested in her. She was so much trouble when we met and only changed her tune after she found out how useful I was. Yeah, I did save her from the King, but that was just being a good party member, Drake thought, mulling over what to do.

"If I did, is that a problem?" Drake finally asked.

"N-No," Chelsea muttered, but then she seemed to muster up enough courage to say what she was really feeling. "A-Actually, yes! You know how I feel about you! So why is it only Claire? Am I not good enough?"

Drake sighed. "No, and don't even go there. You're very attractive. But I don't need conditional affection. You hated me right from the get-go when we met, remember? I didn't just forget that because we're closer now. I'm not even sure what's going to happen with Claire at this point, but I do know I don't want a girl who's as combative as you are and who only started having feelings for me because I'm the best option now. I'm not going to get preachy about it, but you aren't what I'm looking for. I've said it before and I'll say it again. I don't want a relationship with you, Chelsea."

Chelsea recoiled from the assault of words Drake directed at her, but she couldn't speak, let alone refute the words. He was right, after all. Even if what she felt now was true feelings of attraction, it only stemmed from the fact that he had saved her. And after the way she'd treated him at first, it was obvious what he would think of her.

She tried to speak, but she couldn't find the words. Eventually, she began to sniffle as her eyes watered from the sting of the truth she had been struck with. Unable to speak her mind, she turned and walked back to the camp in tears.

Drake looked up for a moment, sighing.

"It is good that you set her straight, though I am surprised you did so. I took you for someone to be more lazy with things like that," Natto hummed.

"Yeah, well, I'm learning that I have a bad habit of putting things off until they become problems. It's time I nip things in the bud," Drake said, looking at the rising sun. "Even if I don't want to."

* * *

Savannah desperately tried to gather as many remaining people who would support her as she could. All of them waited outside of her tent patiently as she did her best to calm herself before they left.

"Why did things turn out this way... I knew I had a bad feeling about that guy! Why did I listen to that moron, Adam! I was sitting comfy at the top just listening to Shigure! It's always like this... I get into a good position and always want more!" she cursed. "At least that psycho left us alone for now. That gives us some time to get out before anything else happens. I swear I never want to see any of these fucking monsters for the rest of my life!"

"Time's up," a voice said from the other end of her tent.

Savannah turned quickly in the direction of the voice, but she was unable to identify the person, his face shrouded in the shadows of the rising sun.

"W-Who the fuck are you? Who let you in here?!" she stammered.

"I'm the consequences of your own actions. And no one *let* me in," Drake said, stepping into the light.

Savannah grimaced and stumbled backward, realizing just who was in the tent with her.

"Please! It was all Adam's idea! I only went alon—" she tried to explain, but Drake was already on her, his hand wrapped around her neck.

"See, that's the important part. You went along with it. And that's all I needed to know," he said coldly. He raised his hand, an earthy brown magic circle forming at the tip of one of his fingers.

Pointing it directly at the shrieking and mumbling woman in his grip, Drake fired it between her brows unceremoniously. A small bead of red trickled down from the wound.

You have killed participant Fire Grace - Savannah Shepherd Level 14. Experience earned. 29,420 TP have been awarded.

Drake cringed from the deed, but he knew he had to make sure it was done. Refusing to look away from the action, he made sure to pay respects to the woman. He waited for her equipment to drop as well as the skill stone— that still rubbed him the wrong way, but he pocketed it regardless. He then lit her body ablaze with white fire, making sure to not let a single piece of her remain.

"Well, at least it's all finished now... Now I just have to keep an eye out for the remaining ghouls, if there are any," Drake thought, looking at the quest.

Subjugation Quest: 72 of 100 Converted Ghouls [F-Rank]

"I certainly believe it is better to assume that there are some strewn about the tutorial, but it should be a tertiary concern. You now have nearly two thousand people to take care of thanks to your little maneuver, and there is still the matter of the King's hoard you wished to settle. Not to mention the crafting that will take up a majority of your time much like the 'training' you have been doing," Natto reminded him.

Drake turned around, walking out of the tent to an empty area that he had cleared out, piles of ashes here and there. He had forced his way into this part of the ramparts which housed many of the coalition leaders, including Shigure's tent, but the teen's saving grace was the contract Drake had entered with him earlier.

If Drake was being honest, the teen had worn on his patience well past what he was worth, especially after yesterday.

"That's true. But that's why Shigure is still useful, even though he's been more trouble lately. We are going to put him to work for real by delegating supervision of what I want from this place. From what I've seen from the outside, almost everyone is a non-combat class or a crafter, with only a small percentage actually being fit for combat. Most of their fighting force was controlled by the coalition leaders, and they all went turncoat." Drake scoffed, walking out of the ramparts and toward his own camp.

"Now, most of the people capable of fighting relatively well are under Shigure. Unsurprisingly, when it's this skewed in power, most of the people in charge aim to stay in charge when given the chance, resulting in me having to clean up most of them... It's sad, but I'm becoming a one-strike kind of guy recently," Drake huffed.

The sun had been out for several hours now, and Drake moved closer and closer to their camp outside of Shigure's, now his, outpost. He could already hear the nagging from Sherry about where he was and why he wasn't making breakfast before he got within earshot.

"*While I am rather upset that we skipped an immediate breakfast, that still leaves the crafting, training, and eventually the hoard of treasure that I am sure is protected by very very numerous ants who will not be friendly,*" Natto continued.

"I know, I know. I'm keeping the timeline in mind, don't worry," Drake conceded, looking at the tutorial time limit.

Time remaining until tutorial's conclusion:
92 days, 15 hours, 28 minutes, 45 seconds.

Drake planned to stay for around thirty days total at the outpost, not only to learn crafting to increase his variety of accessories, but also to increase his fighting ability through training the fundamentals and, hopefully, by meeting the mysterious master martial artist Shigure had mentioned when they first came. Especially now that he had access to the outpost.

He was being conservative with the amount of time he was going to spend here, and based on Natto's best guess on how large the Ant Nest had become, Drake believed it would take him nearly a week or more to clear it depending on how strong some of the higher tiered monsters had become and where the hoard was located relative to the nest's layout. Particularly where the Queen's nest was. With Drake's current luck, he knew exactly where the hoard would be relative to the nest.

Drake sighed, hoping he was wrong, but he wouldn't know until they scouted it out and went there in person.

"Then there's also the remnants of the Goblin Lieutenants we have to deal with, but at this point, they might as well be standard mobs. At least to me," Drake thought aloud. "To everyone else in this tutorial, they might be trouble—well, excluding Bjorn and Shigure. I think Tom could probably take a few hits from a lieutenant at this point... I haven't checked in on all their progress lately, actually," Drake said aloud. He made a note to do so in the future before they left for the Ant Nest.

"*So, you are planning to bring the entire party with you?*" Natto asked.

Drake spotted a few people exiting their tents and a particularly frustrated girl with a side-cut bob giving him the evil eye as he walked closer to the camp.

Waving to them, he talked absentmindedly to Natto. "I think I have to at this point. After what happened with Claire, I don't have a choice if I want to keep them all safe. Thankfully, Bjorn seems to be willing to tag along, although I won't be able to put him in the party. I need to minimize the amount of experience he gets. The slower we can make it for him to reach level 30, the better," Drake reminded her.

Finally coming back to the camp, he received the welcome he was expecting.

Theodore shimmered into view next to him in a slight bow.

"Thou hast returned, my lord. How dost thou feeleth? This one hopes it was not too heavy on one's heart..." Theodore said, trying to be considerate.

"No, Theo, it's about what I expected. But it's my cross to bear, and I'm fine with that," Drake said, giving him a smile of thanks before turning to the little glutton drilling a hole into the side of his head. "Can you stop with the staring? I know I'm good-looking, but jeez, get a picture or something. It'll last longer," Drake said, trying to joke around his absence in the morning.

Sherry didn't say anything, pointing to the empty fire pit at the center of the camp. Her eyes bulged as the rumble of her stomach spoke for her.

"Okay okay. I'm going, Mom!" Drake spat, trudging to the fire pit and table. "I swear! That little woman is scarier than any monster I've ever faced!"

"Are you talking about me?" a sudden bump to his shoulder asked.

"Ah, Claire, you're up? Are you sure you're feeling well enough?" Drake asked, stopping what he was doing to check her head and looking around to see if anything looked out of place.

"Y-Yeah..." she muttered, surprised by his response. "A-Are you that worried about me?" she asked sheepishly. She pulled out her cookware and placed it on the table.

"Nah. Just wanted to make sure you weren't turning into a ghoul or someth—Ow! Hey, that's a knife!" Drake said, rubbing his arm.

"I know it is! You're lucky I don't have the stats to stab you!" she huffed.

Well, it seems like she's fine... Drake thought, giving a smile.

"Is your standard of 'okay' for women them wanting to hurt you? I must say you have awakened to quite the inclination there," Natto giggled.

Hey, we don't kink shame here. Safe space, Drake said sagely.

"I'm glad you're doing well; I'm going to have some healers look at you just to be sure, alright?" Drake said seriously.

"Uh, uh-huh..." Claire mumbled, her ears turning scarlet.

Drake pulled out some ingredients, ready to start cooking, and ignored the smoke coming from Claire's ears.

Soon there were others gathering around ready to eat and help, Sherry the first one after Claire. Harley and Theo stepped up next, Harley falling in line next to Claire as they helped with the prep. Eventually, Hudson, Amir, Tom, and Bjorn joined as well.

"Oh, now you show up. Am I only important when I cook?" Drake asked.

"Yes," Bjorn said plainly.

"Hey..."

"Hey, you're the one who asked, bro," Bjorn said, shrugging and yawning as he took a seat next to Theo.

Drake shook his head with a smile on his face, glad that Bjorn at least knew to joke to keep a sliver of normalcy after what had happened yesterday and what he assumed Bjorn knew he'd done this morning.

But Drake soon noticed two storms rolling in.

One was a massive ball of fury that looked like it wanted to tear him limb from limb. The other was Lamar.

"Shit, Megan doesn't look happy..." Drake sighed.

Chapter 31
Shut Up, Bitch, I'm Cooking!

"Why did you say those things to Chels?!" Megan snapped, throwing her finger into Drake's face and slamming her other hand onto the table.

"First, put that thing away," Drake said, using his hand to gently move her finger out of his face. "Second, what things exactly? I said quite a few."

Megan's face deepened into a scowl. "You know exactly what I mean! Why would you dismiss her feelings like that? She was crying all night!" she shouted, drawing the eyes of everyone around the room save Sherry, who was staring at the food prep unperturbed.

"Dismiss? How did I dismiss her feelings? I was very forward and upfront with what I said," Drake said evenly.

"You couldn't have let her down more easily? Your words hurt more than you think!" she spat.

Drake sighed. "That's exactly why I said what I did. Chelsea is a good woman, she was a bitch to me at first but deep down I know she's a great and loving person. She was willing to sacrifice herself for her friends with no care for her own safety multiple times."

"Then why would you tell her she has no chance?!" Megan shouted again, getting closer to Drake.

Drake didn't budge and moved her back with one arm despite her digging in to stand her ground.

"Because she has no chance with *me*. She's a good girl and deserves a good man. But that man won't be me. And I know my words hurt, but what would you have me do? Lie to her and give her even a sliver of hope that she might have a chance? If anything, that's worse. She might be hurting now, I'll concede that, but I won't be a part of stringing along someone who I don't see as a potential romantic partner. She deserves better than that. And if you think I should go back on my word and tell her she *does* have a chance, you're more of a shit person and a shit friend than I thought," Drake said, looking down as he sneered in disgust.

Megan's mouth opened up, ready to retort, but Jacqueline stepped in.

"That's enough, love, just go comfort Chels now. You're stepping in where you shouldn't. The man may be an asshole, but he isn't mad. Wouldn't you want someone who has no intention of being yours to tell you so? Or would you like to be used and strung along for weeks, months, maybe even years?" she said, holding Megan back by the shoulder.

Megan's eyes widened before she ground her teeth, knowing Jacqueline was talking about her and Chris. It was still a fresh wound in her mind and heart, but both Jacqueline and Drake were right. She had enough sense to know that if Chris was anything like Drake, none of what had happened to their group would have passed.

Megan reluctantly conceded the point, turning with her head down and walking back with Jacqueline in tow to their tent.

"What was that all about?" Tom asked, saying the question on everyone's mind that they weren't rude enough to ask.

"Just unneeded drama." Drake sighed. "But that's how it is in life. There's no getting around it, not even in a death tutorial it seems."

"Is it because of me...?" Claire asked.

"Yep, and 'cause of me. So don't get a stitch about it. All's fair in love and war, and you can't expect to have one guy hoard all the good women. Or *can* you... Wait, I may have made a mistake, someone go ge—Ow!" Drake complained in faux pain as an elbow hit him from the side.

Drake grinned and looked over to a pouting Claire. Her cheeks were puffed up as she chopped away at the ingredients on the table, pushing them off and into the pot on the side while refusing to look at Drake.

"I feel like I'm being hit quite a lot lately, and I'm not getting the good kind of hit."

"There's a good kind of hit? The fuck are you saying?" Lamar asked from behind Drake as he towered over everyone at the table.

"Of course!" Drake said, turning to look up at the cyclops. "There's getting hit in the—You know what, never mind. We don't kink shame here, it's poor manners. You wouldn't want to be like that nasty construct who zapped me in the introduction."

"You got zapped in the introduction, Mr. Shot?" Harley asked from his left, her face lighting up in surprise.

"Long story, but yeah, I got tasered in the introduction room," Drake said casually.

"Haha! How did you manage that, bro?" Bjorn asked from his seat, barking a laugh.

"*Long story*. Do I really have to say that again?" Drake snorted.

"So your smart ass did something ta get yourself tased, and it's too embarrassing to admit. Is that right, ya idjit?" Hudson surmised.

"You know, some people say EQ is a curse, but for you, Hudson, it might be a very funny comedic gift at my expense." Drake laughed.

"Thank ya kindly. Wait..." Hudson's face turned pensive as he went over what Drake said in his head again.

"Either way, good morning ya big lug. You here for breakfast, or you want to just get to it?" Drake said, turning back to Lamar.

"Always down for some grub. Don't exactly get decent meals in the outpost, and after what I heard happened last night... I don't think we will at all anymore," Lamar said wryly.

"Okay," Drake said, holding up both hands. His face turned steely. "Yeah, that was my fault, but the people in charge didn't give me a choice when they decided to try and kidnap someone important to me and hurt another. If you come for what's mine, you have to understand there will be consequences tenfold."

Lamar, as large as he was, still shivered under Drake's not-so-idle threat even though it wasn't directed at him, but said in general.

"Right... I'll keep that in mind. Just stop staring at me like that, it's freaking me out."

"Then let's get some food in us. I'm ready to start crafting! I need some new bling!" Drake shouted, waving two finger W's in front of his face.

The only ones who cheered along were the small garbage trucks, Sherry and Natto. Everyone else sighed and continued to either wait or help with the prep.

* * *

After finishing breakfast, Lamar and Drake moved to the outskirts of their small camp.

"So, how is this going to work? Do I read a book, are you going to impart knowledge on me? Or is it the old-fashioned way?" Drake asked, getting a little excited.

"Don't know, I've never helped someone with it before. I kinda assumed you knew more than I did," Lamar said as he began to take things out of his own inventory.

First Lamar set a tent next to him, then he pulled out more craftsman-type equipment. He pulled out a kiln, forge, whetstones, hammers, files, clamps, stacks of wood, measuring tools, you name it. The large cyclops had everything out and ready within a few minutes.

"You will have to do it the old-fashioned way if the larger-than-life oaf does not have a skill book prepared, which I assume he does not," Natto explained.

There we have it, then. Thanks for the info, even if it was a little late, Drake jabbed.

"You did not need it until now. Do you not have enough problems already dealing with monsters and women, fool?" Natto retorted.

There's no need to be so snippy. One of those lovely ladies might one day be your pseudo-mommy. Drake smirked and wiggled his eyebrows.

"I will never call you or any ill-minded woman either of those words. And

they better not get in my face, 'cause I will unceremoniously drop that mother-fucker!" Natto shouted.

Wow, that escalated quickly. And technically it would be a she who is… yeah… so it would be a fatherfucker…? Never mind, Drake thought, shaking his head.

"Okay yeah, old-fashioned way it is!" Drake said, trying to get the very disturbing image he had come up with out of his head.

"Who told ya that? The little birdie?" Lamar asked as he put some black-smithing tongs on his shoulder.

"Why yes, yes she did in very colorful and endearing words," Drake replied with a smile on his face.

Lamar sighed. "That's not creepy. But whatever. I have things to do, so let's get to cooking."

"Let him cook!" Drake cheered, his hair shimmering to a vibrant orange. Lamar looked back over his shoulder, confused.

"Sorry, couldn't help myself." Drake shrugged. "So what's first then, big guy?"

"First you're going to heat and mold a large slab of regular iron," Lamar instructed, pulling a huge darkened rod from under the table.

Drake looked at it and smiled. "Oh, this should be easy. I've been doing this for most of my life," he said, snickering as he wiggled his eyebrows.

"I don't need to hear that, you fucking freak. Get to beatin—hittin—" Lamar sighed, trying to change the word every time Drake leaned in closer, his eyebrows going up and down. "Just fucking smack the stupid piece of metal with the hammer after you heat it up! Fucking weirdo…"

Drake saluted and moved over to the unlit forge, where he quickly encountered a problem.

"Hey, Lamar," Drake said over his shoulder as he looked at the forge.

"Yeah?"

"How do I set this thing on fire? And I don't have any tools…"

Lamar sighed, his hand covering his one eye.

"That's right, I forgot you're a newbie. Can't you do some sort of magic thing? And the forge... I'll do it. Just watch so you know for later." Lamar thundered over to the forge.

Drake stepped back a bit, watching the hulking cyclops do something he didn't expect.

Breathe fire into the forge.

"How am I supposed to do that? Is that a skill or something?" Drake asked incredulously.

"Yeah, it's a blacksmithing skill. You'll get it later," Lamar explained.

Drake looked at the forge, a thought coming to him.

"Wait. I want to learn how to make rings and necklaces, why are you having me hammer iron? I don't need a weapon," Drake asked.

Lamar looked back at Drake, both silent for a moment.

"Oh," Lamar said.

"Oh?"

"Hmm..."

"Hmm...?" Drake parrotted.

"Well, that makes stuff more simple," Lamar said, pulling an item from his inventory and handing it to Drake. "Here."

Drake looked at the large circle of measuring rings, confused.

"What's this?" he asked.

"Exactly what it looks like, you idiot. They're finger measuring rings." Lamar scoffed and pulled a few more items from his inventory. "Here's some armor you can cut to replace the thin sheet metal for now until you get it down enough to use mana iron strips. This is a mandrel: you're going to be bending the metal around it until it's a circle," Lamar said, throwing the spike-like thing to Drake.

"Whoa," Drake said, catching the piece of equipment. "What comes after that?" he asked.

"That's all you need for now. Once you get good at molding metal to the size you need, we can move on. But before that, you need to get used to bending metal," Lamar explained.

Drake took the piece of armor, a chest piece, and ripped a piece from it with his bare hand, scrunching the strip he had torn around one of his empty fingers.

"Done," Drake said, giving a smile.

"No *not* done, you fucking idiot! Do it how I told you!" Lamar roared.

"Jeez, take a joke." Drake laughed, then spotted a notification.

New profession quest: Create 250 Simple Metal Bands [No Grade] and 100 Simple Chain Necklaces [No Grade].

Reward: Profession experience, Low-Grade Crafting Manual, Mana Infused Tools [F-Grade].

"Oh, look at that." Drake chuckled.

"What?" Lamar asked indignantly.

"I got the quest I needed," Drake replied snidely.

"Bullshit," Lamar spat.

Drake willed the quest window to open and turned it so Lamar could see.

"Read 'em and weep, big man." Drake sneered.

"That's horseshit. You didn't even do anything!"

Drake held up his finger, holding the crushed metal around it. "Nuh uh!" Drake joked, wagging his little digit.

Lamar groaned, but he waved Drake's childish games off, needing to go back to his own work.

"Fine, whatever, do what you need to. Once you get past it I'll help with the more intricate details for better craftsmanship." He sighed. "Stupid fucking system... What was all that work I did for years for?!" He grunted and walked off to his workbench, grabbing some tools and continuing to grumble.

Drake smiled, satisfied that he had annoyed the cyclops well enough for the rest of the day.

Pulling out a few more similar-looking pieces of equipment he still had on hand, Drake got to work pulling them apart for the metal, easily stripping them down into smaller pieces for the rings.

At first, he made each ring just by bending it around his own finger with raw strength, but then he thought better of it.

I'll need to do it properly eventually anyway, better not to take shortcuts I guess, he thought, admitting to himself he was cheating the quest.

Sighing, he pulled out the mandrel and a piece of stripped metal, fiddling around with the best way to bend it. He tried heating up the strip, but he was unable to get it to bend as precisely as he wanted around the tool.

"Damn it, why is this so hard?!" Drake grumbled under his breath.

"Hey," Lamar said from behind him.

Drake turned quickly, saying the first thing that came to mind.

"Shut up, bitch, I'm cooking here! Oh, my bad. Yeah? What is it?" Drake said, chuckling nervously.

Lamar just raised his singular brow in confusion, but he chalked it up to Drake being an idiot like usual.

"You need to hammer the metal around the mandrel lightly to form it. I can't believe I needed to say that. Are you really an idiot? And act like one to cover it up?" Lamar asked incredulously.

"I plead the fifth, thank you very much," Drake said, hearing a snickering in his head from Natto.

"Right, well, get your dumbass over to the table. It'll be easier if you use an elevated surface," Lamar suggested, jabbing a thumb to a spare workbench.

"Thank ya kindly, big guy," Drake said. He tipped an imaginary hat.

Lamar cringed. "I fucking despise you."

"That's what everyone says at first, but don't worry. I grow on you." Drake smiled.

"If only that were true..." Natto sighed.

Chapter 32
So Many Distractions!

Drake sat back down at the workbench after serving lunch for the camp, his mind mulling over how difficult it actually was to craft properly.

He had made a show of pissing off Lamar in the morning and somehow gotten the crafting quest, but he'd quickly noticed that if he didn't go through the correct processes using the system-approved methods, he would not proceed with the quest in any way. He was left with only a crumpled piece of metal on his finger that couldn't even be identified.

The first time he'd tried it, it gave him the quest, but the item itself was just a piece of scrap metal by that point. Drake being Drake, he'd tried it again several times to see if he could cheat the system, but he'd soon found out it was impossible. Which left him with no choice but to make it properly through painstakingly long and arduous work.

Drake found that it was akin to when he'd done his Mining Quest. Somehow, the system was able to make the distinction between when he was crafting with intent and when he was doing tomfoolery to cut corners. If he didn't follow the correct process, the resulting piece of metal would only be that. Scrap metal.

So, Drake took to doing the task seriously and slowly. Which, much like his mining, didn't allow him to take advantage of his overwhelming current status. Bending the metal around the mandrel wasn't difficult in the sense that it took a lot of strength, but because it was a long process of slowly and meticulously hammering the metal to form.

Drake messed up many times, going through trial and error to figure out the process. Each time, he wished the system had given him the internet.

What I wouldn't give for a 'how to' video right now, Drake had thought.

But eventually, Drake reached the finish line just before lunch.

Poorly Made Metal Band [No Grade]

A poorly made ring of metal made by a novice crafter. A pretty shit first attempt.

Drake kept the ring and placed it on his thumb. For sentimental value. The system had oh-so generously given it a unique description, after all.

After completing the first of many, *many* items he needed, Drake was called to help with making lunch by Claire and Sherry.

While preparing lunch, he used the break to go over what he had done wrong and what he needed to do better. He was caught up in his thoughts, but not so much as to not notice the absent Chelsea.

She must have taken it pretty hard... But there isn't much I could do about that one, Drake thought.

After some small talk, Drake quickly made his way back to the workbench to continue crafting.

Which led to the present.

Drake had finally sat back down and was ready to return to his single-minded work, but Bjorn stopped him.

"Yeah, what is it? Didn't have enough to eat?" Drake joked.

Bjorn shook his head. "Naw, food was good as always, bro, but did you forget you did a hostile takeover yesterday? You still have things you got to see to," Bjorn said.

Drake sighed, giving himself a mental slap.

"Oh, that's right. I *did* do that, didn't I..." Drake said reluctantly. "Alright, I'm going to go see Shigure then. Any idea where the little kid is?"

"Probably in his tent. He's been holed up there ever since you gave him the ultimatum. Why do you need to see him?" Bjorn asked.

"I've got to figure out how his outpost used to work, and it's easier to go through him since he's obviously going to be so willing." Drake smiled.

* * *

A few minutes later, both Bjorn and Drake arrived at Shigure's tent. Looking around, Drake noticed quite a decrease in the number of tents surrounding him.

Must be from all the cleaning we did yesterday, Drake thought.

"You did kill quite a lot of their upper echelon, so I would venture that their management and such is in quite the disarray," Natto pointed out.

Drake pursed his lips thoughtfully, mulling over how he was going to go about conscripting Shigure's assistance in keeping the outpost running.

"Well, guess I'll just wing it," he finally said. He began to march toward Shigure's tent.

"Wing it? Have you ever managed anything before?" Bjorn asked, following a step behind.

"Nope! I did run a guild before, but not sure that counts. Either way, the outpost was running fine before we came, right?" Drake said rhetorically.

"Yeah...?" Bjorn answered skeptically.

"Then we just need to put the head back on the snake. Metaphorically speaking. But this time the snake answers to me, and no more dumb fighting for power," Drake said as he opened the tent entrance.

"And why would they suddenly decide not to vie for power?" Bjorn asked.

"Because. The strongest one here, without debate, is me. So why bother?" Drake smiled, his eyes finding a lump of blankets on top of a bed on the other side of the tent.

"Shigure, honey, I'm home!" Drake said, swinging his arms wide.

Shigure, as expected, did not respond, but he did hear Drake as the blob of blankets on the bed flinched slightly.

"Aw, don't be like that. We're best buds, aren't we?" Drake offered, walking closer to the bed only to be held off by Uta in a bloom of black smoke.

"Have you not done enough? I ask that you please leave!" she said through gritted teeth.

"Oh? Gotten very polite, have we? But don't worry, I'm not going to do anything. I can't anyway, remember?" Drake said, crossing his arms. He raised his chin, and a light green magic circle filled the room. The next moment, a gust of wind pulled the covers off Shigure, revealing his gremlin-like form on the bed.

He was no longer in his usual attire, instead in casual wear, and his hair was disheveled and his eyes were sunken in like he hadn't slept in days. Yet, it had only been a single one since his removal from the leadership position.

"What do you want," Shigure asked, his eyes turned to slits. His face was scrunched into a pruney wrinkle of flesh, much like Drake used to look when he saw the sun for the first time after a 24-hour gaming session.

"Aren't you just a face only a mother could love? Have you slept?" Drake asked.

"I have not... I've been up. Thinking," Shigure said reluctantly.

"And what exactly are those things you've been thinking about?" Drake asked curiously.

"Just... things..." Shigure said, his eyes wandering to the floor.

Drake rolled his eyes. *I guess I should be happy he's at least reflecting on things for once. So it's a start,* Drake thought.

"*Yes, but he certainly looks like a shriveled snail,*" Natto added.

Sure, but you didn't have to say it. Drake laughed, drawing eyes from both Uta and Bjorn, which forced him to cough.

"Right. So, let's get you cleaned up first; I got work for you," Drake said, pulling a large tub from his inventory.

Shigure's head raised, and his eyes weakly looked back up at Drake. "What more do you wish to take from me? Is stripping all my accolades and accomplishments not enough?"

Drake snorted. "Don't be so dramatic. I need your help for once."

He jabbed a thumb at the bath. "But first, clean up. You look like death's fourth cousin twice removed from the street no one wants to visit," Drake said, almost too seriously.

He then pulled a table and some leftover food from his inventory, placing the food on the table.

"Might as well get some real food in you while we're at it, kid."

Shigure was stunned, unsure of what to do. His eyes finally found Uta on the side of his bed.

"Do I really look that bad?" he asked.

Reluctantly, Uta nodded, her eyes looking sympathetically at her now-dethroned lord.

"I am sorry, Lord Shigure. I have not done my duty properly as an Assistant..." she added.

An emotion other than sad depression appeared in him for the first time since yesterday. Shigure's face flared up slightly with the heat of anger at her words.

"You have not failed anyone! If anyone has failed, it is I. There is no reason for you to apologize, Uta!" he shouted, quickly getting to his feet to grab the girl by her shoulders.

Drake clapped his hands, breaking up their moment before it got uncomfortable for Drake and Bjorn.

"Look, I know he's finally up and about after being knocked down and all that, but there's only one anime protagonist with an origin story in this tutorial, and it's me. So get your ass in that tub." Drake laughed as he filled it with warm, steamy water. "Clean up and eat, then we'll talk. And make it quick. I won't wait for you two to 'make up,'" Drake added with a wink.

Uta's face quickly flushed red, and Shigure ground his teeth, turning to Drake.

"Have you no shame? I would never think of Uta in such a manner!" he shouted back at Drake.

Uta visibly deflated, her posture sinking.

"Y-You wouldn't...?" she muttered.

"N-No! I mean! I-I think that I'm not capable—" Shigure tried to amend.

"Okay, I've seen enough," Drake said. He made a vomiting noise. "Come get us outside when you're done doing whatever. But don't take too long; I have shit to do."

Walking out of the tent with Bjorn in tow, Drake made his way to a slightly open area, pulling his tools and a spare table out from his inventory to work silently on his crafting while they waited.

"Hey, Shot," Bjorn said. He pulled out his own seat from his inventory and sat down, the wood creaking underneath his weight.

"Hmm?" Drake hummed, not looking away from his crafting.

"I don't get it, bro. You're a good guy; I knew that way back when. And I know you understand this new life well enough to be hard when you have to. But it seems like you're really soft on Shigure. There a reason for that?" Bjorn asked, seemingly to fill the time.

Drake paused, looking up, then returned to his light tinkering.

"Honestly? I'm not sure. I guess he reminds me of my younger brothers. He's just a kid, Bear. He should have never been here to begin with, but here he is, forced to do things and go through a tutorial he never should have," Drake mused. "I'm not absolving him of what's happened, but I get how he's fumbling and how hard-headed he is. I was sixteen a few millennia ago, if you can believe it."

Bjorn shook his head. "Really? I thought you were still, like, fourteen with the way you act, bro," he joked.

"Ha ha." Drake laughed sarcastically. "All I'm saying is, it's hard to punish him when he's all bright-eyed and everything, but I do know it has to be done. I don't pretend to be the moral authority on anything, and I make plenty of mistakes, but the least I can do when I throw my weight around is help him not make the same mistakes."

Drake was about to continue his explanation when Shigure and Uta came out of the tent. Shigure was now in a more fitting state, his hair washed and now in his usual armor.

"About damn time, Bear was talking my ear off." Drake snorted and put his things away, Bjorn shaking his head with a smile.

"What is it exactly that you want, Sir Shot," Shigure asked pensively.

"I want you to go back to doing what you were before: administering this place," Drake said flatly.

Shigure stayed silent for a moment, stunned once again.

"You want to give back what you took from me?" he asked.

"Not exactly," Drake amended, wagging his finger. "I want you to basically do what you were doing before, but now you answer to me."

Shigure raised a brow. "Okay...?"

"What I want is for you to be the figurehead of the outpost for the rest of the tutorial. I'm assuming you had at least *some* knack for this leader thing, seeing as you got it in the first place while being so young. So now you get to do it without people constantly looking to stab you in the back," Drake explained.

"Why do you think people would now no longer want to seek power?" Shigure asked.

"Well, that's because I'm here now, and there's no bigger fish in this pond at the moment. Discounting Bear, but Bear isn't into things like leadership. Right, Bear?" Drake said, looking over his shoulder.

"Yeah. Been there, done that, leader stuff isn't my bag, bro," Bjorn agreed.

"See? So now that's out of the way. You get to actually run the outpost, and if anything goes even remotely wrong, you can come get me and I'll fix it," Drake elaborated.

Shigure's face turned thoughtful, but he quickly began questioning as the offer sounded too good to be true.

"What's the catch?" he asked.

Drake shook his head.

"Why does no one believe me when I give them the benefit of the deal!" he grumbled. "I just don't want to deal with it, alright. What happened the other day was a result of you not addressing the problems that were building up, but now I'm saying that that won't happen again since I'll be here to fix it. Think of it as a probation period for you. Until I leave in a month's time, you are going to prove to me that I don't need to worry about this place or the people here. I don't think you're a bad kid, Shigure, I just think you're a kid," Drake snorted.

Shigure recoiled slightly, surprised at the words Drake offered. He looked into Drake's eyes, trying to discern his intentions, but when he was unable, he sighed. Shigure then seemed to go into an internal debate with himself as his face shifted from one emotion to the other.

Eventually, Shigure opened his mouth to say something, then coughed to clear his throat.

"I agree," he said, offering a hand.

"Hm... Just like that?" Drake said, now the one suspicious.

Shigure gave a wry smile, trying not to form a scowl. "Y-Yes, just like that."

Drake looked warily at Shigure for a moment.

"Hmm..." Drake hummed briefly. "I'm not sure if I should be wary or not..." Drake grasped the hand, then pulled Shigure in close. "Just remember I'm watching. Always watching, Wazowski..."

Shigure grimaced. "I don't know what that is from."

Bjorn laughed. "You get used to it."

Chapter 33
Beware of Tropes

Drake looked around from left to right, making sure the only person near him was Lamar, who could hardly be called 'around' as he was also fully preoccupied in his own work.

"Okay, no more interruptions! This quest is getting done!" Drake shouted, his hands raised. He looked down at the workbench, his materials and tools he had received from Lamar on it.

"Rather eager to do work, are you not?" Natto asked.

Well, yeah. I need these items done ASAP. Not just for myself, but everyone is in need of these accessories. Vitality rings, earrings, and whatever else I can make could be the difference between someone living or dying, so there's no more time to waste. After Claire was kidnapped, too, I need to do all I can to help everyone be strong enough to not have that happen again if possible. I'm more worried about the people close to me than anything... Drake thought, shifting in his chair.

"Drake, you can not save everyone. I have told you this. And you are also not a god; it is not your responsibility to protect every last person that you have interacted with," Natto reminded him.

Drake tilted back his chair, throwing his hands behind his head as he sighed.

At least not yet, he thought.

"What?" Natto asked.

I'm not a god yet, he thought again. He felt Natto roll her eyes.

What? Who's to say you can't technically become a god? You already told me I'll basically live for thousands of years already. Why wouldn't I basically be a god when I reach S-Rank? Those Primordials you're so scared of seem to be just as good as gods.

"That is completely different! They were born as a higher race! They can even bend some of the system to their wills!" Natto shouted back.

That's cool, but I have the power of anime and friendship on my side, and we know who always wins in those fights, Drake joked.

Natto sighed and went silent, knowing that arguing with him would lead to only more of a headache. Drake smiled and leveled his chair, looking back at his materials and focusing on the task at hand.

"Okay, back to it, then," he said excitedly.

For the next few hours, Drake tinkered with making rings first. He went through the process from before and continued to improve on it, ring after ring.

Hammering them to fit around the mandrel was the easy part. The next few steps were much more tedious. He had to figure out how to meld the metal together without proper solder, which he couldn't figure out surprisingly enough. He thought he could manage by just doing his best to heat the metal to a point where he could stick them together, but it only ended with the metal becoming a lump of unworkable mush.

Eventually giving in, he lugged his way over to Lamar and gave the best impression of puppy dog eyes that he could. Which served to creep Lamar out enough to help Drake, if only to get him the hell away from him.

The cyclops gave Drake a frustrated look once he went over to see the process Drake was going through.

"You fucking moron. You're overheating it! And you aren't forging the metal!" Lamar roared as soon as he saw what Drake was doing.

"Not what?" Drake asked.

"You aren't forging the metal! Ahh... It's ruined." Lamar sighed, looking at the lump Drake had just overheated. "You have to heat it just right, then strike it to merge the metal into a single piece!"

"How was I supposed to know? Don't you use solder for that type of thing?" Drake asked, confused.

"Do you think we have fucking solder?! You're thinking of modern-day practices! We don't even have sand and borax, you tool!" Lamar shouted.

Drake was thoroughly confused now.

What do we need sand for? And what the hell does borax have to do with crafting?

"Idiot... Here, just watch."

Lamar took one of the strips from the table. He sized up the strip first, then found his key ring holding his sizers for fingers. His one eye shifted over to look at Drake, then his hands, quickly guessing the approximate size of his thumb. He then placed the strip on the mandrel, marking the position with some charcoal.

After that, he quickly got to work bending and hammering the metal lightly, eventually getting it into a perfect ring. Once he was finished, he looked over the ring's position briefly and nodded to himself.

Lamar took in a deep breath and exhaled slowly, a small, constant flame exiting his mouth as he turned the ring over in his hand, apparently unaffected by the fire. Then, once the ring was a radiant orange-red hue, he began to lightly hammer the piece again on the mandrel.

After a few minutes of dunking the ring into a bucket of water, then heating and dunking some more, the cyclops had a ring of metal between his large sausage-like fingers.

Nodding to himself again, he quickly pulled out a file and rubbed down the edges. After that, he took out a piece of sandpaper that looked like it shone with a color Drake had never seen before. Quickly taking a few swipes at the ring, Lamar huffed in satisfaction and threw it to Drake.

Perfectly Made Metal Band [F-Grade, Uncommon]
A near-perfectly made ring of metal made by a Master Artisan. The system praises the Craftsman for producing a masterpiece out of such shoddy material.

+5% to Strength.

"Well fuck you too..." Drake hummed aloud looking at the piece, his eyes briefly moving to the paper still in Lamar's hand.

Blacksmith's Mana Sander [F-Grade, Common]

Drake wasn't able to get any more information from his Magic Sight skill, but the item's name spoke for itself. The sander must have been a pretty decent item that contained some sort of magic that made it easier to rough down the metal to its smooth appearance now.

Drake rubbed his thumb over the metal band, honestly impressed. Not that he would tell Lamar that.

"Get it now, freak?" Lamar sneered. Drake blew a raspberry.

"Bitch, please. I can do that." He scoffed and slipped the ring onto his thumb.

Wow, perfect fit... Drake thought.

Drake heard a snickering in the back of his mind at the thought, but he did his best to keep a straight face.

"Then let's see it, tiny," Lamar provoked, giving a big, sharp, toothy grin.

Drake moved back over to the bench and gave Lamar a sidelong stink eye before sitting down.

"Just 'cause you're freakishly huge doesn't mean I'm small... Everyone is small to you! Stupid, dumb, stinky, one-eyed—" Drake muttered, pulling a strip of metal from the pile.

"Hit you in the non-six-foot sore spot, did he?" Natto giggled.

Drake ignored Natto and found the ring sizer instead. He fumbled around with the instrument for a bit, eventually finding a snug enough fit for his ring finger.

Going through the same process as before, he reached the point where he had to heat up the ring.

Drake glanced at Lamar, who was looking carefully over Drake's shoulder. Smirking, he formed a scarlet red circle in front of his mouth, allowing him to almost breathe fire in the same way Lamar had.

"That's not funny," Lamar said behind Drake.

"It's kind of funny," Drake replied. He turned his head, but the fire still spewed forward since he wasn't actually spitting fire.

Turning back to his task, Drake willed the flame to move and spread the heat around the joint he was going to hammer. Unlike Lamar, Drake wasn't able to hold the piece with his bare hands, instead using one of the clamps he had been given.

Satisfied with the glow of the heated metal, Drake got to work hammering lightly on the mandrel, turning the ring every so often. Once Drake saw the metal begin to dim, he placed it into the bucket of water, then repeated the process.

Eventually, Drake sweated his way to completing the ring. Or at least, a circular-shaped equivalent.

Adequately Made Metal Band [F-Grade, Common]
A ring of metal made by a novice crafter. It's... alright.

+1% to Strength.

"Ha! Told you I could do it!" Drake shouted in triumph. Lamar scoffed, crossing his arms.

"Let me borrow that sandpaper now, it's still rough around the edges," Drake said, reaching his hand for Lamar.

"No! It's mine—get your own!" he shouted back.

"Come on, just for a minute! It's my first real item I crafted; I wanna make it look good, man," Drake pleaded.

"Stuff it," Lamar spat.

"Uh... what's going on in here?" a voice said from outside the working area.

Both Lamar and Drake turned their heads, Drake pulling at Lamar's arm for the sandpaper and Lamar shoving him away with his other.

"Oh, Claire, what's up?" Drake asked, not bothering to stop pulling.

"I came to get you for dinner," she said, looking from Drake to Lamar curiously.

"Tell this moron to let go. He's trying to steal my shit!" Lamar growled.

"Am not! Jesus man, I just want to *borrow* it," Drake spat.

"That's what people say, then they never give it back!"

Drake was about to shout back, but then he tilted his head. "Yeah, that's true. Alright, fine! Keep your stupid magic sandpaper!"

"What are you two arguing about?" Claire finally asked as she walked up to Drake.

"Oh, I finally finished my first ring," Drake said, holding up the *adequately* made piece. "I wanted to sand it down since it was my first properly made one."

Lamar scoffed behind him.

"Properly made. Ha!" Lamar mumbled indignantly. Drake ignored the sulking cyclops and placed the ring in front of Claire.

"You want it? It doesn't give exactly what I want in terms of stats, so I wasn't going to use it," Drake said, pursing his lips.

Claire's eyes perked up looking at the ring, her hands opening up for Drake to drop it into them. She brought the ring to her face, looking it over, and a smile creased her lips.

"Can I really have it?" she asked.

"Yeah, don't see why not. Like I said, it doesn't have the best stats, and I'll give you better ones once I can make them. But hey, maybe you can get something for it in the outpost if you trade it," Drake said casually.

"No!" Claire shouted, holding the ring. She looked at the ring with stars in her eyes. "Why would I give it away?!"

"Okay... that was a *weird* response," Drake said, shifting on his feet and looking at her with a raised eyebrow.

"*Idiot*," Natto mumbled.

Claire continued to look at the ring before lifting up her left hand. The ring was kept between her right pointer finger and thumb as she slowly moved it to put it on her left ring finger.

"Whoa whoa whoa! Stop, stop!" Drake said, grabbing the ring. "That's not what this is for." Drake laughed nervously.

Claire pouted, blowing out her cheeks as her ring was taken from her.

"I'm just wearing it! It doesn't mean anything," she mumbled.

"Don't play with me! We both know what it means on that finger!" Drake shouted.

"What's the big deal... We're already dating..." Claire said in a hushed tone, bringing her hair behind her scarlet-colored ears.

Drake sighed, his hand going to his forehead. "We are not—Okay I guess I *did* say all that stuff and kill a bunch of people... Susmaryosep..." Drake huffed a long puff of air.

God damn it. Did I trap myself into a love trope? Drake thought, looking at the fidgeting Claire.

"*Duh.*" Natto laughed. "*How does one, with so much weeb experience, not realize saying all the things you did would result in this outcome? Absolute buffoon.*"

I don't like you telling me the obvious. It's very rude. True, but very very rude.

"I'll give you the ring back," Drake said, looking down at Claire. "But it stays *off* that finger."

Drake brought the ring above Claire's hand, and her face brightened again.

A moment later, he spotted her bringing her right hand up this time.

"No! Damn it!" Drake shouted.

Chapter 34

The Butterfly Story

"Okay, that sucked." Drake sighed, shaking his hands from the monotonous work.

For the past week, Drake had been going back and forth to the outpost to catch up and help manage it with Shigure. The teen had put a few more people into the jobs Drake had given the pink slip to.

This back and forth had only been one of the interruptions he'd been having since trying to complete the crafting quest.

The other *interruption* had been Sherry and Claire. They had both come in to hassle him regularly for food. Drake understood Sherry was driven only by one thing, but he knew Claire just wanted to spend more time with him. Their relationship—or more like situationship—had taken a very middle school turn.

Drake was too busy to do much of anything, especially at this point in the tutorial. He couldn't allow himself to be distracted by anything if he could manage it. Food had been one of the few distractions he allowed because he also needed to eat—and to satiate the never-ending black hole that took up home in his head.

So his time had been limited already, which led to Claire trying to take up his remaining time whenever she could and for whatever reason. Drake didn't blame the girl; she was very fond of Drake, and he could tell. But her idea of dating apparently was out of romance novels and tv shows.

What he hadn't known was that she came from a very traditional background, and from what she'd told him in their passing conversations since she'd been kidnapped, she hadn't had a boyfriend before.

The first is always the clingiest, Drake thought, looking at the item in front of him.

It wasn't as if Drake hated the attention. In fact, he was practically touch-starved at this point save for beating the shit out of people and monsters every so often. But that wasn't the point. He had a duty to the people he held in his circle: to keep them safe and to keep getting stronger and moving forward. So right now, he simply didn't have the time to dedicate to her, even if he admittedly wanted to.

Claire's background had started to become a bit more clear to Drake once she became a little more loose-lipped about her past, although she still wouldn't speak about what had happened to her brother. She had just gotten out of college a few months prior to the tutorial. She was from a small town in Colorado where her family helped run a church.

Drake had laughed and thought she was joking, but she had insisted it was the truth. She herself was not very religious, but the old-school traditions held steadfast in their home and under her father's roof.

Which led to the awkwardness of moving their situationship forward.

Everything had been new for Claire, and every step made her blush and squeal with the ferocity of a high school girl in her first relationship because it *was.* Drake remembered those girls from his days in high school. The only difference here was that there was no gaggle of them to gossip with her about him afterward.

Eventually, Drake pushed it all to the back of his mind and limited his time with her. It was ultimately a distraction at the moment.

Drake's hand went for the necklace he had just completed that was lying on the table.

Roughly Made Metal Chain [F-Grade, Common]
A necklace of metal made by a novice crafter.

The necklace was the hardest thing Drake had made so far. It was meticulously slow to link the chains together one by one, and he'd failed for an entire day until this one. It wasn't good enough to give stat bonuses, it seemed, but it did count towards his quest all the same.

Drake sighed and rubbed his hands together, trying to get feeling back in them.

"I should've just learned to pick flowers like Bear... This shit better be worth it. I could've just picked up a cooking profession... Wait, shouldn't I have already gotten one by now?" Drake suddenly thought as he spoke.

"*You are too good at cooking already. The system probably did not want to give you something so easy,*" Natto conjectured with a laugh.

Drake frowned, but he honestly wouldn't put it past the sadistic system.

"Well, only a few hundred more to go," Drake huffed, bending back over the work table.

The rest of the day went by much like the others. At lunch and dinner, he was pulled away reluctantly by Claire and Sherry. When night fell and everyone slept, Drake remained in the work tent with Lamar, pounding away rhythmically on his anvil.

He did leave periodically to check the surroundings, but lately, no one would dare enter the camp unwanted. Surprisingly, many of the monsters had either gone into hiding, waiting for the increase in tutorial difficulty, or they were amassing some sort of army again far off in the forest.

Drake was honestly hoping monsters would wander in; he'd been building up frustration in a number of ways lately and needed to beat the crap out of something.

But he digressed on most nights, instead returning to the workbench and slaving away to complete the quest.

* * *

"Finally!" Drake cried, holding up the last necklace in the morning sun.

It was his second consecutive week in the work tent, and Drake had hammered down on completing the quest.

New profession quest: Create Simple Metal Bands and Simple Chain Necklaces.

Quest completed

Accept rewards?

"Yes, dios ko!! Please give me my shit already!" Drake howled.

Congratulations! You have unlocked the Jeweler Profession.
You have learned system skill: Delicate Craftsman.
You have been awarded profession experience.

You have reached Jeweler Proficiency 2.
You have reached Delicate Craftsman Proficiency 2.

Drake reveled in the new notifications passing by his screen, shouting as loudly as he could.

His voice only grew louder as tools and a leather-bound book dropped in front of him on the table.

Low-Grade Crafting Manual [F-Grade, Uncommon]
Contains basic instructions for crafting beneficial jewelry in F-Grade.

Drake also looked over the handful of Mana-Infused tools that were laid out on the table, his eyes sparkling with thanks for the wondrous bounty.

"Thank fuck for these tools," Drake said, holding them up and looking over the descriptions briefly. "All of these are going to cut down the time to make things by so much!"

"Don't let the tools fool you. They're only as good as the craftsman using them, you idiot," Lamar said from the side, hammering away on the claymore he was working on.

"Damned party pooper..." Drake grumbled. He stowed away the tools.

His excitement rekindled, however, when Drake took hold of the Crafting Manual. His fingers flew across the pages, looking for a particular piece he was hoping to find.

"No, no, no, no. Nope, that's not it either... No, no, no—Ah! Yes, that's what I've been waiting for, baby! Woooo!" he shouted with excitement, plopping the book down as he frantically pulled materials from his inventory.

"Little bit of this, little of that, need one of these... Okay! All set!" Drake mused.

His eyes scanned the page once more to go over the instructions and materials needed, not wanting to miss a thing. He nodded to himself, double-checking everything to a T.

"Alright, I have enough materials for an almost endless amount, so that's good. The problem is I don't know how to make prongs for the gem. Well, those are just little thingies holding the gem, shouldn't be too hard, but making a halo with the other gems is going to be tough," Drake said, thinking aloud.

"Just going to have to muddle through it like always. Good thing we cleared out that mine before we came. Good job, past Drake!" Drake said, patting himself on the back.

"Bet you have not heard that often." Natto snickered.

"Is everyone cranky today?" Drake snorted and pulled the Mana Ore from the pile of stuff he'd brought out.

"I do crave violence on a daily basis. But no, I have not had the opportunity to talk for quite some time. You have been so focused on crafting that I did not want to interrupt," Natto conceded.

Why, that is very nice of you... Drake thought, a little suspiciously.

"That is why I have filled my time with the most embarrassing moments from your memories! And after two weeks, I still have not even cracked the surface. It truly astounds me that you can have such dark history! The thing with the aquarium and the butterfly? How did you manage to get your leg stuck?" Natto cackled.

Drake's face turned red.

Okay, that's not so nice of you... Please forget about that, I was a kid! I just wanted to keep the fucking bug in a big cozy place! Drake retorted.

"That does not explain why you had to use your foot," Natto stated.

I had my hands full with holding the thing, and my brother wouldn't help get the sand out of the aquarium!

Drake moved over to the forge to melt the ore down into a workable metal, his face turned into a scowl.

"What's your problem?" Lamar asked.

"Don't fucking worry about it!" Drake shouted. He stared at the ore melting, the usable metal sinking to the bottom and the impurities rising to the top.

"And the face on your friend when he walked in on you holding your bloody leg! Is there anything more funny?! He even said, 'Oh bad time?' before he left!" Natto laughed.

I get it, haha... That car ride was not fun. Not that I remember most of it, I was so drugged up. At least it was better than the time I broke my hand on the floor...

"No, no! Do not spoil that one, I just got to it!" Natto pleaded.

Drake pulled the cooled ore from the holder, then placed it onto his own new fancy anvil, heating it up again for a red glow before hammering away to flatten it as well as remove the unusable gunk that had risen to the top.

It wasn't anything funny. My brother and I had a fight. He wanted to smoke pot with his friends, and I tried to stop him, being the big brother and all. But I was the one who got yelled at in the end, and he went anyway. His friends were worthless trash that only got into trouble, Drake reminisced, his face frowning again.

I got frustrated and beat the shit out of the floorboard. The floorboard won. It was a really awkward conversation to have with my mother when she had to leave work to come to get me in the ER, Drake thought, giving a mirthless grin.

"That does not sound fun, but the guild master for your game chewing you out for being dumb was quite hilarious. I have never heard someone so upset that someone broke their hand and could not play from the injury. The man actually asked if you broke it on your brother's jaw at the very least! What a savage ape! I must meet that man!" Natto cheered.

Oh, I totally forgot about that. Yeah, Grumps was very crude but a great guy. Honestly, I hope we don't meet him. I don't want to get hit in the face for ruining that server first... Drake thought, trailing off.

"Alright," Drake said, just about done with his preparation for the necklace. "Let's get failing so I can get to the good part: succeeding. I needed this equipment like a month ago."

Chapter 35
Good News, Everyone! I Have Presents!

"**N**ow *that* is an accessory! Holy, if I ever have to make another one of these, it'll be too soon!" Drake exclaimed, slumping back in his chair and looking at the jewelry on the table, satisfied.

Mage's Necklace of Disruption [F-Grade, Rare]
The Mage's best weapon is information. This necklace encompasses the wish of every Mage by giving out false information at the behest of its wearer.
+15 to Intelligence and +10 to Wisdom.
Extra Effect: This necklace contains the power of the elements, disrupting the mana flow of the wearer. Identification effects will be impeded and results changed to the wearer's desired information. This does not affect Identification skills or spells above Rare Rarity or F-Grade Quality.

"Finally, some good equipment!" Drake laughed. "With all the other stuff we made with it, I'd say it's been a productive month!"

Drake looked at the new colored rings on his hands, their blue sheen glowing with a hint of red from the fire of the forge behind him. The sound of Lamar hammering away on something or another rang in the background.

"Are we finally done with this dreary place? I may have passed the time by watching your memories, but even your embarrassing black history is not inexhaustible." Natto sighed.

You really went through most of my past just like that? I feel like I should feel violated you didn't ask for permission... But eh, I'm sure I'll make more embarrassing mistakes, so it's whatever, Drake thought, shrugging as he swiped the colorful silver chained necklace from the table and stood up.

Drake felt the cool metallic surface of the necklace in his fingers before placing it around his neck. A screen interface popped up immediately after he did.

"Oh, that's new. It reminds me of the introduction. Hmm," Drake hummed, looking over the options. "Well, it looks like most of the options are pretty basic. I can choose from any of the basic classes and a few low-rarity advanced classes, or I can also just choose to block the information altogether... Good to know. We'll block it all for now, then deal with it when we get out of the tutorial when we need to spread more misinformation. No point in doing it now, since I assume most people know who I am and what I can do."

"Can we eat now? It is getting near dinner time; I am surprised Claire is not here with the small glutton to haul you off to the kitchen." Natto snickered.

Drake was about to respond before, as if on cue, the blonde and black-haired pair walked into the tent in sync.

"Speak of the devils." Drake snorted.

"Who's a devil?" Claire humphed, turning her head.

"I want my food, dude. It's like a *minute* after dinner already," Sherry complained.

"Are you still mad?" Drake asked Claire, ignoring Sherry for the moment. "I'm not going to apologize for prioritizing making sure everyone's safe. I made that very clear weeks ago. But I did just finish, so here." Drake smiled, moved behind Claire, and placed a necklace around her neck.

"Huh? What's this?" she asked curiously, her face blushing as she tried to keep her scowl.

"It's a vitality necklace I made while working. It'll make sure you don't get one-shot by anything unexpected, at least in the tutorial," Drake said, satisfied.

Claire turned her hand on the purple gem in the middle of the necklace's pendant.

"Oh, it's beautiful... Did you make one for everyone?" Claire asked hesitantly, knowing Drake cared for the group and would have made accessories for everyone.

"Nope," Drake said, waving his hand dismissively. "Yours is one of a kind. Has to be at least *some* benefits to dating the boss, right?" Drake smiled.

"Everyone else just gets regular rings; I have a set for everyone," Drake explained. He plopped several sets of rings into Sherry's hand.

Drake looked at Claire. Her brilliant blonde hair was slightly past her shoulders now, having grown over the past month of their 'break' from monsters and fighting. It glowed with a red hue from the fire.

The necklace was cast in gold, and the large purple gem was placed in a mana-infused silver inlay for a beautiful contrast with the overall design. Drake wouldn't tell her, but it was the best piece he'd crafted over the month and honestly the most intricate.

"Alright, time to eat! I also have to hand out all this shiny new bling I got everyone!" Drake shouted. "Lamar, you coming?"

Lamar didn't look up from his work, just giving Drake a terse grunt.

"Alright, don't take too long or there won't be any food left," Drake responded, giving the cyclops a wave as they all moved out of the tent.

After exiting the tent, Drake and the girls were met by a very tall red-headed man.

"Yo," Bjorn said. "Ready for dinner?" he asked, another person hiding a bit out of sight behind him.

"Yeah, I'm getting to it. By the way, do you need any accessories? I made enough for everyone," Drake offered, giving a smile.

Bjorn took a moment to think it over. "I could definitely use better strength equipment, but everything else is kind of useless for me, bro."

Drake pulled the strength rings he'd made from his inventory—not the ones he'd been getting from the gnolls. Drake's were slightly better, giving fifteen to each stat instead of the ten that the gnoll equipment gave.

"What about you, Chelsea?" Drake asked, addressing the woman behind Bjorn.

"I-I'm fine," she mumbled, not wanting to meet Drake's eyes.

Drake sighed and shifted his weight to his right leg, giving Bjorn a questioning look.

Bjorn shook his head. "She needs dexterity, vitality, and probably a bit of strength. Ya know: normal archer stuff."

Chelsea fumed and punched Bjorn in the side, but she ended up hurting her own hand rather than hurting him.

"Right... Since when were you two so close?" Drake asked, pulling the sets out and putting them in Bjorn's open hand.

"Dunno. I spotted her moping around, so I tried to cheer her up. Now she follows me around like a lost puppy." Bjorn laughed, pointing a thumb at Chelsea.

"Shut up! I do not do that! I just have nothing better to do until we get to the Ant's Nest!" she howled, her face blushing.

"Okay, that's for sure the real reason." Drake cringed, then looked over to Claire, thinking that she was also like a lost puppy.

Claire looked up from her necklace, meeting Drake's eyes, then realized what he was insinuating.

"I do not do that! Shut up!" she yelled.

Drake and Bjorn laughed together then walked towards the campfire area where they usually ate. Chatting a bit back and forth about nonsense, they all arrived at the campfire where the rest of the group had already gathered, ready to cook.

Drake scanned the area, happy to see the rest of the group accounted for. Even Julia and Megan were there instead of waiting until the food was done to come.

It had been a full twenty-seven days since Drake had decided to lock himself up and craft, only taking breaks to practice his martial arts and to cook. He'd also practiced his skills regularly, and he was able to make considerable progress.

Drake Wallen

Tutorial Alias: Shot

Race: Human [F-Rank]

Profession: Miner P5 (0%) [F-Rank], Jeweler P5 (0%) [F-Rank]

Class: [Unique] Elemental Miller Level 20

VIT: 322 (15%)
STR: 338 (20 +15%)
DEX: 280 (40 + 25%) + (40)
INT: 700 (15 + 20%)
WIS: 332 (29%)
END: 274 (20 + 20%)
Free Points: 40

Titles: First Blood, Two Versus One, One Versus Many, Monkey Slayer, Living on the Edge, Close Call, Dead Man Walking, Dual Class, Punching Up, Improbability, Rounded, Dog Hater, One-Man Army, Dog Killer, Battle of Attrition, First of Your Kind, Goblin Hater, Goblin Slayer, Murderer, Serial Killer, Well on Your Way, Highest Contributor, Vanquisher of Kings, Tutorial Forerunner, First of Many, Glory of the Patriarch, Expectations of the Host, The Dawning of a Tyrant

Drake had made significant progress on almost every skill, completing a majority of the skills that he could actively manipulate. Sadly, his other combat skills were slow-moving. His passive skills for the most part had been steadily increasing with little help from him, but only just recently being able to make a necklace to fully utilize his 'Fully Loaded' skill meant it had certainly lagged behind along with his other active debuffs that needed enemies to progress.

For some reason beyond them, the participants of the tutorial hadn't encountered a single monster within their area for several weeks. What was worse was that groups were going further and further out to find food as well. The upgraded beasts were becoming just as scarce.

From what Shigure had kept Drake up to date with over the month, people were becoming more and more apprehensive about the food situation—wondering if they had enough resources to survive the remaining time in the tutorial.

Time remaining until tutorial's conclusion:
65 days, 7 hours, 49 minutes, 4 seconds.

Drake wasn't concerned for his own group; he'd gathered enough food and resources from the goblins to last them well into next year. But if he was to share with the rest of the remaining participants, he didn't think supplies would last more than two months—if that.

It posed just another problem he would have to figure out. It was something they were going to discuss soon, as in today. Because Drake had finally finished his preparations.

"So, good news everyone!" Drake began with, hunching his back and pushing up invisible glasses.

"Oh, I know this one!" Tom shouted.

Jacqueline sighed. "No one cares, Tom."

"Hey, that's not cool." Tom frowned.

"Oh? Finally have your balls drop, yeah?" Jacqueline snickered.

"Now, now, children, not at the dinner table," Drake interjected.

"You're the last person who should say something like that." Megan scoffed.

"Maybe so"—Drake chuckled—"but regardless, this is more of a serious day. We need to go over who is coming with me into the Ant's Nest," Drake said evenly, looking at everyone in turn. "Oh! And I have presents."

Drake smiled and gave out a set of whatever he thought people would need for accessories. Receiving their gifts one by one, the air remained frank and casual.

"So pup, who do you want on this little treasure hunt of yours?" Hudson asked, raising one of the rings he'd gotten into the firelight.

"Honestly, I'd like to have everyone come if I could make it that simple," Drake said with a sigh, "but we simply don't have a support class that can extend the party limit, so we would have more than we could handle on the way. I'm confident I can protect everyone now that some of my skills have improved, but there aren't any certainties, and I don't want anyone to feel obligated to come just to put themselves in danger."

"My lord, this one would follow thee into the dark abyss if but asked,"

Theodore said as he took his set of intelligence gear. "May this one say it even goes without being uttered!"

"I appreciate that, Theo, but you have Harley to think about, and I want everyone to be willing to go after giving it some thought," Drake said, looking around again. "I still have to scout out the area myself, and there's still the problem of the food shortage that's happening. After what happened, I'm partially responsible for the people left in the tutorial, so I have to find a solution to that as well. And with the dwindling number of monsters that's been made apparent over the past weeks, I think there might be a real problem brewing."

"Why is that, Mr. Shot?" Harley asked as she put on her gifts.

"Well, I think everyone's noticed that after a certain time period or event, the monsters have increased in both power and numbers, right? Almost incrementally," he explained. Everyone nodded back.

"But," he said, pausing as his expression turned thoughtful, "after the Goblin King, we didn't see either. No increase in monsters, no new hordes, no upgrades to existing monsters. So either there's something else going on, or we have a big problem."

Everyone's face turned confused, not following the conversation anymore.

"You don't think that's where this is going, do you bro?" Bjorn said, chiming in.

"Going where?" Amir asked.

Bjorn leaned against a tent pole, the metal creaking under his weight.

"He thinks the monsters have gotten intelligent enough to band together and not attack us until we're weak from starvation."

"Is that really the case?" Julia asked, her face painted in surprise.

Drake took a moment, going back and forth in his head on whether or not to divulge what he'd refrained from telling the group about the King. Finally, he sighed and steeled himself to explain.

"When I was fighting the King, something happened I didn't expect," he began. "The King could speak."

Chapter 36

Planning the Nest

"What do you mean, speak? Like, ask you where the bathroom is?" Tom asked.

Drake gave him a side-eye.

"What? It's a serious question. Even I can ask where the bathroom is in a few different languages," Tom said incredulously.

"No, I mean that he fully understood what I was saying and even responded to me. He said some very concerning things, but most of all he was actually intelligent. At least enough to gather an army," Drake explained. "Honestly, he wasn't the strongest thing I've fought. The lieutenants and the royal knights were much stronger, but he was apparently the most intelligent if he was able to control them. Or perhaps sly is a better word. But my point is, if that worthless piece of shit can do it, what do you think ants are going to be able to do if they increase in strength and intelligence?" Drake asked.

"Oh. That's pretty concerning now that you mention it, bro," Bjorn said, nodding in agreement.

"I don't get it," Jacqueline said, speaking up.

Bjorn leaned back off the tent pole he was resting on.

"Regular ants already have a hierarchy or a command structure. Queen at the top, everyone else below protects the queen," Bjorn explained. "If they've increased enough in intelligence, that means their hive could expand and grow exponentially. Normally ants communicate through pheromones, but if they can now use speech or whatever else the system is able to offer the monsters, it could mean something far more devastating... Just think of how large a hive was from Earth before the system."

Some of the group's faces paled.

"We aren't certain it's going to be that large, but Bear's right. That's why I want to make sure of it by scouting ahead myself, and I need to make sure everyone who's willing to come along is going in knowing that it's life and death at all times. This isn't the same as when we were held up behind the safe walls of the outpost. This is nit and grit, taking the fight to them for our own profit. Anyone who is coming needs to know that," Drake said firmly.

Bjorn walked forward. "You already know I'm coming. Things seem to have settled down around here, so I think it's time to move on anyway."

"Then I'm coming too," Chelsea said without hesitation.

Wow, she jumped from ship Drake pretty quickly... Well, at least she isn't trying to sneak into my tent anymore. Drake snorted.

"I'm going to be going as well," Julia said from her seat next to Megan and Jacqueline.

Megan looked as if she had bitten on something sour, but she raised her hand after some hesitation. "I'll be going as well. I can't let them go with you without supervision."

"What, are you the camp mom now or something?" Drake laughed, finding her excuse rather childish. He snorted. "If you want to come to make sure your friends are safe, you should just say so."

Megan crossed her arms, huffing as she turned her head.

"Right, anyone else? I would like to make Amir and Hudson join at the very least; you're both valuable classes that need to be nurtured, after all," Drake said, turning to the pair.

"I ain't no fucking child, pup. Don't need none of your 'nurturing' bullshit. We ain't got much to do here but wait anyway, and I said I was coming a while ago. No sense in going back on my word now," Hudson said grumpily.

"I as well agreed to follow you, Sir Shot. And I intend to do just that. After everything you've done to keep us protected, it just wouldn't feel right to stop here," Amir added, giving a wry smile.

Drake smiled back. "It's okay to be nervous about it. I may have said I don't know if I can protect everyone, but that doesn't mean I won't die trying. Everyone here is family to me. We've been through more in these past months than most in a lifetime. So yes, even you, Jacqueline, I will protect with my life," Drake teased.

"Up yours, bloody asshole." Jacqueline sneered.

"Never lose that girlish charm." Drake laughed, then looked at the others of the group. "Tom, Sherry, Harley, Jacqueline?"

"I'm going wherever you go, dude, I need that food," Sherry answered lazily, her hand going to her stomach.

"Can't say that wasn't expected... Okay, the rest of you?" Drake asked again.

"I will go anywhere my love goes, so I am coming as well, Mr. Shot," Harley said, squeezing Theodore's arm.

Drake looked at Jacqueline.

"Are you mad? I ain't going nowhere near a ting like ravaging smart bugs by the tens of thousands! Count me out. I'll sit my pretty dark ass right here and wait." She scoffed.

Drake smirked. "Okay, you stay here alone then. You can cozy up to little Shigure. The same guy who doesn't like me or anyone who associates with me. Who also had most of the people around him turn on him, forcing me to kill them. I'm sure it will be a great sixty days for you," Drake explained, keeping his smirk.

"Yeah, but you already set him straight, didn't you?" Jacqueline asked, her face beginning to sweat.

Drake shrugged. "He's young, who knows."

"That's just bloody great innit? And you said I had a choice!"

"You do have a choice. But there's only one good one." Drake laughed.

"Fine! I fucking better not die, or I swear to god I'm going to shove my mace so far up your ass, it'll make you look like a bloody sock puppet!"

Drake laughed, looking at Tom now.

"Well?" Drake asked.

"Do I have to?" Tom asked.

"No, but you're going to be alone if you don't come," Drake admitted.

"But I hate bugs, man..."

"No one said you had to go into the nest. We'll probably set up outside after we clear out some space. I need you to protect the base of operations anyway."

"Do I get some of the loot?" Tom asked curiously.

"Yeah, sure. I'm sure there will be something for everyone. Don't see why not," Drake answered.

"Alright, I'm in then. I've seen how the people in the outpost look at us anyway."

"Tom, we all look at you that way," Jacqueline added.

"Yeah, but at least I know you all, so it isn't as bad," Tom explained.

"That's kinda sad, I'm not even gonna lie, Tom. But at least you're making progress; that's all I can ask. And don't mind Jacqueline. She only teases you because she thinks you're cute," Drake said, winking.

"You're off your rocker!" Jacqueline screamed.

"Why so defensive? It was only a joke... Unless?" Drake mused, wiggling his eyebrows.

"I lied! Come here, asshole, I need a cozy place for my mace!" Jacqueline roared.

"Now, now." Drake laughed, letting her hit him. Her strength wasn't enough to even scratch his defenses.

Eventually, Jacqueline gave up and Drake had finished asking everyone. He clapped his hands together. "Alright, now that that's over, let's get to cooking. Which I also don't understand what you need me for. Don't some of you have a cooking profession by now?"

"We do," Chelsea said, standing up as well, "but you just make better food. It's weird and unfair, really."

Everyone nodded in agreement, even the exhausted Jacqueline.

"That's kind of endearing... But please cook yourselves," Drake said, slumping forward.

"But we like your cooking, Mr. Shot. That should be a really big compliment. Your food is even better than the system recipes, even if they don't give the same buffs," Harley added.

"I appreciate the compliment, but I do have other things to do," Drake said, grumbling, but he still broke into a grin.

Drake was about to walk off to help with the cooking despite complaining, but Claire was staying behind and unusually quiet. He turned back and walked over to her.

"What's up?" he asked.

"You didn't even ask me..." she mumbled.

"Huh?" Drake said.

"You didn't ask me to even come!" Claire said, raising her voice slightly.

"What? Of course I didn't," Drake said matter-of-factly.

"Why? Are you just going to leave me here alone?!" she asked, concerned.

"No," Drake said. "I don't need to ask. If I'm going, you're going. I told you not to leave my sight; it's the only way I can keep an eye on you." Drake grinned. "So of course you're coming. Where I go, you go."

Drake gave a goofy smile and pulled Claire into him, his arms around her in front of everyone. Her face lit up like a Christmas tree.

"Ew, get a room!" Jacqueline shouted.

"Go talk to Tom, Jacqueline," Drake jabbed back.

"Fuck you!"

Drake snickered, letting go of Claire as she stepped back a bit, her face a deep shade of red.

"What, don't tell me you don't want to come?" Drake asked leadingly.

"S-Shut up, I'm going," Claire mumbled.

"Good girl," Drake smiled, giving her a pat on the head. He then extended his hand. "Let's go, then. Got food to cook and all that."

Claire nodded, but she continued to look at the very interesting ground.

"Hmm, we should really get some aprons. Love a girl in an apron... Well, only if the apron is the only thing she's wear—" Drake thought aloud, but he was cut off by a surprisingly strong grip around his hand.

Looking back, he saw Claire's face smiling, but the smile did not reach her eyes.

"What? I was going to say you would look good in an apron. Naked aprons are one of the things on my bucket list."

"I will not wear something like that!" she said firmly.

Drake smirked. "We'll see."

"I said no!" Claire shouted, running past Drake towards the table and finding a spot next to Harley.

"She is going to dump you before you ever start actually dating, you know." Natto snickered.

Maybe. But it's better if she knows about how weird I really am if she wants to actually date me. Drake chuckled.

The rest of the night went relatively normally. Food, jokes, laughs, and of course, making fun of Jacqueline and Tom. Everyone turned in early because tomorrow would be the day the scouting of the Ant's Nest began.

Theodore, Drake, Bjorn, and Chelsea were going to be surveying the area. They would not only have to find the nest and make sure it lined up with the map Drake had, but they'd also need to find an entrance. Once they had done that, next would be fixing the food shortage problem.

Drake had a few theories on why the food was so scarce, and many of them connected with the ants. If he was correct, he could kill two birds with one stone.

The morning came quickly. Drake had decided to actually sleep the night away as he'd been up for longer than a week now, hammering away at the crafting quest and the subsequent necklace that dangled from his neck.

He stretched as he saw the light bleed through the tent canvas, doing his best not to wake the snoring and drooling Natto who'd decided to occupy the pillow next to him.

"If only she could always be this quiet..." Drake thought aloud, going for the tent entrance.

Opening the canvas so he could walk through, the sun blinded him momentarily, forcing him to shield his eyes.

Once he wasn't star-struck anymore, he took in a deep breath, ready to start the long day.

"First, a chat with Mr. Teen Angst."

Chapter 37
Little Talking, Little Walking

"Good morning, Shigure!" yelled Drake, storming into the tent. Shigure grumbled, not even reaching for his weapon as he pulled the covers over his head.

"Rise and shine, stinky! I'm leaving soon, so we ne—"

"You're leaving?!" Shigure shouted. He pushed the covers off and leapt out of bed, running over to Drake and grabbing him by the shoulders.

"Y-Yeah... I'm going to be assaulting the Ant's Nest. Come on, man, we talked about this like a week ago." Drake sighed.

"Do you think I listen to anything you say?" Shigure said seriously as he released Drake, then walked over to the bed to begin equipping his armor and weapon.

"That's not something you should be saying to your manager. Haven't you ever worked before?"

"I'm seventeen; I haven't had a chance to work. I was going to get a summer job, but the tutorial happened." Shigure sneered.

Shigure had become much more coarse and casual with Drake over the past month, not particularly wanting to speak to him with respect or courtesy.

"Oh, I thought you were sixteen?" Drake asked.

"My birthday was last week. Don't you remember crashing the party that Uta had set up for me?" Shigure asked back incredulously.

"Did I do that?" Drake smirked.

"I hate you."

"It's okay, I'm leaving so hate me while you can. Anyway, about the food shortage you mentioned on your birthday," Drake said changing the subject.

"So you do remember!" Shigure yelled, pointing the end of his sword at Drake.

"I never said I didn't." Drake laughed and pushed the sword away from his face. "Now to business. I have to go scout the ants out later, so I don't want to waste any time. I think they are part of the reason the animals have become scarce."

Drake began explaining his theories with Shigure. The teen yawned but listened along, attentive enough to understand.

"So you are saying the ants ranked up?" Shigure asked.

"Not necessarily, but at the very least they are smarter and possibly larger than before. I killed a few juveniles before and still have the quest for it, and they weren't exactly a problem. But then again, the goblins had captured those ones and removed their fire sacs, so it's hard to tell," Drake explained. "But basically, I think the ants are the ones hunting the tutorial clean. So my idea is to wipe them out and hopefully the food will be fine then."

"And what if that isn't the reason?" Shigure asked pointedly.

"Then we have to survive somehow on what we have for the next sixty days," Drake said, shrugging. "Honestly, I don't really need to eat, is what I found out, or at least very little now after ranking up. It's mostly for the taste."

"That may be true for you and your abomination-worthy stats, but you are forgetting that a good portion of the tutorial participants left are just crafters and sub-level ten. They don't have the same physique the upper-level people have. They would starve long before the tutorial ends," Shigure said, sighing at Drake.

"We'll cross that bridge when we get to it. We can only hope I'm right for now and killing the ants solves our food problem. How much do we have left?" Drake asked, his face turning serious.

Shigure scratched the back of his neck, holding his hand out. The next moment, an inky puff of black smoke bloomed next to him, a hand with a clipboard appearing and handing it to him.

"Thank you, Uta." Shigure smiled.

"It is my pleasure, my master," Uta said, bowing and moving to the side of the tent.

"I have to see if Theodore can do that," Drake grumbled, holding his hand out open and palm up for a moment.

Nothing and no one came. Drake shook his hand briefly to cover up his embarrassment.

"*Moron.*" Natto giggled.

It was worth a shot. You have to admit that it would've been pretty cool, Drake thought.

"It looks like we have enough food for around two more weeks at most. Our stockpiles are fine, and everyone contributed enough up until the sudden absence of monsters that no one will have trouble using their points to trade for food," Shigure explained.

"Trade points? You have a point system?" Drake asked, astonished.

"Of course we have a system. How do you think people are able to buy anything here?" Shigure replied.

"Trading?" Drake offered.

Shigure grumbled, mumbling something like 'moron' before explaining briefly.

"No. There's only so much you can trade outside of non-perishable items. Sure the skill stones are worth something, but that is only for those who have the slots to use them. And any rare or better stone usually won't find their way to the market since people would rather hoard them or use them themselves. So instead, we have to have a point system based on what you contribute to the outpost. Food and perishables are a certain amount of points. Skill stones, weapons, armor, and services rendered are another. It took a lot to make this outpost work. Are you telling me you didn't have something similar at your own outpost?" Shigure asked.

"Nope. I just gave everyone everything," Drake said flatly.

Shigure slapped his hand to his face.

"How did you ever get this far..."

"Sheer grit, good looks, and luck!" Drake smiled, ignoring the insult.

"*I think you mean dumb luck,*" Natto amended.

I won't deny that. My skills are based on a random rolling system, after all. But credit where credit is due; while I did luck out, I did have to learn the skills and assimilate them. Not to mention actually survive until we got to that point... Twice I might add. Drake snorted.

"Why is it that the more time I spend with you, the more I despise you." Shigure sighed.

"Sounds like a personal problem. But is there anything pressing we need to deal with before I leave? Bear will be going as well, so you need to have all the security and defenses tight. Don't want another Adam happening," Drake pointed out.

"Bear is leaving as well... I see," Shigure murmured, pursing his lips in thought for a moment. "I believe we have all our bases covered, and I remain the strongest after Bear, so there should be no problem with people trying anything this time around. Are any of your own people staying?"

"Nope. Everyone loves me too much to stay." Drake chuckled.

"I highly doubt that, but that does make it easier. I've already placed and invested in the leaders that replaced the others you... *fired*, so there should be no problems outside of the food," Shigure said, reaffirming his confidence in Drake leaving.

"Oh, wait. Lamar is staying. Can't very well bring him into a hive of monster ants, though I do want to level him up," Drake lamented.

"That is not how that works," Shigure said wryly.

"Hmm?"

"Craftsmen—pure craftsmen classes and non-combat classes—gain experience and level through performing their work, whatever that may be. How did you not know this? Haven't you been with Lamar for over a month?" Shigure said in disbelief.

Drake quickly remembered the Farmer class he had seen during his rank-up, realizing that Shigure was correct and the description had mentioned a different way to level up.

"Well, the big man doesn't talk much except when he's insulting me," Drake said, chuckling wryly.

"Reminds me of someone," Shigure jabbed as he got up from the bed.

"Please, I'm the picture of a nice and respectful person," Drake countered.

Shigure didn't respond, only scoffing and walking past Drake to the tent entrance. He pulled back the canvas so he could go into the morning sun. Drake followed behind him out of the tent, Uta waiting until both had left the tent to exit as well.

"I'll be back by nightfall, so if anything comes up, just make sure to stop by the camp outside the outpost and tell me," Drake instructed. "You've done a good job building the outpost back up after everything, so I'm honestly not worried. Keep it up and you'll be going places once this whole tutorial ends, I'm sure."

Drake gave Shigure a clap on the back, harder than he should have, and pushed the young boy forward.

Shigure grunted in pain and scowled back at Drake.

"Oh, by the way," Drake said. He threw some jewelry back at Shigure—enough for him and Uta. "Happy birthday, you little shit."

* * *

Drake walked through the outpost instead of going straight back to the camp, wanting to see how the situation inside was for himself.

He was surprised to see how homey it felt inside, between the pop-up street stores on each side of the dirt roads offering this and that and the sections carved out for tents and even some crudely constructed buildings for the occupants to live in. There was even a small inn that was towards the center of the outpost that used points for admission.

Drake wasn't interested in how the point system worked, but he was interested in seeing if there was anything he could trade for that would be useful.

Moving from street to street casually, people made room for him, or at least most of them did. Many of the people inside the outpost knew who Drake was from his earlier escapades or had seen him rubbing elbows with not only Shigure but Bjorn as well.

Drake didn't mind it, and he also didn't mind the people who paid him no mind. It wasn't as if he needed to be given special treatment or anything. He was just casually browsing, after all.

After a bit of perusing, Drake found the shops he was looking for in the Crafters District of the outpost, a small stone's throw away from the center and towards the north end of the area.

Finding a rather short person, Drake walked up to the street stall, looking at the rings and various accessories laid out on the counter.

"Hmm..." Drake mused, inspecting one after the other, honestly unimpressed.

"See something you like, laddy?" the man said, the top of his head peeking over the counter.

"My, it is a North Rock Dwarf. That is interesting," Natto mused, seeing the man poke his head out.

A what? Drake asked.

"It is a variation of the dwarven race. They are found on a planet that is frigid and cold to the point that not much lives there on the surface. The environment is as hostile as it gets, and the monsters on it are even worse. Many of the intelligent races, if you can call them that, live underground in caves," Natto explained.

Oh... Where do they rank on the fantasy ladder? Drake asked.

"Below what your perception of real dwarves are? While they are skilled at crafting, they do not hold a candle to the real thing." She scoffed.

As Drake looked at the items on the counter, he couldn't help but agree.

"Not really," Drake answered, "but I was wondering if maybe I could trade or sell some of these." Drake pulled out the extra accessories he had made. They ranged from rings to earrings to necklaces of each stat.

The dwarf's eyes bulged when he spotted them.

"Where did ya get these treasures, boy?" he shouted.

"Made 'em. And have you always been a dwarf? I thought there were only humans in this tutorial," Drake asked.

"Yeah, found me an item that changed my race. Didn't care much though since I got to tinker with things," the dwarf said, dismissing the question. His hands went for the accessories in Drake's.

"These are for stats I haven't been able to come across yet... Where did you even get the materials for this?"

"Killed a bunch of gnolls. Why, is it rare or something?" Drake asked.

"Wouldn't say rare, but we haven't had much stat equipment come through here besides the strength and dexterity kind. Lots of the youngins want intelligence and vitality ones, and for good reason."

"Oh, why's that?"

"They don't want to die. And a Mage has a long cast time, so the stronger the spell, the better for the cost of the cast. Not sure what I can give you for this, though. It's beyond what I can trade for... Hell, I don't think most people can trade for this equipment right now. The monsters're all gone, and the animals too. No one is doing much of anything except waiting out the tutorial." The Dwarf sighed and handed back the ring.

"Hmm, how about this then. I don't have time to trade all of these. What do you say about trading them for me? I'll give you a 50-50 cut of whatever it sells or trades for," Drake offered.

The dwarf's brows raised in surprise. "You sure about that, boy? Seems like too good a deal to be true. And why me?"

Drake smirked. "Yeah, I'm sure, and is it bad if I say you just happen to be the first person I talked to?"

The dwarf snorted, looking at Drake incredulously.

"You're a dumb one, but it's a deal. When are you going to come back for your half of the loot?"

"It's what I'm told." Drake chuckled. "And I think maybe a few days before the tutorial ends, so make sure you get some good deals for me, old man."

Chapter 38

First Contact... Again?

Drake strode out of the outpost followed by some very lackluster stares after he had talked to the dwarf at the stall, but he was used to being looked at by the original residents of the outpost with some form of hate or fear after everything that had happened. Thankfully he wasn't *technically* in charge of the outpost.

No, he outsourced that to Shigure, and he had been doing a smashing job of it. Everything at least on the surface had been running smoothly, and Drake was frankly very impressed.

Kid might need a lot of growing, but it's surprising to see how well he can lock the outpost down when given the reins, Drake thought, passing the rampart of the outpost and waving as he passed the paling guards.

"It seems he is growing on you rather than the other way around. And your reputation is very poor amongst the people who have seen you fight the oaf and the weak-willed teen," Natto quipped.

I would never call Bjorn a weak-willed teen, that's just uncalled for, Natto, Drake thought, smiling.

"That is not—Ugh," Natto grumbled.

Drake chuckled and made his way back to the camp, seeing quite a few busybodies.

"So, are we all set to scout this place out?" Drake asked, looking at Theodore and Chelsea who were checking and double-checking their gear. Bjorn, on the other hand, sat relaxed on the ground, his claymore on his shoulder.

"These ones are as prepared as they can be, my lord. We have stocked potions enough to support a small army, thanks to Sir Bear," Theodore answered, twirling his mustache.

"Yep! He gave us all we needed for the trip, so we're just making sure all our gear is in order and waiting on Lamar to repair some stuff," Chelsea added.

Drake raised a brow. "Why are you so proud? Isn't Bear the one supplying everything?"

Chelsea's face turned red. She scowled and made a screw-face at him.

"My lord, could this one bother you to partake in said potions?" Theodore asked, taking a few steps towards him.

Drake raised a hand. "I still have plenty from the earlier quests, Theo, thanks. You guys keep them. I think Bear and I have enough vitality to manage. Which reminds me, you have a health regeneration skill, right Bear?" Drake asked, addressing him.

Bjorn waved his hand. "I do. Well, kind of. Remember the skills I told you about?"

"Yeah."

"The skill wraps them all up into one, pretty much. It's kinda crazy bro." Bjorn laughed.

"Oh, to be so privileged..." Drake sighed.

All three of them looked back at Drake incredulously.

"What?" Drake asked snarkily.

"Can you really say that?" Chelsea asked.

"I can say a lot of things," Drake replied, sticking out his tongue.

"My lord, I would be inclined to agree. Thou art the epitome of lucky and privileged by class and skill if nothing else," Theodore chimed in.

"Hey, whose side are you on, Theo?" Drake said, recoiling in faux hurt. "I worked very hard for my class and skills; I think I almost threw out my arm when I cast the die when I rolled for them," he joked.

"Hey man, I'm not complaining. I'm happy with what hand I was dealt." Bjorn smirked and leaned back until he fell onto the grass, his armor clanking slightly. "Most of it at least."

Drake could relate in all seriousness. He and Bjorn had been given great power, but that didn't mean it didn't come with cons. Bjorn was about to turn into a universe-ending giant, and Drake was most likely slowly losing his mind from the overwhelming number of skills he was consuming and still had to consume.

"Well, once we're ready, let's get to it. Earlier the better. I allocated enough time to be able to conquer the hive, but it's only speculation until we see it firsthand," Drake said, pushing the conversation forward. "I'm going to do some clowning around before we leave. It's been a while since I fired off some spells."

"Sooo, you're just going to do what exactly?" Chelsea asked suspiciously.

"I'm going to blow up stuff," Drake said flatly. He looked at Bjorn. "Come with?"

Bjorn raised his head from the ground, looking down his body at Drake through his legs.

"Sure," Bjorn replied, shrugging slightly.

"Alright. Where can a guy get some open land to let loose around here?" Drake mused.

Drake waited for a moment, letting Bjorn get to his feet.

"You know, for someone who can follow me at my speed, you sure move real slow," Drake joked, giving a snide grin.

"Hey, I'm conserving energy bro. You think this body can move like that all the time?" Bjorn threw back, smiling as he got to his feet.

"I just thought you were too big to move that fast unless it involved food or fighting me." Drake shrugged.

"You calling me fat?"

"I'm not calling you skinny."

"But I'm not skinny," Bjorn said, raising a brow.

"Exactly." Drake smiled.

"You're right, I'm large and in charge, bro." Bjorn smirked back.

Drake rolled his eyes. "Can't you let me insult you for once?" He laughed and moved past Theodore and Chelsea to the back of the camp toward the forest.

"That was supposed to be an insult? I thought you were complimenting me for my gains?" Bjorn laughed and flexed an arm.

"I wasn't—whatever. Now I really need to blow something up…"

Drake and Bjorn walked together out and into the forest, leaving Theodore and Chelsea behind.

"Did we just become invisible? You didn't cast your concealment spell, did you?" Chelsea asked, her face turning into a pout.

"This one certainly did not. It would seem that my lord and Sir Bear most definitely moveth at the beat of their own drums," Theodore said, pushing his broken monocle up.

Chelsea looked over and sighed. "You should really get Lamar to fix that for you."

Theodore nodded and picked up his cane while giving Chelsea a slight bow.

"This one bids you a lovely evening, Miss Chelsea."

Chelsea gave a wave as Theodore left, her eyes fixed on the backs of Bjorn and Drake. When Theodore was well out of earshot, she mumbled to herself.

"Why do all the men I chase seem so far away…"

* * *

"So, Bjorn," Drake started once they were finally away from the camp, "what's going on with you and Chelsea?" he asked, twirling Morning Glory around in his hands.

"Whatcha mean?" Bjorn asked innocently.

"Come on, even you said she's following you around like a little puppy. She's got the hots for the fire crotch now. Honestly, I'd say she's downgrading in her tastes," Drake said, giving a smirk.

"Oh, that's what you mean. Not sure bro. She's nice and all, but I'm pretty full up on figuring out how not to turn into a big world-eating monster in a few levels," Bjorn replied.

"Honestly I'm in the same boat with Claire. She's wonderful and a good one, that's for sure, and that's not even counting how well her class meshes with mine. But I have my hands full with everything. Doesn't feel right to be as committed as I want to be," Drake mused. He put Morning Glory behind his head, his arms hanging over the shaft.

"I think we're on different pages here. I don't have any interest in her right now, and if she has a thing for me, it's one-sided. I've never had time for relationships even before the system," Bjorn admitted.

"Yeah, well, she's persistent if nothing else, so be prepared for that." Drake sighed, remembering the whole situation with her, Claire, and Megan trying to defend her.

Drake and Bjorn walked for a good distance, both having sensory skills in one form or another and looking for an area they could relax for a bit.

But nothing ever went to plan, not with Drake there.

The pair's heads snapped in the same direction in tandem. Both noticed the beings entering their fields of perception.

"I thought we were having trouble finding monsters and food?" Drake said curiously.

"We were… Coincidence?" Bjorn asked, raising a brow himself.

"Has it ever been?" Drake snorted.

"Got me there, bro. Let's go see what trouble you brought on us now." Bjorn chuckled and pulled his sword from his back as he walked in that direction.

"Who says it's my fault?!" Drake replied incredulously.

"It's always your fault, bro. It's like part of who you are." Bjorn laughed.

"I resent that comment." Drake frowned and walked behind Bjorn.

I resent it as well! I am forced to be associated with you; it is not my fault you are a troublemaker! Natto spat.

I am not a troublema—Okay, I'm kind of a troublemaker. But it's not like I'm trying to be… Drake conceded.

"How does your sensing skill work, Bjorn? Can you see who or what it is we're walking towards?" Drake asked, changing the subject.

"Only if I get a line of sight on it. My skill gives me a detailed description of the person, their stats, and I can see through most concealments. And a few other really nice perks that I'm not going to tell you." Bjorn smiled.

"That's really unfair… I can tell where people or beings are, but I don't get anything like that. Maybe later my identification skill will, though. Wait, so that means this necklace I have is useless against you?" Drake asked, grabbing the dangling jewel on his neck.

Bjorn didn't answer, but he smiled.

"Man, that's fucked up… What did I work so hard for, then?" Drake grumbled.

"It's a legendary skill, so don't feel bad bro. It's not like everyone has one," Bjorn said, consoling Drake.

"That's true, I guess. What's the skill called by the way?" Drake asked casually.

Bjorn embarrassedly scratched the side of his beard with a gloved finger, hesitating to answer.

"Well?" Drake pressed.

"It's called Eyes of Heimdall…" Bjorn finally said.

"Like Norse mythology? All-seeing eyes, can't hide anything Heimdall? Keeper of the Bifrost in the movie, Heimdall?" Drake said, his mouth agape.

Bjorn chuckled. "I think so. What's yours called?"

Drake flinched. "It's, um, part of my Aura skills. It's called Tyrannical Aura," Drake answered, just as embarrassed.

They both walked silently for a few steps before they both began to laugh.

"How did we get stuck with such ridiculous skill names?" Drake snickered.

"The more ridiculous the name, the better the skill I guess?" Bjorn laughed.

Bjorn and Drake chuckled to themselves for a few more minutes as they closed in on the now-group of beings they were following. When they got to a reasonable distance, they both switched from their casual demeanors to the jaded fighters they had become during the tutorial.

"Aren't they a bit close to the outpost? How did they get away with not being found for so long?" Drake whispered to Bjorn.

"They have to be passing by; there's no way they would go unnoticed. Shigure would have heard about people going missing or spotting them," Bjorn replied, looking at the group of goblins.

"Are people just not bothering to go out anymore? What gives?" Drake grumbled, spotting a named goblin at the head of the pack. "Looks like there's one of the leftover Knights or Lieutenants here. They seem pretty geared up… Are they preparing to raid the outpost?" Drake thought aloud.

"Not sure, but it won't be hard to wipe out this many. Haven't fought a Knight before, though. Are they tougher than the lieutenants ?" Bjorn asked, pursing his lips.

Drake shrugged. "They're about the same, I guess. The Royal Knights were the *real* pains in the ass," Drake explained, remembering the fight with the King.

"So do you want to take care of them? I can't exactly keep racking up experience if I don't have to right now," Bjorn asked.

Drake thought momentarily, scanning the rest of the group of goblins. Like Bjorn said, it wouldn't be difficult to wipe them out, and Drake was looking for an excuse to blow stuff up. But he didn't notice any prisoners with the goblins this time around, and he was curious as to what they were doing here.

"I want to see what they're up to. I don't sense any single ones patrolling, so I don't think they have many scouts around, if any. I think we wait and see. Take care of any stragglers that cross us," Drake explained.

"Fine by me. I don't have anywhere to be for another sixty days, bro." Bjorn smiled, taking a seat at the tree they were behind.

Drake snorted and refocused on the group of goblins.

Now, what exactly are you green bastards up to?

Chapter 39

And the Chase Is On!

Drake and Bjorn waited patiently, watching the goblins busily prepare for whatever it was they were endeavoring to do. They were only able to fill the time with sparse, hushed conversation and Drake making goofy faces that Bjorn couldn't see behind his mask.

This is getting boring. We should have just killed them. Drake sighed.

"Did you not want to see where they could be going? There are more than one Knight that may have survived, you know," Natto suggested, a yawn accompanying it.

Of course. It would be a good idea to see if they know something we don't, but I've never been one to be very patient... Drake thought, feeling out the goblins with his aura sense.

"Yes, I know. You are quite the hothead and leap-before-you-can-look type of ape, but it is curious that the goblins have decided to set up camp here and prepare, is it not?" she asked.

Yeah, it is. But it's also boring. I came out here to relieve stress and let loose a bit. Not babysit little green monsters and a man three times my size, Drake thought, chuckling at his own joke as he looked at the sitting Bjorn across from him.

"What's so funny?" Bjorn asked softly.

"Oh, nothing," Drake replied.

"You're doing that telepathy thing with the little lady again, aren't you?" Bjorn smirked.

"Probably."

"Well, it's almost sundown. Really don't want to have to wait much longer," Bjorn lamented.

"Why, getting hungry?" Drake snorted.

"Yeah, I'm starving bro," Bjorn said seriously.

Drake stared blankly at Bjorn for a few seconds, blinking to help process the brutal honesty.

Chuckling lightly, he pulled some food out from his inventory.

"Here, this able to hold you over for a bit? I swear everyone I know just likes to eat." He sighed.

"Thanks, bro. And it isn't like I need to eat, I just like eating your cooking. Like have you remembered the last time you used the bathroom, by the way?" Bjorn asked suddenly.

"Um, now that you mention it..." Drake thought aloud, becoming a little worried.

Natto, that normal? Drake asked.

"*Yes, it's normal,*" she replied.

Wanna explain?

"*No, not particularly.*" She snickered. "*It is far more fun to see how it bothers you.*"

Drake's eyes thinned, and he pursed his lips, his face turning into a scowl. Shaking his head, he refocused on the situation at hand. Not that much was going on still.

The goblins had begun to slow down their preparations, and Drake was hopeful that they would be moving out soon, but instead, they waited.

Drake clicked his tongue, deciding to finally sit down against the tree he was pressed against.

"Looks like they might be waiting a little longer. Maybe till nightfall? That would make more sense if they're planning to ambush the outpost, but we should have been back hours ago," Drake mumbled.

"Ish fine, bro, I'm shoor everyone just assumed you got into more trouble," Bjorn said, scooping up the food into his mouth.

"Am I really that predictably mischievous?" Drake asked.

Bjorn nodded and stuffed another handful into his cheeks.

Drake sighed and cozied up against the tree. Making sure to keep his senses fixed on the large group behind them, he closed his eyes and rested for the moment.

* * *

Night had finally fallen. The torches of the goblins lit the surroundings as Drake and Bjorn both let out a yawn and stretched.

"They're finally packing up and doing something, huh?" Bjorn said, standing up and moving over to Drake's tree.

"Looks like it. Problem is they don't seem concerned with being very stealthy, so why wait until nightfall?" Drake wondered aloud. He felt the goblins begin to move and wander out of his Aura perception.

Drake and Bjorn waited a few moments longer as they both felt the goblins move out of the area. Even without their senses, the goblins didn't seem concerned with the torches giving them away as they continued to walk with the bright beacon-like flames.

"They're moving away from the outpost?" Bjorn asked, confused.

"Huh, would you look at that? Guess it was a good decision not to murderhobo them all earlier," Drake said, pleased with himself.

He felt Natto roll her eyes, but he skillfully ignored it, instead walking forward to follow the fires in the night.

The trio walked along, trailing the monsters for several minutes before the pack of goblins finally came to a halt.

"Oh, have we finally reached our destination?" Drake asked in wonder.

"Looking like it. Must be getting ready to do something; they're putting out the lights," Bjorn observed.

Drake and Bjorn watched with interest as one torch after another winked out and plunged the surroundings into pitch-black darkness.

"You wouldn't happen to be able to see in the dark too, Bjorn?" Drake asked hopefully.

"I got it, bro." Bjorn smiled, and his eyes flickered to an ethereal white hue in the deep black background.

"Oooo, I'm kind of jealous. Your eyes turn white? Mine only glow green, blue, and yellow."

"Can't win all the time, Drake."

Drake shrugged. "Ain't that the truth."

Drake fell in line and followed Bjorn, who had taken the position of leading them. His ability to see in the dark allowed him to navigate the brush as they slowly followed the pack of goblins.

He couldn't see what was going on with his eyes—though he was still able to tell where a sparse few of the goblins were thanks to his Aura—forcing him to rely on Bjorn. He followed the large redheaded man like a lost blind puppy.

"Feels like I turned into a lost high schooler. Maybe I should hold the hem of your shirt with my fingers, give you the total anime test of courage experience," Drake snickered behind Bjorn.

"What are you talking about? Just don't get lost. Wait, they stopped again, but I can't tell why because of the treeline," Bjorn said in a hushed tone.

After a few still minutes of waiting, Bjorn began to move again.

"Okay, they're moving. Let's go. Goddamn, that is a big pile of dirt..." Bjorn said in amazement.

Drake snorted.

"I'd agree with you, but"—Drake waved his hands in front of his face, a big toothy grin behind his mask—"blind right now."

"Oh, right." Bjorn chuckled. "Looks like they led us right into the Ant's Nest, or at least one of them... There's quite a few of these dirt pillars sticking out of the ground. Looks like they cleared some of the forest while they were at it."

A light flicked on in Drake's head.

"Are they going after the King's Hoard? That would make sense to wait until night then. I think I remember hearing that ants don't work at night and just return to the colony, right?" Drake thought aloud.

"Actually, you're the opposite of right," Bjorn corrected.

"Isn't that just saying I'm wrong without saying it?"

"That would be correct." Bjorn laughed. "Ants use chemical trails, so they're actually more active at night since more predators and other animals are usually asleep."

"Then why wait for nightfall?" Drake asked.

"Maybe they don't want to be seen? But the ants, if they're anything like the old ones, will be able to pick them out right away through smell. There are usually warrior types at the entrances screening the workers for everything."

"So the ants have stronger border control than most countries? That's kind of ironic." Drake laughed sardonically.

"Hold up, it looks like they're trying to enter," Bjorn interrupted.

Bjorn began to walk forward a bit, stopping at the treeline that Drake couldn't see. Bjorn observed the monsters entering the seemingly inactive entrance.

"That's weird... There's no traffic in or out of this entrance," Bjorn explained to the temporarily blind Drake. "There should be a constant flow of workers if the hive is active."

"Maybe they really aren't coming out at night?" Drake proposed, raising a brow.

"Can't rule it out now, I guess."

Bjorn fixed his eyes on the last goblin as it entered down into the top of the mound.

"Last one just went in. What do we want to do: follow or wait?" Bjorn asked.

Drake pursed his lips, thinking for a moment.

"Well, we scouted out the goblins and the Ant's Nest in one go. So mission accomplished there. And even if the goblins get to the hoard, we can just hunt them down, but I would lose the quest rewards... No, I don't want to go and risk it right now. There will always be other quests, and I've gotten quite a lot so far. Let's take it slow and bank on the goblins taking longer or failing. Time to go ba—" Drake tried to finish before he was interrupted by the sound of the earth splitting.

"What's that?!" Drake exclaimed.

"The mound is splitting open!" Bjorn replied.

Bjorn watched as the mound of dirt split down the middle. Some of the goblins that had just entered screamed and ran out of the cracks, not bothering to look back.

A moment after, a tidal wave of ants followed behind them, the sound of their legs scraping the ground and their mandibles clanking ringing in his and Drake's ears.

Drake covered his head, and Bjorn did the same.

"What the actual fuck! I hate bugs and their sounds, like there are literally thousands of them," Drake grumbled.

"I would say there has to be more! I think we're in for a really long couple of weeks, bro!" Bjorn said, still watching the flood of ants chase down and consume the remaining goblins without a problem.

"And that guy... That guy gives me the creeps," Bjorn added. He looked back at the open wound in the earth that the cracked mound had created.

Rasha Trikk
Race: Tyrant Ant - Royalty Prince
Class: [Epic] Ruler of the Nest Level 29
VIT: 538 (150%)
STR: 411 (150%)
DEX: 515 (150%)
INT: 373 (150%)
WIS: 254 (150%)
END: 605 (150%)

In the wake of the destroyed entrance, a bipedal ant cast in a humming glow of dark blue chitin armor looked back at Bjorn, its eyes flashing red.

The next moment, it gave out a loud guttural chitter as its head whipped back, roaring into the night.

Chapter 40

More Trouble Than It's Worth

"Where exactly have you two been?" Chelsea asked, her arms crossed as she stared at the two troublemakers coming back into camp.

"You know, this whole camp mom thing is getting out of hand. My own mom isn't even this nosey," Drake said, giving a tired sigh.

"Who said I was your mom? Do you know how long Theo and I have been waiting here for you two? We were about to go out and search for you instead of the Ant's Nest!" she answered back.

"No need for that. We already found it," Bjorn said evenly.

"What?" Chelsea replied.

"Yeah, we found it already, and it's big. Like *Texas* kinda big," Drake added.

"What? That doesn't even make sense. Texas isn't even the largest state." Chelsea snorted.

"Doesn't matter, their line is 'everything's bigger in Texas' and the internet never lies, so." Drake shrugged.

"My lord," Theodore interrupted, "if we hath found the nest, shall we depart with all due haste?"

Drake shook his head. "Nah, we have a slight problem," Drake began explaining. "Looks like there're far more and far stronger monsters inside than we thought. From what Bear saw from one of their stats, it's about as strong as him. At least stat-wise."

"I didn't say that; I said it had a lot of stats," Bjorn corrected.

"A lot of stats translates to strong in my book, and since we're screwed if it's as strong as I am, it has to hopefully only be as strong as you. Therefore it's about as strong as you are," Drake reiterated.

"Who says you're stronger?" Bjorn asked.

"I won the fight, didn't I?" Drake snorted.

"You didn't win. It was a tie, bro."

"Really? I canceled that last spell. You know what, never mind. Fine, it's very strong. Happy?" Drake laughed.

Bjorn nodded. "Okay, as long as we have that straight, you may continue."

"Right... So the problem is we have one ant that is *very strong*," Drake said, looking at Bjorn, "but that isn't the half of it. Rather, it's a third of it."

Drake looked at the quest they had both gotten since finding the monster, and it was indeed a problem if the ant was as strong as its stats said.

New Subjugation Quest: Subjugate the Three Princes of the Ant Hive
The Hive has grown to monumental proportions and, as such, birthed three heirs of the Hive. You must enter the Hive and subjugate the royalty inside.

Reward: Experience, TP, choice of Epic Grade equipment.

"This is the first regular quest we've seen that has flavor text, which is bothering me for one. And two," Drake said, scratching the back of his head, "the monster was level 29 and named. I expected there to be strong monsters, but this level of strong might be too dangerous for anyone but Bear and I."

"Doth my lord then expect us to waiteth here? Surely not?" Theodore questioned.

Drake pursed his lips, taking a glance at Bjorn.

Sighing briefly before answering, Drake turned back to Theodore. "That is exactly what I'm saying."

* * *

"No. No, no, no! I'm coming with you! You said you're just going to protect us anyway, right?" Claire pouted.

Drake looked at the rest of the group present at the campfire. He had gathered everyone to explain the situation, and it was going sorta okay?

"I did say that, but stop being a child. Plans change," Drake responded.

"I'm not a child. I'm angry and stubborn. I don't see how this changes anything. Can't we just stick together like we planned and go?" Claire asked.

Drake sighed. "It's not that easy. The Hive is filled with more monsters than we expected, not to mention they're stronger as well. There are three powerful ants already on the brink of ranking up to E with who knows how many more."

Drake paused for a moment, looking at everyone in turn.

"I simply don't know the extent of the monsters' capabilities and strength," he added.

"Seems like a shite plan either way. That bloody treasure that important?" Jacqueline asked.

"Yeah, what's so special about the loot in there?" Tom asked as well.

"I don't have any idea what's in there," Drake said honestly, "but we—*I* need to go in there."

"Why's that, pup?" Hudson asked.

"I'm glad you asked, my emotional support hillbilly!" Drake smiled.

"Your what now?" Hudson replied back, confused.

"Never mind. But the reason I have to go is because I need to keep up my growth. I don't know what's waiting for us as the tutorial progresses, for one, and I also don't know how strong the rest of the world is going to be coming out of their tutorials. The only measure I have against that is getting stronger myself. And seeing as these are the only monsters around right now, I don't exactly have a choice," Drake explained.

"That doesn't mean you have to go alone!" Claire interjected.

"It does if it means keeping everyone else alive. I won't put everyone near danger that I'm not sure I can protect you from," Drake said evenly.

"I make my own decisions, and I'm going," Claire said, glaring at him.

"Fine," Drake replied.

"I said I'm fu—What? You agreed?" Claire said, astonished.

"Yeah, Sir Shot, did you not just say it was too dangerous?" Amir asked.

"I did," Drake said, looking Claire in the eyes. "If you want to come along,

I can't stop you. But if you're coming along, that means I have to be twice as careful to make sure I protect you. That means I'm always looking over my shoulder, always having to think about if a monster is lying in wait to get at you. This isn't like with the goblins, like I said. And because of what we saw at the entrance, we can't even set up a base near the Hive. There are just that many of them. But if you want to create more trouble for me, fine. You can come."

Claire looked back at him incredulously.

"That isn't fair..."

"No one said it was," Drake replied.

"Then you expect us all to wait here and just await your return?" Julia asked, stepping into the conversation.

"Unfortunately, yes," Drake answered.

"That seems rather selfish," Julia stated.

"I'm not saying it isn't, but I care too much about everyone here to put the odds against us. And look," Drake said, his eyes going soft, "I'm not saying I won't come back when we have more information. I'm just saying that now it's too dangerous."

"But not too dangerous for you?" Megan scoffed.

"Yup. I'm a one-man wrecking crew." Drake chuckled and threw up a strong flex.

Bjorn coughed behind Drake.

"Okay, two-man wrecking crew," Drake amended, putting up both arms.

"Aren't you worried about something happening again? Ya know, like with Claire?" Tom asked, concerned.

"They would be stupid to try. After what I did last time, I don't think anyone would even entertain the thought," Drake answered.

"But there is still the possibility, ya idjit," Hudson said.

Drake smiled. "That's why we have you. Lots of guns to stop the bad guys."

"So we're supposed to stay in the camp at all times until you come back or, what, the tutorial ends?" Megan asked.

"Yeah, that about sums it up." Drake nodded.

"So you want to cage us?" Julia asked.

"Pretty much," Drake agreed.

"Fuck that, I'm going," Chelsea spat.

"Damn right. I'm going as well; I've been sitting on my ass here long enough," Hudson added.

"You're all being incredibly selfish right now," Drake said.

"Then why are you smiling, Mr. Shot?" Harley asked, laughing.

"I was hoping everyone would come regardless, but I thought I'd give discouraging everyone a go." Drake sighed.

* * *

The rest of the night was very relaxed despite the discussion the group just had. Eventually, the group was dismissed to sleep for those that needed it. The plan was to reconvene in the morning to assess the Ant's Hive and their plan of conquering it.

Drake was slightly uneasy for the first time in a while. Not because he feared for his own safety, but as a result of having more to lose now that he held the group dear in his mind.

He didn't want to see anything happen to any of them regardless of how some of them still held animosity for him. They had all been through a lot recently; the Goblin Horde was a great hurdle they'd all overcome, some going through more hardships than others, but each one had to carry the burden of suffering in one form or another.

Drake was aimlessly thinking and playing with his elements, the motion of practicing now deeply ingrained in him even if he couldn't advance his skills further at the moment. The mindless practice almost calmed his senses as it helped him focus.

"You could have just forced them to stay if you felt this concerned, could you not?" Natto asked.

"I could have, but I don't want to impede on their rights as people. It wouldn't sit right with me." Drake sighed, crushing and reforming a ball of water.

"Even if they could perish?" Natto added.

"I will do everything I can to not let that happen. But yes. I can't control their lives and how they want to live them. It's a weird feeling. Comforting to know they want to come despite the danger, but also frustrating they won't see reason for the obvious. I don't want to see any of them get hurt. So..." Drake mused, trailing off.

"*So?*" Natto asked.

"So. I'll just have to go Super, Plus Ultra, and the whole shebang to make sure everyone gets back in one piece. Shouldn't be too hard, right? It's only a couple of bugs," Drake said pensively.

"*Are you trying to convince yourself or I?*" Natto scoffed. "*It will be difficult, Drake. The ants' hierarchy is even more extensive than the goblins. There will be almost no end to their ranks, and who knows if one has reached E-Rank already. I advise you to also be cautious, if not abandon this altogether.*"

"You know I can't. There's too much I don't know about what's going to happen when we leave the tutorial, and too much you can't tell me for some reason," Drake said irritably, "so my only option is to grow no matter the risks. I've already proven power is everything when they took Claire. It just cemented it. There's nothing I won't do to protect what's mine. Not against goblins, bugs, or even this godforsaken system."

Drake gritted his teeth. His elements flared with mana briefly before he squelched them all.

Sighing, he moved to his bed and fell face-first into the comfortable sheets.

"Ha... I miss my bed. And my anime... and my minifridge..." Drake heaved another sigh, turning over and placing his hands over his head. "I hope mom and the others are okay... Wish there was a way to tell."

Drake needed no sleep, but he closed his eyes all the same—doing his best to let his mind relax as he waited for time to pass and for the sun to rise the next day.

Chapter 41

A Mother's Love

"**S**uesmaryosep, diyos ko… That lady was not nice!"

The woman shimmered into a brown bricked room, many others appearing in flashes of light around her.

"Jesus, holy god, what is going on?" she said in a hushed tone, looking around. She gripped the club she had gotten in her hand, her fist shaking ever so slightly in fear of the abrupt situation.

The woman was surprised to see people of every ethnicity speaking a multitude of languages around her. She could understand some of them thanks to her years of volunteer work across the world.

Turning her head to the sudden screaming, she frowned.

"What the fuck is going on here? Where did that stupid bitch put me? You answer me! Do you know who I am? I have an important meeting in an hour. I can't be bothered with this nonsense!" the man howled.

The woman saw the man grab a younger boy by the scruff of the neck, the boy terrified and shaking.

Her shivers from before vanished as her motherly instincts kicked in.

She surged like an angry wave through the crowd, running as fast as her four-foot-ten-inch length legs would take her. And they took her right in front of the boorish man holding the teen.

"What do you think you're doing? Didn't your mother teach you any manners?!" she yelled, grabbing the man's hands.

"Who the fuck are you?! Get off me, you old hag! Don't you know who I am?" the man shouted back.

"I don't give a *pucking shit* who you are! You respect your elders!" she growled, raising her cudgel. "I'll beat your ass like your mother was supposed to! Don't you know you shouldn't hurt children?"

"What?! Wait!" shrieked the older man, raising his hands up in his defense. "I'm sorry!"

But it was too late—the woman was set on punishing the man. But instead of bringing down her weapon like he thought she would, she instead pulled the man forward, bending him over one knee.

"Mmmh! I'll teach you, la loko!" she screamed, raising her hand, then hesitating as she realized she was using her open hand. "Where is my belt? Sige! I just use my slipper!"

The woman pulled her flip flop off her foot, holding it in a firm grip before bringing it down on the older man's bottom.

"Sige! Now you know who the puck I am! Sige!" she shouted again, bringing down the slipper. "Talk to me like that! Who the puck you are? Sige! Talaga ne puta ne damo! Sige!" she shouted once more, bringing down the deadly slipper.

"I-I'm sorry!" the man cried, his face beet-red in embarrassment.

"I teach you what is sorry! Sige! Hitting children—you should know better!" she roared, about to bring down another swat of the slipper, but she was stopped by a hand.

"Mom, Mom! Stop! The guy gets it!" the voice behind her said.

"Travis? Oh, Travis! Thank the lord you're safe! Where is your brother?" She beamed, getting up and forgetting about the man. She wrapped her arms around her son, tears filling her eyes.

"I don't know, mom, but we should search for him. I don't think Drake will be here... He's off in a different city, but Dillon was right next to me when we got—I don't know, transported?"

"What do you mean transported? We were kidnapped!" She scoffed. "I don't know who did it, but they are going to be sorry they ever messed with your mother!"

The boy sighed and shook his head, knowing his mother actually meant it.

Whenever it involved kids or her family, she was relentless, always picking a fight over hearing the reasoning.

"Mom, let's just find Dillon first..."

"Miss?" another voice said from behind the woman.

Turning, she looked at the boy she had saved.

"Aye ditto, what is it? Are you okay?" she asked.

"Yes, thank you very much... um?"

"Ah. You can call me Mrs. Wallen or Nanay," she responded with a gentle smile.

Chapter 42
Storming the Beach

"Wakey wakey, eggs and bakey!" Drake shouted loudly as he exited his tent, the sun just passing the horizon.

He continued to shout until people began to exit their tents. Some who needed sleep left their tents with groggy expressions, rubbing their bleary eyes. Others who had not slept left their tents with more subtle expressions, yawns and some light stretching.

"W-What is this wake up call," Chelsea grumbled, rubbing her eyes as she brushed her hand through her hair.

"It's time to get going! Ants aren't going to kill themselves, and we have breakfast ready!" Drake smiled.

"Breakfast...?" Sherry said in a zombie-like tone, her eyes suddenly brightening at the end of the word.

"Yup!" Drake said excitedly. "You get," he announced, pulling a bowl from his inventory, "porridge! And it's happy to see ya!"

Drake smirked and handed her a bowl of food.

"Really? How long have you been wanting to use that one, bro." Bjorn chuckled as he walked up behind him.

"Not too long. Okay maybe a while, I'll admit, but it's still a good one." Drake laughed, pulling out the real breakfast he'd prepared overnight. "Eat up quick, everyone. We have a long day ahead of us, and the magic school bus will only wait so long before Mr. Liz Ard gets angry."

"It's too early for this many references," Megan mumbled, exiting the tent behind Chelsea.

"It's never too early! And get used to it, you all decided to hitch your wagon to mine for the next 60 days. That means my jokes for 60 days, 24 hours a day, 1440 minutes, 86,400 seconds all day every day." Drake smirked and nodded his head, satisfied.

Megan's face paled. "What have we agreed to…"

"You really knew those numbers off the top of your head, bro?" Bjorn asked, taking a portion of the breakfast and sitting down.

"Nope, I had to count. Used all twenty of my digits—took most of the night." Drake smirked.

"I can believe it." Bjorn laughed.

"I was joking…"

"I wasn't!" Bjorn laughed even more loudly, an enormous smile on his face.

Drake snorted and turned to the latecomers who were trickling in.

"You all need to wake up faster, you missed my jokes," Drake said, disappointed.

"Oh no," Claire said sleepily. "Whatever shall we do…"

"Well aren't we cranky," Drake said with a smirk.

"I didn't get any sleep… Sorry," she amended, embarrassed.

"S'all good," Drake said. He walked up to her and brought her in for a hug. "You don't have to worry so much; I'll be there to protect every one of you."

Claire's face flared red as she blushed, her head nodding slowly.

"Y-Yeah…"

"Awake now?" Drake laughed as he looked down at her.

"Ugh, get a room. It's too bloody early for that hogwash," Jacqueline said, coming out of the tent.

Drake smiled and shot a ball of lukewarm water at her, drenching her head to toe.

"What the fuck?!" Jacqueline screamed.

"Oh, my bad, thought you wanted me to wash the hog." Drake smiled.

"I bloody loathe you! Suitcase-head looking, rubbernecking, insufferable cunt—" she roared, only to be cut off as she turned to go back into the tent to change.

Drake laughed. "So I've been told."

The rest of the group gathered relatively quickly and finished their breakfast before Drake rounded them up. The group was finally ready to depart a few hours after dawn.

Drake looked at them all, his face serious for once as he addressed them.

"Listen up, we are going to split into two groups. Only the essentials are going to be with me. That's Claire, Amir, Megan, and Tom," Drake began, looking at each of them.

Tom perked up, surprised to hear his name. He pointed at himself and smiled.

"Yes, Tom, I'll be *needing* you this time around to protect the supporters. So don't screw it up," Drake chided. "The other group will be everyone else. Theodore will be in charge, and Bear will stay as auxiliary support for the landing pad we are going to be setting up. First I will go in and clear as much as I can and gauge how many and how strong the ants are. I didn't plan to have everyone come at first, but that's changed and we are going to do this right. Once I've cleared enough of the Hive to confidently say we have good ground, I'll come back and we'll move further into the Hive."

"From what Natto has told me, this will be a battle of attrition like I've never seen before. I allocated around thirty days for this whole adventure, but it looks like it's going to take much longer," Drake explained.

"So what's the plan when we get there? Ya just gonna kill everything?" Hudson asked.

"Pretty much. We can't have Bear help actively unless he absolutely needs to," Drake explained.

"Why's that?" Chelsea asked, concern in her eyes as she looked at Bjorn.

Drake cursed, having to take the fall for his slip up. "I want to hoard the experience, honestly. And Bear has been nice enough to let me so I can catch up."

Chelsea snorted, crossing her arms, but she nodded.

"When we get there, I'm going to sweep the place. Theo, Chelsea, I'm going to need you both to scout the area. Let me know if there is anything dangerous around I need to flatten," Drake instructed.

They both nodded back at him.

"After that, I'm counting on you and your boys, Hudson, to set up a base of operations that we can work out of. I'll set up an earthen fortress, but the defenses are all up to you. Got it my man?" Drake explained.

Hudson sucked on his front teeth with a snap and nodded his head.

"No worries there, my boys'll take care of it. Haven't been up against no ant yet, but I'm sure we'll handle it smooth as a possum's backside," he assured.

"Everyone else, your job is to stay safe until we're done. The goal is the hoard, but I won't risk anyone's life but my own to obtain it. Even if I have to knock you out myself and carry you back here before I go do it," Drake said sternly. He looked each one in the eyes, making sure his determination to do so was conveyed.

Drake waited a moment for anyone to say their objections, but when no one did, he turned and shouted.

"Alright! Let's get this field trip on the road!"

* * *

After a few hours of walking, making sure to not tire out the people in the group who didn't have physical-type classes, they made it close enough to the ant's nest that both Bjorn and Drake were able to sense groups of beings in the distance.

"Alright, here is where we stop," Drake announced, turning to face the group. "Hudson, can you and your boys set up a perimeter? I want your drones scouting at all times while I'm gone," Drake instructed.

"Sure thing, boss man." Hudson nodded and began to summon his completed drones, his two Large Robot Bodyguards taking to the edges of the group.

Drake looked over to Bjorn. "I'm gonna get going; don't you go killing anything unless you have to, alright?" he said in a whisper.

"No worries, bro. I could use a little vacation." Bjorn smirked. "Don't go getting yourself dead. I don't want to have to go on a rampage and become a planet-eating super-hulk anytime soon."

Drake chuckled and gave one last look at the group before snapping his mask into place. His hair and tattoos flared to life, shimmering to a brilliant yellow hue.

"I'm off; everyone stay alert!" Drake ordered before taking a step in the direction of the ants in the distance. He disappeared from sight in an instant.

"Always so dramatic." Chelsea snorted.

"Really? I thought that was pretty tame for him, honestly," Tom countered.

Jacqueline scoffed from behind Tom. "Bloody simp."

"Hey! I don't want to sleep with the guy! I'm just being observant!" Tom yelled in defense.

"Could have fooled me." Jacqueline laughed.

* * *

Drake rushed forward, his aura picking up more signatures of what he assumed were the ants than he could make out. The sheer number of them almost caused their auras to meld into one large blob.

"That is seriously a lot of monsters," he said excitedly despite the number of them. "I guess they like being out in the sun? There weren't any out and about when we came here yesterday."

"I am not sure on the behavior of the ants, but that certainly could be the case. I urge caution; there are quite a few of them," Natto explained.

"A few? There has to be thousands just here on the surface." Drake snorted. "At least I can blow them up and hope it starts a chain reaction."

Drake continued to run forward, quickly bursting out of the treeline as he saw an ocean of red in front of him. He heard a sigh in the back of his head.

"Please do not tell me that was your plan..." Natto grumbled.

"Yeah, they have explosive sacs for butts, why wouldn't I think I could blow them all up?" Drake replied honestly. He touched down on the head of a Tyrant Warrior.

You have subjugated Tyrant Ant Warrior Level 24 [F-Rank].

Experience earned. 5,000 TP have been awarded.

New Subjugation Quest: Subjugate 3000 Tyrant Ant Warriors [F-Rank] Reward: Experience, TP, 2 random Warrior skill stones, and 20 strength pills [F-Grade].

"You imbecile, they are born with fire resistance! They have a fire sac; why would you think they would not be resistant to their own method of attack?!" Natto shouted at him.

"I don't know... I guess I thought about it like snakes? They aren't resistant to their own venom," he explained honestly, looking at his surroundings that had now turned into an endless sea of pincers and red carapaces. "Also... isn't three thousand a bit much? Did the quest adjust itself or something?"

Natto sighed once more but explained nonetheless.

"Yes, it would seem it has adjusted because of the influx of monsters. That should not normally happen. This tutorial is quite the anomaly," she mused.

"I don't think that makes me as happy as it should." Drake snorted and clapped his hands together.

"Yes, well, you have more to worry about than that for now. Drake, please! The ants!" Natto screamed, the ants beginning to convene around Drake.

"Huh? Oh yeah, I got it," Drake mused. He casually summoned lances of ice, and they began firing rapidly in multiples of ten in every direction as he walked forward, stacking up both experience and kill credits as many other quests began to pop up as he did so.

New Subjugation Quest: Subjugate 5000 Tyrant Ant Workers [F-Rank] Reward: Experience and TP.

New Subjugation Quest: Subjugate 1000 Tyrant Ant Nursers [F-Rank] Reward: Experience, TP, and 20 health, mana, and stamina potions.

New Subjugation Quest: Subjugate 1000 Tyrant Ant Foremans [F-Rank] Reward: Experience, TP, and a random piece of F-Grade equipment.

New Subjugation Quest: Subjugate 2000 Tyrant Ant Foragers [F-Rank] Reward: Experience, TP, and 100 various seedlings.

New Subjugation Quest: Subjugate 500 Tyrant Ant Reapers [F-Rank]

Reward: Experience, TP, and a random F-Grade weapon.

Drake continued to very slowly whittle away at the ants' ranks. After a few minutes, he was left unable to think as more and more flooded forward toward him.

Another half an hour later, he was forced to bring out his staff, in need of the regeneration and buffs.

An hour more and he was regretting not asking for buffs from Megan and Claire, having wanted to save them for a more urgent fight that could possibly happen.

One more hour passed and Drake had killed thousands, but his status was spent and there was no end in sight. He had begun to lose to himself. Not realizing just how many ants there truly were, he hadn't rationed his status appropriately.

"God damn it, there's just no end!"

Chapter 43

No End in Sight

Drake heaved a long sigh as he blew past another group of ants, his body beginning to truly feel the exhaustion catch up to it.

He'd been at it for hours, killing and killing ants to no end, and he'd already finished the majority of the quests that he had received. To his dismay, the ants didn't seem to be giving adequate TP or experience even with their substantial numbers.

"Fucking god damn it, they could at least give enough experience for me to level up! This is getting absolutely ridiculous!" Drake cursed. "If this doesn't end, I'm going to be forced to run."

"I think it wise to retreat and regroup for now. You've exhausted your mana several times already, and there seems to be a reason as to why the ants have not dwindled in number," Natto said, observing from within him.

"I don't want to back down and run from a fight... but I guess it's the best decision. I have to reevaluate how I'm going to do this if they're just going to throw endless monsters at me that are worth less than dirt," Drake spat.

He turned in the opposite direction of where his group was, putting Morning Glory back into his inventory as he pulled his rings from the same place, simultaneously slipping them all on.

His hair shimmered to a crimson red while his tattoos flared, coloring themselves in a bright red as well.

"I am the wall on which my enemies billow! Bulwark!" Drake chanted, boosting his defenses to their current limit through the skill.

"Time to make an exit!" he shouted with a grin behind his mask.

Drake dug in, bending down into a sprinter's form before roaring forward, destroying the ground below him as he shot off like a gun. He quickly plowed through the sea of ants, kill notifications piling up as he threw ant after ant to the side, punching through hordes of thoraxes and fire sacs alike.

Finally he was able to exit through the other side of the large dirt hill that acted as one of the hive entrances. He looked back. His entire body was covered in goo from the ants, the Fire Oil sticking to him like hardened grease.

"Ugh, how do I get this stuff off me? I don't exactly have soap. And it... Oh my lord! It fucking reeks!" Drake turned his head as far away from his own body as he could, his face grimacing.

"I do not know, but please remedy it. I can smell you from inside you, and I did not even know that was possible..." Natto whined.

Drake did his best to wash himself off using hot water, but to no avail. The sticky mess had somehow remained intact.

He sighed, reminding himself that he now had to be more careful with his fire magic unless he wanted to flambé himself. Raising his head from the momentary embarrassment, he saw the other towering Hive entrances in the distance.

Drake was unable to see them before in the dark of night, but in the midday sun, they were unmistakable and easily seen. He quickly counted five that he could notice from his position and gave a short whistle.

"Wow, no wonder there's nothing left in this tutorial. They have to be on the level of a plague of locusts at this point; I can only imagine how large the Hive is underground. This might take more than the time we have," Drake mused. He put his hand to his chin, then realized it was covered in sticky oil. He shook it off in disgust.

"Well," he lamented, frowning at his oil-covered hands, "guess it's time to make it back to everyone and come up with something else."

* * *

After a few more minutes of skidding around the angry mob of ants, Drake made it back to where he'd left everyone. He was embarrassed he wasn't returning a triumphant victor, but at least he was more colorful now and not dead.

"What in the world are you covered in? Oh my god, it stinks!" Chelsea yelled, pinching her nose.

"Yeah bro, might want to take a few steps back," Bjorn agreed, giving a chuckle.

"It's not like I planned on being covered in ant juice… This shit won't wash off. You got any potions that can do something about this?" Drake asked desperately.

"Naw, don't have anything like that, bro. Besides, I don't even think industrial soap could clean up that mess." Bjorn snorted and took a few steps back.

"Are you alright?" Claire asked, concerned, but she was also staying a few feet away.

"You too? You would let this rancid odor come between us?" Drake said jokingly.

"O-Of course not… I just have a sensitive nose," she replied.

"I have a sensitive heart!" Drake shouted, running towards her with his arms wide. "Come give me a hug!"

"No! Stay away!" Claire screamed, her face twisting in panic.

"Bloody weirdo," Jacqueline mumbled.

"What was that?" Drake smiled and turned to her. "You feel left out? Aww, come here Jacqueline!" Drake ran to hug her.

"AH! What the fuck is wrong with you? Stay the fuck away from me, you bloody wanker!"

"Don't be like that; we've gotten so close!" Drake shouted, laughing the entire time as he kept pace with her.

"My lord, this one believes you have chaffed quite enough. May we ask thee how the skirmish resulted?" Theodore asked, raising his now-fixed monocle with his hand.

"Right, right. But Theo…" Drake said, turning his head to the mustached man, "why are you so far away?"

Theodore coughed. "This one believes this to be the correct distance to be from their lord. To show utmost respect," he said, coughing again. "Yes. Respect."

Drake's eyes thinned briefly before he shrugged, having enough fun before needing to seriously address their dilemma.

"Right," Drake said, scratching the back of his head only to feel his sticky hair from before. "Ew... Anyway, it's not going as planned, to say the least," Drake admitted as he tried to scrape off some of the oil.

"Whatcha mean?" Hudson asked from where he stood next to one of his hulking robots.

"Exactly what it sounds like." Drake snorted. "I really underestimated how fast these things reproduce, or maybe they just had so much time since we were dealing with the goblins that they exploded beyond control. From what I saw while I was out there, there's a never-ending supply of the bugs. And their Hive is far more expansive than I expected."

"Any trouble with the monsters themselves?" Bjorn asked.

"With killing them? Not yet. I've basically been able to one-shot all of them, but the problem is there's so many that large area of effect magic would just exhaust me faster. Honestly? I've been having to fight in a way I really don't like the last couple hours." Drake sighed.

"Oh? How's that, Mr. Shot?" Harley asked.

"Well... Correctly...?" Drake snorted.

"What do you mean, correctly?" Tom asked, his face painted in confusion.

Drake moved his mask so he could smirk wryly.

"It means I have to use more standard spells and tactics. It's really very regretful; I spent so much time learning to fight just to have to fight hordes of monsters where it's essentially useless," Drake lamented. "But that means no large area spells, and I have to properly fight while weaving my spells. And close-range fighting might be out altogether, depending on how strong the monsters get later on deeper in the hive. There's so many right now that I can easily get surrounded."

Drake sighed.

"Which brings me to the next point," he continued. "I don't think I'll be able to bring anyone inside unless we can get to the bottom of why they keep sending endless monsters at me or how they're replenishing their ranks so quickly. Oh... Wait, I might have a solution, actually!"

"*No... Did you not just finish saying you could not do that anymore?!*" Natto shrieked.

I did, but that was past Drake. Present Drake has a more fun and better overall plan, Drake thought.

"*It is not better!*" Natto protested.

"Whan eggsagly are you planning?" Claire asked, coming back somewhat close to Drake. Her hand pinched her nose, making her speak in an awkward tone.

"Well"—Drake smiled—"I have two ways of going about it. One, I push through into the Hive alone and figure out what's going on by hoping I find the Queen or whatever is birthing these things so quickly," Drake said.

"I'm voting no on that one," Chelsea said, raising her hand.

"Same, seems like a good plan to get yourself dead, pup," Hudson echoed, also raising his hand.

The rest of the group began raising their hands as well, silently voicing their rejection of the first plan.

"Okay, since I'm apparently outvoted, " Drake said, snorting, "the second idea I had was big boom."

"What?" everyone said in unison.

"Ya know, big boom. Like kaplow, boom, large explosion, excessive amounts of serotonin," Drake said again, explaining with his hands and some sound effects.

"Oh!" Bjorn raised a brow, "*That's* your plan?"

Drake pointed to Bjorn, smiling. "Yep! I knew you would get it. Know me so well, look at you!" He laughed.

"I don't get it," Jacqueline said, shifting her weight to one side.

"He plans on blowing up all the entrances to the Ant Hive but one. That way they don't have as many ways to reinforce their groups outside," Bjorn explained.

Drake shook his fist. "He gets it."

"Are you a Shot interpreter or something?" Chelsea snorted. Bjorn shrugged.

"Well, that's the plan." Drake nodded.

Amir raised his hand. "What about just waiting until they all go back to the Hive? Didn't you and Bear say they weren't active at night?" he asked.

"Good question," Tom said, agreeing. "Why don't we just wait?"

"We want to whittle their numbers down as much as possible while also cutting off their reinforcements," Drake explained, "and we can't do that if they're all inside. By the way," Drake interrupted his thought to look at Amir, "everyone was able to get the notifications from here?"

Amir nodded. "We all got the quests and everything, but no one has leveled yet. It would seem the ants don't give much experience, sir," he reported.

"Yeah, I must have killed thousands by now, and I haven't leveled myself. Even with the experience penalty, I would've expected one level by now," Drake lamented. "What about the stones? I assume since everyone got experience, the stones were obtainable as well?" Drake asked.

Amir nodded, once again pulling up a screen as his eyes went distant for a moment. "You've almost filled my bags with them, sir. If it continues at this rate, I don't believe I can hold them all. Everyone will have to start carrying some as well," Amir said with a wry smile.

"Well at least the ants are good for one thing, then. Let's start giving a majority to Hudson," Drake instructed, turning to the surly young-old man. "How are you on materials for sentries?" he asked.

"After emptying that damned mine? You'd have to give me a few more lifetimes to get to the bottom of my bag, pup." Hudson smiled.

"Good, that's what I like to hear," Drake replied. "Start moving forward when I tell you, then," Drake said, throwing Hudson one of the communication crystals he had. "I'll let you know when I've blown up the entrances and gotten enough ground for you to start."

Hudson nodded. He held up the crystal to his eyes, then tested it.

"Can ya hear me, ya damned idjit?"

Drake snorted and gave a wry chuckle.

"Yes, sire, I can hear you loud and clear. It's like you're right here with me," Drake replied.

"Really like makin' it weird, don't ya?" Hudson answered back. He stuffed the crystal into his pocket.

"It's one of my greatest skills, just ask all my high school girlfriends." Drake laughed.

"You had girlfriends in high school?" Claire asked, her eyes thinning.

"Yeah, at least kind of. It's complicated."

"Why is it *complicated,*" Claire pressed.

"Don't fucking worry about it." Drake chuckled.

Claire puffed out her cheeks and crossed her arms. Drake laughed once more before turning, going toward the end of the treeline.

Before he dashed off to the ants again, he had a few things to prepare.

Quest Complete: 5000 of 5000 Tyrant Ant Workers [F-Rank]
Accept rewards?
Yes < No

"Yes, please!" Drake smiled, looking at the pending quests. "Always love new shit!"

Chapter 44

First One Down

Drake went through his quest prompts as he walked closer and closer to the Ant Hive. Surprisingly, he had completed all but one quest.

Subjugation Quest: 231 of 500 Tyrant Ant Reapers [F-Rank]

To his frustration, he still hadn't leveled up.

"This is pissing me off. I've killed like over five-thousand of these bastards, and all I've gotten are the title, some very scary sounding seedlings, and potions. At least this isn't bad..."

Drake looked down at the ring in his hands, its glowing red bloom pulsating gently.

Crimson Fire Welp Ring [F-Grade, Rare]
Made from the scales of the Fire Welp, this ring is infused with strength and enduring vitality. While the juvenile dragons are of no comparison to their adult counterparts, they are still a monster you would wish not face alone.
+40 to Strength, +10 to Endurance and Vitality.
Limited to one per hand.

He laughed wryly.

Great, another piece of equipment made from dragons. Is the system intentionally helping me piss them off? he thought.

"*Perhaps they are. The system thrives on conflict, after all,*" Natto surmised.

Drake sighed, but he had to agree. After replacing one of his old rings with his new and improved one, he double checked his status.

Drake Wallen
Tutorial Alias: Shot

Race: Human [F-Rank]
Profession: Miner P5 (0%) [F-Rank], Jeweler P5 (0%) [F-Rank]
Class: [Unique] Elemental Miller Level 20
VIT: 322 (10 + 15%)
STR: 338 (60 +15%)
DEX: 280 (40 + 25%) + (40)
INT: 700 (15 + 20%)
WIS: 332 (29%)
END: 274 (30 + 20%)
Free Points: 40

He was happy to see the raw increase in his stats, and he was still holding onto some free points for a rainy day. Drake could feel that he was most likely on the cusp of another level up, but the ants were doing anything but being accommodating to their guest.

"Maybe once we've cracked open the Hive entrances and completed this quest, I'll at least get a few levels. There's still a bunch more variants we haven't seen yet, and I'm getting impatient with just playing a hack and slash right now."

Drake finished looking at his status, seeing that he was comfortably topped off on his resources.

"*Before you begin, I must suggest you start holding onto the monster corpses,*" Natto said suddenly.

"Corpses? Why? I thought we couldn't use anything from monsters of this rank?" Drake questioned.

"*While it is true that it will not be the most profitable, you may use any monster remains. But the purpose for the moment is not the materials; it is the corpses themselves. Did you not read the seedlings' description?*" Natto asked.

Drake scratched the side of his face. He pulled one of the seedlings out of his inventory discreetly.

Man-Eating Fruit Tree Seedlings [F-Grade]
A plant that consumes the flesh of anything to produce fruit with nutritious properties. The seedlings of the Man-Eating Fruit Tree are quick to grow given the

correct sustenance. Planters beware, the flowers have an eye for all kinds of human flesh and may eat you.

Drake cringed slightly reading the description.

"Are these straight out of a horror film? This isn't going to turn into that one light novel with these trees, right? I have some RTS experience, but I'm no grand StarCraft II player. I only reached low gold!" Drake grumbled.

"No, you fool! These are just a larger version of a Venus flytrap. They eat anything within arm's reach to produce food and propagate. They can be trained to eat only monster corpses, at least so I have heard..." Natto admitted.

"You don't know?" Drake asked, laughing sarcastically.

"Of course I know! I know everything. I just do not believe you can do it," she said, almost making the sneer in her voice materialize.

"Well, that was just rude." Drake snorted.

Placing the seed back into his inventory, he walked for a few more minutes, the clearing coming into view and the chittering of mandibles entering earshot.

"Is it just me, or are there more?" Drake said, looking out into the sea of red.

"It is quite possible. Regardless, how do you plan on getting close to the first Hive entrance? Even with all your killing earlier, you barely put a dent into their numbers—let alone got close enough to the entrance," Natto said.

"Easy!" Drake smiled. "I wasn't trying to get there before, but now? I can just punch a hole right through them."

Drake first summoned a ball of fire. It quickly shimmered from red to blue, then from blue to white. Next, a ball of water began revolving around the fire. It shifted from a light, clear blue into a more green aquamarine. Finally, he summoned the last element he needed: a gust of wind that trapped both the fire and water inside, tightly packing them together so that they produced steam that desperately wanted to escape.

Looking like the kid in science class who'd just figured out how to make the assignment exciting, Drake's eyes curved upwards with his smile. He quickly pointed his hand forward, the ball moving with it.

"Always enter with a bang!" Drake shouted. "*Impact.*"

Drake chanted a single word, and the mass of elements turned and spun with such force that it began to suck in the air around it. The ants suddenly noticed the intruder and turned, but it was too late.

The condensed spell of magic shot forward, creating a temporary vacuum as it surged toward the ants, sucking in and displacing anything in front of it until it finally met the first unfortunate ant.

In the instant the ball made physical contact, a deafening boom rocked the area, throwing earth and ants in all directions. Drake immediately took position in a sprinter's pose, a ball of thunder materializing in front of him.

"I've always wanted to use this one." He smiled.

"*Oh god.*" Natto sighed.

"Don't ruin my fun!" Drake shouted. "*Gear, Second!*"

Drake roared his spell. The lightning disappeared, and his hair and tattoos glowed with a brilliant yellow vibrance.

The moment the magic was completed, he was off, stepping forward while the ground underneath him crumbled from the force. Drake shot off like a fired gun, a thunderous snap sounding as he roared forward and followed the devastation his spell had just caused, running straight for the enormous Hive entrance that towered over the area.

Drake ran through Tyrant Ant after Tyrant Ant, throwing one after the other to the side or crushing them underfoot. He used every element at his disposal in its most minimalistic iteration to kill anything in his path to the entrance.

"Move move move!" Drake shouted. He chuckled, happy to finally fight monsters again.

"*Are you enjoying this?*" Natto asked, concerned.

"Maybe a little bit, why?" Drake asked back.

"*You do realize you used to abhor killing, do you not? You are changing once again, and not in a way I thought you wished,*" Natto stated.

Drake flinched slightly, but she was right. Drake had never before enjoyed battle. The growth of his stats, sure, but killing in general? He didn't have a taste for it. When was it that he'd changed? Was it the stones or maybe the levels that he'd gained? Or was it something deeper inside him, that feeling that had been gnawing at him since his fight with the King.

Was there something more going on, something like what was happening with Bjorn?

Drake wasn't sure, and apparently, Natto wasn't either.

"I don't know, but I can't worry about it right now," Drake deflected. "These ants might be small fry, but you never know when the big fish are going to come out. I have to stay alert, so that's just something we'll have to deal with when we cross that bridge."

Drake rapidly closed in on the Hive, his speed unmatched by the ants he was trampling. Before many of them could even react, he was able to dismember or crush them underfoot. Those that did put up the slightest fight were silenced by a barrage of spells that left no room for them to even retaliate against him.

He was a fox in a hen house, and there was nothing they could do to stop him.

Within seconds, Drake traversed the area, reaching the first entrance on his list. Glancing at his status, he still had resources to spare.

"Good, now just a little fireworks, and we'll be out of..." Drake trailed off as he heard loud thumping coming from inside the entrance. He had cleared the opening of the hill, but he wasn't close enough to enter just yet.

Drake stood and watched as he saw and felt the rubble shift with what he quickly assumed to be something moving.

He looked over his shoulder. There were other Tyrant Ants moving about, but the sound was completely out of sync with them.

"This isn't going to be a T-Rex-type deal, is it? I already had it with the Vampiric Ape, so I kinda have some PTSD about it," Drake joked, shivering in faux fear.

He continued to wait and observe the opening in the hill as the steps became louder, the ground rumbling with more motion than he cared for.

"Can it just hurry up and come out... I'd like to get to the part where we fight." He sighed.

Drake's lament turned to hilarity quickly when what popped out of the opening was the small head of an ant, its beady eyes looking back and forth before it locked onto Drake. The mandibles on the monster clicked furiously.

"Awww, aren't you just the cutest li—Okay, you're not so cute," Drake amended as the walls of the hive began to fracture and the monster's mouth began to chitter louder and faster.

The monster was pushing against the entrance. And eventually, it pushed past it.

Tyrant Ant Guardian Level 28 [F-Rank]
New Subjugation Quest: Subjugate 5 Tyrant Ant Guardians [F-Rank]
Reward: Experience, TP, and 5 Rare skill stones.

Drake's eyes and head followed the ant as it pushed out of the entrance and towered over him.

"You know, the last guy who was taller than me ended ass-up on the floor. Wait, that didn't sound right... I killed him. I meant that I killed him, like with a spear and fire. Like pewpew," Drake said absentmindedly, miming with his fingers.

The Guardian was anything but amused. Its hulking figure stood nearly as tall as the Hive Hill, and its small head glared down—or what Drake took as a glare—from on top of its massive body.

The Guardian Ant had six legs like the rest, but its thorax was many times the size of the others, and its front two legs were at least five times larger than its remaining legs.

But Drake didn't fail to notice the smaller ants which were chirping behind it.

Tyrant Ant Mender Level 20 [F-Rank]
New Subjugation Quest: Subjugate 500 Tyrant Ant Menders [F-Rank]
Reward: Experience, TP, and a Rare accessory of your choice.

Drake raised his brow at the name he'd identified, but his thoughts were interrupted by the loud screeching above him.

Looking back up at the massive insect, its front legs were raised in a motion to come down on Drake.

Drake scoffed and stepped forward, the sound of the monster's legs crashing into the ground booming behind him as he moved in front of them through the first Mender he came in contact with.

Like before, the moment he did, the creature's insides and wonderful juices splattered and covered him.

"Ugh! This shit feels... Wait, it feels good?" Drake said, confused. He held his hands up.

Drake expected to be a sticky mess of disgusting innards and fluids once more, but instead, he was met with a soothing feeling from the fluid.

"Wait, Mender right?" Drake thought, pointing at the remaining nine in front of him. He then looked behind him. "Guardian," he said, putting the two together.

"He has solved the mystery! Hooray!" Natto shouted sarcastically.

"Hey, I learn." Drake snorted and turned back, quickly killing the surrounding Menders before the Guardian could turn its hulking body to defend them. "See? Killed the healers first this time. Learning," Drake stated proudly.

"Impressed with yourself, are you?" Natto snickered.

"Always." Drake smirked under his mask.

He turned to meet the Guardian Ant, the monster now noticing that its support had been killed in less than a few seconds. It shrieked in frustration and reared back its legs again.

"See, that's why you always protect the healers," Drake chided the monster. He summoned a ball of fire that quickly disappeared as his hair and tattoos shimmered with a crimson-red glow. Drake looked up, ready to meet the monster with his own punch.

"Heretical Attunement, Fire," Drake chanted, winding back his own fist as another ball of fire entered his vision. *"Normal Series, Normal Punch."*

Drake threw his fist forward through the ball of fire as it wrapped around his fist, meeting the two legs of the giant Guardian Ant in a collision of power.

The two beings connected for just an instant in what could only be called a pathetic excuse for a battle of power.

The ant stood no chance against Drake's overblown status and the subsequent buffs he'd placed on himself.

In the fraction of a second that their fist and legs connected, Drake overwhelmed the ant, blowing its legs clean off and punching a hole right into the monster's thorax.

You have subjugated Tyrant Ant Guardian Level 28 [F-Rank]
Experience earned. 100,000 TP have been awarded.

"You call that a normal punch?" Natto sighed.

"If it's good enough for a man in a mustard-colored leotard, it's good enough for me," Drake said, laughing loudly.

Chapter 45

Dattebayo!

"That should be enough," Drake said, looking back through the cracked entrance the enormous Guardian Ant had broken through.

"*I do not believe that this is a good idea. Are you not expending too much mana?*" Natto asked.

"I have to make sure it falls. Remember, this is a marathon to the end, not a sprint," Drake said, looking over his shoulder into the dark of the hive tunnel. "I don't like the feeling I get from this place, too..."

"*Afraid, are we? That is a first,*" Natto replied, surprised.

"It's something else. The hair on the back of my head is standing on its end, but I can't sense anything from my skills or aura."

Drake gave a quick shake of his head to remove the feeling, then walked past the large balls of fire he had placed all over the entrance of the Hive.

"I'm not going to like this. Whenever I hit empty, it feels like I haven't eaten in weeks and I have vertigo." Drake sighed and pulled a blue-colored potion into one hand, the other raised as he looked back at the entrance he had just exited.

"Time to make it flashy!" Drake smirked and popped the cork of the mana potion, his tattoo rings disappearing into his inventory as Morning Glory materialized above his hand.

Drake twirled the staff dramatically before slamming the bottom into the ground. The sounds of the sea of ants chittering behind him reached a new high as they tried to rush him from below the hill.

"The power of the sun within my hands, burn bright, illuminating the unworthy blasphemers that stand before you! Roar in your cacophony of great expanse!" Drake chanted, swinging his hand as if conducting an orchestra. He pulled his staff from the ground and finished with the last word, pointing it directly at the hive.

"Ex-plosion!"

Drake roared the final word, the sound of multiple thunderous explosions going off within the hive as cracks began to splinter all over the outside of the towering structure.

He turned to face the sea of monsters closing in on him, not bothering to look at the handiwork he knew he'd succeeded in producing. Downing the blue potion in his hand in one go, Drake threw the bottle to the side while his staff disappeared into his inventory.

Drake's Tattoo Rings then materialized in front of him. He spun around, equipping both in one smooth motion. The Hive crashed down in flames behind him as debris and wind pushed his clothes, the fabric whipping back and forth in the gusts.

His tattoos flared to life, cascading up his arm as he pushed mana into them. His hair and tattoos shimmered once more with a brilliant yellow as he changed to his Lightning Endowment.

"I will ask again: impressed with yourself?" Natto sighed.

"Come on, you got to admit that was a cool equip scene. The fire, the spinning, the flawless execution, then the changing forms!" Drake said, trying not to smile.

"Please just kill the ants. That is if they have not already keeled over from the amount of cringe they just witnessed," Natto said, fake gagging.

Drake smiled. He was happy to still be able to have some fun with Natto despite the foreboding feeling he had whenever he looked down into the tunnel of the entrance.

He quickly switched to a more serious demeanor. The ants were becoming too close for comfort.

"I have to store these, right? Think I have enough space?" Drake said, pointing to the ants.

"Yes, that would be what I suggest. I would not worry about space; you have an absurd amount as it stands. I do not think you could fill it even if you tried," Natto advised.

Drake nodded, her explanation good enough for him. If he filled up, he could just hand the corpses over to someone else for a bit. He had given out quite a lot of inventory bags to everyone.

The first of the ants finally reached Drake as he nodded to Natto's explanation.

"Time to put a dent in the population of ants here, then!" Drake laughed, and his arms flared with blue and red mana, his open-palmed hand extending to meet the ant.

The ant chittered loudly as it charged at him, but it stopped abruptly.

Drake smiled at the seemingly confused ant as it continued to try to push forward, its mandibles snapping angrily at Drake while the rest of the ants closed in around him from all directions.

"Has your mother ever told you not to play with your food?" Natto chided.

"All the time." Drake laughed and picked up the monster with one arm. His fingers embedded into the chitin armor of its head, small beads of green ichor spilling down its red outside.

Drake deftly spun around, using the monster as a club and slamming it into the surrounding ants. Eventually, the force of the spin launched the rest of the monster's body from both its head and Drake's hand.

Drake looked at the still clamoring head in his grip in disgust. "Ugh, I forgot insects did that..." He grimaced and summoned small balls of water around him.

"Almost summoned fireballs out of habit," Drake said nervously, looking at the tyrant oil not only around him, but still sticking to his clothes and body. "Just going to have to get more creative than destructive."

Drake willed the five balls of water to flatten and begin spinning. The water disks spun, slowly picking up speed until a low hum was steadily heard from them.

"Now for another collaboration," Drake said, smiling, *"Destructo Disk! Plus Spirit ball!"*

Drake stowed the bodies of the fallen ants around him, picking up both corpses and skill stones alike as the disks shot out, passing through ants left and right with ease. Rushing forward, Drake followed his spiraling disks of death, getting just close enough to the ants they passed through to place them into his inventory.

"So handy!" Drake laughed, keeping pace. "And reusable! I should use my water magic more often!"

Drake was making good time through the sea of ants, killing hundreds of thousands with minimal effort and mana expense. The large army of Tyrant Ants was slowly reaped like grain from a field.

The resupply of ants did not falter, but thanks to Drake destroying the Hive entrance, there was a forced direction to the reinforcements. His surroundings slowly began to clear—save for the insect blood and dismembered parts here and there.

Drake was slowly but surely pushing back the tide of the ants, clearing out a good section around the remains of the Hive entrance behind him.

He looked up, noticing a small flying object.

"Oh, looks like Hudson is keeping track of us. He really is a good guy despite how he talks." Drake smirked, pausing his onslaught for a moment as he pulled a crystal from his pant pocket. "Can you hear me?" Drake asked.

"Loud and clearer than I'd like. Looks like you been busy there, pup," Hudson answered through the crystal.

"You and the rest of the group can start moving forward. Tell Bear to be on his toes and have Theo, Harley, and Chelsea keep their ears and eyes open for stragglers," Drake directed.

"Sounds good, boss man. I'll let the big guy know," Hudson replied. The drone in the air zipped off in the direction of the group.

Drake stashed the crystal back into his pocket, looking up at the sea of monsters still before him.

Tyrant Ant Reaper Level 27 [F-Rank]

He looked over the line of monsters speeding forward past the rest, their front legs replaced with scythes and their chitin skeletons darkened to a navy-blue sheen.

"Oh, don't they look dangerous... I was wondering what they looked like when their quest showed up," Drake thought aloud.

Drake casually held his hand up, his water disks ceasing to spin and converging into one large ball of water in front of Drake as he placed his Tattoo Rings into his inventory. Once again, he switched them out for Morning Glory.

"Time for a little experimenting now that we have some time," Drake mused.

"*Heretical Attunement! Water!*" he shouted. The water spell coalesced around the staff, forming a large double-edged scythe.

Drake grinned behind his mask as he gripped the staff with both hands.

"*Witch Hunter's Crescent!*" he said with glee, shooting forward with the scythe in hand right up to the approaching Reapers.

"Let's see what this baby can do!"

Drake began swinging the large scythe wildly, using its large reach to compensate for his lack of technique. The blade of water connected with the forearms of the first few Reapers who'd rushed ahead of the others. The spell passed through the monsters in what could hardly be called a contest—the sharpness of the water was unmatchable by the beasts.

"Wow, that's sharper than I thought," Drake said, his eyes widening as the monsters instantly fell to pieces in front of him. But Drake didn't have time to admire his work, as he was soon swarmed by other ants.

Swinging his staff-turned-scythe like he was a spinning top, Drake used the momentum to bisect the surrounding ants. Their bodies hit the floor in squirming halves.

After a few more full turns of swinging his scythe, Drake planted his foot and embedded it into the ground. He shook his head.

"I'll have to practice that one. Interesting concept, though. I do wonder if my Weapon of Choice skill applies to magically made ones. Naw... that would be broken, right?" Drake hummed.

Canceling the attunement and endowment, Drake reformed his disks, this time using wind.

Wanting to diversify his options, he changed his Endowment to Water so that he could continue to use his spells while he helped clear out a section for his group to set up on.

"I don't need to overextend myself anymore," Drake said aloud. He glanced over his shoulder, seeing a good portion had already been cleared out around the collapsed entrance. "Now let's just take it slow and get some good ol' practice in."

Biding his time and stacking up kills for his weapon's unique buff for wind magic, Drake continued to clear out the surroundings. Every now and then he checked over his shoulder to make sure nothing was getting past him.

Drake moved methodically through the open area, wiping out every ant that moved too close and picking up and storing the bodies as he went.

I can just let everyone else pick up the skill stones at this point. I need to focus on making more room for now.

Drake had been going for several hours in total at this point, surprising even himself with his tenacity. He once again thanked his overblown stats. Suddenly, he felt people—or things—enter his sphere of aura perception behind him.

Taking a brief look back, he saw a familiar redheaded giant leading the way followed by the sound of gunfire from above as Hudson's drones let loose hell on the ants below.

Drake began solidifying his position and doubled his disks from five to ten right as a notification appeared in his peripheral vision.

100th Wind Kill Stacked

Drake pulled his disks back and raised his staff high above his head. The disks moved to his will, lining up parallel with the weapon.

He pushed more mana into the disks, expanding all of them until they became turbulent spinning blades of death that covered a significant amount of the area.

"*Futon! Rasen Shuriken!*" Drake roared. He wheeled his staff arm in a circle, the blades of wind increasing in speed until their sound overtook the chittering of the ants.

Drake threw his arm forward, the blades responding and snapping ahead, cutting down thousands of ants in their wake.

In only a few seconds, Drake had cleared out hundreds of feet of open land thanks to his staff's effect.

He pumped his fist as another notification passed his eyes.

Congratulations! You have reached Elemental Miller Level 21.
40 FP have been awarded.

"Hell yeah! Believe it!" Drake whooped.

"*Ughhhhhh,*" Natto screamed, grimacing all the while.

Chapter 46
He Is Not a Man, He Is Not a King, He Is a God!

"Let go of me, damn it!" Aono shouted, her eyes wild as she tried to wrench her hand from the man.

"Mistress, I cannot let you go out there and follow him! He has even taken that man Bear with him! This is certainly beyond us!" her guard chided.

"Who fucking asked you?! I watched him kill the King of Goblins! I'll be damned if I let anyone stop me from recording the greatest history in the making! I will be with my dazzling knight!" Aono quipped.

The man fell limp as he heard the words leave her mouth.

"B-But I thought *I* was your knight..."

Aono didn't even dignify the man with a response, instead taking the opportunity to run forward through the forest.

"I have to catch up with them! Oh, I hope I haven't missed any of the good parts!" she howled, pushing up her glasses as she sprinted.

Huffing and puffing with a small entourage behind her that she barely paid attention to, Aono tracked Drake and his party through the forest. She stopped only briefly to sniff the air like a tracking hound.

"Sniff sniff, sniff sniff," she said aloud as she pointed her nose to the air.

"Hmm, my knight seems to be low on electrolytes. He must not be getting enough salt in his diet... Oh! He is low in Vitamin K as well! Oh, my poor knight!" she lamented, licking her lips like she had just had a meal.

"Mistress!" one of the men said from behind her, breathing heavily. "Please at least let us protect you! We cannot let our one and only goddess be harmed!"

Aono wiped her brow, throwing the sweat to the ground, and sneered back at the man.

"You're only going to slow me down."

She quickly bolted forward in the direction she'd obtained Drake's scent until she felt the hair on the back of her head stand up. But it wasn't the same pleasant feeling she'd gotten when her knight had pressed his will upon her.

Stopping, she ducked behind a tree, peering out just enough to see who it was.

Sitting against the trunk of a tree, a huge red-haired man leaned against his massive sword, his eyes closed.

"Oh, is that…" Aono mused, pulling out her mana paper and stylus while snickering to herself. "Hoho, the plot is thickening."

She giggled, a mischievous sheen flashing on her glasses. Turning around again for a look at her subject, she spotted more of Drake's party.

"OooooOOoo…!" she screamed in a hush. "Is this the harem arc?!"

Aono quickly drafted page after page, looking at the people waiting and pacing around. Her eyes landed on a gruff man who continued to fiddle around with small machinery. "Yes, yes! It has to be this, doesn't it?! Wondrous! Simply, *wondrous…*"

Aono's hand sped across page after page, almost in a trance as her concentration became unbreakable. A line of drool formed at the corner of her mouth.

When she was finished, Aono wiped her mouth on her sleeve, a satisfied grin on her face.

"Oh no, no… We aren't done yet. Where is my wonderful shining knight?!" she reminded herself. She inched out behind the tree, carefully walking past the group to follow her nose which apparently had a Drake-dar.

A few minutes later of slowly navigating the forest, she came to the remains of ants.

"Ah!" she shrieked. "Oh, never mind, it's dead."

She sighed in relief until the head on the ground moved slightly.

"Ah! Okay, not dead! Not dead!" she panicked and ran off, passing it, but she was quickly impeded by a sea of red. Halting and hiding behind the tree-line, she tried to still her breathing.

A few seconds later, her posse caught up with her, sweating buckets and breathing heavily.

"Mistress, ha ha. I understand that he is important to your work, but your talents are not worth the risk," one of the group members said.

Aono scoffed and peeked out from behind the tree, her nose telling her that her prey—no, *knight*—was close.

After a few moments of scanning, she saw him.

Standing in front of a towering mound of dirt, he seemed to be waiting for something. Or someone.

Aono could feel it in her bones that something was about to happen, her Drake instincts telling her to prepare for greatness. Pulling out mana paper and preparing her stylus, she pushed up her glasses, ignoring the incessant nagging behind her.

What she saw did not disappoint.

The rumbling of thunder started to rhythmically strike, only to increase in tempo until Aono saw the walls of the hive crack and splinter. The feeling of something oppressive welled up from inside the hive entrance.

Then, a small head poked out of the entrance.

"Aww, cute," Aono cooed.

But it only lasted a second before the rest of the ant pushed out through the entrance, shattering the sides of the opening to reveal a massive hulking figure accompanied by two massive legs. It was built like a battle tank on steroids.

"Okay, not cute," she said, deadpan. She struck something from her mana paper.

She didn't take her eyes off her knight. Suddenly, he disappeared as the monster reared its legs up, attempting to bring them down on Drake. Only for the man in question to abruptly walk out from the entrance the monster had just exited, his body covered in green goo, but a satisfied look in his eyes.

Aono tilted her head, pausing for a moment as she tried to process what she'd just seen.

"He's... covered... in... slime...?" she said slowly, her brows rising with each word. She snickered as her stylus began to race across the paper. "Ohohohoh!"

Her enjoyment didn't stop there as she saw the monster ant raise its legs again, but instead of disappearing this time, Drake's hair changed color.

Her knight took a stance and pulled back his fist. His hair cascaded into crimson red. Aono's eyes widened, seeing Drake then use some spell to cover his arms in red flames.

"*Heretical Attunement, Fire! Normal Series, Normal Punch,*" Drake muttered. His voice somehow reached Aono, and she drank in every second, every moment of the scene, her hand never stopping as pages and pages of mana paper fell from her skill.

In a fraction of a second, it was over. Aono missed how, but in one moment the massive ant was whole, the next it donned a massive hole in its chest, its arms incinerated from its body.

"Magnificent..." Aono mumbled, tears beginning to form in her eyes.

Drake turned and entered back into the hive, but not before he put the corpse of the monster away.

"Where is my knight going?! I must follow, I must—" Before she could finish, Drake exited the hive once more, this time his staff appearing before him.

"*The power of the sun within my hands, burn bright, illuminating the unworthy blasphemers that stand before you! Roar in your cacophony of great expanse! Explosion!*" Drake roared, filling Aono's ears with bliss incomparable to anything she'd ever heard before. A smile crept across her face, her hand never ceasing to record the wonder in front of her.

The moment after, explosions and thunderous booms sounded in the area, the hive beginning to crumble as Drake spun. His hair changed once more, his staff dematerializing as he somehow brought out rings and equipped them in one smooth motion. The black flames from the rings turned into a wondrous yellow as Drake stood in front of the crashing Hive, his garb fluttering in the wind of the explosion.

Aono's lip quivered as she cried, her last stroke crossing the paper, completing her masterpiece.

"He is not a man, he is not a king, he is... *a god*!" she shouted through blissful sobs.

Chapter 47

Pop Up Fortress

Drake looked over his shoulder, his party small dots in the distance compared to where he'd pushed forward.

"Guess it's good enough for now; we have a bunch of stones to pick up on the way back," he said aloud, spotting the shining stones on the ground in the now-fading orange sun, the color like the flashing of car headlights.

Drake looked at the still-healthy sea of Tyrant Ants in front of him and sighed.

"It's going to take a lot longer than I thought to push them back..."

"It is very curious how they are able to produce such numbers. It is possible there is a variant queen in charge of this hive," Natto explained, proposing an explanation.

"Variant?" Drake asked. His hand moved in an arc, a disk of water slicing through another row of ants like he was mowing an overgrown lawn.

"Yes, it is the only thing I can possibly imagine giving these ants the reproductive ability we are witnessing. They should not appear in the tutorial at all as they are too much for an introduction, but after everything we have seen, this tutorial itself is beyond any standard that should be allowed. Whoever is in charge has bent many rules." Natto sighed, concern beginning to bleed into her voice.

Drake pursed his lips, conflicted on whether to feel upset he was thrown into an even harder tutorial than was the standard or happy that he was here and not his family.

He was glad that, at the very least, they would have an easier time than he was, and he had no qualms about getting stronger now that it was something he decided for himself.

The disk of water moved to stop next to Drake. He then crushed it, changing his current Wind Endowment back to Water to recover his status. Turning around, he shot forward, running toward the group in the distance and picking up stray skill stones as he went.

He arrived a few moments later in a burst of dust as he stopped a few feet away from them.

"Yo," Bjorn said, raising his hand.

"Yo," Drake replied. "Miss me?"

"Never," Megan scoffed as she put down a bag of something.

Drake ignored her, instead pointing to the bag. "What's that?"

Megan huffed and wiped away some of the sweat that had formed on her head.

"It's all the monster cores we can't carry because you've killed so many." She sighed.

"Oh? That many, huh? I didn't notice," Drake lied, whistling.

"Sir, there is simply no place to put them," Amir admitted, placing down a similar bag.

Drake chuckled. "Well, better than not having enough. Here. I bring presents."

Putting his palm face down, he began taking out many of the skill stones he'd collected. Tyrant skill stones, healer stones, warrior, fire, and new variations he hadn't seen before.

Subtree Stone: Hand-to-Hand [Uncommon]
Unlocks the Hand-to-Hand subtree branch.
Requires 1 open subtree slot and an unlocked Warrior main class tree.

Skill Stone: Assassin [Uncommon]
Unlocks a random skill from the Assassin tree.
Requires 1 open skill slot, unlocked Warrior or Ranger main class tree.

Skill Stone: Stealth [Uncommon]
Unlocks a random skill from the Stealth tree.

Requires 1 open skill slot, unlocked Warrior or Ranger main class tree.

Skill Stone: Sensory [Common]
Unlocks a random skill from the Sensory tree.
Requires 1 open skill slot.

"It was a good haul. Everyone look through and pick the good stuff up. I want everyone in tip-top shape while we clear out the rest of these Hive entrances. It's going to be a long couple of days."

"My lord, there art rare variety stones here as well. Thou art sure we may consume them after my lord hast done such labor?" Theodore asked.

Drake waved his hand. "Don't worry about it Theo, I'm holding out for better stuff. I'm a nice guy, but I'm not that nice. I'm selfish when it suits me; don't have to worry about that," he said, smirking.

"Who's a nice guy?" Chelsea asked. She bent down to rifle through the stones, but she didn't fail to give him a side stink eye.

"Me. I'm him. The nice guy," Drake said. He pulled down at his eye, his tongue sticking out. "I'm so nice, I'm going to build us a fortress."

Drake looked over to Hudson. "Hey, you ready to put up some pea shooters?"

"Idjit, I was born ready," Hudson huffed, crossing his arms.

Drake laughed, clapping his hands together dramatically before throwing them to the floor. He made a scene of his magic, the earthy brown circle expanding all around them.

"*Earth Make Magic! Grand Fortress!*" Drake shouted, the ground beginning to rumble around them.

The next moment, walls sprang upward and stairs formed to reach the ramparts that had just been built, a small gate at the bottom of one of the walls. Drake tilted backward, exhausted, his hands going to his head.

"Okay, moving established earth is still ridiculously draining..." he grumbled, trying to shake his head to dismiss the exhaustion. He felt a hand touch his back through his robes.

"Don't overwork yourself," Claire said, her face pouting slightly.

Drake chuckled. "This is light work; I'm just a little tired." He smiled. "How you holdin' up?"

Claire smiled slightly, her head tilting down and away from his gaze. "I'm alright. Just wish you didn't smell so... *potent*." She snorted, pinching her nose.

Drake raised a brow, and his face creased in a wry smile as he realized she wasn't looking away from him because of being embarrassed. She was looking away to pinch her nose.

He gave himself a whiff. "Oh man, this stuff is gonna stink for weeks, isn't it..."

Chelsea walked up to the pair. "Let's hope not. I don't want to go anywhere near those ants if that's what's going to happen. Do we have a plan to go out as well, now that we have a base getting set up? You aren't the only one who wants to level up, you know," she said, placing her hands on her bow.

"Eventually," Drake said, turning serious. "There's a few more things I want to confirm before I risk anyone else. I managed to close the first Hive entrance, but it took just about all of my mana and status to do so. So it's going to be slow going there," Drake explained. "Then, I want to confirm if the ants are going to be inactive outside of the Hive once night falls, but so far I haven't noticed anything different while the sun is setting."

Drake crossed his arms and looked around, the group's attention now on him since he had started explaining. The only ones who weren't listening were the grumbling and sleeping Sherry and Hudson, who was at the top of the earthen rampart and setting up sentry after sentry for their defense.

Drake quickly glanced at the tutorial panel before addressing everyone.

Time remaining until tutorial's conclusion:
59 days, 7 hours, 21 minutes, 44 seconds.
Remaining Participants: 1,907

"I want to continue with the plan of shutting down and closing the Hive entrances until there's only one left. Then, I'll be bringing everyone that can go in into the Hive and helping you all level up. I know I've been the main force so far, but we're closing in on the end of the tutorial here, and I want everyone to experience not only working as a team, but also the dangers you might all face once we're out. Not everyone is in the same area as I am in the outside world, so you can't always count on me until you find your way back or join up with another group. And I want everyone to be safe," Drake said, finishing his explanation.

"So…" Jacqueline said, chiming in, "we sit put, yeah? Fine with me, don't want to be smellin' like a pig's backside like you any which way."

"Really? I thought you would want the improvement, Jacqueline?" Drake smirked.

"I'll show you an improvement, you bloody clown!" Jacqueline shouted back, raising a fist up.

Drake soundly ignored her, their banter running its course as he looked up toward Hudson. Seeing that the gruff man had gotten a good amount of sentries down, Drake decided to focus on recovering after putting up the fortress. His spell had left him somewhat depleted, and honestly he just wanted to take a break for a moment to gather his wandering thoughts.

"I'm going to take a breather on the wall. Everyone can settle in themselves? If we need more space or rooms, you know where to find me," he said, making his way to the stairs.

Without a word, Bjorn followed him upward until Drake decided to stop just out of earshot of Hudson, who'd noticed them both but continued to finish putting up the defenses.

"You good, bro?" Bjorn asked. He looked out into the distance, seeing the ants still skittering towards them and slowly closing in.

"Never better," Drake lied.

"Come on. If I'm not allowed to fight, the least you can do is bore me with your problems." Bjorn smirked.

Drake didn't meet Bjorn's eyes. "It isn't a problem; I've got a handle on it. Don't have a choice but to."

Drake wasn't trying to act tough or stoic. What he was saying was the truth in his eyes. He didn't have any options right now other than 'being fine.' Whatever it was that was slowly scratching at the back of his head, corroding his mind and taking away his sense of empathy even past his Indomitability skill—he would just have to deal with it.

He'd made too many promises, and Drake intended to keep them all. Regardless of what it was doing to him currently.

Drake paused, waiting for a remark from Natto that never came.

"Little miss staying quiet?" Bjorn asked, not pushing his previous line of questions.

"How could you tell?" Drake asked, finally turning to Bjorn.

Bjorn snorted. "You get a small smirk on your face and your eyes go distant when you're talking to her. It's hard to miss, honestly. And you don't check your stats nearly as much as the rest of us. Surprised Claire isn't getting jealous with how much you talk to her." Bjorn laughed.

"Man, don't bother me with talk about Claire. Especially when you won't even go after Chelsea," Drake said, tipping his head back. "You and I can both tell she's burrowing a hole into the back of your head from here."

Bjorn and Drake stood quietly for a beat, both looking out into the oncoming torrent of monsters barreling down on their newly-formed doorstep.

"The monster we saw the other night," Bjorn asked, his tone serious, "did you see it while you were out here?"

Drake let the question sit for a breath before answering.

"No, but I got a bad feeling when I collapsed the Hive entrance," Drake said evenly.

"Bad how?"

"I don't know. It just felt like whatever was down there... was looking at me. Wanted me to come down there."

"Do you think it was the same monster we saw that night?" Bjorn asked.

Drake clenched his hand around the jet black earth of the wall. "No Bjorn, I don't think it was. And that's what's worrying me."

Chapter 48
Death to the Tainted

"Ram uu crux encii! Rap! Rap!"

"Oh! Poor soul tainted by the foul magic of this new world, may the sun cleanse you!"

A man stood over a kneeling woman, but she had the ears of a wolf and the tail of one as well. In her arms, she held another beastwoman, one with feline features and bright orange hair.

"May the sun purge your everlasting soul. Be blinded by that of the brilliant dawn! Giant's Dawn!" the man chanted, holding his arms wide as a glowing orange magic circle formed in front of him.

The pair of women shrieked in terror, both clinging to one another as they wept and screamed.

The next moment, a miniature sun formed from the magic circle. Instantly the heat in the surroundings spiked upward, a blaze of red hot flames singeing and charring the area. The searing spared nothing and no one as the grass, trees, animals, and the two women were burnt to a crisp.

"Ah! My lord is good, my lord is great! He gives me solace and power to do what is needed to cleanse this world. I thank him every day for the passion he instills in me to walk my righteous path," the man said, his face showing just how difficult he thought his actions were.

"By his will!" the man shouted. He turned around and spread his arms dramatically, his staff of pure gold in one hand. In the other was a ball of glass, a brilliant yellow and orange flame inside it.

"By his will! For the emperor! For our lord!" shouted the men kneeling in front of him.

The man smiled down on his believers, nodding his head as a tear fell from his eye.

"Bring the next abomination to be cleansed!" he shouted.

"Yes! Right away, my emperor!" one of the devotees replied.

Soon another beastman appeared, this time a man looking to be in his early twenties. His hair was blue, and his furred bear-like ears had streaks of silver on top of his head.

The beastman roared and snarled at the man even while constricted by the restraints around his arms and legs. He was forced to kneel despite his struggle, the devotees overpowering him.

"Kneel, beast! You are in front of the true leader of the Sun God's Devotion!" one of the men sneered.

"Now now," the leader said, his face soft and sincere, "we are here to help these filthy monsters. We are here to cleanse them of their tainted bodies and blood. By being cleansed in fire, flames, and the brilliance of our god, they shall be reborn. Remember that, my loyal followers. We are right, and we are helping these lost beasts find their way."

The men on their knees shouted in agreement, a loud cry and cheer sounding out.

The beastman, on the other hand, continued to struggle, fighting against his constraints as he bared his teeth and stared daggers at the man in front of him to no avail.

"Do not worry," the leader said. "It will be a painless passage. Do not struggle, for my god is kind." He smiled, his left hand raising with the crystal ball. "I will purge you of your disgusting form and blood. Worry not."

"In the light of my sun there is no shadow! May the world be cast in brilliant rays!" the man chanted, the ball in his hand glowing brighter with each word as a magic circle formed above it. *"Cleanse this darkened land, illuminate it with your grace! Bear your power in my hand!"* A ball of flames formed from the circle, condensing until it turned into a white hot dwarf star.

"*Guiding Star.*"

The man completed his chant, and the miniature star stabilized above the crystal in his hand.

"Open his mouth," demanded the leader.

"Yes!" replied the men restraining the beastman. They moved to wrench his mouth open with their knives.

The leader looked down at the beastman, talking to him one last time.

"May you be cleansed. From the inside out." His eyes opened, and his face twisted into a sneer as he thrust the sun into the mouth of the beastman.

The beastman roared in pain, his voice quickly burning out as he began to glow in a white light. The men holding him backed away.

In the next moment, the beastman began to tear and rip. His insides burned him alive with light escaping from the cracks and tears in his skin until he exploded in a cacophony of wondrous bright white flames.

"He has been saved!" the leader shouted.

"He has been saved!" repeated the crowd. "And so shall more!"

The man smiled. "And so shall more."

"All hail the Emperor of the Sun! All hail the true leader!" they shouted loudly, raising their fists and arms into the air.

"All hail! *Atticus Wallen the Grand Sun Mage!*"

* * *

"Haa..." Shigure sighed, looking at the reports on his desk. "These are all just complaints about the food. There is not much I can do to change it, unfortunately," he said aloud. "We still have plenty of food for several more weeks, but we have started to ration already. It is understandable that some people are unhappy with the change."

"My lord, perhaps we should go out in search of more wild game? The current hunting parties may not be going far enough out in fear of monsters and the like," Uta proposed from his side, carrying another stack of papers.

Shigure gave it some thought then shook his head.

"It has only been a few days since Shot and Bear's group left. I would like to give them a little more time," he explained. His face darkened. "There is also the issue of the people he brought in on the day he came."

Uta's face turned into a scowl. "You mean the criminals?"

Shigure nodded with a steely expression while he got out of his seat.

"Because of all the commotion, we haven't had time to deal with them, but now things have calmed down for the most part. And I hate to say it, but thanks to Shot I now have more agency to get things done," he admitted reluctantly. "No one questions the man backed by a tyrant…"

"Please do not say it as such, my lord! You are a great leader! What happened with Adam was… regrettable," Uta shouted, trying to console him.

"Uta…" He smiled. "Thank you, but I have to own up to my mistakes if I am to continue leading after we exit the tutorial. But enough of that. I should get going and deal with these criminals. The paperwork can wait until later."

"Yes, of course," Uta said. She bowed, shimmering away in a puff of inky smoke. Shigure exited the tent a moment later, assuming Uta was trailing him while concealed.

He moved through the outskirts of the outpost quickly, making his way to the other side. Passing through the outpost and greeting people along the way, he finally made it out the other end where they were holding the men and women that were branded as criminals by Shot.

Shigure greeted the guards who were standing in front of the wooden cages that Shot had provided.

"Good evening. Has there been any trouble with the prisoners?" he asked briefly.

"None, Lord Shigure!" one answered. "They have been treated humanely and given food as well as rights to use the bathroom and shower in private… Though some of them don't deserve it," the guard added.

Shigure raised a brow. "What do you mean?"

The guard coughed, getting elbowed in the side by the other.

"It's just… We've heard some of them talk. Some are bragging about what they did. And a few of the people that monster, Shot, brought," the guard said, visibly shivering at mentioning the name, "they came by asking when justice was going to be done, telling us about some of the things that happened."

"I see," Shigure said in a low hum. "Uta."

"Yes," Uta replied, appearing in a bowing position from a puff of smoke next to Shigure.

"Please find these witnesses. Bring one of the guards as well, then also bring several people who do not know the victims or the criminals," Shigure instructed.

"By your will," Uta answered. She stood and grabbed one of the guards, going back into the outpost with haste.

"What are you going to do, Lord Shigure?" the remaining guard asked.

"We are going to have a trial, one we should have had a long time ago," Shigure answered.

Shigure paced the cages, waiting for Uta to return. His eyes observed the men and women inside.

"Hey! You're the leader of this place, right? Please just let me out! I shouldn't be in here!" a woman cried out, her hands pushing through the holes of the cage.

Shigure recoiled, not used to seeing such desperate pleading.

"W-We will see. You were brought here by Shot, so you must have done something," he stammered.

"I was forced to! Please!" she pleaded.

Shigure turned, not wanting to hear her before the trial. Walking away and separating himself from the cages now, he moved back to where the lone guard was, waiting for Uta.

He didn't have to wait long. Soon she arrived with several tens of people in tow.

"I have brought the people you requested, Lord Shigure," Uta announced with a bow.

"Thank you. I did not expect so many?" Shigure said in surprise.

"Yes, there were many affected by the people who were captured. And many who wished to speak on behalf of those who were... killed and unable speak for themselves."

Shigure flinched at her words. He had expected as much, and he had dealt with these types of people before, but he wished for better.

"I see... Then, let's start. Bring out the first prisoner," Shigure instructed, his face clearly showing how uncomfortable he was with the situation.

He looked to the crowd that had followed Uta to the cages.

"We are going to judge these criminals today. I ask that everyone please be as objective as possible when laying down their judgment. Those who were brought here and are unrelated to the crimes, please move to one side. You will be given time to hear and deliberate for each case. Once this is finished, you will be rewarded for your time and honesty regardless of the outcome," Shigure instructed.

Shigure finished his instructions just as the guard brought out the first to be judged. He was a man of about twenty, if Shigure had to guess. His face was somewhat sunken from his time in the cage and the rationed food.

"Does anyone know this man?" Shigure asked the crowd as he looked at Uta.

She moved to him, pulling out the documents that held what every person had done according to what the man Theodore had told them when the criminals had been handed over. It included their names, levels, and what the perpetrator had committed or was accused of.

While he waited for someone to step forward, he flipped through the papers and found the individual's name.

Harrison Regan Level 12

Just as he did, a woman stepped forward.

"I-I know who he is," she said in a hushed tone.

Shigure looked pensively through the file, then steeled himself as he recited the accused crimes.

"This man is Harrison Regan, he is accused of aiding in the sexual assault of a woman during his time in Shot's outpost." He looked to the man first. "How do you plead?"

"Not guilty, damn it! I was forced!" the man shouted.

Shigure then looked over to the woman. "What is your evidence against him?"

The woman looked fearfully at the man being held by the guard.

"I... I'm the woman that was assaulted..." she said, her shoulders shaking. "Th-That monster and his friends tried to do something unspeakable to me! But Mr. Shot, he stopped them. He should have died with his friends, but he was on the lookout making sure no one—" She stopped for a moment, her voice cracking. "—no one interrupted. I still wonder why Shot didn't just kill him on the spot for what he helped them try to do!"

Shigure raised his hand, stopping her.

"I've heard enough," he said solemnly. "You don't have to relive that anymore; I'm sorry for what happened, and I'm sorry that you had to remember it," Shigure said, his face grim.

He hadn't realized just how bad some of the people in the tutorial had it. Was he just blind to the truth? Shot had told him many things, but he didn't want to believe any of it because he was the source.

The woman interrupted his thoughts, responding to his consoling.

"If you want to be sorry, then give that man what he deserves! He tried to take advantage of me! What they tried to do was unforgivable! My name is Gracy Morgan, but I'll never be the same Gracy after that. Why should he get away with that..." she said, sobbing.

Shigure opened his mouth to say something, but he couldn't find the words. Instead, he deferred to the makeshift jury they had assembled.

"You have an hour to discuss," he said, handing the piece of paper to one of the members. "This is his file; use it in your discussion. If you decide before the hour, you may announce your decision as a group. There are ten of you, and it must be a unanimous decision," Shigure instructed.

The man nodded and brought the file to the others as they moved a small bit away, discussing.

During the time, Shigure looked at the woman who had spoken, still in tears and body shaking.

He turned to the accused man, his face and body language showing just how much he didn't care for the woman. It instead painted the undeniable truth that he was guilty, and he knew it. His only concern was what he was going to do about his punishment, and it was obvious on his face.

The jury didn't even take thirty minutes to reconvene, the time passing quickly as Shigure became lost in thought.

Looking up, he nodded to the person they had chosen to represent their findings.

The woman took a step forward from the group. "We find this man, Harrison Regan, guilty on all accounts," she announced. She then looked to Shigure somewhat hesitantly. "But we are not sure what his punishment should be..." she said, trailing off.

Shigure took a step forward this time, his mind and body steeling himself for what he had come to a decision on.

I hate to admit it, but Shot was right... and now even as a temporary leader of this outpost, it is my responsibility to see justice done for these people under my care, he thought.

"His punishment will be death for his crimes. This is a cruel world we live in now, and there is no room for people like him," Shigure said, gripping the sword at his waist. "Release him."

Shigure motioned for the guards to let the man go, even throwing the man a spare sword to his feet.

"Choose to die like a warrior with a sliver of respect still remaining, or you can die like the dog you are painted as. I only give you this last service because you are a human and not a beast," Shigure said. His own hand unsheathed his sword, but an ever so slight tremble accompanied it.

Harrison looked down at the blade, then at the surroundings. He chose to run instead of face Shigure.

"A filthy coward till the end... You will have no quarter from me. *First Strike...*" Shigure chanted his skill, his blade painted in a red glow that hummed with power as he stepped forward, his blade bisecting the man. His corpse fell to the floor.

Shigure swung the blade, cleaning it of the blood as he sheathed it, then turned to the guards. His face looked as if it had matured several years.

"Bring out the next criminal."

Chapter 49

Wait, You're Actually Useful?

Drake swung his arms, trying his best to get rid of the guck that had begun piling up on them from the day. Looking at the Guardian he had just killed, he sighed.

"Ya know, I used to love these rings. But now? I wish I was a damn sword or gun wielder. The insect stuff sticking on my arms is getting on my nerves," he mumbled.

"The blood never seemed to irritate you before?" Natto questioned.

"Yeah, but that's one thing I never liked. But something about the insects gives me bad vibes, ya know? Call it a preference, but I'd much rather have red blood than this green goo..."

"I do not believe having a preference on blood is something you would originally have... Are you sure you are well?" Natto asked.

"No, probably not. I've been on a killing spree for about two weeks now with no sleep or rest," he said, picking up the body and placing it into his inventory. "Before I would probably deny it, but at this point I don't think I can hide it anymore. I've become numb to it all, but it isn't like I'm complaining. I've got a job to do right now, and as long as it stays that way, my failing psyche can sit on the back burner."

"Drake, you are not some battle-hardened veteran. A few months ago you were sitting at a desk doodling to make wage."

"You know, I don't appreciate you calling my illustrations doodles... I was pretty good at what I did," Drake grumbled as he set up a fire mine spell to detonate the Hive entrance.

"Regardless, my point still stands. You are not prepared for the life you have been thrust into. I will help you as best I can, but you cannot expect to be fine after taking as much life as you have in such a short time. Even with the skills the system provides, it will take its toll if you are not careful, Drake. I understand and agree with your decision to forge your path forward, but lest you forget who you are, you will turn into another oppressive dictator and killing machine made by the system once you reach the end."

"Wow, Natto, that was profound," Drake said, walking out of the entrance.

"This is not a joke," she admonished.

"Never said it was. I've always made mistakes as I went forward. I never said I was perfect. And just because there's some system here now spelling out a few things doesn't mean I still won't. We all have our problems, we all have our vices. Mine are just, you know, mental insanity from killing well over a few thousand bugs that may or may not have sentience," Drake said, waving his hand. The Fire spell behind him did its job of collapsing the last of the four Hive entrances he was set to destroy.

"When will you ever give yourself credit not veiled in self-loathing jokes. It does the opposite of being humble when it is every time, you know." Natto sighed.

"Coping. *Coping*, remember? I thought you were part of me; you should understand I bottle things up inside by now. Stoicism and all that. My problems are mine alone—I don't need to puke my mental state on everyone I see." Drake chuckled.

"You say that, but you really should share your troubles with at least someone, even the oaf would be fine at this point in time!" she grumbled.

"Natto, you are privy to everything in my head at all times whether I want you to be or not. I think that's good enough, don't you?" Drake laughed, walking down the hill.

Drake and Natto may have been casually speaking, but outside the Hive entrance Drake had just destroyed was a still very full sea of Tyrant Ants. All were more angry than ever that their Hive was constantly under attack.

Their party had waited until nightfall, anticipating that the ants would retreat back into the tunnels underneath during the dark. Unfortunately that was not the case, and every single ant stayed on alert into the night.

You have reached Elemental Endowment Proficiency 3 (MAX).
You have reached maximum proficiency with skill: Elemental Endowment.

You have reached Elemental Conflux Proficiency 3 (MAX).
You have reached maximum proficiency with skill: Elemental Conflux.

You have reached Weapon of Choice Proficiency 3 (MAX).
You have reached maximum proficiency with skill: Weapon of Choice.

Drake raised a brow as he looked out onto the sea of red in front of him.

"Nice, some skill ups, but I don't really have anything to select for weapon of choice... I only use the rings and my staff, so I guess we put it on hold for now," Drake said, some of the skill upgrades tasting bittersweet. "Now I just have to get back to everyone else."

Drake looked back, his way blocked by a few Tyrant Ants that had filled in the opening he'd made to get to the entrance.

"*We are not done with our discussion, Drake,*" Natto said firmly.

"We are for *now*. Seriously, I'll deal with it after the tutorial is over. I'll last another couple weeks; we don't have time to waste about the voices in my head," he joked.

"*You have voices in your head other than I?*" Natto asked seriously.

Drake coughed and ran forward, breaking through the Tyrant Ants.

"*Drake! Drake I am talking to you, ape!*" Natto yelled.

I'm busy! Drake thought, throwing an ant to the side as he made his way to the group's fortress.

It wasn't as if Drake didn't want to talk to Natto about his problems. In fact, he would like nothing more than to dump his mental payload on anyone he could. He had been feeling an ache that he couldn't get rid of for quite some time now.

Thankfully, it wasn't the voices he had joked about, but it might as well have been. And they could still be on their way if he was being honest.

It had started when he ranked up and began taking in skill stones, but if Drake had to say, he noticed it the most when the Goblin Invasion began. He was becoming more and more cold to the feeling of taking life, but not only that, he was actively enjoying the thrill of fighting, of getting stronger.

Drake remembered the words Bjorn had said and cursed inwardly as it made more sense now. Drake couldn't fathom just how much mental fortitude it took for Bjorn to stay sane, assuming the effects were that much more with two legendary skill stones.

But the time Drake had given into the feeling, the urge, was when he fought the King. Seeing such a monster of complete and utter low quality put on the title of King, one who was supposed to be above all else, had lit something instinctive in Drake. Something that wasn't there before.

Drake shook his head, pushing it to the back of his mind since he had just arrived back at their base.

"All done?" Bjorn asked, greeting him at the fortress wall with a wave.

"Pretty much," Drake said, giving a wry grin. "The ants keep coming, but for now all we have to worry about is the last entrance and the one direction for their reinforcements. I'm concerned, though."

"About?" Bjorn asked.

"Well, one about this nagging voice in my head." Drake smiled.

"Fuck you! Fine, go insane! See if I care!" Natto shouted.

"And about the ant we saw that night. I haven't noticed it at all since we came here, and it doesn't make sense. Wouldn't it want to defend its territory or just fight us in general?" Drake pondered aloud.

"Voice in your head, huh?" Bjorn mumbled. "You treating that young lady right, bro?" Bjorn asked.

"Yeah, of course," Drake said flatly.

"No he is not!" Natto answered in Drake's head.

Bjorn looked at Drake skeptically, but he moved forward with the conversation.

"I'm not sure either," Bjorn answered, shrugging his extremely large shoulders. "I haven't seen or noticed anything on our end. There've been a few strays that found us early on, but nothing even close to the level we saw."

Drake crossed his arms thoughtfully before sighing. "Guess we can only prepare and move forward then. But that's good timing; I left the last Guardian for everyone to practice against."

"Practice?" a voice asked behind Bjorn.

Drake smiled mischievously. "Oh, Tom! Yes, practice." Drake snickered.

* * *

"This is not practice!" Tom screamed. "Do you enjoy putting me through shit like this, you maniac?!"

Drake stood behind Tom, making sure he was actually fine, but he only stepped in if he was becoming overwhelmed.

"Would it make you feel better if I said yes?" Drake laughed, throwing an ice shard into the head of an ant sneaking up behind Tom.

"No! Ah! Don't bite that, you red bastard!" Tom shouted, throwing his shield into the head of an ant that was gnawing on his leg.

"Shouldn't we help?" Claire asked next to Drake.

"In a bit. I won't let him get seriously hurt. I need to regauge how well he can deal with large numbers before we go down into the tunnel," Drake said, not taking his eyes off Tom in case he needed to step in.

"Why's that, Mr. Shot?" Harley asked as she walked up to them.

"Well," Drake said, throwing another ice shard out, "we can think of the hive as basically a large system of tunnels. So if Tom, the party's main tank, can deal with the amount of monsters here, he should theoretically be able to handle the ones in the tunnels when they're only coming from one direction and have limited access to him."

"Is that why you're killing all the ants that are attacking him from behind?" Claire asked, looking on.

"Yep. I want him to get comfortable with leaving his back to his support, which will be all of you and me, of course. But for the purpose of this—we'll call it dungeon dive—it'll be everyone else," Drake answered.

"But what happens when it isn't us or you behind him, like after the tutorial?" Chelsea asked.

"We'll get to that. Baby steps though. In games, it's easy enough to know what's going on around you. There's third person perspective when you're playing, and you have numerous notifications telling you what's going on. Here in real life, we have a status bar, but your vision is limited. It's one of the things that I had a hard time dealing with when the tutorial started. Blind spots are not something you get used to quickly," Drake explained.

"So you're letting him practice with multiple enemies. Makes sense. But aren't the monsters too high above our level to be using them as practice?" Harley asked, looking a little worried.

"True, but that's only on an individual basis. When we work as a team, that level gap is bridged pretty easily. All the ants that are here right now are just small fry. Warriors, foragers, and more of the basic variants. I'm keeping an eye out for the dangerous ones. And surprisingly, Tom is a pretty good meat shield. Takes hits like a champ," Drake said. He frowned. "Wait, maybe Tom enjoys it. Is he an M...?"

"I can hear you!" Tom shouted, throwing his shield into another ant and splattering its head against the ground and his shield.

"Keep it up, buddy! No kink shaming here!" Drake shouted back. He looked over at Jacqueline. "Make sure you keep an eye on his health. I don't want him getting seriously injured, alright."

Jacqueline scoffed. "I know my bloody job."

"Good," Drake said, looking over to the rest of the support squad. "Julia, make sure to keep your buffs up on him. But don't go overboard; maintain the spell enough that your natural mana regen is keeping up. If you need to break that for the spell to maintain it, it's fine. We have Jacqueline here for emergency heals. Your job is just to buffer the blows as he works through the monsters."

"Got it, Lord Shot," Julia saluted then refocused on Tom, her brow beginning to sweat.

"And you..." Drake said, looking over at Megan. "Do you do anything useful...?"

"I'm useful!" Megan shouted, her hands gripping her staff angrily.

"Then, what exactly do you do? I've yet to see your skills or spells. Chelsea told me you have a pretty good buff, but I've only briefly noticed it when we were on our way here. What exactly does it do," Drake asked flatly.

"I'm not sure if I should tell you," Megan said pensively.

"Well," Drake began, having to pause to rush forward when a Tyrant Ant Reaper snuck out of the crowd. "Sneaky little bugger," he grumbled. He walked back to the group. "Right, where was I? Yeah, well, either you tell me, or I send you back to Shigure's. I don't have the time or luxury of dead weight on this one. There's too many things about this Hive I don't know to be catering to people anymore."

Megan ground her teeth, staring back at Drake, but eventually she opened something and walked closer. The next moment, a window opened, showing Drake a skill.

Foster of Light Proficiency 2 (23%) [F-Rank]
You are the tool in which the Goddess of Light works through.

Bringer of Light: *"In the name of she who is the light in the dark, to which all are welcome, these unworthy servants seek sanctuary. Foster of Light."*
Increases defensive proficiency by 100%, increases all stats by 20 points, and all damage is converted to Holy. Increases based on proficiency.
Duration: 10 Minutes. Increases based on proficiency.
Cost: 50% of maximum mana. Reduced based on proficiency.
Cooldown: 5 minutes. Cooldown begins once cast. Reduced based on proficiency.

Drake's jaw dropped. "Wow, you really *aren't* useless..."

Chapter 50

What Was Going Through My Head?

"Megan?" Chelsea asked next to her, breaking her out of her thoughts.

"Ah, sorry Chelsea. What is it?" she asked back timidly.

"You just seem distracted. Did Chris say something to you again?" Chelsea asked, her face turning serious.

"What? No! He's been nothing but supportive since the start. I don't know what I would have done if he didn't bring me into the group. I was a mess when we all teleported in."

"Ha... I won't say I don't appreciate being part of a well organized group, but something throws me off about him," Chelsea replied, putting her arms behind her back.

Megan turned her head, confused. "He seems fine to me? He's gotten us out of some tough spots already."

Chelsea moved in closer and brought her voice down to a whisper.

"Yeah, sure. But you're telling me you didn't catch him pushing Smith into that pack of monsters? Smith lived, but only barely," Chelsea murmured.

"What? He would never do something like that! He said so himself; we're in this together!" Megan exclaimed.

Chelsea waved her hands and put a finger to her mouth. "Shh. I get it, you like the guy, but come on Megs. Don't tell me you don't see what he's doing?"

Ah... Why am I remembering this now? Megan thought, flashing back to a conversation she had with Chelsea time and time again during the tutorial.

What was going through my head? Was I really that blind? If I had just looked past the nice smile and my desperate cry for security, I wonder what would have happened? Would all those people he ended up killing have survived?

Megan snapped back, briefly looking at the man in front of her. He was wearing slightly tattered black robes with gold trim, and his arms were crossed as he read over the skill window she had just presented him with. His hair ended slightly above his shoulders as if he hadn't had a haircut in weeks.

But then again, no one probably had.

Her mind wandered as she waited for him to read the skill window. She thought back to the first days of the tutorial, where she made the biggest mistake of her life.

* * *

"W-Where am I?! I'm supposed to be at my boyfriend's condo!" a voice shouted.

"Tyler? Tyler this isn't funny, buddy! Come on out!" another yelled.

W-What is going on? I'm supposed to be at home preparing for the semester! Megan thought, panicking.

In her hands, she held a mace and a pair of socks.

"I-It's real... That whole thing w-w-was real?!" Megan mumbled. She was barely able to get out the words, her voice cracking.

Soon her mind went wild. Looking around, she saw more and more people appearing in motes of lights. Some were just as confused as she was, but she didn't have the mental capacity to worry about them. Her mind was slowly collapsing in on itself.

What is happening... Where are my parents? What about my boyfriend? We were supposed to get married! What is going on! What is going on?! She screamed in her head, grabbing at her sides. She dropped the mace and socks in her hands and slumped to the ground, the sound of deep sobs the only thing she could make out.

Megan was having a mental breakdown. She slowly realized what the person in the room had told her was real, that everything she knew was changing and that the world had turned into something else.

She couldn't handle it. Her life was all planned out; she was going to go to college, finish her degree, get a nice house in the suburbs with her high school boyfriend. They had promise rings. She'd planned what was going to happen every step of the way.

But now?

That was all gone. Her world was shattered. Everything was for naught.

"Are you alright?" a voice asked.

She slowly raised her head, her eyes dead and lifeless.

What she saw was a blue-eyed blond man reaching out his hand to her with a smile.

"Looks like you're just as confused as the rest of us. Are you hurt?" he asked. "It will be safer if we stick together. Stay with me, and we'll get through this no problem. I promise."

Megan reached out to the hand almost subconsciously, the man's words and tone bringing her back.

"I-I... Who are you?" Megan asked, slowly getting to her feet with the man's help.

"My name's Chris," he said, keeping his smile. "Guess I'm a Warrior now? Don't worry, we have a few more people with us. Everyone is going to get through this together. May I ask your name, miss?"

"M-Megan."

"Glad to have you with us, Megan." Chris smirked. "I won't let anything bad happen to you."

From that point on, Megan only saw Chris. She had imprinted on him to a maniacal degree. Anything he said was the truth, and he could do no wrong. Even the things she saw him do that were obviously wrong, she buried deep in her mind, stowed away in the corner in a box and never to be seen again.

He was all she had. All that was grounding her to the world.

* * *

How desperate was I... Megan thought, coming back to the present. *Shot on the other hand...* She looked at the man in front of her.

He was blunt, unapologetic, rude. But also truthful, helpful, and caring to a degree that she wasn't sure she could understand.

Why is he so complicated...

"Oh wow," Shot said, looking up from the skill window. "You really aren't useless."

And why is he such a dick?!

Chapter 51

Buff Magic Is Pretty Good, Huh...

"Hey! Please! Can I take a break? This is torture—I'm tired!" Tom shouted from the front.

"Well that's *too damn bad*!" Drake shouted back, turning back to Megan. "Okay, this buff is very good. Can you keep it up indefinitely?" he asked.

Megan shifted a bit before answering, obviously not sure if she should tell him or not.

"Y-Yes. I have a mana regeneration skill that allows me to keep it cast as long as it's the only spell I'm using," Megan answered.

"Seriously! I could really use a break!" Tom yelled again.

"You're fine! Suck it up!" Drake told him. He turned his attention back to Megan. "Oh? What are these other buffs, then?" he asked.

Megan pursed her lips, moving her head slightly to look at Tom behind Drake.

"Are you sure he's alright?" she asked.

"He's fine; Jacqueline is watching him. And I can see where everything is with my aura sense. If you're that worried, why not cast some of those buffs on him like Julia is doing?" Drake told her, raising a brow.

Megan's face scrunched up slightly at the jab. "My other spells deal with stamina and combat effectiveness... I say stamina, but it also includes regeneration. The latter is a longer cooldown, so I rarely use it," she explained reluctantly.

"Does it have drawbacks?" Drake asked seriously.

"No… Just a large amount of mana and a long cooldown. The regeneration spell can be used with my main spell without problems," she clarified.

Drake put his hand to his chin in thought. "You're basically a pure buff class then, huh… Could have really used that type of information earlier." He sighed. "What's done is done, though. Alright, let's see them in action," Drake said finally. He then pointed to Claire. "Claire, you have a new water buffing spell also you said? Let's see it."

"Are you sure? It has a pretty big cost and cooldown as well. I won't be able to cast it for a while," she answered, stepping up next to him.

"It's fine. I get the gist from the descriptions, but reading them and experiencing them is a whole different thing. I also want Tom to experience them as well; he needs to get used to buff magic sooner or later, being a tank," he explained. "First up, Miss Grumpy." Drake smiled and extended his arm out as if giving her the stage.

Megan grumbled to herself, but she stepped forward nonetheless.

"I'm not grumpy… I just don't *fucking* like you," she mumbled.

After cursing out Drake, she took a breath and held her staff in both of her hands as she closed her eyes and began to chant.

"*In the name of she who is the light in the dark,*" she began, a white magic circle forming below her, "*to which all are welcome, these unworthy servants seek sanctuary.*" Another magic circle formed above Tom's head. "*Foster of Light!*"

Beads and rays of angelic light were cast down on Tom, bathing him in brilliant white light as his body glowed momentarily before dimming. He shouted in joy.

"Oh hell yeah!" Tom shouted, throwing his shield into an ant. It flew backward several feet compared to before when he would only knock them back a few inches. "This is amazing! I feel great!"

Megan heaved a breath, exhaling and wiping her brow.

"Don't forget it only lasts so long, Tom!" Drake shouted to him. "Don't get too far ah—lost him already. I'm going to have to go get him, susmaryosep…" Drake sighed, walking forward into the sea of ants.

A few moments later, Drake was dragging a flailing Tom by the scruff of his armor.

"Why are you holding me back? I can take this whole damn place on!" Tom shouted, flailing his arms and shield wildly.

"Yes, yes, you're very strong with buffs." Drake sighed. "But stay where I can see you."

"I'm not a kid, dude!" Tom retorted.

Drake narrowed his eyes. "Ten, nine, eight, seven..." Drake counted aloud, looking at the confident Tom, "two, one."

And then Megan's buff ran out. The duration passed and Tom deflated, his brows raising as if he had just realized what he'd said and who he'd said it to.

"M-My bad..." Tom said, scratching the back of his head.

"Right. Just reel it in. I can't have you dying; I don't want to have to go find another comic relief character this late into the game." Drake snickered.

"Hey, I do more than just that..." Tom sighed and turned to the ants.

"I know you do, Tom. Keep it up, and keep your head on next time." Drake laughed, patting him on the shoulder.

Drake walked back to the group with a smile on his face. "Okay, where were we before I had to go catch a runaway? Oh yeah. Megan, second buff now."

Megan had recovered from casting the previous spell, and she nodded.

"This one affects a group instead of just one person, but it is an area of effect," she explained.

Drake gave a nod, understanding what she meant as he walked back over to Tom. He then gave a wave, signaling for her to cast the spell.

Megan closed her eyes again, a magic circle forming at her feet as she began chanting.

"*Tired soldiers, may the grace of the Mother touch your weary bodies so that her light will replenish you on your beaten path. Fortifying Light!*" Megan cast.

This time, a luminescent bubble formed around Drake and Tom that was filled with rays of bright light before popping.

You are under the effect of Fortifying Light.

50% increase in Stamina Regeneration for 4 minutes and 53 seconds.
25% increase in Vitality and Mana Regeneration for 4 minutes and 53 seconds.

Drake whistled. "Wow, now *that's* a buff. Is it just me, or are buffing classes ridiculously strong..." Drake mused.

Next to Drake, Tom roared again, raising his shield high into the air. His triumphant shout only lasted a few moments before Drake pulled him back again, forced to drag him to the group as he took care of the ants for the remaining duration of the spell.

When Drake finished, he walked back to the group, looking down on the sitting Tom.

"I'm sorry..." Tom said in a mumble.

Drake sighed. "It's alright, you're still getting used to it." He laughed. "We have to get it right, so just work on it bit by bit."

Tom nodded seriously, getting to his feet before walking back over to the oncoming wave of ants.

"You're being surprisingly nice," Chelsea said.

"I'm always nice, what are you talking about?" Drake replied.

Drake turned around, finding several pairs of skeptical gazes pointed in his direction.

"What? *I'm nice!*" he said again, unable to hold back his smile. "Never mind that. Claire, are you ready?"

Claire moved forward from the rest of the group, her face puffed up into a pout. "Finally addressing me? Aren't I supposed to be your girlfriend," she huffed, turning her head.

"Haha," Drake laughed wryly. "The spell please," he asked.

She gave him a cold glare, but she began chanting her spell.

Claire's new spell was one that affected water magic, somewhat the same as what her other buff did for lightning. It was niche and only benefited one element type at a time. And from what she had told Drake, the cooldown and cost was similar to her Storm Caller's Rising.

"Let my voice rouse the tides, hear the storm that brews deep within my

heart!" Claire hummed, a blue magic circle forming underneath her. *"Let the waves crash against the world like all of her fury! Let us be your tools that flood the earth!"* she continued, the rumbling of the spell reaching a fever pitch as water began to surface from the ground, ebbing out of the magic circle around her feet. *"Tempest's Beckoning!"*

Claire finished her incantation, the roar of waves against the coast sounding as the magic circle beneath her vanished. She stood triumphantly but shakily, a smile on her face. A far cry from the girl who collapsed performing her first spell on the rampart just a few weeks ago.

You are under the effect of Tempest's Beckoning.
All water affiliated magic and spells will deal 100% more damage for the next 2 minutes.
All water affiliated magic and spells will have their cost reduced by 50% for the next two minutes.
All water affiliated magic and spells will regenerate 1% of mana cost on kill.

Drake smiled and snapped his mask back into place. Putting his hand on Tom's shoulder, he pulled him back behind him.

"Can't let this buff go to waste. Don't worry, I got this one Tom," Drake said, cracking his knuckles and turning over his shoulder to Claire. "Knew I could count on my girl for the big finale." He smiled.

Claire turned her head, still upset, but she couldn't hide the red on her ears that poked out from under her dirty-blonde hair.

Drake turned back to the monsters that were ever present, even with them reducing their ways of replenishing their numbers.

"Playtime is over! Time to clear the board!"

Drake clapped his hands together, a shard of ice forming in between them. He threw the shard into the air, crushing it with another clap of his hands. His hair and tattoos shifted over to white.

"Heretical Endowment! Single! Ice!" Drake roared, changing his endowment to boost his magic damage further.

Spreading both his hands forward, Drake's eyes turned fierce.

"Hunt!"

Instantly, ten instances of blue magic circles formed in front of Drake, each one forming a ball of water that shifted into a jagged tooth.

"*La!*" Drake shouted loudly, the teeth rippling with power as he infused more and more mana into them, each one becoming a small torrent. "*Gota!*"

Finishing the chant, the spells fired off small serrated rockets in water form. They tore and sliced through every ant in their wake, slowly drenching the entire area around them. The water spells even went as far as the last Hive entrance in the distance.

Drake continued to relentlessly fire off the spells one after another as his mana continued to replenish with each tens of kills, eventually stacking to hundreds.

Soon the entire field was soaked, and water began to pool around the ants that were spared. The new ones began to run out of the entrance to replenish their numbers. Drake placed his rings into his inventory, a sleek wooden staff replacing them in his hands.

He willed the magic circles to converge, forming a larger ball of water. He pointed his staff forward and chanted again.

"*Cascada.*"

The ball rippled and frothed, the water shimmering with a faint green light as he dumped his replenished stores of mana into the spell. The ball of water roared forward through the army of ants before it, swallowing up anything and everything in its wake before it reached the center of the battlement.

"*Burst.*"

The spell exploded in a cascading ripple of thunderous booms. The water flew out in sharp pointed needles that pierced everything in the surroundings, once again covering the field in water.

A trail of water led back to Drake's feet. Most of the ants on the surface had died, and notifications flooded his peripheral vision, but he wasn't done yet. He needed to wipe out every single one on the surface so they could begin their assault on the hive below.

Drake kneeled and touched the trail, a snow-white magic circle forming on the tip of his index finger.

"Ice Age," Drake whispered. His finger touched the water as it instantly froze, spreading out onto the field in front of him and covering everything that had been touched by water into a frozen statue of ice.

The frost continued to spread, immediately killing and freezing every ant in place. The ground became a slick reflective sheet of glass; the only imperfections were the ants frozen in time on the surface. The ice continued forward to the Hive entrance, freezing the ground before shooting upward and covering it with a door of thick ice.

Drake stood, taking in his handiwork for only a moment.

Throwing the end of staff into the line of ice below him, he shouted once more.

"Shatter!"

A crack shot out from the impact, spreading like a spiderweb on the glass-like surface until it covered every inch of the ice he had just made. Then, with a snap of Drake's fingers, the ice shattered into pieces, becoming small specks of snow. The remnants of the ants were converted to flecks of white on the ground.

Congratulations! You have reached Elemental Miller Level 22.
40 FP have been awarded.

You have gained the title Insectocide.

Insectocide
Kill over one thousand Tyrant Ants in under a minute.
+20% damage to Insects.

"Really? You couldn't have done that before putting me through an entire day of getting insect goo all over me?!" Tom grumbled.

Chapter 52
Cut Off

"So what exactly was all that abuse I just went through for?" Tom asked.

"Oh come on." Drake laughed. "That was hardly abuse."

"I have bites in places I didn't know I had! Not to mention insect juice!" Tom rebutted, throwing his arms into the air.

"Don't be so dramatic, a little blood never hurt anyone." Drake snorted.

"Maybe for you, but I'm normal! I'm not used to being covered in... whatever this is," Tom lamented.

"He does have a point there, bro," Bjorn agreed.

"Are you calling me abnormal?" Drake asked, raising a brow.

"We're both freaks, don't even play." Bjorn gave a chuckle.

"Okay, fair. But he's a tank and he needs to get used to it. I was babying him during the Goblin Invasion, but the monsters are getting exponentially harder and more numerous. Not just Tom, but everyone needs to deal with it." Drake sighed. "I've been too protective of everyone..."

"Aw, he really does care." Chelsea snickered.

"Sure I do." Drake turned to Chelsea, flatly looking into her eyes. "Some more than others though," he said, smirking and looking over to Claire.

"I—I..." Chelsea tried to say. She frowned.

Too far? Drake thought.

"I would think so, but she cannot complain. She knew from the start that you and her were a long shot. I am still surprised you are even entertaining the other one." Natto sighed.

What do you mean? Drake asked, turning back and looking at the massive ice door that still blocked the ants' last Hive entrance.

"Well, for one, do you even know where Claire is on the outside? Once the tutorial is over, she will be taken away from you and placed back to where she was previously, the same as you. Do you think a class such as hers would not be coveted, let alone safe?" Natto explained.

Drake flinched.

Okay, I see your point. But are you really telling me to not become attached to people I've spent so much time with? Drake thought.

"Of course not. I know how sappy and soft you truly are, Drake Wallen. Just do not be surprised if not everyone you hold dear is here once the tutorial has ended. I just... I just hope you are prepared for the reality of the world."

I understand... Thank you, Natto, but that is what this whole thing is about. I'm doing my best to prepare them all for it.

"But you can only do so much, Drake. You must see that."

Drake paused, not wanting to really answer the last question. A touch on his shoulder pulled him out of his conversation with Natto.

"Are you alright?" Claire asked. "That was a pretty big spell you used earlier..."

Drake smiled. "I'll be fine. What about you, how are you feeling after using your new buff?" he asked.

Claire smirked back. "A little tired. It does take half of my mana to cast, but looks like it was worth it."

Drake looked behind her, seeing Sherry, Hudson, and Amir still picking up the monster corpses and skill stones that peppered the ground around the area.

"Yeah, seems like it. AOEs always give me chills." Drake smiled.

"Chills?" Claire asked.

"Back in the day when I used to play games, AOEin' was the only way to do anything in my game of choice. Every time you would be on the brink of dying, only a sliver of health on every pull. Dying then didn't mean really dying like it does here, but it still gave me a rush every time," Drake explained.

"Did you use to play games a lot, Mr. Shot?" Harley asked.

"Yeah, I loved games. It's where I met a lot of my closest friends, actually. In a game, everyone is from a different background, has different experiences, looks and sounds different. But that doesn't matter in the game, or at least it didn't used to. All that mattered was game skill, how well you could perform your task, and if you could do it better than the other guy." Drake laughed. "I miss those guys from back then. Hope they're doing alright."

The small pause in the conversation was filled by a slightly depressing feeling as Drake looked down, reminiscing for a moment. Finally, he pulled out a black die from his inventory.

"Well, enough being worried about those two. I'm sure they're fine. Games with systems like this, they probably have all Legendary skills and are breezing through their tutorials. Now, what weapon are we going to get?"

Quest Complete: Subjugated 500 of 500 Tyrant Ant Reapers [F Rank]
Accept Rewards?
Yes < No

Experience earned. 1,200,000 TP have been awarded.
Please roll for weapon rarity.

Drake rolled the die in his hand, the glass-like surface cool and smooth on his fingertips.

Throwing it out, the die bounced against the ground, eventually tumbling into the ice door that held the ants at bay. Their chittering and scratching behind it did little to break the thick sheet.

The die rolled back, stopping on 10.

"Damn, was really hoping for a 20," Drake cursed, clicking his tongue.

"You do know 20 is hard to get, right?" Chelsea said incredulously.

"Always aim high. Dream big or don't dream, I say!" Drake snorted and picked up the die, a staff dropping to the ground out of a mote of light.

"Damn, I already have a staff. And this one is only uncommon..." Drake sighed and stowed it away.

"So what now?" Julia asked, looking at the door with the rest of the group.

"Well, honestly?" Drake said, still looking at the ants behind the ice door. "I'm surprised the Guardian isn't breaking through the door for one. And"—Drake looked over his shoulder to Bjorn—"we still haven't seen the big bad boss since the first time we came here. Which is really starting to bother me."

"So? We going in?" Bjorn asked.

"I'd like to, but I don't think everyone is ready yet. And there are still variants that we haven't faced yet inside, I'm sure," Drake thought aloud.

"Well, are we safer with you or out here?" Megan asked.

"Good question." Drake sighed, tapping on the ice door with his finger absentmindedly. He took a moment to look at the remaining time they had left.

Time remaining until tutorial's conclusion:
41 days, 13 hours, 45 minutes, 12 seconds.

We have a decent amount of time still, but the Prince Quest is what's bothering me, Drake thought.

"I advise against bringing anyone not beneficial or necessary inside with you, then. As you have said, there could still be powerful variants within that they are holding in reserve," Natto explained.

You think they're smart enough to trap us? Drake asked, surprised.

"I know they are. You are dealing with monsters that are close to breaking through to E-Rank, if not already there. The difference from F to E is not something quantifiable in only stats. Race passives increase, intelligence, and even skills, depending on your race's purity," Natto warned.

And you didn't want to tell me this earlier?

"I did! Did I not warn you to kill that oaf?"

Is that even the same?

"Of course it is! The titan race is one of the primordial races, meaning it is of the highest order just like the others! Changing into one will have effects on that person and their abilities beyond what you can imagine. I implore you, Drake, this is not the same as the King."

Drake pursed his lips, thinking on the warning.

Do you think I can at least escape an E-Rank? And there's still no guarantee that they've even ranked up. Shouldn't there be a quest or something for stuff like that? Drake asked.

"*For mana vessels, yes there is. But for monsters, they work on an entirely different system and can forego that all together. All a monster requires is experience,*" Natto explained.

So it's like an anime power up? Instant, huh... Well, that's a little unfair, Drake grumbled.

"*That is a horrible analogy, but yes it is instant. If a monster were to gain enough experience while you were inside the Hive, I fear you would stand no chance even at your current status. And the rest of your so-called party? They would be wiped out, Drake,*" Natto said flatly.

"Then there's only one thing to do," Drake said, sighing.

Drake placed his whole hand on the ice this time, melting a small doorway into it before stepping through quickly. He filled it back up instantly. "Guess we're going it alone for now."

* * *

"Drake! Drake?!" Claire shouted, slamming her fists onto the ice wall. "What is he doing? He said we were all going to go together!"

"He must have been talking to the little miss," Bjorn suspected. "She must have told him it was too dangerous, so he decided to go in by himself to see if she was right."

"What? Can't you just break the door down?!" Claire shouted at him.

"I could, but what good would that do?" Bjorn said, crossing his arms. "If he thinks that anyone here would be in danger if they followed him right now, I'd have to agree. Everyone besides him and I are still under level 20; most of you aren't even combat-proficient classes. Wait," Bjorn said, breaking from his explanation, "where's Theo?"

* * *

"*Impact!*" Drake roared, throwing a fist through an ant's head. His other arm aimed behind it as a burst of air and ice shot out from the combination of magic circles, pelting the ants in the tunnel.

"Still no Guardian, just runts. And no new variants yet. Think we're in the clear?" Drake asked.

"*You have not gone deep enough, Drake. It has only been a few minutes. Do you really miss your companions that much?*" Natto asked, snickering.

"Oh, you like our quality time alone that much? I didn't know you cared like that Natto," Drake countered.

"*If I could be rid of you, I would...*" Natto sighed.

"Aw, don't be shy now, it's only us here!" Drake shouted, his voice echoing in the tunnel before it was overtaken by the chittering of ants once more. "Okay, I lied. Us and some insects, but close enough."

Drake leapt forward, summoning two disks of water on either side of him. He used his Wind Endowment to speed himself up and wade his way through the massive cluster of ants, the spinning blades doing their job of thinning the pack.

A third blue magic circle formed at his feet, summoning water all around him and blocking the insect splatter as he moved.

"I don't know why I didn't think of this before; now I don't worry about getting any on me." Drake chuckled.

"*While I am sure you are impressed with yourself, we still have a problem,*" Natto reminded.

"Problem? But things are going so smoothly. Oh," Drake said, understanding her meaning.

"*Exactly. It should be going anything* but *smoothly. I fear there is more to it than just a Variant Queen. This may have more surprises behind it than we are prepared to deal with. Again, I advise you to give up, but I know you will not.*" She sighed.

"Glad we got that out of the way, then. So, how far should I be going down?" Drake asked, stopping at an intersection of tunnels.

Ants on every side of him, he still breathed easy. After such a long marathon of repeatedly clearing out the field above for the other Hive entrances, these few minutes felt like a breeze.

"It's a bit annoying that I can't use fire though, love blowing stuff up,"

Drake grumbled, his water-like bubble shifting into another disk as he sent all three down different tunnels, slicing through ants with ease.

Drake suddenly raised a brow, feeling his spell canceled.

"That's new," Drake said in a low voice, his head turning to the right tunnel.

"*Was your spell canceled?*" Natto asked, unsure as well.

"No, it felt like it was... absorbed?" Drake said, unsure himself.

He quickly raised his arm and threw another disk of water down the tunnel, only to feel the loss of his spell again. But this time, he heard the impact of the disk.

"That can't be good..." Drake mumbled.

Chapter 53

That Was Unexpected...

Drake began chanting his defensive skills, preparing for the worst as something unknown was able to apparently absorb his magic.

"Is there any ant variation you know of that can absorb magic?" Drake asked, his eyes flashing to a deep blue as he tried to see anything down the dark tunnel.

"*Not in F-Rank, there is not. Even the most extreme variations will not begin to show nullification skills and abilities until much later. It has to be an item!*" Natto shouted.

"An item? Are you saying the ants are using equipment? Could they be using the items from the Goblin's Hoard?" Drake wondered aloud.

"*It is possible and the only way I can explain this with any hope of us getting out. If it is anything but...*" Natto said, trailing off.

"What exactly?"

"*It would have to be a C-Rank or higher monster. And that should not be possible. Not only that, I am restricted from telling you anything if that is the case.*"

"Great, so we're either safe because they're using an item, or we're flat-out dead. What wonderful options," Drake grumbled.

The tunnels suddenly stopped humming with the chittering of ants, giving Drake an eerie feeling that something was about to happen.

"Does it always have to be with the suspense?" Drake asked.

Soon, as if on cue, the sound of tapping rang through the mute tunnel. But it was different from what Drake would think of as normal walking; this sounded like multiple people or monsters.

In the next moment, the monster came into view.

Standing in front of Drake was a pitch-black ant, four small white dots on the crown of its head. It had deep crimson eyes, and the ant was standing on four legs. Two arms crossed each other, decorated with golden jewelry.

Obiteron Trikk Level 29 [F-Rank]

"Oh, looks like royalty really does get the best stuff. Raid the whole treasury?" Drake scoffed.

The ant prince chirped in a language Drake didn't understand, then raised a hand as if asking him to follow.

"What the... I'm not sure what to do here. Any ideas, Natto?"

"*Do not follow it, obviously.*" Natto sighed. "*The monster is higher level than you are by a fair amount, and apparently it has equipment that can nullify half of your abilities as a mage! Do not be fooli—Drake!*"

"I'm not going to do anything," Drake teased, stepping forward before stopping and turning around. "See? We are just going to—Ow! What the?" Drake shouted, rubbing his forehead as he felt himself bump into something that was invisible.

Drake looked down at the tuft of dirt that pucked up, hearing a familiar voice grunt.

"Theo?" Drake asked, raising a brow.

Shimmering into view, Theodore bowed his head slightly. "This one apologizes, my lord, but it would not be proper if thou went in alone. This one does not wish to see my lord continue to stand alone when this one can offer aid."

Drake reached out a hand, offering to help Theodore up.

"It's alright, Theo, I was just about to go back anyway." Drake sighed, but he couldn't help but smirk at the man's loyalty. "Next time, just let me know where you are. I could've killed you plenty of times by accident with some of those spells," Drake said, shuddering.

"This one begs for forgiveness. I would also like to address, you did come close several times," Theodore said, gulping loud enough for it to be heard.

But before Drake could say something, the chittering of ants began again.

"Well, looks like they're on the move again. Let's backtrack and get out of here... How did they get behind us? There's only one tunnel down to this intersection!" Drake said in amazement. He looked back down the tunnel.

"I do not know! They could possibly have burrowed in from another tunnel?" Natto replied hurriedly.

Drake cursed and looked at the new variants he'd been searching for down here.

Tyrant Ant Emulsor Level 23 [F-Rank]
New Subjugation Quest: Subjugate 1,000 Tyrant Ant Emulsors [F-Rank]
Reward: Experience, TP, and Key to the Royal Nursery.

Tyrant Ant Bombardier Level 20 [F-Rank]
New Subjugation Quest: Subjugate 500 Tyrant Ant Bombardiers [F-Rank]

Reward: Experience, TP, and 100 Explosive Tyrant Sacs.
Tyrant Ant Foreman Level 22 [F-Rank]
New Subjugation Quest: Subjugate 250 Tyrant Ant Foremans [F-Rank]
Reward: Experience and TP.

Tyrant Ant Flame Spitter Level 25 [F-Rank]
New Subjugation Quest: Subjugate 500 Tyrant Ant Flame Spitters [F-Rank]

Reward: Experience, TP, and 5 rare fire skill stone.

"They have a Flame Spitter? Don't they all have those oil sacs? What makes them so—" Drake tried to joke before he pulled Theodore up forcefully, throwing him behind him as he made a wall of earth in front of him to block the incoming blast of fire that was just thrown at them.

The ants came out in full force from behind Drake, unwilling to let him pass or exit. He was able to keep his wall solid as the flames blazed against it, reinfusing mana into the wall to keep it from melting.

In the brief moment the flames stopped, Drake peered past his glowing red-hot wall to see the last hulking figure he'd also been curious about finding.

Tyrant Ant Guardian Level 28 [F-Rank]

"Oh, now he decides to show up. They really pulled out all the stops on this one." Drake sneered before he was forced to pull back his head again, unable to move because of his need to protect Theodore.

Drake cursed, suddenly feeling movement in his aura sense. The ants were charging him and Theodore.

"Time to wave a big gun around and shoot in the dark!" Drake shouted, trying his best to pinpoint the monsters through his aura.

Throwing his free hand out to the side, he summoned five blue magic circles, trying to form water from them only for the water to evaporate from the flames' heat.

"Fucking damn it!" Drake cursed again. He condensed the circles into one and forced his Water Endowment out. "*Heretical Endowment Single! Water!*" Drake roared, his hand pointing outward again now that he had gotten his Endowment.

"*Mizu no kyoku! Ni no kata!*" Drake roared. A dense ball of water swirled at the end of his hand, flecks of green sparkling in the dark of the tunnel against the light of the fierce flames. "*Mizu Guruma!*"

Drake pushed a significant amount of mana into the spell, using his regeneration to enforce it even more, then arced his hand from right to left. Slashing with all his might, the spell shot forward, extending and carving a line into the walls of the tunnel and cutting through everything.

The spell sliced deep into the walls of the hive, through the fire, and through Drake's own earthen wall, but it also cut through all of the incoming ants.

Normally this would be a good thing, but this time around it ended in horror.

Instantly as Drake received kill notifications, the deafening sounds of explosions rang out throughout the tunnel, the walls beginning to rumble.

"Fuck! Great thinking, Drake, kill the monsters that have bombardier in their names!" Drake cursed and scooped up Theodore in his arms. He changed to his Lightning Endowment, then bolted down the tunnel the Ant Prince had beckoned him down before. The tunnel collapsed quickly behind him.

* * *

"What was that?!" Megan shouted as she tried to keep her balance against the shaking ground.

The other members of the party were also doing their best to keep themselves upright, the sudden trembling surprising them all.

"We need to get back to the fortress!" Bjorn shouted.

"What about Drake?!" Claire yelled.

"And we still don't know where Theo is!" Harley added, pleading with Bjorn.

"We don't want to be here right now; we just have to trust Theo is with Shot, and they can take care of themselves right now. I don't know what is going on! Get moving!" Bjorn shouted. "We don't have a choice!" he yelled, gritting his teeth.

"Dang it! That idjit better be fine, or our meal ticket is punched!" Hudson shouted, running for the fortress.

"Yeah! He promised to make some good food when we get out of here! Dude better pay up!" Sherry grumbled.

"That's what you're damned worried about?" Hudson said incredulously over his shoulder. "I meant that man is the only one keeping us alive, you damned little garbage disposal!"

"Yeah! With his food, dude! It's correlated!" Sherry snapped back.

"I don't think this is the time to be arguing over that!" Amir stammered as he ran with all his strength.

"Everyone just run, I won't let anything happen to any of you! We need to regroup on solid ground; then we can figure out what's going on and how to find Theo and Shot," Bjorn yelled, picking up the slow Sherry in a fireman's carry.

The party sprinted for the fortress in the distance, the ground behind them as well as the towering Hive beginning to collapse with the numerous booms sounding beneath the ground.

* * *

Drake stopped. The collapsing tunnel behind them had finally finished barreling down. He let Theodore down onto the ground and heaved a sigh.

"So much for getting out... You think they planned that?" Drake asked.

"If not them, then who?" Natto replied.

"The enemies this time art using unusual tactics to thwart us," Theodore nodded, brushing off the dirt from his clothes.

"Unusual to say the least. I'm sure they can rebuild tunnels, but I never expected them to throw kamikaze-type monsters at us," Drake cursed.

"What shalleth we do now, my lord?" Theodore asked.

"Only one direction to go. Guess we walk down the yellow brick road?" Drake said evenly. He began to walk forward down the tunnel.

"That was an awful joke." Natto sighed.

I tried. More importantly, I think we might be in for some real trouble here if we have to worry about ambushes from behind and wherever else these ants can dig from... Coming in here might have been a bad idea. Drake sighed and switched his endowment back to water.

"You are just now realizing this? How many times did I warn you!" Natto screamed.

I said might, not that it is. We still haven't died yet, so it's a win.

"Dying and not dying are not the only two options here! That is a horrible way to think about it!"

Drake shrugged. *Yeah, but it's the most simple.*

Drake and Theodore remained on their toes as they walked down the tunnel. Drake made sure to keep his Magic Sight peeled for anything that might be coming at them in the dark, almost pitch-black, tunnel. He didn't want to illuminate them so as to not give themselves away, so he relied on his skill and aura sense to guide them.

"There hasn't been any ants so far since we started walking," Drake mused.

"It is quite peculiar indeed," Theodore agreed.

"How you doing on mana, Theo? Good on potions?" Drake asked over his shoulder.

"This one has adequate resources, my lord. No need for alarm," he replied.

"Good, we might be down here for a while... I'm going to hopefully assume the ants made another exit somewhere, so we just need to walk around until we find it," Drake said, continuing to scan the tunnel as they moved forward.

Several minutes passed of the pair walking forward. They eventually found bends and turns in the tunnel until they suddenly came upon a dim light at the end.

"Oh? Did we find it already? And we don't even have a luck stat to help us! I'd say we're—" Drake began saying, then paused as he looked at what was causing the light.

Out in front of them was the opening to a large cave, the walls covered in glowing stones. On the floor, thousands and thousands of ants meandered in and out of tunnels, parting only for the exits and the dirt columns that were supporting the cave. The columns were extensive and wide, with holes along the sides from bottom to top. Ants came and went through the holes just as frequently as the exits to the cave.

Drake whistled. "This is bigger than I thought, it's like a goddamn city down here."

Chapter 54
The Need To Be King

"Your Majesty, do you think it wise to allow the human into the nest?" chittered the attending guard.

Walking up one of the columns of the cave, Prince Obiteron fiddled with a gold pendant around his neck.

"It is the only option I have left to outperform my brothers. There is no other way," he chittered back. He continued to walk, several more Royal Knights falling into line with the entourage.

"But... it will be the end of the nest! Surely you have seen the destruction that lone human has caused the Hive? Is becoming king above your brothers worth destroying the entire kingdom we have built up since being transported here?" the attendant pleaded.

With a snap, the attendant was pinned to the wall, a pitch-black hand pressing him against it. The prince looked into the black eyes of his attendant.

"Yes," Obiteron hissed, only one emotion in his crimson eyes.

Ambition.

* * *

"Sire!" shouted a Royal Knight skittering into the chamber. He bowed before an ostentatious throne.

"Speak," said the second prince.

Bulkier than his brothers, he toted wiry muscles under his chitin armor, his callous armor bending to form around them.

Braxor Trikk, the second prince, was the most likely to ascend to the throne through his sheer power and command of the Hive.

"The human that has been decimating our forces on the surface has just infiltrated the Hive entrance. We lost track of him in the tunnel collapse caused by the third prince, sir!" the knight reported.

Stepping off the throne, the ground cracked under the weight of the prince's mighty body. Braxor patted the slightly nervous Royal Knight on the shoulder.

Every prince was assigned six Royal Knights to serve them, and Braxor was no different.

"I see," he said in a deep chitter. "What is my little brother up to now? Bringing such an opponent into the Hive... is he so desperate to usurp the throne from me that he would use that filthy walking abomination as a tool?" he thought aloud, still holding the knight's shoulder.

"There is something else you should be informed of, Your Majesty," the knight added.

"What?"

"The human was spotted in the tunnel leading to the main chamber before the collapse," the knight reported, only to be cut off by the crunching of his shoulder under the prince's sudden grip.

"Ready yourselves," announced Braxor. "My brother's games have gone too far this time."

* * *

"Haha! So the human is in the main chamber now? Sounds like a fun time," Rasha, the first prince, chittered. He let the skull of an animal fall from his hand as he sat lazily on his throne.

"Prince! Your Majesty, this is no laughing matter! This human is dangerous!" a Royal Knight informed.

"Dangerous? Because he can kill a few of the footmen, you're saying he's strong? He's just a single puny human, fleshy skin, only two hands, two feet, two *stupid* eyes. How could he be more dangerous than I?" Rasha said, sneering back at the knight.

"B-But even so, even if he is no match for the prince, the Hive is still in danger! The man single-handedly—"

Rasha rushed forward, grabbing both of the knight's mandibles and stopping him from speaking.

"He's not stronger than I am, so it doesn't matter. *Right*?" Rasha said in a hushed chirp.

"N-N-No, he pales in c-comparison to the p-prince!"

Rasha snapped one of the mandibles off the knight, throwing it down to the ground as the knight dropped to the floor in pain.

"Good, that's what I thought." Rasha walked to the end of the chamber. "Get your lousy asses ready; I'm in a bad mood. *Now*, let's go have some fun..."

* * *

"Ackchoo!" Drake sneezed. He sat up against a wall of earth he'd made to close the tunnel, leaving a small crack for air at the top.

"What is the matter, my lord? Doth thee have a sickness? Can my lord even acquire sickness?" Theodore asked.

"Not sure... Maybe someone is talking about me? Probably Jacqueline... Actually, it's almost dinner, so it's probably Sherry," Drake said, shivering slightly.

Natto sighed next to Drake, spooning the little amount of food she had been given into her mouth.

"Why is this portion as pitiful as you are?" she asked.

"That was uncalled for." Drake smiled and rolled the black die in his hand. "We don't know how long we're going to be down here. Have to ration."

"Why do you not just build upwards and create your own exit?" Natto said, putting the spoon into her mouth once more.

"Well," Drake started, throwing the die against the wall, "for starters, I don't know anything about structural integrity, so I have no idea if something is going to collapse again if I try."

Drake waited for the die to settle, clicking his tongue when it turned up a 5. A glass-like stone dropped from a flash of light that illuminated the closed tunnel they were currently in.

"Fuck, another dud. Three more rolls to go..." Drake sighed. "Also, the ants are better tunnelers than I am. The amount of mana it takes for me to move earth I don't create is so large that I would exhaust myself instantly. Not to mention that because they're also making tunnels, we don't know when or where we might run into them."

"This one sees your point, my lord, but dare this one ask just what art we doing staying in a singular location, then?" Theodore asked. "Will it not just be a matter of time before our quarry finds us?"

"True!" Drake agreed. "But if we're here, I can better tell where they can attack from, so it's more defensible and that's the most important right now," Drake explained. "I also want to roll for the Guardian Quest I just finished, if I'm really really lucky," he said. He pulled the die back to his hand with a wind spell by creating a vacuum in his hand.

"I'll get something good, maybe..." Drake sighed and threw the die again.

"That does not answer this one's query, my lord. Why must we be in a defensible position?" Theodore asked again.

The die bounced, tapping against the stone of the floor and eventually the wall before tumbling to a stop at 1. Another flash brightened the dark tunnel. The light revealed Drake's face, bent down into a frown.

"Because I'm not sure I can protect you if we go out into the open. I already almost killed you in the tunnel, and with everything, I'm not sure if they have more variants that could possibly see through your concealment skill. I don't want to risk your life so I can go on a rampage," Drake said, gripping the die before tossing it at his feet once more for the final roll. "I don't want to make a preventable mistake... again."

It had been weeks since Theodore had been taken hostage by Stewart, but the memory of it, and then the same thing happening again to Claire under his watch, still burned the image of both deep in his mind.

Drake wouldn't allow it to happen again if he could help it. If that meant staying in a hole for a little bit and clawing their way out, waiting until he was able to inch his way toward a higher level, or their last resort, waiting out the tutorial timer, he was prepared to do so.

His party on the surface was safe; he knew that. Bjorn would keep them safe until the tutorial ended. And they had enough food to last until the end even without rationing.

"My lord," Theodore said in a hushed tone, "such events were not thy fault. Such a monster. No one except the creator themself could have foreseen it. Please do not trouble thyself with such guilt. This one chose to follow my lord no matter what may happen and regardless of happenstance."

Drake sighed, looking at the last roll. Another dud. Picking up the die and stone, he walked over, extending his hand to Theodore.

"You're a fool, Theodore... but I can get behind that." Drake smiled.

"This one would have it no other way." Theodore smiled back.

They both grinned in mutual understanding in the dark, only the faint glow of crystals from the main cavern peeking in through the air hole and illuminating them.

The sound of crunching broke up the moment. Both turned their heads to a scowling Natto.

"You two were made for each other. I am truly on the edge of my seat as to what will happen next," she said as she chewed her food, slurping another bite from her spoon.

"Aww, missing out on the touching moment Natto?" Drake said, walking over to her.

"What are you doing? No, do not touch me!" she shouted.

"Don't be shy. Come here for a nice big hug!" Drake laughed.

"Cease! You still reek of insect filth!" she screamed, trying to push herself away from Drake.

Their moment was abruptly broken as the wall Drake had put up began to crack. His head snapped to it, and his arms glowed an ethereal blue. Drake instantly shot forward and grabbed Theodore, his endowment changing his hair to a deep orange glow.

The wall began to crumble, revealing a pitch-black ant of a stature incomparable to the previous ones. Its crimson eyes locked onto Drake.

"Fuck."

Braxor Trikk Level 29 [F-Rank]

The prince's mandibles chittered, the sound ringing throughout the tunnel as its arm tore at the walls.

He's trying to take down the tunnel! Drake cursed. He quickly identified his only option.

Shooting forward, he placed a carrier bubble made of wind around Theodore. Natto had just enough time to fuse herself into Drake's body, her utensils and food dropping to the floor.

Drake rocketed forward, trying to grab the prince's arm that was gripping the wall, but the prince was fast. At least faster than Drake was currently without his endowment.

Flying past the prince who dodged his grip, Drake whistled when he saw the entourage around him.

Nibyu Kikk Level 29 [F-Rank]

Vimyr Kikk Level 29 [F-Rank]

Uucyu Kikk Level 29 [F-Rank]

...

New Subjugation Quest: Subjugate 18 Royal Knight Tyrant Ants [F-Rank]
Reward: Experience, TP, and a rare weapon of your choice.

Suddenly out of the tunnel and careening for the base of the cavern, Drake spotted several Royal Knights but no other new variants.

He was halfway to landing before another ant stopped in front of him, its mandibles spread wide as it chittered loudly.

Drake's eyes widened at the monster that had seemingly appeared out of nowhere. He'd had no time to register the blip on his aura sense.

Rasha Trikk Level 29 [F-Rank]

Scowling, Drake flexed his aura. The monster flinched under the increased pressure from his Tyrannical Aura and the titles that boosted its effects.

"Hold on tight, Theo!" Drake shouted, his hair turning to black. He flipped 180-degrees around to grab Theodore in a fireman's carry, and the wind bubble disappeared.

In its place, a bolt of lightning shot out—aimed right at the prince.

The bolt flew forward, crackling with power as it traveled the short distance toward the creature's head before the spell suddenly vanished. Another ant appeared in front of Rasha.

Obiteron Trikk Level 29 [F-Rank]

"Where the fuck did you come from?!" Drake shouted, but he didn't stop his plan. Another magic circle of bright yellow formed as a bolt manifested and vanished, Drake's hair shimmering with the same brilliant color. "Doesn't matter. Smell ya later!"

Drake flexed his aura again. He expected Obiteron to freeze as well, but he was unpleasantly surprised when the monster instead clacked its mandibles together, almost sneering. It reached forward for Drake.

"Does this fucker have an item for everything?!"

Chapter 55

Not All Is Right at Home

Drake shouted and threw Theodore into the air above them. "Hang on, Theo! It's going to get bumpy!"

The instant Drake pulled Theodore in and released him upward, he stepped under the Ant Prince's reaching limb.

"M-My lord?!" Theodore screamed.

Obiteron's crimson eyes widened as Drake stepped in, pulling the monster over his shoulder. A brown magic circle formed on the ground adjacent to them.

Drake summoned a spike of black earth right where he was going to throw the prince, his goal to impale the monster. Obiteron couldn't resist Drake's current strength, thrashing over Drake's shoulder and just moments away from being skewered.

But Drake wasn't only against one opponent.

In the next second, Braxor moved, his fist smashing the spike at the base.

"Fucking ant..." Drake cursed. He clicked his tongue.

Drake instantly switched it up, forcing the earth down into a pool of mud. Obiteron careened, and the Ant Prince sunk into the floor with a splash.

A flame sparked in the next moment. Drake threw his fist forward at the gaping Braxor, the creature's focus still on the floor where the other prince had just been thrown. That instant gave Drake just enough time.

Punching through the flame, Drake's endowment switched again. His arm and hair shifted to a crimson red that lit up the dim surroundings.

"Marked!"

In the last second before impact, Braxor came to his senses, barely putting up his guard before Drake's Martial Skill-enhanced fist collided with him.

The impact sounded throughout the cavern. Braxor's thick chitin arms cracked and splintered as he was thrown backward.

"Tough bastard." Drake grunted.

Rasha had finally shaken off Drake's fear, and a chittering howl sounded from his maw. He lowered his stance and rushed Drake from behind.

Feeling the movement with his aura, Drake dropped to the ground, dodging the ant's arms. Drake's legs extended as he swept the monster from beneath, knocking the prince into the mud with his brother.

The next moment, Drake summoned another brown magic circle at his feet and bent his legs from his sweeping position.

"You know, there *is* such a thing as too many people at a party." Drake sneered. The earth magic below him formed a platform and pushed him upward toward Theodore.

Drake quickly grabbed Theo, manifesting a ball of wind around the man once more. Another wind spell shot Drake and Theo off for the other end of the room with a boom.

The three princes hissed and shouted into the air, but Drake had already left the area.

* * *

"You imbeciles! Your jokes and plots have gone too far this time!" Braxor clacked as he walked forward, tending to his shattered arms. Obiteron and Rasha pulled themselves from the pool of mud. Obiteron's expression was even and unperturbed.

"I have not the slightest idea what you are speaking of, brother."

Braxor snapped his mandibles together in anger. "Do not play me for a fool! I know you led him to the Hive! Are you so desperate for the throne that you would condemn the entire colony?"

Obiteron scoffed, wiping the mud from his body and trinkets. "As I said, I have not the slightest clue of what you speak. Was it not Rasha who met them but a few weeks ago on the surface? Perhaps they simply followed him here after *you* chose not to deal with them."

"What did you say, weakling?" Rasha hissed. "Are you saying it was *my* fault? If you two hadn't gotten in my way, that filthy flesh-ridden human would be dead!"

"Oh? Is that why you were knocked on your thorax? Because you were doing *so* spectacularly? If I hadn't intervened, you would be nothing but ichor on the floor, *brother*," Obiteron chirped.

"You think a waste of a larva like you, who is only as good as the filthy trinkets you took from the hall, could ever *help* me?!"

Rasha walked forward, still covered in dirt, and gripped Obiteron by the golden necklace that adorned his neck. He laughed.

"Take away your trinkets and what are you? Weak! You should be ashamed to call yourself a Prince of Tyrant Ants!" he spat.

"Enough!" Braxor roared. "The human is stronger than I thought. He will become a problem if he is allowed to rampage through the Hive. We will assign blame later, unless you both wish to rule a broken colony!"

Rasha released the necklace with a scoff. He jumped in the direction Drake had run, his Royal Guards following suit.

Braxor waved a guard to him. "Get the knights and the trackers. Find them. They can't hide his disgusting pheromones in our home."

The guard nodded and moved toward another tunnel exit, the Royal Knights following as more and more ants gathered around them.

"You and I, brother, are going to have a long talk after this is over." Braxor sneered, then turned to follow his knights.

"I wouldn't have it any other way, *brother*," Obiteron chirped back.

Once Braxor left, a knight from Obiteron's guard walked forward.

"What would you like us to do, Your Majesty?"

"Do as we planned. I showed us fighting the intruder. Now, we must use him to our advantage..."

* * *

Drake was still using his wind magic to propel Theodore and himself through the air, trying to reach the opposite end of the cavern as fast as possible.

Below him, the skittering of ants still sounded, and he saw movement constantly. They'd obviously been alerted to his presence and were following. More and more ants began to gather, forming a horde below. Some even poured out of the columns that supported the cavern.

"This is a bit of a pickle." Drake sighed.

"M-My lord! Allow us to pause in our escape so that this one may conceal us!" Theodore screamed over the blistering wind.

"Oh! Good idea!" Drake agreed.

Looking down, Drake canceled his Fire Endowment, switching to Water for the regeneration. Summoning a handful of orange magic circles, Drake smirked under his mask.

"Time to sow some chaos."

The circles fully formed as droplets of red-hot glistening magma began to drip from them while Drake continued to propel forward.

Huge bombs of liquid fire rained down on the ant horde gathering below them, kicking up dirt. The ants instantly burst into flames.

"We don't want to leave a trail… Do we think they need so many columns? They can go without one, right?" Drake thought aloud.

"*Do not dare! You said yourself the place might collapse again!*" Natto screamed.

"That was then, this is now. Before we didn't have three high-level monsters on our tushies. Besides, we aren't staying here. We have to find the treasure room or at least another place where the princes aren't!"

Drake slipped his rings into his inventory. Morning Glory shimmered into existence in front of him. Pointing his staff toward a pillar in the opposite direction they were going, he began casting.

"*Bring down the house!*" Drake smiled. A flame formed in front of him, quickly changing colors as it flickered from red to blue to white.

"*Howitzer.*" A brown magic circle came into existence, and a jet-black barrel of earth formed around the condensing flame. A green-tinged magic circle then flashed into place behind the flames at the end of the barrel.

"Impact!" Drake roared, finishing the spell. The flame bullet pushed through the barrel, melting it as it went screeching forward toward its target. The force of the recoil was more powerful than Drake had expected, flinging both him and Theodore backward. His magma magic circles were barely able to keep up as they were launched toward the cavern wall.

A thunderous boom pierced through the noise of the cavern as the spell ripped from the barrel. A second later, it slammed into the column.

At the moment of impact, an explosion sounded with an earth-shattering pitch, deafening the surroundings as the column broke apart. It tumbled and cracked at the point of contact.

The column broke and snapped from its support, crumbling down to the ground in large pieces that crushed whatever was underneath without discrimination or care.

Drake and Theodore were pushed with such force that Drake struggled to reorient them. He had to cancel his magma spells and quickly form wind spells around them instead to cushion their impact.

The wall quickly encroached on them as they sped forward, Drake gritting his teeth. Instead of slowing, Drake chose to shoot forward in front of Theodore, orienting his feet toward the wall.

"Legs! I know you haven't liked me recently, but don't break, damn it!" Drake shouted, his hair switching to a fierce orange.

Drake braced for impact, his legs almost buckling as he hit the wall. But he didn't have time to care about the pain or wonder if he'd shattered every bone in his legs. His head shot up just in time to see Theodore flying toward him.

Drake aimed his staff upward, summoning a pillar of water to cushion Theodore's landing. Stowing his staff, Drake raised both arms.

Theodore screamed loudly as he tumbled into the pillar of water, eventually slowing down and coming out the other end. He landed right in Drake's arms in a princess carry.

Drake chuckled, his legs still stuck in the wall.

"That was fun. Wanna go again?"

"M-My..." Theodore tried to say, but he coughed up a mouthful of water.

"I'll take that as a no." Drake laughed and pulled his feet from the wall with some effort and pain. They fell to the ground.

Drake again used his wind magic to cushion their fall. He then pulled a health potion from his inventory and downed it in one gulp.

"Fuck, I didn't pull one Bjorn made. I really wanted the grape juice-tasting one, bleh..." Drake said, sticking out his tongue.

Theodore righted himself, still soaking wet and coughing up water.

Drake watched and spread his aura to make sure no one was following them while he waited for his broken legs to heal.

Once Theodore was done expelling the water, he spared no time in concealing them with his spell.

"So hopefully this keeps us safe for a bit. I can feel the potion working on my legs, but I need a few more minutes. Can you use some illusions to get them off our trail, Theo?" Drake asked.

"Certainly, my lord. But a moment." Theodore nodded.

"*My enemies see not the world through a lens of clarity but as I make it. Breath of Nightmares,*" Theodore chanted. Tens of inky black figures formed around them, slowly condensing into identical versions of Drake and Theodore.

"You know, I don't think I've said this before, but you're taller than I am aren't you, Theo," Drake said in a hushed grumble.

"Y-Yes? This one believes so...?" Theodore answered as he sent the illusions out in different directions.

Drake clicked his tongue.

"Of course you are, bastard..."

Chapter 56

This Map Isn't Helping...

Drake and Theodore were still stuck waiting for Drake's legs to heal. Theodore offered to carry him, but Drake refused.

"We should be fine for now since you're concealing us," Drake said in a hushed voice. "It's open, and we can tell where the ants are coming and going. We'll know if we're in danger beforehand. If we went into a tunnel, there's no telling if we'd be ambushed. I'm not sure how they found us, but somehow they tracked us to that tunnel, and my Aura sense can't penetrate the cave walls."

Drake sighed and rubbed his itchy legs. The healing process was thankfully painless to a degree, but the sensation coming back felt a lot like when your legs went to sleep.

"What is our plan of attack, my lord? Shalleth we scour the tunnels until we find our esteemed prize?" Theodore asked, his fingers tapping his cane like he was playing on a keyboard.

"Ah ah ah," Drake chided. He waved his finger, then remembered he and Theo couldn't see each other. "We have a map, remember?" Drake chuckled and pulled out the piece of paper. "And what's with the hands, I can hear them from here. Are you nervous, Theo?"

"Certainly not," Theodore said, not ceasing. "'Tis but an effect of the skill. This one must control the puppets like a puller of strings. Please pay this one no mind."

"Oh? That's kind of cool... Okay! So let's see what this map can—damn it," Drake cursed, looking at the wall across from them on the other side of the cavern.

"Is there a problem, my lord?"

"Yeah. I don't know if the ants built on top of where the goblins put the hoard, moved it, or sunk it, but"—Drake pointed to the opposite wall—"that is where the map says the treasure hoard *should* be."

"Then...?" Theodore asked.

"Then this map is fucking useless!" Drake scoffed and threw the map back into his inventory.

Crossing his arms and scowling out into the dimly lit cavern, Drake sighed, waiting for his recovery to complete. He hummed.

"I guess we just have to do this the old-fashioned way."

"What, might this one ask, is the old-fashioned way?" Theodore asked.

* * *

"My lord... This is not what this one anticipated when thou stated he was going to take the old-fashioned way..." Theodore sighed, obviously disappointed.

"What way did you think I meant, Theo?" Drake laughed slightly, his left hand on the tunnel wall.

"This one expected black magic, divination, or possibly another wondrous means of predicting our journey, not..." Theodore trailed off, walking behind Drake.

"Not what? Left hand on the maze's wall?" Drake snorted. "Hate to break it to ya, Theo, but I don't have unlimited skills or spells for things."

Drake and Theodore were now walking down a tunnel they'd found and hugging the left side as they followed its bends and twists. They did their best to avoid the coming and going ants that skittered to and fro throughout it.

"Man, so much experience just passing by... My gamer heart is aching!" Drake mumbled.

"You can kill them all later. Remember, if you alert them to where you are, you will be stuck in another skirmish with dear Theo exposed," Natto reminded.

I know, I know. I was just hoping to let loose a bit more. I didn't get to really use everything in that last fight. Maybe once we find the treasure room, it'll be more secure. And on that note, how the fuck did the ants move a whole what I'm assuming is a vault? Drake thought, asking the burning question.

"*I would assume they simply moved the earth. There are tens of thousands, if not more of these vermin. Ants on your planet can lift one hundred times their own body weight, if I am not mistaken. It would not be surprising that a human-sized ant would be able to do the same.*"

Then what was with the weak one earlier? I threw him like a paperweight, and I was using my Fire Endowment.

"*Abnormality?*"

Come on, abnormality? Things are considered rare because they are. *What're the chances of one of the three princes being one of the ones who happen to be extra super weak?*

"*Then what are you proposing?*"

Drake grit his teeth, accidently carving a chunk out of the wall as he gripped his hand too tightly.

Fuck, he cursed, sighing.

I think he was holding back, like he wanted to look like I overwhelmed him, Drake thought. He walked forward, suddenly needing to take a left turn.

"*Impossible. These monsters want to kill you. For what reason would they wish to hold back?*" Natto asked.

That's what I'd like to know...

"My lord," Theodore suddenly whispered, bringing Drake out of his conversation with Natto.

"Yeah?" Drake replied. He turned out of habit but didn't see anything.

"We seem to have intruded on some sort of nursery," Theodore whispered.

"A what?" Drake said, confused. He turned around again. "Oh, would you look at that..."

Drake held back the urge to whistle in amazement. Covering every inch of the walls were eggs, Tyrant Ant Nursers tending to them here and there. Piled high in between every few rows of eggs were the beasts that had once been running about outside.

"That explains the food shortage... But aren't they also exhausting their food by doing this? They're going to run out eventually," Drake thought aloud.

"Indeed. This one cannot fathom how they are replenishing their stores if everything on the outside hast been pushed boneth dry," Theodore agreed.

"Another thing to add to the long list of mysteries right now... This sponsor is doing a real shit job of administering this tutorial." Drake scoffed.

"Ah," Theodore said in surprise.

"What?"

"This one just received a quest to stab my lord. It doth not specify a reward..."

Drake raised a brow and looked to the sky, raising a hand and a single finger.

"You think you're funny, prick? Better hope I don't catch you outside," he grumbled.

Looking back into the room, Drake began to ponder his options. If the nursery was here, that meant the Queen should be relatively close as well.

A plan began to form in Drake's head.

"Alright, lets scout this out a bit," Drake said, hushed. "So far your concealment has been doing wonders. They can't seem to track us at all like before. How are you doing on mana?" Drake asked.

"As long as this one does not have to cast any subsequent spells, this one dares say he could keepeth the spell indefinitely," Theodore replied in a chipper tone.

Drake assumed Theodore was also twirling his mustache, although he couldn't see it.

"Good, that's perfect for us. Let's look around a bit more. I want to find out if we're near the Queen's throne or if this is just one nursery of many. I'm hoping for the former because I'd rather not have more bugs on our hands..."

"Indubitably, my lord. It shall be done. Would thou like to separate, or shall we proceed together?"

"Let's keep as a pair. If you somehow got caught by one of those princes...

Sorry, but I don't think you could hold your own right now, Theo," Drake explained.

"Think nothing of it, my lord. This one understands their position. And to be forthright, this one would prefer to make it back to his beloved by the end."

"Theo…"

"Yes, my lord?"

"You can't drop a death flag like that, man." Drake sighed. "Susmaryosep, now I have to try extra hard to make sure you survive."

"Apologies."

Drake waved his hand and chuckled.

"Don't worry about it; I never planned on letting you get hurt again anyway. Let's get going. My Mark on the prince just faded, and he was sitting down just a ways off from us."

"Sitting down?" Theodore asked.

Drake nodded out of habit, then snorted as he caught himself. "Yeah, I couldn't see what he was sitting on, but he's been stationary for a while now. I can see an outline of whatever I mark to some extent, and I get a general sense of where they are. The big lug was on the other side of the nest, it seems."

"Drake," Natto interrupted.

Hmm? Drake replied.

"You need to find a place to rest," she instructed.

What? I feel fine?

"Not you, ape. Theodore!"

He just said he was fine?

"Of course he did; he does not wish to be a burden again! Why do you think he came here in the first place! Or was that 'I know why you came' all hot air?"

Oh… I forget sometimes that other mage classes aren't like me. Damn it, Drake cursed.

"Theo," Drake said.

"Yes, my lord? Are we moving now?" Theodore replied.

"No, we're scrapping the plan for now. We need to find a place for us to spend the night."

"But my lord, what of finding the treasure room?"

Drake waved his hand dismissively, not that Theodore could see it.

"It's fine, we have a lot of time. There's no need to rush. I promise we'll get to it in time—and safely."

"*Now who is raising death flags…*" Natto snorted.

"My lord's will is my command. Speak it and it shall be so," Theodore answered in a brief hushed tone.

Drake imagined Theodore bowing at the waist in a butler-esque pose and smirked slightly.

"Then let's get a move on. Need to find a place to hole up tonight," Drake affirmed. He began to walk along the wall through the nursery, assuming Theodore was following not far behind.

Drake and Theodore were passing the pile of monster and animal corpses when Drake abruptly stopped, Theodore running into him.

"My lord?" Theodore asked.

"I just got a great idea…" Drake sneered and held out a palm, pulling an item from his inventory. "I guess I really *am* an asshole." He laughed.

Man-Eating Fruit Tree [F-Grade]

"*Even these ants do not deserve this…*" Natto said, but she couldn't hide the slight glee in her voice.

Please, they're monsters. They would kill us without a second thought. Least they can do is help us solve our food problem, and to be honest, I just want to fuck with them. That prince pissed me off, Drake thought.

"*Because he did not take you seriously and held back?*" Natto asked, snickering.

Yeah. Fuck that guy. Or insect. Whatever, screw him is all I'm saying. Drake scoffed and dropped the seeds onto the corpses.

"Alright, Theo. Let's get the hell out of Dodge," he urged.

"Sire, we are in the Ant's Hive, not Dodge," Theodore replied, confused.

"I know what I said. Just hurry the hell up, Theo!"

* * *

"We need to do something about it!" Claire screamed.

Bjorn looked out onto the land that was cleared, some of it sunken in thanks to the tunnel below collapsing.

"There's nothing we can do. Without knowing where the tunnels are or where they are, we could just collapse another tunnel on top of them," Bjorn said, gritting his teeth.

"You're the strongest in the tutorial! Can't you do something?!" she shouted again, gripping at his arm. "I can't lose him! I can't lose him... not like I lost my brother. I don't think I could stand losing him and being all alone again... Please..."

Bjorn didn't say anything, unable to give her comfort or a solution. Soon Harley and Chelsea came to pull her away.

"Why aren't you angry? Theodore is missing and probably with him too! How can you be so calm?!" Claire said, ripping her arm away from Harley and shouting in her face.

Harley shook her head. "That is exactly why I am not worried," she said evenly, although her hand shook subtly. "I know that he is with Mr. Shot, and he will not let anything happen to him. If you believe in him," Harley said looking back at Claire, "you will have to trust he will come back safely, one way or another."

Claire lost her gusto and collapsed to her knees, Harley and Chelsea helping her back up to her feet after a few moments comforting her.

With them leaving and going back to the fortress, Bjorn continued to look out, waiting for something, *anything* he could use to help find them. His eyes were trained on the horizon, and his ocular skill was on constantly.

Soon footsteps came from behind him, but he didn't bother to move.

"What ya thinking, big guy? I know that idjit ain't gonna die lying down, but this one is a doozie if I ever seen one. Might as well be a bear caught in the living room. Everything's a mess, and I don't know up from down right now," Hudson said, giving a tense sigh.

"We wait. It's all we can do right now. We wait until there's something we can use and go from there. That collapse didn't just trap them inside, but also the ants. Sooner or later they'll need to come up, whether it's for food, air, or whatever else. And when they do, I'm going in and bringing them back. I should have never let him get close to the damned wall alone in the first place. He's nothing but a reckless bastard..." Bjorn said, sighing.

"That's true," Hudson agreed. He gave Bjorn an awkward pat on the shoulder, having to step on his toes to reach him. "But, that damned bastard is a stubborn one too."

Hudson walked back to the fortress with the others, deciding to go to the top of the rampart to get a better view since he didn't have an ocular ability like the rest.

Bjorn continued to stay vigilant, searching for anything.

"Don't worry, bro, I'm coming. Just stay alive long enough for me to get there. Can't have you dying before you put a stop to me..."

Chapter 57
Okay, so It Wasn't the Best Idea I've Had!

"How you holding up, Theodore?" Drake grunted as he turned his head over his shoulder.

"Th-This one is managing, my lord!" Theodore grunted back from on top of Drake's shoulder.

"Why is this place so fucking complicated! There isn't any rhyme or reason to any of the tunnels! It's like they *want* us to get lost! Oh." Drake roared and ran at full speed, jumping off the heads of some of the ants and blasting them here and there in the tunnel.

For the past week, Drake had been looking for a 'place to rest' for Theodore, but unfortunately for them, there was no secure location.

They had tried holing up in a small cave Drake had made for them overnight, but they were quickly found once Theodore fell asleep and his concealment spell was canceled.

"You do understand it would help if you did not constantly leave a trail of destruction wherever you went," Natto shouted.

It was a good idea at the time! And it did get them off our tails for a little bit! Drake shouted internally.

Drake's plan to use the Man-Eating Fruit Trees to cause chaos for one of the nurseries they'd found had been a good idea at the time. He was striking the ants at the heart of the problem.

What he hadn't known, unfortunately, was that there were many more nurseries in the nest. His impulsive idea had now caused them to be chased through the Hive for the past week.

On his tail currently were trackers and some of the Royal Guards. Normally this wouldn't have been a problem, but with Theodore here with him, Drake was limited in what he could do. Theodore was barely a fraction as durable as Drake was, and he was a very delicate class by nature of being a mage variant.

Drake was also at a loss on what to do about counterattacking the chasing ants. He'd been able to and did use a large area spell in the main chamber, but this tunnel was obviously not the large cavern. Drake was also wary of blowing up tunnels since they still hadn't found the treasure room or the new exit that he'd expected the ants would build to reach the surface.

"You would think they would've made an exit to the surface by now! What's taking them so long?!" Drake growled, rushing forward through the tunnel and jumping from ant head to ant head.

"*It is possible they already have and we just have not found it as of yet? Lest you forget, we have yet to find the Queen's Chamber, any of the princes, or the treasure room,*" Natto reminded.

"It would be nice if you had anything helpful to say." Drake sighed, then clicked his tongue as he looked forward. "They're blocking the tunnel again!"

A few feet in front of Drake stood a barricade of ants with weapons and shields at the ready. A phalanx of guards and Royal Guards chittered in anger, waiting for Drake.

"Another blockade. Theo, brace up!" Drake shouted. He stepped down on an ant's head and brought it to the floor with a crunch this time.

"Y-Yes, my lord!" Theodore said nervously.

Drake planted his feet, throwing his free hand in an arc in front of them. Multiple brown magic circles formed as well as one snow-white and one dense blue circle.

In one motion, a whip of water formed, bisecting the ants around Drake before falling in a small encirclement on the floor. A spike of ice formed from the white circle only to be crushed as Drake's hair and tattoos cascaded to white. The brown magic circles formed spikes of jet-black earth pointed right at the blockade.

"Earth Spike Repeater!"

Drake willed the spikes of earth to condense into smaller bullets, then fired them off like a gatling gun as he anchored himself in the tunnel.

The bullets of black earth sped forward, piercing through the air, the blockage, and anything in between in moments.

Drake sprinted ahead with Theodore on his shoulder, following the bullets. He picked up stones, armor, and corpses along the way.

He was able to deal with some of the ants when necessary, but Drake was limited. He was forced to stay at long-range with his magic, and he couldn't use anything explosive or too large. Right now, he couldn't risk getting in too close with Theodore not safe and still exhausted.

"It would be nice if we could find this treasury soon." Drake sighed and dashed forward past where the blockage had been.

"'Tis only a matter of time before we find it, my lord. Thou hast footed a myriad of travel for days; tis bound to be hither in but a few breaths!" Theodore encouraged over his shoulder.

Drake raised a brow. "Wait. It *has* been a few days of running nonstop. Are they playing with me?" Drake suddenly thought.

"My lord?"

Drake jumped up, beginning to jump from ant to ant again now that they swarmed the tunnel once more.

"What if the ants are actively changing the tunnels? It's been, what, twenty-four hours since we found a new nursery, right?" Drake said aloud.

"*That seems to be a stretch, no? How would you even test that theory?*" Natto asked skeptically.

Only one way, Drake thought. He turned his head to a random worker ant. "*Marked,*" he whispered before continuing to run.

Drake quickly switched his Endowment to Lightning, increasing his speed. Running forward as fast as he could, he ignored the screaming Theodore on his shoulder. Drake followed the tunnel, keeping a mental note of where the ant he had marked was.

A few minutes into running, he began to scowl, feeling the ant's position close in.

"Those bastards are screwing with me!" Drake growled, eyeing the worker ant in front of them. "Then new plan." Drake smiled and put Theodore down.

"If they're using the same ants in this tunnel to keep us here, that means no new reinforcements. So I get to clear out the tunnel!"

* * *

Obiteron played with the ring on one of his clawed hands, waiting patiently for news of the human that had entered the Hive.

"Your Majesty!" a guard shouted, scrambling into the room.

"Yes, what is it?" he asked somewhat expectantly.

"The human has killed another blockade and several guards. It seems he has figured out our means to stall him," he reported, bowing his head.

"Seems he is not completely dull... Inform the workers that they are to tunnel him to the second chamber. I believe my brother is becoming impatient enough as it is," Obiteron ordered in an even tone before going back to his jewelry.

"But Your Majesty, that is right next to the Queen's birthing chamber! We can't possibly—"

Obiteron waved his hand. The blood from the guard's head splattered to the floor. He then pointed to one of the remaining standing guards in the chamber.

"You, tell the workers. I don't believe there is a problem, yes?"

The guard nodded and scrambled out of the room just as fast as the now-deceased guard had scrambled in.

Obiteron focused back on his jewelry, playing with it in his claws.

"Good, everything is going to plan. First Braxor, then Rasha..."

* * *

"My lord, what, may this one ask, is the plan now?" Theodore asked. He was sitting down on a comfortable seat that Drake had placed in the tunnel.

"Not sure. I can't exactly go blasting through walls," Drake replied, sitting on a similar chair as they both took time to relax. "But take a nap if you can.

The tunnel is cleared for now, and they don't seem to be sending in more reinforcements for whatever reason, so I guess we just wait for now," Drake surmised, shrugging.

"This one fears that they cannot find solace in slumber just yet. The events that have unfolded art but a fresh wound on this one's mind after all, my lord," Theodore said wearily.

"You won't get another chance until we find a really secure place, Theo. Might as well try. Want a bed instead?" Drake asked jokingly.

"This will suffice, my lord..."

Drake chuckled and went back to focusing on his senses. He tried his best to stretch his aura past the rocks of the tunnel, but he continued to fail each time.

Sighing, he took a break. He made sure to stretch his aura wide enough to cover as much of the tunnel as he could, waiting for something, *anything* to burrow through and give them something to do.

"*Quite curious,*" Natto chimed in.

What is? Drake asked.

"*That you are being so patient with this. Normally you would run in head first and worry about the consequences later. I understand you have dear Theo to worry for, but even still, it has not stopped you before. What is different this time?*"

Well for one, I can't dig us out. Two, whoever is directing us has me by the twig and berries. So might as well go along for the ride.

"*You believe this to be best? Let the artificer of our doom direct you as they will?*"

Not exactly. I know I can beat anything in here—at least anything we've met so far. That, I'm sure of. The problem is I can't have Theo taken hostage or let us both get buried under who knows how many tons of rock if they decide to collapse a tunnel on us. There isn't a need for anything drastic just yet, so I'll let whoever it is pull us around. We got nothing but time for now. And hey, they were nice enough to let us rest after chasing us for a week. Can't be all bad?

Natto remained stunned in silence, unsure of how to answer Drake's laid-back position.

Drake put his arms behind his head and closed his eyes, focusing on his aura sense fully. He could feel and hear Theodore breathing slowly as he apparently finally fell asleep from exhaustion. Drake smirked slightly and continued to monitor the tunnel.

Hours passed while Drake remained vigilant. He kept focus on anything that could change at a moment's notice within the tunnel.

"My focus has skyrocketed," Drake mused. "If I had this kind of focus when I was an artist, I would've been the best there ever was... Is this a result of my status increasing?" Drake wondered.

"*Yes,*" Natto replied flatly.

"Oh. Well, that solves that mystery." Drake laughed. "If only that introduction construct was that concise."

Drake slumped slightly in his chair, growing tired of waiting for hours, when what he'd been waiting for finally happened. He quickly turned his head, hearing the moving of gravel and dirt from the wall further down the tunnel.

"Strange... I don't feel anything entering the tunnel. They're running away. Guess we're being led by the nose again," Drake thought aloud as he sat up. "Let's go see what killer Tyrant Santa brought us."

Drake moved over to Theodore, gently pushing the man to rouse him from his sleep.

"Wakey wakey, Theo."

"W-What is it my lord? Hast thy enemy found our quarry?" Theodore answered blearily.

"Not quite," Drake said. He offered him a cup of water. "More like we're being led out of here. Come on, wash up. Let's go."

After a brief minute, Theodore and Drake moved through the tunnel and found one side collapsed. The wall opened into another tunnel.

"Shall I conceal us, my liege?" Theodore asked.

"No need; they know we're coming. Keep yourself concealed, though.

Once we exit the tunnel, I want you to try to get to a position where you can use your illusions again safely," Drake instructed as he started to walk down the tunnel.

Minutes passed, then an hour as the pair walked pensively, unsure of whether they'd be ambushed or led out of the hive.

"This is getting really theatrical, don't you think? What's with all the cloak and dagger they're putting us through? It's like it isn't even about us being here." Drake sighed.

"That is what you are upset about? The fact that it is not centered around you?" Natto scoffed.

Well yeah... I mean you would think they would be more adamant about trying to get rid of us, right? It only makes sense, Drake thought.

"I suppose it does. It is quite strange that they did not send a full-force suppression party after you two. It does beg the question."

I don't like begging.

"That is not what I was suggesting, you moronic dullard!"

Oh sorry, I thought it was about me again. Drake smirked.

Their back and forth was cut short when the sound of chittering and movement resounded in the tunnel. A dim light glowed in the distance.

"Looks like we've reached the end of the line. Took long enough." Drake sighed.

Theodore remained silent, wanting to conceal himself before they reached the tunnel's exit.

"And behind door number one?" Drake said, running out.

Bursting out of the tunnel, Drake was met with the unexpected. Looking out, he saw the forest. Ants continued to skitter about the forest floor, but there was no sun. The sheer expanse and magnitude of the cavern put him in awe.

"Well, wasn't expecting that one..."

Chapter 58

The True Tyrant

"This is not what I was expecting at all," Drake said, looking out at the expansive forest underground. "Did they decide to sink half the forest in here? How did we not notice that much of the land missing?"

"Perhaps they had sunk it from the beginning, and it regrew above before anyone noticed. Or they grew this underground on their own. Regardless, it is irrelevant right now. What is important is why we were led here," Natto posed.

Inside the dense trees lower down the slope leading up to their tunnel, there was movement.

Drake focused and tried to inspect the movement, stretching his aura as best as he could to reach the trees. There were things moving in the forest. A lot of things.

Forest Deer Level 10 [F-Rank]

"Well, that explains where all the wildlife went. If we ever get out of here and release these back above ground, I think we'll be in good shape until the end of the tutorial," Drake mused.

He continued scanning the forest, seeing ants coming and going as well.

"So they're basically domesticating the wildlife here to feed their numbers? Is that even possible on the scale of what they've been producing?" Drake wondered aloud.

"The reproduction rate of the animals in the tutorial after ranking up is faster than normal by leaps and bounds. You will notice more of this on your planet once you leave the tutorial as well. Ranking up affects all beings differently, including

Mana Vessels. It is why we are lucky your oaf of a friend is seemingly so resilient..." Natto explained, trailing off.

Drake raised a brow as he began walking down the slope toward the forest. He needed to see what he was dealing with and figure out where to go from there. Theodore was safely hidden away for now; Drake assumed he was staying within trailing distance of him.

I'll have to keep the spells and such in my back pocket for now. Don't want to accidentally hit Theo, Drake thought before speaking again.

"Care to explain more of that? It's the first you've mentioned of it, and what was that stuff before with Uta and a King Vote? You've been dodging me about that for weeks."

"Unfortunately, I cannot divulge further about the things outside until we are out of the tutorial, as I have told you multiple times! And do not worry about the vote. All will fall into place where it should, fear not," Natto said, her smirk coming through in her voice.

"Okay... You know when people say that type of thing, it's never good, right? But fine, can you at least explain what you mean by Bjorn and the change?" Drake asked, adjusting his question.

Drake reached the treeline before Natto spoke, the construct seemingly hesitating on how to explain it.

"The... oaf... has shown remarkable resistance for ingesting two legendary stones, if what he said is true. In most instances, there is an immediate change within the vessel, whether that is their race or in the function of some of their skills. Purer lineages receive more potent benefits from an earlier rank. Primordials in particular receive such things at F-Rank, and even more at E and so on. In some cases, though, they do not manifest until E-Rank, but no later. Which is what will happen with the overgrown ape."

"So what would happen to someone with less resistance? Turn into a cyclops like Lamar? Or a dwarf like the old man back at the outpost?" Drake asked.

"Precisely. Normally, as I have said, the change is instant. For the more extreme cases or pure blood Primordial races, even more so." Natto sighed. *"Which*

makes the fact that he has not changed even more distressing. It would mean that he is just that much more powerful."

"So the longer he takes to change, the more powerful he is?"

"Not necessarily, but the delayed change does more accurately indicate such. But that is for later."

"Don't try to dodge me again! We were just getting started!" Drake snorted, raising his hands up in the air.

"I am not. You have a guest, if you haven't noticed," Natto spat.

"Oh, I noticed, I'm just more interested in what's going to happen to Bjorn than some oversized cockroach." Drake sighed.

Drake had meandered through the trees for some time now and somehow only been met with the animal life that inhabited it. Surprisingly, he hadn't come into conflict with any of the ants he'd seen earlier.

Instead, he'd picked up on something in his aura sense that was casually moving closer to him. Alone.

Braxor Trikk Level 29 [F-Rank]

"Were you the one who led me here?" Drake asked, stopping.

Braxor did nothing. The Ant Prince had stopped and was what Drake could only call glaring back at him.

"Don't understand me? I sure as hell can't understand you. Seems we're at an impasse," Drake said casually. "You know, last time we met you tried to kill me only to get your ass handed to you. Or wait, is thorax handed to you better?" Drake said, pausing to think for a moment.

Braxor again did and said nothing, seemingly waiting for Drake to do something. Although Braxor wasn't moving, Drake could feel the ant's gaze and the pressure around it increasing with every word he said.

"For someone or something that doesn't understand me, you seem to be getting pretty upset with every word I say." Drake chuckled.

"It can only be your grating voice," Natto huffed.

Drake rolled his eyes and snorted, but his focus remained on the ant. He waited for the prince to make some kind of move.

"You don't seem to be one to carry accessories like your other brother,"

Drake mused, looking at the hulking figure of the ant in front of him. "Don't like bling, or is gold just not your color?"

Braxor remained stoic, his forearms crossed.

"I'm getting nowhere with this guy..." Drake sighed and opened his palm, a crimson magic circle forming on top of it. A flame sparked.

"KREEEEE!!!" Braxor screeched.

"Oh? Fire bad?" Drake said, pausing.

Braxor hadn't moved, only howled and tried to suppress Drake with its own aura. But Drake was far out of the ant's league.

The Ant Prince raised a limb toward Drake, curling its claws into a fist. The chitin around it creaked.

"Hmm, you want to bump fists?" Drake thought absentmindedly.

"*You fool, why are you even entertaining this monster? Kill it!*" Natto instructed.

"There's something telling me not to... How do I explain this? Instinct? Warrior's honor?" Drake thought aloud. He scratched the back of his head. "I don't know how to explain it. Besides, the prince came here all by himself." Drake smiled. "The least I could do is give him his last rites and show him what a *real* tyrant is."

* * *

"Your Majesty, we have found the location of the human! It took us longer than—"

"I do not care for your excuses. Where is the disaster in human flesh?" Braxor asked evenly.

"Y-Yes! He is currently being led into the Food Chamber!" reported the guard.

Braxor stood up from his throne, heaving a chittering sigh.

"So, brother, it's come to this. You would jeopardize our mother, our food, and our entire foothold in the new universe just for a chance at being King?"

"Your Majesty?"

"Nothing. I will meet with the human abomination."

"Then we shall call for the rest of the guards—"

"No," Braxor said sternly. His voice boomed throughout the chamber and shook the walls. "I will face him alone as the Second Prince. None of you would be anything more than a hindrance in any event. Bring the guards to the Queen's Chamber. It is your duty now to keep our colony alive and remain after all the scheming is finished."

The guard tried to protest, but he was met by the backhanded claw of Braxor.

"I am the Second Prince of the Tyrant Ants, and my word is still law here until I take my last breath. And I am yet breathing. You will do as you are told." Braxor sneered and exited the chamber.

Braxor walked down the tunnel, his head held high as he flexed and relaxed his claws, checking for any lasting damage from the previous fight a week ago.

"That human was able to take on all three of us... He played with us like we were but fresh larvae, hatched but moments ago." He sneered as he spoke aloud, his voice echoing in the tunnel.

"Can I kill him..." Braxor mused, his mandibles clacking. "It matters not. I am a prince, and I will do my duty for the Hive regardless."

Braxor's mighty mandibles clacked once more, sending a rumble through the tunnel. His Tyrant's Aura became palpable in the air.

He walked for some time before he found the exit, but with every step, his legs felt more and more heavy. The weight of his colony, of the hive and its future, weighed on him.

Looking out into the green forest that they'd brought down below the surface to feed their brother and sisters, Braxor steeled himself.

Seeing ants turn their heads in his direction, he chittered, commanding them all to return to the tunnels and close them off. He enforced his command of protecting the Queen's Chambers that were close by.

Once done, all that remained was to find the human, but it was not hard.

Braxor walked through the forest toward the pressure he felt. He scoffed, his claws gripping the air in anticipation.

"Their Aura feels much like our own, but it is more... I did not notice it before," he muttered. He brought his hand to his face. "Am I afraid?" he asked.

Braxor's hand subtly trembled, but it was only for a moment before he gripped tightly and laughed to himself.

"A human more oppressive than a Tyrant Ant?"

Braxor scoffed once again, feeling the weighted aura in the surroundings. The human would find him soon.

So he waited.

Soon the human found Braxor just as he'd expected. The human wore black robes trimmed in gold, his flesh exposed from the shoulder down on both sides, and his face seemed to be covered by something.

Odd armor. How does he move with such hindrances? Braxor thought.

The human seemed to be ignoring him, only now stopping and speaking to Braxor.

Braxor could not understand the human, but the tone of his voice and his body language told him all he needed to know.

He is not taking me seriously. He does not even see me as a threat.

The human then lifted his hand, forming fire from nothing.

"NO!" hissed Braxor.

A moment later, Braxor raised his fist and aimed right at the human. The human then squelched the flame and tilted its head slightly as if confused.

"We will fight like tyrants, the honorable way!" Braxor shouted. "*Your strength against mine!*"

Braxor knew the human did not understand, but he hoped his plea would work.

If this human is able to use magic, he should be weaker physically. He did get the upper hand when we fought, but I could sense magic behind his blows. He must be using a skill. But I am prepared for it now, and I have skills of my own. I will topple him. I will win! For the colony!

The man nodded, the hair on top of his head shifting from blue to black. He then stood as if waiting for Braxor.

"So I get the first blow then, human?" Braxor sneered. "It will be the mistake that costs you your life!"

Braxor screeched, pulling his arms to his sides as he prepared his own Martial Skill. He pressed and condensed the aura around him.

"You are overconfident! You must not know that princes of the Tyrant Ants have a special ability!" Braxor screeched. "For every ant that is under our command, we gain a status bonus. And I am the strongest prince! This whole colony is loyal to me!"

The ground around Braxor cracked and dented. A whistle came from the human.

"Prepare to die!" howled Braxor.

Pushing against the ground, Braxor crushed the earth below as he shot forward, his every step denting the dirt underfoot into craters while he barreled ahead. His outstretched pitch-black claw glowed in crimson red from his Martial Skill, the chitin armor around his arm cracking and splintering from the increase in status from his skill. His claws roared, moving faster than even Braxor himself could see.

But he was stopped dead in its tracks.

The human's hands intertwined with Braxor's, holding his claws at bay with seemingly little effort.

"W-What?!" Braxor screeched.

The human had embedded himself into the ground somehow, the earth beneath him pushed inward as it took the full force of Braxor's blow. But what was more astonishing to the prince was the eyes of the man.

Braxor's hand struggled to push forward to no avail. Instead he was moved by the human, his face slowly coming into view from behind Braxor's claw.

His eyes shifted color from blue to yellow to green.

"No!" Braxor shouted again. He threw his second hand forward, but he was met with the same result. The human stopped the blow without effort.

Braxor tried to push forward, digging into the ground with his four legs and carving deep divots into the earth.

"No, no, no! I won't let it end like this!" he shrieked. "It is impossible for a Tyrant Ant to be outmatched by a human! I can't—Ahhhh!"

Finally, the sound of crunching reverberated throughout the area as Braxor dropped to his knees.

His hands were being crushed by the human's bare hands.

Suddenly, it felt as if the world was put on Braxor's shoulders. The pressure from the human's aura increased to a level that made anything else he'd ever felt pale in comparison.

Braxor stiffened, feeling cold even through the pain. His mandibles clattered in fear.

The human pressed down more, looming over the prince. His eyes glowed with glee and malicious intent.

"B-Brother, *what have you done.*"

Chapter 59
No Choice

You have defeated Tyrant Ant Prince - Braxor Trikk Level 29 [F-Rank] Experience earned. 5,000,000 TP have been awarded.

Congratulations! You have reached Elemental Miller level 23. 40 FP have been awarded.

Drake loomed over the now-dead body of the prince, his breath ragged as he continued to throw fist after fist into the corpse.

"Dr...ak... D...ke!"

"M... l...rd?! Cea...e! My lo—"

Drake had gone into a stupor, his body moving on autopilot after facing off against the prince. He'd beaten the monster handedly, but like several times before, his body had reacted in a way he could not control.

It was instinctual. Drake only saw red, only saw the feeble creature in front of him challenging him and his authority as the stronger being. Something deep inside him wouldn't allow it. It wouldn't allow this pitiful creature to pretend to be royalty. Pretend to be strong.

"My... L...o...r...d!"

"Drake! Stop! You are killing him!" a voice screamed in Drake's head.

Drake blinked, the feverish stupor he'd entered fading away slowly. He heard his own heavy breathing. His arms raised, holding a familiar person in his hands by the throat.

"Th-Theo?!" Drake stammered, releasing him immediately.

Theodore dropped to the floor, his breath coming in chaotic coughs and heaves as he held his neck. Drake's hands had left prints around it.

Drake quickly brought out a health potion and held it for Theodore to take, but his face was quickly becoming blue, and his eyes were hazy.

"Fuck! Is his windpipe crushed?! He can't breathe or swallow! What do I do!" Drake panicked. "Natto! What is going on!" Drake shouted.

"I-I do not know, but we have to save Theodore first. You need to force the potion down his throat or somehow get the liquid inside his body," Natto explained warily.

Drake gripped the flask in his hand, looking at Theodore hesitantly, but he finally came to a decision.

"Theodore! Can you hear me, buddy?" Drake shouted.

Theodore nodded weakly, still gripping at his neck.

"This is going to hurt," Drake said tersely before throwing his hand into Theodore's side, opening up a small finger-sized wound.

Theodore gave a muffled scream of pain and dropped to the floor, but Drake was forced to ignore him as he uncorked the flask and pushed the potion into the wound.

Within seconds, Theodore's neck returned to a normal color along with his face as he began to breathe again. Drake pulled the flask from the wound and sprinkled the remaining fluid on the injury, closing it up.

"M-My lord... Art thou alright...?" Theodore asked in huffs.

"Shut up, you idiot. I nearly killed you twice, and you're worried about me? There's something wrong with your head..."

"Loyal to a fault is the way of the gentleman, my lord."

Drake was angry, furious even, but he couldn't help smirking slightly before the anger returned.

"What exactly is going on, Natto? I knew I was having problems, and the skills, even with the resistance some of them gave, were deteriorating my personality. But this... This is something else! I nearly killed Theodore!"

"I am unsure... There should be no reason you are having these personality switches. You have not consumed a legendary stone, and you are human. I suppose it is possible that keeping the legendary stones in your personal inventory could be

resonating with you, but that is an extreme and should not be possible..." Natto explained pensively.

"Then I'll just get rid of the stones. I don't give a shit about them anyway, especially if it's making me nearly kill someone close to me," Drake growled. He pulled the stones from his inventory.

Drake reeled back his hands, ready to throw the stones, but he was interrupted by the loudest chime he'd ever heard in his head. It was so loud that apparently even Natto could hear it.

Attention! Urgent Quest!

Urgent Individual Quest: The sponsor of the tutorial implores you to retain the Legendary Necromancy Skill Stones until the end of the tutorial period. Reward: Meeting with the sponsor.

"Susmaryosep, why was that so loud? A meeting? As if I give a shit about a meeting!" Drake shouted. His hair changed to crimson red as he launched the stones into the air.

But the unexpected happened. There was no crashing of the stones into the cavern wall. Instead, a flash of light covered the stones as they left his hands, another pair of lights materializing next to Drake and dropping the stones at his feet.

The sponsor of the tutorial implores you to retain the Legendary Necromancy Skill Stones until the end of the tutorial period.

Drake bit his lip, picking up the stones and throwing them again as hard as he could.

"I don't care what you want! I won't hurt someone close to me because of some fucking glass rock!"

Again motes of light covered the stones as they left Drake's hands, and they reappeared at his feet.

The sponsor of the tutorial implores you to retain the Legendary Necromancy Skill Stones until the end of the tutorial period.

"No, damn it!"

The sponsor of the tutorial implores you to retain the Legendary Necromancy Skill Stones until the end of the tutorial period.

The sponsor of the tutorial implores you to retain the Legendary Necromancy Skill Stones until the end of the tutorial period.

The sponsor of the tutorial implores you to

...

Drake ground his teeth and gripped the stones in his hands with all of his strength, unable to crush the shining pieces of glass.

"So I don't get a fucking choice?! You can't do this! Isn't this interfering with the rules or something? Hey! Are you listening to me, you insufferable piece of shit? You think I'm going to do what you want when you can't even talk to me face to face?!" Drake roared, pointing into the air.

Drake was furious. He looked at Theodore, who was still recovering from the injury that Drake had inflicted on him. Drake dropped the stones to the floor.

"I would rather sit here and do nothing and wait for the tutorial to end, then. I won't do what you want. If they aren't in my inventory, that probably means they won't come with me when I leave. So you lose." Drake sneered into the air.

"Drake... this is foolish. Do not argue with a sponsor. As far as we know, it is still a Primordial race like we imagined!"

Don't care. I've reached my quota for being jerked around this week. And if what you said about the stones is true, I want no part in holding onto them. I won't risk hurting people I care about for some piece of glass, Drake explained as he crossed his arms.

"That is hardly what those stones are, and you know it! Those legendary skills are things entire worlds and solar systems would wage wars for!"

Are you saying they're worth more than Theo? Than Bjorn, Claire, Sherry, Harley, than everyone on the surface? I was this close to snapping Theo's neck, Natto, Drake thought angrily, shivering slightly at the thought.

What happens the next time I snap? The next time I black out in a violent rage because of it? Will I kill someone and not even know?

Natto was forced into silence, but Drake could tell she was uncomfortable with not speaking. He knew she was pragmatic about things of this nature. She wanted him to keep the stones; it was the best course of action for their future. But Drake didn't care. He wouldn't put his friends and loved ones in jeopardy.

"If that is what you wish," she said finally.

Thank you, Drake thought honestly.

Turning around, Drake sat down in front of Theodore. He left the stones where he'd dropped them, only for them to move in a flash of light to his feet again.

Drake smiled.

"So you can't put them directly in my inventory? Checkmate, idiot." Drake sneered and looked up.

"My lord, doth thou think it best to antagonize whoever it is that thou is provoking?" Theodore asked gently, rubbing his sore neck.

"Nope. But that's tomorrow Drake's problem. Right now, I just want to make sure you're alright. I'm sorry I did that, Theo... I-I don't know what happened."

"This one would like to ask that my lord please refrain from nearly killing him in the future." Theo smirked, his mustache twirling upwards. "But it is of no matter. Thou hast saved my life countless times. This one thinks it only right that my lord put it in danger now and again."

Drake looked blankly at Theodore as he sat down to get eye level with him. He then began to chuckle.

"You have to have something wrong with you, Theo."

"Perhaps. But only someone as insane as this one could follow such an eccentric lord."

Drake sighed, pushing the legendary stones on the ground away from them.

"Got me there..." Drake agreed.

Drake and Theodore continued to sit and wait while Theodore recovered from the muscle pain of his injury. Theodore was a mage class, and his recovery was not nearly as fast as Drake's. Theodore may have had a recovery skill, but it only pertained to his mana recovery.

For an hour, Drake was pestered by the sponsor. The stones appeared on his lap, and he brushed them away again and again until finally a new quest appeared.

Urgent Individual Quest: Accept to hold the legendary stones until the end of the tutorial.

Reward: Skill Stone Container [S-Grade]

Drake scoffed at the quest. He picked at his ear, trying to reduce the ringing from all of the forced notifications.

"Trying to bribe me now?" Drake said, looking up as he leaned back on his arms. "How about fuck off."

"What bribe, my lord?" Theodore asked.

"Sponsors want me to hold onto those stones, the legendary ones I mentioned a while back," Drake explained, using his chin to point to the stones. "Gave me a quest to do it. But I won't. From what Natto said, the stones are the reason I'm having such violent changes in personality and almost... well, almost killed you."

Theodore looked over at the stones pensively, obviously thinking over what Drake had just explained.

"What is the reward for such a quest, my lord?" Theodore asked.

"A meeting with the prick. And they're offering a 'skill container.'"

"*You should take—*" Natto tried to say.

No. I'm not doing anything for some asshole just to meet the bastard face to face. Drake scoffed.

"My lord," Theodore said, picking up the stones, "thou should agree to it."

"W-What? I nearly killed you because I was holding those on me, and you want me to go ahead and keep them just because some sponsor is asking me to?" Drake asked incredulously.

Theodore nodded. "This one understands better than most that my lord cares for those around him and would go to great lengths to do so. But this one also trusts my lord. This one would not be able to forgive oneself if he was the reason my lord was not able to take an opportunity to reach the top where his lord belongs."

"Theo, no. I won't take those stones," Drake said firmly.

Theodore's eyes dimmed slightly after hearing Drake, going distant for a moment.

"My lord…"

Drake frowned, knowing what had just happened.

"They didn't…" Drake growled, looking up. "How slimy can you get?! You can't get me to do it, so you give him the quest? Are you just going to do that with everyone until you find some schmuck that accepts it?!"

Drake was thrown into a state of rage again. He snatched the stones from Theodore's hands. Wrestling with what to do, Drake went back and forth on if he should accept the responsibility himself.

But the decision was made for him.

"M-My lord… The quest is saying… The quest is saying if this one does not accept, i-it will kill Harley…"

Drake's eyes turned to points, and his face twisted in fury. Drake gave a guttural scream of frustration.

Drake Wallen
Tutorial Alias: Shot
Race: Human [F-Rank]
Profession: Miner P5 (0%) [F-Rank], Jeweler P5 (0%) [F-Rank]
Class: [Unique] Elemental Miller Level 23
VIT: 358 (10 + 15%)
STR: 362 (60 +15%)
DEX: 280 (80 + 25%)
INT: 736 (15 + 20%)
WIS: 356 (10 + 29%)
END: 274 (30 + 25%)
Free Points: 120

Chapter 60
Boiling Over

"How is this allowed?!" Drake shouted, his aura and mana going wild for a moment. "It can't possibly be something the system is okay with!"

"Drake, you need to calm down. You are becoming erratic!" Natto pleaded.

"I'm fine!" he shouted back. He did his best to take a deep breath.

"You are not fine! The stone should not have degenerated your mental state this much... It is possible your skills have affected you beyond the point of repair, permanently changing your underlying personality!"

"I said I'm fine!" Drake shouted again before realizing he had started manifesting a fireball in his hand.

"I-I don't know what's happening... It's never been this strong of a reaction before. Is it the Tyrant Ant's Aura? It has to be, right? I can still feel the disgust in my stomach of when that prince tried to challenge me..." Drake said, chuckling wearily.

Natto exited Drake with a light pop, resting on his shoulder as her hand went to the back of his head.

"Drake... I-I am sorry. This is my fault. I knew the risks I was putting you through when we began consuming the skill stones, but I never thought that it would catch up to you this quickly. I fear that this may not be reversible," she explained solemnly.

"What? Are you trying to say I'll always be stuck on a knife's edge between going mad and killing anyone around me whenever I fight now?" Drake asked.

"For now, yes… With time it can be managed and controlled, but right now, unless you wish to risk further deterioration by speeding up the process of ranking up, I believe it would be difficult for you to control any impulse you have."

"That's just fucking fantastic." Drake sighed, his shoulders slumping.

"It is not your fault. I should have been more adamant about spacing out your skill stone intake. I trusted that you would be able to handle the strain, but I suppose I was wrong."

Drake chuckled. "So you're saying it was wrong to put faith in me? Thanks for the kick while I'm down… Great vote of confidence."

"I am not saying I do not still trust you, but I have failed as an Assistant by allowing you to have your way. I should have known better based on your personality that you would go too far and outstrip your tolerance for the mental effect on yourself," Natto explained, a look of sympathy on her face. "I know you wish to be a hero and save everyone, but that just is not how the real world works. The fire that burns brightest burns out the quickest."

"That was really morbid." Drake snorted.

"This is not a joke!"

"And I'm not saying it is. I've calmed down a bit thanks to you, and I know what needs to happen," Drake said. He exhaled a long breath. "Are those stones really affecting me the way you think they are?" he asked, pointing down.

"Yes, I believe they are at least exacerbating your problem. We know now that powerful foes are also a trigger. It would seem you have obtained one of the Tyrant Ant's traits in that way, possibly even one of the Goblin King's."

Drake recoiled with a grimace.

"Going a bit far, don't you think?" he said, frowning.

"You were nothing but arrogant with that Tyrant Ant Prince. Fighting him on his terms? The Drake I first met would have fought him with everything he had at his disposal. If not a trait from the King, what is it? Are you naturally inclined to be condescending?" She scoffed.

Drake pursed his lips, unable to argue.

"So in the end, I don't have a choice about the box or the stones for now. With what's happening to me and the shitty fuck upstairs threatening Theo, I have to accept," Drake cursed.

"Yes, unfortunately, it seems you must. But this is also for the best. At least with this, we can control at least one variable that is affecting your personality," Natto agreed.

"Fine." Drake sighed and mentally accepted the quest. "I don't like it, but for Theo, I would have done it anyway."

With that, a box materialized in a mote of light, clanking to the floor. It was a porcelain-colored chest of small size. It looked like it was possibly made of ivory or some other bone.

Mir'phyra's Personal Chest [S-Grade]

A small personal chest of the Dragon Matriarch Mir'phyra. Anything contained within the chest is sealed off from the world.

Made of the bones of her predecessors, this chest is of the highest quality known to the multiverse—priceless in both craftsmanship and material. It is one-of-a-kind.

"Natto...?" Drake asked hesitantly.

"Yes?" she answered, looking down at the same chest.

"This is really bad, isn't it."

"Certainly..."

"How expensive is this box?"

"You do not wish to know..."

Drake laughed uncomfortably. "Well, at least we know for sure who the sponsor is now..."

* * *

"That wretched, worthless brother of mine! I'm ashamed to even call him a Tyrant Ant! He wears the tools of those lesser beasts to compensate for his own weakness!" Rasha screeched, throwing his fist into the throne. "How dare he even suggest that I am weaker than that filthy human?"

"Your Majesty!"

"*What?!* This better be good!" Rasha sneered.

"We've just been told Prince Braxor has sent all of his guards and personnel from the Main Chamber to protect and seal off the Queen's Lair!"

Rasha screeched and stood from the throne. "Why would my brother do such a thing?!"

The guardsman looked at the prince hesitantly, not wanting to die like his predecessors.

"W-We..."

"Out with it, fool!"

"We have heard reports that Prince Braxor was killed in combat by the human..."

The room chilled the moment the words left the guard's mouth. The prince's aura was thick within the room, his emotions spilling into the oppressive pressure.

"You are lying, my brother would not die to some worthless human flesh bag. The only one who could kill him is me. *I* will be the one to take the place as king," Rasha said evenly. His voice was calm, but the aura surrounding him was anything but.

"I... I... My sincerest apologies, my prince, but we have confirmed as much—"

The guard's head rolled to the floor. Rasha howled inside the chamber.

"I'll kill him! I'll kill that filthy human!!"

* * *

Obiteron leaned back on the throne inside his chamber, his jeweled claws intertwined with one another as he awaited the expectedly good news.

Soon the guardsman that he was expecting passed through the open archway into the chamber.

"Well?" Obiteron asked.

"Th-The prince has fallen... The human has slain Prince Braxor."

"Good, and what of his guards? Have they moved as expected?" Obiteron asked again, raising a hand.

"Yes, they have been instructed to seal off the Main Chamber and to protect the Queen at all costs."

"Perfect," Obiteron mused. He stood from the throne, his arms swinging open wide. "Then all troops to the Queen's Chamber. It is time to defend her with our lives!" he announced, his mandibles clacking joyously.

* * *

"My lord, what is it that we shall doeth now?" Theodore asked pensively, getting to his feet now that his body was healed.

"You," Drake said, pointing at Theodore, "will stay out of sight and will not come out of your stealth unless we find a safe place to rest or it's absolutely necessary," Drake said, sighing slightly.

"But, this one can be of service! There is no need—"

"Theo, there is no telling when my next freakout will be. And I have no idea if next time I'll be able to stop before I do something I regret."

Natto had already merged once again with Drake, deciding to stay silent for now as she did her best to go over the information they had at hand. Her goal was to figure out a way to help Drake, but until the tutorial ended, she was limited in what she could access and divulge to him.

"My lord," Theodore said beginning to protest, "this one understands that thou may be pensive about what mayhaps in the future, but do not cast this one from thy side," he said. His hand gripped and rubbed the top of his cane in nervousness. "This one knows full well what art the perils of continuing forward. And I would have it no other way."

Drake sighed. His appreciation for Theodore's loyalty and honest devotion was hard to reject. They had been stuck in the Hive for a little more than a week already, and it may have been fine for Drake, but death was always just a stone's throw away for Theodore.

Not to mention Theodore had just as much—if not more—to lose than Drake did. Theodore had Harley waiting for him, his wife. For Theodore to be so devoted despite that made Drake all the more certain.

"No, you will stay at a safe distance. Away from me," Drake said sternly. "Our priority is to keep you safe until then or until we're out of the tutorial. I may have wanted to come here, but not at the cost of losing good friends."

"But—"

"No buts! Don't make me knock you out and carry you around like a mustached handbag!" Drake shouted.

"This one understands... if it is thy will, my lord," Theodore responded. His arms slumped to his sides.

Drake sighed again, putting his hand on Theodore's shoulder.

"I appreciate your resolve, Theo, I really do. But I won't have Harley chasing me down to the ends of the earth because I let something happen to you. Especially if it was me that did it. I'm not myself right now, and I don't know when I'm coming back. So please, if it helps, just do it for me. For my own sanity."

Theodore's jaw visibly clenched, but he nodded, quickly casting his spell and disappearing from sight.

"Rather harsh to step on a man's resolve like that, do you not think?" Natto asked softly.

Not now... I'm really not in the mood. And he'll thank me later when he's back with his wife in one piece, Drake countered. He began to walk to the chamber's wall.

"Do not think you can save everyone, Drake. Was it not you who said as much? You must let them live their own lives and make their own mistakes eventually. Or do you plan on being with them every second of every day?"

I said not now! I'm not delusional enough to believe I can keep every single person I hold dear safe, but that doesn't mean I can't aspire to. That's what this whole mess was about in the first place! Drake roared back in his head.

I'm not going to say you're wrong, but I'll be damned if I admit I won't prove you wrong! And if that means I have to push them all away for now while I get a handle on my shit, so fucking be it!

Drake had finally walked to the edge of the large chamber.

He felt the wall using his Magic Sight to try and see if he could identify anything of use, but it seemed the ants had closed every entrance or exit using real labor and not magic, giving him no hints as to where to go.

"Fuck! They basically buried us alive... I can't exactly go blasting holes into the wall," Drake cursed with a click of his tongue. "At least there're trees down here, so I don't think breathing will be a problem."

Drake eyed the forest again, seeing the deer and other animals move within.

"I guess I should at least grab some deer for later. Those food buffs would be a welcome sight; I can't remember the last time we had F-Grade food... The kobolds and goblins barely had any."

Disappointed with not getting anywhere after inspecting the wall of the chamber, Drake decided to change it up and do something that always calmed him. Cooking food.

"Theo, I know what I said, but do you want to rest and eat? I don't think we'll be going anywhere anytime soon," Drake said into the air, but he got no response.

Well, that's to be expected... Drake thought with a sigh. *I'll just save him some food then.*

Drake took to the forest, taking out a few deer and other animals that he hadn't even known were in the forest above. He was able to capture deer, rabbits, small fowl, and even a bear.

"This should be good for now. Time to set up a little roast, then," Drake said in a damper tone, taking out a fire pit and some cutlery.

Sitting down, Drake took to preparing the food and lighting the fire. His mind was somewhat clearing and calming down as he did so. He let out a relaxed sigh, the background noise of the forest taking over his senses.

"This... This is actually nice. Maybe taking a break was all I nee—"

His solace was short-lived. The sound of breaking rock reverberated throughout the chamber. The ceiling began to crumble just above Drake and his fire. He looked up.

From the ceiling, the dirt began to fall in small patches and then in large boulders. The fragments of the ceiling fell around the sitting Drake as ants suddenly began falling with them.

Soon Drake was surrounded by Royal Guards and a very pissed off-looking prince.

Rasha Trikk Level 29 [F-Rank]

"Aaaaaannnnd now the moment's gone." Drake sighed.

Chapter 61
Little Kids and Bug

"I'm in a very unfriendly mood right now, and you just stomped out my dinner," Drake hissed. He got up slowly from his seat on the ground.

"KREEEEE!!!"

Prince Rasha screeched loudly, flexing his own aura on the surroundings in response. The prince's guards shirked under the sudden pressure, backing away slightly.

Drake sneered back, unaffected thanks to his skills. Instead, the challenge from the prince slowly began to spark his personality once more. But Drake was aware this time, and he tried his best to clamp down on the change.

"Let me ask you," Drake said coldly, flexing his own aura, "was the last time I put you on your ass not good enough? You came back for more?"

The prince froze again, shaking as he struggled against Drake's aura. His dramatic entrance only served to make it easier for Drake to find him.

"I was never one to pull the legs off insects as a kid. Too busy playing video games and sneaking candy from the pantry. But I think it's time to catch up on lost opportunities," Drake thought aloud, walking forward toward the struggling Rasha.

Drake quickly produced a white flame in his hand. He quenched it as his arms and hair went crimson. His every step forward forced the prince to flinch subtly.

"Regret your own arrogance for challenging a true tyrant," Drake spat, his hand moving to grip Rasha's shoulder and arm with his hands.

The next moment, Drake wrenched the appendage from the prince's socket. Ichor splattered over the ground. The surroundings suddenly came to life as the guards thawed from their fright, jumping into action.

Drake threw the arm away casually, his hair changing to a bright yellow as sparks cascaded from one of his arms to the other.

"*Heretical Endowment, Single, Lightning,*" Drake muttered. His speed shot through the roof as he weaved and dodged the oncoming onslaught of weapons from the Royal Guardsmen coming to defend their prince.

Drake moved, dancing in and out of the strikes from the Royal Guards. He took his time to move out of the encirclement.

"Sadly, I can't do anything flashy to put you in your place. But the over a hundred stat points I put into strength to beat your brother should be a nice consolation prize for you." Drake looked directly at Rasha who was holding his missing limb, his mandibles clattering wildly. "*Weaklings.*"

Drake knew Rasha couldn't understand him like his brother, but the tone of Drake's voice and the condescending manner in which Drake delivered it was more than enough to convey his feelings.

Rasha screeched again in anger, throwing off the Royal Guards left and right with his still attached arm.

"Touchy," Drake chuckled. His palms opened, and two white flames manifested in each. "*Heretical Attunement, Fire.*"

Drake summoned his flames to enhance his tattoos further, the glow of his Martial Skill, Lightning Endowment, and the Fire Attunement cascading together for a magnificent light show.

"Time to squash a bug." Drake sneered. He planted his back foot into the ground, crushed it below, then shot forward.

Drake took no time to appear next to the first Royal Guard ant, his fist millimeters from its serrated jaw. Following through with his jab, Drake took the monster's head clean off, the body falling limply to the floor.

You have subjugated Yu'zik Kikk Level 29 [F-Rank]
Experience earned. 650,000 TP have been awarded.

"One," Drake counted aloud.

In a flash of colors, Drake sped forward to the next guard, throwing an uppercut into its abdomen before it could react. His hand passed through the natural armor it had like it wasn't even there.

You have subjugated Vidmyr Kikk Level 29 [F-Rank]
Experience earned. 650,000 TP have been awarded.

"Two."

Drake grabbed the lifeless ant this time and threw it at the rest of the group. Using the monster's body as cover, he quickly chanted a small spell, but the density and power of the spell did not diminish with the size.

"*Ouka Houken*," Drake whispered. The fire on his arms rushed forward and condensed in front of him into a small bright white ball.

Drake shot the spell forward. It passed through the ant's flying body and landed at the feet of the three other guards and the prince, exploding and taking out two of the guards' pairs of legs.

Not stopping there, Drake moved while the explosion distracted the evading guards and panicked Rasha.

Digging his feet into the ground once again, Drake pushed forward and caught one of the jumping ants mid-air as it tried to dodge the explosion, one hand on its neck.

"*Heretical Attunement, Magma, Revised Gauntlet*," Drake chanted in a murmur.

In Drake's free hand, an orange magic circle quickly manifested. A blob of gooey red and orange moved over his outstretched fingers in fractions of a second. With his next motion, Drake threw the magma-covered hand open. Slamming his palm into the ant's head, he sent it spinning mid-air as the body crashed into the ground below.

Dust and debris exploded from the impact, clearing with a quick sweeping motion from Drake.

The remaining guards and the prince stood stock still, staring back at him.

Drake brought his other hand to his attuned one. The slimy magma slowly moved to cover his other hand as well while the guards and prince looked on.

The prince howled and screeched again, trying to assert some sort of reprisal for Drake's one-sided slaughter.

You are under the effect of Tyrant Royalty's Dominance.
Your skill Tyrant's Indomitability has negated Tyrant Royalty's Dominance.

"Looks like I'm the winner," Drake said, smiling beneath his mask, "and you *lose*."

Drake rushed forward again, making a beeline for Rasha all while dodging and weaving through the remaining guards.

But he was suddenly interrupted by the crashing of the chamber wall. An army of ants flooded the forest, eleven figures shooting out ahead of the rest.

Drake halted, waiting for the newcomers to reach them. Not because he couldn't reach out and kill Rasha, but because the small rational part still left in him told him to hold back.

Natto had been silent ever since they last spoke, and she continued to be, leaving Drake to his own thoughts and will. He understood that the increased amount of monsters in the chamber would mean more fights, more destruction of the land, and possibly killing the food they needed for the rest of the participants to survive for the remainder of the tutorial.

Drake also considered that he had no idea where Theodore was at the moment. He couldn't risk accidentally getting him caught up in the fight if the number of monsters increased and forced him to start using large spells.

Landing down moments later, Drake felt the new ants enter his Aura Field. He stared back at the last prince who screeched something at Rasha.

Drake held firm and waited for them to finish. The pair of Princes stared back at him.

"Go run with your tails between your legs. Don't worry, I'll wait." Drake scoffed, crossing his arms as his magma attunement faded away.

"Antagonizing them when we wish for them to leave is rather stupid," Natto said, finally speaking up.

Oh, are we talking now? Drake thought.

"I have been busy. But it seemed this act of foolishness needed my immediate attention..."

Drake continued to watch the back and forth the princes were having before they finally looked to be ready to move. The thirteen other Royal Guards—Obiteron's, Braxor's, and Rasha's remaining three—all waited for the princes before helping the pair of guards Drake had blown the kneecaps off.

Moving, Rasha was pulled away by Obiteron into the opening of the wall, but not before Drake Marked the prince to track where the pair was going.

"Now, I just need to figure out where the hell Theo is and stuff his curly mustached tushy into a safe place so I can go wild." Drake sighed, then looked out into the sea of ants that had flooded the chamber.

* * *

"It's been more than a week already!"

"There's nothing I can do about it. We have to wait until there's another entrance. If I go around cutting into the ground, I risk burying them alive."

This back-and-forth had happened several times over the week.

Megan stood on the rampart like the rest of the party, waiting for something to happen so they could do something. Anything.

She looked on as Bear and Claire went back and forth again. Claire was desperate to find Shot even after being reassured by Harley and Bear that he would be fine, and Bear was again trying to calm her down while looking for any openings into the Ant's Hive.

Megan had been going over the events in her mind again and again: everything leading up to this point in the tutorial, all her mistakes, all the blunders she'd made until she found her friends again as well as someone who was actually honest for once.

"And I really believed him for a second..." she muttered.

"Believed who?" Chelsea asked next to her. She was sitting on top of the rampart, her legs dangling off the edge.

"O-Oh, just thinking out loud," she muttered again with a nervous chuckle. "You aren't worried like Claire? I thought you were head over heels for Shot."

Chelsea flinched briefly from the sudden question, but she sighed and resumed her casual surveying.

"It's not that I'm not worried," Chelsea explained, her eyes flashing green for a moment before turning back to her natural brown. "It's just I understand there's no use in getting worked up about it."

"And the falling for your boss?" Megan snickered.

Chelsea coughed before answering. "He isn't my boss… He's our party leader. And I already know I don't have a shot with him anymore, so I moved on."

"To bigger and better things, yeah, love?" Jacqueline suddenly said, stepping into the conversation.

Chelsea's ears turned red, and she clammed up at the pointed question. Megan and Jacqueline laughed lightly before Jacqueline pointed a new question at Megan.

"You worried about the dumb sod, Megan? Julia's been pretty worried about the bloody guy despite usually being calm."

Megan looked down at the barren land below the rampart before responding, taking a moment to think.

"It isn't that I'm worried about him, it's that I really believed he was what he said he was. After Chris… I really wanted to hope he was being honest," Megan admitted.

"Honest?" Chelsea and Jacqueline asked together.

"Yeah, honest. He's everything I thought he was: brash and arrogant. He's also strong, protective, and works hard despite always joking around. But he said he would stay with us and protect us all until the end of the tutorial, and then he left…" Megan explained, turning sullen.

"Love… you sure you don't have the hots for this guy? You seem to be pretty right with noticing them small details," Jacqueline joked.

Megan blushed, but Chelsea also spoke up to add, "Shot didn't leave us."

"What do you mean? Of course he did," Megan countered.

Chelsea shook her head. "He didn't leave us to abandon us, Megs. He isn't Chris. If Shot left us behind… it means we just couldn't follow. If I've learned anything from being around that guy for this long, it's that he always puts us first. I don't know why and honestly, I don't know why we deserve it, but he always protects us. So I'm sure he's doing just that."

Megan looked back out into the barren field where the Hive entrances used to be, the collapsed rubble of the tunnels underground forming jagged fallen crevices in the earth.

"I hope you're right. I don't know if I can deal with losing another hero..."

Chapter 62
Not For the Colony

"Theo! Theo, where the hell are you?" Drake shouted as he passed the numerous ants converging on him in the forest. "Damn it, that guy's concealing skill is just broken," he cursed.

"Perhaps he has already left the chamber? Or is simply taking your advice and staying close by and silent?" Natto proposed.

"I can't exactly take that chance with so many ants here. If they swarm me, I can always get out, but if they catch him… I don't see how Theodore would be able to survive. I have to be sure of where he is," Drake said, concerned.

Drake shot through the ants, only killing those necessary for him to scour the area in search of Theodore. But Drake's time was limited in a sense.

Looking over his shoulder, he saw the entrance that the ants had made being plugged up once more.

"At least I know where to start digging once I find Theo. I just hope he wasn't reckless enough to go in there without me."

"You mean you hope he is not like you?" Natto corrected.

"Not the time!" Drake spat, running past another group of ants.

* * *

This one doth believes he is lost… Theodore thought to himself as he stood plastered to the wall, watching ants passing by him in the tunnel.

Theodore had done exactly what Drake hoped he had not. While under the effect of his concealment, he had snuck into the chamber opening, wanting to prove that he was a valuable asset to Drake.

He was currently stuck in the flood of ants that were surging through the tunnel, all of them rushing in one direction.

It doth beg the question, hitherward art these formicidae bound?

Theodore, although curious about where the flood of monsters were going, had another goal that took priority.

This one must find the treasury whilst my lord battles. It is the only way to put him at ease. Unfortunately...

Theodore wished to move from his position stuck to the wall, but it was impossible for him to go anywhere with the crowded tunnel packed by ants. If he was to try, he would surely bump into one of them, giving himself away.

So despite his best efforts, Theodore was stuck waiting for the massive flood of ants to cease.

Minutes, then hours passed by as Theo remained where he was. He waited for the flood to slow to a trickle so he could get on with his personal quest to prove his worth.

Finally, the tunnel opened up. The ants coming in full force slowed down to a calm stream, giving Theodore enough space to peel himself from the wall.

At long last, this one is allowed to move. Now, onward to thine goal. The treasury! Theodore shouted inwardly. He began to run in the opposite direction of the ants.

Theodore moved through the tunnels quickly, his stats finally beginning to compensate for the class he was hoping to produce.

After talking with Natto, Theodore realized he was not a combat mage, and had no hopes of becoming one. His class relied on misdirection to fool enemies, and his skills allowed him to be the perfect scout. That is what he had decided on, splitting his free points into wisdom and endurance. For now, he was slowly increasing his stamina. This was a benefit he thanked Drake for, as he had leveled up significantly because of the party system, even passing his wife now that he was level 17 to her level 16.

Theodore moved through the tunnel, taking its bends and turns and stopping only briefly to look into whatever opening he happened upon. But alas, each and every room bore no fruit to his quest.

He was almost desperate to find the Treasure Room. Theodore understood Drake's hesitance with keeping not only Theodore, but also the others near him when things became dangerous. For whatever turn of fate, many of them were not direct combat classes.

Even more, it was a surprise to all of them that the jump in levels and difficulty from the goblins to the ants had left them all in the dust. But Theodore didn't want to allow that to force him to give up his service to Drake.

Drake had saved Theodore. When he was a fresh level 10 unable to gain experience or resources, searching hopelessly for some way to gain power, Drake had lent him a helping hand. It may not have been completely pure reasoning, but he was Theodore's benefactor nonetheless.

Then when Theodore was in the process of repaying his debt, it grew larger. He had found his wife and once again had no means of helping her from the horde of goblins. That was when Drake had once again helped him.

Again and again, Theodore was helped. His pride wouldn't let the relationship remain one-sided.

Theodore ran through the tunnels, determined to find the room that would ease his lord's mind and allow him to, if only minutely, pay back his generosity.

Passing through the tunnel, Theodore finally came to a crossroads.

If this one is not mistaken, my lord said in passing that the treasury was meant to be in this direction. Or was it this direction... Curses! Theodore snapped. He looked left and right.

Theodore went with his gut, turning right and running down the tunnel. He made sure to dodge the incoming ants.

The chambers and small caves he passed piqued his interest.

The chambers art becoming smaller... There is no room for the young in these places. Is this one getting close?

Passing chambers more and more frequently, Theodore was convinced he had gotten to a part of the hive that was away from the nurseries. It was at least somewhere else. Finally, he stumbled upon a door that all but confirmed his suspicions.

Huzzah! 'Tis the heart of the beast and the destination of thine wealth!

Theodore looked from the other side of the tunnel into a large archway where there were ants standing in front instead of marching with the rest of the fold.

Beyond them, he looked into the chamber. There, a stone throne was placed on a platform with several stairs leading to it. Behind the throne lay golden doors three times the size of the room, the face of a monstrous goblin carved into the handles on each section of the door.

* * *

"Brother, why did you stop me?! That human needs to die!" Rasha hissed, leaning on Obiteron as they ran through the tunnel. Both headed with their entourage of guards straight for the Queen's chamber.

"I should leave you to befall the same fate as Braxor, then? Do not be foolish; you could have done nothing there alone," Obiteron chided, practically pulling his brother along. "We must regroup at the Queen's chamber first. Mend your wounds, then survive until we can kill that flesh-ridden nuisance."

Several minutes passed as the pair bickered back and forth while running through the tunnel. Eventually, they reached the Queen's Birthing Chamber.

Entering through the massive archway, they both kneeled briefly with the rest of the guards.

"Your Highness!" the arriving ants all shouted at once.

"What is it, my children?" the Queen asked in a soft chirp from her imposing position high atop a pedestal.

The Queen sat elegantly with her four legs crossed over one another, her abdomen swollen to such a size that it dangled down to the floor. There, Royal Nursers took care of the constant stream of eggs being laid.

Obiteron was the first to speak. He raised his head and addressed the queen.

"Mother, I assume you have heard the news. Braxor has died in battle, and there is a human within the hive," he explained calmly.

"I have. Braxor was a good and loyal son; it is a tragedy that he has perished in battle. But it is life, and it is your duty as princes to take care of the intruder," she responded pointedly. "Why is it that you have not? You will not be telling me he is stronger than my sons, will you?" she chirped calmly, but her commanding tone weighed heavy over the ants in the room.

"I would be remiss to inform you that sadly that is the case... We have fought with the human several times, and we have been routed each time," Obiteron informed.

"Then why are you here!" she shouted back. "You should be continuing to defend the colony! A single mere human stronger than Royal Tyrants?! It's unheard of, and I will not affirm such false pretense! Bring his head here even if you must throw every last worker at him. I will not hear that you have failed again, *son.*"

Rasha remained kneeling, his taloned hand shaking with frustration at the words of his Queen and mother.

Obiteron, on the other hand, stood arrogantly, contrary to the other ants in the room.

"*No,*" he announced soundly.

"No?" The Queen scoffed. "You are going to defy your Queen?"

Obiteron flashed out of sight, appearing next to the Queen in an instant. "No. I'm going to *remove* the Queen. I don't need you anymore, mother!"

In one swift motion, Obiteron threw his talons forward, the serrated fingers covered in pitch black light as they passed through the thorax of his mother, killing her instantly. She fell from the top of the pedestal to the floor.

"W-What are you doing, Obiteron?!" Rasha shouted from below. He stood and leapt to catch his falling mother.

"I'm taking charge! After that muscle-bound loyal dog Braxor finally died thanks to that human, it was all I needed to take the throne by force! Now there is only you left, and because of your injuries, you're no match for me!" Obiteron shouted. His head tilted backwards as he screeched in joy, his ambition laid bare.

"You are a disgrace to our race! I always knew you were a weak scheming fool *who* didn't even deserve the mandibles you bare! Do you feel nothing as our Hive dies right before our eyes?! Our brother fought and died! How... How could you not feel the need for vengeance in your very thorax? And now you kill our Queen?!" Rasha roared in anger, holding his lifeless mother's body in his arms.

"Of course I feel nothing, because I want to take it all! Is it not in our very essence to stand above all else? The moment we were sent here, I put my plan into action. And that human helped me do it. I should thank you and him, really, for without either this would have all been for naught. And I would never have had the opportunity to reach my *goal*." Obiteron sneered.

"To what? See the fall of our colony?!"

"*No,*" Obiteron mused. He moved down and punched his hand through guard after guard that surrounded Rasha and the Queen, killing almost every Royal Guard in quick succession.

"To become more. To become stronger than anyone. Than you, than our brother, than that filthy human!"

Obiteron cackled, his arms shimmering with dark light as he threw them both forward, bisecting his brother and the Queen's body that he held.

You have killed Rasha Trikk Level 29 [F-Rank]
Experience earned.

You have reached Ruler of the Nest Level 30.
Race Evolution is now available.

Would you like to accept Race Evolution to Tyrant Ant King?

Chapter 63
Struggling With Loyalty

Drake had been shouting and hollering in an attempt to find Theodore for the past several hours. He ran back and forth throughout the forest from end to end.

"Alright, now I'm getting annoyed. Where in the world is Theo?! Theo! You mustached bastard, come out!" Drake shouted into the air, throwing an ant to the side as he went.

"*At this point, I believe we can say he is not here. Even if he was thoroughly angry at you, I do not believe he would take it so far,*" Natto proposed.

"Yeah, but we don't know that. If there's any chance he could still be here, we need to get him before we leave—"

Quest Update: The Queen of the Tyrant Ants has been usurped by the Third Prince Obiteron Trikk.

Subjugation Quest: Subjugate the Three Princes of the Ant Hive Failed.
New Subjugation Quest: Prevent the Third Prince Obiteron Trikk from evolving their race to [E-Rank].
Reward: Experience and 1 epic skill stone

Time remaining: 23 hours, 59 minutes, 58 seconds.

"That is not good." Drake sighed.

"*I would think not! This is beyond disastrous! You must leave immediately. Run, break through the walls, the ceiling. Whatever it is you must do, do it! Drake, you have to run with all haste!*" Natto entreated.

"Whoa whoa, not without Theo. I'm not going anywhere," Drake answered back.

"Drake, this is no longer a hypothetical or some form of weird egotistical entertainment for you. You will die if you try to fight an E-Rank monster at your current stats and level!"

"Ha." Drake snorted. "Says you. And like I said, I'm not leaving Theodore and that's that. I guess his stupid blond butt went in with the other ants when they made the opening in the side of the wall."

Drake stopped on his heels, pivoting before running back the way he just came. He tore through the ants as he went, beelining for the aforementioned wall.

"Drake, please listen to me! Do not make more mistakes. I am advising you so you can live and so that you have a chance to recover your broken personality! An E-Rank monster has stats in the thousands; even with your endowment skills, you would need buffs of incredible magnitude to match them!"

Drake smiled, finally reaching the wall where the ants had plugged up the hole. His hand reared backward as an orange magic circle formed above his open palm.

"It's a really good thing I happen to have so many support classes waiting for me up top then, huh? It's almost like fate is on my side or something!" Drake shouted. He threw his hand against the wall, the magma inserting itself into the rock as his mana plummeted.

Drake forced his spell into the wall, burrowing out with hot lava. It soon melted a human-sized opening for him.

Breathing out a sigh of slight exhaustion, Drake's hair shifted to blue in an instant as he changed endowments to recover.

"Okay, if I was Theo, where would I go?" Drake thought aloud, looking from left to right.

The tunnel was dim, but the light from the chamber housing the forest bled into the tunnel from behind Drake. The sound of scurrying ants came from the same direction.

Surprisingly, the tunnel was empty where Drake would have thought it would be packed full of ants. The only indication of life was the moved rubble from what looked like thousands of ants passing by.

"I'm going to guess they went that way," Drake said, pointing to his left, "so I think it's safe to assume that Theo went the other way."

"*What makes you so certain?*" Natto asked.

"Well, that's the direction the prince went when I marked him before it wore off," Drake said, "and Theo just isn't the type of guy who goes looking for a fight. I'm sure he went in the other direction."

Drake, convincing himself that what he was saying was true, began sprinting down the tunnel in the other direction.

"You know, this feels a lot like it did with the Goblin King with the timer for the quest and all. But I'm pretty miffed I failed the quest because some bozo decided to off his family tree GoT style." Drake sighed, running down the tunnel.

"*This is nothing like the previous monster. The King was hardly a fight compared to the Royal Guards, but this is entirely different. Certainly, you see that! An E-Rank is nothing to be trifled with!*" Natto yelled back.

"So you keep saying," Drake replied, turning a corner, "but can you really say for certain that with everything I've done and all the support I have from my party, I couldn't beat a single E-Rank?"

"*In certain circumstances where there were multiple of you catching a freshly evolved E-Rank monster off guard, I would concede that there is a possibility. But that is only due to your increased stats as a Dual Class being. Normally rank is absolute, the only exception being pure races of the Primordials or possibly a race rank below. And that is only because of their increased statuses and the effects their race has on their skills and stat growth!*"

"So, you're saying if this treasury has something that can change my race to something better than just a human, I'm in the clear to win?" Drake snorted.

"*No! Not unless you wish to bend your mind to the point of breaking! A change in race in your current condition... I do not even wish to think of the result. You may suffer something irreversible.*"

"But I thought you hated my personality? Maybe it will get me to stop making jokes and referencing anime." Drake smirked behind his mask.

Natto went silent then, making Drake pause and stop for a moment.

"Natto?" Drake asked.

"I-I do not... entirely despise your personality..."

"Hmm?" Drake mused. "Is that so?"

"I said nearly entirely! I still hate a majority of you! If all it took to cease your incessant references was a change of race, I would have suggested it long ago!" she shouted back.

Drake began chuckling, hunching over as he held his stomach.

"I may not be in my best form now," Drake said, standing upright and turning slightly serious, "but I'm not going anywhere. I refuse to let the system, or anything for that matter, change my goals and aspirations now. Maybe I'll have to bend in this new world, but I refuse to break."

Drake didn't wait for Natto to reply. Changing his endowment again now that he'd fully recovered while running, his hair cascaded into a vibrant green. The tunnel filled with a brief gust of wind as Drake took off.

The next few minutes sprinting down the tunnel were muted, Drake's head spinning on what to do about the quest he had just received. On the outside and as far as Natto was concerned, he was the same confident laid-back manchild he had always been throughout the tutorial.

But deep within his subconscious, even Drake was slightly shaken by the news.

Would he be able to beat the prince? Could he protect everyone with how strong he was now? What would happen if he couldn't? Was this tutorial doomed to have no survivors? Was that what the sponsor intended?

These questions stirred within his rational mind with every step forward he took in search of Theodore. But the uncanny thing was that a part of him, a small part that was slowly getting larger and more loud, looked forward to it.

That part of his consciousness almost *wanted* to fail the quest.

Would the fight be fun? How much stronger would he become after defeating an E-Rank named monster? How much closer would it bring him to standing at the top?

Drake's mind paused, coming back to reality as he hit a crossroads. There were still no ants in sight yet, confusing Drake even more.

"Well... where do we go now? I can't sense anything nearby, and it's a 50-50 chance if I'm right or wrong on where he went." Drake sighed. "Do I just guess or roll the dice... or make a coin to flip?" Drake thought aloud.

Shaking his head, he eyed the timer for the prince's evolution and decided to just guess. Turning left and readying to step forward, Drake was stopped when he bumped into something invisible.

The sound of something hitting the ground thumped through the tunnel before Theodore shimmered into existence, his rump on the floor and his hand rubbing his bruised nose.

"Mhy lhord! Ahs strhong ahs ahlwhays!" Theodore said through a bleeding nose.

"Theo! Damn man, are you okay? Why in the world were you just standing there?" Drake asked, offering a hand.

"This one wished to search for our grail, and in doing so, this one hast found it!" Theodore proclaimed.

"What?" Drake asked, surprised. "You found it already? Where?"

"'Tis but a small distance hitherward." Theodore pointed down the tunnel, his other hand still rubbing his bruised nose. "Thine treasure is guarded by but a meager few within a chamber. This one is sure it will be of no trouble for my lord's strength."

"That's great, Theo," Drake said somewhat hesitantly. "You got the quest notification too, right?" he asked.

Theodore turned to look at Drake as he stood, nodding. "Yes, my lord. Would thou allow this one to join in this fight? This one is sure he would be of use in some—"

"Theo," Drake said, gripping Theodore's shoulder, "this isn't a fight I'm sure I could win if the prince manages to finalize his evolution. I couldn't ask you to—"

"My lord," Theo interrupted, brushing off Drake's hand, "this one's life and choices are his own. Please, allow this one to aid his lord and benefactor."

Drake saw the determination in Theodore's eyes, but he struggled with allowing him to join a fight that Drake knew would be not only dangerous for Drake, but most likely fatal for anyone outside of Bjorn and himself.

"Let's focus on getting to the treasury first, my man," Drake said deflecting. "Maybe we can find some goodies in there to help us out."

Theodore looked as if he had swallowed something bitter, but he nodded while his gaze pointed downward.

Drake could feel the tension between them, but he had no choice but to delay answering Theodore. Theodore had made his point, and it was true. But Drake was not prepared to send the man who'd been with him almost the entire tutorial to his death.

"Good, let's get going then," Drake asserted.

Theodore cast his concealment spell once more, and Drake ran down the tunnel in the direction that Theodore had instructed.

After a few moments of following some bends in the tunnel, Drake sensed and spotted several guards ahead of them.

Not needing to change Endowments, Drake summoned a blade of water and quickly dispatched them in one swift motion. Their bodies dropped to the floor as his spell fell to the floor with them.

"Looks like a throne room," Drake observed, peering into the room and walking toward the lone large chair in front of the double doors.

"Hmm," Drake mused, moving past the throne and to the doors. He looked them up and down. "So what's behind door number one?" Drake announced, pulling a key from his inventory.

"Now... where is the hole I put you in?"

Chapter 64

When Gold Is Worthless

The night was waxing. The sun slowly disappeared from the outpost as Shigure made rounds on the wall rampart.

"Another quiet night. I am curious if it is Sir Bear and Shot's doing…" he wondered.

It had been weeks since the pair and Shot's party had departed with no news back from either. However, there had also been no new conflicts throughout the entirety of the tutorial as far as the outpost was concerned.

There had been nothing. No fights, no new monster species, no increase to the strength of the current monsters. Monsters which Shigure noticed that he hadn't seen in many weeks.

"It is as if the tutorial is drying up," he said, looking out into the forest slowly being eclipsed in the night.

"It's not the only thing drying up, Kenzo," a voice said from behind Shigure.

"Sato? I haven't seen you in quite some time. Where have you been?"

"There haven't been any monsters around lately, so I got held up in the part of the outpost you never want to visit." Sato smiled.

"Ugh, that place is filthy. I hope you showered." Shigure grimaced.

"Oh please, are you really still on about that after everything?" Sato sighed.

"After what?"

"After that guy trounced your ass left and right while spouting reference after reference." Sato chuckled.

Shigure went to snap his refute, but he was stopped by Sato's hand.

"I'm saying it's surprising that's the only thing you're fixated on with him," Sato said pointedly, "especially after how much you've changed after meeting him."

"Changed? I do not see how I have changed in the slightest, Sato." Shigure scoffed.

"I may have been locked up playing cards for the past two weeks, but that doesn't mean I haven't seen the effects of what's going on. 90% of the coalition is gone, and so is that scum that followed them. And I've seen the cages cleaned of prisoners. You would never have had the heart to do that before that guy came," Sato said, pausing for a moment. "We've both seen and done things since coming here, more things that we're not proud of than things we are. But it was always a reaction to something. Now? You're finally taking charge. It's what you've needed to do all along, and I'm proud you finally realized it."

"I don't need praise from a person who thinks lines from cartoons count as morals." Shigure snorted.

"Excuse me for having a hobby..."

"It isn't a hobby for you! You have figurines of fictional characters all over your room!"

"Don't remind me... Please, Taka-chan! Be there and unharmed when we come back! I've done all of this for you..." Sato said, bringing his hands together in a prayer.

"That! That is what I am talking about! It's disgusting!"

"Hey, you have posters of Kendo and archery olympians in your room. You don't think that's any worse?"

"Those are real people with real accomplishments! It's entirely different!"

"But you've never met them, so they might as well be fiction to you! So, same thing!"

"That is a leap in logic that makes no real sense! W-Why am I even arguing this with you?!" Shigure sighed.

"You're no fun, always have that giant stick up your ass. Anyway, with the food dwindling, it's starting to get worse, but I'm sure you already knew that… Surprisingly the crafters have been doing well even when there's no monsters to gain points and stones from. People are breaking their piggy banks to get some of the stuff on the market," Sato mused, pushing up his glasses.

"What stuff?" Shigure asked, intrigued. This was the first he'd heard of it.

"Remember the dwarf? He got his hands on some really good skill stones and accessories. Won't say from who, but they're better than anything you could have gotten outside of quest rewards right now."

"Is he still open?" Shigure asked.

"Old guy lives in that stall, so I think so." Sato shrugged.

Shigure didn't say anything and walked past Sato. Sato chuckled a bit before following his friend.

They passed through the outpost, ignoring the wandering eyes here and there. Shigure headed straight for the old dwarf's stall.

Reaching there relatively quickly, Shigure knocked on the front of the stall to get the man's attention.

"Hello! I heard you have some new merchandise to sell?"

"I swear to god, if you bastards came back again to haggle, I'll break my hammer off in your ass—Oh, Lord Shigure! What a surprise…" The old dwarf grimaced.

"The merchandise?" Shigure asked, ignoring the dwarf.

"Yeah, sure thing. Give me a moment."

Waiting a few seconds while the dwarf rummaged through some things further back in the stall, Shigure began feeling anticipation well up slightly.

"Here they are; have a good look."

Shigure eyed the pieces of jewelry on the counter as well as the skill stones that had just been placed there.

"Where in the world did you get these? We don't even have intelligence accessories available at this stat increase," Shigure said in amazement.

"Can't say—business partner wants to stay silent. So you buying or just window shoppin' again, Sato?" the dwarf asked, pointing to behind Shigure.

Sato raised his hands in defeat. "Can't, lost all my money in 'Tales of the Tyrant Knight' and there aren't any more monsters left to hunt."

"What about selling one of them pistols you got?"

"What?! Never! I could never sell Little Maru!" Sato shouted, recoiling from the stall.

Shigure ignored his friend, picking out several strength and dexterity accessories as well as a few rare skill stones that looked promising for after the tutorial.

"How much for all of these?" Shigure asked.

"Hmm..." grumbled the dwarf, grooming his beard. "I'm thinking—"

Before he could announce the price, a notification popped up in all of their heads, silencing them and their surroundings.

Subjugation Quest: Subjugate the Three Ant Princes of the Ant Hive Failed.

New Subjugation Quest: Prevent the Third Prince Obiteron Trikk from evolving their race to [E-Rank].

Reward: Experience and 1 epic skill stone.

Time remaining: 23 hours, 59 minutes, 58 seconds.

"What?! E-Rank?" Shigure growled. "What have those fools done?"

The next moment, a puff of smoke appeared next to Shigure, a woman clothed in shinobi attire kneeling in a half bow.

"My lord," Uta said in an even tone.

"Gather everyone that can fight and reinforce the ramparts. We won't be able to get to wherever the Ant's Nest is in time to help or search. Our only hope is to defend until the tutorial is over!" Shigure ordered.

"As you command!" Uta announced. She disappeared again in a puff of inky black smoke. Shigure turned again to the old dwarf.

"How much? I'll be needing these sooner than I imagined."

The dwarf smiled. "Everything you got, boy."

"W-What?! You're going to rob me!"

"Supply and demand. You demand and are very much in need of what I supply."

"This is highway robbery!"

Sato laughed from behind Shigure.

"Ha! Now we're both broke!"

Shigure turned to growl at Sato before turning back to the dwarf.

"This is bullshit!"

* * *

"Ahhhhh!!! This is bullshit!!" Drake shouted into the vault.

Drake and Theodore had finally managed to find the keyhole for the double doors and eventually wrenched them open, only to find, well, nothing much.

"Is this supposed to be a joke?! There's nothing here but scraps! It's been picked clean!" Drake howled, picking up a few loose gold coins and rubbish accessories that didn't compare to his own.

Looking upward, Drake cursed at the sky. "What the fuck kind of quest reward is this? I had to trudge through an army of ants for weeks! For this?!"

Drake sighed, then began placing whatever he could into his inventory as he grumbled curses. Theodore went through and picked things that could be useful as well.

"This truly is an unfortunate outcome, my lord, but it may not all be for naught. We have indeed found the treasure, which would allow for a safe space in the future of overcoming this fortress and these insectoids!" Theodore mused, trying to lighten the mood.

Drake bit his tongue, not wanting to hint at his uneasiness for the future. He'd been expecting something else, something *more* from the treasure of the Goblin King. Something he could use to help increase his fighting strength or at least something for everyone else. With the timed quest and the looming evolution of the prince ahead, Drake needed some sort of bone thrown to him.

Shuffling through the room, Drake was again amazed that a place this large was brought underneath the surface. The walls were made of what looked to be gold, or they were at least gold-plated.

Who knows if the King skimped on the decor, maybe it's even fake gold. I wouldn't put it past the scumbag... Drake mused.

"*I believe it is gold. Gold is not as valuable in the multiverse as it was on your singular planet, at least not regular gold. Mana infused minerals and materials go for a much higher price,*" Natto explained.

Thanks for the commentary... I thought you might have gone for a walk or something with how silent it got.

"*I am simply busy trying to figure out what to do to save our lives. You have put us in a right mess this time...*" She sighed.

It's not my fault the ants decided to stage a coup right as we entered the Hive. How was I supposed to know? Drake thought.

Drake heard Natto sigh within his head. His hands continued to go over item after item in the room, trying to find something useful.

"No, that's worse than what I have. Gold? Worthless right now. Potions? Have that. Man, there's nothing here right now. I'm guessing one of the princes somehow got in and swept the place clean..." Drake sighed.

"My lord! I found some status pills in a box! Would thou care to take them?" Theodore suddenly shouted from the other side of the room.

"Are they F-Grade? One stat per pill?" Drake shouted back.

"Indubitably!"

"It's fine unless it's fifty or more. You can use them, Theo. A few won't help me right now."

"Understood, my lord! I will save them for Harley then!"

Drake shook his head and continued to rummage through the worthless gold coins, chuckling slightly.

"Guy always thinks of his wife," Drake mumbled.

"*And of you. Perhaps he thinks of you as his second wife?*" Natto snickered.

"That's very disturbing because it honestly might be true," Drake said shivering. "But man, I never thought there'd be a day I would see so much gold and money and not have any use for it... This is pretty depressing in a way."

"*There will most likely be nothing here if we have not found it already. I suggest we leave and run very very far away,*" Natto proposed.

"If I run, who's going to stop big and scary when he wakes up or evolves or whatever?" Drake asked, his hands pocketing some status pills he found.

"*It is not your job to defend the whole place from this monster, Drake. You have not even set foot outside the tutorial yet. There is much more for you to do in the days to come. Do not extinguish your flame now before it has had time to burn bright.*"

"Wow, that was almost poetic." Drake chuckled. "But sorry, no can do. What happens when the ant decides to kill everyone then comes after us anyway?"

"*Then we would have delayed for a time so that you could survive!*"

"Okay, I'll play along," Drake said, reaching through more piles of items. "What if rough and ugly decides he wants to screw over my day? Comes right for the strongest person in the tutorial. Or what if he just wants vengeance on the person who killed his brother?"

Natto became silent.

"See? There might be a bunch of reasons you don't want me to die, and contrary to what you might think, I don't want to die either. But this boils down to there only being three people in this tutorial who can maybe, kind of, possibly do anything about an E-Rank. And I don't plan on asking Shigure. A kid that young needs to survive. And Bjorn... I wouldn't feel right asking for his help, so I've got to do it myself."

"*They are not your responsibility,*" Natto mumbled.

"Technically they are. I signed a contract, remember?"

"*You can always annul it!*"

"That would just be underhanded, though. I gave my word, and that's that," Drake said finally. His hand went for a pine box he saw on top of a chest.

His hand halted as he approached it. Drake noticed a slight shiver in his arm.

He was nervous, he was unsure, but he still had to put on his strong face. Because if *he* didn't, then who would?

"My lord! Outside!" Theodore shouted.

"What is it?"

Chapter 65
The King Of Tyrant Ants

Drake rushed to the entrance, making sure to put himself in between it and Theodore. His defensive skills went off in rapid succession.

Outside of the Treasure Room and beyond the throne chamber in the tunnel, thousands of stampeding ants ran past them.

"What's going on? They're all running to something? Or running away…?" Drake said absentmindedly.

Drake didn't let down his guard, motioning to Theodore to go invisible once again. Drake moved in closer to the tunnel, curious about why the ants were so adamant in their sudden fleeing.

He was close enough that he was sure the ants could smell and see him, but not a single one stopped to turn toward him or fight. They all continued to run at maximum speed in a single direction.

"They're ignoring me? Theo, you can come out," Drake said, not taking his eyes off the ants. A sinking feeling enveloped his stomach.

Theodore wisped back into view next to Drake, a curious look on his face as he too looked at the stampeding passersby.

"What is occurring, my lord? Art thy enemies completely and utterly foregoing us?" Theodore asked.

"No, I think they're all running from something. My best guess? It's the prince's evolution. But he still has…" Drake paused to look at the quest. "He still has about 19 hours left. Could be that because he killed the others and the Queen, they're just running away?"

"Should we depart as well?" Theodore asked. "We have already searched for riches within the treasury; this one doubts we will find more."

Drake pursed his lips in thought for a moment, watching the never-ending trail of ants as they passed the chamber.

"Damn, this means I won't be able to finish the last of my quests either. I'm just a few away from the guard and Royal Knights being finished. I was really hoping I could at least finish those for a level-up, but levels are starting to slow as it is… I still have time to stop the evolution. I just have to backtrack to where the ants are running from."

"Then shall we be on our way, my lord?" Theodore asked, raising his cane.

"No, Theo. Sorry, but I can't bring you on this one. I need you to go to the surface. Follow the ants to whatever exit they're using and get back to Bjorn and the others. I don't know if I can beat this prince if he finishes his evolution before I get to him."

"M-My lord, please do not discard this one in your time of need! This one can certainly help! Do not remove me from your side!" Theodore pleaded.

"No! I can't and won't ask you to do this, Theo! I don't want to see you get hurt like last time. This monster is possibly out of my league, so it's *definitely* out of everyone else's. I *need* you to get to the surface and prepare the group in case I need to fall back and get help from everyone's support buffs. Please, I need you to do this for me. This is how you help me," Drake said firmly, looking into Theodore's eyes with determination.

"My lord…" Theodore murmured, unsure of what to respond with.

Theodore didn't want to leave his benefactor to fight on his own, but he couldn't refute that he may not be able to help and may, in fact, be a hindrance. Theodore was above average in level compared to the rest of the tutorial, but he wasn't made for direct combat. He was also a supporting class mage, which made it nearly impossible for him to compete with the prince—a monster nearly twice his level that even Drake was worried about defeating.

Biting his lip, his cane creaked as his gloves gripped the wood.

"By your command, my lord. It will be done," Theodore said solemnly. He chanted a spell and shimmered out of sight.

Drake gave a smirk and moved his mask, speaking to the empty room.

"Thank you, Theo. Be safe and don't die."

"Thou as well, my liege. Come back safely."

With that, Drake re-entered the treasury, giving it one last look over for anything he could possibly use. But alas, he only found some scrounges of decent armor and weapons as well as a few status pills that he pocketed with the rest.

"Well, at least we have a small boost. That's ten pills per stat, but I doubt it'll be enough..." Drake sighed.

"Anything will help at this point, Drake. You are taking on something far out of your realm of experience. Are you sure you will not heed my warning and leave?" Natto asked one more time.

"No can do. *Manners maketh man.* And I'm a man of my word. I'll get stronger and protect those I care about, or I'll die trying."

* * *

The surroundings were muted. Muffled scratches and chittering reached Obiteron, but he was unable to make out anything coherent enough to understand.

The moment he'd accepted the sounds of the world in his head, he was thrown into a dark place.

But he didn't fear it. Obiteron knew the darkness that had enveloped him was nothing more than the process of the world cementing his new power.

The power of a newborn King.

He didn't know how long the process would take, but he could slowly feel himself changing within the confines of the dark place he'd been submerged in.

Reveling in the feeling of growth, the anticipation was enough to run him ragged even before emerging into the world as the victor. Finally, he was the true King of the Tyrant Ants. The strongest of them all.

He'd planned for years, even before the voice of the world took them into this new landscape. His brothers had always mocked him for using all the tools at his disposal, saying it was unlike a Tyrant Ant to seek help through means outside oneself.

But now they were both dead, along with their mother. And it was his doing.

Obiteron felt his carapace flex and mold to his growing body within the dark. What felt like an eternity to him continued, and he fell back into thought.

After his increase in rank, he would no longer need the trinkets the goblins had left. He would be the strongest being within this new land. When the tutorial's time was over, they would move to a new prosperous land where he could grow a new Hive. His own colony in his image where he stood at the top. Just like the voice of the world promised him.

Obiteron flexed his body and aura, feeling them like new muscles wanting to be tested.

Soon, very soon, his evolution would be complete. He could feel it.

The sounds of the outside had quieted, but he could feel something approaching. Even within his dark prison, he could feel it.

The human.

Cracks began forming in the dark, light spilling in from every direction and blinding his sight momentarily. Obiteron felt the pressure of something hitting him and his body, but he felt no pain.

Coming out of the dark, he saw the human throwing spells at him with considerable force and potency.

Looking down, Obiteron saw that his necklace had shattered.

The human overloaded the magic-negating trinket. Impressive, if futile.

The pressure Obiteron felt was the human's spells hitting him harmlessly.

Obiteron shook his body, releasing himself from the molted body he'd emerged from. He stretched, and he felt new muscles and the strength within them. He had grown wings.

Appropriate for a King. Why should I be confined to the ground like a lowly larva? he thought, snapping his mandibles.

Once he was done flexing his new body, he began observing it. His chitin armor had turned from dark black to a silver hue. Red streaks ran down the length of his body, pulsing with vital energy and power.

Clenching and unclenching his serrated fingers, Obiteron let out a screech of joy.

He was complete. He was finally the King he'd always wished he could be, and all for the measly cost of his worthless family.

Looking up, his eyes fixed on the human that could have killed him easily before. One word reverberated in his mind.

Weakling.

* * *

Drake heaved. He continued to throw spell after spell at the dark cocoon in front of him that he'd finally found after searching with no rest. But it was too late.

Subjugation Quest: Prevent the Third Prince Obiteron Trikk from evolving their race to [E-Rank] Failed.

New Subjugation Quest: Defeat the King of the Tyrant Ants, Obiteron Trikk [E-Rank]

Reward: Experience, a large amount of TP, and 1 legendary weapon of your choice [E-Grade].

"Fuck, I'm in danger..." Drake cursed with a self-deprecating smirk behind his mask.

Drake had followed the nearly endless trail of ants back to the Queen's Nursing chamber, which he was able to get inside using the key he'd gotten from the Nursers.

But instead of finding Obiteron in a vulnerable state, after 18 hours of searching the Hive, he had stumbled upon a jet-black cocoon.

Drake immediately began pummeling the cocoon with everything he had, expending his status in chunks as he pelted the thing with spell after mana-charged spell.

But the cocoon held strong against Drake. Even at full power, it resisted his onslaught.

He lost count of how many times he'd cursed as he sent spell after spell at the thing over the course of the remaining hour. Drake eventually convinced himself that the cocoon must have increased defensive bonuses while the prince was evolving inside. Drake continued regardless.

At least, that was until his time was up.

Once the last second ticked by and the quest failed, Drake felt something he hadn't in a very long time since beginning the tutorial.

Pure dread.

Fear.

With the cracking of the cocoon, Drake felt the immense pressure of the being inside push against his own and the world around it.

He could also feel that the aura wasn't malicious. It was as if a child had found a new toy and was testing it, which made Drake all the more nervous.

"Drake..." Natto mumbled nervously, her teeth chattering.

I... I know. I threw everything I had at it, and there isn't a scratch on him or the cocoon... Drake stammered.

"You need to run! You don't stand a chance!"

Where am I going to run? I doubt he's just going to let us stroll out of here...

Drake joked while sweat began to pool down the side of his face. His status was still recovering from the bombardment of spells he'd used to assault the cocoon earlier. And now the prince was emerging.

From inside the cocoon, Drake felt the air pulse almost like a heartbeat. Cracks rippled through the sleek black covering of the cocoon, splintering it more and more with each pulse.

Finally, one large crack split it down the middle, and the prince emerged slowly from the shell.

Obiteron Trikk Level 30 [E-Rank]

The prince took in his surroundings slowly, flexing here and there as he apparently tested his new body and extremities. With a flutter, the new wings on his back buzzed briefly, shaking off the excess shell of the cocoon.

"This guy looks like one of the old school Big Bad Beetleborgs... silver edition," Drake muttered under his breath. He lowered his stance, ready for a fight.

Obiteron flexed his claws and then let out a loud howl.

"Shit, did he hear me or just not like the reference?!" Drake shuddered. He raised a hand at the burst of aura pushing down on him with the screech.

Looking through his hands, Drake saw the prince snap to Drake, their eyes glaring at one another.

From the prince's eyes, Drake could tell what he was thinking. It brought fury into every fiber of his being, overtaking the previous fear.

He thinks... He thinks I'm weak?!

Chapter 66
The Surface

Drake was furious at the insinuation to his very core.

Weak?

It went against everything he had worked for. He'd climbed from the ground up to where he was now. Endless life and death struggles led him to this point. But this insect called him *weak*.

Drake knew that the prince was a rank above him, and after feeling the aura from the prince, Drake also realized that Natto was right all along. Rank was absolute, or at least it felt like it.

But he couldn't let the insult slide. Something within him wouldn't allow it. Wouldn't allow the slight from another being.

"Drake, please run! You simply cannot win!" Natto pleaded.

Drake straightened. His arms raised as he dumped mana into his rings.

"A wound on a warrior's back is disgraceful."

"You are a weeb, not a warrior! Please, enough jokes! Run!"

Drake's rational mind heard and wanted to flee as Natto suggested with every fiber of his being, but his subconscious wouldn't allow him to budge.

Only move forward.

"I am the wall on which my enemies billow. Unbreakable! I am the shield, I am the rampart. Bulwark! On blessed wings. Guardian's Reprieve!"

Drake roared as he rushed forward. His body flashed in three bright flickers of green as elements formed in an instant in front of him.

"Heretical Endowment! Serpentarius! Heretical Attunement! Lightning!"

With one great lunge, Drake flew forward toward the stone-like prince. The aura surrounding the prince was thick and oppressive.

Drake flexed his aura moments before meeting the prince with his thrown fist.

Tyrannical Aura has failed. Target has resisted the effect.

Drake clicked his tongue, but he surged his fist forward nonetheless. The electrified violet twirled with the red of his Martial Skill, combining and connecting with the side of the ant's head.

Once the fist connected, Drake quickly backed away, cursing as he did.

"Damn it! I hit him, but I felt no give! How sturdy did he get?!"

While Drake did his best to analyze the situation quickly, he summoned two magic circles of lightning on both his sides. He clenched his teeth in frustration.

Obiteron didn't move. Instead, he seemed to still be flexing his body here and there, feeling out the new power within him. Almost mockingly ignoring Drake. The impact from his previous strike smoldered harmlessly on the ant's cheek.

"This fucking bug is looking down on me again!" Drake growled.

"*Asura! Twofold!*" Drake chanted. The two lightning circles formed arms at the base of his shoulders.

Drake roared again, stepping forward and maneuvering to Obiteron's blind spot. He threw two fists at him in quick succession with all of his might.

Each pair of arms hit their mark with no resistance, but there was also no effect.

His shell can't be this hard! I'm using attunement and penetrating spells! I almost have over a thousand intelligence! What is this stupid fuck made of?!

Drake began to feel pangs of fear slowly creep into his mind once more. The anxiety of his previous thoughts inside the treasury room resurfaced.

His brow began to sweat, not from exhaustion, but from an inability to do any damage to the prince. His assault on the newly ranked-up ant had no effect.

Drake backed up once more, getting space on the edge of the cave and bringing his palm up. His attunement lightning and two lightning arms formed into a spear of dense mana.

"*True Lightning Magic!*" Drake growled, the spear pulsating as more magic circles formed around it, adding layer after layer of violent violet crackles of threading light.

"*Pierce him! Ceranos!*"

Drake opened his status window and hurled the spear forward with all his physical might. He dumped the last of his points into his intelligence, brought out the pills he'd found in the treasury, and swallowed the sixty small pills whole.

His status spiked as his intelligence shot past 800. The spear of lightning ripped through the air between them, igniting the surroundings and turning the chamber into a hot sauna.

Drake wasn't willing to bank on just the spell. He snapped forward with the spear, getting above Obiteron in the same swift motion.

With his Adrenaline Acuity on full throttle, Drake couldn't help but let out a gasp at what ensued.

The spear of lightning was moving faster than anything Drake had thrown before, careening right for the ant prince's chest. But it was stopped like a plaything in one hand, the magic struggling to move forward between the ant's smoldering claws.

The prince held the lightning spear as if it were nothing but a stick he'd picked up off the ground. He looked up at Drake as if waiting expectantly for his next move.

Drake ground his teeth. He wrenched his fist backward, winding up for a full power straight to the ant's head. He chanted two spells in quick succession as he threw it forward.

"*Cower! Atrophy of the Mind!*"

Drake hoped the spells would be enough to do something, have some effect on the ant long enough for him to do some kind of damage. But he was met with the cruelty of reality and rank.

Cower has failed. Target has resisted the effect.

Atrophy of the Mind has failed. Target has resisted the effect.

In the next moment, Drake saw the prince snap the spear of condensed lightning like a twig. His eyes never left Drake as the prince's other arm swatted him away like a bug.

Drake was reminded of the first time he'd felt the effects of his Adrenaline Acuity skill when he'd fought Bjorn. This was the near mirror image of it. He saw the ant's hand moving toward him, but his body refused to react in time. It collided with his face.

The impact thrust Drake to the side. He slammed against the wall with such force that it brought the cave down on top of him. The sound of glass breaking rang in his ears as his defensive skills were triggered.

Gained Reprieval charge.
Gained Reprieval charge.
Gained Reprieval charge.
Max charges stored, charge lost.

Drake did his best to maintain consciousness as the rubble began piling on top of him.

"*Drake!*" Natto pleaded.

I know! Drake agreed reluctantly.

Pulling two vials of red and blue from his inventory, Drake managed to wiggle his arm free from under the rocks to bring them to his mouth. They replenished his status, if only slightly.

Drake quickly summoned a magic circle of orange and canceled his Heretical Endowment. He opted to use his Earth Endowment for the defensive boost, minimizing his mana use while his defensive skills were down.

Using the magma to melt through the rocks behind him, Drake wrenched himself from the rubble and tumbled into the space he'd made, cursing at himself.

"*You can chew yourself out later! Please just get to the surface!*"

Drake clenched his fist and teeth together, but he moved forward, melting away the stone as he attempted to find a tunnel. Within the short time it took, he did his best to minimize the effects of using two potions at once. A small smirk reached his melancholy expression as he praised himself for his internal mana manipulation.

With barely a sliver of his mana left, Drake finally reached an empty tunnel and tried to orient himself.

Looking down in disappointment, he managed to find the tracks of the ant swarm that had retreated previously. He wordlessly followed them, using his Reprieval stacks to teleport as far away as he could from the prince.

* * *

Theodore ran in tandem with the ants escaping from the Hive, keeping his invisibility on as long as possible as he sprinted with all his might.

He had his reservations about leaving Drake, but he couldn't deny that what he had said was true. Theodore was not strong enough to stand next to his lord currently, but he knew who was. And his aim was to reach that person with all haste.

Theodore ran and ran until he was out of breath and mana, then ran some more. He was just as unconcerned with the ants as they seemed to be with him. He ran, ran until his body refused to move another step before drinking a stamina potion and beginning again.

For hours he repeated the process, following the trail of ants to whatever exit they were vying for. Until finally, he reached it. The light of day.

Casting his spell and unsure if the ants would suddenly turn on him once they tasted the freedom of the surface, Theodore was pushed forward by the flood of monsters behind him. They exploded out of the newly-made Hive entrance.

Shooting out and tumbling forward, he was met with the stink of spilled ichor on the ground. Looking up, he saw a giant in gray matted armor with a sword the same size as his body.

"Sir Bear!" Theodore shouted in joy.

"Theo?!" Bjorn said, surprised as he heard the voice. The man shimmered into view on the floor. "Where is Drake?"

Theodore looked pensive as he tried to steady his racing mind, recounting the events. Slowly, he told Bjorn of the events that had ensued while deep within the Hive and what led up to him parting ways with Drake before coming to the surface.

"That stubborn asshole..." Bjorn growled. "I'm going down there right now!"

"This one beseeches thee, Sir Bear. Please do not insert thouself into the Hive. This one believes that it is already difficult for my lord to fight as it stands within the confines of the tunnels. He hast directed me to wait for him on the surface with the rest of our camp."

"You expect me to just wait while he's down there fighting an E-Rank? We all got the notification for the failed quest. He could be fighting right now for all we know, bro!" Bjorn scorned.

"But he is not yet dead! This one understands your need to go to my lord more than thou knoweth, but it is his decision and command that we stay above and await his return. Could thou very well risk the danger of the entire Hive collapsing down upon the rest of us?"

Bjorn ground his teeth. His hand gripped the creaking metal of his sword.

"No! He isn't my keeper, and he isn't my boss. I'm going down there to help him whether he likes it or not. It's been weeks!"

"Not without me!" Claire shouted, followed by the rest of the group.

"Theo!" Harley shouted as she ran to him, launching into his arms on the ground. "I was so worried! I'm so glad you made it back safe! What happened with Mr. Shot?"

"Exactly!" Claire demanded, her usual calm and demure aura replaced with abject concern and anxiety. "Where is he? Is he hurt again?!"

Theodore raised his arms in surrender and recounted the events once more for the party that surrounded him. Bjorn and Hudson took care of most of the ants as they set up a closer perimeter with Hudson's sentries and big boys.

"He did what?!" Claire shouted. "Why is he always running off without us... Why doesn't he understand we're all worried about him," she sobbed. "That *I'm* worried about him!"

Harley reluctantly removed herself from Theodore, moving to console Claire in her arms. The rest of the group also voiced questions.

"Bloody idiot's still alive though, yeah? He hasn't disappeared from the boards just yet, so that's a good sign," Jacqueline said, pushing her weight to one leg. "Let me see ya, love. Ya hurt anywhere?"

"This one is uninjured. The ants, you all see, are fleeing in droves from something. Our lord suspected it was the evolving prince below. We must all prepare for—"

Theodore was cut off by the sudden feeling of unadulterated dread that seemed to pierce through the surroundings. The party all froze as they felt it as well, the only one able to move under the pressure being Bjorn.

"Everyone run! Get back to the fortress!" Bjorn roared as he was covered in a black aura. Everyone heard the instruction, but no one was able to move under the assaulting pressure.

Moments later, the sound of rumbling from the Hive entrance that the remaining flood of ants were barreling out of overtook the skittering of the scrambling insects.

With an explosive, thunderous bang, the entrance flew apart. And out of it came a man, bloodied and bruised.

Claire was the first to recognize the man. She screamed at the top of her lungs.

"DRAKE!!!"

Chapter 67
Fight of Our Lives

Drake gasped out in a fit of pain, his body thrown from the tunnel as he tried his best to escape.

Gained Reprieval charge.
Gained Reprieval charge.
Max charges stored, charge lost.

"*Drake!*" Natto shouted in his head, trying to keep him conscious through the pain.

"I know!" Drake shouted back, looking down at the Hive entrance he was just expelled from. A silver-sheened insect slowly walked out of the wrenched-open entrance. An oppressive aura stilled even Drake's heart as he moved in defiance.

Looking down, he spotted Bjorn and the rest of his party fleeing backward. He heard a shout from Claire in the distance, her face contorted in concern and fear as she screamed his name.

"Fuck," Drake cursed.

Using a charge, he teleported down next to Bjorn in an instant and fell to his knees in a heap. He scrambled to pull another health potion from his inventory.

"Drake?! What happened? What is—That's the Prince... What... What are those stats?!" Bjorn said suddenly, having just realized what they were up against.

"Oh hey, yeah I'm fine. Thanks for asking. These grape-flavored health potions have been a great help; think I can get more of these?" he joked. He tipped his head back and downed the vial in one go.

"How can you joke in this situation, bro? That thing is crazy." Bjorn scoffed and held his claymore at the ready, the weapon quickly enveloped in a black aura.

"No, don't attack him! He won't go on the offensive unless you challenge him!" Drake shouted, stopping Bjorn.

"What do you mean? Look at you, you're a mess! We need to get you to Jacqueline!"

"No, I need Claire and Megan right now. If we want any chance of fighting, we need their buffs. Get Julia up here and Tom as well. I don't know when that prick insect will change its mind and attack again, so we need to be beyond our best if we want to kill it."

Bjorn clenched his jaw as he watched the Tyrant Ant Prince walk from the entrance down the hill. It then seemingly waited, uninterested.

"If it isn't going to attack us, why don't we just leave?" Bjorn asked.

"He will give chase... He seems to like the hunt, but he won't attack first unless you turn to run. From what I can get from his Aura and what he's done so far, he thinks even *I'm* weak," Drake said admonishingly.

"With the stats I just saw, I can see why... Is the jump to E-Rank really that great?"

"He's an anomaly just like this entire Hive. He's a higher-tiered mob, from what Natto told me. Normally E-Rank monsters are strong, but with our stats and class rarity, we should be able to fight them on even ground. I'm hoping with both of us and the buffs, we'll stand a chance..."

"And if we can't? What then, bro?" Bjorn scoffed.

"Then I don't need to worry about stopping you from reaching E-Rank." Drake smirked.

Bjorn smiled, but he kept his eyes trained on the prince.

"Theo!" Drake shouted.

Theodore had been close by but not invisible as the prince exited with

Drake. Coming over from his position next to the rest of the group, he shakily ran up to Drake.

"Y-Yes, my lord?"

"I need you to get Claire, Tom, Julia, Megan, and Jacqueline here. Bjorn and I need their buffs to deal with the prince. If we don't have them, it'll be over in a second," Drake instructed, not taking his eyes off the lackadaisical Tyrant Ant.

"A-Art thou sure, my lord? Wouldeth it not be safer for them to stay at a distance?"

"I'm sorry to say this, but this guy will chase down anyone that flees. So if we fail here, we're all dead anyway. Please just bring them here; don't tell them what might happen. I'll put my life on the line to make sure all of them are as safe as I can possibly manage. Now get going."

Theodore nodded and turned on his heels, heading for the group slightly farther back.

"It really isn't moving. Why is it looking at us like that?" Bjorn asked.

"I told you, it thinks I'm—*we're* weak. I guess it's just using us to test its new strength? I think it knows something we don't. I would've expected it to kill us right away and just move on, but it's been toying with me... just like the Goblin King did," Drake explained.

"And we both know how that turned out, huh. That's good for us then, right?"

"Only if it doesn't decide to do anything as we're preparing. I don't know how patient it's going to be."

A few moments later, the people Drake had called for came up behind them—some if only reluctantly.

"Drake! Are you okay? You're hurt! Jacqueline, heal him please!" Claire shouted, grabbing onto Drake's arm.

"You ain't my boss, Claire. And I can't believe I agreed to come along just to die to some bloody insect..." Jacqueline sighed.

"You seem rather calm about it though." Drake snorted.

"Whatcha mean? I was scared shitless just like the rest of us when the thing started coming out of the hole in the ground! I just rightfully gave up... If you two monsters can't kill it, we're bloody dead anyway, innit?" she said dejectedly, but she walked up to Drake all the same.

Drake waved her off. "I'm fine for now; you're just here in case anything really really bad happens," Drake explained.

"And the rest of us?" Julia asked.

"I need you guys to buff Bear and me so we can squash the bug," Drake said, jabbing a thumb at the prince.

"Are you sure you can even beat it...?" stammered Megan. She gripped her staff for dear life, her arms shaking.

"Pretty sure!" Drake laughed and lied through his teeth.

"Where does that leave me?" Tom asked, holding onto his shield.

"Meatshield," Drake said flatly.

"Come on! Really?!" Tom yelled.

"Yup! You better make sure you die before any of our supports die or, well, we all die. Important stuff, yeah?"

"Drake! This is serious! You're already... already so injured. Are you sure you and Bear can do this? We can't just run? Can't we just get away from here and wait out the tutorial?!" Claire pleaded, her face a mix of every emotion of concern and fright that Drake could imagine.

"I *am* serious," Drake said softly, gripping her hand. "That thing won't let any of us leave. So I have to kill it. But don't worry"—Drake smiled and moved his mask—"I'm not going to let him harm a hair on your head."

Drake patted Claire on the head, then looked to the others. "That goes for everyone here. I won't let this bug harm any of you; I bet my life on it just like I said. Except you, Tom. I might let him hurt you a bit." Drake smirked and placed his mask back.

"Have I ever told you I hate you?!" Tom growled.

"Probably."

Claire gripped his arm tighter, and Drake looked down into her eyes filled with concern.

"Trust me," Drake told her. "I'm going to win."

Drake turned and returned to stand next to Bjorn while the girls and Tom moved back slightly. They all began to chant their support spells.

"You ready, Bjorn?" Drake asked evenly.

"Don't you remember what I said, bro?" Bjorn answered, his sword again painted in a black hue. "My life's been one fight to the next. This is just the next fight."

Behind them, the chanting continued.

"*In the name of she who is the light in the dark...*"

"*Let my voice rouse the tides, hear the storm that brews deep within my heart!*"

"This is going to be harder than when you kicked my ass the first time, Bjorn." Drake snorted.

"Believe me, that first time"—Bjorn laughed—"wasn't that hard."

"Let's hope you're telling the truth about that... If you have some secret skill, now's the time to tell me," Drake said evenly. He lowered his stance as Claire and Megan finished their chants, Julia not far behind with her barrier spell.

"*Foster of Light!*"

"*Tempest's Beckoning!*"

They both shouted, and the spells enveloped both Drake and Bjorn. The prince finally showed something other than sloth as his crossed arms went to his side.

"It's time to go at it with everything we got! Everyone else get back!" Drake shouted. He began to chant his own skills. *I am the wall on which my enemies billow. Unbreakable! I am the shield, I am the rampart. Bulwark! On blessed wings. Guardian's Reprieve!*"

Bjorn stood stoically and waited, watching Obiteron closely as Drake buffed up.

Drake flashed in three consecutive shimmering waves of green. His eyes began cycling through his skills, his aura flexing to the fullest.

"Debuffs don't work on him, and my aura hardly affected him at all," Drake whispered over to Bjorn. "My spells won't dent his natural armor, so I'm leaving the damage up to you and your sturdiness. I'll hit him with a big one once we can break it."

Bjorn nodded, his stance tightening as he bent his knees and readied to charge.

"My magic won't affect him, but I can at least try to slow him down and keep him contained. Time to pull out all the stops!"

"*Heretical Endowment! Single! Ice!*" Drake growled through his teeth. He pulled a blue and red vial from his inventory, downing them quickly before bending to the ground.

Throwing the vials to the floor, Drake clasped his hands together. A massive white magic circle formed below him, Bjorn, and the prince.

"*Ryoiki Tenkai. Ninth Circle of Hell!*"

Drake's hands plunged into the ground. Ice cascaded in all directions as a massive structure of frozen waste was constructed around the three of them. Flecks of purple glowed in the deep blue sheen of the ice. The mist from the suddenly cold air covered them in a light fog.

"Don't worry about it breaking, I'll put my all into it! Go!" Drake shouted, his hair swiftly changing to blue for the regeneration.

Bjorn took the cue and rocketed off from his spot next to Drake, a small dent forming from his step forward. He quickly got into position right in front of Obiteron, his sword coming down like retribution from the heavens.

But the first strike didn't hit home. Obiteron raised his arm upward, blocking the blow. The sound of the weapon and natural armor clashing sent out an ear-shattering screech.

Obiteron immediately went for a counterattack this time, his other arm reaching out to claw at Bjorn's side. Bjorn's automatic defenses kicked into high gear, and he went to grab the incoming clawed hand by the wrist.

Snatching it, the two were locked into a power struggle that Bjorn was slowly losing.

Bjorn reassessed and planted his feet firmly. His defensive skill was beginning to ramp up, and his sword hand wound backward, coming back down in a blur of strikes. The prince's hand blocked each one while his other struggled with Bjorn's.

Drake used his last Reprieval charge to teleport behind Obiteron. His hair was now a bright crimson red, his arm tattoos flaring to life and twisting with his fire attunement magic, Martial Skill, and the mana infused into the tattoos.

He threw his fist forward at the back of Obiteron's head. Drake was sure he'd landed a solid hit, only for him to be met with one of the ant's four other appendages not currently busy with keeping Bjorn at bay.

"I'm getting really tired of blind spots not being useful!" Drake cursed, coiling his hand back and throwing another fist forward in a battle of strength and speed against Obiteron's backside.

Both Drake and Bjorn were stuck in a constant exchange of blows back and forth with the prince. The prince was obviously playing with them, and he stood his ground willingly.

This continued for several seconds until the prince screeched, his wings unfurling. He pushed Drake backward, and he skidded against the icy floor. Bjorn, on the other hand, was able to stand his ground thanks to his skills, allowing him to bring down one more strike with his black aura-infused sword.

But it did nothing. Obiteron parried the blade with a single finger, the blade instead finding home in the icy ground.

Drake saw the ant's arm pull backward, black aura surrounding its serrated fingers.

"No!" Drake howled. His hair changed colors to an electric yellow as he rushed forward.

But the prince was faster. He swiped to the side, hitting Bjorn straight in the ribs.

Drake arrived a second later, his palm to the back of the prince's head. A spinning disk of black obsidian earth aimed right at its nape.

"Sables!"

Drake launched the spinning disk. It connected with the chitin of the prince's neck, sparks flying as it eagerly tried to dig into the armor.

He wasn't allowed to see if the spell dealt any damage, however, as the prince gripped Drake's arm, his claws ripping flesh from it.

The prince screeched and pulled him forward, throwing Drake over his shoulder and toward the ground in the same direction he'd sent Bjorn.

Drake careened through the air, colliding with the ground before skidding to a stop right next to Bjorn. Looking over, Drake saw that Bjorn's shoulder guard was completely ruined. It had been sliced into pieces, and blood dripped from his wound.

"So..." Drake huffed. "I think the fight's going great."

Bjorn growled instead of responding. He got to his feet and launched himself forward once more toward the prince, his sword in both hands this time.

Drake pulled two new vials from his inventory, one red and one blue.

"Drake! You've already had six in the past hour! You will kill yourself!" Natto implored.

Not if he kills me first, Drake thought. He drained the vials in one go.

"Heretical Endowment! Septenarius! Asura! Magma, twofold!" Drake screamed as he stepped forward, crushing the ground below him and charging behind Bjorn toward the prince.

The three clashed again with a thunderous boom. The mist surrounding them scattered as if in fear for its life.

Bjorn's speed had increased now that he was using both hands on his claymore. He threw a flurry of strikes in every direction at the prince.

Drake followed up, striking from the side in tandem with his own four arms.

But it was to no avail. They couldn't land a solid blow on the prince, and anything they did land had little to no effect.

"Drake!" Bjorn shouted.

Drake glanced at Bjorn. Bjorn's body was suddenly enveloped in a bright white mana.

Understanding what was coming, Drake stepped in, his hands glowing with dirt-brown magic circles.

"*Chains of the Earth!*"

One of the two magic circles anchored onto the prince's chest. Dropping down, Drake touched the ground with the other. Jet-black chains formed from the circles and latched onto the prince.

The prince either couldn't break the chains or decided to ignore them as Bjorn chanted his skill.

"*The world has borne witness to my absolute power,*" Bjorn muttered. He raised his sword, the density of white mana spiking. "*Rend the skies! Heaven Splitting Blade!*"

Bjorn brought his blade down on the prince, the powerful white mana bending the air and light around it as it passed through on its way to the prince.

Only to be stopped by a single arm.

Obiteron flexed his wings once more, breaking Drake's chains of earth with ease.

The prince was done playing.

Snapping Bjorn's blade in half with a turn of his hands, Obiteron reared his other arm backward and thrust it right into Bjorn's stomach and out the other side. He raised him into the air.

"You fucking oversized cockroach!" Drake shouted, his anger hitting a feverish pitch as he surged forward.

The prince threw Bjorn to the ground, his lifeless body skidding to the side.

Drake screamed and howled as he threw everything he had at the prince: spells of every combination he could think of, magic-infused fists and spell-covered jabs. But nothing affected the ant.

Finally, Drake was stopped mid-thrust, his body freezing mid-air.

Drake looked down. A silver arm covered in red protruded from his body.

Gazing back up, he saw the crimson eyes of the prince looking back at him as if sneering.

Drake and Bjorn's struggle was just that—a joke to Obiteron. A worthless, meaningless, inconsequential fight that they couldn't possibly win.

Obiteron threw Drake to the ground, the ice structure Drake had created shattering into pieces around them as he collided with the floor.

"*Drake!*"

Drake could hear the shattering of glass as his skills were broken one by one, Natto's cries slowly drowned out as the sound faded around him.

He looked up, seeing one last glimpse of the prince before his body was thrown across the ground.

The distant chime of a new notification reached him before his vision began to close in.

New Personal Quest: Do you seek power?
Accept the meeting with the Sponsor.
Reward: Meeting with the Sponsor. Unknown.

Drake's jaw clenched. His eyes scanned the surroundings, seeing Bjorn's limp body on the ground while Obiteron slowly approached it. To the side, he saw Tom and the rest of the party holding Claire back from running forward, their faces covered in abject, horrifying dread.

In the fraction of a second it took to take it all in, tears began forming in Drake's eyes. One word escaped his blood-drenched mouth.

"*Yes.*"

Chapter 68

Chapter 64: Forced Change

"Drake! Drake!!! Dr...ke...!?" Natto screamed out desperately at the lifeless body on the floor, struggling to shake him awake.

Her voice was suddenly caught in the back of her throat as she felt an overwhelming presence in the room.

"Rather rude, is it not, to ignore your benefactor?"

Natto broke out into a cold sweat. Her body shook uncontrollably as she turned toward the voice.

"It seems that the mud monkey has passed out from blood loss. *Here.*"

Natto fully faced the being that spoke, her body shivering at every word. Her hair and tail stood on end.

Standing in front of her in full view was a woman with porcelain skin. A flawless white robe draped over her perfectly, its long sleeves reaching the floor. Adorning her body were golden streaks of lightning running up her arms, exposed leg, and neck until they converged in a golden circle around her neck. Upon her head lay two magnificent ivory-like antlers jutting out from her glistening silver hair.

The eyes that looked back at Natto were a fierce golden hue with the slitted pupils of a predator. Her thin lips curved into a slight smile, and a single fang protruded from her sealed rose-colored lips.

Reaching out, the woman held a clear vial with a golden choker. Red liquid filled it. A health potion.

"Take it," the woman said softly.

Natto was forced into shock, her mind simultaneously stumbling over itself and going blank out of fear.

"W-What do you want... in return...?" Natto asked, struggling to force out the words.

The woman's smile broadened, her fangs on full display.

"Why? Must I need something in return to help a promising participant?" she mused.

Natto looked down at Drake. His body was turning cold under her hands as she ground her teeth with indecision.

"Hurry now, the poor thing is going to perish soon if you do nothing. And you along with it."

Natto bit her lip and lunged for the potion, her fright disappearing as she snatched it from the woman's hand.

Immediately popping the cork, she forced it down Drake's throat and poured the rest onto his open stomach wound. His body mended instantly, both the color and warmth returning to him.

"Who are you...?" Natto asked, turning again to the woman.

The woman raised a brow. Her smile disappeared as she waved an arm.

"Your insolence is noted, *Assistant*. Now sleep. I have much to discuss with my new little toy."

* * *

Drake's body felt heavy—worse than any other time he 'd been injured. His consciousness returned slowly, and his eyes struggled to pry open. But once he realized he wasn't dead, he shot upward with a painful gasp.

"Fuck! Mother... *God* that hurts! Where is that fucking bug! I'll kill it!" Drake growled as he winced, his hand nursing his stomach.

"*Now, now*," a soothing yet horrific voice cooed from behind.

Drake suddenly felt the air chill, his breath and blood running icy cold. The presence of whatever else was in the room choked the life from him.

"Oh. I sometimes forget how fragile common F-Ranks are."

The choking pressure soon receded, and Drake's breath returned to him.

Coughing, he gripped at his throat and chest. Blood came up in chunks with every heaved cough.

"You are getting my floor dirty. At least your Assistant had the decency to not bleed all over it."

"My Assistant...?"

Drake suddenly remembered Natto. He scanned the room quickly. His eyes finally found her in the corner of the white room leaning up against the wall, her eyes closed.

"Natto!" Drake shouted. He tried to get up, but he collapsed under the weight of his own body, forcing him to crawl over on the floor.

Finally able to reach her, he checked her breathing and saw that her chest moved up and down normally.

She's asleep...

"What did you do to her?" Drake growled, finally turning to the voice. His eyes flashed different colors.

"I put her to sleep. This is a private conversation, at least for now."

Looking at the owner of the voice, Drake saw a woman like none he'd ever seen before in reality, fiction, or any medium. It blew him away. Looking at her was blinding, like he was looking at the sun.

"The... sponsor?" Drake mumbled, his mouth agape.

"Mir'phyra. It is incredible how ill-informed you are," she said softly.

Drake tried to identify her, his eyes turning blue.

ZxW121nC@tn

He clicked his tongue, unable to identify anything.

That means she's got some sort of interference item.

"Sit down," Mir'phyra commanded, sitting at a table. "I have much to tell you."

"Wait. If I'm here, does that mean I died?" Drake asked. "And what about Bjorn?! The others? Claire!"

"Quiet," Mir'phyra growled. Drake's mouth snapped shut.

Mir'phyra stood from her seat, the pressure returning as the air was squeezed from Drake's lungs. His hands reached for his throat. He struggled to breathe under the pressure, his body buckling as he slumped to the floor. Saliva dripped from his mouth, and he started to asphyxiate.

"I tire of your questions. This is a space created by me. Your tutorial is of no concern. Listen well and do as I say, and you will return soon enough." She smiled.

Drake clawed at the floor, doing his best to resist the pressure and speak.

"S-S-Screw you!" he growled.

Mir'phyra's smile broadened. "I love a toy that's a little rebellious. Worry not, I will train it out of you soon."

Mir'phyra snapped her fingers and sat down once more. The pressure in the room vanished.

Pushed into another coughing fit, Drake stood, refusing to not look the terrible woman in the eyes.

"What do you want." Drake coughed.

"Sit."

Drake reluctantly moved over to the table and sat down.

Finally having a moment, he glanced down at his attire. His robes were thrashed, a bloody hole going through them. Opening up his inventory, he saw that the item armor was grayed out, indicating that it was useless. His set bonus was also gone.

"Damn it," he mumbled.

"Enough of that. I will get straight to the point," Mir'phyra said, propping her arm up with her hand. Her elegantly long fingers rested on her cheek.

"You have something you should not. I would appreciate it if you would relieve yourself of them."

Items... the Necromancer stones? Drake thought.

"No. Why should I?" Drake snapped, remembering how the sponsor had threatened both him and Theodore.

"This is not a discussion." She sneered, and the pressure in the room bubbled. "I will give you the only legendary stones provided in the Tutorial Shop in exchange for them. Free of charge."

Mir'phyra waved her hand. Six stones dropped onto the table, each one a fiery crimson. Flecks of orange as radiant as the sun appeared to move within the blood-colored glass stones. Drake's eyes widened.

"Do you seek power…" Drake mumbled. "Why are they so important to you?"

"It isn't your business." She sneered. Her arms dropped to the table to push the stones forward. "Bring out the Necromancer stones. *Now.*"

Drake paused for a moment, unsure of what to do.

She's willing to give me six stones for the price of two? That doesn't make sense, Drake thought, looking down at the stones to identify them.

Subtree Stone: Asuran's Warbook [Legendary]
Unlocks Asuran's Warbook subtree branch.
Requires 1 or more empty subtrees and an unlocked Warrior main class tree.

Skill Stone: War God [Legendary]
Unlocks 1 random skill from the War God tree.
Requires 1 open skill slot and 1 Warrior main tree or subtree branch unlocked.

"Asuran Stones? Not Dragon?" Drake asked curiously.

Mir'phyra bared her teeth in a snarl, the room chilling as the oppressive aura came down even more potent than ever before. It slammed Drake to the floor through the chair.

"You think I would give a filthy monkey the ability to turn into such a grand race?! You receive more than you deserve, and yet you still question it? You will bring out those stones now, or I will crush her like the worthless trash that she is."

Somehow Mir'phyra lifted Natto from the corner despite never leaving her seat.

"N-No!" Drake shouted from the floor. His head struggled to turn so that he could see her. "Fine!"

Drake used his shawl to summon the box from his inventory, the item falling to the floor with a thud.

The pressure remained as Natto was lowered to the floor. Mir'phyra got up to pick up the box, and it disappeared into what Drake could only assume was her inventory.

"Good," she said tersely, moving to lift the stones on the table.

"N-Now l-let me go," Drake growled, trying to resist the pressure.

Mir'phyra smirked. She pulled the subtree stone from the pile, hovering in the air.

"Oh, but the fun is just beginning, my pet. For all the things you take from me, you will pay me back handsomely. After all, you are a promising Dual Class as well. Play along with me, and I promise you will have no trouble in the future. That is... until I come to collect." She snickered.

"Fuck you." Drake sneered from the floor.

"Unfortunately, I was not asking. You haven't seemed to realize within your small monkey brain that you have no choice in the matter. Thankfully for you, I will be turning you into another mud-brained pet. Asurans are a joy to watch..."

Mir'phyra's eyes glowed, and the world constricted under her power. Drake was pushed into the floor as it cracked around him. Mir'phyra showed no signs of needing to put effort into doing so, displaying just how large the gap in power was between them.

"Try not to break, my little pet." She laughed and licked her thin lips with an elongated tongue.

Mir'phyra gripped the stone, and it began to radiate a red brilliance as she kneeled down. She thrust it into Drake's back.

You have consumed Subtree Stone: Asuran's War Book [Legendary].

You have unlocked the secondary subtree Asuran's War Book [F-Rank].
Passive effects applied.

You have unlocked 5 new skill stone slots in Asuran's War Book.

Subtree stone potency has forced a change.
Your race will be changed in accordance with the stone.

Asuran's War Book [F-Rank] P1 (0%)
The lineage of the prideful Asurans runs strongly in your veins. Since ancient times, fighting with bare fists was the way of the Great War Gods.
200% increase to hand-to-hand combat.

Increased learning curve of all fighting styles and forms of hand-to-hand combat.

Drake roared, his body suddenly free from the pressure of Mir'phyra's gaze. Instead, he was gripped with unfathomable pain as he felt his body light on fire like never before. His ears throbbed, and he heard his heart race. The sound of snapping bones and muscles tearing reverberated in his ear.

Drake screamed in agony, his body contorting in pain as he scrambled on the floor, gripping and clawing at anything he could.

The pain felt like it lasted for days to Drake. Pools of sweat and black excrement covered the floor.

Finally, it stopped.

Drake was barely conscious, his breaths shallow and ragged.

Congratulations! Your race has changed from Human [F-Rank] to Asuran [F-Rank].

Drake saw the outline of what he could only assume was Mir'phyra in his blurred vision as new notifications continued to flood him.

Your race has interacted with Primary Skill Tree Elementalist [F-Rank]
Your race has interacted with Secondary Skill Tree Internal Mastery [F-Rank]
Your race has interacted with Secondary Skill Tree Soul Mastery [F-Rank]
Your race has interacted with Secondary Skill Tree Weapon Mastery [F-Rank]
Your race has interacted with Skill Magic Sight [F-Rank]
Your race has interacted with Skill Heretical Mind [F-Rank]
Your race has interacted with Skill Multi…

Every one of Drake's skills flashed in his blurred vision, passing by faster than he could read them. Mir'phyra's faint voice snickered above him. "Oh, this is going to be most fun!"

Raising her hand, she gripped the remaining five stones. They began glowing in a similar light before she thrust her hand once again into Drake, forcing the stones on him.

Drake writhed in agony, twisting and screaming in pain on the floor as he tore and ripped at his body, begging for the pain to end.

You have consumed Skill Stone: War God [Legendary].

You have learned Skill War God's Battle Right [F-Rank].

War God's Battle Right [F-Rank] P1 (0%)

By birth and blood, an Asuran's right is to thrive in combat and fight to their last breath in beautiful glory!

200% increase to Strength, Stamina, and Vitality during combat.

Drake roared once more, his voice becoming hoarse.

You have consumed Skill Stone: War God [Legendary].

You have learned Skill Asuran's Constitution [F-Rank].

Asuran's Constitution [F-Rank] P1 (0%)

As one of the Primordial races, those closest to the Originators, your body is one that is of ancient power and origin. You are capable of living through the eras.

200% increase to Vitality, Endurance, and Wisdom.

Screaming, Drake's voice became faint, echoing in the room as Mir'phyra looked down in joyful curiosity.

You have consumed Skill Stone: War God [Legendary].

You have learned Skill Asuran's Punishment [F-Rank].

Asuran's Punishment [F-Rank] P3 (0%)

Your blood boils and your body trembles at the insult of being challenged. Show the pride of the Arbiters of the Multiverse. Give them their rightful punishment.

Asuran's Punishment: *"Death is nigh. Asuran's Punishment."*

Effect: Deals 1000% increased pure mana damage to a target under 15% health.

Additional Effects: Should the target not take lethal damage from this skill, they will be inflicted with 250 pure mana damage + 10% of current Strength over the next 30 seconds.

Cost: None

Cooldown: 48 Hours. Decreases with proficiency.

You have consumed Skill Stone: War God [Legendary].

You have learned Skill Line in the Sand [F-Rank].

Line in the Sand [F-Rank] P1 (0%)

You demand one-on-one combat with a worthy opponent. It is your right by birth as an Asuran to fight with honor to the death. "To the death."

500% increase to all stats against Marked opponent during one-on-one combat.

Duration lasts until the Marked target is killed, you are killed, or the skill is canceled. Skill cannot be cleansed or resisted.

Cost: None

Cooldown: 48 Hours. Decreases with proficiency.

Drake howled in pain. The ground shook around him as he slammed his fists into the ground. He turned over, lashing out in an attempt to lessen the pain in any way.

You have consumed Skill Stone: War God [Legendary].

You have learned Skill War God's Battle Fervor [F-Rank].

War God's Battle Fervor [F- Rank] P1 (0%)

As is your birthright, you revel in the carnage of the battlefield. Every moment within it is a breath of fresh air. Everything is for the thrill of battle. "For the thrill of battle."

100% increase to all stats. Can stack up to 3 times every 10 minutes for up to 30 minutes. Increases with proficiency.

Cost: None

Cooldown: 12 Hours

The last of the skills finally settled within Drake. He drooled on the floor, his every breath pushing steam out from his loosened mask.

Finally, it was over. Drake could feel his body's heat slowly reduce, but his anger spilled over.

He surged forward, his hands reaching for Mir'phyra's neck in an attempt at retribution for the forced change. Drake howled and shouted as he clawed at her, only to be held back at arm's length. Mir'phyra's face suddenly scowled, uninterested.

"Did I break him...? Pity."

Mir'phyra was playing with Drake like a newborn. Now as a Primordial race, his race and skills had changed and bloomed into something incomparable to before. But it meant nothing in the face of the Dragon Matriarch.

"I look forward to how well you will increase my returns, mud pup. You are now that world's problem."

Mir'phyra snapped her fingers, and Drake disappeared from the room along with Natto.

* * *

"That was entertaining," the chattering of bones said from behind Mir'phyra.

Mir'phyra didn't turn, knowing who it was. She sighed in disappointment more than offense.

"How did you know?"

"I have my ways. Everyone owes the God of Death a favor or two... or twelve."

Mir'phyra scoffed, turning to face the voice.

In front of her was a hideous creature. Beggar's clothing draped over bones, a crown adorning its head. Here stood the only High Lich in existence.

"Vandelu, what lovely clothing you are wearing today..." she mused.

"Oh, this old thing? I had to move in a hurry. No time to change, Mir'phyra," Vandelu teased. "The stones," he demanded. He reached out with bony fingers, each one covered in numerous jeweled rings.

"I have no idea what you are talking about."

"Do not play this game; we both know who will win."

"They are property of the Dragon race. Why should I release them to your wretched ilk?" She sneered, her lip raising and revealing her teeth.

"You wouldn't want to go to war over this, would you, old friend?" Vandelu said pointedly. "After all I have done for you and your *son?*"

Mir'phyra flinched. Her anger vanished, and she clicked her tongue. A box dropped to the floor and snapped open.

"Take them, you snake. We are even-handed after this."

Vandelu moved to the box, picking up the two stones and inspecting them in the air.

"Yes, but of course. And as you say, this is going to be most *enjoyable...*"

Chapter 69
Return of the Tyrant Asuran

Claire watched from outside the massive structure of ice with the rest of the party. Chelsea had run up to join them, concerned for Bjorn as they looked on in anxious anticipation.

Megan, Julia, Jacqueline, and Tom held their breaths. They could hear the clashing resonate throughout the ice structure, the sound beating deep in their chests.

"W-What's going on in there?" Chelsea asked.

"Them kicking that ant's ass if we're lucky," Tom said, tightening his grip on his shield.

Megan shuffled next to the group, unsure of what to do. "Do you think they're beating it? It's an E-Rank, we all got the notif—"

Claire turned and glared daggers at Megan. "Be quiet! They won't lose! Drake won't lose! He promised us!"

She turned back to the ice, clenching her hands in prayer after snapping at Megan. Claire closed her eyes and pleaded for Drake to make it through.

The ground shook as another thunderous impact sounded from inside the structure, rocking everyone close to the ice.

"A-Are we sure it's safe to be this close? Maybe we should move back," Tom stammered.

"Don't be such a bloody sod, Tom. Ain't you the one who's supposed to be protecting us?" Jacqueline scoffed.

"We can't go anywhere. What if they need our support and we're too far to help," Julia interjected.

"I'm not going anywhere!" Claire shouted.

"Neither am I!" Chelsea added, gripping Claire's hands.

Nodding to each other, the pair looked in concern at the ice, the sounds of fighting continuing.

The feeling of a dead weight suddenly pressed down on them, a guttural screech piercing the surroundings and pushing them all down to their knees.

"W-What was that?!" Megan eked out.

The next moment, Drake's unmistakable scream reached their ears through the ice. Multiple booming impacts went off in quick succession.

Then—silence.

In the blink of an eye, the ice structure shattered, revealing the aftermath of the fight.

Claire's hand snapped to her mouth. She gasped in horror.

Standing with its hand through Drake was the ant prince. Bjorn lay a small distance away, bleeding on the ground.

The prince then threw Drake to the floor before kicking him across the field.

Claire's eyes followed his lifeless body through the air as she struggled to scream out his name.

"Dr-Dr-Drake!!!!!!!!!!!"

But before she could move or watch him collide with the ground, his body disappeared in a flash of white light.

"W-What?! Where did he go?" Claire yelled, looking around in desperation.

"Bear!" Chelsea shouted from the side. She sprinted to him before anyone could stop her.

She barreled forward across the field, reaching for him only to be stopped by the ant prince suddenly appearing in between them. Chelsea was immediately frozen in fear, her body stiffening mid-step in front of the ant.

"Chels!" Julia yelled. She cast her barrier spell, a white luminescence forming around Chelsea.

The prince lightly arched his hand, sending Chelsea flying backward. Her body curled and bent as she collided with the ground. Jacqueline immediately ran to her and cast a healing spell.

The prince chittered, and his mandibles snapped. One moment he was by Bjorn, the next he appeared in front of Jacqueline, his hand raised.

"No, stop!" Claire yelled. She raised her staff and cast her only attack spell in a feeble attempt to stop the monster. "*Spark!*"

The bolt of lightning shot out from her staff. It fizzled out on the back of the prince's head.

He snapped around and singled out Claire. With a screech, the prince disappeared again.

A light flashed. It was accompanied by an impact that sounded like a bomb going off. Claire raised her hands, trying to hold back the gusts of wind.

Her eyes opened, and she saw the back of a man she didn't immediately recognize. He wore a familiar black and gold trimmed robe that was tattered and worn. His skin was a caramel tan.

Claire's eyes began to water as she scanned him, a familiar mask on the side of a sharp face framed by shoulder-length bangs and hair that reached his waist.

"D-Drake...?" she murmured.

Drake didn't reply right away. In one arm, he held a sleeping Natto. In the other, he gripped the prince's arm, sparks of blue mana cascading off his infused Tattoo Ring.

"Take care of her," Drake said evenly, handing Natto to Claire.

Claire began to break down, the floodgates opening as tears fell.

"I-I thought you died... I thought you lost! You don't have to keep trying! It's alright as long as you're okay! As long as you don't get hurt anymore! You've done enough! Please! Drake!"

A shit-eating grin creased Drake's face. He turned, his hair shimmering into a kaleidoscope of colors as he applied multiple endowments.

"You heard her, Obiteron. Looks like I can't afford to lose any longer."

* * *

Drake held the prince at bay, surprising himself as he gripped his claws with relative ease.

These new skills and body have put me on another level. I hate to thank that Dragon Bitch, but I wouldn't be able to win if I wasn't forced to change... he lamented.

"To the death."

Drake cast his new skill. The prince's head tilted back as he felt the skill's effect. He looked confused, watching both Drake and his now-stopped hand.

Drake instantly felt his status surge even further from its already ridiculous increase since his race change. Surprised by the sudden influx of power he felt, Drake gripped his hands out of instinct. He immediately crushed the prince's hand in his grip.

The prince screeched and howled in pain. It shot backward, nursing its shattered hand as ichor leaked from the broken armor.

Drake scoffed, then looked over and saw Bjorn still on the ground. His teeth clenched at the sight of his friend in such a state.

Moving with increased speed, Drake appeared next to Bjorn.

"Hey, you're still with us, right bud?" Drake asked, putting his hand on Bjorn's neck to check for a pulse.

"I-I'm still kicking, if only barely, bro..." Bjorn chuckled wearily.

"Did you take a potion yet?"

"N-No. What happened to your hair? It get longer in the last five minutes?" Bjorn asked, almost delirious.

"My hair?" Drake parroted. He saw his bangs sway in front of him, painted in a myriad of colors. "Oh, would you look at that. I turned SSJ3."

Drake popped a red vial into his hands; thankfully his shawl was still in working order. He quickly uncorked it and poured it over Bjorn's open wound, then flipped the man on his back to tip the rest into his mouth.

"You alright from here? Even with my new strength, I don't think I can carry your fat ass over to Jacqueline." Drake chuckled.

Bjorn wearily got on his feet, shaking slightly. Using his giant claymore as a crutch, he leaned into it and gave Drake a wry smile.

"I'm not fat, I'm just big boned. And yeah, I got it from here. What... What happened to you though, bro?" Bjorn asked.

"It's a long story, man..." Drake grimaced. "I'll tell you all about it after I deal with this bug."

Drake stood back up and faced the obviously irritated ant.

The prince's hand had since healed from Drake crushing it; Obiteron's natural healing ability proved tenacious. He looked at Drake with newfound hate.

Drake smiled as he somehow saw the emotion in the prince's Aura change. It was no longer looking at Drake like a weak toy, but now as a threat.

A problem.

"Oh am I a problem. The whole problem. I'm *the* problem!" Drake snarled. "*For the thrill of battle!*"

Drake's body bulged and surged with power, but it wasn't over yet.

"*Marked.*"

Asuran Battle Instincts: Weak Point [F-Rank] P3 (0%)

This skill allows you to gain insight into your opponent through your knowledge of internal mastery. Your insight guides you to vulnerable locations on your marked opponent. Your newfound instincts further push your knowledge of your opponents.

You may mark up to 3 opponents by saying "Marked."
Increases with proficiency.
Passive increase in critical chance of 10% to Dexterity.
Increases with proficiency.
Active increase of critical chance to marked targets by 150%.
Increases with proficiency.
Cost: A small amount of Mana and Stamina.
Cooldown: 10 minutes or until Marked target is killed.

With Drake's improved skill, he narrowed his focus on Obiteron. In this moment, there was nothing else. There was no one else.

Drake's eyes subtly changed from their natural baby blue to a deep aqua, then to a serene verdant green, and finally to a brilliant piercing yellow.

He bolted forward, crushing the ground around him while the prince did the same, meeting him in the middle. They clashed, sending out a pulse of destruction as debris was kicked up all around them.

Drake began channeling his mana into his rings, his improved Martial Skill going to work while his improved Adrenaline Acuity allowed him to fight well beyond his peak from before.

Asuran's Battle Acuity [F-Rank] P3 (0%)

A passive stacking skill that allows the user to increase the effect of adrenaline to the limit, increasing their cognitive ability and tolerance to pain over the course of a fight. The skill increases as time passes while in combat.

Increases the potency of adrenaline over the course of 10 minutes, ramping up from a 5% increase to 50% potency. Increases with proficiency.
Passive effects last for a duration of 30 minutes. Increases with proficiency.

War God's Martial Prowess [F-Rank] P3 (0%)

A skill that allows the martial artist to infuse their body with inner energy to harden themselves.

Increases the damage done by physical strikes by 200%. Increases with proficiency.
Cost: A small amount of Stamina.

Drake collided with Obiteron in a cross guard, then quickly gripped the prince's extended arm as it passed his right side. He threw his own right fist into the prince's side, forcing the ant a few inches into the air.

The prince recovered quickly. Healing the wound, he tried to pull his arm from Drake, but he was unable to do so. Obiteron threw a fist and a kick with his free arm and leg.

Drake reacted swiftly, seeing the strikes easily with his skills in full effect. Dodging the clawed arm, he gripped it under his own, then jumped into a spin as his leg began glowing a sinister crimson red.

He brought his Martial Skill-infused foot up and into the side of the prince's head, throwing him to the ground.

Drake landed deftly on his feet, bending at the knee and beginning to channel his new and improved, nearly bottomless pit of mana into his rings.

"Saisho wa guu."

Drake chanted in a hushed breath, his hand beginning to radiate a blue glow that bent the light and air around it. The infused weapon began to snap and whip around him as it condensed within the ring and tattoo.

Inner Sanctum of the Asuran Soul [F-Rank] P3 (0%)

Your soul has gone through a monumental change, and with each improvement, it will become purer. Your body is the envy of every martial artist, for it reaches further toward the peak of perfection.

Passive Effect: Your maximum mana capacity is increased by 7 times. Increases with proficiency.

Extra Effect: You now gain an additional 10 Intelligence per level.

The prince wrenched himself from the ground just in time to see Drake above him, his skill manifesting in his drawn right hand.

Drake threw his fist into the center of Obiteron's chest, shoving him deeper into the ground with the strike. The sound of shattering glass sounded as Drake saw his ring snap and break in front of him from the overflow of mana.

Clicking his tongue, he moved his left-hand ring to his dominant right side.

"Still alive? That regeneration of yours is impressive, if nothing else. That explains why I thought I was doing no damage earlier... You were regenerating it in real-time. But"—Drake sneered and pulled his staff from his inventory—"*playtime* is *over.* Sit still, and I will show you what a *true tyrant* is."

"*Fear is binding. Cower.*"

Cower Before the Mighty [F-Rank] P3 (0%)

A spell that uses your Aura to forcibly make a target immobile by producing fearful hallucinations based on your Aura's strength.

Cower: *"Fear is binding. Cower."*
Target is placed under Terror Debuff for 20 seconds. Damage beyond the threshold will break the effect. Increases with proficiency.
Debuff can be cleansed with high-level Holy Magic.
Cost: A small amount of Mana and Stamina.
Cooldown: 10 minutes.

Drake mumbled his improved fear spell, allowing the inky mana to drip down his arm. It enveloped Obiteron, who suddenly lurched and began clawing at his body. Drake then bent down before throwing himself upward into the sky as countless magic circles formed around him.

Asuran's Magic Prowess [F-Rank] P3 (0%)
A passive skill that allows the caster to create separate instances of spells.

This skill allows the use of multiple instances of any spell.
Limit: 55 additional spells. Max 56 instances including combined forms. Increases with proficiency.
Cost: None
Cooldown: None

Taking advantage of his now almost fifty-fold increase in spell count, he used his wind magic to keep himself afloat while manifesting numerous elements around him.

"Heretical Attunement. Earth."

Drake whispered, and his earth magic formed around his outstretched Morning Glory staff. It shaped itself into the massive arch of a bow that was the color of his obsidian black earth.

"Heretical Attunement. Duo. Lightning. Fire."

Adding more magic to the spell, a swirl of fire and lightning coalesced into a taut bowstring crossing from one end of the bow to the other.

Using his right hand, Drake opened his palm. Forming at the edge was a pure black arrow made from earth magic. Drake began chanting, pouring his status into every fiber of the spell.

"O' sacred Lord in Heaven."

The magic began infusing itself into the bow and arrow, the arrow now crackling with power.

"Radiant Lord, merciful, who bestowed upon me wisdom and strength."

Drake nocked the completed arrow, aiming it carefully down at the still-writhing Obiteron on the ground.

"I call upon thee to witness my heart, my thoughts, and everything I have achieved."

He pulled back on the string, and more elements snapped into being and attached to the arrow. It swirled with a vortex of every color.

"Now, creator of the moon and the stars!"

More! Push more into it! Dump everything you have! I'll kill this bug here! Drake cursed as he looked down at the prince inside the crater. He was still tearing and clawing at himself and the ground around him.

"Behold my deeds, my death, and my Spenta Armaiti which I must carry out! After I unleash this last arrow with all my strength, my iron body shall shatter and annihilate me where I stand!"

Drake pulled harder on the string, putting every last drop of his new status into the spell. It crackled and snapped with power, the magic swirling and screeching in his ear in a contest to drown out his voice.

"STELLAAAAAAAAA!!!"

Drake released the string. The arrow roared forward with jubilation, screeching and tearing through the air toward its target. The now-shattered bow in Drake's hand disappeared in the wind.

The arrow seemed to move slowly in Drake's improved perception. It finally hit the ground, lighting up the surroundings in a kaleidoscope of colors as it spiraled forward.

Drake was drained, but he smiled all the same when he saw the prince finally come out of the fear. He screamed in one last defiant moment before the spell impacted with the ground like a lone meteor.

You have subjugated King of the Tyrant Ants Obiteron Trikk Level 30 [E-Rank]

Experience earned. 24,000,000 TP have been awarded.

Quest Complete: Defeat the King of the Tyrant Ants Obiteron Trikk [E-Rank]

Chapter 70

Coming Down

Drake lowered himself to the ground, entering the large chasm his spell had created. His hair had already turned a deep majestic blue to recover. His skills had moved leaps and bounds beyond what he could ever imagine, and the recovery speed proved such.

He eventually made it to the impact at the bottom where the light of day didn't reach the end of the chasm. There, he finally found a small crystal stone lying next to the scattered remains of the monster that had nearly killed him and his party.

Drake scoffed.

"Why does it feel like such an empty win... I feel—It feels like it isn't enough. This must be one of the changes the stones made; I hope there aren't too many side effects. I'll have to give that Dragon bitch a piece of my mind next time I see her," Drake said, grinding his teeth as he bent down to grip the stone.

Subtree Stone: Massive Regeneration [Rare]
Unlocks Massive Regeneration subtree branch.
Requires 1 or more empty subtrees and an unlocked Warrior main class tree.

Drake stowed the stone and jumped to climb out of the deep chasm, traveling the distance to the top quickly. Once he got out, he saw his party gathering.

"Hey," Drake said awkwardly. "Well, we won!" he announced.

"Are you serious? What was that? You disappeared for a moment after I saw you thrown! I thought you died!" Claire screamed, tears still in her eyes.

Drake raised his hands in defeat.

"Okay, okay! I obviously have some explaining to do, but first, is everyone alright?" Drake looked, seeing Bjorn move to help Jacqueline carry Chelsea over.

"I got to say, idjit, that was some entrance. Didn't even recognize ya. What's with the long hair and tan?" Hudson asked, crossing his arms and raising a brow.

"L-Long story..." Drake sighed.

"Look around, pup. We ain't got nothin' but time," Hudson pressed.

"Indeed, my lord! Thou hast changed a great deal externally! This one would also like to be enlightened on your formal change," Theodore added.

"Fine, but first everyone gets treated. Let's get back to the fortress at least."

Before they moved, Drake addressed Amir. "Amir, you got the E-Grade Monster Core, right? Give it here."

"Of course, sir," Amir said. He pulled the stone from his inventory. "Here it is. I am surprised it is still so small."

Drake pursed his lips, picking up the stone. "It *is* a little weird it didn't get bigger, but I can sense the mana inside is far more dense. I'll have to give it to Natto as thanks."

"Sir, might I ask something?" Amir said after handing over the stone.

"Of course," Drake replied.

"Are all E-Ranks going to be this strong...? I fear we will stand no chance outside the tutorial if this is the standard we are to meet," Amir said warily.

Drake chuckled. "No, no. Natto already told me that the prince is a little, well, a lot different. Obiteron and his brothers were named high-tier F-Rank monsters, so when Obiteron evolved, he made a larger leap than what a regular E-Rank would be. Sure E-Ranks are going to be strong, but he was closer to mid or high grade because of his status already."

"That is comforting... I think." Amir laughed nervously. He turned to walk to the fortress.

"I'm glad you didn't die," Julia offered, clasping him on the shoulder.

She paused a moment, then began gripping him more strongly. "Jesus, are these made out of steel? Marble? Titanium?!"

Drake looked at her, his eyes thinning. "You do realize the double standard here, right?" He snorted. "And yeah, I'm glad I didn't die either."

Julia let go, giving Drake a wave and a smile before walking away as well.

Theodore and Harley were happy to be reunited after everything, and they took off without waiting. Sherry mumbled about food as always even after the whole ordeal, following the forming crowd.

Megan looked pensively at Drake, her hands rubbing together around her staff.

"Out with it. I may not look it, but I'm tired," Drake said, addressing her.

"U-Um, I'm just happy you kept your promise in protecting us. Seeing you get hurt and still give it your all really... really showed me how different from Chris you are," Megan explained, her cheeks reddening slightly.

"Right... Thank you I guess? But I could've told you I'm not like that guy right from the start. I'm pretty sure I did too..." Drake answered, scratching his head.

Megan looked more embarrassed than she probably should have been. She scurried off to where Bjorn and Chelsea were, looking over her shoulder as she went.

"That is going to definitely be trouble later." Drake sighed.

"I'm going to get going too... Ya know, before it gets awkward again because you forgot about me for the fourth time. Glad you didn't die, too. Cool hair," Tom said. He sprinted off after the rest of the party.

Drake raised his eyebrows in surprise. "Even after a race change to a Primordial, he still has such an absence of presence that I don't notice him. That has to be a special skill or something..."

Drake shook his head.

Finally, he was left alone with Claire. He turned to her. Her head was slightly dipped, and she was looking down.

He scratched his cheek, not sure how to go about consoling her. She did just see him die and come back to life in the last few minutes. And when he returned, he'd been an entirely different person. It would confuse and traumatize anyone.

Drake lifted her chin, seeing her blue eyes reddened by tears. Her face was a mess from crying. He looked her in the eyes as she tried to turn away. He smiled.

"I'm back. And I won, just like I promised."

"That isn't the point! I was worried about you. I thought you died! I don't want to see you get hurt like that ag—" Claire's angry and concerned tirade was abruptly stopped.

Drake had stolen her lips, pressing his against hers. She hit him with her free hand that wasn't carrying Natto, but she didn't pull away. After a few moments, she leaned into him as well.

"Wow." Drake smirked. "If I knew shutting you up was that easy, I would've done that a long time ago." He laughed.

Claire growled and pushed him away.

"I'm still angry! Don't ever do something like that again!"

"Yeah, but if you're so angry, why are you smiling?"

Claire pressed her hand to her face, checking herself only to turn her grin into a scowl. Pushing Natto to Drake, she huffed and stormed off.

"That went well." Drake chuckled lightly, looking down at the still-sleeping construct.

Drake took the E-Rank Monster Core he'd gotten from Amir and waved it in front of Natto.

"Wakey wakey, I have a nice treat for you," Drake said in a light tone, wafting the stone in front of Natto's nose.

Natto's nose began to twitch. Her ears tilted back and forth, following Drake's hand.

"Come on, it's a really nice treat," Drake said, waving the stone closer.

Suddenly Natto lunged forward, her mouth opening at a near 180-degree angle to clamp on the stone, but she took some of Drake's fingers in the process.

"W-Whash ish dish...?" she said, her eyes fluttering open as she chewed mechanically on Drake's fingers and the stone. Drool spilled everywhere.

"Those," Drake said, wrenching his hand from her mouth, "are my fingers. And good morning sunshine."

"W-We are alive? Wait, who the hell are you!" Natto yelled, suddenly spitting. "Uhh... I had a stranger's hand in my mouth... What vile joke is this?!"

"Hey, I'm still me," Drake said, hurt, "and I'm not sure what the Dragon bitch did to you, but I'm glad you're safe."

"D-Drake...?" Natto stammered. She made sure to hold the E-Rank core tightly in her hands as she looked him up and down. "W-What happened to you?"

"Come on." Drake chuckled. "I'm going to go over the story with everyone else. Don't drop that stone; it took a lot of effort to get it."

Natto looked from Drake's face down to the core in her hand, her eyebrows scrunched in a thoughtful expression. Drake left her to her thoughts and instead walked over to Bjorn, Chelsea, Jacqueline, and Megan.

"Need a hand?"

"Who the hell," Chelsea asked before coughing, "are you?"

Megan nudged Chelsea, explaining to her in a soft whisper, "That's Shot..."

"What?! The bloody hell happened to you? Change teams?" Jaqueline shouted.

Drake raised his arms and looked at his body. "Oh, now that you mention it for the 100th time, I am lightly toasted, aren't I? See a snack do you, Jacqueline?" Drake chuckled and wiggled his eyebrows.

"Hell I do, you knob. You can turn into whatever right bronze-looking god you'd well like. I ain't turnin' up anywhere near your batshit crazy self."

"That's just hurtful." Drake frowned then turned to Chelsea. "You alright?"

Chelsea nodded and looked to Bjorn, leaning on him for support. "Yeah, I got smacked around, but thanks to Jacky I'll live. What happened to you and Natto?" she asked.

"Long story—I'll explain later. Let's get everyone to the dinky fortress before anything," Drake instructed. They began walking along.

"I'm guessing you beat the bug?" Chelsea asked during the silence as the group walked.

"You didn't see it?" Drake asked.

"I was knocked out cold by the thing…"

"Didn't do much to fix your mouth though, did it." Drake snorted. "Yeah, I killed it…"

Bjorn noticed the lament and slight regret on Drake's face.

"You don't seem happy about it, bro. Doesn't look like you leveled up either."

"Not from the kill, yeah. I'm expecting or at least hoping the quest will give me a level up. I want to reach E-Rank as fast as possible, but I don't think I'll have time for it…"

Drake looked at a screen in front of him, viewing the current leaderboards as well as the remaining time and participants.

Top Level Leaderboard
Rank 1, Level 27: Bear
Rank 2, Level 24: Shigure Kenzo
Rank 3, Level 23: Shot
Rank 4, Level 19: Super Megan
Rank 5, Level 18: Theodore Rotwood
Rank 6, Level 17: Jimina Seinen

…

Tutorial Points Leaderboard
Rank 1: Shot [51,246,505 TP]
Rank 2: Bear [11,735,355 TP]
Rank 3: Shigure Kenzo [3,283,945 TP]

Time remaining until tutorial's conclusion:
35 days, 16 hours, 57 minutes, 21 seconds.
Remaining Participants: 1,889

The level rankings hadn't changed much, which was understandable considering the lack of monsters outside of the ants, but Drake had again made leaps forward on the tutorial point ladder.

He still had a lot to do before they left for the world ahead of them. New skills, new limits to test, and most of all, relaxation and hopefully a fun time with his girlfriend now that he'd made it past first base.

"Or is that second base? I can't remember how that analogy works..." Drake mused aloud.

"What?" Bjorn asked.

"Oh nothing. Anyway, I should mention I'm beyond impressed that you didn't change with your stones, Bear."

"What do you mean? Is that what happened to you? Thought you were gonna wait, bro?"

"I'll go over the story later, but right now I'm more concerned and frankly suspicious of why you haven't changed yourself. I was force-fed six legendary stones, so it makes sense I changed, but even one of those stones... I can't believe you endured it..." Drake said, his face turning serious.

"I don't know what to tell you or how to answer that, Shot. I used the stones because they were there and powerful. It isn't like I didn't struggle with them when I consumed them. I had my own demons for a while, and you know I still do."

"I know, Bear," Drake said, his face softening.

Drake and the group continued to walk, this time in silence after the small conversation. Drake caught up in his own mind.

I know he has his own problems, and now that I'm... not human, I know I can deal with them when the time comes. But... what is this anticipation? It's almost as if I want him to change. Like I'm looking for the next fight.

Drake clenched his hand, unsure if it was the stones talking or just him. The future Drake had been aiming for felt further away than ever.

Chapter 71

Big Announcements

"Will you stop touching it already?"

Drake sat down in the fortress, Natto on his shoulder as he looked at the rest of the people currently pulling at his new long hair.

"I'm just checking if it's real," Claire shushed.

"Certainly this is fake, but changes of this manner often do manifest in such physical alterations," Natto added, yanking on his hair.

"Ow! What the hell? Punyeta! And checking for over twenty minutes?!" Drake chided.

"It is fine, continue with your story." Natto waved and began to braid his hair with a snicker.

"Right..." Drake sighed and gave up. "After I woke up, there was the sponsor of the tutorial. The Dragon bitch."

"So the one in charge of everything was a Dragon after all?" Bjorn said, scratching his beard.

"That's like, really bad for us, isn't it?" Tom added.

"Well sure as hell won't be no walk in the Dairy Queen parking lot, that's for damn sure," Hudson added, giving a low whistle.

"Th-That... doesn't even make sense," Tom mumbled, a look of pure confusion on his face.

"What exactly does that mean for us?" Chelsea asked.

"Well for one, it's bad," Drake started. "Two, it wasn't just *a* dragon. It was the Matriarch."

Drake paused for effect, waiting to hear some astonishment, but it never came.

"Really? I say it's the big bad leader of the Dragons and nothing?" Drake snorted.

"Yeah, get on with it already bro. We all know you like to be dramatic." Bjorn chuckled.

Drake grumbled a bit but continued. "Anyway, I was transported into that small room, you know the one from the intro? And she was there. I couldn't identify her, but she was strong. I couldn't even compare her to anything we've faced so far."

"One could not compare her to the ant prince?" Theodore asked curiously.

"If I'm being completely honest, I don't know how many Obiterons it would even take to get in the ballpark," Drake said, scoffing in self-loathing.

"Even after your power up?" Claire asked. She paused for a moment to help Natto braid his hair.

"Let's just say it's more than a lot of me."

Drake heard gasps around him.

"Really?" He sighed.

"What? It was surprising." Bjorn smiled.

"I can confirm that it would be impossible for anyone on Earth to be able to stop Mir'phyra. Most likely it will be hundreds of years before you are able to, possibly thousands," Natto explained, not looking away from her work.

"Seriously?" Drake asked.

"Please... Do not tell me you could not guess her rank?"

"If I say S-Rank do I get a prize?"

"Correct. She is not only an S-Rank, but the epitome of such. She is the original Matriarch of the Dragon Race."

"Wait, you mean like OG OG? Wouldn't that make her..."

"Yes, she is very, very, very ol—" Natto was about to finish her sentence when her tail stood on end. She coughed. "Experienced."

"You mean old?" Drake corrected. He felt pressure suddenly hit him as a cold sweat formed on his face.

"She is one of the most powerful beings in the multiverse; there are seldom few who could truly challenge her. A fight that involved the Matriarch of Dragons would destroy whole thousands of systems."

"So you're saying we're screwed."

"In the long term, yes. You are rightfully her little *toy*."

"Toy?" Claire said, pausing.

"I'm not guilty of anything. She did look really good for being as old as she is, though," Drake said, remembering the woman's appearance.

Drake pretended to lurch forward as Claire's hand passed over the back of his head.

"Don't dodge!" Claire shouted, puffing out her cheeks.

"I didn't do nothin'!" Drake smirked.

"So, what exactly did she want then, Shot?" Bjorn asked, getting the conversation back on track.

"Right," Drake said, sitting back up straight. "Honestly, I don't know. She didn't mention anything outside of getting a better return on her investment. Those stones I got way back when apparently were really valuable. So much so that she traded six other stones for them."

"Just like that?" Bjorn asked.

"Just like that."

"Then what happened with the stones? You just decided to use them all at once like some crazy person?"

"N-No, not exactly," Drake said embarrassedly. "I basically told her to eat a"—Drake coughed—"to stick it where the sun don't shine. And she found that disrespectful, I guess?"

Jacqueline burst out laughing in the corner. "Bloody brilliant! You piss off someone who can snuff us out like she's blowing out a candle. And what happens? She gives you legendary stones? This world is mad! Mad I tell ya!"

"Well, she didn't only give them to me," Drake corrected. "She forced them on me."

"What do you mean?" Megan asked, finally entering the conversation.

"I mean she physically threw them into my body," Drake explained. His hands clenched and unclenched. "It was the most painful experience I've had so far. It felt like my insides were being ripped apart cell by cell for hours and then pieced back together with molten metal."

"That... That should not be within the realm of her powers as a sponsor," Natto stammered. "That goes beyond what is allowed for the tutorial. She will receive severe repercussions for those actions. The system is all for entertainment, but it is also the pure expression of free will and choice. It never allows anything to be truly one-sided. Why would she break those rules?"

"Does that mean she's getting an ass spanking? Cause I'd like to watc—N-ever mind, it's good she's getting punished," Drake added, laughing nervously.

Claire and Natto had finished playing with Drake's hair, and the rest of the party was slowly digesting the information.

"So what now?" Julia asked, piercing the thoughtful silence of the group.

"Now?" Drake wondered aloud. "Well, if nothing else comes up, we have a little less than a month here to relax. If anything does come up, I'll be having a bit of fun." Drake smirked. "But right right now? I think we make some food and relax, then head back to the Shigure's outpost."

"The outpost?" Bjorn asked.

"Yeah, I have a few things to take care of back there. And we need to discuss where to meet back up. That is, if everyone can still tolerate me." Drake smiled.

"We could never tolerate you," they all said in unison.

"Gasp," Drake said in faux offense.

"Can we eat yet... It's been weeks since we had a good meal..." Sherry interjected, her eyes sunken and red.

"Oh! Speaking of food, I found out what happened to all the wildlife." Drake held the food zombie at arm's length. "I just need to get back down there and corral them back up."

"The ants took the animals underground?" Harley questioned.

"They took a lot of stuff underground, which is both surprising and amazing at the same time, but yes the animals we were looking for are all underground. I'll probably just tell Shigure to deal with it. Yeah, let's do that."

* * *

The group made a meal out of the fresh food Drake had gotten while down underground. It had been quite some time since they had roasted venison.

When everyone was served, Drake slipped away to go over his new status and his changed skills. He had also gained a few new titles, not to mention he still needed to accept his quest rewards.

Drake was at the top of the fortress right now looking out onto the open wasteland. It seemed to only have gotten worse as the weeks passed.

"We really did a number on this place..." Drake said, giving a light chuckle. "I can't believe we're almost out of here too."

Drake digressed and opened his full status.

Drake Wallen

Tutorial Alias: Shot

Race: Asuran [F-Rank]

Profession: Miner P5 (0%) [F-Rank], Jeweler P5 (0%) [F-Rank]

Class: [Unique] Elemental Miller Level 23

VIT: 358 (10 + 215%)

STR: 362 (60 + 25%)

DEX: 280 (80 + 35%)

INT: 916 (15 + 20%)

WIS: 356 (10 + 229%)

END: 274 (30 + 235%)

Free Points: 0

Skills Branches

Primary

Elemental Master of Asura P3 (0%) [F-Rank] 5/5

Asuran's Magic Insight P3 (0%) [F-Rank]

Mind of the Mad War God P3 (0%) [F-Rank]

Asuran's Magic Prowess P3 (0%) [F-Rank]
Elemental Battle Endowment P3 (0%) [F-Rank]
War God's Elemental Conflux P3 (0%) [F-Rank]

Secondary

Shield Bearer of the Battle Hall P3 (0%) [F-Rank] 5/5
Asuran's Inner Ki P3 (0%) [F-Rank]
War God's Movement P3 (0%) [F-Rank]
Command of the Mighty P3 (0%) [F-Rank]
War God's Martial Prowess P3 (0%) [F-Rank]
Indomitable Ruler's Constitution P3 (0%) [F-Rank]

Primary Subtree

War God's Inner Roadmap [F-Rank] 5/5
Apex P3 (0%) [F-Rank]
Asuran Battle Instincts: Weak Point P3 (0%) [F-Rank]
Tempered in War P3 (0%) [F-Rank]
Asuran's Prideful Aura P3 (0%) [F-Rank]
War Tyrant's Indomitability P3 (0%) [F-Rank]

Secondary Subtree

War God's Soul Roadmap [F-Rank] 5/5
Asuran's Mana Mastery P3 (0%) [F-Rank]
Five Point Inner Atrophy P3 (0%) [F-Rank]
Cower Before the Mighty P3 (0%) [F-Rank]
Honed Asuran Physique P3 (0%) [F-Rank]
Inner Sanctum of the Asuran Soul P3 (0%) [F-Rank]

Tertiary Subtree

War God's Weapon Blessing [F-Rank] 5/5
Weapon Vault P3 (0%) [F-Rank]
Battle Ready P3 (0%) [F-Rank]
War God's Chosen Armament P3 (0%) [F-Rank]
Asuran's Battle Acuity P3 (0%) [F-Rank]
Submission of Magic P3 (0%) [F-Rank]

Quaternary Subtree
Asuran's War Book [F-Rank] 0/5
War God's Battle Right P1 (2%) [F-Rank]
Asuran's Constitution P1 (4%) [F-Rank]
Asuran's Punishment P1 (0%) [F-Rank]
Line in the Sand P1 (2%) [F-Rank]
War God's Battle Fervor P1 (4%) [F-Rank]

Titles: First Blood, Two Versus One, One Versus Many, Monkey Slayer, Living on the Edge, Close Call, Dead Man Walking, Dual Class, Punching Up, Improbability, Rounded, Dog Hater, One-Man Army, Dog Killer, Battle of Attrition, First of Your Kind, Goblin Hater, Goblin Slayer, Murderer, Serial Killer, Well on Your Way, Highest Contributor, Vanquisher of Kings, Tutorial Forerunner, First of Many, Glory of the Patriarch, Expectations of the Host, The Dawning of a Tyrant, Insectocide, Marked by Dragons, Race Change, Birthright, Vanquisher of Kings II, Exterminator

Drake gave a soft whistle, going through his new skills as well as his changed ones.

"Wow, it really did interact with every single skill... The only thing that's left is my original class name. The percentage bonuses are bonkers... I have a few new titles too."

Drake skimmed over the skills. He had all the time in the world to go through them. He instead moved on to his titles since there weren't forty of them to go through.

Let's see...

Vanquisher of Kings II
You have dealt 99% of the total damage to a royal. As the usurper of the Tyrant Ant throne, you are forever hated by the Tyrant Ant race.
+10% damage to royal bloodlines. +50% damage to all insectoid races.

Race Change
You have changed from a lower being to one of insurmountable power: a Primordial. Permanent +10 to all stats for each future level.

Birthright
You are an Asuran, one born of blood and battle. Your honor will not be tarnished, and you know not defeat.
+10% to Strength, Endurance, and Dexterity.

Exterminator
You have killed over 50,000 of a single monster race.
+5% damage to monsters.

Marked by Dragons
You have been marked by the Dragon Matriarch. She awaits your growth and return on her investment in the coming years. She always collects her debts.

"Wow, again. These are some serious buffs to my status, and I haven't even accepted the last quest. And let's just ignore that last title..."

Drake pulled up the prince's quest notification and finally hit accept. He heard a gong go off instead of the usual ring as notifications began filling his vision.

Quest Complete: Defeat the King of the Tyrant Ants, Obiteron Trikk [E-Rank]
Accept rewards?
Yes < No

Experience earned.
Please select your E-Grade weapon from the following options.

Congratulations! You have reached Elemental Miller Level 24.
40 FP have been awarded.

System-Wide Announcement!
Tutorial #1,294,007 is the first to complete their tutorial. Rewards will be awarded based on Ladder Standing in 34 days, 13 hours, 27 minutes, and 10 seconds.

Completionists will be awarded the First Completionist title when exiting the tutorial.
Early access to the Tutorial Shop will be granted in 34 days, 13 hours, 27 minutes, and 2 seconds.

First Completionists will be awarded an allowance of one item from the designated rewards based on tutorial performance.
Completionists have the option to leave their tutorial early, but they will relinquish their right to rewards. Leaving the tutorial early will suspend you until all tutorials are completed.

You have gained the title Named in the System.
You have gained the title Dawning of a Tyrant II.
You have gained the title Hated by Many.
You have gained the title The Awe of Many.
You have gained the title Bounty.

"*Fuck.* What do you mean a bounty...?"

Chapter 72

Reluctant Disappointment

"What did you do?!"

A shout came from below the rampart. Drake looked over and down to see Chelsea right as rain, Megan next to her looking slightly confused and flustered.

"I didn't do nothin'," Drake replied evenly.

"What about this announcement, then?!"

Drake shrugged his shoulders. "I dunno."

"What do you mean you don't know?! Why can't you take—"

Drake slowly began to tune out Chelsea's yelling as he looked at the new titles he'd just received.

Named by the System

As one who has contributed to the closing of your tutorial, your name has rung throughout the multiverse.

+50% effect to your Aura Suppression on beings of your rank or below.

Dawning of a Tyrant II

Your will and ideals have been thrust upon the world. Your views will not be opposed, and those that do have perished underfoot. Your rule is law under penalty of death.

+20% to all Aura skill effects. +20 to all stats.

Hated by Many

Envy can be a poison that gnaws away at those who endure it. Peace was never an option after your name became known.

+5% to Aura Effects.

The Awe of Many

Inspiration through rivalry is the first step in leadership. Through your deeds, you have inspired and awed many.
+5% to Aura Effects.

Bounty

Your name has been placed on a high-profile kill list and exceeded the price of several high ranked Mana Coins and Monster Cores.

"A b-bounty? Really? What did I do?" Drake laughed hesitantly. "Though these buffs to my Aura are insane; that brings me over 100% effectiveness overall. Speaking of effectiveness..."

Drake trailed off, looking at his now completely tattered rags of armor and the missing tattoos on his left arm. He sighed.

"I really went overboard this time..."

"That you did!" Natto said, tapping along the side of the rampart with food in her mouth.

Drake gave a doting smile, glad to see her up and about already.

"Did the core rank you up?" he asked.

"Certainly not. It is only one core; I will need several. There may be some in the Tutorial Store, so remember that when you are purchasing items. Speaking of which, do remember that you are to save a few hundred thousand points for our needs outside of the tutorial."

"I got it. Shouldn't be too hard with the amount I managed to rack up."

"You say such, but you underestimate the amount of stores the Dragons have and are willing to part with. What have you been doing up here alone? Sulking over your forced racial change?" Natto asked, biting down on the last of her venison.

"No, surprisingly not. It's a big change and I haven't gotten used to it exactly, but I feel... I feel good. I feel stable. I hate that she forced it on me, but it's unfortunately a net positive. I'd call it an absolute win even. Every skill powered up, my passive effects went through the roof, and I got a rocking tan. I haven't been this dark since I stood out in the sun as a kid when I was in the Philippines."

Drake shook his head. "No, I was going through the new titles I received mostly. And just being glad I can take a moment to breathe finally."

"Enjoy it while you can, ape." Natto snickered. "You will now get even less rest than I presumed before. Completing a tutorial first is quite the feat."

"Someone had to do it, and I'm sure there're plenty of integrations based on what that announcement said when we first got into the introduction room," Drake proposed. He looked out again and saw Chelsea still yelling at him from below.

"It may be that there are many tutorials, but there is only a title and announcement for the first completion. There are none for the ones after. Do not underestimate how petty the beings of the multiverse are."

"Is that so?" Drake replied.

Looking down at the yelling Chelsea, Drake began forming water effortlessly at his fingertips. He then gave a small grin as he dropped the water down on her.

Chelsea dodged the first water ball with her speed as an archer, but she failed to dodge the second. She sidestepped it, expecting it to fall down to the floor, but instead the ball of water took a hard turn and splashed into her face. The next hit her on the top of her head, and another hit Megan who'd begun snickering. She ended up just as soaked.

"Asshole!"

"You know it!" Drake yelled back with a smirk.

"Hey, take on someone your own size, huh bro?" Bjorn smiled and walked out to the front of the fortress, looking up at the midday sun.

"With pleasure." Drake grinned widely, something bubbling up inside him that he didn't expect. He forced his eyes wide. "What was that?"

"What was what?" Natto asked, hopping up to his shoulder.

"I just felt, I don't know, some sort of primal anticipation."

"Ah... I see. You are an Asuran after all," Natto said in understanding.

"Is that supposed to mean something to me?" Drake asked, confused.

"Inspect your race. If you are confused, I assume you have not yet."

Drake opened his status and looked at his race.

Asuran

One of the Primordial races. Known as one of the races with the most blood-thirst, they are also called the race of War Gods. They rule over others with pure force and combat prowess. Seldom do they know defeat, and they will always be found improving their martial abilities in combat.

Asurans have been known to plunge head-first into battle regularly, fighting for the honor of grand single combat to hone their abilities. Nothing is more important to an Asuran than a good fight; they have been used as weapons of war for many of the other races.

Primordial Racial Effect: 100% increased status during single combat. +5 to all stats per level. Increases based on overall rank.

Drake let out a breath.

"Great. So now I'm some sort of bloodthirsty battle junkie?"

"Were you not before? Now it is simply official as well as a biological imperative." Natto laughed loudly.

"This isn't a good thing... I was hoping to not have some sort of weird quirky personality change after all of this. Ah, don't say it! I know already. 'You were already quirky before, moron.'"

"While true," Natto snickered, "there is nothing to be done. With strength comes at least some demerits. You could not improve this quickly without a few."

Drake sighed again, his back slumping.

"You coming or what, bro? I'm growing a beard waiting here!" Bjorn shouted.

"You already have a beard, you idiot!" Drake snapped back.

"Oh, true." Bjorn chuckled and leaned his sword on his shoulder.

"Just give me a minute; I don't want to forget about this," Drake said over the wall. He turned back around.

Please select your E-Grade weapon from the following options.

Drake scrolled through the list, but he was immediately disappointed.

"There aren't any ink tattoo weapons..." he lamented with a sigh.

Going back over the options, he found the next best thing and selected Fist Weapons.

In an instant, a flash of light sparked and disappeared, leaving behind a dark-colored box with a flat top that was at least a foot and a half tall and a few feet wide.

Drake didn't waste time and opened the chest lid, revealing the shine of golden light from the weapons.

"This is… These are so badass! What are these?!" Drake squealed.

Asuran Initiate Chained Gauntlets [E-Grade, Legendary] Set Piece 1/6
These gauntlets are the culmination of Asuran ideology over eons of countless battles. Only those who have completed their initial training in the Halls of the Furious Asurans are given the chance to wield such weapons. Forged from the mana-infused gold wrenched from the hands of their defeated, the engravings on the chains and gloves are a constant reminder of the trials and battles each Asuran has overcome—and of the battles yet to come.

4000—5092 Physical Damage.
3500—4115 Magic Damage.
25% increase to critical strikes and 25% increase to damaging skills.
+100 STR, +150 DEX, +100 INT, increases Aura Effects by 100%.
Full Set Effect: *Increases flat defense proficiency by 250%, increases all stats by 200%, reduces abnormal effects by 115%, and increases regeneration by 200%.*
2 Set Effect: *Increases flat defense proficiency by 40%, increases all stats by 30%, and increases regeneration by 30%.*
4 Set Effect: *Increases flat defense proficiency by 100%, increases all stats by 80%, reduces abnormal effects by 115%, and increases regeneration by 80%.*
Requires a minimum of 2 pieces to activate set effect.
Requires a being of E-Rank or higher to be wielded.

Drake was in awe of the weapon. He picked them up from the chest and the felt cloth that housed them inside. The Golden Gauntlets gave off a sheen of power unlike what Drake had felt from other weapons. They were formed to be large gloves, each finger and joint interlocking seamlessly to the next. Connecting the two were four lengths of chains hooked to the pointed spikes that would cover his elbows.

The moment Drake stood up with the weapons, they flashed a crimson fire as markings were etched into the gold in a burning, pulsing red on the surface.

Forced to shield his eyes momentarily, he gazed back and saw new symbols and images carved on the chains. They were cool to the touch as Drake brushed his fingers along the gold.

"These are awesome... Wait. I can't wear them?!" Drake howled in physical pain.

"Of course; you are still F-Rank, you mongrel." Natto sighed, slightly disappointed as well.

"It's a set item as well. Where am I supposed to get the rest of these?"

"I wonder," Natto said evenly. Her face showed that she knew but either would not or could not tell Drake as of yet. "Let us hope you will not be extorted on your way out."

Drake took the hint and placed the gauntlets as well as the box into his inventory very reluctantly. A tear ran down the side of his face as he did.

"Are you crying?" Natto scoffed.

"Only a little..." Drake sniffled, wiping away the single lonely tear and getting up.

He moved to the edge and looked over. "Alright all ready—Wait, where'd he go?"

Julia stood where Megan, Chelsea, and Bjorn had been.

"Oh, they left. They got tired of waiting, and Bear went for food. Megan and Chelsea went to dry off!" she hollered.

"Aw, I was looking forward to testing stuff out." Drake sighed. "Well, I have another thirty-some-odd days left to do whatever I like. There's no rush!" Drake said, his shoulders finally relaxing. "I wonder what Grumps and Wow-fi are up to..."

Chapter 73
They're My Best Friends

"Is that it?"

The man or beast removed the spear from the corpse, cleaning the blood from the tip with a single stroke to the side.

"That was the last of the monsters in the area, sir," a woman said, casually strolling up to him.

"Damn, that's all that's left? Really? I didn't even get to work up a sweat! Ari, find me more would you?"

"Sir... Leon, I just said that there are unfortunately no more monsters in the area. My scanning skill is not picking up anything."

"Ari, I'm only joking. You really need to lighten up." Leon snorted.

"Sorry... It's just hard to tell sometimes," Ari replied. She pushed up her glasses by the brim.

"I'm kind of pissed we didn't get that first achievement, but nothing can be done. Wish it told us who contributed the most to that completion. I'd like to have a name to hunt down once we're out."

"We, sir?"

"Of course. You think I'm going to give up a great-looking woman and an amazing support class just because we're out of the tutorial?" Leon smirked, his canines peeking from his lips.

Leon placed his spear behind his head, his two wolf ears flickering. He let his arms hang over his weapon. His short aquamarine hair and fierce yellow eyes stared back at Ari.

"Th-That would make me very happy, sir," she mumbled, her face turning slightly red.

"I told you, it's Leon when it's just us. I don't like the sir shit, but that moron Luke won't take no for an answer."

Leon moved forward and pulled Ari close, only to be interrupted by the shout of a man coming out of the trees and onto the battlefield.

"Oi! What kind of ruckus you been up to ova here? Looks like a bloody good time there, sir!"

"Luke..." Leon sighed.

"What? Boys and I just got done sweepin' the area. Thought I'd give you an update," Luke said, walking up to the pair. "What in the fuck is this cunt?! You do that, sir? Right thrashin' if I've ever seen. Sure a croc ain't get his ass? Seen those things pull a man apart in a few seconds flat, I have."

"Bro, Luke. Do you see any crocodiles?" Leon growled.

"Alright, alright. Don't get your panties in a twist there, sir, just makin' conversation."

"Then make it elsewhere. I've killed the last of them; tutorial's over. You can leave."

"No can do, sir. The boys and I came to an agreement that we wouldn't be leaving even after this shindig. Seems like the world's gone to shit, eh? So we're sticking with ya!"

"Oh, joy..." Leon sneered.

More men and women came out of the treeline, explaining and shouting as they raised their weapons and firearms, cheering and hooting at Leon.

"Yeah, Leon! That was some good shit!"

"Glad we all decided to stick with him. Knew it was a good idea."

"Dumbass, you were the one who said we should just shoot him!"

"Yeah, and I'm saying I'm glad we didn't, 'cause we'd be dead if we did, smartass."

Leon sighed and shook his head, letting go of Ari who now wore a similar scowl at the group.

"Where the hell were all of you? Just watching?" Leon asked.

"You told us to stay out of your way, mate. We're just along for the ride!" Luke chuckled and gave Leon a slap on the back.

"If I ever needed Shot to run something, it would be now..." Leon mumbled, putting his spear away.

"Say something, mate?" Luke asked.

"No. And it's sir to you, motherfucker. That was the deal: you pick shit up and I kill things. So go pick it up."

"Alright, alright." Luke scoffed, shouldering his gun. "You heard him, you lazy cunts. Pick up after our puppy!"

Leon pressed down on the surroundings with his aura, a chill washing over the people.

"You've been getting a bit mouthy lately, Luke," he growled, "and I'm all out of things to hunt..."

"I-I got it, boss," Luke eked out. His face paled. "No more jokes for a while, yeah?"

Leon released the pressure, and everyone gasped in unison. Leon turned away, followed by Ari.

"Didn't have to do that in front of everyone, did ya? Bloody hell..." Luke said, rubbing his throat. "Always need to show you're top dog, eh?"

Luke complained, but he did what he was told, turning to the battlefield as Leon moved away with Ari. In front of him were thousands of monsters strewn across the ground, all with a single puncture wound to the head.

"If he wasn't such a prick, I'd have called him an artist... Alright, you lazy bastards! Get to cleaning!"

"We already are! You're the one slacking, dipshit!"

"Oi! Watch your goddamn mouth!"

Out of earshot, Ari and Leon walked back toward the outpost that he'd made his own early on in the tutorial.

"So where are we going to go once this is all done?" Ari asked, breaking the silence.

"I was thinking of finding an old friend. I owe him a smack, and I'm pretty sure he'll be doing just fine in this whole mess, so I'm sure it'll be fun. Just like old times," Leon said, smiling.

Leonardo Velcruz
Tutorial Alias: Grumps
Race: Silver Wolf [F-Rank]
Profession: Scribe P5 (0%) [F-Rank], Enchanter P5 (0%) [F-Rank]
Class: [Unique] Spear Bullet Scholar Level 24
VIT: 361 (10 + 15%)
STR: 823 (20 +210%)
DEX: 952 (80 + 220%)
INT: 340 (10 + 215%)
WIS: 226 (10 + 15%)
END: 386 (30 + 225%)
Free Points: 40

Titles: First Blood, Two versus One, One vs Many, Croc Slayer, Dual Class, Punching Up, Improbability, Rounded, Croc Hater, One Man Army, Croc Killer, Battle of Attrition, First of Your Kind, Troll Hater, Troll Slayer, Murderer, Serial Killer, Vanquisher of Kings, Tutorial Forerunner, First of Many, Well on Your Way, Glory of the Patriarch, Highest Contributor, Highest Contributor II, Expectations of the Host, Dawning of a Hunter, War on Beasts, Marked by Kirins, Race Change, Hunter's Calling, Vanquisher of Kings II, Exterminator, Named in the System, Dawning of a Hunter II, Hated by Many, The Awe of Many, Bounty, Ill Made Leader

* * *

"Yo man, where's the dude at?"

"Aye, shut up will ya? He said he would scoop us up. Guy said he got a new toy from that last kill. You know, upgraded his baby."

"Wha—Oh shit! Get up! Move!"

The men scrambled to get off the rock they were sitting on. It stuck out of the sand, located in the shade of the cliff. In the distance, the low sound of what seemed like a jet taking off rumbled while dust kicked up.

Dodging out of the way, the two men tumbled in the hot desert to the side.

"What the fuck, dude! You could've ran us over!"

Charging past them and slamming into the cliff face was a black suit of armor five times the size of a person. It slowly backed up from the indent it had placed in the wall, sand gliding off its armor.

Turning around, the black monstrosity's eyes shone in red, green, blue, and yellow. On its shoulder was a large cannon, its arms two large gatling-type weapons.

It creaked and shifted until it stopped and bent down. Its chest opened to reveal a small dark-skinned man with dark hair braided into a ponytail. His beard reached past his waist.

"Got damn! This thing is just like the games! This new baby is like a got damn mobile suit!" the dwarf shouted.

The two men got up, dusting themselves off with scowls on their faces.

"What was that about? All the monsters are dead, dude. What's the point in being out here? Can't we just chill in the outpost?"

"Naw, bro, I have to get these controls down. I won't be doing this for shits and giggles, you hear me?" The dwarf scoffed, sniffing and rubbing his nose. "I got to make sure I keep up; those two bastards're always calling me a leecher and shit! I'll show them that Wow-fi is back in business, baby! I know that asshole Grumps is gonna be jealous I got this thing!"

"R-Right... Man, Damian, we're tired and it's fucking hot out. Can you just take us to the outpost, dude? I don't wanna be out here even if there aren't monsters. There's still those idiots trying to kill us after the last stunt you pulled."

Damian reached out his hand, palm open.

"Really?"

Damian nodded, waiting for his payment.

"Fine, here's your damn cores. Now take our asses back to the outpost, will you."

"You gots it. And don't worry about them dudes no more. I took care of it." He smiled.

"You killed them?!"

"Oh, you know it. You don't fucks with me like that and get to go home. We don't tolerate that bullshit where I'm from," he said seriously.

"Man, when did you get so hard-headed?"

"Since always." Damian snorted. "And I told you to tell that motherfucker to stop eyeballin' me like he can snag my shit. Just 'cause I'm out of the mech don't mean I won't *whoop* his ass too!"

The man turned, seeing the other reaching for something beneath his cloak. He sighed.

"Don't do it, bro. We only have a few weeks, then we're out of here."

"Why? He's out of his big suit and has all the shit from the tutorial! He's robbed everyone!"

"I ain't rob shit. I killed it, it's mine. Only people that get free stuff from me are friends and family, and you're neither!" Damian laughed at the man.

"Fuck you!" the man shouted. He pulled a blade from his side and rushed at Damian.

He was stopped dead in his tracks as a shot rang out, half of his body incinerated on the spot. A burning hole was left in the ground. The cannon of the black marvel behind Damian emitted a faint trail of smoke.

"No." Damian smiled. "Fuck you."

Damian Bellair

Tutorial Alias: Wow-fi

Race: Obsidian Dwarf [F-Rank]

Profession: Mechanic P5 (0%) [F-Rank], Specialist P5 (0%) [F-Rank]

Class: [Unique] Mechanical Puppeteer Level 24

VIT: 271 (10 + 15%)

STR: 210 (20 + 10%)

DEX: 952 (80 + 220%)

INT: 655 (10 + 15%)

WIS: 526 (50 + 215%)

END: 266 (80 + 225%)

Free Points: 0

Titles: First Blood, Two versus One, One vs Many, Spider Slayer, Dual Class, Punching Up, Improbability, Rounded, Scorpion Hater, One Man Army, Scorpion Killer, Battle of Attrition, First of Your Kind, Hawk Hater, Hawk Slayer, Murderer, Serial Killer, Vanquisher of Kings, Tutorial Forerunner, First of Many, Well on Your Way, Glory of the Patriarch, Highest Contributor, Expectations of the Host, Dawning of a Puppeteer, War on Arachnids, Marked by Celestines, Race Change, Puppet Master's Calling, Vanquisher of Kings II, Exterminator, Named in the System, Dawning of a Puppeteer II, Hated by Many, The Awe of Many, Bounty, Rogue Element

Chapter 74

Blindsided

"What are you doing?" Claire asked, looking over Drake's shoulder.

"Just checking up on my skills again. All of them changed, after all; every single one improved or has an extra effect on it now, so I need to make sure I have them all memorized. It's basically relearning my skills all over again..." Drake sighed.

"Don't worry, bro, you got plenty of time to practice. I'm sure Shigure wouldn't mind sparring as well," Bjorn added.

"True. But I'm a little worried I might take it too far... or I just won't be interested," Drake replied with a wry grin.

"What do you mean?" Chelsea asked, popping her head out from behind Bjorn.

"Ah! Where did you come from?!" Drake shouted in faux surprise. Chelsea frowned.

Drake coughed, his joke hitting flat, but he explained, "I mean that after the change, apparently I have some very unhelpful or unlikeable quirks..."

"Like you didn't before?" Jacqueline shouted behind her from ahead of the group.

"I mean *actually* unhelpful," Drake said, pursing his lips. "It looks like I have an all or nothing type of mentality when it comes to fighting now. When I was going to spar with Bear earlier, I felt my body shiver with anticipation. I wanted to fight him to the end, to prove who's stronger, and to have the honor of defeating a strong opponent. But seeing the leftover ants..." Drake sighed.

"What about the ants?" Claire asked.

"Well, I couldn't be more disinterested. It was like that feeling you get before you go to the gym? Or when you look at a salad. A measure of past reluctance. It was almost disgust."

"Hey, I like salads," Tom chimed in.

"And I like long walks on the beach," Drake quipped, "but I'm talking about before and after changing my race, Tom. What I'm concerned with is a serious change to my personality. If the stone can affect me enough that I look down on those who're weaker than me, I could really be turning into a tyrant—not just in title."

"You? Mr. Goofy Weirdo Who Talks about Anime Nonstop and Can't Take a Moment Seriously Guy? Not sure if I believe that one, bro." Bjorn chuckled.

Drake stopped, the whole party looking back surprised.

"No, Bear. I mean it. If we had started fighting, I don't know if I could've held myself back from going all out just to prove I was the better fighter."

Drake's Aura moved and bent around him in a way that it hadn't before. It wasn't just oppressive, it was aching for battle. It wanted for someone to test him, inviting them to stand up to the challenge.

"I think it might be a bigger problem than I gave it credit for," Drake said stiffly, his body going rigid.

"W-What's wrong?!" Claire stammered, looking on with concern.

"I-I don't k-know!" Drake said, his body beginning to sweat as he pushed the words out through clenched teeth. "Naw, I'm just kidding."

Drake waved them off and smiled. Everyone let out a uniform gasp of air except for Bjorn, who had his hand on his sword behind his head.

"Not funny," Bjorn said flatly.

"Most of it was true, but the last bit was in poor taste I'll admit. But that's exactly what I'm talking about. We have no idea how much this change has done to me, and that Dragon bitch forced it on me. There's no telling what else she might've done while rifling through my insides with those stones." Drake grimaced. "Natto said she shouldn't have been able to bypass the system like she did, and she's going to be punished for it. But I'm still questioning why. Why go so far to mess with me?"

"My lord, those art questions we shalt not be obliged to resolve for some time," Theodore said. "We have just overcome a foe like none other we have faced before. Is it not the time to bask in the glory of your felled enemy and taketh time for thyself?"

Theodore said what everyone was thinking. Drake had been pushing himself the entirety of the tutorial, only stopping to rest when he was injured beyond the ability to move or due to the loss of a limb.

"No. That ant prince might be gone—" Drake started.

"Ant *King*. We all saw the notification when he evolved," Sherry corrected lazily.

"Right... That ant *King* may be gone, but what about the next threat or the one after that? I can't let myself rest like I'm on vacation. And that's another reason I'm concerned; my mental stability has been a rollercoaster ride these past few months, and that's an understatement. I wanted... I *want* nothing more than to just sit around relaxing with my feet up, a bourbon in hand on a nice sofa with my girl. But I don't get that luxury."

"What are you saying then, pup?" Hudson asked suspiciously.

"I'm saying that once we get to the outpost, it might be time we all part ways for real. At least for a little bit."

* * *

The walk back was silent. Drake had made a declaration no one really expected after they'd just gone through that last fight together.

Bjorn was quiet, which wasn't that unusual when he wasn't talking to Drake. But Drake didn't start a conversation with anyone either. Instead, he walked silently with the group, Claire by his side.

Claire tried to speak up several times, but she failed to get the words out, her mouth opening and closing. She turned to him but was never able to bring herself to speak.

The rest of the group didn't fare much better. The reality that they soon wouldn't have the person who'd protected and guided them throughout the tutorial hit harder than expected.

Drake finally broke the silence with a sigh.

"It isn't like we'll never see each other again, I just need time to myself to figure out what's going on. I still plan on having everyone come together outside of the tutorial. And there're only a few small remaining groups of ants left, which I know all of you can and should be able to handle as a group. You'll be fine without me for a few weeks."

"It isn't that we won't be fine, it's that we shouldn't have to be," Claire said, looking at Drake. "You always talk about taking responsibility and not taking the easy way out, but aren't you doing just that? You would rather hide away from us, from yourself, than stay."

Claire grabbed Drake's hand and squeezed it tight.

"Don't leave us. Don't leave me—not like this. I know you're worried about what might happen, but... but I'm not. You've saved us more times than I can count, pushing past every wall that's tried to stop you. And when I saw you hurt, disappearing before my eyes, my heart broke. Don't do that to me again by taking yourself away. Don't... Don't do it sooner than you have to."

Her eyes began to water as she looked down at the grasped hand in hers, different but still belonging to the man who'd saved her from the goblins so many weeks ago.

Drake was stunned. He wasn't expecting such a reaction. To him, the temporary retreat was only that—temporary. A way for him to battle with his own traumas and the problems he'd put on hold for so long during his countless battles for survival.

But for her, for them, it was as if he was abandoning them. He'd done so much to build them up, and he'd forgotten that in doing so, he'd forged a connection between them. They were no longer just party members. Their fates, their goals had intertwined.

"Is this how you all feel?" Drake asked.

"I wouldn't put it just like that; I ain't got a thing for ya like the miss does." Hudson snorted. "But it does feel pretty cheap of ya to just off and go on your own. You already did it once, leaving us behind, and it stung like a sore bee sting. We trust ya, idjit, but do you really trust us?"

Drake felt a pang of guilt hit him.

Is that true? Was I just being selfish when I left to search the Hive on my own? Do I not trust them to pull their own weight?

"Well, you did try to have them fight on their own, only to stop halfway the moment you suspected it may be too dangerous. Do you believe them to be chil-dren or people capable of making their own decisions and living their own lives? I have told you before: you cannot protect them forever. If they wish to stand and watch you fall or rise, it is a choice of their own volition, Drake," Natto said softly.

Drake ground his teeth.

"I've been blind, huh. Fine, if you want to risk me turning into a monster right in front of you, I won't complain. I could use the company." Drake sighed, pulling Claire's hand in and wrapping his arm around her.

"Do I get a hug too?" Tom asked.

"No, we aren't there yet," Drake snapped, not turning to him.

"Oh. Okay..." Tom frowned.

Drake released Claire and exhaled a tense breath. "Well, onward to the outpost then. I still have a bunch to catch up on and a short surly dwarf to shake down before I figure out if I'm really going to be turning into something I can't control or recognize..."

"Don't worry, bro. I may not be able to beat an ant, but I'm sure I can throw you around just fine." Bjorn smiled, his hand finally off his sword. "You need people looking after you more than I do, looks like."

Drake snorted, but he smiled back. "You might be right about that... It's going to be an interesting couple of weeks. Just don't let me kill you during sparring. This new body of mine, I'm still getting used to it."

"Couldn't even if you tried, bro." Bjorn smirked back.

"Right, if you two tossers are done with your subtextual bro moment, we need to bloody get on with it. I want to get into a real bed; it's been weeks, you pissin' idiots." Jacqueline sneered from ahead of them.

"Aren't you always the ray of sunshine? No wonder you have such a great boyfriend," Drake replied. He walked forward, holding Claire's hand and pulling her with him.

"I don't have a boyfriend...?" Jacqueline said, aghast.

"Oh, I know." Drake smiled.

"Jacky! *Jacky* put the mace down!" Megan shouted behind them.

"Just one! Just one good smack! I'll put that sarcastic little boy on his bloody ass!" Jacqueline shouted.

* * *

The group came back alive after their little discussion, and they made their way through the forest back to the outpost after half a day of walking. The sun had begun to set, painting the surroundings in a warm orange glow.

"Looks like it hasn't changed much since we left. That's a good sign," Drake observed.

"You thought something would happen?" Bjorn asked.

"Honestly? Yeah, I thought Shigure would be forced to burn it to the ground. Looks like he grew a backbone, though."

"Oh... I see what you mean. The food shortage and the prisoners he'd been delaying sentencing."

"Yup. Dealing with hungry masses is much harder than you'd think; people turn on each other quicker than a penny can drop. But looks like he's managed it just fine," Drake said, seeing a few guards posted at the rampart's gate. "Alright, I'm going to see Shigure quickly and tell him about the food by the hive. I'm sure he'll want to go and secure it. Can I leave the camp to you guys?"

Drake began walking without waiting for an answer, only to feel his hand being tugged backward. Looking back, he saw a worried Claire.

"You're really coming back, right? You won't just run off again as soon as you're out of my sight, right?" she asked.

Drake gave her a doting smile. "I promise."

Claire reluctantly released him, giving a nod as she watched him walk off.

Passing Bjorn, Drake asked him, "Do you want to come with?"

Bjorn shook his head.

"I may not look it, but that bug really did a number on me. My body's been throbbing in pain the entire walk back. I'm going to go take a long nap after a bath. You got any hot water?" he asked.

"No, but I got you covered."

Drake summoned several empty barrels. He snapped his fingers and filled them with a waterfall of steaming water.

"Rest up, I want to be able to kick your ass by tomorrow morning." Drake smirked.

"Yeah yeah, we'll see. You sure those stones didn't make you more arrogant, bro?" Bjorn laughed.

"Could be." Drake shrugged. "Anything else?"

"Yeah, got any food?"

"Food?!" Sherry said from the side, her eyes lighting up.

Drake laughed wryly, seeing the woman make a beeline for him through the group like a golden retriever hearing the snack bag open.

"Y-Yeah, I was able to snag a few bucks while we were underground. Do you want to cook them up?" Drake asked Bjorn.

"I'd rather you cook them," he said flatly. Sherry nodded furiously next to him.

"Fine. If you can wait till I get back, I'll cook them."

"Yay!" Sherry cheered.

Drake held Sherry back at arm's length as she pressed forward and tried to grab Drake, carving a small ditch into the ground below her.

"Right, I'll be back then. Keep her in the camp—I don't need her following me into Shigure's tent." Drake laughed.

Bjorn scooped Sherry up under his arm, her body going limp like a cat.

"Don't take too long, bro," Bjorn said, giving a wave before turning back to walk with the rest of the group.

Drake waved back then walked toward the gate.

"No promises this time, man..." Drake muttered under his breath.

"Who the fuck are you?" one of the guards yelled.

"Really? Again?" Drake sighed and put his hands up.

Chapter 75

Food Stuffs and a Stiff Hand

Shigure sat in his tent going over the same numbers he'd been looking at for the past several days.

"It's not enough… We simply don't have enough food to last us the remainder of the tutorial. Even with the higher levels not needing to eat thanks to their status, it still will not be enough."

Shigure sighed and leaned back in his chair, wondering how they were supposed to get through this. There had already been people trying to force others to give up rations, but it was between the sub-level 10 craftsmen, so it was easily dealt with for now.

But what would happen when the higher-level fighters began to have the same problem? Just because they didn't need to eat as often didn't mean they didn't have to entirely.

Before he could dwell on it much longer, a voice came from the tent entrance.

"Lord Shigure! There is a problem at the south gate!"

"A problem?" Shigure asked, getting to his feet. Uta appeared next to him in a puff of inky smoke.

"There seems to be an unknown person asking to see you. No one can identify him, but he came with Sir Bear and that man's party," Uta explained before they left the tent.

Exiting, Shigure gave a nod to the guardsman. He quickly walked past the guard to the rampart with Uta in tow.

"Is he trying to force himself in?" Shigure asked.

"N-No, he... He is making jokes," Uta professed.

* * *

"So then I said, 'Looks like it's time for this bug to buzz off,'" Drake said in a deep, hoarse voice.

"That wasn't even funny. Did you really say that to a monster five levels and a rank above you? Did it even understand you?"

"Well, I didn't really say that one. I did beat the crap out of it though. Give me a break, I was in the middle of a heated battle! Forgive me if my quippy nature didn't take over!"

Drake fell back on his arms. He was sitting on the ground with the two guards seated across from him.

"So there hasn't been any problems except the food stuff?" Drake asked.

"No, nothing major other than a few people trying to rough others up for food. We did have a few ghouls come around, but Lord Shigure took care of them quickly," the guard answered, tearing into the meat. "Wow, this is good!"

"That's gonna be a few hundred F-Rank crystals there, fella." Drake smirked.

"What?! Now that has to be a joke!"

"Nope, I'm robbing you." Drake laughed and pointed a finger gun at the guard.

Spotting a familiar figure, Drake smiled and moved his finger to point past the guards.

"Put that thing away! You're going to kill someone!" Shigure shouted, scowling at Drake.

"Heyyyyyy buddyyyyyy." Drake chuckled and mimed blowing out his finger gun and putting it away. "How ya been? How's life?"

"Ugh, I thought it might be you... I take it you were the one who took down the monster we received a notification about, ending the tutorial?"

"Aw, don't be so glum. It's been weeks since we've seen each other, Shigure! Aren't you going to tell me how much cuter I look?" Drake grinned and batted his eyes.

The guards had since stood up and moved to the side, hiding their pieces of meat that Drake had bribed them with. They now enjoyed the back and forth that the two were having.

"No, but thank you for defeating the monster. You have given us all an amazing title. What is it you want to speak to me about?" Shigure asked, ignoring Drake's joke.

"Wow, you've really put on some chops," Drake said, giving a whistle and standing. "You sure you're okay with speaking out in the open like this?"

"There is no reason not to; anyone who has any problem with me in charge is long gone. I am curious about what happened to change you to such a degree, I must admit, but is that something you're comfortable speaking about?"

"Nope, I won't be saying anything on it. Inner circle stuff. You understand, I'm sure."

"Fine. If you would be kind enough to make it quick, we are currently dealing with a major food shortage." Shigure sighed.

"What? Not going to try to muscle it out of me? You sure have grown in these last few weeks, little Shigure."

"I am not going to be goaded into fighting someone who can take down an E-Rank. Given it was the last monster needed to end the tutorial, I'm very sure I would stand no chance. But a later spar would be appreciated."

Drake whistled again, crossing his arms.

"Wow, you really did grow up. Good for you. As for what I wanted to talk to you about, I found out what happened with all the animals. And I know where they are."

"Is that so? Are you going to ask me for something in return for the information?" Shigure asked calmly.

"Is that the kind of man you take me for?"

"That is exactly the type of man I take you for, yes."

Drake flinched, stepping back slightly.

"That's hurtful..."

"It was intended to be."

"Fine. It's to the southeast; you can find it if you travel about a day's worth.

You could probably make it in a few hours, given your level. There's a collapsed tunnel leading to the underground Hive for the Tyrant Ants. Most of the remaining ones are around level 20, so be careful on your way there. They travel in swarms. I could tag along if you want," Drake offered.

"No. I alone should be sufficient, and I do need the experience. Thank you," Shigure said, bowing his head slightly. "With this, we will make it to the end easily. Is there anything else?"

"Uhh..." Drake was slightly stunned by Shigure's candidness. Just what had happened to him during their time apart?

"For the moment, nothing, but we should speak about the alliance you proposed earlier," Drake said, losing his playful tone. "There's a lot we need to discuss about what comes next as well. The tutorial sponsor is the Matriarch of the Dragons, and I have a bad feeling about what's coming for us."

"Matriarch of Dragons...? Understood. I will come find you in several days after I've gathered enough food for the outpost."

Shigure bowed again and turned back to the outpost without a fuss. Uta only spared Drake a glare before evaporating into mist.

"Well, that was no fun. I at least wanted him to try something..." Drake pouted, putting his hands behind his head. "Oh well, time to go make food I guess."

Turning around, Drake walked casually back to the camp that was being set up.

"What made you change your mind about the alliance? I believe it to be a poor deal for us," Natto said.

"The world is going to be much different once we're out. We knew that, but now that I know I have a target on my back from a Dragon who can circumvent the system, I'm not sure if it's smart to try to go it alone. I'm convinced more than ever that we'll need stronger people for what's to come, and that I need to be at the top. Until I'm proven wrong, it's going to be my plan going forward. I won't stand for our world to be picked clean by someone who thinks of us as toys," Drake responded, grinding his teeth.

"Quite the change in character indeed... I believe the ambition is good for you

in the long run. But you must get a handle on your changes quickly. Thirty days will pass in a flash," Natto advised.

"I know. I have a lot of skeletons in my closet right now and only so much time to get over them…" Drake sighed, his body relaxing. "I'll be leaning on you a bit."

"It is what I am here for, you stupid buffoon."

Drake smiled and reached the end of the camp.

"Alright, foodie time!" he shouted. The sounds of cheers reverberated throughout the small camp.

* * *

"Mrs. Wallen! Mrs. Wallen!"

"Yes? What is it, honey?" the woman asked.

"The front fighters are getting into an argument again over loot. It looks like it's going to turn into a fight," the boy explained.

"Oh? What have I told those little kids about sharing! Can't they let a woman rest in peace!" Mrs. Wallen's attitude made a 180-degree turn. She got up from her seat, leaving the steaming food on her table.

Exiting her tent, she moved from the dungeon safe room that the rest of the non-combat participants had been camped in. As she weaved through the camp, everyone made sure to say hello and greet her.

Everyone knew Mrs. Wallen; she was like everyone's mother. She was kind when you met her, but fierce when she had to be. The first instance of this, the entire tutorial had almost broken out into a war. She had taken the bull by the horns quite literally.

There were a variety of races in their tutorial: beastmen, elves, and lower celestials. And they were at each other's throats at the start. But no one fought when Mrs. Wallen showed up. They knew better.

The first person to try to challenge her had made it out alive, but not with their dignity intact. The poor man had stood up to her after berating a kid half his age. He got the beating of a lifetime and the shame that came with it. He was single-handedly disciplined in front of the whole tutorial.

More people from every race tried to challenge her for top dog status, only to be put on a metaphorical leash for their troubles. No one knew her class, but they were very familiar with her swift backhand and even quicker chancla trigger.

Mrs. Wallen walked through the dimmed hall, the sounds of yelling echoing down it as she went.

Eventually, she reached the command tent, as they'd named it. The tent was made for the front group leading the dungeon dive of their tutorial. There were a few participants who'd earned an Assistant, and they'd found out that their tutorial was one of the more unique ones.

She entered the tent. The arguing quieted down as everyone's eyes went to the entrance.

"What's the problem, children?" Mrs. Wallen asked.

A large bullman didn't meet her eyes, his brow beginning to sweat.

Mrs. Wallen looked to the side where a beautiful fair-skinned woman was beginning to shirk away, her long ears drooping down.

"Come now, tell Nanai. I'm tired and want to eat my soup in peace. Diyos ko..."

"Mom... We're grown adults. We can figure this out on our own without you—"

Mrs. Wallen raised a hand, and her son's mouth clamped shut.

"I didn't raise you to not show respect to your mother! I asked what is going on that a boy had to come get me to quiet down *adults*! You should be ashamed of yourselves!" she yelled.

Mrs. Wallen's son, Travis, shivered. A wry smile was on his face.

"What is the problem?" she asked again.

"W-Well," Travis began explaining, "we've reached the last floor of the dungeon, but there's only one person who gets to have the kill achievement. We're all debating who it's going to be."

"Ay! Susmaryosep! You all are really getting so upset over a little title!" she huffed.

"It's not just a title, you old—Mrs. Wallen!" the elf in the corner shouted.

"It comes with massive stat bonuses. The previous bosses all gave flat bonuses to stats. This being the last one, we're sure it's going to be much larger!"

"Den, plip a coin," she answered flatly.

"What?" many of them parroted.

"Plip a coin," Mrs. Wallen repeated.

"You want to leave it up to luck, Mrs. Wallen?" a man asked from across the room.

"Why not? Would you rather continue to bicker like toddlers? Sige, yes, plip a coin I tell you. Or maybe I should just pick myself?" She scoffed.

"No!" the whole room screamed.

"Sige! Don't you yell at me, punyeta!" Mrs. Wallen yelled back, her hand going for her cudgel.

Everyone including Travis shrunk back slightly, giving wry laughs and smiles.

"Den, plip a coin and beat that monster. I want to be home already and watch my soaps. See my baby son, yes?"

"Mom... Your soaps aren't running anymore." Travis chuckled.

"Don't tell me what I already know, Travis! I have Teabo!"

Chapter 76
Gauging and Past Grievances

"Hmm... Hmmmmmm..."

"What are you humming at! It is giving me a headache!" Natto shouted.

"I'm wondering if there's a real damage increase with my new main class tree and defense increase," Drake explained with his hand on his chin. He sat looking at his status screen.

School of Fire Proficiency 3 (0%)
The active ability set to control the magic school of fire. Your proficiency over fire is still early at this juncture, giving you only the basics of spells.

Fireball: *"The fire of my heart, take form and sear my enemies. Fireball."*
Basic single target spell. Deals fire damage in a 3 to 1 of Intelligence.
Small mana cost.

Fire Cloud: *"The fire of my heart, disperse and set flame to the world. Fire Cloud."*
Basic area of effect spell. Deals fire damage in a 5 to 1 of Intelligence.
Moderate mana cost.

Drake leaned into the screen, hoping that looking more closely might give him a glimmer of understanding.

"It says the damage has at least doubled, but there's no way for me to really tell since there aren't any monsters around. And I kill everything in one shot already, so I can't really gauge the difference."

"You could use one of the many imbeciles that walk the outpost, no?" Natto proposed.

Drake snorted. "I'm not going to try a spell against a person. I want to test this, not kill people…"

"Then it will remain a mystery until we find our next E-Rank."

Sighing, Drake fell backward onto the grass with his hands behind his head. He stared up at the sun. It was the following day after they'd returned from the Hive, and they still had a few more weeks of the tutorial to go.

He was taking it slow, going over his skills little by little during the remaining time. He still had to talk to the dwarf, but he didn't think it was urgent. It was always better to let investments sit, after all.

Drake's aura sense had rocketed past anything he thought possible with his race change.

Asuran's Prideful Aura [F-Rank] P3 (0%)

The monster inside of you refuses to be below others. It has been honed into a prideful warrior. The world is meant for you to take your place above it. You are the epitome, the apex, the ever-oppressive and prideful Tyrant. Your word is law inside your domain.

This skill gives access to Aura, the passive ability to inflict your will upon the world within a certain distance.

Allows the user to perceive their surroundings within a 65-meter sphere around themselves. Increases with proficiency.

Aura suppresses anyone inside your sphere that is of your rank or lower, inflicting a perpetual 25% debuff to all combat stats and momentary fear. Increases with proficiency.

Aura momentarily disrupts any and all spells or skills being cast when will is flexed. Must be of equal or lower rank.

Devourer: Any target inside your sphere of influence has a beneficial buff removed once per every twenty minutes.

Level Killer: If target is under the effect of Asuran's Prideful Aura for an extended period of time, the aura will slowly deplete their health based on the difference in level and proficiency. Increases with proficiency.

The range of influence had expanded considerably, and with all of his buffs specific to the aura, it alone was a tool he could use to deal devastating damage.

"Might as well be conqueror's haki... Now my looks can kill. Literally." Drake chuckled nervously.

He could feel nearly everyone moving within Shigure's camp, people coming and going from tents, stalls, the gates, and more. He was essentially the FBI agent everyone thought was watching them constantly, but he would rather not be.

Thankfully, the skill didn't overwhelm him with information as much as he would've thought. It was jarring at first, that was sure, but after some fine tuning before bed, reducing the range slightly, he was set.

"I could've gone without being aware of so many people doing the dirty, but not like I can bleach my eyes right now. Would my eyes survive that?"

"*Oh please try. It would be very funny,*" Natto chimed in.

"Okay, so I probably shouldn't do that if you're that eager."

"*Please, it would not kill you. It would... simply sting a lot for a long period of time. You would be fine; your improved regeneration skill would make it fine.*"

"Can't argue there..."

Drake let the conversation die, taking in the sun as he bathed in the warm light. Soon he could sense footsteps approaching, but he could only imagine who it was.

Lately, Drake had been stuck in a pickle. A rock and a hard place. He wasn't sure if it was his constant risking of his life for others, or maybe it was his dashing charms? Regardless, a new storm had rolled in on his life.

"This is where you were?"

Drake craned his head backward to see the source of the voice.

"Megan... Hi..."

"Are you avoiding me?" she asked.

"I am. I thought you'd get a hint after I let down Chelsea that I'm not interested in the whole harem trope."

"E-Excuse me?! I just wanted to thank you! If it wasn't for you coming back and beating that monster, we would all be dead. Gratitude doesn't insinuate romantic interest, you idiot!" she yelled.

"Then why didn't you just say thank you like Julia did and move on? Why are you hounding me whenever Claire isn't around? I'm not *that* oblivious."

"I-I just wanted to make it heartfelt! A simple thank you wouldn't convey what I was thinking..."

"Megan, I'm not Chris. I'm not your hero, and I don't want to take advantage of you. I'm also involved with another woman already; I'd appreciate you understanding that and finding someone else."

Megan's face blushed with a flash of scarlet before she stammered something incoherent and stormed off.

"Is the drama worth not being unfaithful...? And what's with women throwing themselves at me lately? All I'm doing is killing monsters—anyone can do that."

Drake shook his head and resumed his sunbathing, hoping that would be the last of people he didn't want to see for the day.

A few minutes later, more footsteps crushed the grass underneath.

"Who is it this time? If you're going to confess your love to me, at least wait an hour please!" Drake shouted.

"Who is going to confess anything to you...?"

Drake turned his head and saw an angsty black-haired teen.

"Oh, Shigure? You sure? With how much you seem to hate me, I kinda thought you were playing the tsundere angle. But I'll have you know I don't swing that way. Tom might, though."

"Your jokes are noted. But I have business matters to discuss."

Drake looked the teen up and down, noticing how unperturbed he was with the jab. Then a lightbulb lit up in Drake's head.

"Oh, you sly dog you! You confessed to someone, just not me, huh?" Drake shouted, wiggling his eyebrows and standing up.

He seemed to have hit the nail on the head. Shigure's face turned rosy.

"I-I don't know what you mean! I have no idea what you're speaking of! Regardless, please drop the matter. I have something important to discuss!"

"Oh come on, I already know who it was. So does everyone else; it's hardly a secret, if I'm right." Drake smiled. "But I'll let you off the hook for now. So? What is it?"

Shigure coughed, trying to regain his composure.

"The Hive you mentioned, we are having difficulty gaining access to the tunnels you detailed. It seems whatever monstrous display you and that ant put on has destroyed the entrance and made it nearly impossible to get in without a talented earth mage."

"So you could only ask me, huh? Okay, let's get going then."

Shigure looked surprised.

"Just like that?"

"Just like that."

* * *

"So, Shigure, tell me more about what's going on with the outpost since we're doing this," Drake asked as they walked, a line of people behind them.

"There is nothing of significance that you don't already know from talking to the guards," Shigure answered.

"No, I don't mean the stuff they know. I mean the things you did that changed you."

Shigure's brow lifted at the question.

Drake snorted. "I know something big happened. You changed from a hot-headed kid to a budding leader. You haven't taken any of my bait, and now you're concise with what needs to be done. I'd say that's a major step up. And that doesn't happen for no reason."

Shigure looked like he was struggling with addressing the topic. Both they and the group behind them walked in silence to the Hive for some time.

Eventually, Shigure spoke up.

"I sentenced the criminals you brought."

Drake looked over but didn't speak, allowing Shigure to unload.

"I hadn't known the extent of how far some people had fallen. I thought what happened... what happened to my friend was a tragedy done by an insane individual. I thought people would be more..."

"More like you? Bright-eyed and idealistic? Out for the good of others just because?" Drake interrupted, not able to help himself.

"Y-Yes. I thought people would understand that we could not make it alone, that we needed to band together to survive. But I underestimated how greed and a thirst for power would affect the minds of those who had a taste for it. I was blind."

Drake hummed, thinking back on his own realization a day ago. "Seems like we were both blind to some things, but there's always room to grow. That psycho who did something to your friend, this is the first I'm hearing of it. Do you know who it was?" Drake asked leadingly.

"I do. His name was Kohoo. He seemed like a normal man when we met, but I was soon proven wrong..."

Drake turned to Shigure, stopping them both.

"Then there's no worries there. I killed that sorry piece of scum months ago."

"You what?!" Shigure shouted.

"Ow... Dude, my ears. I'm standing right next to you."

"What proof do you have?"

"Do you really need proof? The guy disappeared from the leaderboard a while ago. Shouldn't that be enough?"

"I suppose that's true... What did you do to him?" Shigure asked.

Drake turned and began walking again.

"Well, he and a couple of his goons tried to kill me for my TP when it happened. It was almost right out of a cliché villain scene. They took Theo hostage after I'd just fought Bear."

Shigure put his hand to his chin in thought, then spoke of his realization.

"This was when Sir Bear had just returned? That means you had to have fought with the debuff his skill produces."

"Right you are. Thankfully, it was ending just as they got to me. I knew Kohoo from before the tutorial. I won't get into the details, but I learned some very depressing stuff. So the fight ensued, and I took my first human life that night. And many more. Stewart, Kohoo's real name, got the drop on me as I was escaping with Theo, who was badly injured."

Drake pulled his ruined robe's sleeve back, displaying the scar from his previously missing arm.

"That's when he took my arm from me. And then I used that same arm to beat his face into the ground. Rest is history," Drake explained.

"Just like from Hunter x Hunter..." someone behind them mumbled.

Shigure turned to the voice.

"Sato? Why are you here?" Shigure asked, surprised.

"Oh, I wanted to tag along. It's not everyday that the strongest person in the apocalyptic tutorial you're in is an otaku who can literally turn anime into real life." Sato smiled.

"I like him! He's spot on, this guy." Drake laughed. "Come, brother! Let me regale you with my tales of wondrous anime battles!"

"Hai, shishou!" Sato replied with extensive gusto.

Shigure sighed and trailed behind them, but he said nothing. He looked at Drake's back with new eyes. He never would've thought that the man would be the one to avenge his friend. Strange how the world worked.

Chapter 77

Letting Off Steam

"So, shishou! What exactly happened here?" Sato asked as they reached the open area littered with destruction.

"I am also curious how exactly you managed to wreak such havoc... Even if you're strong, this is quite something," Shigure added.

"Aw, you're making me blush here, guys," Drake joked. He walked out in front of the group. "It was just a spell. The ant king had a regeneration ability that required a spell that would pretty much kill him entirely in one blow. So I obliged." He shrugged.

Sato and Shigure looked over with slightly opened mouths.

"That isn't very descriptive... What kind of spell?" Sato asked, wanting clarity.

"A noble phantasm," Drake answered flatly.

"Which one??!!"

Drake pretended to pull back on a bow and release an arrow.

"A lone meteor that I put my heart and soul into."

Sato's eyes shone like stars, and he nodded up and down.

"I do not understand the reference." Shigure sighed. "May we please just move along now if you don't wish to speak plainly? More people will grow hungry as we dally. After the last rant you two went on about how strong magical girls really are in comparison to Dragon something or other characters, we'll be here well past the tutorial..."

"That was a vital discussion!" Drake and Sato shouted in unison.

Shigure rolled his eyes and walked past Drake, moving toward the crushed Hive entrance.

"This is the entrance you spoke of, yes? Are you sure there are no others?" Shigure asked.

"Nope, I destroyed the rest while we were going after the Goblin King's Hoard. Still some stuff down there if you want to give it a look," Drake offered.

"If you do not mind. We could use all the help we can get. I would like to ask something of you privately, though," Shigure said suddenly.

"Oh? Sure, right after I open this up first."

Drake moved next to the entrance, his hand outstretched. Five orange magic circles formed in a flash in front of his fingers. Drake braced himself for the drain in mana that was expected from moving established earth, then fired off five magma spells into the broken entrance.

Within seconds, the orange pellets embedded themselves into the rock, heating up the ground in a fiery orange glow as they burrowed their way through the dirt. The hissing sound of the melting stone was accompanied by the heat of the smoldering earth.

Drake raised his other hand, a blue circle quickly forming as he felt his mana take a hit. Thankfully, his enormous mana pool had tripled in size since his race change, allowing him to manage well enough.

He soon felt the earth's resistance fall away, letting him know he'd punctured through into a tunnel. He sent down a wave of water, cooling the stone he'd just melted through. His hand shifted from glowing orange to an earthy brown as he reinforced the tunnel with his own earth magic, even going as far as forming steps for them to go down.

Finalizing the tunnel, he switched to wind magic and blew the smoky air clean from the tunnel.

"Give it a few more minutes to air out; don't want people dying from some weird gas. There might still be ants down there, so I hope you have someone who can light up the tunnel or see in the dark."

Drake pointed a thumb to Shigure, motioning to move away slightly. Shigure nodded and followed him.

"Then, what's this question? Thought you wanted to wait on the alliance talk?" Drake asked, getting straight to the point.

"I will hold off on the alliance. No, my question is more of a personal favor..." Shigure said, looking uncomfortable. "What I would like to ask is if you would spar with me again."

Drake was surprised. He hadn't expected Shigure to ask him to train. After all, Shigure had often expressed his hate for him.

"I don't think that's a good idea," Drake replied.

"What? Why is that?! I assure you I only wish to get stronger!"

Drake shook his head. "I said it was a bad idea. I didn't say I wouldn't do it."

Shigure looked confused.

"Right now, I have my own problems." Drake sighed and pointed to his skin. "I had a bunch of things happen when I fought the ant, and I'm still getting a handle on them. Give me a week or so to work through things, and then we can talk about sparring."

"I... I understand. Thank you. And I am also grateful you obtained vengeance for my fallen friend, even if it was a coincidence. I am truly thankful," Shigure said, bowing lower than a 90-degree angle.

Drake would normally blow off the heartfelt gratitude, but Shigure had never thanked him like this before. He knew it must have been hard to admit that someone Shigure hated so adamantly had helped him. It was growth that Drake didn't think would happen so soon.

"It's alright. Stewart did unthinkable things, and he got what he deserved. I bear no regret in giving him justice. Even before learning about your friend, he was scum. I want no thanks for taking a man's life, but I'm glad you can have the solace of knowing that he'll never commit such an atrocity again. You are welcome," Drake said solemnly, placing his hand on Shigure's shoulder.

Shigure did not raise his head. His shoulders shook.

Drake smiled.

I guess he really cared about his friend. To bring a man to tears, even a young man, is a lot.

"Ah, it looks like it's beginning to rain," Drake said.

"N-No? I don't feel any rain," Shigure answered, his head turning slightly.

Drake raised his hand, a flash of blue forming in front of his outstretched palm. A ball of water shot up far into the clear sky.

"No, it's raining alright." Drake smiled. The ball of water burst and brought a downpour down on the area.

* * *

A few minutes after the rain had stopped, Drake saw Shigure and his group off into the tunnel. He handed them the key to the Goblin's Hoard as well, then set off in the other direction.

Drake wanted to be alone for a spell, and he ran for some time through the forest.

"It's amazing how large this place actually is..." he mused aloud as he weaved between the trees. "It's also crazy how those ants literally picked it clean... Ow!"

Drake rubbed his nose as he hit something face first. He placed his hand forward, feeling a glass-like substance.

"Oh... Looks like we've reached the end of the world. I wouldn't have guessed there was really an end. Is it the end of the tutorial? Or is this just a barrier?" Drake wondered, knocking a finger against it.

Natto rolled out from the side of Drake's head, finding a spot on his shoulder.

"I believe it is the end of the spatial dimension that houses the tutorial."

"A separate dimension? So what would happen if I tried to crack it open?" he asked.

"You would not be able to. The dimension is created by the system, and only those who have reached the peak of S-Rank could even hope to scratch it."

Drake smiled. "Then you wouldn't have a problem with me letting off some steam now, would you?"

"N-No. But I do not think that is a good—"

Before Natto could object, Drake's arm flared with mana. His last tattoo ring crackled with power as it shimmered blue, then coated itself in a fiery red followed by another layer of his Martial Skill's bright crimson.

"Heretical Endowment! Fire!"

Elemental Battle Endowment P3 (0%) [F-Rank]

A spell that allows the user to use elemental magic to perform extraordinary feats through endowing aspects of their magic into their body and weapons.

A spell that places a buff based on the elemental magic used with the spell for the user. While the spell is in use, the user may not perform magic with said elemental magic. This is not limited to base elements and includes magics of confluence.

Cost: Use of Elemental School of Magic while the spell is in use.

Cooldown: None

Fire: *"The power of Fire is not thine to possess, but mine to adhere. Endowment."*

Effect: Increase in Strength by 150%. Increases with proficiency.

Water: *"The power of Water is not thine to possess, but mine to adhere. Endowment."*

Effect: Increase in Active Regeneration by 60%. Increases with proficiency.

Earth: *"The power of Earth is not thine to possess, but mine to adhere. Endowment."*

Effect: Increase in Defense Effectiveness by 150%. Increases with proficiency.

Wind: *"The power of Wind is not thine to possess, but mine to adhere. Endowment."*

Effect: Increase in Dexterity by 150%. Increases with proficiency.

Cost: Use of Elemental School of Magic while the spell is in use. In cases of confluence magic, all included Schools of Magic will be locked.

Cooldown: None

Lightning: *"The power of Lightning is not thine to adhere, but mine to possess. Endowment."*

Effect: Increase in Dexterity and Strength by 150%. Increased reaction time and visual acuity. Increases with proficiency.

Ice: *"The power of Ice is not thine to adhere, but mine to possess. Endowment."*

Effect: Increase in Dexterity by 150%, increase in Active Regeneration by 30%, and increase in Magic based damage by 50%. Increases with proficiency.

Magma: *"The power of Magma is not thine to adhere, but mine to possess. Endowment."*

Effect: Increase in Strength and Defensive Effectiveness by 150%. Increase in resistance to debuffs by 60%. Increases with proficiency.

"Heretical Attunement! Fire! Heretical Attunement! Lightning! Heretical Attunement! Wind! Trifold! Asura!" Drake shouted, magic twirling around his arm as Natto fell backward onto the dirt from the pressure of the mana he was exuding.

"1,000,000%! United! States! Of!" Drake roared. His fist flew forward, his tattoo ring screaming in protest from the infused mana.

"Smashhhhhhhhhh!!!"

Drake's punch collided with the dimension's invisible barrier, crackling with the mana he'd infused into it as he tried to force his way through. The sound of a bomb going off rang out from the impact, the force of the blow forming a gust so strong that it threw Natto backward. The leaves on the trees were torn from their branches as the trees close to Drake bent backward, desperately gripping at the earth below them.

"Dr-Drakeeeeeee!!!!" Natto shouted as she flew backward, grabbing onto whatever she could.

The battle against the barrier finally calmed down, and Drake was left standing against an unblemished invisible wall.

"Fuck! It hurts!!!" Drake wailed, holding his hand. He fell to the ground writhing around in pain, his hand a pulpy mess.

"What in the fuck!" he shouted, pulling a health potion from his inventory and changing his endowment to water. "Why is it so tough?!" Drake growled, tears in his eyes.

The sound of footsteps pushing down dirt quickly tapped closer to Drake. He felt something hit the back of his head.

"At least give me a warning before you do something so idiotic! I could have died!" Natto roared, throwing her wooden sandals into the back of Drake's head.

"Hey, I'm wounded here!" Drake snapped back. He sat up and watched his hand heal slowly.

"Whose fault is that?! You gain no sympathy for inflicting such a dumb injury on yourself, you dolt! I told you that barrier was something even S-Ranks could not match normally! How idiotic are you?!"

"Hey, I graduated. Took me an extra year, but I passed…" Drake smiled.

Natto let out a frustrated groan and kicked him again in the side.

"Ahh!" Drake stretched his mostly-healed hand. "I feel a little bit better now. I've had nothing but pent-up frustration since the fight, and being able to let it all out on something I can't hope to break was a welcome outlet."

He stared out into the sky.

"I can't wait to get back home… I feel like I've been out here way too long."

"You miss the outpost already? It has hardly been a few days," Natto pointed out.

"No, not the outpost. I mean Earth, or whatever it is now. I miss my cramped apartment, my cheap coffee maker, my barely-working rice cooker. My overly expensive bed. The computer I was on 12 hours a day. I miss the normalcy…"

Natto moved to look at Drake's face, her own turning to surprise.

"Drake? Are you alright?" she asked.

Drake's face was contorted into a desperate smile. His shoulders moved up and down as he heaved long drawn-out breaths, his eyes locked in a battle as he tried to hold back the tears in them.

"I lived, damn it… I made it to the fucking end! Fuck you!" Drake roared at the sky. "I made it through every dumb stupid situation you put me in! And now in a few days, I'm going home! Whatever stupid bullshit is waiting, go ahead and throw it at me! I'll survive just like I already have! I'll live, you hear me! I'll beat the shit out of everything in my way and come out on top!"

"Drake…" Natto said in a hushed tone.

"I'm alright…" Drake whispered back, coming down from his rant. "I just… I just needed to be weak for a moment, one last time." He smiled mockingly. "From now on, it's only forward. And before we go, I want to say goodbye."

"Goodbye? To whom?"

"To my weak old self that I buried a long time ago."

Chapter 78

The Grand Return

Aono had been following her knight across the entire tutorial. Her body was ragged and injured, but she still persevered through the staggering number of ants that had chased her through the tunnels when she'd followed him into the Hive. She had proven that she was stout of heart, needing to capture every moment of her dashing, dazzling, magnificent knight.

"I will never let a moment pass unrecorded! Unillustrated! Every galant moment in my knight's story must be put to paper for others to be in awe of and adore!" she exclaimed, spreading her arms wide.

Alas, even her knight was put to the test. The newly-hatched monster proved to be a trial he had to go through. Aono had witnessed her knight defeated once, but it was only for a moment.

She'd managed to exit the Hive to the surface once more through a small, almost collapsed tunnel. She then circled around to the trees in view of his battle.

Aono watched on as her blazing, dazzling knight fought tooth and nail with one of his companions, the large one with the red hair and beard.

"This shall make for a lovely scene..." she muttered, pushing up her glasses with the back of her mana stylus. "This may be the turning point of their relationship! Will the giant win? Or will the gorgeous ladies of the camp?!"

Aono began to drool with anticipation as her stylus hit the mana paper, illustrating the pair's standoff against the newly-hatched monster. Its body looked as if it was carved from pure silver and was still heated from its formation, red streaks of crimson pulsating throughout its natural armor.

But she was interrupted once again by the charlatans who wanted to call themselves followers of the true knight.

"Milady! Where have you been?! You've been missing for almost two weeks! When you plunged in after the man—"

Aono turned, her eyes fierce.

"You mean after I chased down the true knight! You false, half-wit, lily-lipped, single-celled, frightened, indecisive, cowering, uncourageous, pond scum! You would not follow and risk yourselves for the true history of the land!"

The group flinched, berated by her coarse words.

"But milady... We surely would have died had we followed him down into the depths of such a place. Do you not see the monster in front of you? What you do rivals stalking..."

"S-Stalking?! I am *observing*! Ob-ser-ving! And what of it?" She sneered. "If you are not prepared to give your all and die for your art, can it truly be called *ART*? He is true *elegance,* and he will overcome this lousy bug like the rest!"

She lifted her chin confidently as she shouted at them. She then heard the end of a spell chant and saw the beginnings of the ice that filled the plains.

"Ryoiki Tenkai, 7th Layer of Hell."

Aono's head whipped back to the fight, catching the last glimmer of her knight's grinning face before it was obscured by the ice.

She and her group looked on and waited with bated breath as the sounds of battle continued from within the ice.

"W-What is going on in there?" Aono said. She bit down on her thumb in frustration.

"I do not know... but I must!" she shouted, running for the ice domain.

"No, milady!"

Aono charged out of the trees, aiming for one of the small windows that opened into the structure. She finally reached the window, but she was too short to look in. Her followers arrived a moment later behind her with ragged breaths.

Looking back, she pointed downwards.

"Get on all fours! Quickly!"

"W-What?"

"On your knees! So I can look into the ice!" she repeated.

Some of the followers began moving to get into a pyramid on the ground so she could reach the window, their faces saying just how much they were enjoying the assignment.

"Stop smiling, you disgusting perverts!" she shouted.

"B-But our goddess is stepping on us..."

Aono growled, kicking one in the face as she stepped up. "Keep it up and I'll do it again," she began saying, then grimaced when the man smiled more wildly.

"P-Promise...?"

"Kimoi..."

Aono flinched momentarily from the sheer disgust welling up in her stomach, but she shook her head. She needed to reach the top so that she could record her gallant knight.

Once there, she looked inward, seeing the battle resume.

Her knight and his companion were on the back foot, fighting for their lives against the insect.

Aono's hand flew across the mana paper, capturing the fight as best as her unenhanced eyes could manage. They appeared as if they were teleporting across the battlefield. One moment they were at the edge of the ice chamber, the next they were clashing with the insect.

Aono began to froth at the mouth at the material she was witnessing.

"Yes... Ha... ha... Yes!!! Good... Goood!!!!" she shouted with glee.

"S-She's drooling on me!"

"Lucky..."

"Shut up down there! You are breaking my concentration!" Aono growled.

She refocused, seeing Drake jump backward as he summoned chains of earth around the monster. His companion raised his sword with both hands.

"Witness... Heaven Splitting Strike!"

Aono gasped as she felt the power from the strike, her breath taken from her, but still she kept her eyes locked on the scene.

Her stilled breath was released only after the impact of the strike. The low mist inside the ice was blown away, and the insect was left standing.

She heard her knight's voice ring out.

"Noooo!!"

The red-headed man was suddenly thrown to the ground, a hole in his midsection.

Drake flashed forward, battling desperately with the insect, but he couldn't land a substantial blow even to Aono's untrained eyes. The insect was toying with her knight.

"Ki-sa-maaaaaa!!!!" She seethed in anger, her stylus snapping in her grip. "My Dazzling Knight! Put that sorry excuse of a cicada back in the ground!" she screamed, becoming fully immersed in the fight.

But she witnessed something she never thought would happen.

Drake was struck, his chest pierced by the insect.

Aono gasped in pain. Her eyes turned to points.

"NO!"

The icy chamber that had been erected now disintegrated, crashing apart in small shards of ice as the insect threw Drake's limp body to the ground. The creature followed it up with a swift kick to the stomach, sending him flying across the field.

Time slowed down for Aono. Then, Drake disappeared.

"Milady! We must retreat! It is not safe here!"

Aono tumbled to the ground from the pyramid, the group circling around her, but she didn't move. Didn't speak. Her world was muted.

Her body shivered, unsure of what had just happened. The sound of screaming and gut-wrenching blows reverberated in her chest and ears.

Then, a shiver.

She looked up and saw a man on the field. He was holding back the monstrous insect like a child.

The man's smile ignited neurons in her mind like a lightning strike of the highest order.

"My Glorious Knight! My Dazzling Tyrant!" she squealed, blinking away the onslaught of tears, his clear visage in her gaze once more.

She looked at Drake. His skin was tanner, his hair reaching past his knees, and his body seemed to be made out of chiseled marble. He said something in a whisper to the woman behind him, then turned to the insect.

"Sorry. Looks like I can't afford to lose anymore."

Aono held back a girlish squeal, only to leak out a few words.

"It's the return scene!!!!!!"

Instantly the insect backed away, nursing a broken arm. But Drake did not let up. He shot forward in a flash, closing the distance with a swiftness incomparable to his speed before.

"S-Such speed?!" she muttered.

Drake reared his hand backward, the air and light around it deforming and bending, before throwing his fist forward. He thrust the ant into the ground, creating a crater so large and deep that it obscured her view of them.

"S-Such power?!"

The next moment, something shot out from the crater and into the air. Aono's head snapped upwards more from the sense of mana in the air shifting up rather than her eyes being able to follow.

Her gaze focused, and she managed to make out Drake in the air. He held a large black bow with a string of lightning in his hand. In the other, an arrow formed of the condensed elements encircling him.

The arrow finally manifested with each element swirling in tandem around its jet-black base. Drake nocked the arrow and drew back on the bow string, chanting something she couldn't make out over the crackling of magic in the air.

"We must get away! Milady!"

"No! I have to see it!" she shouted.

Drake's voice pierced the thunderous surroundings, entering her ears.

"*Stellaaaaaaaaaaa!!!*"

Aono looked at the tempest of magic molded into an arrow as it careened toward the ground. Her eyes blurred, and she realized she had begun crying, a maniacal smile on her face.

"Ha... Haha! Hahahahaha!!!! Beautiful! So beautiful!!!!!!!!!!!!!!!!!!" she screamed.

The impact of the arrow resonated throughout the area, wind, debris, and lashes of mana spreading out—kicking up and blowing away everything nearby.

Aono was still screaming in joy as she was flung backward into the trees.

"BEAUTIFUL!!!!!! AHAHAHAHA!!! WONDROUS ELEGANCE!!!!!!"

Chapter 79
Finally, Some Good Relaxation

"So, uhhh, what's your take on pizza there?"

"Pizza? The hell are you talking about? It's the apocalypse; there isn't any more pizza. Come on, we're supposed to be watching the entrance in case any monsters show up."

"I know, I know. Just humor me. I swear to god, you can't have a pizza unless you've got some nice fucking wings too, ya know?"

"Man, you're making me hungry. I could go for some wings. And ranch dip..."

"RANCH DIP? The fuck are you? Some kind of animal?! I should put you in the trunk and drive you into the desert! Fucking ranch sauce!"

"What? I like ranch dip! I'm not a fan of blue cheese."

"Blue cheese or go fuck ya motha!"

"Fine, whatever. Blue cheese with the wings. But I was just thinking with, ya know, the early monsters—how did you get by?"

"What? You calling me fat?"

"Joey... I'm not calling you athletic, that's for sure. Are you really going to those jujitsu classes?"

"Of course I am! Haven't missed a session."

"Okay, sure. But back to what I was saying, Jamie can you pull up that video of a bear fighting with an ape monster—fuck Jamie didn't make it now that I think about it—Anyway, you heard those apes, right? They sounded just like I said on the show, didn't they?"

The two guards idly talked outside of the entrance that Drake had made.

The sun was still coming down on them, and there was plenty of daylight for them to relax for now.

They were so relaxed that they didn't notice Drake walking up behind them.

He poked his head in between the pair. "Hey guys. Watcha talkin' about?"

Spooked, the pair nearly jumped out of their armor.

"Ah! Who the fuck is this guy?!"

"Oh, it's that dude Shigure was talking to," the other guard said. He brought his voice down to a whisper. "You know. The one who can kill us all with his pinky toe..."

Drake's eye twitched slightly. "Man, I can hear you still..." He sighed. "I'm not going to do that. But if you keep talking about ranch dressing, I might."

The pair nodded, but Drake could tell they were still wary of him. He didn't exactly want to return to the camp in a rush—he wanted to spend some time away from the rest of the group. So, Drake made a stool out of earth and took a seat next to the guards.

Drake pulled a deck of cards out of his inventory and waved them.

"You guys know the Tyrant of the Forest?" Drake asked.

Both of the men's eyes sparkled. "Yeah, we know it. We betting?"

"Only if you want to lose." Drake grinned and moved his mask.

"Hey... You're actually pretty human under there, aren't ya? Always thought you'd have some kind of monster face or somethin.'"

"No, still—Well, not human, but human-like." Drake laughed wryly. "Alright, I'll even give you guys a handicap. I'll take turn three."

"Oh, confident huh. You ain't gonna snuff us if you lose, right?" one of them asked, sitting down.

"Of course not." Drake smiled.

Both of the guards looked at him suspiciously, but they pulled their own cards from their inventories.

* * *

"Have you found the forest that Shot spoke of yet?" Shigure asked.

"No, Lord Shigure. The hive is incredibly large; it may take days at this rate."

Shigure sighed. "What about you, Uta?"

In a flash of smoke, Uta appeared kneeling.

"I have had no luck as well, my lord. As they have said, the hive is vast. I hate to admit it, but should we not ask that man for his help in finding it?"

Shigure grimaced, but he admitted that they needed to get the food as fast as possible.

"Fine, I'll return to the surface. Continue searching. I'll be back as fast as I can."

Shigure turned, backtracking through the tunnels as Uta disappeared once again to do her own reconnaissance.

"I feel I am becoming far too comfortable with asking that man for assistance... I'm sure his amicable cooperation will run out sooner or later, or he'll soon ask for something in return."

Shigure sprinted through the tunnels, following the trail of torches that his group had left to track their way through the maze of tunnels. It was a boon that he was traveling alone; his stats allowed him to cover the distance in a fraction of the time it took for them to explore downward.

Within an hour, he'd reached the exit. He stepped out into a more dimly lit surface, the sun falling behind the treeline.

"It's already this late?" Shigure mumbled, scanning the surroundings where he'd left the guards to watch the entrance.

"What! How do you even have that card? My last three turns are useless now! That's fucking insane!"

Shigure turned to the noise, seeing a table lit by hovering lightning and white fire. One of the guards was throwing his hands up.

"Ha! I didn't trade that many weapons back at the outpost for nothing! Fear my power! Fear the Dazzling Tyrant!" Drake shouted.

"Wait, doesn't that picture look a little like you?" the other said, leaning down to look at the card. "Wait, this is fucking holographic! There's less than ten of these things in the tutorial!"

Drake pushed the guard backward. "Yeah, and that's why you need to keep your grubby hands off it! Don't even breathe on it; you'll get it dirty!"

Shigure placed his head in his hand, sighing. He then moved over to the group.

"What are you three doing... And Shot, I expected you to have gone back to the outpost by now. What are you still doing here? Playing games, no less..."

Drake turned around and waved to Shigure, a ball of lightning moving over to illuminate his face.

"Oh, just, ya know, chillin'. Needed some relaxation for a bit. By the way, what's your take on blue cheese on wings?"

"Hey, I thought we were over this! Let it die, dude."

"Blue cheese or fuck ya motha!"

"Well?" Drake asked, smiling at Shigure.

"What is blue cheese?" Shigure asked. All three gasped in unison.

Shigure shook his head. "Never mind your games. I need your assistance again to find the chamber you spoke of. We are having trouble locating it."

"What? I gave you the map, didn't I?" Drake replied, confused.

"Many of the tunnels have collapsed for one reason or another. The map is useless to us."

Drake cleaned up his cards and grumbled. "Alright, I'll come down then."

"You will?" Shigure asked, surprised.

"Yup, I will," Drake answered.

I need to burn some time anyway. I can only imagine how mad Claire is that I skipped out again when I've been gone a few days already... Drake thought while keeping his picturesque smile.

"F-Fine. Then let us be on our way quickly," Shigure said tersely.

Drake put a hand to his head, saluting. "Yes cap-i-tan!" He turned back to the two guards. "It was fun while it lasted, guys. And no, I've never played Quake. I'm not *that* old..."

He smiled one last time, scooping his winnings and his priceless cards up into his inventory before following Shigure down the deep dark hole.

***

"So," Drake said, breaking the silence after the first few minutes, "since we have time, what're your plans after the tutorial? We're making an alliance for the summits, but I assume we'll be worlds apart, so I won't be of much help early on if at all. I doubt there'll be any planes that are still working. Not to mention, what if there's flying monsters? Don't really want to deal with that inside a metal tube..."

Shigure slowed down his pace, looking over his shoulder.

"I intend to do what I have always planned. My parents expected much from me ever since I was a boy. It is my job to carry on the Kenzo legacy, now more than ever. I will most likely establish one of those system-sanctioned towns that have been mentioned and go from there." He paused, looking down for a moment. "Although I hate to admit it, the burden of being placed in charge has helped me grow greatly... Thank you for that."

Drake whistled. "Wow, two thank yous in a few days? Are you sure you're really Shigure and not some body snatcher?"

"I am being grateful! Can you not just accept it without the need to joke?!"

"Of course I can, but it wouldn't be fun if I didn't tease you a bit. Lighten up!" Drake said, putting his arm around the disgruntled Shigure. "Look, you've grown a lot somehow. I'd like to take credit, but it was all you. Don't go ruining it by saying thank you to someone you don't like. Makes me all itchy. You might be a disrespectful little brat, but it works for you."

Drake let go, moving the subject forward.

"Then once this is all over, our first goal is what we already have planned. Make a town. Then find a way to communicate before the summits, whenever those'll be." Drake crossed his arms. "I don't know what's ahead, but I won't be happy if you somehow croak early. So I'll be beating your ass this time around till we're out of the tutorial!"

Shigure brushed his shoulder off. "I can do without you telling me to do what I'm already planning," he said, finally giving a snide smirk. "And since you've become so strong, you won't be opposed to me going all out during our sparring, will you?"

Drake smirked back and chuckled.

"No problem there. Remember, you're pretty weak, Number 3." Drake laughed again.

He continued to laugh as he passed Shigure, who was grinding his teeth together as his hand went for his sword.

"Don't be so stiff—we just had a good rival moment! Come on, this way. I can feel the mana in the air, and someone's ahead. We must be close to your people. Let's get this food; I need to take my licks from the missus."

After a few brief minutes, Shigure and Drake came upon the group Shigure had left. One of them held a map and a torch to the collapsed tunnel.

"Ah, Lord Shigure, you've returned. It seems we've reached another dead end."

"So you have," Drake said, talking over Shigure.

Without waiting for the argument to start, Drake walked up to the collapsed tunnel. He placed his hand on the rubble like he'd done before above ground. His hand glowed with a vibrant orange hue as each finger held a magic circle on its end. Beads of magma inserted themselves into the dirt.

"Alright, give me some room. It's going to get smoky in here. Any mage that can use wind magic is free to aerate the place with me."

Drake lifted his other hand, a green-tinted magic circle forming as a gust of wind began sucking up the smoke from the smoldering rubble. It formed a twister of gray clouds that spun past the crowd of people behind him.

He made sure to reinforce the wall with more earth as he went, managing seven different magic circles easily. Even before he'd received his new skills, the task would be trivial, but now it was second nature. His mana easily could keep up without effort.

Drake quickly burrowed through the rubble, coming out the other side. He heard oohs and aahs behind him.

"Alright, where to next?"

Chapter 80
My Favorite Meal

The sound of smoldering, molten rock bubbled through the tunnel for only a moment before a large separated chunk crashed to the floor from the other side. The smoke parted quickly as a gust of wind cleared the area, revealing a man in torn and tattered gold-trimmed robes.

"And here we are. Welcome to the underground forest, ladies and gentle-ladies! Well, and Shigure." Drake smiled.

Shigure gave Drake a steely glance before walking through the hole, his eyes widening at the sheer vastness of the underground area.

"My, this is expansive... They really submerged this much of the land above, and we didn't notice?" Shigure said.

"That's what I said," Drake parroted. "Well, there weren't nearly as many animals when I was here a few days ago. Looks like they've been busy." He snickered. "That, and not being eaten by the ants probably helped. Should be more than enough here for the rest of the tutorial. Just need to get them to the surface."

Shigure nodded. "That is quite true. I can see many animals; there shouldn't be a problem feeding the outpost with this quantity."

"Good," Drake said, stretching. His mana pool was still surprisingly healthy after all the digging. "I'll be going then. I have a feeling if I wait any longer, I'm going to be in very deep trouble."

Drake's hair shifted to blue. He gave a wave over his shoulder, then turned around and re-entered the tunnel they'd just exited.

Walking down the tunnel, he took a breath. He had been through a lot, and helping Shigure had helped him steady himself once more. He was thankfully still *mostly* the same person he was before, but he couldn't shake the feeling of anxious anticipation in his gut. The feeling of wanting to fight the next strong opponent. The fear that crept within his mind that he might not be able to keep his new, baser instincts in check when the time came.

Drake's hair shifted again, shimmering to a light green as he took a deep step forward, then vanished. He ran so quickly that he became a blur, the backdraft of his movement putting out the torches in his wake.

Oops... Well, I'm sure Shigure and them will be fine finding their way out. Drake laughed and continued to traverse the tunnels.

"You seem to be in a better mood." Natto hummed.

"I *am* in a better mood. I'm ready—ready to take on the world outside this small pond."

Time remaining until tutorial's conclusion:
32 days, 17 hours, 57 minutes, 2 seconds.

"There's only so long before we're let loose. Is there anything you can tell me before we get out?" Drake asked.

"Unfortunately nothing I have not already spoken of. I apologize..."

"It's fine. One foot in front of the other, as my old man used to say."

"Certainly quite the saying."

"He also said you should kiss your ass goodbye if you get caught out in the open in a thunderstorm." Drake smiled, remembering the conversation on their porch as they'd looked out one night from their home, one very loud thunderstorm raging outside.

"I-Interesting..."

"He was quite the character." Drake laughed, turning and running up the stairs he'd made earlier. "He used to purposely mispronounce things we liked because we would correct him."

"Oh? Such as?" Natto asked.

"Poke'man, Harry Pothead, things like that." Drake laughed. "I miss him quite a lot. My whole family does."

Drake smiled, but a small storm brewed in his heart as he remembered how his father had passed—the feeling of helplessly watching him deteriorate in a hospital bed right in front of his eyes. The smell of medicine had been constant in the room, the stream of doctors and nurses reassuring him all for naught.

His hand clenched subconsciously, his last tattoo ring creaking under the pressure. The noise brought him back to the moment.

"*Drake?*"

"I'm alright; it's always been a sore subject for me even after all these years. I'm not proud of how I handled it, but that's something I can't worry about right now. I wanted to relax, but I still have a lot to get a handle on."

Drake shot out of the tunnel from the stairs, leaping from the entrance onto the empty plains. He kept running as he hit the ground, moving right for the outpost.

The sky had turned light again, the sun peeking out over the trees to the east. The sun warmed his body as he covered the distance in a matter of minutes thanks to his speed.

"I'm glad I lived until now; this place is beautiful. Well, at least it is without all the killing and monsters and stuff, but yeah, you don't get to see stuff like this all the time," Drake said. He paused, seeing a lone woman standing at the edge of the camp outside the outpost.

Her eyes were steely, and her arms were crossed and currently unloving-looking. Dirty-blonde braid pulled to the side, the woman glared daggers at Drake.

"*Well*, it was nice while it lasted."

Drake stopped a few feet out from the camp and walked casually up to Claire.

They stood there silently for a few moments, just looking back at one another, until Claire broke first. Her eyes teared up. She leaned forward and rested her head on Drake's chest, her arms wrapping around him.

"You *promised* you wouldn't go anywhere."

Drake gave a wry smile. "Sorry, I needed time alone to figure things out."

She continued to look down, her arms squeezing tighter.

"Did you...?"

"Did I what?"

"Figure it out?"

Drake smiled, his hand going to rest on her head. "Yeah. Yeah, I did."

"Don't do that again, okay?" she asked. Drake was able to hear the cracking in her voice.

"I promise."

"Are you lying again...?"

"No, this time I'm not. I promise."

"Good... I don't want to lose you like I did him..." She sniffled, squeezing tighter again.

Drake felt at ease, his arms now wrapped around her as well. He was grateful that she wasn't as mad as he'd expected.

"Do you want to talk about it?" Drake asked finally.

Claire rubbed her face on his clothes and nodded into his chest.

Drake took her by the hand and led her to his tent. They walked silently, no one bothering them as they went.

Once inside, Claire began to unload her past. How when she first got into the tutorial, she was with her brother and they both had no idea if the experience was real. That was until the first ape entered their group, sending them into a panic.

She told him how her brother had protected her through the first part of the tutorial. They had joined a smaller group, surviving the apes thanks to her support as a Mage while her brother as a Warrior was able to frontline well enough.

Then the goblin hordes had started coming for them. The story progressed with Drake listening intently in silence on the bed. Claire fiddled with his hand in hers. She sat in front of him, leaning her back against his chest.

She detailed how she and the rest of their group were captured. The disgusting things that ensued after. Drake squeezed her hands in frustration at not being there, but then she began explaining how she was forced to kill her brother. How he had saved her by giving up his own life.

There was a long pause after that. Claire cried in Drake's arms.

By the time the tears dried, the sun had already begun setting. They'd spent the whole day together, just them. Claire began telling the rest of the story, how she was saved by Drake. How she felt like it wasn't real.

She saw him as more than someone who'd saved her. He'd given her purpose. Vindication.

"When you came back that day, bloodied and wounded, passing out on your feet after you gave me my justice, my revenge... I knew I loved you. I mean—I already knew, but that was when I realized it, I think..." Claire giggled slightly. She rubbed Drake's hand.

"Why, because I look good in red?" Drake chuckled, only to receive a pinch on the back of his hand.

"No." She smiled. "You kept your word. You kept me safe and gave me what I needed most. You barely knew me, but you did all that. I knew I wanted to support you then. But," she added in a mumble, "I also knew I didn't want to see you hurt again..."

Drake pressed his head on top of hers, letting their bodies comfort each other for a moment before she began talking once more.

"When you fought that monster ant, when I saw you hurt like that..." she said, beginning to cry, "I thought I was about to lose everything again. My heart ached, my heart broke when I saw you disappear!" she snapped, her voice raising as she turned around to face him. "And when you came back, came back to me... I don't know if I can bear that happening again. Seeing you hurt to protect everyone. I want you to live, Drake! I want you to be able to make memories with me, have a life with me! Even if that means you can't protect everyone!" she shouted. Her voice quieted to a whisper. "I-Is that selfish...?"

Drake wrapped his arms around her, pulling her in close.

"No. That isn't selfish, Claire. But I'm going to keep doing it. I'm sorry. I can't let anyone get hurt. I'll keep putting my life on the line over theirs because I'm strong, and I'll become stronger," Drake said, his voice even as his eyes looked out into the distance. "And I dare anyone to try and take what I care for most, because they'll be begging for the end before I'm done..."

Drake released Claire enough to lift her face to his with his hand, giving her a kiss. She blushed.

"It's getting late; you should get some sleep and something to eat. Thank you for telling me about your brother. I'm glad I was able to give him the justice he deserved. When we get back to the real world... I want to make a marker for him somewhere. No, I want to do it where the new city is going to be. My city. *Our* city."

Claire nodded. "That... that sounds nice. But I don't want to sleep alone tonight. I don't want you to slip away again," she mumbled, embarrassed, gripping onto his torn robes. "C-Can I stay here tonight?"

"Sure you can stay. My parents won't be home for a while." Drake chuckled, getting a punch to the ribs, but he smiled through it. "You just have to join me for my favorite meal."

"What's that?" she asked, her cheeks puffing out.

"You."

Chapter 81

Morning After

"Ah! Good morning, everyone!" Drake shouted as he came out of his tent. He was holding a mug of something. "And what a wonderful morning it is!" he shouted. Bjorn passed by, stopped, and looked at him like he was ready to be entertained.

"Why are you looking so glum, friend?" Drake smiled at Bjorn. "Get some 'experience' too. It'll put a smile on your face!"

"Everyone and your mother heard your experience last night, bro, and I'll pass for now. I got training to do." Bjorn snorted, shouldering his claymore.

"Aw, you're a party pooper man." Drake sighed. "Fine, I'll be there in a little. You going to snag the kid?" Drake asked, deflating.

"Yeah, I got Shigure. Don't worry about it. Remember, aftercare is important." Bjorn winked.

"Hey!" Drake snapped. "It wasn't like that! Yet. I *meeeeean*, we don't kink shame here, dude."

The sound of the tent flaps opening sounded behind him, and a sheepish Claire walked out. She pulled on Drake's clothes.

"Oh, you heard all that?" Drake snickered.

Claire nodded silently, her face slightly scarlet.

"I'll summon some hot water. You can take a bath first in the tent if you'd like, Claire," Drake offered, to which she nodded again.

"Boarish ape..." Natto sneered in his head.

Hey! I was very gentle. And it's kind of weird to think about now after the fact, but you were technically there for that whole thing weren't—

"Ahhhhhhh! Say no more! I beg of youuuuuuuu!!!" she screamed at the top of her lungs.

Drake guffawed.

Did you want to take a shower too? Wash the disgust from yourself? Drake smirked.

Natto rolled out of Drake's head and onto his shoulder, then hopped down. Without a word, she entered the tent.

"Enough water for a bath, you foul-smelling, bipedal, single-celled, sad excuse for a man." Natto cringed.

"Hey Natto," Drake said, stopping her. Natto turned around, her head cocked in a curious look.

"*I won the bet.*" Drake sneered.

"Ahhhhhhhhh!!! Shut up!" Natto screamed, covering her red-furred ears.

Drake reared his head back, cackling and almost dropping to the floor before recovering a few minutes later. He wiped tears from his eyes and finally got around to filling up the buckets of hot bath water and bringing them into the tent.

Inside, Claire was still clothed, and she was speaking to Natto about something. Drake dropped the barrels down and brought out a larger tub-like wooden barrel, pouring the water into it.

"Here's some extra to rinse off. I'll be outside when you're done."

Drake left, understanding that they most likely wanted to talk about something privately.

Once outside, he quickly began practicing. He'd been slacking on assimilating his new skills and on checking the extent of the upgrades that came with his new race.

His magic felt more natural than ever, and the energy within his own body felt cleaner and more accessible. Flexing his hand, his arm began to glow in a red hue, his Martial Skill brimming to life before dissipating. The skill felt more in tune, much like his other skills.

Not only had they become more powerful, but Drake could feel how they'd grown more in line with his imagination.

His magic had jumped leaps and bounds in strength. It had also become more adaptable thanks to his increased control and his mana pool helping him in ways he didn't think should be possible.

"I'm still F-Rank, and I can take down a mid E-Rank... I don't think that's supposed to be normal," he thought aloud.

"What's not normal? I never thought you were normal for a second anyway, bro," Bjorn said, returning.

"Well, that's just rude. I was talking about my strength increase from the change that happened. I'm wondering if yours could be the same?"

Shigure stood silently behind Bjorn, his brow raised as he listened in.

"I suppose it's fine to tell him now?" Drake asked.

"I don't really mind. I haven't exactly been hiding it, I just don't bring it up." Bjorn shrugged.

"Well," Drake began, looking at Shigure, "I'm not human anymore, but I'm sure you could guess that based on the skin tone change and the hair. And no, I'm not a saiyan," Drake said with a little disappointment in his voice.

Shigure looked only slightly shocked, but he seemed to have already guessed what Drake had revealed.

"I guessed something had changed, but a race change is quite substantial... Was it an item?" Shigure asked.

Drake shook his head. "No. I won't give you specifics, but it wasn't an item, and it wasn't by choice."

"Not by choice?" Shigure questioned.

Drake nodded. "It was forced onto me when I met the tutorial's sponsor," he explained, shivering slightly as he remembered the feeling of the Dragon woman's hand inside his back.

"What? I thought consuming skill stones had to be by choice?"

"That's what I thought too, but apparently an S-Rank being can do whatever they want." Drake scoffed. "I was told the system will punish her for doing it since it's still against the rules. But back to what we were planning: do you think you could get your friend Sato? I'm going to be bringing some of my party as well. Might as well make this a group exercise—we want everyone to survive out there, after all."

Shigure winced, but he nodded. "Yes, I'll go see him." He then mumbled, "Damn it, now I have to hear more stupid show references..."

Bjorn followed Shigure with his eyes until he was past the tents.

"Surprised you trusted him with that. Something happen?" Bjorn asked.

"Not really. I just think I should trust him a bit more since we're going to be partners for what's to come," Drake explained, twirling some of his spells in his hand.

"Decided to work together then, huh."

"Yup. What about you? What are your plans after the tutorial?"

Bjorn placed his hand on his chin. "Hmm, not sure if I'm being honest."

Drake looked at him, a little confused. "Well, you have to at least come find me. I'm sorry to put it this way, but the world can't have you running around unsupervised."

"You sound like a mother worried about her kid going off for the first time." Bjorn snorted. "I wouldn't worry about that; I'm sure I'll find you. I'm just not sure about what my goals are. I've always just wanted a quiet life, but I don't think I'll be able to manage that..."

Drake stood up and placed his hand on the big man's shoulder. "I'm sure we can work something out. Come find me after the tutorial, and I'll carve out a little home for you where no one will bother you. Promise."

Bjorn pushed Drake's hand off, placing a closed fist in front of him. "Sounds great, bro."

Drake met his hand with his own fist, bumping Bjorn's just in time for Claire to walk out of the tent. Her hair was still slightly damp, and Natto, seated on her shoulder, looked just as watered down.

"Ah! I am alive again!" Natto shouted, raising her arms. "You ape, enough of your dallying. Dry us off," she demanded.

Drake looked at Claire and smiled.

"Yes, yes, right away your highness," Drake said, complying as he waved his hand. A warm, gentle breeze blew toward the pair. "Something about a woman coming out of the shower is special..." he mumbled.

"What? I can't hear you over the wind!" Claire shouted.

"Oh I know, that's why I said it." Drake grinned.

"That's foul, bro." Bjorn frowned. "But I can't help but agree."

"I knew you had some stories to tell!" Drake said, snapping back to Bjorn.

Bjorn shrugged and began walking off toward the other tents. "I never said I didn't, but you won't be getting them out of me, bro," he said, laughing as he walked into the distance.

"How was the bath?" Drake asked after a few minutes of drying Claire and Natto off.

"It was heavenly... I wish we had some proper soap, though," Claire admitted.

"We had a long talk." Natto nodded. "The bath was adequate as well."

"Oh, a talk, huh? About what?" Drake asked, raising an eyebrow.

"N-Nothing..." Claire said, slightly embarrassed, but Drake was also able to make out a bit of sadness in her eyes. He turned to Natto, his eyes burrowing into her for an answer.

"W-What? I did nothing uncalled for! But I will not speak of it out of respect for the zappy zappy girl."

"My name is Claire..." Claire whimpered.

"That is what I said," Natto replied.

Drake shook his head. "Right. Well, let's get some breakfast. We have a long day of sparring ahead of us."

* * *

"Everybody here?" Drake shouted, looking around.

"Hai, shishou! Thank you for including me in this!" Sato replied with gusto.

"Who is this guy?" Chelsea mumbled to Jacqueline.

"Looks like another tosser. Man probably brought him just to have a laugh, yeah?" Jacqueline whispered back.

"No whispering in class!" Drake yelled, pointing at Chelsea and Jacqueline. "Serious time!"

"When have you ever been serious, ya twit?" Jacqueline laughed.

"Fair! But serious time is now. We have thirty days to help everyone's combat abilities improve as much as possible, and I plan on forcing every last one of you to do so. I don't want any dead party members once you're out of my sight, alright?" Drake explained.

"So what will we be doing then, sir?" Amir asked.

"Good question, Amir! You will each pair off with someone who is relatively close to you in level and spar. Everyone should focus on hand-to-hand combat for now. We'll move on to honing your skills and spells after," Drake instructed.

"But why would I need hand-to-hand if I can use my damn lil 'uns?" Hudson said a little grumpily.

"Well, Mr. Scrooge, if you fight something that can tank your bots, what are you going to do? Drop your pants and turn around? Hope for the best?" Drake scoffed. "No, first thing is foundation. Most of you were warrior or ranger-based classes before your upgrades, which means you'll need to be skilled in a few areas regardless of how strong your current class is with its skills. You'll one day find a monster or person you can't beat with your skills alone, so you need to take measures to learn how to survive even when your skills are ineffective or on cooldown."

"Wouldn't we just die if we met someone like you or Bear?" Julia offered.

"True, but we're talking more about the slightly above-average people and monsters. We shouldn't be your baseline for strength. Both Bear and I are freaks."

"Not cool, bro," Bjorn added.

Drake chuckled, but he continued. "The opponents I'm referring to would be people and monsters who are slightly above your level, possibly 3 to 5 more. And who might be a bad matchup for you. The point of these sparring sessions is how you handle a situation that isn't in your favor. But to get to that, I need all of you to have alternative means to survive without your regular classes. That means kiting, delaying for cooldowns, deception, pulling your pants down. Whatever it is, it needs to be honed to help you overall."

"We can skip that last one, right?" Sato asked, some paper and a pen in his hands.

"Yes, you can skip the last one." Drake laughed.

"My lord, what wouldeth be the next part in our said regimen after the sparring?" Theodore asked, his brow already sweating from the expected answer.

Drake smiled widely and spread his arms. "Theo, my good boy! You will be fighting us three!"

"That's a joke, right?"

"I'm going back to bed."

"I didn't think I would make it out of the tutorial, but not like this…"

Grumbles and complaints came from the group, but Drake ignored them. He opened up his inventory to show some of the goodies he'd gotten from the Goblin Hoard that he still had yet to use.

"Stay and do it, and you get your pick. Also Bear is supplying the potions."

"I'm in!"

"Why didn't you say so, you idjit!"

"Bloody tosser always leaves the best bit till after we're angry proper!"

"This one would have stayed regardless, my lord…"

"Shh love, just grab the good stuff alright?"

Drake smiled and whispered, *"Suckers."*

Chapter 82

The Three Monsters

"Hey! I told you to move when you're charging your skill! Stand still and you're an easy target!" Drake roared, throwing a water ball at Chelsea.

"Ah! That's bullshit! It's hard to focus on the skill if I have to run!" she shouted back, taking the waterball to the face and then shaking off the water.

"That's why you have to do it. If you can do what others can't, you're a league ahead of them already! Your skill doesn't specify that you can't move while charging. It might be hard, but you won't always have us to help you after the tutorial," Drake replied.

"You're open!" a voice shouted. The sound of several bullets rang out.

Drake turned to see the mana-filled bullets traveling toward him.

"Bulwark."

Shield Bearer of the Battle Hall Proficiency 3 [F-Rank] 2/2
A battle-tested frontliner of the furious halls of the Asurans.

Passive: +15% to Vitality and out-of-combat stamina regeneration. +15% to Endurance. Increases based on proficiency.
Active: Bulwark P3 (0%), Unbreakable P3 (0%)

Bulwark Proficiency 3 [F-Rank] (0%)
The active ability to summon a temporary shield around yourself based on your Vitality. The Shield Bearer of the Battle Hall is the shield that takes on and advances through any adversity.

Bulwark: "I am the shield, I am the rampart. Bulwark."
Skill can be quick-cast for half benefits: *"Bulwark."*
Temporary Shield skill. Creates a barrier of health based on a 1 to 1 per

Vitality. Shield lasts 10 minutes or until broken. Cooldown does not start until the shield has expired. Increases based on proficiency.
Cost: A moderate amount of stamina.
Cooldown: 5 Minutes

In a flash of green, a shield was made around Drake. The bullets were stopped in front of him, battling with the shield before sputtering out, unable to penetrate it.

Drake pointed his fingers back at Sato with a smile on his face behind his mask. "Nice try. Next time don't shout out and ruin your ambush. This isn't an anime, Sato." Drake laughed and shot two bullets of water right at the man, hitting him in the forehead and stomach. He doubled over.

Sato rolled over on the ground in pain, but he was still in good health.

"Ahhh, shishou... Why the stomach! And it isn't fair! You out level me by so much!"

"True, but who said your enemies were going to be fair and pull their punches!" Drake shouted back.

"Weren't you the one who just said he was going to go easy on them? Come on, bro, you're supposed to be helping them," Bjorn reprimanded as he deflected Tom's shield with his hand. He threw a punch for him to block.

"Okay, I might have gone overboard letting off some steam." Drake shrugged. "What can I say. I'm a man-child and I saw an opportunity for pay-back."

"What did I even do?!" Sato shouted from the ground.

"Don't remember, but I'm sure it was something worthy of the punishment you received." Drake smirked.

"Shishou..."

"Haven't you bullied poor Sato enough?" Claire asked, walking up to Drake.

"Not nearly enough. That bastard won one of my rare cards off of me earlier," Drake grumbled.

"So it *was* something! I won it fair and square!" Sato shouted.

"Yeah, and that's why you still have it! I didn't take it back, did I?!" Drake yelled.

"I think maybe it might be time for a break." Claire laughed. "It's almost dinner time either way."

Drake sighed and nodded. "You guys can go eat. I want to do my own thing some more."

He looked over to Bjorn and Shigure, who were still sparring with some of the others. "Are you two going for lunch, or do you want to spar some more?" he asked.

"Are you cooking first?" Bjorn asked.

"Naw," Drake replied.

"I'm good to wait then. No offense," Bjorn said to Claire.

"None taken. No one can really compete with his food; it isn't just me." She sighed.

"If you are staying, I will stay as well then. I do not wish to fall further behind than I already have," Shigure added, walking to the forming group.

"Alright then." Drake nodded. "Guess you guys are eating without us. How about two on one?" Drake grinned.

"Oh no, I'll be staying as well. I'm not letting you out of my sight after what happened before." Claire smiled, looking at Shigure and then at Drake.

"R-Right..." Drake grimaced.

"What makes you think you can take on both of us?" Bjorn frowned.

"Why don't you prove me wrong then?" Drake sneered. "I did beat the big bad bug, after all."

"True, but that was after a Dragon lady put her hand inside you and played around with the parts, bro. That's hardly just you winning. We both got our asses handed to us before that, if you don't remember." Bjorn snorted.

"Sorry, I don't remember that part. Only remember saving the day."

"Really?"

"Lalala, I can't hear you!" Drake yelled, covering his ears.

Bjorn laughed. "At least your dumb personality is intact."

"I don't find that to be a good thing..." Shigure sighed. "I am fine with two on one. I suppose you have no problem with us going all out then?"

Drake smiled. "No problem, kid."

* * *

Drake, Shigure, and Bjorn took to an open space outside of the camp and outpost. A small group of onlookers formed from Drake's party as they returned with food in hand.

"So who's winning?" Tom asked.

"Would have to be the pup, wouldn't it? Can't see him losing nothing after whatever happened. He did kill that damned bug, after all," Hudson answered, forking his meat.

"No way, it's two on one! Shigure and Bear have this in the bag!" Chelsea sneered and raised a spoon.

"Alright, let's bet on it then. 1000 F-Rank cores on shishou." Sato grinned.

"I'll take that bet, ya daft idiot. Shot is strong, but he ain't strong enough to take on two of them monsters at once!" Jacqueline yelled.

"I don't know, he did take on the bug all by himself... And he did beat the crap out of Shigure already," Julia offered.

"Damn." Jaqueline clicked her tongue. "I forgot about that. You shoulda landed earlier with that, Jules! I take it back!"

Sato laughed. "There's no take backs here! What about you four?"

"3,000 stones on Shigure," a voice said next to them.

Everyone's heads turned to see Uta, her arms crossed as she looked out onto the field.

"Y-You sure about that, Uta? Do you even have that much?" Sato asked.

Uta only nodded.

"Okay... anyone else?"

"1,000 on Shot," Megan said, surprising everyone.

"What?" She shrugged. "He's strong, and it's a good bet. That's all..."

"You know he's dating Claire, right?" Tom told her, only to get hit by Jacqueline. "Ow! What?!"

"It's a bet—nothing more!" Megan said embarrassedly.

"Theo? Care to bet?" Sato asked.

"This one would findeth it most unhonorable to bet in such a fixed game. It is impossible for my lord to lose in any capacity!" Theodore explained only to get hit by Harley.

"What are you saying, love? Here, cough up your stones. There's nothing wrong with free money; think of our future!" Harley demanded.

"Y-Yes, dear..."

"Oh! We have some pretty skewed odds here! Looks like four to one on shishou," Sato announced.

* * *

"You hear that? Looks like I already won." Drake smiled.

"Yeah yeah, say that when you actually win, bro." Bjorn laughed. "I may not have leveled up, but I did get quite a few quest items from those ants," he said, wiggling a new ring on his hand.

"Oh, I didn't see that before. Did you have it when we fought the prince?" Drake asked.

"I did, sadly. Didn't do much against him. But I'm sure it will help against you."

"Why's that?"

"You're human."

Drake gave a forlorn grin. "Sorry man, that ship has sailed. Don't think I count anymore. Don't you remember? I'm a whole other beast now."

"Yes, well, you were quite the animal before, so I suppose it matches now." Shigure scoffed.

"That's not nice. Also, bad form to insult the one who's going to beat the crap out of you." Drake sneered back.

"Whoever said we were going to lose lying down? This is practice to push past our limits, isn't it?" Shigure said calmly. He lowered his stance.

"We'll see about that. I have someone to show off to now, so no hard feelings, alright?" Drake replied, cracking his knuckles. "Damn it, I forgot I only have one ring... Oh well, I've been there before."

In an instant, Drake summoned a layer of earth to cover his left arm. It solidified above it in the color of obsidian.

He flexed his earthen arm. "Been a while since I've done this. You two ready?"

Bjorn removed his claymore from his shoulder and shifted it to a guard position in front of him. "Oh you know it, bro. Unfortunately, I was born ready."

"Kenzo, Shigure. Kensei! Maeru!" Shigure shouted.

"I am the shield, I am the rampart. Bulwark! I am the wall on which my enemies billow. Unbreakable! On blessed wings. Guardian's Reprieve!"

Drake lowered his stance, putting up his own guard as well and pushing mana into his sole tattoo. His hair and tattoo shifted to a vibrant yellow.

"For the thrill of battle!"

Chapter 83
Containing the Beast

Drake waited, allowing Bjorn and Shigure to make the first move. His goal was to assess his newfound strength and to see how his new skills would allow him to deal with situations he would've lost before.

Bjorn and Shigure didn't take the bait right away. Bjorn opted to stand where he was, building up his passive stats as his skills allowed his stats to grow over time. Shigure moved closer to Bjorn, using him as a barrier between him and Drake.

"If you won't come to me, I'll just have to come to you!" Drake yelled, stepping forward. "Let's see how well your self-defense skill works against my new speed!"

In a blur, Drake moved forward, reaching Bjorn and Shigure at record speed.

Bjorn may have not increased his level since their last fight, but his skills were still progressing along with him obtaining new items. But he was still half a second behind Drake.

Drake threw his mana-infused fist forward, passing Bjorn's claymore as it careened right for his face. Bjorn's body reacted a half-second later, moving to intercept the punch and only barely managing to deflect the blow. Drake's fist passed Bjorn's cheek, singeing it.

"Still that fast even after my step up in stats, huh? How good is that ring you got?" Drake smirked and stepped to the side in an instant, throwing another punch into Bjorn's right blindspot.

"Do not forget that I am here as well!" Shigure shouted. He stepped into Drake's fist with his katana bathed in a red light.

Both of Drake's tattooed fists glowed with the intense mana he infused into them. Shigure's radiant blade was covered in the red hue of his skill, and the two's clash sent sparks flying everywhere.

"Fast as well there, Shigure. Those accessories I gave you must have been a big help!" Drake shouted, overpowering the teen.

"I'm still here, bro!" Bjorn smiled and brought his sword down on Drake's hand, but to Shigure's and Bjorn's surprise, Drake's hair shifted in an instant to red. He easily held back the two's blades.

Drake smirked. "No aura behind the strike means I can take it head-on!"

His eyes shifted, focusing on Shigure first. "*Marked.*"

Drake threw back Bjorn's blade, his jet-black covered hand moving to grip at Shigure's throat only to be stopped by Bjorn.

Bjorn gripped Drake's wrist, roaring as he lifted him up into the air. He slammed him down onto his backside with all his might, crushing the ground below them.

Dust kicked up from the impact while Shigure repositioned himself behind Bjorn, his blade ready. Bjorn raised his sword again, a white aura swirling around the blade as he motioned to bring it down like a hammer.

The dust settled just before the blow. Drake was unharmed, his barrier having increased to the point where one blow could not break it anymore.

In slow motion, Drake saw Bjorn's bright blade come down at him, and he saw it as an opportunity to see what would win out: Drake's mana pool or Bjorn's unique aura.

"*Armament, Earth!*" Drake shouted. His earth arm shifted into a dense blade of earth magic at the end of his hand.

Drake's eyes widened as Bjorn's blade passed right through the dense blade of mana like a hot knife through butter.

His new adrenaline skill went into overdrive. He saw the blade inch closer, his sword severed at the base now flying off into Narnia. With a quick shot of air to his side, Drake slipped out in the opposite direction. Bjorn's blade met nothing but the ground below.

Drake waved the cut blade with a frown as he looked back at Bjorn. "How is that fair?"

"It's not." Bjorn grinned.

"So I have to hit you without being hit, huh. Sounds like a good test of speed." Drake chuckled, his hair turning back to black as he summoned three balls of lightning. Each one was speckled with flecks of purple from his increased Magic Exposure skill.

"Heretical Endowment, Lightning. Asura! Twofold!"

Before Drake finished his sentence, he was already rushing back toward Bjorn. The extra two balls of lightning attached to his shoulder to create two more arms.

Reaching Bjorn in an instant, they went into a fierce melee, moving in a blur as he threw punch after punch at his friend. He then moved to reposition himself as Bjorn's auto defense began to ramp up the more time went on in the fight.

But he wasn't the only one with time-gated increases in speed. Drake began to ramp up as well, and within a few seconds, he was overtaking Bjorn.

The fight lasted only a minute before Bjorn began receiving more damage and strikes to his armor than his auto defense could account for. Singes and burn marks appeared on his armor with every second that passed.

Drake had not forgotten about Shigure; he kept tabs on him with his Mark. The teen seemed to be struggling with finding a moment to strike, his eyes straining to follow Drake and Bjorn in their brawl.

"Any time, Shigure!" Bjorn shouted, sweat evaporating off his heated armor.

"First Strike, Blood Moon—Nitoryu no Ogi, Mugen Ketsu!" Shigure clenched his jaw and sheathed his main blade, his hands moving to draw both katanas at his side.

Drake paused for only a second to give Shigure the moment he needed. Thankfully the teen took it, but he had fallen for Drake's trap.

"*Iai!*" Shigure shouted as he stepped forward. In a flash, he moved across the field, both of his blades drawn.

But instead of passing through Drake, he was stopped.

One of Drake's lightning hands had changed to ice, his hair also shimmering a pristine white now. In the hand's grasp were both of Shigure's swords.

Shigure's eyes met Drake's, and the teen could imagine the smile under the mask.

"Nice try, good initiative!" Drake roared and threw Shigure into the air, the teen screaming something obscene as he was lifted weightlessly.

But Drake's win was short-lived. A white claymore passed down, cutting off the two arms, and he was forced to detach them.

Jumping away, Drake distanced himself from Bjorn for a moment, re-assessing what he could do to beat the man.

I know I can win at this point if I just overpower him, but I don't want to kill him. I guess this is the time I start testing some theories? Drake thought.

"*This is quite stupid.*" Natto sighed in Drake's ear.

Drake ducked, dodging a swing from the falling Shigure, then stepped to the side for the follow-up.

What do you mean? Drake thought.

"*You are simply playing with them. Is it not disingenuous?*"

I wouldn't say that. I'm giving it my all, but in a different aspect. I have to learn my own limits again; I don't want to hurt them.

"You are certainly faster than before!" Shigure roared.

"You ain't seen nothing yet!" Drake laughed, still dodging the blade swings.

Drake summoned another bolt of lightning, using it to battle with Shigure. He wasn't nearly as skilled with a blade as Shigure was, but his speed easily compensated for his lack of experience.

As they fought, Drake began pumping more and more mana into the bolt of lightning. It crackled with power with each second that ticked by until he was finally satisfied with the amount.

Reverting back to simply dodging the swings, Drake crushed the bolt in his hand.

"*Gear, second!*"

And with that, Drake moved with unprecedented speed. Shigure's mouth widened as his eyes failed to track Drake.

With his increased speed from the spell, Drake struck Shigure several times before the teen could react—once in each hand to knock his swords from his grip, another to the side of the head, and yet another to his solar plexus.

When time resumed, Shigure was caught in a tidal wave of pain as he was thrown backward, spinning to the side from the blow.

Drake grimaced. "Oh shit, I went too far…"

But he received no kill notification, which meant that he could be healed.

Drake sighed and refocused on Bjorn, who had raised an eyebrow in the direction Shigure had blown past him.

"Little overkill, bro, don't you think?" Bjorn snorted.

"I'm still learning? It's hard to keep my will to fight down right now. It's an entirely new feeling, like I need to win and display my strength…" Drake paused for a moment, reflecting on it.

It felt as if a pot was boiling in his gut, and every passing moment in the fight forced the temperature to rise higher and higher—the steam clouding his judgment so that he could only see the next move. The next way to win.

Drake's eyes turned to Bjorn, and he pushed more mana into his tattoo. The ring screamed in protest at the influx.

Bjorn looked and smiled back at Drake. "Don't keep me waiting, bro."

Drake laughed and shot forward, his right hand leading the charge right for Bjorn. The giant's sword was coming down as if he'd already anticipated the challenge, but Drake wasn't about to back down.

Instead of dodging, Drake's aim for the last part of the fight was to see if his resistances could overtake Bjorn's Divine Curse debuff.

Drake's arm raised in a colorful swirl of yellow, blue, and red from his skills and mana. He met Bjorn's white-coated claymore in the middle.

The weapons clashed, pushing out dust and debris from their point of impact. An intense thunderous boom let out a shockwave from their position.

War Tyrant's Indomitability has resisted Divine Frailty.

Bjorn's eyes widened, and Drake smiled. He pushed back the blade with the back of his hand as he reared back, ready to throw another punch.

Bjorn was pushed off balance slightly, but he dropped his sword, caught it with his other hand, then used the flat of the blade to block the punch.

Drake's hand collided with the blade, pushing Bjorn back several feet. A trail was left in the ground where he'd dug his shoes in.

But what happened next wasn't Drake's victory. Instead, he fell to the ground screaming in pain.

Drake's head was on fire. The feeling was bubbling over, and he felt himself battle with it.

"*Drake!*" Natto shouted.

"G-Get out of my head!"

"*W-Who?! I'm the only one here!*"

Drake screamed and threw his fists into the ground, writhing in pain. The sheer agony was comparable to the feeling he'd had from the forced racial change. And what sounded deep in his subconscious was even worse.

Kill him. Fight with honor and defeat the greatest opponent. Defeat the Titan!

"N-No!"

You will find glorious victory in this battle! Take his life! Fight!

"Arggghhhh! N-N-No!!!"

Drake screamed, his aura and mana going wild as he heard the muffled voices of people around him.

"G-Get away!" Drake shouted, his head snapping upward as he clawed at his head.

But what came into view was Bjorn—not the same Bjorn he was so used to seeing. No, he saw the monster he would become. He saw the titan in him.

Kill the Lonely Mountain! Bring pride and glory to your bloodline!

Drake's head felt like it was splitting in two, his body refusing to listen to him.

The monster before him was massive, a gray mountain of insurmountable size. Its eyes were pure hot white fires that looked back and down at him. Massive black spikes protruded from its back, cutting through the clouds in the sky like fingers through water.

In its hands, it held two massive swords only matched by the monster's size. They glowed with a white aura.

Before he knew it, Drake was on top of Bjorn, his hand raised. But Bjorn's face didn't hold any malice, anger, or surprise in it. It looked understanding.

"It's alright, bro. No hard feelings." Bjorn smiled.

"N-No! Not... N-Not like this! I won't let it happen!" Drake yelled.

Kill him! He will endanger your family! Put a stop to the Titans! Fight!

Drake released a mana and aura-powered scream. "I said no, damn it!" He then threw his fist into his own stomach, praying that the pain would make him come to his senses. Instead, the sensation only battled with the pain of his splitting head.

He reared back his hand one more time as he slid off of Bjorn. His back on the ground, he threw another punch to his stomach, ripping through skin and viscera. He snapped his fingers and caged himself in earth and ice. He felt a stream of something warm leak from his mouth and body.

Drake coughed, smiling as the voice subsided and his head returned to normal.

"*Fuck you.* I won't... be... your... monster..."

His last words parted from his lips, the world going dark as screams and voices failed to reach his ears.

Chapter 84

X-Force

"So does this mean Bear technically won?"

"Is that really important right now?"

"I'm just saying. I put a lot of money on this bet, so I think it's relevant..."

Drake heard whispers around him as his consciousness began to come back. Slowly the sounds came into focus.

"What was that, anyway? It's kind of scary just how strong he's gotten. I mean he was strong before, but that was on another level."

Drake struggled to open his eyes, barely able to make out the blurred visages of people around him.

"You think it was only scary for you? I lost control of my body for a moment..." Drake eked out.

"Drake!" Claire shouted. Her hands wrapped around his neck uncomfortably.

Drake looked around and saw that he was still encased in his spells from earlier.

"No one thought it was a good idea to get these off me?" Drake asked.

Jacqueline stood over him and shrugged. "We didn't know if you'd go full psycho mode again, damned bloody idiot you are. You nearly tore out your own guts there, ya brilliant knob. Don't be doing it again; I got a week cooldown on this spell, ya know."

"Noted," Drake grumbled. He dismissed the cage around him and struggled to bend and sit up. With a little help from Claire, he found himself upright again, his party grouped around him.

"Where's Bear?" Drake asked.

"Right here, bro," Bjorn said from behind him.

Drake looked at the ground, embarrassed that he had lost his mind and body for a moment.

"Sorry about that, man. I don't know what happened."

"All good. If I was going to go out, I'd rather it be by you than someone else." Bjorn shrugged.

"That's morbidly comforting..." Drake sighed.

"Drake, what exactly happened?" Claire asked.

"I'm not sure... I heard a voice, and then I got a splitting headache. Oh, is Shigure alright? I might have gone a bit overboard with him."

"I am fine." Shigure scoffed from the side. "The last blow was substantial, but I managed. More importantly, are you going to be a problem with those outbursts?"

Drake frowned.

"I don't know. I've always had something eating away at the back of my mind, but this is the first time something's *said* anything to me. I feel like Eren right now..."

"Who?" Shigure said, confused.

"Never mind, not important. But I think for now, it's safe to say I won't be doing any more sparring. If I do any more practice, it'll be on my own," Drake explained, his face wincing from the pain in his abdomen. "Ah... this is going to sting for a while, isn't it..."

He received a smack to the back of the head.

"Of course it will, you dolt! You nearly killed yourself! Again!" Natto yelled from his shoulder. "How can you still do such things!"

"Hey, this one wasn't really my fault," Drake said wearily. "Took everything I had to stop myself from going out of control. Know anything about that?"

Natto pursed her lips with her arms crossed. "I have an idea, but I do not have enough information on race changes while inside the tutorial. Even at

E-Rank, I do not believe I will have enough access. As I have said, Primordial races are very special. Most start off at C-Rank when born."

"Primordial?" the group said in unison, questioning expressions on their faces.

Drake scratched the back of his head. "Oh, guess I forgot to mention. I changed races to an Asuran. *Oops*?" Drake chuckled and stuck out his tongue.

"So you're in my same boat then, huh?" Bjorn sighed.

"Not exactly," Drake said. "I had a total of six stones forced into me, thank you. And you somehow have resisted or delayed your change until E-Rank. Whatever Dragon bitch did to me forced me to change, or I just wasn't as mentally strong as you were. But it's the former, of course."

"Yeah, of course." Bjorn smirked.

"What doth this mean for the rest of us, my lord? If thou is to say we should part ways or distance ourselves once more..." Theodore said, looking grim.

Drake shook his head. "I'm not—I'm past trying to micromanage you all. You're grown adults, and you'll make up your own minds. That said, I'm not sure if or when I'll have another... episode."

Some of the group looked concerned, but Claire clung to Drake firmly, her eyes saying 'I'm not going anywhere.'

Drake smiled and looked at the rest of the group. "If it makes you all feel better, it seems like only really strong opponents trigger it. So you all have nothing to worry about since, ya know, you're all weak."

"Not cool." Tom frowned.

"It's a joke, Tom, but you're all objectively weaker than I am. It's kind of why we were doing all this training in the first place, remember?" Drake struggled to stand up even with Claire's help. He addressed the group again. "Don't let my freaking out stop you all. Back to it. We only have a few more weeks of this before you're sent out into the world. I'll be observing."

Claire helped Drake to a seat he'd summoned from his inventory, then pulled a similar one from her own and sat down next to him.

Drake looked over. "Thanks, but you need to practice as well. Now that

I've thought about it, we never did talk about where you're going to end up once we get out of here, did we?"

Claire pursed her lips, slightly annoyed that Drake was deflecting from his problems and pain again, but she gave in and answered him.

"I'm towards the center of the United States, the Idaho area... I'm not sure where I'll be once we leave, though. The introduction told us several planets were combined to make our new one, so we might be even further apart..."

Drake smirked and moved his mask. "Miss me already? We haven't even left the tutorial yet."

"I just don't know if you're going to get yourself into trouble again while I don't have my eye on you." She frowned.

"Hey, I'm supposed to be keeping *you* out of trouble, not the other way around."

"And you are doing a great job..."

"So are you." Drake laughed and pointed to his stomach which was now exposed through the hole in his robes that he'd carved out himself.

"Fine, we're both terrible at it." She smiled.

Drake motioned to the rest of the group that was forming pairs. "Go on, I'll be fine over here. I think Bear and Shigure want to talk anyway."

As if waiting their turn, both Shigure and Bjorn kept a sidelong gaze on Claire and Drake, not wanting to interrupt.

Disgruntled, Claire reluctantly got up. "Fine, but no more stupid stuff. You hear me!"

"Aggressive, I like it. Reminds me of last night," Drake joked, wiggling his eyebrows.

Claire's face turned scarlet before she ran off, smoke practically coming out of her ears.

Shigure and Bjorn took that as their cue to walk over, Shigure with a slight scowl.

"Have you no tact?" he spat.

"She knows how I am; I don't apologize for it." Drake smiled.

"Mystery how you managed to not have her stab you in your sleep." Bjorn laughed.

"Well, being a handsome and funny man helps. And we've only slept in the same bed once so far." Drake chuckled. "But back to the point. I don't know if I have a handle on this anymore."

Drake looked down at his wound. The skin had closed, but the pain from the fatigue of it being healed was still fresh. Remembering the splitting pain in his head also made him wince, even from the vague memory.

The day was waning, and dusk was falling swiftly. Drake summoned fireballs to light the area for the rest of his group, the white fire illuminating the space brilliantly.

"And what are we supposed to do about it? When you were in control, we stood no chance. You expect us to handle you if you go on a rampage again?" Shigure asked skeptically.

Drake shook his head. "No, I don't think I'll go on a rampage again as long as I don't fight directly. I think what spurred it on was the heat of battle when Bear challenged me. I can't say for certain, though, and Natto isn't saying anything either."

"Then what do you want, bro?" Bjorn asked.

"I just want you both to do what we'd planned: help everyone get stronger and cap out their skill proficiencies before we leave as best as you can. I'll do my best to get a firmer grasp on my own problems without getting into any fights. But what I want to get underway right now is to figure out how we're going to meet up outside the tutorial. I still need to talk to the rest of the group, but I'm stationed in New York on the east coast of the United States. And I can only guess how out of whack everything will be once we return."

"You already know my position on the matter," Shigure offered.

Drake nodded and turned to Bjorn.

"I'm up in Canada, bro, near the Yukon. It's more than a few steps away from you." Bjorn chuckled.

Drake pursed his lips. "And that isn't including the new space that might be there thanks to the other worlds assimilating into ours. Unfortunately

Natto is also mute on most information involving things outside the tutorial, but I do know about a quest to start system-sanctioned towns. And I have the perfect name for mine."

"Oh, what's that?" Bjorn asked.

"ReUnite," Drake replied. "It also happens to be the name of my guild from an old friend; I'm hoping they find their way there once I get the name out. I'm sure they're going to be a handful for the world, just like me." He smiled.

"That's a dumb name, bro." Bjorn chuckled.

"I agree, it's rather childish." Shigure nodded.

"Hey!" Drake gasped in faux hurt. "Are you insulting my naming sense?"

"Yes," both replied.

"Fine." Drake sighed. He looked at Bjorn, singling him out. "I know I can't keep an eye on you when the tutorial is over, man, but promise me you'll keep yourself safe and in check until I find you or you reach me, alright? I don't want to have to find you as that thing I saw…"

"What thing?" Bjorn asked, raising a brow. His expression was serious.

"That voice I heard, the one that tried to get me to off you. It messed with my head and showed me something. I guess it was what you would be if you went through the racial change. Let's just say it wasn't pretty. And I don't think something like that… I don't think I'd be in a position to hold back, man."

"That bad, huh." Bjorn snorted.

"All that and a bag of chips. Like family-sized."

"You spoke of racial changes before. What exactly is the race Sir Bear is meant to change to? Is it a Primordial race like yours?" Shigure asked.

Drake looked to Bjorn, waiting for him to make the decision on whether to answer or not.

"The race my skill stones will turn me into is a Titan," Bjorn explained. "Apparently they're at the very top of the list for bad guys in the multiverse. If I reach E-Rank, I'll turn and destroy the world and everything else in our system."

Shigure's mouth opened and hung there for a minute. He shivered. "This is true?" he asked, looking over to Drake.

Drake nodded. "Yup, every word. But we're not gonna let that happen, right?"

Shigure paused for a moment, his arms hanging on his swords by his hip as he thought. He nodded.

"Surely a musclebound idiot and I can manage enough to keep you from destroying everything. Drake has not failed us so far, despite the odds and hate." Shigure coughed.

Drake chuckled and pushed out his hand. "Good, then it's decided. Grow strong enough to stay alive and keep Bjorn from destroying the whole world. Go, X-Force!" Drake shouted.

Both Shigure and Bjorn looked at Drake incredulously.

"What?" Drake asked.

"I am not saying that." Shigure sighed.

"Yeah man, I'm used to you being cringy, but Deadpool? Really?" Bjorn laughed.

"Why are you both ruining the moment? Just go with it! Fine, whatever." Drake frowned and bumped his own fist, whispering to himself, "*Go X-Force!*"

Chapter 85
Playing With Myself

"That's the way, good! Remember to step in with your shoulder only when you're using that skill, Tom. The skill will do most of the work for you, but remember you have leeway when using it," Drake shouted from the sidelines.

Keeping his eyes on the party as they practiced in pairs, Drake lamented at not being able to join them due to maybe having another mental episode from his sudden change.

It had been a few days since it had happened and he'd almost killed himself and Bjorn. He'd been relegated to sitting a fair distance away on a chair, Claire checking up on him every now and then in between her own practice.

Surprisingly, he also had some visits from a very embarrassed Megan and a not-so-embarrassed Julia.

"What are you doing there?" Julia asked, taking a sip of water.

"I'm trying to quicken the speed I'm able to temper my mana." Drake hummed, summoning and extinguishing spell after spell.

"Tempering?"

"Yeah," Drake said, keeping his focus on the pairs practicing as he felt the mana from his manipulation skill. "You know how for some of my spells, the color changes on the elements?"

Julia nodded, fixing her glasses as she looked on.

"I'm trying to make it happen instantaneously, but I'm getting hung up on a few places, so it's taking a while. I guess I just don't have talent with it..." Drake sighed.

Drake was attempting to make his spells more condensed and powerful now that he had the excess mana to do so. His Magic Exposure skill—now Submission of Magic—increased the amount of mana he used for his spells while increasing their penetration ability. But the process did have a delay, and his goal was to, as he said, lessen that. He could always use larger spells and give himself time to charge up through his Heretical Chanting, but he was sure there would come a point when fights would be so decisive that a single spell or action could decide the outcome.

He wanted to prepare for that.

Thanks to the tutorial timer quickly approaching zero, in the back of his head Drake began feeling more and more anxious about the future. The number of tutorials alone told him just how wide the system was for this induction of worlds.

His thoughts continued to fall on just how many powerful people would possibly be coming out of these tutorials. Their tutorial may have only had him as a Dual Class, but who was to say the other tutorials didn't have at least one or more? And then there were the other planet's tutorial members.

The system promoted and seemed to enjoy forcing conflict. He knew this just from his own experience and the fact that Natto had mentioned there would be a summit to decide a leader of their planet. It always seemed to be a competition in the most primal sense.

"Survival of the fittest at its best, huh…" Drake mumbled.

"What now?" Claire asked, bending down over his shoulder. "Hearing voices again?"

Drake snorted. "Only one annoying one." He smiled.

Claire placed the hot bowl of food on Drake's head.

"Ow! What the hell, woman?!"

"Serves you right." She laughed and sat down next to him, Julia taking her cue to begin walking back toward the pairs to practice.

"I was just thinking about the coming events that might happen. Natto still can't give me many specifics, but I know there's more to it, and I'm not looking forward to it." Drake sighed, taking the bowl from his head and gripping it in both hands.

"Oh?"

"I'm sure it'll be a bloodbath even if I'm prepared for it. I don't particularly like it."

Claire's expression softened as she took Drake's hand in hers. "Don't worry, you have friends around to share the burden. And me. We'll get through it together."

Drake laughed. "Are you sure you haven't watched anime before? That's a pretty heroine thing to say."

"I've watched cartoons on Sunday... My brother used to have them playing after church when we came home." Claire smiled with a bit of sadness. "Our mother would always scold him for it."

Drake gave an endearing smile, gripping her hand tighter.

"You wish to correct her on cartoons versus anime, do you not?" Natto snickered.

Oh you know I do. It's taking all my willpower not to scream, but I'm glad she's opening up about him after everything.

"Yes, it seems your... nights together have allowed her to become more relaxed."

It has *been fun. But that's also why I'm so hard on her to get this stuff down. I want her to make it on the outside until I can come find her or she comes back to me. Thankfully she's been a good sport about it.* Drake smiled.

"Bjorn was right," Claire said, narrowing her eyes.

"Bjorn huh? And about what?"

"You do that thing when you're talking to Natto, the distant look thing," she said, pointing at him. "What were you talking about?"

"About how much I'll miss you when the tutorial is over." Drake smirked.

Claire's mouth opened to say something, but it quickly closed, her hand squeezing Drake's slightly harder as her ears turned rosy.

"You better go off and train. Mage classes have it the toughest," Drake said, letting go of her hand as he went back to casting magic.

Claire nodded and walked back to the group as well. Drake watched her as she went. Well, parts of her.

"I'm a lucky man."

"Calm down there, Romeo," Bjorn said from behind him. "Don't let the rose-tinted glasses get you this early, bro."

Drake turned his head, splashing some water on Bjorn. "Debbie downer as always." Drake snorted.

"I just don't want to see you turn into Tom." Bjorn slicked his wet hair back. "Last time he confessed to someone, he was crying for three days. I thought the tutorial introduced banshees..."

"*Last time*? You mean three days ago?" Drake laughed.

Bjorn sat down and nodded. "Yeah, bro. I'm sure Hudson regrets bunking with the guy now if he didn't already."

"Maybe you should give him some dating advice then. I'm doing alright over here." Drake chuckled.

"I can see that. You know where she's coming out?"

"I thought I told you? She's around the central states, so might be a long way depending on how large the world got after the introduction and merge."

Bjorn put his hand to his chin. "Oh, that's right. I wonder how I'm going to get down from Canada. At least I won't have to worry about a visa anymore."

Drake raised a finger. "That's not entirely true. The world's gone mad, but I'm willing to bet whatever remains of the people in charge are gonna want to stay that way even though they probably shouldn't."

Drake shivered. "Damn, that means longer career politicians, doesn't it... People are going to be living for thousands of years. Might have some Darth Sidious-level stuff on our hands."

"That's a good point, but I'm optimistic. I don't think it's going to get that bad. We have magic powers now, bro."

"Yeah, but so do they. It will all depend on who comes out and just how strong they are. All we can hope for right now is that the right people come out on top and that the losers are the bad ones." Drake sighed.

"Don't be so down, man! Have some gratitude!" Bjorn said, slapping Drake on the side. "We just lived through this mess, and you beat an E-Rank. How many other people are going to be able to say they did that?"

Drake smirked. "I can think of at least two."

"Your friends again?" Bjorn said, raising a brow.

"Yeah, I'm convinced they're going to be coming out even stronger than I am. I just hope they haven't changed too much."

Drake and Bjorn watched the others train, letting the conversation die down as Drake spun spells in his hand and continued to practice.

This was the pattern for the past couple of days. Everyone would practice, Drake on the sidelines. Then when everyone was finished, he would practice again on his own only to return to his tent when Claire retired for the night.

Despite his wanting to have fun and not stop, he restrained himself in lieu of training. All that was on his mind were the foreboding feelings eating at the back of his head.

Bjorn a stone's throw away from E-Rank turning into a monster with no solution other than to kill him. The possible state of the world after certain unscrupulous people gained magic powers. The location of his family.

He had to master his new skills and perfect them to a knife's edge.

Drake in the night would continue to drill and practice, pushing himself to his newfound limits. Today was no different.

Once the day waned and everyone was back in camp to retire for the night, he would let Claire fall asleep in his arms, then sneak out using his wind magic to gently let her down as he slipped out from under her.

In the pitch black of night, far away from the camp, he would let himself practice.

"I'm glad I watched DBZ, this training method lets me stretch myself thin while practicing so many different things..."

Drake raised his hand, a myriad of colors cascading from it as several magic circles formed beneath.

"*Summon! Primal Elemental!*"

Drake concentrated, first forming a body of earth, then a shroud of fire and lightning around it. Containing the mass of magic and spells was a thick sheet of ice that constantly reformed around it.

Once it was finished, Drake wiped the sweat from his brow. He pulled two vials out from his inventory and downed them both in a quick gulp.

"Alright, Steven, ready to go again today?" Drake asked the mass of magic.

It didn't answer, of course. It couldn't. It wasn't a sentient elemental but just a mass of spells that Drake controlled.

That's what made it quite fun for Drake, though. He both had to control the elemental to an extent and also fight against it. He'd packed it full of so much mana that it was a struggle to even form the spell at first, but now after a few days of practice, he was able to manage quite well.

The elemental contained so much mana that Drake was surprised himself. Because of the amount of mana within it, the makeshift elemental was able to cast spells as well.

"Good to hear it, buddy. Alright, same thing as yesterday. Anything goes. No hard feelings, right?" Drake said, jumping back a few paces.

Drake began counting down to himself. "Three! Two! One! Start!"

On his word, the elemental spell activated. It began to fight, straightening both arms and aiming at Drake while firing off masses of ice.

Drake shifted into his Endowment, his hair shimmering into a peerless white as he raised his arms as well and dodged to the side.

Throwing out an equal amount of condensed fireballs, Drake tried to circle around the elemental. The impacts of the blasts between the ice and fire covered the field.

Drake lost track of the elemental in the explosions of magic, even with his enhanced eyesight. He ceased his assault of fireballs, waiting for the debris to clear only for the elemental to burst out of the cloud of magic.

"Cheeky!" Drake smirked. His arms glowed red, and he braced for impact.

The elemental increased its speed similar to how Drake had done so previously, using a combination of wind and fire magic to propel itself.

Drake pushed mana into his remaining tattoo. It hummed with power.

"Attunement, Lightning!" Drake shouted, throwing his fist forward to meet the elemental's.

The elemental's fist evaporated and reformed, the spell contesting with Drake's raw power thanks to the amount of mana he'd funneled into it beforehand.

But the elemental didn't wait for its mana to be exhausted. It wasn't cast for that. It began a flurry of blows matched by Drake's one arm, both a blur of speed.

The elemental then took the advantage, casting spells before Drake did and forming magic circles in Drake's blind spots.

Drake was only able to see the bloom of spells at the last second with his Magic Sight. He didn't bother to turn his head as he cast a defensive skill.

"Guardians Reprieve."

The spells collided with his back and sides, bombarding him as they continued to exchange blows. It only lasted long enough for Drake to hear the crackling of his shield.

Gained Reprieval charge.

Drake quickly teleported behind the elemental, his hand already charging a spell of white-hot fire.

"Blaze Palm!"

Drake's hands were engulfed in fire, and he threw them forward, evaporating the elemental at a reckless pace.

The elemental shot forward, taking the damage Drake dealt as it tried to escape. Ice slowly reformed over its raw earthen skeleton.

Drake rushed after it, pursuing the elemental, his hands shooting out blasts of white fire all around. The spells missed their mark and careened past the elemental, cutting off its escape.

Unfortunately, it was now at a disadvantage. It couldn't travel instantaneously like he could.

The elemental quickly turned, unable to escape further. The ice on its arms shimmered to a purplish sheen as it pushed mana to its icy outside.

Drake smiled, keeping himself from using too many of his innate buffs to keep the fight as difficult as possible. Instead, he pushed mana into his tattoo once more, matching the elemental.

On cue, they both surged forward, meeting each other as they exchanged punches and kicks. Drake wove in and barely evaded the pointed ice-tipped strikes as his hands continued to throw out balls of fire all around them.

Quickly the exchange became heated. Literally. The area was soon covered in glowing balls of white flame, the elemental slowing down as its mana couldn't keep up with regenerating itself anymore.

"Looks like this is the end of the session, Stevie," Drake said, jumping backward out of the encirclement of fireballs. His hand reached out, his palm up and open.

"Crush and Bloom!"

Drake roared and balled his fist, the fire around the elemental convening into one location. A massive explosion sounded off with a thunderous boom that rocked the area.

"Good fight, Stevie. See you again in a few hours." Drake smiled.

Chapter 86

Rewards

Drake fell backward onto the grass, looking up at the black night sky. It had been just one of the numerous training sessions he'd had after everyone else had retired for the night.

Taking a moment, he looked at the timer counting down. He felt slightly less anxious about the future now that he'd put the last thirty days into strict practice.

Time remaining until tutorial's conclusion:
1 day, 23 hours, 52 minutes, 43 seconds.
Remaining Participants: 1,881

"Only two more days, huh? Time flies when you're beating the crap out of yourself repeatedly." He laughed and splashed himself with some water.

Natto rolled out of his head and onto the grass next to him.

"It would seem this part of the initiation is coming to a close. Do you remember what I said about the tutorial shop? Have you thought about what you will be selecting?" she asked, pulling a bag of food from her sleeve.

"I haven't forgotten; I'm just curious to see what's in there. I know I need to get whatever quest item you were talking about or the quest itself, was it? Either way, I know I'll be needing better equipment." Drake sighed, looking at his tattered mess of clothes. "I'm surprised they didn't even last a year. Shouldn't there be some kind of self-repair function or something?"

Natto scoffed. "No, you do not receive equipment with things like that until much later. You expect to have the best right at the beginning? Even that weapon you acquired was something special, and you are still dissatisfied?"

"Hey, we always want the best gear. It's how we are!" Drake said, defending himself.

"We?"

"Yeah, gamers. I need the next new shiny thing. More numbers, more damage, numbers go brrrrr!" Drake said, rolling the "R" as he threw his hands into the air.

Drake laughed to himself, then quickly opened his inventory, seeing the massive number of items, equipment, stones, and monster cores that filled it. And at the very bottom, he saw his current TP.

35,723,553 Tutorial Points

"That's a crazy number." Drake whistled even after having seen the number several times before.

"Yes, well, you did kill the technical boss monster of the tutorial. Imagine if you did not fail in killing the queen; you would most likely have more."

"Really sticking a knife where it hurts right now, aren't you..." Drake chuckled wryly. "That's another thing, isn't it? We may not have rounded up all the PKers, but at least the participants stopped dropping." He sighed. "Just wish we could've saved more... It seems like the more I think about it, the more I should have done. I mean, over half the tutorial participants we started with are gone."

"We have been over this many times, Drake. They were not your responsibility. You cannot save every person, nor should you require it of yourself. You may be strong, but you are not that strong," Natto explained. "If you wish so much to protect others, then create a new place where you can do so. Outside of the tutorial, I can aid you there. I am a Territory Assistant, after all."

"Then, I'll work you to the bone." Drake snorted.

"As long as I am fed, I will not disappoint you. Remember I require only the best meals and, let us not forget, E-Rank cores. I expect great things."

Drake waved his hand. "Yeah, yeah. That also reminds me: what are the monster levels going to look like when we get out? There are kids who haven't even had their classes selected, right? There can't be E-Ranks right off the bat, can there?"

Natto looked a bit pensive before she answered, taking small bites of her food.

"It is honestly hard to say. Each area will be different. Drake, you should be prepared for what you will see when you leave. The system is not unfair, but it is unforgiving. Your priority must be to establish the first town. No matter what."

Drake turned his head, looking at her curiously. "Why so serious and specific? And I won't know until we get there. You already know I won't abandon kids."

"I know. But I must say such things as an assistant regardless." Natto sighed.

"Don't worry." Drake grinned, feeling more at ease now than before thanks to her concern. "Whatever may come, it'll work out. I'll *make* it work out."

* * *

Drake returned to the camp a few hours before dawn, sneaking back into his own tent as he prepared a tub of hot water for both him and Claire. The sun began to peek into the cracks of the tent just as she started to stir.

"Uunn... Are you up early again? You smell like burnt... burnt *something*," she said, scrunching her nose.

"I was out training again. Got hit with a lightning bolt." Drake laughed.

"A-A lightning bolt? Aren't you training by yourself? How did you get hit?"

"Oh, I'm not by myself. Stevie was there."

"Who's Stevie?"

"Stevie the elemental. Now, are you going to wake up or stay in bed asking me twenty questions?"

Claire grumbled and took off the covers, revealing her in nothing but a slightly tattered T-shirt that forced a whistle from Drake.

"Wow, maybe I should stay in more often..."

Claire giggled as she pushed him out of the tent. "Maybe you should. But then you wouldn't be you, would you?"

Drake raised a brow, processing her words for a bit. "Okay that's true," he admitted, turning around. "Are you saying you wouldn't like me if I changed—"

But she had already gone back inside the tent. The sound of water splashing reached his ears.

"She might be the one changing... She used to get so embarrassed at me seeing her, but now she doesn't even bat an eye... Oh well." Drake shrugged, summoning some elements to mold as he passed the time.

The few weeks until the end of the tutorial had passed peacefully since Drake had killed the ants. Whatever remained of the stragglers were hunted down quickly by the parties inside Shigure's outpost as well as Drake's own, securing what little experience was left within the tutorial.

With the time waning, he'd been making sure to check in with everyone. Where they were outside the tutorial, what their plans were, and would they be coming back to rejoin Drake?

"Oh, I have to see that old man about my cut, don't I? Wonder how much he got for all the stuff I gave him. Oh! That gives me an idea..." Drake mused, thinking about the tutorial shop and his inflated TP.

"Early to rise once again, my lord?" Theodore said, shimmering into sight next to Drake.

"Morning, Theo. And yup, night training has been going well. Just wake up?" Drake asked.

"Indeed, Harley and this one have just risen. Unfortunately this one's stamina is no match for my lord's."

"That's not exactly something you should compare. You're a pure mage class, Theo. Isn't exactly fair." Drake chuckled. "But you're improving with all the sparring we've been doing. Well done, man."

Theodore bowed with a smile. "It pleases this one to hear such praise, though it pains this one to think we shall be apart for so long, my lord."

"Oh don't be like that. You're pretty close, right? Somewhere in Maine?"

"Tis indeed somewhat close, but this one fears just how far the distance will be due to the new world we face. But!" Theodore said loudly, pointing a finger into the air. "This one shall not be disheartened in finding his way to his lord! This one assures thou!"

Drake chuckled wryly. "Right. Good to hear, Theo."

"Theo, it's too early to be that loud..." Claire said, walking out of the tent in her cleric armor.

"Forgive me, m'lady. This one was simply excited to meet his lord in the world outside," Theodore said, bowing.

"Don't call me m'lady. We've been fighting together for months now, Theo," Claire said sheepishly.

"This one cannot! Once you have been with my lord, it is natural that my lady is to be seen with respect!"

"Drake..." Claire pleaded, looking at him with puppy eyes and asking for help.

Drake raised his arms. "Not my problem, I'm taking a bath. I smell like burnt"—Drake sniffed himself—"burnt *something*, remember?"

Claire frowned and gave him a glare as he laughed and entered the tent.

A few minutes later, Drake came back out revitalized. A crowd had gathered in front of the tent.

"Yo," Bjorn said, raising a hand.

"Yo," Drake replied.

"Same stuff different day, bro?" Bjorn asked.

"Yup. Going to see a dwarf about some loot later, though. Everyone have breakfast or?"

"Dude... Fooddddddddd..." a voice growled from behind him.

"Oh, Sherry... Ow! Don't bite me! I get it! I'm going! Ow! I said stop it damn it!" Drake cursed and moved with the rest of the group to the kitchen area by the fire pits.

"You would think you guys could do this without me at some point." Drake sighed, pointing his knife tip at the others at the table who were preparing food.

"We've been over this, you make the best grub. We just like to help. You should just think of it as quality time with your friends!" Chelsea snickered.

"True, I guess. We *will* all be separated very soon... Might as well enjoy it while we can," Drake reluctantly agreed.

"I can't wait to be rid of this bloody tosser." Jacqueline sneered.

"Aw, don't worry. I'll miss you too Jacqueline." Drake smiled.

"As if! Thank god there's an ocean in between us!" she cursed.

"Oh? You're not in North America on the outside?"

"Nah, I live in the states, but I was back in my hometown in the UK when this all happened. I just happened to get into the same tutorial as everyone else," she said, looking at Megan, Chelsea, and Julia.

"Huh, that's interesting... I wonder if the system did that on purpose?" Drake thought aloud.

"Who knows." Chelsea snorted. "I'm glad they were here, but I won't be thanking the damned system for anything."

"Well, just remember you're all welcome to come back and settle with me in the town or whatever it's going to be. I won't be hard to find," Drake said honestly, his face serious. "And if you ever need help, all you need to do is ask."

"That's sweet, Drake. Is that a promise?" Julia smiled.

"My party is my family, we've been through too much not to be. And I'm sure there'll be more to come once all is said and done," Drake answered, finishing his meal prep and sliding the food into the pot.

"You all still have one day left of training, so no slacking," Drake instructed, looking at the line of helpers and the peanut gallery waiting by the other tables for their food.

"Don't you worry about that, ya idjit. Don't plan on dying anytime soon after all this!" Hudson shouted from the tables.

"Agreed, I am excited to make my way back to the party as soon as possible," Amir added.

"I just want the food I was promised..." Sherry grumbled, rubbing her stomach.

"Yeah, I'd like some food too please," Tom agreed, waving a fork in the air.

"You keep it down over there before I give you a whoopin', Tom!" Drake shouted.

* * *

The day continued to progress normally for the group. After eating and calming heated personalities at the table, the party took to their practice area.

Drake didn't observe this time around as he needed to speak to the old dwarf. After a bit of protest, he managed to keep Claire from joining him and skipping practice. He'd rather she use all her time available to improve her chances of surviving. She very much disliked him for it, but he was willing to make her angry if it meant increasing her chances of staying alive without him.

Drake walked through the dirt-worn paths in the outpost after a bit of trouble at the gate which was quickly cleared up by Shigure and Uta. People were still able to recognize him from his striking mask, and they cleared a way for him.

I don't know if I like this attention or not. On one hand, it's nice people don't bother me. I'm an introvert at heart. But on the other, I'd rather not have people look at me with such fear... he thought.

"Well, it was bound to happen. You are simply in a different league of strength than most people, being a dual class. I would venture to say that only very specific epic classes and above would be able to compete with you at the moment if in the same rank. But that should be for the best for when the tu—Damn it!" Natto snapped, clicking her tongue.

System stopping you again?

Drake felt her nod, affirming his suspicion.

Can't you just, ya know, ignore it?

"If I wished to be harmed as well as placed within a debuff penalty for my trouble, yes. But you will know once we have left the tutorial, so it is not urgent."

Drake was reminded of the Dragon bitch after Natto mentioned the debuff.

Speaking of that, Drake thought, walking toward the crafter's district of the outpost, *what do you suppose the penalties will be for the Dragon lady?*

Natto scoffed. *"Nothing pleasant, that is certain. But when you are at the apex of rank, the system does treat you more favorably. She will most likely receive a stat debuff that will be inconvenient for her for many years, and a large portion of her experience will be taken from her."*

Large portion, huh?

"Yes, around 5%."

Really? Only 5%?

"5% at S-Rank is equivalent to dropping from B-Rank to F-Rank, you mongrel. If not more depending on how far she has progressed into the rank, which I assume is quite far as she is one of the oldest Primordials in existence."

Good. Fuck her. And not in the good way, Drake spat, his face grimacing.

"What's with the sour face there, youngin?"

Drake stopped, his face relaxing when he saw the old dwarf at the stall.

"Nothing important. Just thinking about a woman who did me dirty." Drake chuckled.

"Ain't that always what it is. Ah, to be young again!" The old dwarf smiled.

"Yeah, I'm having a blast... So what about my cut?" Drake asked.

"Cut? Oh! You're that guy who gave me all that stuff to sell, aren't ya! I hardly recognized ya with the long hair and the, well, darker skin."

"Yeah, I had an upgrade. Longer hair means stronger, right?" Drake laughed.

"Where did you hear such nonsense? Either way, I didn't get all of it sold, but that's because no one could pay what it was worth. I did get a bit from the leader of the camp, though!"

Drake smiled. "You don't say?"

"Darn tootin! Milked that youngin for all he was worth for some of those accessories you gave me. Made most of the profit there. Give me just one second."

The dwarf turned around, pulling some things from under the counter and placing them in front of Drake.

"Here's the unsold stuff, and here's your cut. I know we agreed on 50%, but you sure you're alright with this?"

Drake smiled and pulled the items, skill stones, and cores into his inventory.

"Yup. Glad you could get a good chunk out of it, old man. Stay safe out there; hope to see you again," Drake said, waving to him.

The dwarf shrugged. "Strange kid."

* * *

Drake chuckled to himself, happy to have made a good amount from the stuff he wasn't using. Which also gave validity to his later plan.

He'd spent a decent amount of time casually walking the outpost before he decided it was time to get back to their camp.

Walking back, he eventually made his way to their practice area in time. He spotted Shigure and Uta training as well, having come from their duties to improve with the others. That made Drake smile again as he thought about how many monster cores he'd gotten from them for his accessories.

Drake eventually turned to Claire, calling in everyone else as well now that the time was coming up.

"Alright, we only have a few minutes, but I'll be going for the last day. There's somewhere I want to be when this is all over, so this is finally goodbye," Drake said solemnly. "At least for now. May we meet again and be ReUnited!" Drake shouted.

"I still think that name is lame." Jacqueline sighed.

"Yeah, it isn't the best, is it..." Megan agreed.

Drake tried to ignore them as he kept his fist raised, his eye twitching.

"It's okay, Drake. The name isn't... Well, it isn't *too* bad," Claire said, trying to console him.

"Damn it... I like the name though!" he screamed.

Before the rest of the party could pile on him, the voice from the introduction along with a high-pitched ring reverberated inside their heads.

Tutorial #1,294,007 has been completed. Rewards will be calculated based on current leaderboard positions.

You have gained the title First Completionist.
You have been granted early access to the Tutorial Shop.

Ladder positions calculated.

You have finished #3 on the Level Leaderboard.
Experience earned. 3,000,000 TP have been awarded.
You have gained the title Top 3.

You have finished #1 on the Tutorial Points Leaderboard.
Experience earned. 10,000,000 TP have been awarded.
You have gained the title Top 1.

Congratulations! You have reached Elemental Miller Level 25.
40 FP have been awarded.

Extra title Top Finisher has been awarded.
Extra title Lucrative has been awarded.

Overall placement has been assessed.
Overall tutorial contribution has been assessed.
Extra rewards are being distributed.

You have received Epic Armor Box x2.
You have received Epic Weapon Box x2.
You have received 20x Strength, Intelligence, Vitality, Stamina, Wisdom, and Dexterity pills.
5,000,000 TP have been awarded.

This concludes the tutorial. May you gain insight, power, and renown. And most importantly, survive.

Chapter 87

Hey Again

"So where exactly are we going?" Claire asked, following along with Drake.

"Nowhere special. I just want to go there when we leave," Drake said, turning his head slightly to answer her.

"Sounds special, if you want to leave everyone early to go there... Did something happen there?"

"Could say that. But just enjoy being alone with me, alright? We get to just relax for the last day, browse the shop."

"That's true, I guess..." Claire said suspiciously.

Drake snorted and guided her through the forest at a casual pace, looking at the various items in the tutorial shop. He'd already found the items that Natto had mentioned earlier, worried about them possibly getting sold out if he didn't grab them immediately.

Language Book of the Myriad Races [S-Grade]
The use of this book allows one to understand all spoken and written forms of languages throughout the multiverse.

Quest Voucher: A Land All Your Own [E-Grade]
A quest voucher able to be redeemed at any system-sanctioned center help building.
Expires after one year.

The two items had already cost him a pretty penny, easing his worry of them being sold out. It seemed that certain items were only available to certain people. Natto explained that it was based on a combination of accomplishments, titles, and max TP earned during the tutorial.

For example, he, Shigure, and Bjorn could see the Quest Voucher whereas everyone else they knew could not. As for the Language Book, it seemed to be available for everyone in the tutorial to purchase if they wished. It was also relatively affordable for everyone at a price of 5,000 TP, whereas the Voucher was 100,000 TP.

Drake was sure he'd be able to get the other items he was eyeing on the way to their destination, so he was taking his time and enjoying the walk with Claire. The last thirty days had been mostly training for the both of them, giving them no time to be together outside of a few select days and nights.

They talked and walked comfortably through the forest that Drake remembered vividly from his time trying to improve and level up rigorously. They even passed by many of the same routes he'd fought through. Outpost B that Drake had single-handedly taken. The fake army he'd left within the forest outside of their old outpost.

Drake even thought they'd passed the place where he'd first met Bjorn. He could have sworn that part of the river looked familiar, but all the rocks were the same, so who could tell for certain.

"These are places you fought at before you met all of us?" Claire asked as Drake pointed them out casually.

"Yeah." Drake smiled. "I was alone for most of the beginning. The first person I met was actually Bjorn, then Natto came out of an egg. That was a weird one."

"An egg? Like a chicken egg?"

"It was bigger, more like an ostrich? I had to use some blood sacrifice thing to get her to hatch, too. Spooky stuff," Drake said, giving a flutter of his fingers.

"So you've just always had one thing happen after another since coming to the tutorial," Claire said.

"Suppose so. I roughed it alone for the most part until I somehow got Natto, then I met Theo and rescued everyone else."

"Hmm..." Claire hummed, putting her hands behind her back. "So, are you going to keep me in the dark about where we're going until we get there?"

"Yup." Drake smiled and pointed to a clearing in the forest. "And we're there."

Drake's face turned solemn as he looked into the clearing. In the middle was a mound with no marker that had become overgrown by the grasses around it. Beneath it lay the nameless person he'd met on the day he became a Dual Class.

This was where Drake had decided to push forward and give it his all.

He left Claire at the edge of the clearing, walking up to the mound as he pulled a sword from his inventory.

"Hey there. Remember me?" He chuckled wearily. "As promised, I came back at the end when I changed who I was. Literally," he said, giving a bit of a listless laugh. "This sword isn't the original, but I think it's just as nice."

Drake slipped the sword into the mound of dirt, the gravestone replaced.

"Who's that?" Claire asked gently.

"No idea," Drake answered.

Claire paused for a moment, looking at the mound pensively.

"Were they important?"

"You could say that." Drake smirked. "This is where I killed my weak self. If it wasn't for what happened here, I might not have ever gone on to be so strong and save everyone I did... Thinking back, I kinda wish it happened sooner. Maybe... Maybe I could have done more."

Claire squeezed Drake's arm, no words needing to be said.

That was because Natto said it for her. Popping out of the side of Drake's head, she slapped him.

"Will you stop this self-loathing! It is becoming insufferable! How many times must I tell you, it is not your fault nor is it your duty to protect every idiotic buffoon that walks this tutorial! You are not a god!" she yelled.

"Not yet." Drake smiled.

"You are not even E-Rank yet! Leave your dreams for when you are asleep!"

"But I don't sleep anymore, so I only have when I'm awake?" Drake laughed.

"Ahhh!"

Drake gave a genuine smile and laugh before pulling out some supplies and placing them nearby. Water, food, camping gear—if you could call a luxury bed that—chairs, and flooring.

"Might as well be glampers at this point." Drake nodded, looking at the setup. He looked back toward the mound where Claire and Natto were still talking and moved to grab their attention.

"Alright, about time we see what this tutorial shop is all about, yeah?"

"I don't have that many points, so I'll just watch along with you. Is that okay?" Claire asked.

"Of course. Do you want me to get you something? Speaking of something, did you get any bonus rewards?" Drake replied, throwing the question right back at her.

"Bonuses? No, I didn't get anything like that. I wasn't anywhere near the top, after all," she answered with empty eyes.

"It's okay, we can't all be special like me. Ow!"

Claire had punched him in the gut. Obviously it hadn't hurt, but Drake felt like acting the part was necessary for these moments.

"Ass..." she mumbled.

Drake just smiled and pulled the boxes from his inventory.

"Guess we look at these first."

Epic Armor Box [F-Grade]
Contains a class-specific random piece of non-set armor or accessories.
Roll using the black die before opening for use.
Bound to participant Drake Wallen.
Cannot be traded.

Epic Weapon Box [F-Grade]
Contains a class-specific random piece of non-set weaponry.
Roll using the black die before opening for use.
Bound to participant Drake Wallen.
Cannot be traded.

Drake currently had two of these in his possession as well as twenty of each stat pill. The pills weren't bound to him like the boxes, so he'd given the vitality pills to Claire ahead of time. The more health for a mage or support class, the better.

"It's been a while since I used this," Drake mused, pulling out the die from his inventory. "So what happens to this thing after the tutorial?" Drake asked.

"Disappears," Natto said snidely.

Drake frowned. "Really?"

"Were you expecting it to be a key item of some sort? Change into an epic weapon maybe?"

"Well, yeah, kind of." Drake nodded.

"It is an item created specifically for participants of the tutorial so that the new inductors of the multiverse can intentionally make it more difficult. How skills are gained outside of the tutorial is completely different. I have told you this."

"I know, just wanted to make sure. Geez." Drake snorted and threw the die to the floor.

Drake was less stressed over rolling than he'd been previously. He had the ability to get exactly what he wanted now that he had his massive pool of TP at the tips of his fingers.

But, there was one thing a gamer always kept.

The need for better loot.

His eyes bulged as his skills took hold, increasing his perception. He saw the die roll slowly to a stop.

First it landed on a 17, then a 5, then it turned slowly and bounced twice to a 19 before finally halting and skidding to the ground. 12.

"FUUUUCKKKKK!" Drake yelled.

Claire pointed at Drake, this being the first time she'd seen him roll for loot. "Has he always done that?"

Natto nodded.

"That's cute... In a weird sort of way," Claire mumbled.

Natto looked at Claire incredulously. "Are you broken? Never mind, I take that back. To love a man like him you must be. I lost a bet for wonderful candy over this... It was rigged! Rigged, I say!"

Drake ignored them, sighing before opening the chest to his first Epic armor.

"Oh, that's pretty..." he swooned.

Ice Wyvern's Crystal Eye Earring [F-Grade, Epic]
Well-made jewelry made from the crystalized iris of a fully grown Ice Wyvern.
163—208 increase to Ice-based damage.
+40 to Intelligence.
+10% to Spell Critical Rate, +20% to Spell Critical Damage.
Equipt Limit: 1

"Oooo... Spell Crit..." Drake drooled, holding the item to the fading sun. The crystalline blue captured the orange spectacularly within the earring.

"That is gorgeous, can I see it?" Claire asked with hearts in her eyes.

"Sure," Drake said, tossing it to her.

He quickly bent down and picked up the die, ready to keep the process going.

One after the other he rolled, getting relatively average numbers for each chest. For the last armor chest, he rolled a 13. For the two weapon chests, he rolled a 15 and a 9 respectively. The results were better than expected, but the weapons were honestly not suited for him.

"Is it because I'm a dual class?" Drake wondered, looking at the weapons.

"Yes, that is exactly why." Natto sighed and sat down next to Claire, a bag of food popping into her hands.

"Damn. Makes sense, but... Damn," Drake lamented.

Lower Basilisk Wrist Guards [F-Grade, Epic]
Battleworn wrist guards made from the tough hide of the basilisk species. +30% defense proficiency.
315—364 Physical Damage Reduction.
282—290 Magic Damage Reduction.
15% Critical Hit Reduction.
+20 to Strength, +15 to Dexterity, +50 to Endurance.

Mana-Infused Knuckle Claws [F-Grade, Epic]

Well-crafted three-bladed gauntlets made with a basic smithing technique and infused with mana to improve the efficiency of the blades and the durability of the weapon overall.
628—644 Physical Damage.
110—125 Magic Damage.
10% increase to Critical Strikes.
+20 to Strength, +25 to Dexterity.
Reduces consumption of Stamina for skills by 1%.

Lightning Storm in a Bottle [F-Grade, Epic]
Bottled storms from the planet Arabath, the home of the never-ending storm. Mages of the planet often gift this to fledgling mages to supplement their growth.
4—12 Physical Damage.
568—700 Magic Damage.
10% increase to Spell Critical Strikes.
+20 to Intelligence, +15 to Wisdom.
Reduces consumption of Lighting-based spells by 1%.
Can only be worn in the off-hand.

"So these are kinda awesome, but set items are significantly better, huh?" Drake asked, slipping the wrist protectors on. "Oh, comfy..." He smiled.

"By design, yes. Set items will always give better effects while the set effects are in full use. You may find unique items that surpass them, but they will be far more specific in use. That orb, for instance. It is rather strong for an F-Grade item, even at epic grade, but it is only effective for lightning spells," Natto explained.

"Well," Drake said, looking at the shimmering and crackling bottle, "it isn't all bad. I can use this for my disguise on the outside."

"Disguise?" Claire asked, finally done admiring the earring and handing it back to Drake.

"Yeah," Drake replied, taking the earring and placing it on his right ear. "I'm going to be a Mage on the outside until I can't be. I don't want people to know just yet that I'm a Dual Class. I'm strong, but I don't know who else might be able to take me. It's better to sow misinformation for now, at least until we all get back together and can start building up our strength as a whole.

Figuring out who the real enemies and allies are once we're outside is a good way to pace it, too," Drake explained, fiddling with his necklace.

"Well? What do you see?" Drake asked, opening up his hands.

Claire was confused, then realized he meant identify.

"Um..." she said, squinting. "Drake Wallen... Level... 13?" she said, confused. "You picked a pretty low level, didn't you?"

Drake smiled. "Yep. I want to know who will pick on the little guy, for one. My inner Cid Kagenou is coming through... But also, this is relatively the average level, I think, if our tutorial is anything to go off of."

Drake heard a snicker come from Natto, but he didn't think anything of it.

"Imbecile till the end..." Natto muttered through bites.

Drake opened the tutorial shop, now ready to start buying with his deep pockets.

"Alright, let's see what this baby has to offer!"

Drake and Claire sat down at the table a few feet away. Natto trotted along as well until she took a seat on the table with her bag of snacks.

"Let's see, there's quite a lot here... But the price goes up exponentially for the rarity... That's really—Wow, that's a ripoff! One million points for a single Stat Pill?! I found like fifty of these in the King's Hoard!"

Natto laughed and shrugged. "It is the Dragons. What did you expect? Do you believe they would give up their treasure for mere shekels?"

Drake ground his teeth, his expectation of coming out with a bunch of good stuff shattered.

"Well, I can still get a lot... I just have to be more selective, I suppose." He sighed.

Paging through the large selection, he browsed the profession books, seedlings, skill stones, weapons, armor, potions, anything and everything.

He paged through the entirety of the shop, not wanting to miss a single opportunity for something that may be useful for him now or later. The sun had long passed below the horizon even before he'd added a single thing to his cart. The night took hold of the area, and Drake summoned floating fireballs to illuminate the surroundings.

"Hmm," he mused. He then noticed Claire fast asleep on his shoulder, forcing a smile from him. He quickly picked her up and put her to bed inside the tent, hearing some small grumblings from Claire as he did.

Coming back out of the tent, he got back to his shopping, finding a few things he knew he would need right away.

He looked over at Natto. She had long since finished her snacks and was now slightly drooling on the table, asleep. Drake poked her awake.

"Hey, Natto."

"W-What?" she said groggily.

"There seems to be a pack of set equipment here, rare grade. Is it worth getting? It's giving me limited access to what's inside, but based on the labeling I think it's good."

"What is the name?"

Drake turned the screen around and pointed at it. "Asuran War Garb Set, rare grade. It's thirty million points, though."

Natto looked over the item for a moment, then nodded. "Yes, it does seem to be made for you based on the name. Unfortunately, I cannot tell you either way if it is an advisable purchase. I can tell you that it is worth much more than mere tutorial points, at the least."

"So that's a yes," Drake said. He hit the 'add to cart' button. "What about this?"

Spirit Ink Tattoos of the Asurans [F-Grade, Rare] 10,000,000 TP

Natto looked at Drake like he was dumb. "Do you really need me to answer this? It has Asuran in the name, Drake."

Drake smirked. "Just making sure."

He continued to add things to his cart one by one as he paged through the store.

Lesser Fire Drake's Burning Eye Ring [F-Grade, Rare] 3,000,000 TP
A well-made ring crafted from the crystalized iris of a juvenile Fire Drake.
180—131 increase to Fire-based damage.
+10 to Intelligence.
+5% to Spell Critical Rate, +5% to Spell Critical Damage.

Equipt Limit: 1

Lesser Earth Dragon's Petrified Eye Ring [F-Grade, Rare] 3,000,000 TP
A well-made ring crafted from the crystalized iris of a juvenile Earth Dragon.

100—110 increase to Earth-based damage.
+10 to Intelligence.
+5% to overall spell damage.
Equipt Limit: 1

Large Dimensional Compartment [F-Grade] 5,000,000 TP
300x50 Dimensional Space Bag.

Requires one inventory slot. Must be placed in inventory to be equipped.
Stores items in current state indefinitely, does not include living entities.
Drops on death.
Equipt Limit: 1

"Okay, that does it for accessories, and I know I'll need that inventory space in the future. There's a reason games always charge micro-transactions for space, after all. Now, for the stuff I'm going to be using for my plan." Drake hummed. "Oh wait, there's that as well."

Small Dungeon Dimension Anchor [F-Grade] 500,000 TP
Anchors a dimensional space. Produces a Small Dungeon Anomaly.

Does not provide the monsters within the Anomaly.
Anything trapped within the Anomaly space when anchored will forever be anchored to it.

"I have no idea if this is going to pay dividends, but a dungeon sounds like just what I'll need later on. Too bad I can only get one from the shop."

Next Drake filled his cart with skill stones he thought would be valuable to people on the outside as well as materials and seeds much like his man-eating plant. He lamented not being able to get a particular item he spotted in the process.

World Tree [F-Grade, Legendary] 100,000,000 TP
A growing monument to the elven lineage.

This tree must be grown over centuries, but it gives massive beneficial growth buffs to its citizens.

Only one may be planted on a planet at a time.

"It would've been nice to get this. Really drive home the fantasy feel, ya know?"

"You would be asking for trouble even if you could purchase that," Natto explained. "World Trees are beneficial in many ways. They inspire and encourage growth of all kinds in both the citizens and monsters of the world. They also bear fruit to all kinds of surprising things, not to mention that items made from the tree are always in demand no matter the grade. You are better off not having one right off the bat, especially with no elves to properly care for it."

"Hmm, well that's unfortunate." Drake sighed. "But I got almost everything I wanted regardless. Thankfully the skill stones I picked up were duplicates from stuff I had before, so they weren't too much, and the profession technique books were pretty inexpensive also, for some reason. Anyways, time to blow my load!" Drake chuckled and hit the purchase button. Natto rolled her eyes at the joke.

But she could only scoff and look at Drake in contempt for so long before a large box appeared and crashed into the table, snapping it in half and sending her flying off into the distance.

"Isn't that just karma." Drake laughed, then frowned, looking at the table. "I really liked that table though..."

Chapter 88
Cheers to a New Chapter

Natto walked back over, disgruntled. She dusted herself off while picking pieces of grass from her hair. She patted her ears gently and glared at Drake, who was still cackling.

"You could have warned me!"

"Hey, I didn't know it was going to happen." Drake shrugged, smiling.

"To be stuck with you for the rest of my life..." Natto whimpered.

Drake kept his smile and picked her up, pulling a large venison skewer from his inventory.

"Now, now. You're alright here."

"Hai ham nawt foreghiving shew!" she said, chewing on the skewer.

"Yes, yes. Isn't it time you get to bed too? I set up a bed for you in the tent." Drake laughed.

Natto yawned as she gnawed on the meat. "I *am* getting somewhat tired. What will you do?"

Drake pointed to the box.

"Going to get familiar with my new goodies."

Natto waved and turned toward the tent. "Do not spend all your time staring at the screens. You will go blind."

"Yes, mom," Drake replied. He picked up the box and put it onto a new table from his inventory, eager to get into his new gear.

"Now what did Dragon Santa give me?"

Drake pulled the surprisingly familiar tape from the box, a little put off by how much it looked like one of the moving boxes his mother used constantly to send things back to the Philippines.

The tape now removed, he flipped open the flaps and saw a kaleidoscope of lights covering the empty space.

"What in the…? Is this like a dimensional space?" Drake thought out loud. He stuck his hand into the light.

"Oh, that feels very weird…" Drake grimaced, moving his hand further and further into the box until he felt something touch his fingers. Grabbing and pulling the thing out, he was surprised to see several items come out of the space and tumble out onto him.

He had pulled out several pieces of armor and clothing that he assumed were the Asuran Armor he'd purchased.

"Well, these are colorful?"

Asuran War Vest [F-Grade, Rare] Set Piece 1/6

The armor of choice for warriors of the Asurans. With mana-infused threads and leather made from the fierce monsters of their homeworld, Ran'tu Kai, this garb offers defense to rival dwarven-made Mana Steel Equipment. +25% defense proficiency.

257—275 Physical Damage Reduction.
202—217 Magic Damage Reduction.
7% Critical Hit Reduction.
+20 to Strength, +10 to Dexterity, +5 to Endurance.
Set Effect: *Increases Health and Mana regeneration by 20%. Increases skill proficiency gain by 2%. Increases defense proficiency by 50% when surrounded by enemies scaling from 10 to 100.*
Requires a minimum of 2 pieces to activate set effect.

Drake's eyes sparkled as he looked at the black and white top vest, the deep, colorless black chains seeming to absorb the light of his fire spells around him. The chains feathered out from a center node in the back and front of the vest.

"Only one problem," Drake said suddenly feeling embarrassed. "It only covers the top half of my body… Where's the rest of the armor?! You don't expect me to wear something that shows so much skin, do you?!"

Drake gave up, sighing. He had no other option but to wear the equipment. His current armor was torn to pieces from the tutorial and his recent training, so much so that they could hardly be called anything but rags at this point. His wonderful armor was no more.

Taking off his robes and undershirt, he suddenly felt incredibly vulnerable. He quickly placed his old clothes into his inventory for sentimental value as he slipped on the vest.

The vest fit perfectly as if it was made just for him. His arms slipped into the holes of the vest as the chains fell into place around him, surprising him further by making no sound despite obviously being made of metal.

Drake picked up one of the chains, jangling it. He still heard no noise.

"That's neat." He picked up the next piece.

Asuran War Leggings [F-Grade, Rare] Set Piece 1/6
The armor of choice for warriors of the Asurans. With mana-infused threads and leather made from the fierce monsters of their homeworld, Ran'tu Kai, this garb offers defense to rival dwarven-made Mana Steel Equipment. +20% defense proficiency.

288—294 Physical Damage Reduction.
212—225 Magic Damage Reduction.
5% increase to Spell Critical Strikes.
+20 to Intelligence, +10 to Wisdom.

Set Effect: *Increases Health and Mana regeneration by 20%. Increases skill proficiency gain by 2%. Increases defense proficiency by 50% when surrounded by enemies scaling from 10 to 100.*
Requires a minimum of 2 pieces to activate set effect.

"Are all of these pieces going to be this dramatic looking...? God, I hope so." Drake smiled and brought the leggings into the light.

To call them leggings wasn't exactly accurate. They looked like torn cloth pants wrapped in some type of hefty leather. The thighs were protected with an interlocking flexible metal material, and on top of that were the bottom coverings of a robe with iconic black fire on a white background, the inseam of the robe a striking bright red. The whole thing was fastened together with a similar pitch-black metal chain for the belt.

Drake looked around briefly out of habit even though his aura told him both Claire and Natto were sound asleep in the tent. He then pulled off his old armor and slipped into the new piece of gear.

"Oh... Oh! That's like silk... Dios ko, I have to remember to get fresh undies when we get back to my apartment, not to mention a bunch of other stuff. Rice, candy, my rice cooker, my PC, my tablet... Will I even have electricity for it? I'll figure that out later." Drake digressed, picking up two cloth wraps in his hands next.

Asuran War Footwraps [F-Grade, Rare] Set Piece 1/6
The armor of choice for warriors of the Asurans. With mana-infused threads and leather made from the fierce monsters of their homeworld, Ran'tu Kai, this garb offers defense to rival dwarven-made Mana Steel Equipment. +15% defense proficiency.

133—142 Physical Damage Reduction.
121—127 Magic Damage Reduction.
+20% to Stamina Regeneration.
+20 to Endurance, +5 to Dexterity.

Set Effect: *Increases Health and Mana regeneration by 20%. Increases skill proficiency gain by 2%. Increases defense proficiency by 50% when surrounded by enemies scaling from 10 to 100.*
Requires a minimum of 2 pieces to activate set effect.

The footwraps were exactly that, wraps of tough silky cloth. There was, however, a large metal frame that fit perfectly into the arch of his foot at the end of each wrap.

Drake looked at it curiously. Through some trial and error, he was eventually able to twine them around his feet, the metal plate at the soles of his arches.

Once he was done, he spotted another pair of wraps, but these were already bundled away almost like a compression wrap.

Drake could already guess which pieces these were, but he inspected them all the same.

Asuran War Handwraps [F-Grade, Rare] Set Piece 1/6
The armor of choice for warriors of the Asurans. With mana-infused threads and

leather made from the fierce monsters of their homeworld, Ran'tu Kai, this garb offers defense to rival dwarven-made Mana Steel Equipment. +15% defense proficiency.

120—135 Physical Damage Reduction.
115—130 Magic Damage Reduction.
+5% to Physical Critical Strikes.
+15 to Vitality, +5 to Strength.

Set Effect: *Increases Health and Mana regeneration by 20%. Increases skill proficiency gain by 2%. Increases defense proficiency by 50% when surrounded by enemies scaling from 10 to 100.*

Requires a minimum of 2 pieces to activate set effect.

Drake whistled, looking at the stats and feeling the effects of the set activate once he finished wrapping the handwraps into place. He squeezed and unclenched his hands, feeling the fabric between his fingers.

"These are incredibly comfortable..." Drake mused. He summoned a spike of earth in front of him, condensing the mana used to do so to harden the spike.

Drake's arm hummed with power as his lone tattoo ring flared to life. Reeling back his hand, he threw a straight right into the spike, smashing it to pieces.

"Wow, I barely felt a thing." He smirked, looking at the wraps. The armor hadn't even wrinkled from the strike, only a bit of dirt covering them.

"Now the problem is, do I replace the rest of my equipment with the set items? There's technically seven pieces. The bracers, shoulders, and headpiece are the ones I'm currently not wearing. Stat wise the shoulders would be better than my shawl, but I don't want to give up the ability to freely use my inventory, and my bracers right now are technically better at epic grade. But the full six-piece bonus is nothing to scoff at... If the tutorial is any indicator, I'm sure there'll be swarms of monsters again at some point. I guess I can just freely equip the other two pieces when I need it." Drake nodded at his self-explanation. He put the three extra pieces away and stuffed his hand back into the box.

Feeling around, he pulled the rest of the consumables and skill stones from the box until he found one of the items he was looking for. His new Dimensional Storage.

"Just put that into place real quick."

Drake removed one of his old "smaller" bags and replaced it swiftly with the new storage, increasing his already monstrous inventory with more space.

After a little more fumbling around in the box, he pulled out his new earrings and rings. He replaced those as well until he finally pulled out a small chest—the last item from the box.

"These are the spirit tattoos then, huh?" Drake wondered, looking at the small golden chest.

Not wanting to wait, Drake opened the chest. It was covered in a red velvet-like material on the inside, and it housed a small vial filled with golden liquid.

Spirit Ink Tattoos of the Asurans [F-Grade, Rare]

The Spiritual Ink Tattoos are a special tool used by veteran warriors in the halls of the furious Asurans. They are forged by skilled craftsmen so that the mana-infused ink may take shape for the fighter. By design, they are perfect for mana control and manipulation as well as the growth of apex fighters within the ranks of the Asurans.

520—552 Physical Damage.
515—530 Magic Damage.
5% increase to Base Critical Strikes.
+10 to Strength, +10 to Intelligence.
Reduces consumption of Mana for spells by 5%.

Magic Spiritual Ink Tattoos of the Asurans: By constantly infusing mana into the tattoos, you may produce Magic Spiritual Ink Tattoos of the Asurans. The increased infusion of mana will increase the durability and damage of the tattoos by 1% per total Mana percentage.

The Spirit Ink Tattoos are made from the reforged materials of fallen rivals of the Grand Asurans. By design, the Spirit Tattoos wish to consume and grow. A limit of 1 weapon can be integrated into the Spirit Tattoos to increase grade.

Drake's eyes bulged at the description, his legendary E-Grade weapon flashing in his mind.

Taking a few audible breaths, he tried to calm himself, his hand shaking as he held the vial.

"Calm down, relax... I can't use it yet. You read the description, right Drake? If you feed it the gauntlets now, you wouldn't be able to use them since it would increase to E-Grade. Just breathe... Take it slow!" Drake forced himself to let go of the box that held E-Grade gauntlets inside them, almost succumbing to the temptation to see the new weapon come to life.

"All in due time... ALL IN DUE TIME!" Drake shouted, trying to bury the voice telling him to upgrade the weapon already.

Letting out another breath, Drake looked at the vial in the light of his spells.

"How do I use this, then? Don't tell me I need to see a tattoo artist to use it first?" Drake wondered.

Drake first took off his tattoo ring, placing it back into his inventory, then ran his fingers over the vial of golden, somewhat viscous liquid.

"I hope they don't want me to drink this stuff; I'm not into that..." Drake cringed, turning the vial over several times. "Well, it's a weapon right? Maybe I just equip it like one?"

Drake shrugged, popped the vial open, and extended one arm.

"Here goes nothing."

A moment later, the gold liquid almost slithered out of the vial in a single blob, snapping to the skin on Drake's arm. He suddenly felt his skin burn with an intensity akin to when he consumed a skill stone.

Gritting his teeth, he forced himself to not flinch away as he emptied the vial, the liquid searing his skin as it slowly entered his body. The next second, his skin illuminated with a golden light. The flash cascaded across his arm and past his shoulders to his other arm. He dropped the vial.

Letting out a breath of relief after the process finished, Drake looked at his arms. He saw the faint, ethereal outline of flames painted on his skin.

"Dope..." Drake mumbled. He pushed mana into his arms, feeling for the weapon.

Once he found the connection to the weapon, the sensation was instant.

His arms flared in a golden light once again. The flames danced with a royal hue of deep gold, almost coming to life off his arms.

"Hahaha! This is amazing!" Drake shouted, feeling his mana smoothly transition into the weapon. He instinctively knew that the amount he could pass over to it was a monumental number—many times more than his tattoo rings could previously hold. It felt as if the Spirit Tattoo was a part of him, not just physically but also spiritually.

Drake pushed his hand out, pointing it to the air.

"I can't possibly not christen this!" he shouted. His hair suddenly turned white, the flames around him bristling as they hardened and formed spikes of ice with a golden flame humming to life underneath.

"*Moeru.*"

The shift in Drake's mana happened quickly. The process of turning his fire into its matured white form happened in a split second as it breathed to life instantaneously, surprising Drake when he saw the dense ball of fire mana continue to build.

Soon the ball was so bright that it illuminated the night like a bright north star. Condensed into the size of a small baseball, it hovered on top of Drake's open palm.

Once it began contesting his control, he smiled and willed it into the air. It shot upward, the sound of the screeching ball of intense heat searing the very air as it reached for the sky.

"*Cheers to the next chapter.*"

The ball of fire imploded, turning night into day for miles around the area and, of course, startling Claire and Natto. They ran out of the tent to find Drake grinning ear to ear.

Turning his head to them, he grinned even wider. "Sorry, did I wake you?"

* * *

"I said I was sorry. It wasn't even that bad!" Drake laughed as he sliced apart some meat for their breakfast.

"I thought we were under attack again!" Claire shouted from the other side of the table, pointing her knife at him. "Don't do that!"

"But I had to test out the new weapon I got. You know how it is."

"I don't! You can basically destroy whole neighborhoods with your magic power, you can't go throwing it around as you want anymore," she admonished him.

"Alright, alright. No more showing off. But I have a present for you," Drake slipped in. He washed his hands briefly before taking out a ring from his inventory.

"I know you can't use it, but I thought you would want something of mine while we're apart. Ya know, to remember me by," Drake explained, holding out his remaining Tattoo Ring.

"Th-This is… This is the last of the rings you always had, right?" Claire asked pensively.

"Yep. I got new weapons, so I don't need it anymore. Do you want it?"

Claire nodded, looking at the ring before trying to slip it on. The system sent her a small zap, informing her that she couldn't wear it.

She wagged her hand from the shock but puffed out her cheeks. "I wanted to wear it!"

Drake chuckled and pulled a strap of leather from his inventory, twining it to make a neat, durable thread. He laced it inside the ring.

"Here, maybe this will work since it won't provide stats this way," Drake said. He moved behind her to drape her hair out of the way so he could fasten the leather.

"No shock, perfect." Drake smiled and gave her a kiss on her shoulder. "Now you won't forget me." Drake laughed.

Claire's face went crimson for a moment before she raised the ring and looked at it endearingly. "I would never forget you. How could I? You're the man who saved my life and the one I love."

Drake embraced Claire from behind, letting his feelings pour over her through it.

"I've never been good at saying stuff like that, but I'll just say it since you won't be seeing me for a while," Drake said, turning her around to look her in the eyes. "I love you too, Claire. I'll come find you once everything is done, so wait for me."

"Only when everything is done?" she said, pursing her lips.

Drake snorted. "There has to be a place to come back to, doesn't there? You're a big strong girl now. I know you can manage a little bit without me."

Claire fell into his embrace once more as they stood silently in each other's company.

"Alright, so one last meal before we're out of here, huh?" Drake said, letting her go and looking at the countdown.

Time remaining until tutorial's conclusion:
3 hours, 2 minutes, 43 seconds.

The rest of their time was spent relatively silently together. They finished preparing the meal, cooking, and sat with one another. Even Natto was pleasant as they ate, the three of them simply enjoying each other's company while they waited for the end of the tutorial to come.

Drake pushed away thoughts of what was to come once they were back. His mind was set on the present, relaxing in the moment for once.

Drake and Claire gazed into the midday sky. They held hands, the clock ticking down.

10

9

8

7

6

Drake turned to her, leaning in for one last kiss.
"I'll see you on the other side, yeah?" Drake said, pressing his head to hers.

5

4

3

2

"You know you will. Can't get rid of me, you stubborn asshole." She smiled back and gripped his hand a little tighter.

1

Claire's hand vanished inside Drake's as they were both engulfed in a spectrum of lights much like they'd been during the introduction of the tutorial. The familiar sound of the robotic woman's voice chimed in their heads.

The tutorial has concluded. You will now be placed back to your original locations on your planet as best as the system can provide. We hope you have enjoyed your experience.

May you gain insight, power, and renown. And most importantly, survive.

Afterword

The tutorial is complete, and Drake is hurled back to his old world. However, it's now merged with several other planets, changing it into an unrecognizable landscape where life-threatening monsters are a constant occurrence. Pre-order the third volume today!

Can't wait for book three? You can read advanced chapters on Patreon and join the conversation on Discord.

Patreon: www.patreon.com/Arthur_Inverse

Discord: https://discord.gg/4MHFtZc5rR

Books You May Like

**When a dragon-blooded emperor reaches for godhood,
Earth reaches back—with bullets.**

The plan was simple: conquer a new realm, harvest its souls, and become a god.

But nothing about Ohio is simple.

Armed with grit, ingenuity, and a lot of guns, the scrappy humans of Earth prove they're not the kneeling type. In a clash of magic and modern firepower, alliances are forged, friendships are tested, and ambitions burn brighter than the skies over the Midwest.

Can humanity stand its ground, or will the emperor's quest for divinity grind them to dust?

Grab your copy of Grimoires & Gunsmoke today! Perfect for fans of epic battles, unlikely heroes, and a healthy dose of fantasy-meets-modern warfare.

Available now on Kindle Unlimited and Audible!

And if you're still wanting to jump into action and madness, check out another MoonQuill original, *The Hiro is a Rubber Duck*.

What if the world's last hope wasn't a brave warrior or cunning mage… but a rubber duck worshiped as a god?

After nearly a thousand years of slumber, Hiro awakens to find he has been reincarnated as the divine core of a living, indestructible dungeon.

Once a failed hero, he must now survive in a post-apocalyptic world filled with corruption, cursed champions, and far too many cults.

With zealots at his side, monsters at his command, and a mysterious system guiding his rise, Hiro isn't saving the world the noble way. He's doing it his way.

Purge the filth. Cleanse the world. And maybe, just maybe, enjoy a bubble bath or two.

Grab your copy today and dive into this LitRPG Isekai Adventure full of dark comedy, wild twists, and enough madness to tip the world off balance.

Available now on Kindle Unlimited and in paperback!

Thank you for reading a MoonQuill original novel. More exciting stories can be found on at www.moonquill.com.

We would greatly appreciate it if you could take a moment to leave a review. Each one helps the author and supports their ability to continue writing fantastic books for everyone to enjoy!

Scan the QR code below to subscribe to our mailing list and be notified of new releases. You'll receive 4 e-books for free!